HAMMADI-NUARI LTD.

MUSA, ABRAHAM, AND JACOB. The founders, praying for their work to survive.

ABDULLAH, IZAK, SOLOMON. The uncles. After a lifetime of toil, destiny gave them a common tragedy.

JUDAH and **MOHAMED.** The partners. Until Judah felt the lure of Zionism, while Mohamed put his faith in their company's profits . . .

JACQUELINE and **RUTH.** The wives. One was a French beauty driven by an insatiable lust, the other a Polish girl forever shadowed in her husband's heart by the ghost of another.

BEN, ANWAR, YASSIR, TARIQ. The radicals. They would risk their lives and even fight one another for their ideals.

ABE, ZED, MAURICE, FRANCOISE. The children, inheriting a world far different from their parents' dreams . . .

Berkley Books by Jesse L. Lasky, Jr., and Pat Silver

LOVE SCENE
THE OFFER

THE OFFER

JESSE L. LASKY, JR. &
PAT SILVER

BERKLEY BOOKS, NEW YORK

This Berkley book contains the complete text of the original hardcover edition. It has been completely reset in a type face designed for easy reading, and was printed from new film.

THE OFFER

A Berkley Book / published by arrangement with Doubleday & Company, Inc.

Printing History
Doubleday edition / July 1981
Berkley edition / October 1982

ISBN: 0-425-05549-3

ACKNOWLEDGMENTS

Our gratitude

To Ronald Sears
for his contribution to the planning and architecture
of this book

and to Sarah Darlôt
for her patience and tremendous courage in typing
the final of many drafts

and to Betty Prashker
for her editorial guidance through a wilderness of
words

For Ronald Sears, whose interest, enthusiasm, research, and imagination helped make this book possible.

J.L. & P.S.

"The Promised Land is the land where one is not."

—Amiel

". . . and the Lord said unto him [Moses], this
is the land which I swear unto
Abraham, Isaac, and unto Jacob
saying I will give it unto thy seed."

—Deuteronomy 34:4

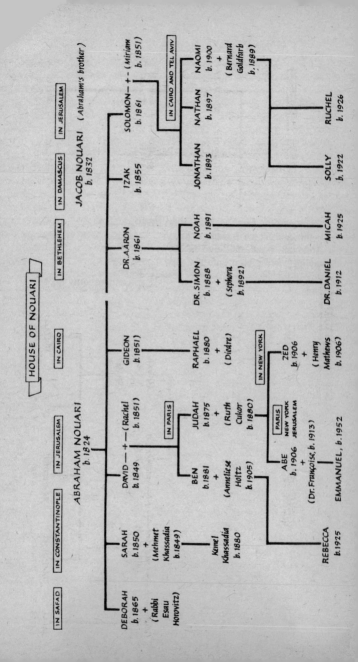

HOUSE OF NOUARI

JACOB NOUARI (Abraham's brother)
b. 1832

ABRAHAM NOUARI
b. 1824

| IN SAFAD | IN CONSTANTINOPLE | IN JERUSALEM | IN CAIRO | IN BETHLEHEM | IN DAMASCUS | IN JERUSALEM |

DEBORAH
b. 1865
+
(Rabbi Esau Horovitz)

SARAH
b. 1850
+
(Mehmet Khassadia b. 1849)

DAVID — + — (Rachel b. 1851)
b. 1849

GIDEON
b. 1851

DR. AARON
b. 1861

IZAK
b. 1855

SOLOMON — + — (Miriam b. 1851)
b. 1861

Kamel Khassadia
b. 1880

BEN
b. 1881
+
(Anneliese Holtz b. 1905)

JUDAH
b. 1875
+
(Ruth Cukor b. 1880)

RAPHAEL
b. 1880
+
(Diedre)

DR. SIMON
b. 1888
+
(Sephora b. 1892)

NOAH
b. 1891

JONATHAN
b. 1893

NATHAN
b. 1897

NAOMI
b. 1900
+
(Bernard Goldfarb b. 1889)

| IN PARIS | | IN NEW YORK | | IN CAIRO AND TEL AVIV |

ABE
b. 1906
+
(Dr. Françoise, b. 1913)

ZED
b. 1906
+
(Henry Mathews b. 1906)

DR. DANIEL
b. 1912

MICAH
b. 1925

SOLLY
b. 1922

RUCHEL
b. 1926

| PARIS / NEW YORK / JERUSALEM |

REBECCA
b. 1925

EMMANUEL, b. 1952

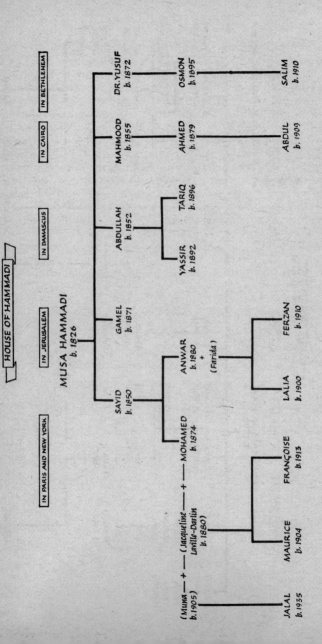

HOUSE OF HAMMADI

| IN PARIS AND NEW YORK | IN JERUSALEM | IN DAMASCUS | IN CAIRO | IN BETHLEHEM |

MUSA HAMMADI
b. 1826

SAYID
b. 1850

GAMEL
b. 1871

ABDULLAH
b. 1852

MAHMOOD
b. 1855

DR. YUSUF
b. 1872

MOHAMED
b. 1874

ANWAR
b. 1880
+
(Farida)

YASSIR
b. 1892

TARIQ
b. 1896

AHMED
b. 1879

OSMON
b. 1895

(Jacqueline
Laville-Darlin
b. 1880)

ABDUL
b. 1909

SALIM
b. 1910

MAURICE
b. 1904

FRANÇOISE
b. 1913

LALIA
b. 1900

FERZAN
b. 1910

(Muna
b. 1905)

JALAL
b. 1935

PART 1

Dreams
and Declarations

JUDAH'S room brimmed with flowers, a basket of fruit, and on the dresser facing his bed a photo of his wife that she herself had placed there. The clinically brushed and scrubbed patient was propped up in the elevated hospital bed. The left corner of his mouth sagged just slightly. His cheeks were hollows, eyes shadowed but open and strongly responsive. When he saw the Arab, Judah's lips trembled as though trying to form words, or perhaps even a smile.

Mohamed knew instantly that Judah would hear and understand. "Don't exert yourself." Mohamed took Judah's hand in his own, sensing rather than feeling the pressure of response. At first they were silent, letting the reunion flow through hands to hearts and minds.

Judah saw Mohamed as clearly as at any time in their lives. He saw how his friend had aged, the mustache white, face weary from the long, difficult flight via Egypt by private Company plane. Judah felt perfectly able to form all the words he wanted in his mind, but he was not really sure if he had actually spoken them. The trouble was that Mohamed kept talking right through what Judah was trying to say.

"I see you've gone into the florist business. Appropriate for an old gangster, eh? They say you'll be up and about in time for the next Olympics."

Cut the bedside chatter, will you? I'll be damned lucky to ever set foot on the floor again. The words rang only in Judah's head, but Mohamed seemed to understand anyway.

"Look, Judah, I didn't take that rotten long plane trip just to watch you being pampered by beautiful nurses." The Arab's face grew serious. "I came to apologize for a terrible wrong I have done you."

3

*Yes, I forgive you, Mohamed. And I agree, it was the
stupidest conclusion you ever jumped to. But it's in the past.
Everything is now. I bear you no grudge. . . .* Only Judah's
expression told Mohamed what was needed. He smiled.

"Then, we are again friends?"

Friends. Jew and Arab. A friendship that had bridged all
the chasms of their days across a widening gulf of worlds. It
had begun in the sun-splashed streets of their ancient city,
Jerusalem. Always there was the closeness of knowing, caring—
even through anger when all that had been between them
seemed forever lost in the rising tides of change.

Toward what?

Soon Mohamed Hammadi would stand before that newly
founded body of nations—called "United"—opposing everything Judah had fought to bring about.

If not Palestine—where, then? The moon?

Judah was unable now to counter with his own arguments.
Reason. Logic. No matter; others could carry on that battle.
Between him and the Arab, all that need remain was love and
memory.

Mohamed blew a perfect smoke ring, letting it drift upward,
change shape, disintegrate. The room smelled of medication
and now the more pungent aroma of his fine cigar. "We have
both lost so much. We are a pair of bankrupts in life. Everything given—everything taken away." He rose. "Now you
must really sleep. And without a troubled mind." He smiled,
and for a moment he was to Judah the young Mohamed,
fearless, unconquerable.

Judah closed his eyes. Their meeting had been a great
strain. And yet he felt his own strength returning.

Mohamed moved quietly from the room.

Judah was already asleep.

One _____

WHO could be certain, that Saturday morning at nine o'clock, January 5, 1895, whether the French artillery captain was marched out to be decorated, or shot? Unless, of course, one had been following the events so highly played up in the Paris newspapers. Evidently the crowd pressing against the railings of the courtyard of the École Militaire, had. They were at this moment poised in tense expectation—an audience who had waited too long for the third-act denouement of a play.

This "stage" had a cast of thousands: an entire French division formed up in an open square five thousand strong in crimson kepis and blue tunics, with the longest bayonets in Europe and the shortest memories—of a war too recently lost against the Prussians. At their center sat a general astride a steaming mount—an imposing figure, stiff with gold braid and authority.

The French captain was of slight build and no more than five feet ten. Short gray hair, going bald in front, now hidden beneath the peak of his military cap, made him appear a good ten years older than his mid-thirties. Against the somber formality of the École Militaire, a small group of privileged spectators watched beneath umbrellas. The captain was marched between four officers to the center of the square and halted before the general, who leaned forward, wiping the rain from his thick mustache.

"Alfred Dreyfus, you are unworthy to bear arms. In the name of the French Republic, I degrade you from your rank. Let the sentence be carried out."

Dreyfus held himself at crisp attention, peering up through pince-nez, voice tight with emotion. "I declare and solemnly swear that you are degrading an innocent man. Vive la France!"

The drums rolled. An officer stepped forward, impersonal, formal. As one following a prescribed, well-memorized ritual, he began to deface the captain's immaculate tunic. The golden epaulets were ripped from the shoulders, the cap tossed aside, the gleaming buttons torn off. Finally, the sword was unscabbarded and broken. A ritual humiliation, ludicrous had it not been accompanied by that steady, persistent roll of drums, adding a terrible solemnity and suspense, as though presaging some death-defying feat of acrobatics: one man hurling himself against some dooming force of official gravity—beyond hope of mercy or salvation.

In a few moments it was over. Dreyfus, divested of all marks of rank and service, was marched around the square of troops through a gauntlet of insults, pausing at one point to wipe spittle from his pince-nez.

"I forbid you to insult me," he said. "Vive la France!"

The military spectacle was finished. Handcuffs were snapped onto his wrists. Civilian police took charge of the prisoner. Behind him now, all the years of careful, devoted service. Ahead, Devil's Island. The play was over.

But not for the audience. The normally stolid bourgeoisie pressed and shoved against the railings, petty clerks in respectable black city suits and shiny stiff collars, plump, self-righteous housewives—metamorphosed into one powerful voice clamoring for blood. Not just for the blood of one man.

"Death to all Jews!"

The crowd seemed to have taken on a life of its own. Dreyfus had already vanished into the gray edifice of the École Militaire. The troops were being marched away, bayonets damp in the soft rain of that cold winter's day.

On the perimeter of that crowd, a few were not shouting. They were frozen by the spectacle. Among those few was a foreigner, a Jewish student. Judah Nouari had only one thought: to get away! But Judah found himself sucked into a frenzied whirlpool, shoved forward and backward in a swirling eddy of bodies. Shouting men beat their way forward with umbrellas. Judah was knocked to his knees. He might have been trampled under, had not a steadying hand grasped his arm firmly and hauled him to his feet.

"This is no place for you or for me, my friend." The resonant voice sounded close to his ear within the clamorous wave. Judah looked up. The face was familiar, intense, serious-eyed above a full beard. A hint of thick black hair beneath a well-worn soft felt hat. The student knew who the man was. A journalist. They had met at the home of Baron Liebermann, but he couldn't recall the man's name, only the piercing eyes, the rich voice.

"I have a carriage waiting. This way, Judah. Hurry!" The younger man allowed himself to be guided away. Behind them, lethargic gendarmes were not overexerting themselves. Riots had always been the cathartic of the populace.

Judah sank onto the leather carriage seat. He brushed the mud from his trousers. He eyed the older man, who was staring out the window in thoughtful silence. The sound of the crowd receded into the clop-clop of hoofs and the bump of wheels over the rain-slick cobbles. Now that danger was past, Judah could feel anger rising. "The whole world knows that Dreyfus is innocent!"

"Perhaps. Perhaps not. Perhaps only you and I know, Judah. And Captain Dreyfus himself. And the real traitor, whoever he may be."

The young man's voice rose almost out of control. "It is not bad enough that one Jew was convicted and sentenced to life on Devil's Island. No, that one could expect from the military. But the fury of that crowd!"

A sad smile touched the journalist's lips. "Citizens of the most enlightened city in Europe . . . prepared to murder every Jew in France because one captain who happened to be a Jew might have been a traitor."

"Yes, yes. Precisely the point, sir!" Judah exploded. "If a Frenchman steals—he is a thief. If a Jew steals—he is a thieving Jew! *We* bear the guilt. We, like the carpenter's son, are expected to die for all mankind. We are punished for the crime of being born Jews. And yet, sir, and yet . . . hardly any of us can even agree what a Jew is! A faith? A political party? A heritage? A race?" Embarrassed at having unburdened himself of so much sound and fury to a virtual stranger, Judah fell silent. Still, the stranger had remembered his name. He returned to the subject. "But surely you believe Dreyfus is innocent?"

The older man—not so old, actually, just coming into his mid-thirties—sighed. A journalist knew the ways of the world. This one had grown up in the little cosmos of the Austro-Hungarian Empire. A continent within a continent. A political union of diverse populations—old as Rome, passionate as the hordes that had once banged sabers on the gates of Vienna, sophisticated and cynical as that parade of sycophants and courtiers who studied survival and prosperity under the Hapsburgs. Oh, yes, Middle Europe was a fine school in which to study man—and form conclusions.

"I ask myself . . . would a Jew who makes a successful career in the French Army, who distinguishes himself by his performance of duty, who has become assimilated in his habits, his beliefs, his whole way of feeling and thinking until he is more French than Jewish, more patriot than zealot . . . is it possible that such a man—who has not even any need of money—could become a spy?"

The student shook his head. He had asked himself the same question. He had even skipped lectures at the university so that he could attend the trial. Until it had been closed to the public. The journalist answered the question in Judah's mind: "They had to close the trial. The evidence was manufactured. The schedule that was supposed to have been in his hand-writing—the 'Bordereau.' . . . Even the handwriting experts would not agree that it was Dreyfus's."

"But why, sir? Why?"

The older man smiled, lighting a thin cigar. "You—a Jew—can ask such a question? You were born in Jerusalem, were you not?"

"I hardly see what difference that should make," Judah replied.

"You will. If you remain in France." The journalist noted his companion's handsome features: straight nose, thick black eyelashes. Semitic. Or Roman? Or Greek? Or Arab? It was all one. The kiss of the Mediterranean on the faces of its children. "Where can I drop you?" he asked.

Judah took out his fine gold watch, opening the case to glance at the Roman-numeraled circle of time. "A friend is waiting for me in the Place de l'Opéra. Anywhere near there will do."

The journalist passed the instructions on to the coachman, then settled back into silence, studying the plumes of his own smoke.

"What, then, is the answer, sir?" Judah ventured.

"Answer to what?"

"To being a Jew?"

"Two alternatives. The first: total assimilation. Intermarriage. Abandonment of the faith."

"Not a very religious answer," Judah said.

The man smiled. "I did not suggest that it was. Only practical. Economic. Political."

"But that alternative would require the cooperation of the Christians, would it not?" Judah asked.

The older man nodded. "And in some cases the *goyim* have very long memories. Back to another trial where the evidence was also falsified, and for lack of a Devil's Island, an innocent Jew was made to bear his own cross." Judah could see the older man's eyes narrow as though looking past some horizon of the mind.

"You said there were two alternatives, sir?"

The man pulled on the cigar. In his answer there was also a question. "Self-preservation, my friend. Unity. The unity that comes from belonging to a nation of people." He turned sharply to Judah. "I met you at Marcel Liebermann's. You are staying with him?"

Judah nodded. "Baron Liebermann is an old friend of my father's."

The journalist smiled. "Marcell. It used to be 'Moishe.' But then, it didn't use to be Baron. What about that young friend of yours? An Arab, is he not?"

Judah nodded. "Our fathers are partners. We grew up together. But you are most observant, to even have noticed us."

"A tool of my trade." The voice trailed off like the passage of some foreign spirit returning to another layer of knowing. "What is his name?"

"Mohamed Hammadi. We came from Jerusalem together." He avoided going into details of the family business founded by their grandfathers, or the curious history of the donkey and cart and how it had become a trademark that had endured for fifty prosperous years. "We are invited to stay with the Baron's family until we complete our examinations at the university."

"The Baron's hospitality is as well known as his bank. You are lucky. . . ." The carriage pulled to a halt and the older man opened the door.

Judah paused before stepping out. "I should be interested to hear more of your ideas, sir."

"Perhaps one day—when I'm more sure of them myself. But don't discuss them with the Baron and Baroness. It won't increase your popularity. And do give them my respects. They are almost the perfect example of my first alternative."

"Assimilation . . . And you think that bad?"

"Not at all. But, in the end, will it be enough?"

Judah cleared his throat with some embarrassment. "Sir— it is stupid of me—but I'm afraid I don't recall your name."

The journalist smiled. "No reason why you should. Am I a beautiful young girl? The name is Herzl. Theodor Herzl."

"I won't forget it again. You remembered mine—when we had met only once."

"Can one forget the name of his own tribe?" Herzl asked gently.

Judah tipped his hat to his benefactor and climbed down. "Thank you for getting me out of trouble."

"Oh, I am much more likely to get you *into* trouble! If we should meet again." Herzl closed the door, tapped his umbrella on the roof of the carriage. It pulled away.

Judah crossed the boulevard to an empty line of marble-topped tables under the dripping canopy of the restaurant. Flower boxes being watered by nature showed no blooms that day. Judah entered the humming, smoky room. A few late customers still lingered over morning coffee and brioches, reading newspapers on long sticks from the wall rack. He found Mohamed Hammadi at a corner table, as always dressed with great elegance, shiny black hair carefully parted and pomaded. Large eyes, brown as olives, took in his approach with lively affection and a touch of annoyance.

"One hour I have been waiting! If I had known, I could have brought my books, or at least found some amusing company. Or stayed in bed a little longer."

"Sorry, Mohamed. But it wasn't entirely my fault." Judah dropped into the chair and signaled the waiter, who came over surly from scooping up a meager tip. "Brandy. Cognac."

"So early in the day? There is no hope for you infidels," Mohamed chided.

"Even less for the world. . . ." Judah frowned.

The young Arab—only a year older than Judah—fixed a long Turkish cigarette into an amber holder. He lit it carefully with a phosphorous match. "I admit that outside there is rain—enough to bring gloom to the heart of any Palestinian.

But since today we have no lectures, Judah, did we not agree to visit the Goupil Gallery this afternoon?''

"What for?''

"To feast our eyes on the naughty posters of this French dwarf who gets his inspiration from brothels and music halls. Like us.''

Everyone was talking about the daring work of Toulouse-Lautrec, and Judah himself had suggested the visit. But now the stubborn, troubling ghost, the face of Dreyfus, the voices, the ugly tide of hatred, had wiped it quite out of his mind.

Mohamed listened with mild interest while Judah described Dreyfus's humiliation.

"You take the incident far too personally,'' Mohamed said. "After all, the uncircumcised followers of the Prince of Peace have always needed somebody to persecute. Did the crusaders not practice by slaughtering the local Jews before setting off to slaughter us Arabs? The only thing that saved us from being wiped off the face of history was that we became better at slaughter than they were. A lion is a lion—and a lamb is a lamb; so let us talk of more important things: like how to cure the boredom of this Saturday night in Paris.''

Despite himself, Judah was forced to smile. He could never make Mohamed take life as seriously as he thought it should be taken. "What did you have in mind?'' he asked.

"I suggest we punish ourselves with a brief visit to Fernando's Circus,'' Mohamed replied. "Then to Maxim's, to force down a Caneton aux Cerises, soaked in cognac. Then perhaps an absinthe—for which Allah forgive me—at the Mirliton and on to the Moulin de la Galette for a bit of low life. If we endure all that, we may end up in bed, and not alone.''

To Mohamed, the two years he had spent in Paris were an advance taste of paradise. Paris turned everyone into a Parisian. One dared forget the dietary laws, his religion's ban on alcohol, the five ritual prayers to be said each day. Mohamed had stored away his customary observances with the loose, flowing robes he'd left behind in his father's house. Perhaps every man must have two countries: his own—and France, he thought.

•   •   •

His own—their own—the land, always the land. Promised to Moses, and used by almost everyone else. Persians, Greeks, Romans, Arabs, French, Turks. Palestine had seemed at times a railway station of history; harsh as the anger of God, yet coveted by so very many peoples in passage. Whole civilizations lay in layers beneath its sands. But, on the face of it, the place appeared always changeless and unchanged.

That was how Musa Hammadi had seen it some fifty years before, in 1843. Musa was Mohamed's grandfather.

Not that Musa ever thought very deeply about the past these days. The land was there, just as he was there—by the will of Allah—and one had to make the best of it. One had to keep the laws and try to survive. And so he had, for sixty-nine years. Time enough for Musa to count births and deaths, until the shallow graves of his father's fathers seemed to outnumber the stars. Time enough to see the family fortunes rise to such peaks of plenty that his grandson could be sent off like some Arab prince to attend a university in France.

The Hammadis had come from Tiberias, and could trace themselves back to the time of Saladin, the Saracen warrior who had fought, and occasionally defeated, Richard the Lion-Hearted. Musa had never known his mother, who had died giving birth to him. When Musa was only two years old, the Turks ended the possibility of his ever knowing his father by flogging him to death for killing one of their soldiers. It was never clear to Musa why his father had killed the Turk—but it was very clear that his father was dead. Try as he might, he had never been able to bring a sure image to mind of this violent parent. The mustached features always dissolved into the face of his own grandfather. Grandfather "Abu," wise man of the village. Musa could still recall people coming to the old man to settle disputes. When not handing out judicial decisions, Abu had been a farmer; but he sowed more of his own seed than melons. Under the olive and fig trees, Musa had shared his childhood with a swarm of cousins. Then, when Musa was sixteen, wisdom died; and it seemed that his grandfather had not been wise enough to foresee that without his venerable protection, Musa was just another mouth to feed. Aunts and uncles, whose seed had also multiplied exceedingly, offered Musa his birthright: the oldest cart on the farm, and the meanest donkey.

That donkey! Tears of laughter came to Musa's eyes when

he thought of him. Named Eblis—the Devil—because that donkey made life hell for anyone who tried to put him to use! Perhaps with a shading of guilt, the uncles stocked Musa's cart with jars of olive oil, olives, dates, figs, and goat cheeses bound into leaves to preserve them from the scorching sun and the plague of flies. Musa tied a turquoise-colored bead painted with a large black eye between Eblis's ears to protect the donkey from the evil eye—though it seemed much more likely that Eblis would *give* the evil eye than receive it. The fattest uncle made the first speech.

"You are sixteen, Musa. The age of a warrior who may fight and win battles in the great world. We have been generous in memory of your father, who, it must be confessed, was not always as generous as ourselves, may Allah rest him in paradise."

Another uncle offered guidance from the fourth sura of the Koran: ". . . Believe in God and his Apostle and the Book which He hath sent down to His Apostle and the scripture which he sent down formerly. Whosoever believeth not in God and His Angels and His Books and His Apostles and the Last Day, hath strayed far from the Truth."

Having delivered themselves of charity and faith, his uncles pointed Musa on the road to Jerusalem, where his hopes could become his fortune. For several days, Musa traveled along the road, speaking to no one, feeling safer in the hills at night than in the villages, slaking his thirst at every friendly well and nursing the resources of his waterskin in between. But, for all of his diligence, he was making poor progress. His arms ached from pulling the reluctant Eblis. Dust thickened on his robe and feet. He had become careless with the prescribed number of his daily prayers.

And then Eblis, in his most diabolical mood, backed the cart into a ditch. Musa heaved and pulled. Then he tried pushing and rocking the cart. This might even have succeeded, except that a wheel split. Vainly he tried to repair the damage, but the ancient wood was too rotten. It was hopeless! The donkey brayed at him in malicious triumph. Despair seized Musa. And then rage. He considered beating Eblis to death—even selected the murder weapon: a spoke from the broken wheel. There would be justice in the act!

But not wisdom. In death, Eblis would be even more the victor. Better to make the devil pay for his crime, decided

Musa, unloading the cart and carefully tying the heavy jars
and bundles to the wretched beast's back. He left open one
bag of dates, to feed himself. And then with the wheel spoke
as inducement, he persuaded Eblis to move toward Jerusalem.
But now it was even harder to drag his overladen donkey, and
Jerusalem seemed to be receding as a possibility.

That night, sleeping under the stars, he considered turning
back. But he knew he would be as welcome as the plague.
Failures were not honored among the descendants of Saladin's
warriors. A lesser youth might well have given way to tears.
But Musa turned his mind to the storytellers. He thought of
that legendary ancestor whose curved sword could slice a
silken scarf floating leaflike in the air. Could the descendant
of such a hero be defeated by the whims of a diabolical
donkey? So he clenched his teeth and counted the stars dancing in their fixed patterns like the houris of paradise.

Next morning, he took to the road, dragging Eblis. Allah
rewarded his courage. There, ahead of him, swathed in dust,
two youthful figures were dragging a cart. One looked no
older than he; one, much younger. The cart was almost new.
As he drew nearer, Musa called out a greeting in Arabic.

The two boys beamed at him with faces as dusty as his
own. They returned the greeting in Arabic, although they
were Jews. The eldest, Abraham, introduced himself. Their
family name was Nouari. Abraham was eighteen; his brother,
Jacob, ten. In their cart they had pots, pans, needles, thread,
and even two valuable bolts of cloth that they were hoping to
peddle through the villages along the road. Musa, anxious to
make a good impression, pretended he knew the road well.

"These villages are as poor as my own. You will find a
better price for your goods in Jerusalem. But, of course, you
could not reach there with only a cart and no donkey to pull
it."

"Have you been there?" asked Abraham, impressed.

Musa shifted his glance. It would be necessary to preserve
his status as a man of the world. "Who has not been to
Jerusalem has seen from only one eye—as my grandfather
always said."

Abraham offered to share some unleavened bread. The
Arab lad graciously accepted. In return, he offered dates and
figs. The three sat down under an acacia tree near the remains
of an ancient wall. Musa squinted up at the sun. It must be

approaching the noon hour. He anointed himself sparingly from his waterskin. A splash on the face and hands, a drop on the feet. Though he had grown lax about his prayers, in the presence of Jews it seemed more important. He excused himself politely and began the simple ritual of the seven movements.

"*Allahu akbar,*" he said with his hands open on each side of his face. Then he recited the *fatihah,* for which he stood upright. He bowed from the hips, straightened, and then slowly fell to his knees and made a first prostration with face to the ground. Musa sat back on his haunches. Then a second prostration. His new friends watched without comment until he had finished. They respected his act of faith. They said the *beruchah* over their own food. Then all settled down to eat.

"Where is your grandfather?" inquired Jacob.

"In paradise. I am sure his soul was admitted into heaven without any waiting. The Koran lists seven heavens. My grandfather would be in the best one."

"You are lucky," replied Abraham. "We Jews have only one heaven, and from what I've seen, almost nobody I know could ever get in there." Indeed, Abraham had seen too much to be contained in a mere eighteen years. The last two of those years, hauling that cart, had given him the strength of a young Samson. The sight of his powerful shoulders would deter the most aggressive thieves. When he smiled—which hadn't been too often of late—his teeth showed fine and even against sun-bronzed features. His nose was small, straight, flaring to thin nostrils; his look was weighted with responsibility, for now he was the sole support of mother and younger brother. Anyone who might threaten Jacob would face the lion with the cub.

For generations, the men of the Nouari family had been tinkers. They had migrated from Baghdad to Palestine more than a hundred years before. The boys' father had left a family circle of brothers in Beth-Shemesh with the vow never to speak to any of them again—which suited Abraham's uncles perfectly. Rifts in Jewish families run deep as the hatred of Cain for Abel: doors never to be darkened; thresholds never to be crossed. Well, let the old men nurse their hatreds, their vows of silence. It was all behind him now—buried in wheel dust.

For, by the age of ten, Abraham was already on the road,

helping his father peddle their wares with a cart and a fine, strong donkey. His father managed to make a living, but he also made life hell for his family. There was a smoldering fire in the man that could explode into beatings and rages directed against anyone who crossed his path. After Abraham was born, his mother, a gentle woman, had suffered three miscarriages. Then Abraham's only sister died. So Jacob's arrival came as a blessing. Two sons now! And the two had grown close in defense against their father's tyrannies and senseless furies. It was as though the world was too small to contain such a man. A man who needed a bigger life than a cart full of pots and pans, he would bellow at the firmament like some Old Testament prophet thundering at the stars when he and Abraham had bedded down beside some wilderness road. A man who might have helped to forge a nation, had he not been born half a century too soon!

And then, one day, as he was trundling his cart through Gibeon, a brick fell off a wall and killed Abraham and Jacob's father. Everything about his life had failed him, even his death.

Abraham had never learned to love that father; but he could miss him. Now life was harder still. When they'd been forced to sell the donkey, Abraham had taken its place between the shafts, with little Jacob running along beside him ringing a bell to call the wares. Two years, and they were still unable to buy another donkey.

Now Jacob's eyes turned longingly to Musa's beast. "What's his name?" he inquired.

"Eblis," Musa replied, adding quickly, "a noble name."

"Does that not mean . . . the Devil?" asked Abraham.

"The name is a joke of my grandfather's," the Arab boy assured him. "Eblis has a nature as meek and mild as the Angel Azrael, who stands beside the throne of Allah." He paused, eyes on Abraham's cart, weighing whether or not all of his goods would fit into it. "Now, if my fine donkey were to be hitched to your cart," he ventured, "the three of us could reach Jerusalem with no difficulty."

The Jewish boys considered the suggestion. It had already occurred to them, but in business it didn't do to be too eager. "He doesn't look strong enough to pull the extra weight," said Abraham.

"He's strong enough! Though I'll admit he needs a bit of

coaxing. But my grandfather always said the donkey that needs no coaxing is dead! Is it not so?'' Musa hastily transferred his goods from the donkey's back into the cart. Then he came up behind the animal, giving him a sharp suggestion with the wheel spoke. Eblis turned his head to the boy and showed his teeth. Musa smiled at his companions and tried again, a shade less gently, to move Eblis into the cart shafts. The donkey would not budge a hoof. Musa brought the wheel spoke down again, hard, on its flank. ''Cloven-hoofed son of a staggering lump of snail manure! Move, will you!'' Then he turned apologetically with a limp smile. ''It's most unusual for him to be quite so stubborn.''

''He probably doesn't like being beaten,'' Jacob said, going to the donkey and stroking his head.

''Why shouldn't he like it? He's always been beaten,'' Musa replied with the plain logic of the desert. But Jacob had begun whispering into the twitching, furry ear. Eblis flicked off a colony of flies with his tail and twisted his head toward the small boy, listening. Jacob whispered a few words more; then, with a gentle pat, backed Eblis between the shafts of the cart. He fastened the harness straps, and at Jacob's touch the donkey moved forward, drawing the cart on down the road.

''Come on, then!'' he called to the others. ''We're going to Jerusalem!''

In absolute wonder, Musa fell into step beside his new friends. Surely there must be mysteries in the world beyond his knowledge. ''What did you do to make him go? You must know better curses than I,'' Musa said with admiration.

''Not curses, Musa. I told him a story. Of Balaam and his ass. How the Lord opened the mouth of the ass to speak.''

''Why would He do a thing like that?'' asked Musa.

''The ass had seen the Angel of the Lord, and Balaam had not,'' Jacob answered, switching flies away from the donkey.

''Hmmm,'' said Musa. ''Such a story is not to be found in the Koran. Perhaps Eblis is a Jewish donkey!''

''What does it matter?'' laughed Abraham. ''As long as Jacob can persuade him to serve us all.''

The three boys didn't know it at that moment, but a partnership had been launched. It was to grow and span the years until, by 1895, their grandchildren would be heirs to a trading empire with ever-expanding interests. Known throughout the Middle East, with head offices in Jerusalem and branches in Damascus and Cairo, their trademark—even on their banking houses—would remain a donkey and a cart. Like the green bay tree, the partnership flourished exeedingly.

Judah Nouari surveyed his new office in the Liebermann Bank of Paris. A sumptuous setting for a rising young captain of finance. Well, "promising" might be more appropriate, since he was scarcely a few months out of the university. Here he would be expected to master the complexities of the international circulation of money: the blood flow of capital, percentages, loans, collaterals, investments. And here he must cross the mysterious invisible bridge from student to man of affairs. He glanced about the room. Too sumptuous for his own taste, really. He would have to grow into it.

Standing at his desk, Judah could just catch a glimpse of the parade of carriages interspersed by an occasional brass-fitted automobile in the boulevard below. It was 1897. The world was changing. He should be grateful to his father for directing his career away from the stagnation of Palestine and into the seething hub of financial Paris. But the responsibility was terrifying.

He turned his attention back to the portrait of Grandfather Abraham. It had been painted on the old man's last trip to France, and Judah had never much liked it. The artist's attempt at flattery had removed all character from his grandfather's craggy features. It diminished the stature of a man who had built an empire from a peddler's cart. But it had taken great persuasion to get Grandfather Abraham to pose for it at all.

The portrait was hoisted carefully by the concierge and his helper, positioned between portraits of Great-uncle Jacob and Judah's father, David, Abraham's eldest son. Three forebears to peer critically at the newest Nouari to take his place in the Hammadi-Nouari holdings. If only Judah could take things more in his stride, like Mohamed, who seemed to revel in any challenge.

"A little to the right," suggested Judah, making a quick eye measure of the distance. The man edged the painting along the wall a few inches.

"Now, monsieur?"

"Yes, perfect."

They lowered the portrait to the thick red carpet and drove a nail halfway in where a thumb had marked the position on the wall. Judah suddenly felt the weight of three sets of eyes upon him. He turned away and caught an image of himself in a mirror, straightened his shoulders, and ran his index finger along the thickening new mustache. But it didn't help.

An efficient knock announced his secretary. Trim, middle-aged, well starched, virginal. She had been selected by the Baron as a suitable guide dog into the monetary maize, now that the Hammadi-Nouari interests had acquired one third of the Baron's bank.

"Your eleven o'clock appointment, monsieur."

He stepped back to his desk, glancing at the open page of his diary. It was empty except for eleven o'clock, with the notation: "Zosia Halevi: Reference, Dr. Herzl." No doubt one of those boring fanatical Zionists with a hand outstretched for contributions.

"I shall wish to be interrupted in exactly five minutes. Remind me that Monsieur Hammadi is waiting in the conference room."

"But Monsieur Hammadi is in Brussels today."

"Yes, well, think of something." Judah took his place behind the polished but empty desk. His secretary signaled the concierge and his helper to leave, and followed them out. She returned a moment later with a young woman.

"Mademoiselle Halevi," she announced. The visitor stood planted firmly in the doorway, seemingly reluctant to enter the room.

"It is Judah Nouari I have come to see. The banker," she said.

Judah rose, coming around the desk. "Judah Nouari is standing before you, mademoiselle."

She peered at him doubtfully. "Are the Nouaris so rich, then, that they can make bankers of children?"

"Their own children." Her rudeness amused him. "Though offices can be deceiving. I'm merely an apprentice banker." He noted her high cheekbones, pale skin, enormous almond-shaped eyes. Were they green . . . or gray? Difficult to tell.

Judah came over and offered her a chair. The young woman sat down quickly, gripping the arms as though he might have intended dragging her out of it. He chose a tall chair facing her and let the tips of his fingers touch each other, as he had

seen the Baron do when interviewing an unpredictable client.
He cleared his throat. "If Mademoiselle will explain how I
may be of assistance?"

"For three weeks I have been trying to see you! But, of
course, you are a very busy man." There was more than a
slight edge to her tone.

"The pressures of commerce. But now you are here,
mademoiselle—with an introduction from Dr. Herzl. And
how is the good doctor?"

"First, I must tell you"—she smoothed her skirt with the
flat of her hand—"that I am Jewish . . . and I am proud of
it!"

"I wouldn't have guessed it. I mean, it is nothing of great
importance." He felt annoyed that she was making him sound
like a fool, the way she held his glance with those powder-
gray eyes, shuffled his words into confusion.

"You, too, are Jewish. Though you are an 'oriental' Jew—
since you come from Palestine."

"You know a great deal about me, mademoiselle."

"The Nouaris are well known . . . for their wealth."

"I hope . . . not only for that!"

"Monsieur, have you ever thought what it means to be
born a Jew?"

"Well, I've never regarded it as a matter of life or
death. . . ." He had meant this as a joke, but she did not
smile.

"For too many of our people, monsieur, it can mean life or
death. But for those of us who live in safety, it is sometimes
easy to be ashamed of our heritage." There was something
aggressive in her tone, as though she expected to be challenged at every turn.

"I'm sure I've never been ashamed of mine," he replied,
annoyed at finding himself on the defensive.

"Yes, you are one of the lucky ones. You who have a
home in Palestine. And a fine position in Paris! You can
choose the world you wish to live in. But most Jews are not
so fortunate!"

Judah had been right. She was going to touch him for a
contribution. Herzl's cause was a bottomless pocket. The
good doctor nudged one's conscience. But this girl—she
attacked with a battering ram. Though far above average in
looks, she seemed to be doing everything to make herself

appear plain. Her hair flew wildly in all directions, her severe dull gray serge suit looked as though she'd slept in it. Her high-collared blouse was frayed at the edges. Her shoes were scuffed. She was too thin. Yes, and her nails were bitten. Yet she radiated an excitement, a glow of inner fire that made it difficult for Judah to take his eyes from her.

"You who have a home in Palestine . . . answer me one thing. Have you ever heard of the Choveve Zion? The Lovers of Zion. No, of course you have not! You are too busy enjoying your position, your power"—she indicated the room—"to care what happens to your own people."

"My people?" he asked. "Why mine? People belong to where they live. To where their careers take them. To their families, their work, their interests."

"Then you, Monsieur Nouari, belong only to the vault of a Paris bank." Her accent was curious. Polish, or Russian?

"I am sure Dr. Herzl didn't send you here to insult me, mademoiselle. He was quite friendly when we last met."

Her eyes fixed him. She looked as though she might spit in his face. "Have you ever been caught in a pogrom? Ever had the Cossacks burn the roof down over your head? Ever had to flee your country?" She struggled to compose herself. "Yes, I am here for Dr. Herzl. Yes, we want something from you! But no more than to put one hand in your pocket. From others we might ask more. Much more. But first we must raise a great deal of money."

He smiled. "So behind all the rudeness is a begging bowl?"

She shrugged. "Why not? And why not you? We are getting support from Rothschild, from Montefiore. Even your Baron Liebermann has given—though he asked that the gift remain anonymous."

"Then, you shouldn't have told me." He smiled. "The Baron is a man of discretion. A banker's trait. It is also a banker's policy to ask what the money is for," he added.

"Zionism."

He sighed. "Yes, of course. It would be that."

"Have you read Theodor Herzl's pamphlet *Der Judenstaat?* No, of course not."

"You know, from the moment you walked in here, you haven't asked me one question that you haven't yourself answered. And you do me a disservice, mademoiselle. I *have* read *The Jewish State*. And I admire Dr. Herzl. In fact, he once saved me from being trampled in the street. Yes, I admire him. A man of fine ideas. But not really practical. A new Jewish homeland? Where? What country is going to offer shelter to a reunion of strangers from all over the world? People who have nothing in common with each other except religion. What has a rug merchant from Baghdad to say to a peasant from the steppes of Russia?"

"They don't need words. They share the curse of anti-Semitism from the hour of their birth. And not only Jews are concerned by it. Zola speaks out for Dreyfus. George Eliot wrote *Daniel Deronda* to direct the attention of the world to our cause. Catholics, Orthodox Russians, Lutherans, Christians in every land concern themselves with our problem. Can a Jew do less?"

"The Jewish problem was not made by Jews. And it will not be solved by Jews," Judah pronounced, fingering his mustache.

"You think we are all too divided by self-interest, like you and your friends? Too willing to assimilate and be forgotten? Well, I'll tell you something. That will never be. Because the anti-Semites will not allow it!"

"And Herzl's answer is Zionism? It has never worked. One might as well throw money into the Seine."

She lifted her chin defiantly. "We shall hold our first international Jewish Congress at Basel next month."

How old was she? Maybe twenty-three or twenty-four. It was hard to say. The lack of personal vanity—so unlike the women Judah had known in the salons and ballrooms of Paris, or the girls in Palestine, protected in the prisons of their families until marriage released them like lambs to the slaughter. The slaughter of the innocents in planned marriage contracts. But this girl! This girl made her own destiny. He longed to ask her questions. Discover more about her. How she had become so serious, so dedicated.

A discreet tap brought the secretary peering around the door. "Your conference with Monsieur Hammadi, sir. You asked to be reminded."

He glanced at her with some annoyance. "Oh, yes. Tell him . . . I'll be a bit late. Tell him to begin without me."

The secretary looked puzzled, then shrugged and closed the door.

"Well . . . what will you do?"

"Perhaps more than give money, mademoiselle. I might even attend your conference. I must be in Zurich anyway, and I could spare a day or two in Basel. I should like to see Dr. Herzl again."

"Why, monsieur?" She leaned forward. He suppressed a mad desire to touch her.

"Curiosity. To see where my investment is going."

For a moment he was not even sure that she had heard him. She seemed to be listening to another voice, within herself. "Palestine. . . . To you, it is only a birthplace." Something of the sternness went out of her face. Her hands relaxed into her lap. Even her voice seemed changed. "The storm bursts on the face of the sea," she said. "But the wind spreads its wings above my homeland. For I shall live high on the hills of Zion, and my heart will forget the troubled voices. Cry, oh, cry, my people. Let your voices echo in all the caverns of the land. Though we have never seen you, still do we reach toward you through our prayers."

"Who wrote that?" he asked.

"I did," she said.

Two _____

FROM an ascension balloon it would have looked like a vast garden of flowers peppered with licorice drops. Then, as one descended, the bobbing blooms would have been transformed into varicolored bonnets and tall silk hats.

Flags and pennants sucked the breeze above the great open grandstand that was Chantilly in 1897, first among palaces of the sport of kings when kings were still available for sport. A sun dance of silver and brass from the military band trailed a waltz of Offenbach in a gala of rhythm. Gentlemen, impeccable in black frock coats, gray waistcoats, and slim trousers promenaded gaudy butterfly ladies in silks and cambrics—who flirted parasols above arched glances and whispered behind kid gloves. Binoculars pivoted to fasten on distant glossy horses being formed up at the starting line with no little difficulty by jockeys in carnival-colored silks that marked their stables.

Baron Liebermann leaned brass binoculars across the railing of his box for a closer look at his horse, Vau-l'eau. Over his shoulder he addressed his guest of the day, Mohamed Hammadi. The young Arab was clean-shaven, darkly handsome, perfectly attired; suit fashioned in London by the same tailor who outfitted H.R.H. the Prince of Wales.

"The finest British blood stock, Hammadi!" Liebermann confided. Vau-l'eau was the Baron's latest addition to a growing stable. Plum, crimson, and cerise were the racing colors sported by his jockey, who at the moment was fighting to keep the spirited Vau-l'eau under control. "He did well at the Grand St. Leger. I'm staking a packet on him today. One thousand louis-d'or!"

Mohamed leaned an elegant elbow on the railing. His

ever-ready self-assurance had mellowed with success in his position with Liebermann's bank. Now he could address the older man as a confidant—even an equal. "You know, Baron, all British blood stock comes from three Arab strains, so you may feel perfectly confident in your horse. I have, indeed, pledged an almost equal amount myself. And if Vau-l'eau wins, I hope you will do me the honor of accepting the finest magnum of champagne the Jockey Club can provide."

"And if he loses, a jeroboam. Curious they should choose such a name."

"Jeroboam? Where does the word come from, sir?"

"A king of Israel of the Jehu dynasty," Liebermann replied, adding quickly, "History has always been one of my hobbies."

But Mohamed's mind wasn't on wine or history. He had caught a glimpse of a profusion of golden ringlets beneath a crimson bed of silk poppies. The girl's beige silk tunic was trimmed with red velvet braiding in the style of a French hussar. Her eyes were green and restless—the eyes of a cat. Probably about eighteen. As the girl entered the next box, she caught Mohamed's glance, held it brazenly for an instant. "Magnificent . . ." he murmured.

The Baron nodded, confident the remark referred to Vau-l'eau. "If he wins, I'm entering him in the Grand Prix de Paris."

The girl was standing almost beside Mohamed now, separated only by the narrow wooden railing. He could not avoid listening had he wanted to—which he didn't. She was accompanied by a man and a woman in their early forties. Her parents? The woman looked something like her. A sister, perhaps?

"Which horse? Which horse?" the girl demanded, green eyes sparkling with excitement. The older woman gestured her parasol to the distant lineup and passed her dainty pair of mother-of-pearl opera glasses. "Number six. There. In the orange, green, and white, my dear."

"Marjolet . . . ! Oh, he is splendid! Coal black! Oh, he must win! Do put a bet on him for me, cousin!" She dipped into her small purse and gave some bills to the man. He drew out his gold-chained watch. "Just time." He excused himself, lifted his hat, and stepped out of the box.

Mohamed ventured another look at her tilted nose. Quite the most evocative thing he had ever seen. He could sense a streak of wildness and daring. An undercurrent of electricity. She was peering through the opera glasses, her breast lifted full and round on a frame that seemed almost too slight to support such bounty.

"But the jockey is so little!" she exclaimed. "He looks like a monkey riding an elephant!"

"My dear, you can't seat a big man on a racehorse. Think of the weight. Every gram slows him down," her cousin assured her.

Baron Liebermann touched Mohamed's arm with the gold head of his cane, feeling particularly expansive. "What a glorious day to be alive! I went this morning to Notre-Dame for morning Mass. Three duchesses beside me on their knees and the Prince de Condé. Quite an assembly. His Highness and I have a private bet on the race. 'Marcel,' he said. 'Marcel.' He calls me 'Marcel,' my Christian name." He flourished his cane like a scepter toward a box some distance away. "There he is—the Prince—with that handsome woman in blue. Not his wife, you understand."

"Naturally," smiled Mohamed. And the Western world was shocked when Moslems had three or four wives. Europeans kept mistresses in discreet apartments. Wasn't it more honest to accept man's polygamous nature as the will of God?

A sudden wave of excitement swept the crowd. The horses were off and away! The man from the next box bustled back. "Placed your bet just before they closed the window, Jacqueline. . . ." He gave her arm an avuncular squeeze.

The girl scarcely heard. "Come on, Marjolet! Come on . . . ! Come on . . . !" Her waving parasol barely missed Mohamed's hat. She was shrieking with exultation, while the Baron was shouting with careful dignity. "Vau-l'eau . . . ! Vau-l'eau! Faster, Vau-l'eau!" He turned to Mohamed. "What's that idiot jockey doing? Why doesn't he give him his head?"

"Holding him in for the bend, sir. Good strategy." Mohamed was wondering by what strategy he could effect an introduction to this delightful 'Jacqueline.' . . . His mind turned over the name, his eyes, her profile. She was trembling as Marjolet pounded up even with the lead horse.

Vau-l'eau was in fourth place. The Baron was losing his poise. "Use the whip, *Dummkopf!*" he shouted.

The horses thundered into the final stretch, a blaze of

colors and sweating, foam-flecked flanks. Vau-l'eau strained forward under the whip, but the Baron's jockey had plied it too late. The horse lunged into third position. Not quite good enough. *"Mamzer!"* shouted the Baron, then caught himself quickly. "A quaint German expression."

Marjolet pulled ahead by a nose, and then, with a burst of speed, won the race by half a length. Amid the shouts and cheers, Jacqueline went quite wild with excitement. She seized her cousin by the waist and danced her around the box with squeals of triumph. "We won! We won! We won! Oh, isn't he marvelous?"

"Contain yourself, cousin Jacqueline. You are making a spectacle," the older woman chided.

"We must go down to the paddock. I want to kiss him!"

"The horse—or the jockey?" The man smiled.

"The horse, of course, cousin Henri."

"You'll find him rather damp, I fear. But we should congratulate our jockey. A splendid win." He glanced across at the Baron, adding pointedly, "The interest on money lending will no doubt rise tomorrow."

As she turned to leave the box, Jacqueline's eyes met Mohamed's.

"Congratulations, mademoiselle," he dared venture. She had regained sufficient poise to avert her glance, but not before their eyes met. And Jacqueline had not missed noting that Mohamed was quite the most attractive man in the whole grandstand. Then she was whisked away with her cousins.

"To the paddock, Baron?" Mohamed suggested.

"No reason now," growled the Baron, tearing up his tickets.

"Oh, but you must have a word with your jockey, sir. The race would have been yours if he hadn't been so sparing with the whip."

"Yes, quite right. And then . . . a glass of champagne." The jeroboam had shrunk.

It didn't matter. Nothing did. In the mind of Mohamed only a single purpose remained. How to effect a meeting with that girl. An introduction. If need be, he would even ask the Baron's help. If the Baron had showed no sign of knowing his neighbors in the next box, the man certainly seemed to know the Baron. By name . . . by reputation . . . by bank.

Mohamed felt a definite surge of confidence. It was as

though a revelation of destiny had come to him, manifested as surely as fate sifted from grains of sand over fortune tellers' leathery palms for a few coppers at the Jerusalem gate. A mystical kind of knowing, of wanting, that reached deep into the roots of his desires and promised a sense of fulfillment. He was a man seeing reality through his dream. He smiled at the Baron, gesturing the older man ahead of him.

"I don't know what you are so happy about!" the Baron grumbled as they walked to the paddock. "You, too, lost a packet on that wretched race, Mohamed."

"What I lost, Baron, was only money. What I gained was my future."

The Baron snorted. An Arabic enigma, no doubt. But a future this handsome young Hammadi certainly would have! It had not escaped the Baron's attention that the Arab had a flair for finance. Yes, the Baron hated to admit it even to himself: Mohamed was proving shrewder in business than young Nouari. More adventurous, more daring, more imaginative . . . more self-confident. And he had a way of insinuating himself into the closed circles of French society that the Baron was forced to admire. An important area for a banker—and one that Judah showed little interest in. Of the two young men, the Jew seemed to be the slow starter.

"Monsieur and Madame Henri de St. Rimaud . . . and Mademoiselle Laville-Darlin!" piped the liveried majordomo.

Henri and his wife made an appropriately sedate entrance, enhanced by the dazzling beauty of their cousin, Jacqueline Laville-Darlin. Months had passed since that notable day at the races when they had met the Baron and young Hammadi in the paddock. And now they had accepted the Baron's invitation to a weekend of shooting, preceded by a formal ball to introduce his daughter Mimi to society—ready or not. His château, just outside Paris, was almost a miniature Versailles. Although they would have died before showing it, the St. Rimauds were duly impressed. Henri's eyes took in the wall of mirrors lining the ballroom, multiplying the dancing couples into a whirling ostentation of jewels and gowns.

"A Jewish Louis Quatorze," Henri whispered to his wife.

"Very grand," she granted. Henri shepherded the two ladies toward the receiving line. Host and hostess greeted guests, the Baroness a blaze of sapphires. Mimi Liebermann's gown was a confection of pink tulle encrusted with lavender roses and bows—a cake overpowered by icing. Henri could not resist another stage whisper: "The daughter could catch a fish with that nose!"

"More easily than a husband," his wife agreed.

"Don't be ridiculous. With his money, she'll land a prince." Henri cast a covetous glance at his wife's radiant cousin. He could not resist fondling her elbow as he guided her to the Baron. They were received with great warmth—a bit too expansive for Henri's conservative taste.

"Ah, St. Rimaud! So good of you to come! May I present my wife? My daughter, Mimi?"

"A great honor to be included, Monsieur le Baron," Henri managed.

Liebermann's eyes lingered for a moment on Jacqueline. "Your cousin is truly a jewel among women. Is she not, Sarah?"

The pillar of sapphires acquiesced.

Jacqueline smiled, her attention drifting toward the ballroom.

Liebermann indicated a long table of refreshments. They stepped out beneath a ceiling jeweled with chandeliers.

"From ghetto to gâteau—in one generation." Henri smirked.

"He did lend you money, my dear," his wife reminded him.

"At a damned good interest rate!" It annoyed him that the Jew—however converted—should have managed a title, and merely by contributing money for the reconstruction of a section of Paris damaged in the Franco-Prussian War. It annoyed him even more that he, Henri, along with Jacqueline's father, had been forced to go to the bank, hat in hand. They had sought and received an extremely generous loan from Baron Liebermann to complete the purchase of a new factory for the production of machine tools. That interest was involved placed the Baron hand in glove with Shylock. No, Henri could not be overgrateful to this converted Hebrew for the largesse—however swiftly the loan had been arranged. Henri's gratitude was reserved for Mohamed Hammadi, who had recommended and sponsored the loan at extremely favorable terms. This Arab had made a great impression on the two business partners. And apparently on Jacqueline, too.

Henri noted his young cousin's expectant air. She had

spotted Hammadi standing with a group near the punch bowl. And Mohamed had seen her, for he quickly excused himself and hurried toward them. He had used the ambitious manufacturer to wangle two dinner invitations.

Those two visits had only whetted Mohamed's interest in Jacqueline. She stood before him now, even more breathtaking than he remembered. In the St. Rimaud house, she had been part of the decor, like a stuffed bird under a glass dome. Tonight she was alive and independent, shimmering in emerald-green satin, hints of iridescent blue in its folds. A single large freshwater pearl accented a slender throat. Long white kid gloves, hair tamed by a band of green velvet ribbon, framed an ivory complexion. A man could drown in those quicksilver eyes. Eyes of the cat-woman, timeless as Eve, tantalizing the mind with mystery, promise, contradiction.

Mohamed bowed to the St. Rimauds, but his gaze didn't leave the girl. Jacqueline pretended surprise at finding him there, though she knew perfectly well he had engineered their invitation.

He swept her away on a tide of music. Henri's wife watched them, frowning. "I hope Jacqueline isn't becoming too interested in Hammadi. After all, Henri, we don't want her to end up in a harem."

"He and that Nouari fellow own a substantial share of the Baron's bank. The Hammadi-Nouari Trading Company . . . worth millions. Our cousin could do worse."

For some half hour, Mohamed had waltzed Jacqueline around the outer perimeter of the polished floor. The music stopped, and he was forced to let go of her.

"Are we to behave like your camels, Monsieur Hammadi, who travel from palm tree to palm tree across the dunes, without ever a drink?" She smiled with a slight challenge.

"At the Baron's oasis, the champagne-skins are never empty," Mohamed laughed. They stepped off the parquet dance floor, and he seized two filled glasses from a passing tray. She had already downed three. He marveled at her capacity. Jacqueline seemed imbued with more vivacity than any woman he had ever known, and was less inhibited by the constraints of society. It was almost as though she existed on another plane, breathed another air, saw only what she chose to see, made her own rules. And she had the ability to infect others with her enthusiasm. They caught it from her like a disease. It had not been easy keeping his own name on her crowded dance card, for every nongeriatric man in the room had tried to claim her. He had watched her cousin's husband, Henri, waltz her away, and the possessiveness of St. Rimaud's look made him furious. What was the swine thinking? Was Jacqueline aware of her effect on her cousin? How could she not be?

Jacqueline's glass was again empty. She let him refill it. The wine seemed to be having no effect at all. But it certainly would not do if the St. Rimauds blamed him for leading her astray.

Again the music stopped. This time the Baron stepped up to the bandstand. "Ladies and gentlemen, I have a surprise for you! Monsieur Claude Achille Debussy has agreed to play for us his beautiful composition, *Prélude à l'Après-midi d'un Faune.*" There was a ripple of perfunctory applause. The Baron went on. "It is only a few years since this music was honored by the Ysaye Quartet. I was fortunate enough to attend the performance and meet the composer himself!"

A coup for the Baron's celebration of his ugly duckling's debut. When he heard about it, the Prince de Condé might even regret that he had turned down the Baron's invitation. The room hummed with anticipation as the young composer stepped to the grand piano.

"Do you think Monsieur Debussy would mind if we pursued his faun through the garden?" Jacqueline whispered. Without waiting for answer, she whisked a bottle of champagne from a silver bucket at a side table and led Mohamed out to the terrace. They moved down the crescent curve of steps into the moon-splashed garden, followed lightly by the cascading ripple of piano notes. She turned, silhouetted against the glow of terrace lanterns.

"This is what we wanted to do, isn't it?"

"Do you always do exactly as you choose?" he asked.

"If I can."

"I doubt if anyone would have the heart to stop you doing anything," he said.

"My father never stops me. And my cousin Henri would like to take me to bed." Her laugh tinkled across the Baron's park. She moved down a row of plumed cypresses dividing manicured hedges. Gleaming white, Diana the huntress cocked her bow at Apollo. Aphrodite posed amid assorted cupids and posturing Pans.

"I think you like to shock," he said.

"Why not? Everyone is asleep. Come on! Why do you wait?" Jacqueline quickened her step down the path. He followed, caught up in her mood. They rounded a clump of trees and entered a secret garden. At its center, a magnificent fountain sprayed glittering droplets across Neptune. His team of dolphins entwined with mermaids in the foam.

Jacqueline caressed a marble snout. "Poor creatures. Always pursuing. Never capturing." She refilled their glasses to the brim and set the bottle on the rim of the pool.

He knew so little about her: only that he wanted to possess her like some peerless gem, to own her, exhibit her, have use of her. St. Rimaud had told him little enough: that her mother was dead, that her father, his business partner, was missing a limb, a souvenir of the Franco-Prussian War. And since Major Laville-Darlin and his beautiful daughter lived in the provinces, it had been arranged that Jacqueline should be advanced into Paris society by her cousins. No doubt they were greasing the rails toward an advantageous marriage—a prize that would bring many offers.

Marriage. To such a woman. A wildly intriguing thought. But would he, a Moslem, even of substantial financial background, be welcomed into this family circle of ambition?

"Irresistibly beautiful. . . . I suppose you've been told that many times?" He was trying to suppress his excitement.

"I know I am beautiful. But if seeing me were knowing me, then everyone would. And nobody does. Are you afraid of the truth, Monsieur Hammadi? Or do you prefer your packages done up in little bows?"

"Should I be afraid of you?" He smiled.

"Most men are. If I ever allowed my cousin Henri to seduce me, he'd die of fright." She laughed, then, caught up in the music as it drifted out to them, began to sway into a slow dance around the fountain.

He was enchanted. "You are like a mermaid in a gown of sea," he breathed.

"Shall I be your mermaid?" she asked.

"With me, you shall be anything you like. I would never stop you."

"Then, you shall allow me to seduce Neptune." She laughed,

turning away. "Old man of the oceans . . . shall I kiss the salt out of your beard? You, with your trident and lecherous eyes, are you like Cousin Henri—all leers, gropes, and pinches? Or are you Mohamed, burning like the fire inside the belly of a mountain—that will one day erupt and bury the world in love?"

Deftly she unhooked her gown. It dropped to her feet in one soft rustle of silk, leaving her standing nude in the moonlight. Mohamed was stunned that she wore no underclothing. Even the whores of Montmartre were tightly laced into corselets. Though the women of his family never showed more than their eyes outside of the immediate family circle, his Paris years had accustomed him to the ways of Western women. This girl could be as abandoned as any Montmartre whore, yet remain chaste and virginal—even untouchable.

Jacqueline stepped into the foaming pool. The water boiled up around gleaming thighs, played across the downy mound of Venus. Arms extended into the spray. She moved; water spilled down breasts and flat belly. She was like a naiad, a water nymph from antiquity, abandoning all restraint to the pagan urges of banished goddesses.

Jacqueline stepped out of the pool, coming toward him, water diamonds streaking pale skin. She stood before him, still as a statue, arms at her sides. For a moment, he could only look; then he reached up and let loose the green velvet ribbon that held her hair. Gold ringlets cascaded down over her shoulders. Still she stood silent, frozen in moonlight. He made no move to touch her, but bent to kiss her. His lips paused before reaching her mouth, then descended to one rose-tipped nipple.

"You are too beautiful . . ." he murmured.

"I am bored with that word. Really, Mohamed, you'll have to do better. We shall return to the ball now," she said. "And we shall dance sedately like poodles at the Cirque Pigalle. And you will never speak of this to anyone." She gathered up her gown and stepped back into it. "Fasten it," she commanded.

He obeyed, trying to control the throbbing in his loins. She tilted her chin around at him. "Your hands are trembling, Mohamed."

"Don't expect too much of a man, Jacqueline."

"My glass is empty—and you have not touched your wine."

She poured from the bottle, then bound her hair back into the ribbon. "Come," she said, starting back to the château. "I'm sure no one has even missed us."

"If they have, I will have compromised you."

"Don't be a child. Don't you know that in life one can do anything one wishes? All it takes is the courage to dare. And that, I shall never lack. I shall not ever allow my life to be bound and corseted by convention. Who knows how long it will last? It could be over in a moment—or it could wither slowly in a century. The gift of life is for taking."

"Jacqueline," he breathed. "I worship you."

"Poor man," she said. "Poor man. What shall we do about it?"

Three _____

JUDAH Nouari wiped his forehead with a silk handkerchief, tilted his black felt hat, creased precisely at the top, took his valise from the rack, and stepped down onto the platform. The Gross-Basel station was crowded for a Sunday. The day was warm for August. The platform seemed to be bobbing with black frock coats vying for a handful of available carriages. At last Judah managed to capture an antique barouche drawn up by a trimly currycombed sorrel, and clopped off toward the city's finest hotel.

No rooms available. They rolled on over the Rhine, across an old wooden bridge.

Six hotels later, there were still no rooms to be had. "Basel is full of Jews today. Jews for the next three days," one of the desk clerks had said. "Jews from Russia, from Germany, from France, Austria-Hungary, England. From everywhere. Not that I've anything against them," he added quickly with a closer look at Nouari. "But without reservations, monsieur. . . ." He shrugged.

Had Judah imagined this conference would be such a popular event, he would have taken the precaution of telegraphing ahead. He was beginning to be sorry he'd followed the whim that had brought him. Well, he was here—and he might as well go where everyone else was going.

The stolid Swiss coachman set him down in front of a somber gray edifice with the unlikely name of The Casino. Above it a sign proclaimed to a moderately interested city: ZIONISTENKONGRESS.

What a city for congresses, this Basel! Balanced on the Rhine, wedged in by the weight of France and Germany, this tidy Swiss bastion of banking and commerce had long offered

an ideal neutral setting for the exchange of ideas, reforma-
tions, conferences, causes, peace declarations. And peace
movements—such as the one in 1891, which generated more
talk than world peace. Today, the cause up for discussion was
"a home for the Jews."

The flag above The Casino surprised him. A blue Star of
David on a white field divided by two blue stripes. The colors
of the *tallit*—the Hebrew prayer shawl. An improvised banner
for Zion. . . . Colorful, at least.

Judah hefted his valise through the crowded entrance, wishing he'd had time for a wash and a clean shirt. A bearded
man stopped him. Had he a delegate's card? No? Well, in any
event he was not properly attired. Dr. Herzl had plainly
directed that black frock coats and white ties must be worn.
The doctor wished the occasion to be both festive and digni-
fied, the man told him, adding that Judah might find a seat in
the visitors' gallery—if he were lucky. But there were more
people than they had counted on. Still, that was the purpose,
wasn't it?

Judah climbed the stairs and edged his way along the
narrow balcony encircling the concert hall's gray walls. He
squeezed past seated spectators. The atmosphere was charged
with friendly elation, strangers beaming at each other as
though amazed that they were actually there together. A man
smiled and made room for Judah on the bench. He spoke in
Polish, and Judah could only nod gratitude. Below them, on
the main floor, an air of expectancy pervaded as delegates
took their places. The platform supported a long green table
with leafy decorations and a raised seat for the president.
Almost every chair was taken. A smaller table at the side was
reserved for journalists and stenographers. That, too, was
almost full. In the gallery around him, Judah could pick up
fragments of conversation in French, German, Hungarian,
and English. A Jewish congress! What did it mean? What sort
of anarchy would it produce? "What possible decisions can
be reached?" they were asking each other in every language.
They were local Basel Jews and even a number of Christians—
even Christian Zionists!—who supported the Jewish cause.
Men who had read Herzl's plea for a Jewish state and had
read into it an answer to the "Jewish problem" that Herzl had
not intended: Get rid of the Jews. Send them somewhere else.

A jungle in the Amazon, perhaps. Why not the Artic Circle? Anywhere but next door.

All had come to hear what Herzl would add to his bold declaration. All but Judah. He searched the faces along the gallery and down on the floor below. He did not find the one that had haunted memory. "Cry, oh, cry, my people. Let your voices echo in the caverns of the land. . . ." Well, she would find a few ears today. But where was she?

Three taps of the gavel brought the meeting to silence. Judah recognized the dean of the praesidium, Dr. Lippe of Jassy. Lippe had come to Judah's house in Palestine to solicit his father's aid for a colony of Jews trying to make a settlement at Midian. That was in 1892. His father had given neither money nor support. Like most Palestinian Jews, David Nouari was not happy about the prospect of Middle Europeans pouring into their homeland. Strangers with little in common except religious tradition. Anyway, the Midian project had been doomed from the start. The colonists had quarreled among themselves, and Turkish administrators, suddenly roused from customary lethargy, opposed the plan. But all that was in the past. Now Lippe was covering his head and uttering the prayer of *sheheheyanu*.

"Blessed art thou, O Lord our God, King of the Universe, who has kept us alive and brought us to witness this day."

This day of August 29, 1897.

This day that had brought so many from the shadows of old ghettos. Here were men in whose memories rang the terrible cries of Cossack marauders. Here were the outcasts who had crouched in the corners of Islam's medinas, tolerated but never loved. Here were the rabbis who had carried the faith forward, like a nation in their minds. Here was a smattering of that vast scattered seed; the children of Israel, who had once marched out of slavery in Egypt bearing the vision of a single God, who had built a powerful nation and seen it blown away on all the winds by the trumpets of Rome's iron legions.

In some areas of the hall, there was a flutter of handkerchiefs, and then a silence of surprise. Lippe had actually moved that a resolution of thanks and devotion be sent to the Sultan of Turkey. Little cause for sympathy with *that* ruler of Palestine—from whom few mercies fell!

And then Judah recognized the stately, elongated figure of

Dr. Herzl moving to the tribune. His dark beard had grown. It made his face even paler. There was something almost kingly in his bearing now, something akin to the image of a Messianic figure. Voices lifted in spontaneous enthusiasm. *"Yehi ha-Melech!*—Hail to the King!"* The voices were underscored by a storm of applause. Herzl made no gesture of acknowledgment of the tribute. Like a latter-day Saul, Solomon, or David, he stood straight as a cedar, composed, quiet, waiting for silence. Judah saw a change in the man since that day in the Paris crowd two years before, when they had met.

A rustle of chairs, a few coughs, then Herzl spoke. "We are here to lay the foundation stone of the house which is to shelter the Jewish nation. . . ." His words flowed easily. He spoke of anti-Semitism but avoided any mention of Russia, which among all nations was, that year, the worst offender. He spoke of the modern, educated, deghettoized Jews, and how each new tide of anti-Semitism had strengthened their sense of identity. "Zionism is a return of the Jews to Judaism even before their return to the Jewish land," he said. He talked of forming a strong organization—but was careful to say that it would not be an "international" organization. Rather, it would be an international "discussion" to solve the Jewish question. "We have nothing to do with conspiracy, secret intervention," he added pointedly.

Why, Judah wondered, was it still necessary to refute that old accusation—international conspiracy—so often brought out, dusted off, and launched at the Jews? It was this sort of imputation that drove men like Rothschild and Liebermann into the safer arms of Christianity; a lie repeated often enough can become more deadly than truth.

Dr. Herzl was talking about the attempts that had been made to form colonies in the Argentine and Palestine. Attempts to create an agricultural class out of ghetto-bred Jews. Was it any wonder that they failed? All such plans would fail, until the people learned to help themselves.

But nothing Herzl was saying added to the more challenging statements in his pamphlet *Der Judenstaat.* In fact, to Judah, his message seemed watered down. Diplomatically couched for the ears of the world—the hostile as well as the friendly. Indeed, the press had many ears present—from London, New York, Paris, Frankfurt. Judah's eyes drifted to the table of reporters.

There she was. Sitting among a small group of stenographers. Zosia Halevi. . . .

She had made an unsuccessful attempt to draw unruly hair neatly to the nape of a slender neck. Still it flew wildly, untamed as ever. Her concentration was intense. He could see by the speed with which she took down Herzl's words, occasionally stabbing at an inkwell on the table in front of her, that she was writing in shorthand.

Herzl finished with a provocative question: "Today we meet on the soil of this friendly nation. Where shall we be a year from now?"

Where, indeed? wondered Judah. Afloat on another sea of words? Herzl was obviously speaking for the world at large. He had become a statesman without a state, an Isaiah turned diplomat.

Max Nordau followed Herzl to the tribune. Nordau, the prodigal returned, for he had strayed so far from his origins that he had even changed his name from Südfeld. He, too, balanced on a verbal tightrope, taking care not to offend the orthodox or trouble the freethinkers. Moderation, it seemed, was the order of the day.

When all the reports were in and the last word had brought its applause, Judah pushed his way downstairs through knots of exuberant conversationalists. He found Zosia collecting her notes into a folder. Her smoky eyes lifted with surprise, and then she actually smiled. Judah felt she might even be glad to see him.

"I never thought that you would come," she said.

"I told you I would." He glanced around the crowded hall and added, "Impressive."

She arched an eyebrow. "And what would you have called the opening of the Red Sea? Noteworthy?"

He laughed. "Perhaps I expected a bit more."

"More of what?" she demanded.

"Well, what happened to Dr. Herzl's 'Promised Land' —for one thing?"

"One must trim one's sails to suit the wind, Judah." The deep voice came from behind him. Judah turned to face Theodor Herzl. "The fact is, that I stand at the head of a mass of youths, beggars, and jackasses. I am"—he smiled— "the leader of an army of *schnorrers*. But it is beginning, and this congress will be followed by greater acts."

"Greater?" Judah asked. "It seems to me that today your idea of a Jewish state was diminished to a hope for a guaranteed reservation—not unlike what America gave its Red Indians."

Herzl's expression was patient. "Did you know, Judah, there are even Orthodox rabbis here today who believe that a Jewish homeland would destroy the sanctity of the Sabbath? Things can't move as quickly as we might wish. But more quickly perhaps if men like you were with us. Don't you agree, Zosia?" Eyes turned to the girl.

"Wealthy bankers can be very useful to the movement," she replied with her usual bluntness.

"As a banker, I felt a little shortchanged—though you must understand, sir, I was only here as an observer."

"Has it ever occurred to you, Judah, that the Jewish people are like a trapezium. No two sides are the same. From this we must make a unity. But if I were to sum up what has happened here today . . ." Herzl's voice dropped to the level of one sharing a confidence, "and I certainly wouldn't make this a public statement, I would say: In Basel I created the Jewish state. It begins in the mind—and it ends on the map."

Other delegates, who had politely stood aside awaiting a word with the great man, were now pressing forward. Herzl extended his hand to Judah. "I am glad you were with us today, Judah. Even if only as . . . an observer." Herzl turned away to greet the impatient cluster of eager questioners.

Zosia glanced at the luggage at Judah's feet. "You are leaving Basel already?"

"Well, I certainly hadn't planned to. But perhaps I should have brought a tent. You see, I haven't found a hotel, mademoiselle. Dr. Herzl's *schnorrers* may force me to sleep in the park tonight."

"There might still be a room at the *pension* where I am staying. But you will not find it very grand," she added.

"I'd be grateful for anything," he said almost too eagerly. "And I haven't eaten since early morning. Perhaps you would permit me to take you to dinner?"

She turned back to gathering up her papers. "No time."

"But even the most dedicated Zionists have to eat, surely," he insisted, helping her collect her notebooks.

"An apple and cheese in my room will do me. I must transcribe these notes tonight." Then her expression softened slightly. "But first we had better see about that room for you. If there is one, it won't last long."

As they moved out of the hall, he noted that a great number of people seemed to know her. Members of the Choveve Zion, no doubt.

Outside, he hailed a carriage. He had been firm when she suggested walking the length of the city. She sat stiffly on the edge of the leather seat, as one unaccustomed to such extravagances. He smiled across at her.

"How long will you be staying, then?" she asked.

"It depends," he replied, "on the length of the speeches...."

Judah heard the clatter of Zosia's typewriter through the thin wall of his bedroom. Nothing at the Schloss Elfenbein suggested an ivory tower. Heavy lace curtains failed to obscure the depressing vista of a Basel back street. The small room suffocated in fading alpine decor: edelweiss-sprinkled wallpaper. A green wooden headboard painted with orange and white wild flowers matched dresser and chair. His eyes climbed the white-cowled Matterhorn in a heavily foxed mezzotint. Switzerland's Mount Sinai. Still, he was lucky Zosia had found him a bed. He sat down on it, tested the mattress. A chorus of iron springs croaked back.

Judah considered his situation. Here was he, and there was Zosia—in a self-imposed prison of work. Zosia—bound and handcuffed to her cause like those fanatic suffragettes who chained themselves to railings. Zosia—a Hebrew Maid of Orléans, leading a charge of typewriter keys against blank pages. Zosia—who lived to serve. Zosia—who had never learned to live. There was Zosia, and here was he. . . .

Had he come all the way to Basel to sit alone in a tiny room? Of course, there were one or two people he could contact: business associates of the Baron's, who would offer instant hospitality. He dismissed the thought, planting his pinched black hat firmly on his head.

Zosia heard the door of Judah's room close. She continued her typing on one of the new "front stroke" machines supplied by the congress. Dr. Herzl would insist on reviewing the notes in the morning before launching the next day's proceedings. She was interrupted by a tap at the door.

"May I come in?" Judah asked.

"I am working . . ." she said.

He looked past her, toward the apple neglected on the bureau. "Just as I thought. You haven't eaten." He beamed across a bulging bundle of provisions. "I've brought us something."

"Really, monsieur—quite unnecessary!"

"A small reward for saving me from the streets." She allowed him in. He glanced around, looking for a place to set down his bundle. Her room, larger than his, was furnished with dark Biedermeier in the Germanic Rheingold tradition. Her only table was already occupied by a typewriter, notebooks, and sheaves of foolscap.

Judah set his bundle on a chair and produced a bottle of wine. "Trockenbeerenauslese. Quite an acceptable hock, they assured me."

"They've sold you a dessert wine, monsieur."

"Then, we shall have it at the end."

"It is against my principles to be wasteful," she said. "Since you have brought the food—it must be eaten."

Judah grinned. "I have had dinner invitations accepted more enthusiastically." He darted toward the door. "Won't be a moment."

Zosia was surprised at feeling pleased by Judah's attention. Surely in Paris his life must overflow with beautiful women. She glanced in the mirror—wiped a smudge of ink from her cheek. Why her? She smoothed her blouse, looked at her hands. Dirty! She washed them hurriedly in the basin, brushed her hair back from her high forehead. So curly! What could one do with hair like this?

Judah returned bearing a small table from his own room and a tooth mug. He spread his silk pocket handkerchief as a table cloth and laid out the food: cooked chicken, paté, a slab of cheese, black bread, and a pastry. He held a chair for her.

"There is far too much food here for the two of us. I don't approve of extravagant gestures, monsieur."

"But tonight is certainly an occasion for celebration, even you must admit!" Judah folded down a corkscrew from a staghorn knife and drew the cork with a comfortable pop. "And occasions should be toasted with the fruit of the vine. Even a sweet one." He poured the pale amber liquid and handed her a glass. "What does the Talmud say? Wine is at the head of all medicines."

"Perhaps you are right, monsieur. This is an occasion. And I will give you a toast for it: Next year in Jerusalem!" She raised her glass to his. They drank.

"Let me tell you about Jerusalem, Zosia. Something you should know. It's a fine place—to get away from. You can love it better from a distance. Oh, name it in your prayers, praise it in songs, but don't make the mistake of living there. It's crowded, it's dirty, it's hot, it's dusty, its streets are narrow. We still draw our water from a well. There are no toilets in our houses. It doesn't matter how rich one is; life is primitive."

"So was the Garden of Eden."

"But the Garden of Eden only had two people in it. Jerusalem has always been overcrowded."

"There's plenty of land in Palestine. Our coming will bring prosperity."

"To whom? The Turks? To the people who are already there? Jews and Arabs? In Jerusalem, you know, there's little difference between Jew and Arab. They eat the same food, they dress the same way. We worship Jehovah, and they worship Allah. But, believe me, Zosia, Arabs and Jews in Palestine are far more like each other than like you. And neither will welcome Dr. Herzl's dream of Zion. Who should know better than I?"

"Perhaps someone who has never been there." She held her glass almost primly in front of her like an unaccustomed thing. Almost as an afterthought, she took a sip. "Because to us—the ones like us—Jerusalem was never just a place. Never just a city. Yes, it is the dream beyond the horizon of our lives. Escape. 'If I forget thee, O Jerusalem. . . .' It was—it is—a haven. Somewhere that we never saw—and probably would never see. And that is its importance, you understand! No," she said. "You don't. You couldn't. Arabs and Jews. Fine. But you were never awakened from your sleep by the cries of 'Hep! Hep! Hep!' The cries of the Cossacks on a Jew hunt through your village. One survived— only to fear the next raid. For inevitably it would come, and it could be your family next time. Your father, your mother left in the street like a sack of old clothes bleeding on the stones! And *you* would be the sobbing child clinging to them." She rose. "Well, then, one grows up in fear. Hounded, hunted from one wretched village to another—from one country to another. Don't talk to me about toilets and Jews who will not want us. When someone says the word 'Jerusalem,' we see a golden city in our minds. 'Next year in Jerusalem' means 'next year . . . life.' "

In this moment, she seemed so small, so vulnerable. And yet so strong. Her dedication was almost suffocating. "What about your own life, Zosia?" he asked. "Is it to be spent as the handmaiden to a prophet?"

Her eyes glistened. "Herzl is the voice of our future."

"But he can't walk on water." Judah smiled.

"We don't need miracles, we need leaders." Her face became intense. "Men who can offer an answer to Russia's solution: liquidation . . . emigration . . . starvation . . . conversion. No, monsieur, Dr. Herzl was not the first voice in the wilderness. There were many. Leo Pinsker, from Odessa, who named his dream 'autoemancipation.' And in the sixteenth century, Reubeni tried to unite the Jews of Spain, Italy, and Turkey."

He put down a chicken bone. "At least they were all Sephardic, which gave them something in common."

"All Jews have that: persecution! And the idea of Palestine isn't Herzl's either. As early as the seventeenth century, Manasseh Ben Israel wanted to resettle Jews in England as the first step toward their return to Palestine."

"You're giving me a list of failures."

"That doesn't mean we should stop trying! There were others. Always others. Sabbatai in Smyrna, proclaiming himself a Messiah to lead a return to Palestine. Moses Mendelssohn in the eighteenth century. It isn't that Dr. Herzl's ideas are new. It's that he's here—now."

"His solution will fail, like all the others. The question, I accept. Yes, the question! But the answer. . . ." He shook his head slowly. "Herzl is a great mind—but even he cannot put himself into the mind of God. He, and all those self-appointed Messiahs." He took her hands. "Do you understand what I am trying to say? You are wasting your life, Zosia."

That night, he lay awake for hours listening to her typewriter, endlessly tapping—until the sound blended into pattering rain falling into his dream and he was asleep. For the next two days, he could not separate himself from Zosia. Judah knew he should be back in Paris, knew the Baron would be furious at his unexplained absence. Perhaps more furious if it *were* explained. But Judah hung on, collecting her for the meals she scarcely touched, trying to find a chink in her personal armor. But it was as though she kept her emotions under lock and key.

One night when he knocked at her door, it was opened by a tall young man who bore himself in an oddly stiff manner. The stranger had a pale, intense expression, small eyes framed in round, steel-rimmed glasses. He half bowed to Judah, then stepped past him into the hall. "Please forgive me, sir, I am already late for where I must be." He headed down the corridor.

Judah watched him go. "Your visitor didn't seem anxious to be introduced. Who is he?"

"A friend."

"Are you trying to make me jealous?"

She hesitated. Then, reluctantly: "Count Alexander Lubenov." She was cradling a stack of pamphlets in her arms and seemed indisposed to elaborate on her visitor's identity.

"Your count walks as though he forgot to remove a coat hanger from his jacket!"

"A riding accident." The way she said it made him think there was much more to explain. "He has delivered these pamphlets; that is all."

He glanced at them as she set them on the table. "The *Narodnaya Volya?*"

She looked at him sharply. "When you read what isn't meant for you, you should not be surprised at what you discover."

"Have the anarchists started enlisting members of the Russian nobility for the Jewish cause?"

She shrugged. "All causes are not fought with money, Monsieur Banker." How pretty she looked when she was being superior! "To you everything must be black or white. Alexei is among those Russians who would like to see a more liberal face on Holy Mother Russia. Which would include a happier future for the Jews." She sat down before her typewriter.

"And is his noble family aware of this dedication to Zion?"

"His father doesn't read Gorky. I doubt if he reads anything."

"Most definitely not his son's pamphlets. Is the Count also a printer?"

"He has access to a printing press in Geneva. Alexei has been helpful preparing propaganda—which we circulate. That is all."

"All?"

"Our relationship is not personal." She added, "Alexei holds a minor position at the Russian Embassy in Paris—which is often helpful."

"In other words, he's a bit of a spy."

Zosia glowered. He took her hand and drew her up. "Let us have one day without argument. I'm taking you out for a walk in the fresh air. And not to hand out pamphlets."

She began to protest, but he was firm. "I want to introduce you to Basel. You haven't noticed it since you've been here. And then I want to introduce you to someone else you haven't noticed: me."

Zosia smiled wanly, shook her head as though giving in to a child. She put on her hat, with a glance in the mirror to set it straight, pushing a long pin through it. "Very well, Monsieur Banker. I will let you introduce me to Basel." She smiled again. "And even to yourself."

It was perhaps the first firm indication of personal interest. Judah seized it. Yes, he had been hungry to know her—and be known. If he had come to Basel to exorcise an attraction, it had worked quite the other way. And this, if he could be honest with himself, had been a secret hope: that Zosia would prove as fascinating as their first meeting had promised. Slowly, through their hours together, he had begun to know her—the shadows that lay behind her eyes, the ghosts that haunted memories. Memories of Odessa, where her family had been caught in one of Count Plehve's well-organized pogroms. Her mind held kaleidoscopic images—of endlessly walking over vast distances, of clinging to her father's back to swim a river that seemed to widen with every stroke, until he had dragged himself up on the far bank and she could remember only the heavy beating of her heart with fear. Images of huddling around a fire and meeting a ragged rabbi who spoke the most beautiful words she'd ever heard: "I am the rose of Sharon, and the lily of the valleys. As the lily among thorns, so is my love among the daughters. . . .''

They had been the lucky few to escape. And to have a destination: relatives in Warsaw. But when were "poor relations" ever welcomed with open arms? The Halevis had brought nothing from Russia but a child. A child that had to be clothed, fed, educated. Zosia could recall that elder cousin, so affluent he used a silver toothpick, drawing it like a tiny sword from an ivory scabbard dangling from his watch chain at the end of every meal. The light would glint on the blade before he inserted it between yellow teeth. Zosia's father, always frail, scarcely had time to taste the joys of comparative safety. He died of pneumonia, leaving Zosia and her mother to the unenthusiastic charity of their Polish cousins.

"The longest distance is to the pocket," the elder had frequently announced between tooth stabs. "Throw a lucky man into the sea, and he will come up with a fish in his mouth. Throw in a fool, and the fish will swallow him." Such pearls of wisdom were offered more freely than second helpings.

Zosia's mother played the violin and could take in a few pupils. Along with needlework, this provided a modest income. "The future of business is in the typewriter!" proclaimed the voice of wisdom. And so Zosia was trained to master it, along with shorthand. But something of her mother's music must have flowed into her pen and spilled out into poems. "The best verse is the jingle in your purse!" her cousin decreed. Then Zosia left for Paris, where a job on a Jewish newspaper led to the interview that changed her life. With Herzl. And the poetry? Oh, that was her luxury now, she said.

When Judah said he was falling in love with her, she replied that love, too, was a luxury. Nevertheless, she let him kiss her. Beneath that composed surface, the shell of poised efficiency, lay sensual depths still unexplored. Her lips felt softer than he could ever have imagined. But she would let him go no further than a kiss, and he would not have forced the matter. Zosia could master passions, suppress hungers, but Judah was relieved to find that she was not without feelings and desires. Nevertheless, the night before they were to leave Basel, he came to her door. It was late. Nearly twelve-thirty. He stood for a full five minutes before knocking. Judah had never made love to a woman—except those he had bought when he and Mohamed had prowled the street cafés. She answered in a faded peignoir, hair falling in a smoky shadow around her shoulders. She let him in without a word, as though she had expected him. He took her in his arms and carried her to the bed. She weighed almost nothing, and he lay beside her, holding the frail perfection of her body tight against his, feeling the pressure of her small, firm breasts and slender thighs against his own. He could feel himself grow hard against her. "Ye shall be mine own treasure from among all peoples . . ." he whispered. He had wondered if her body might be as stiff and unyielding as her dedication. But she was soft and giving, warm and accepting. His hand gently parted her thighs and she allowed him to move inside her. This was fulfillment. The destination of all feeling and wanting. This was the return of man into woman—this, the mating of all things, rhythms, desires. This was the Song of Solomon, the hind springing in the forest, the leap of flame, the surge of life in life. This was the end that was its own beginning. Their bodies were a dance together, a questioning and an answering. And finally they reached the only pure moment of oblivion that humans know before the grave.

"Beloved. Beloved. Beloved," Judah breathed.

She turned her face to the wall. Said nothing.

"I wonder . . . can human beings deserve so much?"

"I think there is always a price. . . . I think that nothing is ever given for nothing."

He raised himself on one elbow. "Aren't we meant to be happy, then? Is this God you expect to lead you back to Jerusalem a sadist, who allows us to lose the burden of the flesh only for brief instants?"

"Judah, Judah. . . ." She stroked him gently, as one comforting a questioning child. "The world does not end or begin simply because a man and a woman find each other in the same bed. The troubles, the wrongs, the struggles—they go on. And yes, it is perhaps those things that matter, not the moments of happiness."

"You said there was a price. . . ."

"Perhaps it could be no more than a single life. Or a multitude scattered across the earth. A people searching the mirrors of all nations—and finding no reflection. Only the masks of their fears, their own needs.''

Judah reached across her slightly glistening body to a glass half full of wine. He emptied it, and tossed it against the wall. The tinkle of falling bits was small music. "There is your libation, Zosia. Your sacrifice to your angry God! There, my beloved, is your payment." His hands cupped her head. They kissed, mouths open, like those for whom no hunger could ever be fulfilled.

Four _____

THE train orchestrated the descending night with a rhythmic beat. Crepuscular flashes—steeples above clinging mountain villages. Mohamed Hammadi swayed in the corridor of the Orient Express, sucking a gold-tipped Melachrino. A tit of Fortune. He still found it difficult to believe that Jacqueline's family had finally hurdled religious considerations to accept him as a son-in-law. True, it had taken two years. But banking connections had weighed in his favor. Her graceful hand—in exchange for financing a second factory; this one to manufacture tools in France that Hammadi-Nouari Cairo would purchase on behalf of Egyptian interests. A bit like a duck eating its own egg. Cousin Mahmood, who ran the Cairo office with Gideon Nouari, had been highly complimentary about the deal.

Major Laville-Darlin had insisted on a Catholic ceremony; Mohamed and Jacqueline, kneeling together before the great altar in the cathedral at Tours, bathed in the pungent aroma of lilies and incense. What tantrums, what intrigues had led to that moment? What torrents of protestations from a headstrong, beloved daughter? Major Laville-Darlin had favored the causes of several "more suitable" candidates from old French families. But he was no match for Jacqueline's determination. Was ever a husband more fortunate? thought Mohamed. To be rich enough to marry for love—and to be loved not for one's riches.

The week before their marriage, Count von Bülow had arrived in Paris with a proposal that would send Mohamed back to Palestine. When Jacqueline heard of it, she insisted on making the journey a honeymoon. "I didn't marry you to have you out of my bed for three months," she had said.

50

They'd departed the Gare de l'Est on Thursday at 6:25 P.M., Jacqueline traveling with three steamer trunkloads of dresses and a bulging jewel case. His engagement gift had been an emerald parure—necklace, bracelet, and earrings of the clearest ice-green facets that set off her changeable eyes. The train would carry them the length of France, Germany, Austria-Hungary, Serbia, Bulgaria—to Constantinople. Traveling with them was Count von Bülow's representative, a highly skilled Prussian engineer and surveyor. Oscar von Leiter was likable enough, but Mohamed did not appreciate the tall, blond German's open admiration for Jacqueline.

Mohamed had married without notifying his own family. He had discussed it with Judah. Judah told him it was a mistake not to inform them. There were sure to be objections. Arguments. But, once home, all would evaporate before Jacqueline's smile; of that, Mohamed felt certain. Besides, he was bringing a project that could change the face of Palestine. He and Judah Nouari had examined the Germans' proposition together. It could mean millions flowing into the Hammadi-Nouari Trading Company.

"Mohamed . . . ?" Jacqueline called through the polished mahogany compartment door. He regretted his frugality in not hiring a private car to be added to the train. He would make up for such economies once they reached Constantinople.

Jacqueline, in the palest blue gossamer negligee, opened the door. He caught his breath, still unable to accustom himself to her beauty. She was more exciting than any woman he could imagine: spontaneously electric, vibrant. All men must sense it, he knew, reading the desire she brought to their eyes. It made him want to veil her—like the wives in his own land. Jacqueline masked by a black *galabia!* The thought made him smile.

"You're laughing at me. Why?" she demanded.

"Most men have to die to reach paradise. I entered through a wedding ring."

She held up a glass in each hand. "More champagne?" He came into the compartment, closing the door behind him. She lifted the glasses higher as he put his arms around her waist to kiss her. "If they had been full, you would be christened at last, Mohamed," she laughed, waving the glasses. They drank. Her capacity for wine always seemed unlimited. But then, so was her capacity for sexual pleasure, for excitement, for living on the peaks. For everything.

She turned away to close the curtains as the train slowed into a station. "Poor Von Leiter," she sighed.

"What's so poor about him?"

"All by himself. Let's send him a bottle to keep him company in his lonely bed."

"He can buy his own bottles—and find his own company." He took the empty glass from her and drew her down to the narrow bunk. Her hand slid under the waistband of his trousers. She kept him off balance with her curious mixture of boldness and elegance—the whore and the princess in one *persona*. No need for wine. With every act of love, she became more intoxicating to him. He was besotted.

Mehmet Khassadia, tall, swarthy, hawklike in a deep red fez, Prince Albert coat, and striped trousers, paced impatiently in the lobby of Constantinople's finest hotel. Judah Nouari's uncle-by-marriage knew his own importance. He also knew his own unimportance in the family hierarchy as "aunt Sarah's husband." Being kept waiting by the Nouaris, or the Hammadis, was a penalty for marrying his way up in the world, which had carried him to a high perch: civil servant in the Finance Ministry, wherein he wielded influence tempered with discretion. In this capacity, he had arranged all the necessary appointments for Hammadi and Von Leiter. Furthermore, he had organized that his son, Kemel, a lieutenant in the Turkish Army, should escort the bride of this Hammadi on a sight-seeing tour: the Mosque of Suleiman, the Blue Mosque, the Aya Sophia, Topkapi, a trip down the Golden Horn—even a visit to the Sultan's harem, with a glimpse of the royal jewels: diamonds, rubies, cabochon emeralds as large as goose eggs. Oh, they might call his country "the sick man of Europe," but one sight of those jewels would make any Parisian lady crawl into the invalid's bed.

He snapped closed his turnip watchcase and produced a broad, gold-capped smile at the appearance of Mohamed and the towering German.

"A thousand pardons, dear Mehmet," Mohamed said. "A cable from the Paris office. Judah sends his warmest greetings."

Not much of an excuse. But then, Arabs were habitually late.

Jacqueline gazed out across a forest of minarets and listened to the muezzins call the faithful to prayer. All afternoon, the humorless Lieutenant Kemel had dutifully guided her, conversing in his stilted French, weaving through a maze of cobbled streets where the human back was used to transport everything from baskets to beds. The Turk seemed oblivious to the filth and poverty of his city. It made Jacqueline feel unclean. But Mohamed belonged to this teeming Eastern culture. For the first time, she sensed the foreignness of her alliance. Secure in her hotel suite, she poured a glass of champagne and slipped out of her clothes. She would have burned them if she could! Instead, she sank into a cool bath scented with cologne.

Wife to a Moslem. . . . What would it mean? Her mind was impaled by images. Black eunuchs padding about the Winter Harem of the Grand Seraglio. The four sultanas, who had each borne the Sultan a male heir, layered in fat, sucking Turkish delights; the Gözde girls, who considered it the highest honor to have their pubic hairs removed before entering the imperial chamber to kiss the coverlet and worm their way up beneath it, fondling their master from toes to testicles. Was she to take her place as a *cariye*—one who serves? Would she, too, be allowed the sight of only castrated males— aside from her Lord Husband? Her bath water caught the chill from her body as she waited for Mohamed to return from corrupting the natives.

"A railroad stretching from Damascus to Jerusalem to Aqaba?" speculated Tahsin Bey. The first secretary to the Finance Minister of Turkey gazed placidly out beneath his fez, a sphinx of calculation. Mehmet Khassadia, who was in fact his assistant, roosted uneasily on a thin-backed chair. He had arranged this meeting; now he could only hope that Mohamed and Von Leiter played their parts skillfully. An attendant stirred the stagnant air with a palm-frond fan. Another poured sticky sweet coffee into minute alabaster cups offered around with glasses of water from a beaten-brass tray. "I ask myself," continued Tahsin Bey, querying the ceiling, "why should my country be interested in such a project?'' His glance drifted down to a fading photo in an ornately painted border depicting medals and decorations. Beneath it, the words *Vive le Sultan Abdul Hamid.* ''And why should I concern myself with offering your plan to our Sultan?'' He invited temptation as surely as the tray of sweetmeats invited flies.

''Railroads will open Palestine like the legs of a houri,'' Mohamed assured him.

''To what, I wonder?'' mused Tahsin Bey. ''Palestine sleeps better without too many lovers.''

''Palestine is a beggar, Excellency—with an empty bowl waiting to be filled. Your great Sultan, Abdul Hamid Khan II, fingers his province like a string of amber worry beads. But are his prayers for it answered?''¯ asked Mohamed.

Tahsin Bey grunted and turned from Mohamed to the German engineer, noting the penetrating blue eyes and clean-cut features beneath closely cropped blond hair. ''And you, Herr von Leiter, your Kaiser paid us a visit only two years ago. The Sultan received him with great expectations. But his words did not weigh heavily in our Sultan's purse. Can you offer more than your Kaiser?''

''Excellency, your Sultan supports a Turkish army to police his province of Palestine. Not so?'' asked Von Leiter. ''And should that army ever need to defend his province . . . then a railroad could carry them to victory.''

Worry beads hesitated in the fat palm, oily with sweat. ''We already have a railroad. From Jaffa to Jerusalem.''

Von Leiter drew out a map, placing it on the Bey's desk. ''We are speaking of a new railroad. A modern one. The finest equipment. Paid not from your Sultan's coffers but by German investment. German marks flowing into the Turkish economy. . . .''

''With all construction equipment supplied through the Hammadi-Nouari Trading Company,'' Mohamed added. ''It is not money we are asking for. It is not supplies. Not manpower. Only a strip of land—wide enough for two camels to walk abreast.''

Tahsin Bey's shrug rippled down to his ample belly. ''*Enchela* . . . !'' he said. ''Perhaps a golden future. But we live in the present.'' He scratched his plump palm with an ivory fork from the Turkish delight. ''Permissions . . . always expensive.''

Mehmet Khassadia had been sitting quietly sipping his coffee. Now he signaled Mohamed with a quick look. "You will see, Excellency, that the matter has not been brought to you without . . . consideration." Mohamed extracted a beautifully tooled leather folder from his portfolio and set it on the first secretary's desk. It bulged with promise. "The Prophet says that generosity is the mother of faith, does he not?" ventured Mohamed, having invented a suitable quotation for the occasion. A nod from Khassadia brought him and Von Leiter to their feet. Tahsin Bey made no move toward the leather folder, but a smile touched the corners of his thick lips.

"The matter shall be weighed," he said. They bowed themselves out, leaving map and money to balance each other on the scales of Bey's conscience.

An opal sunset floated minarets and domes across the water. Jacqueline and Mohamed stood at the rail of the *Emperor Nicholas II*. The steamer nosed out across the little Sea of Marmara threading through pincushion islands of pines. "Beautiful—from a distance," she observed. "Teeming with filth when you are in it. . . ."

"It's the gateway to the Near East, Jacqueline. Gateways always attract beggars." He slipped a possessive arm around her. She turned to kiss him. He felt a tremble run through her, caused not only by the freshening air.

"Tell me, Mohamed," she whispered. "Tell me, my love— will I be happy? Will I belong?"

"To me, always."

"But will you leave me myself?"

He had telegraphed ahead to the Hammadi-Nouari agent in Jaffa. They would require a suite at the Hotel Kamenetz. Preparations would have to be made for the overland journey. "You shall travel to Jerusalem like the Queen of Sheba," he promised her.

"All the way from Jaffa by caravansy? I would have hoped there'd be something more modern. After all, this is 1900."

"Caravansy is still the most comfortable way. Some modern inventions were designed by the Devil. Like that movable oven the Turks call a railroad.''

"But aren't you going to build another railroad?"

"Not for you to ride in, my love. You'll prefer a tent under the stars.'' He glanced up with annoyance at the approaching glow of a cigarette through the dusk.

"Do I interrupt the honeymoon?'' came the affable Teutonic voice.

"Good evening, Herr von Leiter. We were just discussing our trip to Jerusalem. I'm afraid you and I are completely in my husband's hands. We shall have to be allies.'' She smiled at the German a shade too warmly for Mohamed.

"It will be my honor. For I, too, have never before been in this part of the world.'' He bowed, adding, "This color you wear is very suitable to you, madame. But so, I think, are all colors.''

"You'll join us at dinner tonight?'' she asked.

"Honored, madame.'' Heels clicked. "And it will be my pleasure to provide the wine. *Auf Wiedersehen*.'' He left them alone on the deck.

Mohamed's voice was tight, husky: "I do not wish to reprimand you, Jacqueline. But it is the husband's place to offer invitations . . . to a business associate.''

"But we are traveling together! Why shouldn't he share our table?''

"What else would you like him to share?'' His anger was genuine.

She turned away. "And when we come to your country, will you find it suitable for me to walk three paces behind you? Will you open my mail? Forbid me to receive gifts? Lock me in purdah—behind the grille of a harem?'' Her voice had taken on a shrill note he had never heard before.

"My dear. . . .'' His voice was gentle now. "Forgive me.'' He put his arms around her. "We were married in your church, not mine. And we shall live in your world. Not mine. Even in Jerusalem.''

The steamer had carried them through the Dardanelles into the Aegean Sea. They had skirted the Dodecanese, bypassed Rhodes, called in at Cyprus, then crossed to Palestine. Early in the morning of the last day, they emerged on deck . . . into a thunderstorm.

Jaffa offered no harbor. The ship tossed at anchor a mile out. Jacqueline and Oscar von Leiter had come up on deck early for a first glimpse of Palestine. Sand hills stretched beneath low, ragged clouds. Flat-roofed houses, an expanse of orange groves, a minaret—and atop a rocky hill, like a warning finger of stone, Jaffa Lighthouse. The boat rocked and heaved. Jacqueline was glad she had eaten no breakfast. The wind whipped rain into their faces. They became aware of an argument swelling into angry shouts among the steamer's crew.

"What's the matter?" Jacqueline asked Mohamed, who emerged from the companionway.

"The storm. Sometimes the police won't let the boats come out. If we can't be taken ashore, then we will have to go on to Haifa to land. Another fifty-nine miles."

"No! I think they come now!" exclaimed Von Leiter. "Half a dozen of them." Buffeting their way toward the steamer came a procession of open boats, each manned by a dozen bare-legged rowers. Mohamed grunted. "Whaleboats. The camels of the sea. At least they do not tip over very easily." Between jagged rocks, the long boats leaped high on the crests of the waves, then bumped down into the troughs.

"Are we to go ashore in one of those?" Von Leiter asked.

"Unless you'd prefer to swim, Herr von Leiter," Mohamed said.

Jacqueline laughed with excitement. The boats pulled alongside. The chiefs of the crews scrambled aboard the steamer. They began to sort out baggage and lower it to the bobbing crafts below with guttural shouts. Everyone seemed angry. Finally a dusky boatman helped the passengers to climb down the slippery, swaying ladder. Jacqueline leaped into the arms of Mohamed, who had gone down first. Oscar von Leiter followed gingerly, stumbling over the wet thwarts. The three found places in the stern sheets and watched an Italian lady descend with her parrot in a cage. She was so concerned for her pet, she forgot to be afraid.

The boat shoved off. The rowers cut into the choppy waves with long oars, singing as they pulled: *"Halli—yallah—yah hallah!"* High in his place in the stern, the steersman swore at his crew. They swept along on the tops of the waves in the foaming channel between the rocks.

At last the boat edged alongside the little quay. They clambered out onto wet, slippery stones. "So this is the Holy Land!" Jacqueline said.

"Our Kaiser has called it a land with a future." Von Leiter turned to Mohamed. "Now you and I shall make that future begin. Not so?"

Mohamed nodded. "With the blessings of the Sultan. Let's hope my Company will be as easily persuaded."

"Why should they not be? It's money for them."

"The trouble is, they didn't think of it."

The heat lay like a lid over the ancient city of Jaffa. Jacqueline looked from her window across the garden of the hotel with its purple flowering bougainvillea, orange trees, drooping palms, drowsing long-tailed cockatoos on perches. "Is it what you expected?" he asked, standing behind her.

"Everything. But you are not. You are much more."

He glanced out toward the last cloud rags of the thunderstorm spreading westward under a whip of wind toward the highlands of Judea. "In this port, Solomon landed cedar beams from Lebanon to build his temple. The Romans sacked Jaffa, and Richard the Lion-Hearted planted his crusaders' banner on its citadel. And so it goes on, now under the Turks, unchanged as ever. Nothing ever changes Palestine. Nor ever will."

"And you. Will I change you?" she asked.

"You have already, and you know it," he replied.

"I wonder. I don't know. Ever since we arrived on these shores, you seem another person. Maybe somebody you were before I knew you. Somebody who belongs here. . . ." She turned her gaze out the window. "All those civilizations— and Palestine untouched."

Two servants bowed themselves out, having filled the high-backed bathtub for the second time. He shed his Western clothes like an outworn skin and sank into the cool water. "The Romans went down the drains of their baths. One day the Turks will sweat themselves away—in their Turkish baths. One should never become too soft. There are always barbarians around the corner who don't worry about plumbing!"

She watched the ripple of amber muscles as he soaped

himself. "You're magnificent, you know. Men are not meant
to be so handsome. I thought so even that first day I saw you
at the races." She turned away, drawing aside the mosquito
netting that encased the bed; lay down. The heat of the
afternoon made her drowsy. She glanced through the netting.
His eyes were so large—almost like a young calf. . . .

When she awakened, a stranger stood over her. He wore an
abaya of fine white linen, head covered with a loose *kaffiyeh*
and golden braided *agal*. In his hand was a curved silver
dagger. He lifted it and she caught her breath. Then he slid
the blade into its sheath and thrust it through his sash. He
drew back the netting and bent to kiss her.

"What an enigma you are, Mohamed," she sighed, pulling
him down to her. "Yes, in your own land you *are* another
person. Transformed by the simple act of return. The patina
of Paris . . . rubbed away. In your native dress . . . speaking your native tongue, I wonder did Paris really change you
at all? Do I really know you?"

He ran his knuckles along her cheek. "Who really knows
their lover? Or their horse? Or their house? Or even their own
land?"

"What do you feel, coming back here, Mohamed?"

"It makes no difference where I am. Everything I feel is
for you." He kissed her breast. Then her lips. "Never be
unfaithful to me," he said softly. "I love you enough to
murder."

"Me . . . . or my lover?" she asked, removing his curved
dagger from his sash and offering it to him. He slipped it
under the pillow and lay down beside her.

Two victorias rattled through Jaffa's narrow streets, past
odd little open shops. The music of this strange city sounded
in Jacqueline's ears: hammer on brass, street vendors' cries,
donkey bells, the arguments of commerce. Her nostrils were
filled with the smells of spices, tanning leather, the perfume
of flowers from walled gardens. He had told her they would
be driven out as far as Ramleh, where they would leave the
carriages, load luggage onto pack mules and camels, mount
waiting saddle horses, and ride out across the plain. Ahead of
them, in the first open carriage, Von Leiter rode with Telhami,

their dragoman. The Arab cut a trim, alert figure in belted khaki and brown leather riding boots. Her glance caught the glint of Telhami's long Arab musket protruding above the seat like a metallic mast. "Will there be danger?" she asked expectantly.

Mohamed, who shared the second victoria with her, shrugged. "Where there is hunger there is always danger. Many hawks watching for a fat caravansy. But we are prepared."

"How, my love? With Telhami's antique musket?"

"It might surprise you to know that our dragoman can shoot the tail off a scorpion. Or so he assures me. In any event, we shall post a guard each night." He did not mention the Mauser in his own belt holster, nor had she missed noting it. He changed the subject. "By rail to Jerusalem, it would be fifty miles. Forty by carriage road—a trip made by thousands of pilgrims every year. Your first glimpse of my country will not be from the window of any railroad coach, Jacqueline. I want you to fall in love with it, for it is part of me." He glanced down at her jodhpurs with a hint of a frown. "A split skirt would have been wiser."

"Why?" she demanded. "I don't intend to ride sidesaddle."

"It might have caused less attention," he said.

The road straggled through ragged eucalyptus trees, budding figs, mulberries. Past fat-tailed sheep herded along by white-robed women. Past *fellaheen* with overladen donkeys. They brought him a quick image of his own grandfather, Musa, on the road to Jerusalem. How much had come out of that journey. . . . If it had not been for the luck of Musa, he would not be riding now on this journey to Jerusalem with the most beautiful bride in the world beside him.

At Ramlah, fine Arab horses waited in the shade of the tall tower of the Forty Martyrs. Telhami jumped down to complete arrangements. The carriages would be left there. Jacqueline chose a white mare with a silvery mane. Mohamed helped her mount. She swung a jodhpured leg over the horse. "Still worried I'll make a spectacle of myself?" she asked.

"I'm certain of it," he smiled.

She rested a gloved hand lightly on his arm. "Thank you, Mohamed."

"For what?"

"For everything. . . ." For a moment he glimpsed pure exultation in her face. He put his lips to her gloved fingers.

"Tonight I've arranged a surprise for you at our camp. Tomorrow we shall travel leisurely through the hills. And then, by sunset, you will see the gates of Jerusalem." He mounted a powerful horse, and they rode off side by side.

Von Leiter galloped up beside them, an excellent horseman. He rode bareheaded, pale blond hair catching the sun. "You should keep your head covered," warned Mohamed.

"This is a thing I can never understand. Why you Arabs wrap yourselves up like a caterpillar." In high spirits, he spurred his horse out across the gently undulating Plain of Sharon. Mohamed galloped to catch up with him. They rode on together for a moment in silence. Then Von Leiter called over.

"What a country for making war! Nobody here could resist it. Israelites, Philistines, Egyptians, Romans, Persians, Arabs, crusaders, Saracens. All have marched and fought here. And we, Hammadi, shall supply transportation for the next invasion. Not so?"

"Let us hope it is an invasion of commerce," Mohamed replied thoughtfully. "Our railroad could bring the twentieth century to this land." He looked toward the eastern horizon. As far as the eye could see stretched the highlands of Judea bathed in an azure and amethyst haze, rugged and treeless save for the occasional outcropping of oak and terebinths marking the tomb of some Christian or Mohammedan saint. "Yet here time sleeps," he added. "I wonder . . . can even a railroad wake it up?"

The caravansy followed an ancient trail across the basin of an open valley. As night fell, they reached the outskirts of a mud-hut village. "Latrun," Mohamed told them. "No more than a watering place." He turned his horse back for a word with Telhami.

A pack of jackals slunk furtively toward the horses from the shadows of gathering dusk. Jacqueline's mare shied and reared. She cried out, losing her reins, but managed to cling to the silvery mane. The beast was off at a pounding run. Von Leiter spurred after, charging up to catch her bridle. She swayed, almost falling into his arms. He dragged her mare to a stop.

"Lady Godiva in the desert, only with clothes on," he laughed.

"Afraid I'm not the horsewoman I thought," Jacqueline gasped.

"You ride very well." Von Leiter smiled. "But no horse, I think, likes jackals."

Mohamed cantered over. "Thank you, Von Leiter. For being so quick to the rescue."

"My pleasure."

Mohamed kept his horse closer to Jacqueline's as the caravan moved on. Across the plain, an undulating *kafila*—a camel caravan—disappeared behind an olive orchard. It was growing darker by the minute. They had been riding for hours. The horses had begun to stumble wearily. "How much farther?" she asked.

"We are almost to the campsite," Mohamed assured her. He ordered Telhami on ahead. The dragoman spurred his small horse like a jockey and disappeared in front of them. "In this place, the dusk falls like a curtain. People can disappear into it. Or come out of it before you know they're there," he said. A quarter of an hour later, a light bobbed toward them out of the engulfing dark.

"Telhami!" Mohamed shouted.

"It is Youssouf!" came back the answer. The attentive majordomo of the campsite brandished his lantern to illuminate a row of gleaming teeth. *"Salam aleikum, ya ghafir!"* Mohamed called. *"Aleikum es salam!"* Youssouf called back. They followed the dancing lantern through a muddy patch of trail around an acacia hedge to the ruined arch of an old well. Before it, six tents stood waiting with open flaps. Mohamed jumped down, offering a hand to Jacqueline.

"Where are we?" she asked.

"In the Valley of Aijalon, where Joshua fought the five kings of the Amorites."

"Fascinating," she said. "But I'm hungry."

"I promised you a feast beneath the stars."

An hour later, candles had been lighted on small folding tables decorated with wild flowers. Jacqueline and Mohamed sat on carpets spread over the ground. The air was spiced with the pungent aroma of Arab cooking.

"Aren't we waiting for Herr Von Leiter?" she asked.

"Let him follow his nose." Mohamed signaled Youssouf, who herded out a group of musicians. They gathered under a tree near the fire.

"My surprise, Jacqueline. . . . Music you will not hear in Paris!" He named the instruments for her. There was a violin of sorts, a flute, a *deff* (a form of tambourine), the *kanun* (a zither-like harp, which the musician held in his lap). Another sat cross-legged scraping a bow across a *kamanjah*.

"Like a teacup on a stick!" Jacqueline laughed as the musicians began to play.

Von Leiter finally appeared from his tent, his step a little unsteady, eyes too bright. He offered a silver flask. "Schnapps. It removes the aches from the ride, and puts the edge on the appetite, not so?"

Mohamed declined. Jacqueline accepted a small glass. "Prosit!" Von Leiter watched her in the firelight. "If you will not think me rude—and your husband will permit—beneath the stars you are even more beautiful than in Paris, madame. You make me sad I am not also on a honeymoon."

"No woman in your life, Herr von Leiter?" she inquired.

"Always too many, never enough." He sank down on the cushions, exhausted by the weight of amorous memories.

Youssouf, in embroidered jacket and baggy blue breeches, passed steaming platters. Baby lamb bedded on saffron rice. Quail. Spicy condiments. Fresh figs. "I hope the wine will be to your liking, Von Leiter. From a vineyard near Jaffa, at Petach Tikva. It is called Rishon le-Zion—The Treasure of Zion." Mohamed sipped.

"I am surprised to see you drink in Palestine," said the German.

"I drink in Paris. I would not be a hypocrite in my own country," Mohamed replied.

Von Leiter swirled the wine around on his tongue. His lip curled slightly. "For me, this Jewish wine is too sweet!" Nevertheless he emptied it at a gulp. The glass was immediately refilled.

"Isn't this wine from a German colony?" Jacqueline asked.

"German, madame? By my information this colony is financed from Baron Rothschild—who may call himself a German. The Jew has a good nose for money." He emptied his glass again. "Better, I think, than for wine."

Mohamed frowned. "Hammadi-Nouari is a partnership of Moslems and Jews. It has lasted for three generations. Through respect. Here, in Palestine, it would be well to remember that."

"Why not?" smiled the German amiably. He leaned toward Mohamed. "Tell me one thing, my friend. Is it not true you Moslems are not allowed to receive interest on your loans? Just as you are not permitted to drink?"

"By strict religious law, that is true. But, as a banker, I do arrange business loans. Not for interest but for a share in the profits."

"Profits are not—you will pardon me—against your religion?"

"It is in accord with the law of Islam. If the debtor makes no profit, the bank receives nothing from any loans arranged by me." Mohamed tried to control a mounting anger.

"Isn't it fortunate," Jacqueline put in quickly, "that my husband is such a good judge of character?"

"And your partners, Liebermann and Nouari—if the bank makes nothing, this I think is against their religion!" Von Leiter laughed at his own humor. Mohamed's expression hardened to a bronze mask. The tension was broken by Youssouf, passing a tray of steaming meats. He offered Jacqueline two whitish, egg-like lumps.

"What are they?"

"You are honored, my love. Youssouf has brought you the eyes of the sheep."

"I'm going to be ill . . ." she said, starting to rise. He grasped her arm tightly, pulling her down.

"Not before these people. It would be an insult. Eat!" he commanded. She forced herself to pick up one of the lumps. For a moment, she thought she might faint. Von Leiter leaned forward.

"Surely, Hammadi, you are not going to make her swallow that thing?"

Jacqueline stiffened, holding the object up in her fingers. "Of course I shall eat it, Herr von Leiter. After all, it's no worse than a frog's leg, a calf's brain, or a pig's foot." She bit into it, and chewed with a brave show of pleasure. Pleased, Mohamed pointed to one of the tents, giving an order in Arabic. Youssouf clapped his hands.

"I spoke too much, before. You will forgive if I have offended," the German said, sobering slightly.

"In my country a guest is always honored, Herr von Leiter. In keeping with his station in life."

From one of the tents, two belly dancers appeared, a mother and daughter, plump and shiny in spangled costumes glittering with gold. The music loudened with a lively, rhythmic beat. The moment of tension passed. To the bell-jangle of coins, the dancers began undulating to clapping hands and nasal, guttural chanting. Von Leiter sank back against the cushions, eyes gleaming across his wine at pivoting hips and rounded bellies. Mohamed watched, enigmatic.

"I think I should learn to do that," Jacqueline said.

"A gliding of a lily," Von Leiter enthused.

He had shown her the wonderful closeness of stars in the open. They made love in the stillness of the tent, their breathing joining the sound of that faint, restless, creeping breeze. He moved from her narrow camp bed back to his own. His hand was still reaching across to touch her skin when he fell asleep.

The stillness. . . . Something eternal about it here—for where else could it be so still? No movement on earth or in sky but the faint stirring of olive branches.

Mohamed wasn't certain what it was that had awakened him. A sound that didn't belong to the night. Next to Jacqueline in the carpet-hung tent, he had fallen into a heavy, dreamless slumber. Then, suddenly, he was wide awake—listening. Yes . . . there it was again! No more than a rustle of movement somewhere in the encampment. The wind?

Telhami had posted a guard for the night. A young Arab lad wrapped in flowing rags perched high atop the broken arch by the well, a long brassbound musket across his knees. If anything were to approach, the lad would fire a warning shot. Mohamed closed his eyes, annoyed with himself for his nagging sense of unease.

Then it rippled the stillness with a dagger of sound: the anguished, terrified cry of a woman! Mohamed snatched the Mauser from under his pillow, darted out through the flap of the tent before Jacqueline was fully awake. She sat up look-

ing after him, for the first time in her life frightened by the
wild, guttural shouts.

The whole camp was awake now. Men were rushing about
in the dark. At the opening of Von Leiter's tent, the elder of
the belly dancers cringed in a blanket, shrieking incoherently.
Mohamed hurried to her. One look inside the tent said all.
Stretched across the narrow cot lay Von Leiter, naked and
still carrying an erection like a grotesque, phallic joke. His
throat had been slashed. There was blood everywhere, his
features frozen into a look of surprise.

Telhami ran up, shouting, "The guard! He has been
stabbed!"

A rush of feet brought Mohamed in time to see four robed
figures hurl themselves on waiting horses. One twisted around
in his saddle and fired. Mohamed squeezed the trigger of his
Mauser, toppling the rider. His animal bolted away with the
others, blending instantly into the darkness.

Mohamed shouted at two dazed servants stumbling toward
their own horses. Though armed, they seemed in no great
haste to pursue the retreating marauders.

Telhami's lantern beam picked out the bundle of dirty rags.
Mohamed turned the dead bandit face up. A bullet hole
through his forehead was already clotting with blood. The
eyes were open, staring. They were blue! Mohamed closed
them, pulled back the *kaffiyeh*. Sandy hair. He took up the
bandit's revolver. It was a .45-caliber Webley.

He had never killed a man before. He was surprised by
how little he felt.

They carried Von Leiter's body with them to Jerusalem to
be delivered to the German consul, with a full report to
Turkish authorities. There was much that didn't make sense
to Mohamed. Such raids had become rare in this area. The
pistol used by the raider had been British Army issue of 1897.
Not easy to come by in Palestine, particularly for a roving
bandit. If that was what he was. A British Army deserter? But
from where? Egypt, perhaps?

But, most of all, the motive troubled Mohamed. If robbery
had been the objective, Jacqueline's jewel case would have
been the main target. Yet all they had taken were a few brass

and silver trinkets. Hardly worth two murders. The belly dancer confirmed that she and the German had been making love when the marauder burst in, knocked her aside and slashed Von Leiter's throat. The work of an expert—a professional assassin. But why Von Leiter? Who would care about a German engineer?

Jacqueline had barely spoken since the murder. She rode along beside Mohamed wrapped in distant thoughts, moving in a dream, without volition. The shock, Mohamed assured himself. When they reached Jerusalem, the sights of the ancient city would erase the tragedy from her mind. Or had Von Leiter meant something to her? No. The idea was absurd!

There were other implications to be considered. No matter what Mohamed had thought of the German personally, the man was an integral part of the railroad project. His death could delay things by at least six months. Naturally, Mohamed would cable Von Bülow. But it would take time to send another man, and Mohamed was more determined than ever that the deal go through. That Hammadi-Nouari Trading Company should supply Von Bülow's group with everything that would be needed. And the railroad builders would need everything.

Still the haunting question kept returning: Why Von Leiter? Could he have been the target of the raid because someone didn't want this railroad built? If so, who? He hoped the incident would not dampen the Germans' enthusiasm. Or the Company's! If only Judah were here to support him! Judah, too, believed in the project in spite of the risks, the expense, the political implications. He and Judah always saw eye to eye.

The caravan paused on the hill above old Jerusalem. As always, the sight brought mixed emotions to Mohamed. Nostalgia. An ache of remembrance . . . for this was still home. The dusty smell, the heat, the serenity, the lethargy and inertia, the hypnotic torpor of the place also brought a discontent, a vexation at how little it had changed or caught up with the rest of the world. Sometimes, in Paris, he found himself longing for this vista of home. But each time he returned, it was more as a stranger. Never so much as now, with his foreign wife.

"Does it look as you expected?" he asked, pointing across

the narrow strip of the Valley of Jehoshaphat, where olive trees marched in ranks below a hillside plumed with cypresses, towards crenelated walls framing the city.

She was silent.

Jerusalem stood out like the knuckles of a clenched fist, the Church of Dormition, a jewel on Mount Zion. His eyes rested a moment on the El Aqsa Mosque, near the Jewish Quarter, then drifted to the dark shadow of the Wailing Wall. He offered his field glasses, but she didn't touch them.

"Jerusalem is a city where everyone mingles, yet everyone belongs to himself. There . . . that's the Armenian Quarter. There the Moslem, by the Dome of the Rock. Where Mohammed ascended to Heaven—and where on Judgment Day, God's throne will be." He moved his finger to the right. "But that is what will interest you, Jacqueline. The Church of the Holy Sepulchre, the French Convent and the Notre-Dame de France. They should make you feel more at home. And there, the Via Dolorosa, where your Christ bore his cross. Within these ancient walls . . . are man's holiest shrines and bitterest memories. Always my city has been fought over like a carcass in a pack of hyenas."

And still she said nothing. They rode on, breaking with the caravan now, to skirt the wall of the city.

"We shall not be staying in the city. My family owns houses outside the Damascus Gate. It is cooler there." The barest nod of her head was the only indication that she had heard. "What is it that's troubling you so deeply?" he asked, suddenly angry.

"Nothing. Nothing. Nothing. . . ."

"There's a wall around you higher than the city. Are you worried about my family? Or is it me? Or the German— dragging you into his grave? I must know, Jacqueline!"

She shook her head. "I hate to be questioned. I can't stand questions. Why did we come here, anyway?"

"Because you happen to be my wife."

"Happen?" Her voice took on a strange, irascible note. "What happens? Nothing happens. It's waiting for you and no escape. Ever, ever. . . ." She began to weep. He couldn't think what to say. He took the bridle of her horse and led it onward. What had gone wrong? Was this woman ever possible to understand? And then a different sound chilled him.

She was laughing—like someone who had found a secret joke.

"Tell me," he begged, grateful that she had stopped crying.

"Nothing to tell." She smiled. Her face was masked in mystery. The path of tears had dried a trail through the dust powdering her cheek. "Would it seem strange to you," she asked suddenly, "that I don't want to meet them? Not yet. Not today."

"It would," he replied. "And even stranger to them."

A fly made its journey from a donkey turd in the crowded street, up over a whitewashed wall, and hummed its way down into the interior courtyard toward a tray of glasses of sweet mint tea on a low, octagonal, ivory-inlaid table. Its descent was broken by the stinging passage of a whisk. The fly retreated toward the bougainvillea creeping up the wall, there to grumble buzzingly to his careless fly-god, who had let him be so damaged at a moment of fulfillment.

Three old men hovered over a low table in the courtyard in the old part of the city. Three who had once come to Jerusalem with a donkey and a cart full of goods. Now they had been retired for many years, but it was their habit to make their way each afternoon to the offices of Hammadi-Nouari Trading Company. They rarely went inside the building these days, preferring to play a game or two of backgammon, drink a glass of tea, exchange some crumbs of family gossip, or talk about old times.

For the last few years, since his stroke, Jacob, youngest of the three, had been confined to a wheelchair. Bulky, venerable Abraham would collect his frail brother from the rambling house outside the city's walls and drive in to meet Musa. Now that their sons were in charge of the business, they made it a rule never to interfere. Just as it was also a rule that sons-in-law did not enter the business through marriage. A handsome dowry went with each daughter's hand, but the partnership passed from father to sons. If the three patriarchs were asked for an opinion on some matter of business, it would be offered. But that happened less and less these days.

Solomon, Jacob's eldest son, was now chairman of the board. "A weigher of words," Musa called him. "He holds some of the wisdom of the great king whose name he carries—along with the shrewdness of his father!'' Musa would say with a wink at Jacob, and Jacob would politely shrug off the compliment with ''But he thinks too slowly.''

Musa knew his own eldest son, Sayid, to be unbending, inflexible at times. Such had been Sayid's reaction when his son Mohamed arrived with his French Catholic bride. Musa himself had been more lenient on his grandson's behalf. ''It isn't the last days of the world, Sayid,'' he had said. ''For his next wife Mohamed will choose a nice Arab girl.'' Musa had two wives. The Koran permitted four.

And as for David Nouari, he secretly wondered whether he had done the right thing in allowing his son Judah to remain in Paris. For the young, Paris could be a disease. Who knew what kind of girl Judah might meet there? Mohamed's assurances were hardly reassuring. A Jewish girl. All right. But an Ashkenazi! From Poland . . . or Russia. As bad as a French Catholic!

Voices drifted out to the courtyard through the grilled window of the boardroom. Not often did so many members of the Hammadi-Nouari empire meet together. A Company gathering was also a family reunion. This one had brought Abdullah Hammadi and Izak Nouari from Damascus, Mahmood Hammadi and Gideon Nouari from Cairo. Mohamed's arrival from Paris, his marriage, his proposal of their participation in the German railroad project—all were in themselves events of sufficient importance to require the airing of attitudes and opinions, the making of decisions.

Concerning the marriage, there was nothing further to be done. The step had been taken, and even Mohamed himself did not seem very happy about it at this moment. ''A hundred respectable families in Palestine. A hundred orchards from which fruit might be picked. . . . One cannot think that what happened in Paris was by the will of Allah,'' Uncle Abdullah had grumbled.

''The end of the page has not been written. Each morning, the world begins again,'' Musa had assured his nephew. But the project of the railroad, ah, that was something else! A thing to be examined, weighed, analyzed—and finally put to a vote by the Company directors.

''I agree with my nephew, Mohamed, that our first concern

must be the profit!'' It was Mahmood's voice drifting out into the courtyard where the old men sat. Expanding, fleshy, stouter than his brother, Sayid, Uncle Mahmood was devoted to the joys of the table. But he was also a man of practicality.

"Some profits can be too expensive to afford.'' David Nouari's voice sheathed impatience.

The old men listened and nodded. "Always the cautious one, your son David.'' Musa pulled down the corners of his mouth.

"Caution is not always a virtue," Abraham allowed. "One must be willing to take chances.'' They listened again as the next voice sounded through the grilled window.

"I have taken the trouble to find out certain things. Things Mohamed may not know and therefore cannot have considered.'' David's fingers touched the file of papers before him as though caressing musical keys. An impressive figure, Judah's father; slender for his years, thickly maned with white hair.

Mohamed's voice interrupted with impatience. "I have put before you the chance to enrich the Company by millions— and you sniff it, walk around it! What's the matter? Has the Company become so prosperous that you can afford to throw away opportunities?''

"Mohamed, please . . .'' David said. "I have had a communication from a minister in the office of the Turkish governor in Syria. It suggests that no decision for permissions has yet been made. That until His Excellency has been informed how the wind blows in Constantinople, he finds himself reluctant. . . .'' His lips pursed the word, wanting them to share the unpleasant taste. "Yes, reluctant to enter into any agreement that might introduce the influence—influence of a foreign power—by whose presence could be planted a seed of hostility.''

"Hostilities can grow into wars,'' observed Gideon Nouari, who hadn't yet spoken and needed to say something.

"You hear what a voice speaks?'' old Abraham disparaged his second son. "Hostilities grow into wars. . . . What an original conclusion! Could King Solomon have reached it? No, it took our Gideon, all the way from Cairo.''

"We crossed enough palms in Constantinople to buy Topkapi! If your local governor feels neglected, we can rattle a few coins in his direction as well. This issue isn't political!'' Anger tinged Mohamed's voice. ''It is a private German company. Not a government project. Besides, the Germans have already built one railroad in Turkey. They offer us a business proposal, not an international alliance! No matter what the cost—or even the risk—I have brought you the opportunity of your lives!''

There was a muttering and shaking of heads. ''You have also brought a dead body,'' Izak growled. The trip from Damascus had tired him, and he was more irascible than usual. A sour man, corroded by ill health that made him appear older than his forty-four years, Izak was as different from his robust, jolly elder brother, Solomon, as chalk from cheese. To Mohamed, Izak had always seemed devoured by some secret grievance against Musa Hammadi—so beloved by all the rest of the Nouari family. There were stories that, years before, Izak had been in love with Bethena, Musa's daughter. But intermarriage between the families was unthinkable. That was, as Jacob joked, why they always got on so well. Bethena had been rushed into a convenient marriage; Izak, elevated to co-head of the Damascus office.

Now the sour Izak leaned forward in his chair. ''No, I do not write off the German's death as some casual crime. I see it as a clear warning!''

Abdullah Hammadi nodded support to his partner. ''If we involve ourselves—and mind you, Mohamed, much of it must be handled from Damascus—we will be required to accept the Germans' insistence upon fixed estimates for all supplies and services.''

''That's never worried us before,'' said Mohamed.

''Before, we were dealing with merchandise. Now we may be dealing with forces who might not want the Germans to marry the Turks and give birth to a railroad,'' warned Solomon.

''And if we don't get those official permissions for which our cousin Mehmet Khassadia has allowed you to pay so generously,'' Izak crowed, ''nobody will build as much as a shit house between here and Aqaba!'' There was an explosion of voices as order was lost, and the meeting broke into private encounters.

In the courtyard, old Jacob sighed, turned his attention back to the backgammon board. The dice spilled from his cup, and he moved to cover his bar point, cocking an eye at

Musa. "She is not well, you know. His wife. The French-woman."

Musa nodded. "Two weeks they have been here. She sits on the balcony of his mother's house and stares at the hills."

Abraham sighed agreement. "Her eyes. You have seen her eyes? She wears a veil on the soul."

"And she barely speaks to anyone," Musa observed, adding, "although I myself do not speak French, nor does my daughter-in-law, Mohamed's mother, who has told me that the woman takes all her meals in her room. And she doesn't eat enough to give strength to a bird."

Jacob pulled his beard. "You remember, Abraham? When we were young, there was in our village a woman like this French one. Less beautiful, of course. But then, nobody saw her face. For hours she sat. Just sat. And our mother said she suffered from this mysterious thing that comes out of the wind from the desert: the melancholy."

"The melancholy . . ." repeated Musa. "Yes, but the French one must have been all right when he married her. Maybe in Paris they don't catch such things."

"Musa," said Abraham, "do I not recall that your second son, Abdullah, did not agree with the plan of Sayid to send Mohamed for education to Paris?"

"What you recall is true. But I also recall that you did not approve of your own son, David, sending Judah to Paris." Their train of thought was derailed by the voices drifting out again.

"And who would oppose German expansion in the Middle East? I'll tell you: the Russians . . . the British . . . the French. Don't forget the French, Mohamed. The French first of all!" Abdullah considered his nephew's foreign marriage a punishment of fate. "If someone doesn't want the Germans here, enough to kill Von Leiter—then they will sabotage all that follows. And we, who will commit ourselves to purchasing and supplying everything from a labor force to iron spikes, will see the profits blow off like sand."

"Abdullah's point is well made. Our first concern must be profit," Mahmood agreed. There was a murmur of accord around the table.

Out in the courtyard, old Abraham frowned. "Too much caution!" He watched his brother throw the dice. "If the ones in there had been with us on the road to Jerusalem, we would still be sleeping in the fields.''

In the conference room, Solomon lifted his voice with finality. ''We have talked ourselves into circles. Sabotage. Murder. Great fortunes to be made. We have heard of profits and perils. Now we must decide. Are we willing, as Mohamed urges us, to take the risk? It is time to vote.''

Mohamed rose. ''Take your vote. Make your decision. But I want it understood . . . that if you vote my proposal down . . . I will resign. I will accept the German contract. Form my own trading company to supply them—and I can do it! Because I believe that this is the greatest opportunity for the future of our land since the building of the Suez Canal! Now I shall have a breath of cool air.'' He walked out of the room without a backward glance.

''That is what happens when you send someone for education to Paris.'' Musa rolled his dice. ''He comes back like Napoleon!''

Dust rose and settled in lowering sun-flecked motes above the wall. Day aged toward dusk. The old men waited in the courtyard; waited and speculated. But the result, when it came, brought them neither surprise nor wonder. Mohamed had come outside to wait with them. They became silent, as though his commanding presence corked conjectures. He said little. They said less. He smoked a cigarette and watched the goldfish swimming in endless circles in the tiled pool formed like a Moslem star. Street cries of vendors, the croak of wheels turning somewhere near, moved time to a conclusion.

Solomon, last to vote, was first of the little procession to emerge. His smile was the clue. ''Well, Mohamed, you have won. A majority in your favor. It was moved and passed that the decision should be declared unanimous.'' Solomon stepped to the wheelchair and put a hand on his father's shoulder. The old man beamed, pleased.

''Since the project was initiated by you,'' David added, ''we wish you to have full and final authority to see it through. And may God grant you wisdom, my son.'' Indeed, Mohamed could look upon David Nouari as a father, sometimes more of a father in understanding than his own. ''Thank you, my uncle.'' He used the customary term as he had since childhood. He guessed that it had been David Nouari's deciding vote that had won the day. He was wrong. It had been Solomon's.

"I'll do my best to make certain none of you will be sorry." Everyone nodded, voicing good wishes. Some still kept a silent reluctance in their hearts.

"Congratulations," wheezed Jacob, beaming up from his wheelchair. "Sometimes even the younger generation do something sensible. Sometimes, but not always." All laughed. It was a time to bury lingering rancors and share one of those rare moments when the Company could function with the harmony of one body guided by a single mind. Servants appeared; more tea was passed, with trays of sticky-sweet honey cakes. The babble of voices rose—then sharply, suddenly, died.

Jacqueline stood in the gateway, exhilarated, happy, and wondrously beautiful—followed by two young Arab boys carrying a large basket between them. "I've been all afternoon shopping in the bazaar," she said cheerfully. "You won't believe what treasures! Put it down there. . . ." She indicated to the two boys an area near the brightly tiled fountain pool. Then she poured silver coins into their cupped hands and waved them out. The boys ran off, babbling and laughing.

Mohamed stepped to her, noticing that the hem of her white muslin dress was dusty, spattered in places with mud. Her large straw hat was slightly askew, collar ribbons untied. Her eyes had a shiny, overexcited look. There were hectic points of color in her cheeks. He was displeased that she had violated custom by barging in among the members of the Company without a word of apology. Certainly without invitation. But he also felt relief at seeing her looking well again. It was as though a cloud had lifted. She was disheveled, maybe, but the total effect was enchantment. "You did not go into the bazaar alone?" he asked, looking past her through the gateway, expecting to see a carriage with his mother, perhaps, or one of the other female relatives, waiting discreetly in the background—as would be proper.

"But I wasn't alone, Mohamed. Little boys followed me everywhere. Swarms of them. Until I finally selected two—and saw this quite divine basket to hold everything. They're gifts, you see."

"Gifts?"

"Yes. For everyone." She fumbled into a purse and brandished a notebook. "I've learned all the names—I have been studying Arabic, you know. And put small marks beside them to give me a hint of the right choice. So there'd be something for everyone. Don't you hate being left out? I always do. . . ." Her eyes probed the clutter in the basket. "Now, first. Where are we? Oh, yes, Jacob. Jacob, Jacob, Jacob . . . where are you? Ah, here you are! A dagger in a brass sheath!"

Jacob looked somewhat embarrassed as she flourished the tourist souvenir. "Very nice," he mumbled.

"Now—who's next? Abdullah. Yes, Abdullah! For you—a rare Turkish tobacco. And a pouch. See? A yellow pouch! Very handsome. Now, yes. Slippers. Green leather slippers for Abraham to steal into some secret harem. Oh, no, I've got the wrong one, haven't I?" She laughed hectically. "Well, Mahmood, then. The slippers are for you. For padding through the streets of Cairo."

Mahmood glanced down at his own superbly handmade French kidskin shoes. His smile was limp.

"And for you, Gideon, a fly whisk. Then there's a robe to cover my beautiful husband. Look, isn't it a fine, strong color to inspire great feats of love? Red!"

Mohamed took his wife's arm. "Jacqueline, I think the gifts can be distributed later. It is getting toward evening. . . ."

She stared at Mohamed as though he'd suddenly become a stranger. "Are you jealous of these old men, too?"

Solomon came toward her. "Very thoughtful of you, madame, and we are all most grateful."

"Oh, I even have extra things for the children. And your wives, of course. Perfume. A fine piece of silk. And this cigarette holder—for you, Solomon."

"He doesn't smoke," Mohamed snapped.

"Amber. For such a beautiful thing, I would learn," Solomon said tactfully.

"Now, come, my dear. . . ." Mohamed's voice was steely. "No more gifts. Later it will be arranged. You should not have gone alone to the bazaar. It was very wrong, Jacqueline. Anything could have happened. I don't wish to reprimand you, but my concern is for you. Now I'll take you back to the house. I think you should rest."

"Well!" she laughed. "Perhaps you are right, Mohamed. And the gifts—will be more appreciated by the goldfish."

With a sudden motion, she emptied the basket of trinkets into the pool.

Nobody spoke.

The brass sank; the leather floated, ludicrously bobbing about within the tiled Moslem star.

Mohamed put an arm firmly about her. "Come," he said, voice tight. "You're very tired. You're not yourself."

She turned back to the group, and in a last, strange, spontaneous gesture, curtsied deeply to the men of the two families. Then she left with her husband, head high, but moving a little as one might through a dream.

Old Jacob turned slowly to the others. "A man may stand like a giant in the world of his business—yet be more helpless than a little child to manage his own house."

Nobody at this instant could think of anything worth adding. Least of all old Musa and Mohamed's father, Sayid.

Five ─────────────────────────

IT was not the kind of homecoming Judah would have wished. But then, it was not any kind of home, that Paris apartment where Zosia lived, where he visited, and where they occasionally made love. Judah had come directly from the depot. He knocked—heard voices. When no one answered, used his key.

She was seated at her desk, Count Alexei Lubenov bending over her shoulder, his hand on her arm. He straightened stiffly. Every time Judah returned from anywhere, this Russian seemed to be looming over Zosia.

"Judah!" Zosia detached herself, rushing into Judah's arms.

Aside from a sofa bed, the attic room was strewn with papers, every surface cluttered. There were inkwells, pamphlets, as well as notebooks of shorthand in Zosia's slanting, hectic fly tracks trailing across white pages. And rising at the center of all was the citadel of Zosia's war of words, the great crabbed cage of her typewriter. For the past year, she had been carrying on a bombardment of anonymous articles. They appeared in the Narodnaya Volya's underground newspaper under the pen name of Chofesh—Hebrew for "freedom." The paper, distributed throughout Europe, as anti-Czarist. Some people considered it anti-Semitic.

But anti-Czarists and Zionists had a common enemy: the Okhrana, Imperial Russia's secret police.

"I trust your journey to Constantinople was successful, monsieur?" the Count asked in his usual, stilted manner. "For you—and for our mutual cause."

"For neither, I'm afraid." Under Zosia's influence, Judah had become ever more deeply involved with the Zionists. It would be fair to say (and Mohamed had!) that Judah's busi-

78

ness trips for Hammadi-Nouari were mainly fund-raising expeditions for Herzl's cause.

Herzl was always delighted. "A natural ability," he had praised. "A talent to marry the pen to the checkbook."

Mohamed found Judah's efforts on behalf of the railroad project less impressive. He objected strenuously when Judah insisted on accompanying Herzl to Constantinople.

Count Lubenov gathered papers into a battered portfolio. "If you will excuse me, I am expected back at the embassy." He contorted into his odd, rigid-backed bow, lifted Zosia's hand punctiliously a few inches short of his lips, brushed past Judah, and was gone.

"Someday—just one day—I'd like to walk into this room and not find that Cossack practically seducing you."

She laughed. "You are being stupid and unfair, and you know it. If you weren't tired from your travels, I would be very annoyed." She kissed him again. He melted slightly. She helped him off with the heavy, fur-collared coat, led him to the only comfortable chair. "And Dr. Herzl? How did you leave him?"

"Busy sugaring Turkish palms, with the help of my uncle Mehmet. He still hopes to persuade the Sultan to sell land in Palestine for Zionist colonies."

Judah's eyes traced the slim figure in its trim gray skirt and peach bodice. "Tea," she said. "We'll have a glass of tea." She pulled away to fuss over the small gas burner.

"But Herzl won't succeed with Abdul Hamid. Any more than he did three years ago, when he tried to woo the Kaiser. The Sultan hadn't even authorized that visit. Herzl was lucky the Turks didn't take him prisoner or deport him to Alexandria on some cockleshell boat!"

"Well?" she asked. "What happened this time?"

"A lot of double dealing—at which the Turks are expert and the Jews are children." He took her hand and pulled her to him. She sat on the floor leaning back against his knee.

"It's so good to have you back," she whispered.

"Is it?" he asked. "I swear I don't know why I keep coming back, Zosia. Sometimes I think the only reason you care for me is because of what I can do for Herzl." He surveyed her room with disapproval. "You won't let me do anything for you. Look how you live! I've offered to find you a decent apartment. I've offered to marry you."

She rose, carrying their glasses back to the counter. "We've been over all this, Judah. Many times. Isn't it enough that I love you?"

"How should I know that?" he demanded. "Because you allow me into your bed occasionally? Do you also allow Alexei?"

Her hand slapped hard across his cheek. Then she turned away, voice husky. "If you feel that way, I do not want you here."

"It's only because I'm jealous of everything that separates us." He kissed the smoky curls at the nape of her neck.

"Of what is there to be jealous?" she asked. "My articles? They are the voice of our needs. Those documents Alexei was showing me when you arrived—they are evidence against the chief of the Okhrana, General Pyotr Rachovsky, Zionism's worst enemy."

He put his arms around her waist. "Zosia, my darling, you're wrong. We Jews are our own worst enemies. Do you know what the German Reich Chancellor asked Herzl? If he really believed Jews would throw over their stock exchange to follow him to some barren, promised land. And who do you think *would* follow Herzl?"

"The perfect anti-Semite—you, Judah! Can't you understand we are what the ghettos made us? For centuries we were forced into finance. Because Christians wouldn't dirty their hands with money. Except to borrow it—and pay their debts with the sword. Yes, now we are branded with the stock exchange—then hated when we perform our role too well." She began to toss papers in a blizzard of emotion. Her rage excited him. He seized her and kissed her almost savagely. She pushed him away.

"Zosia—why do we always end up in a political argument?"

"Zionism isn't political!" There were tears in her eyes.

"What the devil is it, then?" he demanded.

"Hope . . ." she replied. "For those who do not have comfortable nests in tolerant countries. For those who do not have full bellies."

He sighed. "Another night of debate . . . Zosia, I'm tired. I'm hungry. I'm thirsty. I want to make love. Can't we—just tonight—go out, eat dinner, listen to some music,

and talk about ourselves?'' He tried to pull her to him. Again
she drew back.

"Please, Judah," she said. "I didn't expect you tonight.
My article—I promised Alexei. It must be printed immediately. It is very important."

"And we are not, Zosia?"

"Tomorrow night . . . we will be. I promise you." She
kissed him so tenderly his anger melted into desire. Desire
that would have to wait.

"And if tomorrow night I ask you again to marry me . . . ?"

She smoothed back her hair. "For everything there is a
time, the Bible tells us. Ours will come. I am not yet able to
devote my days to babies. Be patient a little longer."

"How much longer?"

Her face brightened into a smile. "Tomorrow we will dine
anywhere you like. I'll wear my best gown and pretend I am
a pretty woman without a thought in my head."

He allowed her to help him into his coat. "You're getting
me into a great deal of trouble, you know. You and Dr.
Herzl. But then, Herzl once promised me he would. I don't
spend enough time at the bank to answer my mail."

"Yes," she agreed, "you've been wonderful; you are
appreciated. Tomorrow night I shall say thank you properly.
And I will not let you out of my bed until morning." She
pushed him gently toward the door. "Now go, before I forget
how much work I must do tonight."

She returned to the typewriter with a reluctant sigh. He
picked up his bags. "Zosia . . . why, when you make me so
miserable, do I love you so much?"

"There is a limit to Baron Liebermann's patience, Judah. I
think you have reached it."

"And yours?"

"Frankly, yes."

Judah leaned back in the chair that faced Mohamed's desk,
smoothed his hand across his crest of thick, dark hair. He had
made a special effort to be early this first morning back. Early
and waiting in Mohamed's office when his Arab partner
arrived. He had overstayed his Turkish mission by six weeks.
"You want me to feel guilty? I feel guilty," Judah admitted.

"You should. You damn well should." Mohamed caressed the serious dignity of his new mustache. "While you've been trailing after Herzl like an Arab bride, I've had meetings in Germany with Von Bülow's crowd. Three trips to the Lebanon—and what deals I made . . . ! Timber for ties—and no extra charges for cutting or filling in beveling, or putting in frogs and switches."

"Brilliant."

"Don't flatter me!"

"I wasn't."

"It should have been *you* in Birmingham, bargaining for those steel rails and spikes."

"I know. I know."

"What the devil *are* you spending your time on, Judah?" The question was academic. Mohamed knew well enough. But he also felt that Judah's dedication to this cause was superficial. Dedication to the gray eyes of a Polish girl was more like it. The Arab knew how it was to be trapped by a girl's eyes.

And he knew that a moment would come when you were free again.

A year had passed since Mohamed and Jacqueline returned from Jerusalem, to the fine new house in the Avenue Malenkoff. In that house at first it seemed that her illness had been a mirage. A shimmering of desert heat. She threw herself into the chores of furnishing and decorating, in preparation for lavishly envisioned entertainments.

But something had been lost between them. A feeling known only once. With her. He longed to feel it again, could not.

Mohamed dragged his mind back to the thick portfolio on his polished desk. "Do you know what this is, Judah?" His gesture swept across contracts, maps, plans, accounts, blueprints. "The railroad you supported when I proposed it. Hammadi-Nouari is committed to a time schedule—and we're nine months behind now."

"I'm back. What can I do to help?"

"Read that." Mohamed tossed him a letter. "A new explosive being manufactured in Sweden. An improvement on Nobel's ballistite. If you want to help, go there. See it tested. How it performs. If it's all they claim, buy it. It doesn't matter what it costs. It will take most of the danger out of blasting. Save money in the end.''

"And lives.'' Judah scanned the letter. "I'll leave tomorrow.''

The tension eased. "A curious thing . . .'' Mohamed mused. "You and I took ourselves out of Jerusalem—to study, to work, to live. And our first project is a railroad through our homeland.'' He moved to the wall map and traced the proposed route of the railroad with an unlit cigar. "Tell me honestly: do you believe Herzl's colonists will ever come to Palestine?''

"Anything that is necessary is possible.''

Mohamed frowned, decapitated his cigar with a gold cutter in the shape of a guillotine. A gift from Jacqueline. "You know, Judah, the Arabs want Palestine for themselves. Without the Turks. Does Herzl want Palestine . . . without the Arabs?''

"Of course not. There's room for everyone. There always has been.''

"This Zionism—do you really believe in it, Judah?'' Mohamed's gaze was so intent that Judah averted his eyes.

"I believe there's a need for a Jewish homeland. Somewhere.'' He came over for a closer look at the map. "Our two families are spread all over that damned country. Is there one rock or tree you or I haven't had a relative sitting under?''

Mohamed laughed. "And where there's a relative, there's a branch of Hammadi-Nouari.''

Judah folded the letter into his pocket. "I have come to a decision, Mohamed. Tonight I'll ask her—for the last time. Either she marries me . . . or I shall give her up. And Zionism.''

Mohamed considered this. "Can't you sleep with one without the other?''

Judah sat on the edge of the desk. "If it were only just bed with Zosia. At times we're like brother and sister. We row, we argue. That girl sets my mind on fire with ideas. Oh, she's no beauty like your Jacqueline. But she has given me a faith that I need, and yet . . . I cannot totally believe in.''

"Your God gave you a brain, Judah. Use it. You have the ability to weigh a problem and solve it. And you can talk the teeth out of a crocodile. Look what you've done as Herzl's fund raiser." He came around, putting a hand on Judah's shoulder. "If the answer to your life is marrying that wretched girl, maybe you should. Marriage is the best cure for love. But remember, in your religion you can only have one wife."

A third voice turned them. "What an honor, Judah—to see you in the bank!" The bustling figure of Liebermann. "Both partners actually on the premises. We should celebrate!"

"Don't celebrate too soon, Baron. I was just leaving," Judah replied.

"I tell you something, Judah. Like your father, David, you are not." He helped himself to a cigar from Mohamed's rosewood humidor, sniffed it. "I must send you a box of my own Havanas, Mohamed. The girls in the factory roll them on their thighs." The Baron regarded Judah bleakly. "So?" he observed. "Who is going where—and when?"

"I'm off to Sweden in the morning, Baron."

"Judah has learned of an important invention. A new explosive that could revolutionize railroad construction," Mohamed lied protectively.

"Remember me to the Baroness—and of course your charming daughter." Judah inched a step toward the door.

"Ah, so you remember Mimi? Yet you never call on her. Our door is not locked to you, Judah. Use it."

"I'll bear that in mind, Baron."

They watched him go with mixed thoughts.

"And that is a banker?" asked Liebermann of no one in particular, palms spread slightly.

Never had the hands of the clock turned more slowly for Judah. In dark gray suit, hair neatly pomaded, he sat at the wheel of a highly polished, brass-fitted Renault. Beside him on the leather seat a large basket of violets trembled against his thigh. He shifted stiff gears, bumped to a stop at the empty curb in front of Zosia's building, and hurried in with the basket.

When his knock brought no answer, he used his key. The room was empty. With a sinking feeling, he pawed through the clutter on the desk.

No note of explanation. He dropped the violets and rushed downstairs.

The concierge shuffled to her door in carpet slippers, swallowing a mouthful of *saucisson*. No, Mademoiselle had left no message. Yes, she had gone out. Early. With a small hatbox—and the man who walks like a soldier. The Gare de l'Est, they told the coachman. Nothing said of when they might return. "Mademoiselle is paid up to the end of the month. After that," the old woman added, "if there is nobody to pay. . . ." Judah stuffed money into her hand.

Out in the street, he cranked the car, temples throbbing. Easy to guess where they'd gone. What a fool love made of a man! "Tomorrow night I shall say thank you properly. . . ." He had swallowed the hook, all right. . . .

Next morning, he was on the train—but not to Sweden.

He knew the address. Often enough he had posted letters to her when she had gone to deliver her articles in person. Rue des Rires, No. 5, tucked away in a corner of the old section of Geneva.

The horse clopped up the steeply winding cobbles. He thought how it would look: a dingy, oily printing press operated by the Romanian émigré with the forged passport who posed as a tailor. Old, perhaps not blind, but conveniently deaf. He wouldn't hear the creaking sofa in the small back office when she and Lubenov stole moments to make love. Zosia was passionate—how well he knew that. And perhaps between bouts of copulation, she and that Cossack would read *his* love letters. His cries of loneliness from Paris, from London, from Constantinople. How they must laugh at Judah, the adoring, trusting fool.

Judah Nouari—the human cornucopia—composed withering combinations of words to pelt them:

"So you have used me as your pawn?" Absurd.

"You are worse than a whore, who gives value for money. . . ." Too melodramatic. And the hurt was too real.

The barouche lurched to a halt. The driver leaned around. "A tailor shop, you say, monsieur?"

Judah glanced up from his thoughts. All anger and jealousy vanished in that first second of seeing the charred ruin. Black rags of smoke still plumed from cinders. Half-burnt bolts of soggy cloth, twisted metal railings protruding like ribs from the ashes, broken glass catching diamonds of pale sunlight. Barely legible in the debris lurched the heat-blistered tailor-shop sign. Not far from it, the wreckage of the illegal press sank like a battleship under waves of burnt paper and melted lead newsprint. Uniformed police and firemen sifted through files, collecting evidence into sacks.

A plainclothesman stepped over. "You have business here, monsieur?"

"None. That is . . . none," stammered Judah.

Sharp eyes of the law stabbed him.

"I must have the wrong address. . . ." Judah fumbled into his pocket, offering the policeman his card from a gold case. The Swiss scrutinized it with a colorless glance. "As you can see, I am a visiting banker. From Paris."

Respect dulled suspicion.

He tried to keep fear from his voice. "Curiosity only, monsieur l'agent, but what has happened here?"

"A bomb. Somebody has thrown a bomb."

"Into a tailor shop?"

"It appears the premises were used for more than that." His glance tightened. "You knew somebody here?"

"No, of course not. Was anyone . . . hurt?"

"One dead." The plainclothesman returned the calling card to Judah's trembling hand. The scene swam before his eyes.

"Was it . . . a woman?"

The man's face hardened. "I suggest Monsieur take his curiosity elsewhere."

Judah signaled the driver on. "That *was* the address Monsieur gave me," the driver said pointedly.

"We newspaper reporters must find our stories where they happen. Please let me off in the rue du Rhône."

Judah prowled the city. He stopped at every small hotel. Every *pension*. Nobody answering Zosia's description—or even Lubenov's—was recalled. Half crazy, he bought the first evening newspaper. Not a word of the bombing! Obviously the police had reason to keep their investigation secret. Weary and near collapse, he found himself on a bridge over the Rhône staring down into the rush of water. He knew he would never see her again.

● ● ●

She was sitting quietly, eyes down, twisting a ring on the finger of her left hand in the gaslit waiting room.

The name sprang from his throat. Then he was in front of her, pulling her up into his arms. "Zosia. . . . You can't imagine what I thought."

"No names . . ." she whispered.

Then he saw Lubenov. Long face hidden by his hat brim, seated on another bench, an open newspaper in front of him. The Russian rose, glanced at a pair of elderly ladies in the half-deserted station, stepped casually past Judah, murmuring, "You must not be seen speaking to us." He strolled out to the night platform.

"What a coincidence we meet again, monsieur," Zosia said loudly, reseating herself. "Toulouse, was it not?" Then, under her breath, "Wagon-lit 23."

Judah bowed and stepped away to the fruit kiosk. He purchased a bag of apples and walked out onto the platform. Lubenov ignored him, reading his paper in a pool of gaslight.

Alive. . . . At least she was alive. That was all that really mattered. There were questions, of course. But he knew Zosia would explain—and he would be satisfied.

A railroad attendant blew the boarding whistle. Judah realized he hadn't yet bought a ticket.

She sat opposite them, nudged slightly by the motion of the train. He could scarcely hear their explanations. The words. Seething in the back of his mind was a burning frustration. A jealousy. Why had she come with Lubenov? Why, without telling him? Why were they sharing this compartment? Traveling as man and wife. They admitted that. Produced the fact as an occupational necessity. Arranged by the organization. Polish passports—under the name of Lezno. It enabled them to cross borders, keep one jump ahead of the Okhrana.

Only, this time they almost hadn't. The bomb had exploded only minutes before they arrived. They were too late to save the Romanian printer. But still in time to recover vital papers. Lists of names. Places. People. Only time to get out before the Swiss police arrived.

He half heard, eyes fixed on the berths. Made up for the night. Were they so impatient to make love? Alexei's words flowed over him. How nimbly they could use words. Waves of anger flooded his mind. He framed the Russian's face, tight as a skull, in his consciousness.

"It is not the first time they discover our headquarters. Rachovsky's arms are long enough to reach into any corner of Europe.'

"And knowing all that, you still allowed Zosia to risk her life!''

The enigmatic Alexei shrugged. "Do you want the truth—which you have asked for? Or are we to have the tantrums of a tiresome schoolboy?''

"Alexei—Judah has worked hard for us too, remember.'' She took Judah's hand. "Alexei didn't recruit me. I do what I must. What I believe in.''

"Unfortunately, the bombing has drawn the attention of the Swiss police. They turn a blind eye to propaganda, but they cannot ignore terrorism.'' The brooding, longitudinal face became even more thoughtful. "To the Okhrana, blowing up a newspaper is nothing. It is slapping a fly. They know we will start again somewhere else.''

"Vienna, perhaps?'' Zosia asked.

"They have already stopped us there,'' Alexei reminded her.

"That is why I suggest it.''

"True. They would not expect us to return.'' He dug a silver flask from his satchel, poured vodka in the cup end, tossed back his head, and drank.

Their world was so unreal—another dimension in reason. A world with its own rules, its own codes . . . and its own penalties—this world of conspiracy. Here was he, Judah Nouari, locked into this claustrophobic compartment on their made-up bed, speeding toward Paris through the night, the woman he loved, the woman he adored, willing to risk her life with this strange, gauntly handsome man. For a cause. A cause they both believed in enough to die for. He knew there was no way to convince Zosia that she must get out of it. Quit before she, too, was lying in some morgue. He knew her will, knew it was stronger than his own—because she believed. Her belief fed unswerving determination. It excluded the shelter of his love.

"Rachovsky's timing of the bomb was no accident," Alexei continued. "He had to silence our voice—so that there would be no opposition to his master stroke." Heavy lids hooded dust-blue eyes as he explained that the embassy was to hold a reception. To honor a visit from the Minister of the Interior, Count Plehve.

At the mention of that name, tears welled in Zosia's eyes. It was Plehve who had burned her uncle's village, Plehve who had lit his cigarette from a burning thatch of their roof.

Alexei passed her a drink. "Yes, it is necessary to remember—in order to hate. It is necessary to hate—in order to act."

"Plehve isn't coming out of Russia just to lead the toast to the Czar," she said. "He will be present when Rachovsky reveals a document: *The Protocols of the Elders of Zion.*"

"How do you know all this?" asked Judah.

Alexei undid the buttons of his shirt, slipped papers from a pouch strapped to his chest. "I have managed to make a copy." He handed it over.

"The document was signed by a group identifying itself as 'International Jewry.' It purports to be a secret manifesto outlining the takeover of the Gentile world. They intend to say that this is what Herzl was really planning at the Zionist Congress in Basel."

"Nobody will believe it. . . ."

"But the international press will print it! A document like this could be used to justify genocide."

Judah could feel again the frenzy of the crowd that day they took Dreyfus. He knew what this document could stir up in those same mentalities. "But without a printing press—without a voice—how can you make people aware this is a forgery?"

"It is possible to stop a rogue elephant with one rightly placed bullet," Alexei replied.

"Rachovsky's forgery is not even original! He stole it from a play—written over forty years ago, by a Frenchman. Maurice Joly wrote it as a political satire against Napoleon III. *Dialogue aux Enfers entre Machiavel et Montesquieu.* Rachovsky has used Joly's play line for line, barely changed a speech. Merely substituting two words: 'We Jews.' "

Jealousy was gone now, with understanding. Their objective was vital. Nothing must stop them. And if he could, he would help. They had a plan, but it must wait until Paris.

Alexei rose, left the compartment. He would change rooms with Judah for the night.

Alone with Zosia, all confusion of the last few days vanished. In her arms, everything seemed to make sense.

From beneath the filtered light of a gas lamp in the rue de Grenelle, Judah watched the stream of carriages making sedate pauses at the embassy steps. Gentlemen in evening dress, ladies in plumes and tiaras. He did not notice the car parked in the side street, or realize that someone was watching him.

What was he doing here, anyway? A successful young business executive, standing under a chestnut tree, spying on an embassy, with a telephone number muttering through his brain. How had he gotten himself into such an absurd situation? He shifted from foot to foot under the rustling leaves. Perhaps they would not even come. Some last-minute change of plans—and they wouldn't be able to tell him. Well, he'd give it another half hour. His nerves were strung tight. What was he doing here?

It had all seemed so simple when Alexei explained it in Zosia's apartment, his tapered hands forming Gothic gestures. Judah had found himself admiring this strange warrior in a cause that was not even his own. The aquiline features, the sallow complexion—this nobleman could almost pass for a Jew. The thought made Judah smile.

The plan required precise timing. Alexei would escort Zosia to the reception. She would pose as an obscure Polish countess. Paris was full of countesses these days. Judah would be watching for their arrival. . . .

On seeing them, he was to check his watch, hurry to the nearby hotel. Exactly twenty minutes later, he must make a telephone call to the private number of Rachovsky's office. He would insist on speaking to the Okhrana chief personally. Rachovsky would leave the reception and answer—because Judah would use the word "protocols."

"A matter of protocols," he would say.

The number stuttered through Judah's brain: 86–42. He mustn't forget it! He would keep Rachovsky talking—invent a good story. Just hold him there in his office—give Zosia time to reveal the forgery to the press.

Oh, Judah's part was easy enough. But why weren't they there? Had something gone wrong? No, it was still early. He must be patient. Once again he went through it in his mind. She'd be safe, he was sure of that. Nobody would dare touch her in the presence of the press. But Lubenov would have to vanish.

"It will be necessary for me to leave the building—before Zosia produces her evidence. Leave the building. Leave the country. Take a new identity in a new land. South America, perhaps. But this will take money," Alexei had said.

"And Zosia?" Judah had asked.

That was when she had said she would become Judah's wife. Her usefulness to the Narodnaya Volya would be ended forever. Judah had asked how much money would be required? The permanent departure of Lubenov seemed worth any sum; still, he had been staggered at the amount. "10,000 louis d'or would make me invisible for the rest of my life," Alexei had assured him. Judah had promised that the money would be arranged.

One thing more, Zosia requested: that nothing be said to Dr. Herzl. His approach to their problems was too moderate. "When one is dealing with adders, one must have a sharp stick. Herzl thinks dreams speak louder than actions. It is his greatness—and his weakness," she had pronounced in her authoritative way that brooked no contradiction.

Judah savored the memory of the days that followed. Always before, she had refused his presents. Nothing for herself. All for the cause. But now she needed a special gown to play the countess. Her appearance would be altered by a black wig, and heavier eyebrows. They had chosen ice-blue taffeta with wide satin waistband and large, double mutton-chop sleeves. A pearl necklace to confirm the look of nobility. A coat of blue velvet trimmed with sable and a large matching fur muff.

It had to be large. She would be carrying the evidence in it.

Well, he had seen to all that. It was only money. He drew out his watch again. How the minutes were dragging! Slower than the horses pulling up the carriageloads of guests. No matter. They would come. They must.

Another scene swam into mind. . . .

"Are we still partners, Judah?" Mohamed had almost bounded into the office. "I don't care a damn what Liebermann thinks of you, or of me for that matter. But I care very much what we think of each other. I want a straight answer. Now. Is this the way it's going to be?" He was referring to the fact that Judah had scarcely been in the bank for the past two weeks.

"I'm involved in something. I can't tell you now. But it's so important I can do nothing else until it's over."

Mohamed leaned the flat of his palms across the desk. "You don't have to tell me. Zosia!"

Judah avoided Mohamed's eyes that day, and encountered instead the disapproving stares of his three forebears squinting down from their frames. "All I can say is, after Wednesday, I'll be a changed man."

"That sounds familiar. . . ."

"Mohamed, Zosia has promised to marry me."

"May Allah preserve you."

"And I will take her with me to Sweden. We'll spend our honeymoon listening to explosions of dynamite. You took Jacqueline to Jerusalem on Company business. It could become a Hammadi-Nouari tradition."

Judah's attempt at humor had fallen flat. Mohamed had permitted himself a tight-lipped nod. "I'll cable Ledbeck in Stockholm that you're leaving on Thursday."

Thursday. And this was Wednesday evening. Judah, waiting in the rue de Grenelle, hand sweating slightly on the gold watch, was still unaware that others were watching him.

Surely by now they must have left her apartment. . . .

But Alexei Lubenov had no wish to arrive early. It suited his plans for the reception to be crowded. At this moment, he was tapping discreetly at Zosia's door. He wore full evening dress and carried a small package. The sight of Zosia, ivory-pale skin defined by the starkness of black wig, was a metamorphosis from beauty into beauty.

He set the package on the table as though it were a crate of eggs. "Is that all there is to it?" she asked.

"Large enough. Lovingly prepared by our friends. It should fit admirably inside the sable muff. Ready?"

She nodded. He helped her into her coat. She shuddered slightly.

"Afraid?"

"A little," she admitted.

"Good. Then, you will be more careful."

"Can we go over it once again?" she asked anxiously. "The cigar humidor stands by the telephone in Rachovsky's office. . . ."

"It has been emptied. You have only to watch me for the signal. Then walk down the corridor. His private office is through the second door. Go directly in."

"If I should meet someone . . . ?"

"No one will be there." He passed her the package. Her hands trembled as she took it.

"Careful . . . !"

She edged it into the soft furs.

"When you've placed it inside the humidor, you must leave the building as quickly as possible. It is timed to explode while he is talking to Nouari."

"Where will you be?"

"Don't worry. I've told you. I will leave directly I've signaled you. Our friends have an automobile waiting in the side street. Nouari will not notice them, but they will be watching. When he leaves to phone, they will be ready. He will be gone before we come out of the building."

He took her in his arms, kissing her gently. "My beloved wife. . . . I know for you this has been the most difficult assignment. Because of Judah Nouari."

"I'm sorry he has to be hurt," she said.

"A casualty in a war, my dearest. The purpose we have dedicated our lives to . . . ever since ghetto days in Warsaw." He studied her carefully. "Have you perhaps allowed yourself to become emotionally involved with Judah Nouari?"

At first Zosia did not reply. Then she spoke softly: "Where, after tonight? Where to this time, Lolik?"

He smiled. Zosia had called him by the only real name he'd had in a lifetime of incognitos. "Berlin. I hope you will not be too sorry to leave Paris."

"No," she replied. It was true. Staying would mean seeing Judah again. And her own heart was too confused. Alexei was not entirely wrong. The relationship that had begun only as a political expedient . . . had turned into genuine feeling. Zosia would go to Berlin with Alexei. But part of her would remain in Paris with Judah.

"Soon Alexei Lubenov will have vanished as permanently as Rachovsky. Once again, there will be only Zosia and Lolik Lezno," he assured her.

The image of himself on the train from Hamburg flashed through Lolik's mind like a reel of film. He had recognized the man. The man who had been the boy. Recognized him by the birthmark on his cheek. Seeing that birthmark made him feel again the whip blows that slashed across the skin of his own back.

That other man . . . the real Count Alexei Lubenov . . . riding with a stranger into the darkest tunnel of his life. When the train stopped in Paris, only one of them got off. The other was found in the tunnel with the papers of a Jew, Lolik "Persoff," in his pocket—and his face smashed under the wheels. . . .

Lolik drew out his watch. "It is not too soon to start."

She clutched the sable muff to her. "It is like a little package of fate. . . ." He turned out the lamps, bowed his head.

"Sh'mah, Yisroel, Adonoi Eluhenu, Adonoi E'hud. . . ."

She echoed his words: "Hear, O Israel, the Lord our God, the Lord is One. . . ."

They moved outside to the waiting carriage. "I only hope . . ." she began.

"What, my darling wife?"

"That we shall never meet Judah Nouari again."

"The world is large, my love."

Judah moved forward to gain a better view. He saw the stiff-shouldered form of Alexei descend from a carriage. The white-gloved hand reached up to assist the small figure, now so elegantly dressed. Wild, hectic Zosia, the overdedicated zealot, creature of causes; could one ever possess her mind? Her moods were all tints of the rainbow. Her depths hid sensed mysteries—secrets of time concealed beneath the sand of some forgotten desert. This was Zosia, his Zosia—belonging to so much more than one man's possessiveness. Yet she had promised to marry him, share his life from tomorrow on. Would he become her cause? he wondered.

Could he hope for such a future?

They were moving up the steps now. He drew out his Half Hunter. It was 7:03 P.M. Twenty minutes . . . he had twenty minutes to reach the hotel and make the telephone call. They were approaching the liveried footman at the great door.

Suddenly the pavement rose under his feet, lifting him into the air. His ears were deafened by a thundercrack, his eyes blinded by a tameless outrage of lightning. Or so it seemed in that instant's horror.

That instant in which Zosia virtually disintegrated before his eyes. Lubenov was blasted upward like a loosely strung puppet. Then . . . the terrible after-fall of all that the explosion had hurled toward the sky.

That was all that Judah saw before losing consciousness. He did not see the car in the side street speed away.

When he recovered, a few days later, he had no idea how he had come to be in his own room. He only knew that Zosia was dead. That he would live with the nightmare for the rest of his life.

A sober-eyed Mohamed sat by his bed.

"She lied to me. I know that." They were the first words Judah had spoken. "It was because she wanted to protect me from the truth. The truth of how dangerous it would be for her, Mohamed. All through the planning, she never once mentioned a bomb. A bomb . . ." he repeated.

"No cause justifies terrorism," Mohamed said. But Judah wasn't listening.

"She would have married me when it was over, you know. She promised that."

Mohamed nodded patronizingly. "A Boadicea. A Joan of Arc."

Judah swallowed back the tears. "A Jael . . . trying to destroy the enemies of the Israelites." All the emotion seemed drained from his voice. "And, Mohamed, I will tell you this: I intend to devote the rest of my life to her memory. And to her cause. That is the vow I have made."

Mohamed didn't go into the details of what he had done after Judah had been taken to the hospital. He had broken into Zosia's apartment, removed all letters and gifts that could link her with his partner. Bribed the concierge to eternal silence. And all because he hoped that the woman's death would end Judah's devotion to this worrysome Zionism. Now he wondered if his friend ever would get over it.

And if he didn't, what use would he be to Hammadi-Nouari? Or to himself?

Six _____

THE young woman would not have been immediately recognizable by anyone who had known her before. Her yellow dress was cut too low at the bust. Too many black fringes. Too much red silk ankle. Rouge heightened high cheekbones, kohl outlined eyes, traces of color accented sensuous lips. Beyond her smoky Pernod glass, the afternoon dragged by its street traffic. Occasionally her smile saluted some passing stranger. It was a Wednesday afternoon in 1903. Every Monday and Wednesday, she came to sit and fish with her eyes in the boulevard. It had been nearly two months now.

"Oh, yes, she is one of *them*. A recruit to the regulars. You notice, always she leaves with a man—never the same one, you understand," the café owner informed his wife.

He was wrong. She was not one of Maurice's girls.

At first, the others also thought Maurice had enlisted her. But when they mentioned her, he denied knowing her. Why hadn't they told him before?

Maurice had eight girls working. He took good care of them and they were grateful. They paid him promptly—half their earnings. He supplied clients, and generally checked them out. It saved the girls from knives and beatings. One never knew what trouble one might pick up along the boulevard. Protection was worth paying for.

But this *poule* in yellow satin—she ran risks few of them would take.

Maurice was small, wiry, with brick-red hair and sharp blue eyes. He had even features, a cocky, aggressive way of walking—as if he owned not only the eight girls but the whole *arrondissement*. He was strung on sinews tough enough to beat up any rough trade, or any one of his girls who got out of step. Mostly, none did. They all liked Maurice. He had been tutor to many of them.

The woman in yellow watched the approach of tight plaid trousers and high-heeled boots. Nobody had told her who he was, and he didn't bother to tell her himself, at first. He stood over her, the diamond winking in his cravat. "Your name?" he asked.

"Yvette." She attached a smile to it. "You want to come to my room?"

"I'll come. No fear. . . ." He splashed a few coins on the table, hoisted her up by the elbow, and guided her forcefully down the street. "Where do you nest, Yvette?"

She indicated a shabby building up ahead, feeling the animal electricity of the man through his grip.

Her room, on the third floor, had walls that seemed to sweat, and a smoky mirror behind the bed. She began to unbutton her dress.

The sting of his hand surprised her cheek, knocking her to the floor. "That is for working in my district. Nobody works without cutting me in! I'm Maurice."

He pulled open a few drawers in the scarred bureau. Empty. That did not surprise him. Few girls lived where they worked. He peered into the wardrobe. One dress. A subtle shade of green. Hardly her type of plumage. He fingered the material. "Expensive stuff. Where'd you get it?"

"Stole it." She got to her feet. He pushed her roughly down to the bed, holding her there with his knee.

"Stole it, eh? Why? Where'd you expect a dress like that would get you—to the opera?" He ripped open the remaining buttons on her bodice. Then stood back. "Undress," he commanded.

She stripped down to a black corset with red ribbons, stockings fastened up by long black garters on slender thighs. Her waist was small, breasts round. He slid a hand between her legs.

She could feel a growing heat. His eyes seemed to penetrate her corset. Her slender fingers began to unlace it.

"Leave it," he ordered. His kiss was savage, claiming her mouth with his tongue. She did not resist, but pulled him down to the bed. Down, down, like a tigress. . . . A flame of wanting that demanded satisfaction, that made him incautious.

Afterward, he dressed quickly. "Now you are working for me. Fifty-fifty," he told her. To himself he admitted he had never known a whore so sensuously carnal. Usually their pleasure was pretense. But not this woman. "When did you get on the game?"

"When I found out I liked it."

He threw back his head and laughed. "From now on I choose your customers. And you—whenever I want you. Au revoir, Yvette." He left her half undressed on the bed.

She removed all traces of *maquillage*, arranged her hair neatly, then took the green dress from her wardrobe.

The key was left on the dresser. She whispered good-bye to the room, not without regrets. The girl in the yellow dress must find new pastures.

On the boulevard Montparnasse, Maurice emerged from a tobacco shop in time to catch a fleeting glimpse of the woman in a passing cab. Pale skin above a green dress. Something about the face struck him as vaguely familiar. Then she was gone. He struck a match on his thumbnail. The face would haunt him—but not for long.

Inside the cab, Jacqueline gave an address in the Avenue Malenkoff, on Paris's right bank. She had not noticed the man staring at her, although at that very moment she was thinking of him.

A hansom cab lurched through gray drizzle, encased in the dreary London day, a prisoner of climate. Its two occupants were heading for the Foreign Office. Neither of them could feel great hope for what might be accomplished.

"All we needed was ten million pounds. It could have been so easy." Herzl was still plaguing himself with the failure of his mission three years earlier. The Sultan had agreed to sell Palestine to the Zionists, provided the arrangements could be kept secret—and the payment was prompt.

"The money. Always the money. . . ." Judah had personally managed to raise nearly fifty thousand pounds, in francs, dollars, and marks. "It wasn't 'world Jewry's' finest moment," he said. They had failed to rise to the financial occasion.

Since Zosia's death, Judah had filled his hours with work. For Hammadi-Nouari. For the bank. For Herzl and Zionism.

He never slept more than six hours a night. "Driving yourself too hard," Mohamed had told him.

"It was not your fault. It was not mine we failed," Herzl continued. "In Constantinople it is impossible for anything to go right."

"Let us hope, sir, we'll be more successful here in London." Once again Judah had acceded to Herzl's request to accompany him to a crucial meeting. But he was uneasy. Never had he seen the father of modern Zionism more ill, more weary, more dispirited. On the wretched Channel crossing there had been a sea-tossed moment when it seemed entirely possible Herzl might not survive to confront the British Minister.

"And your uncle, Mehmet Khassadia, was not the great help we had prayed for."

Judah wished Herzl would get his mind out of Constantinople with Uncle Mehmet.

"A Turkish-Jewish official who proved more Turk than Jew, more official than Turk. Promises he made, assurances he gave. On the Sultan's behalf. Always on behalf of the Sultan. Everything agreed. Then suddenly, not agreed." Herzl fished in his pocket and then remembered he had given up smoking.

"Just when the world tried to forget the Jewish problem, the Russians provided another massacre. Over a hundred killed at Kishinev. More than a thousand injured, almost all Jewish property destroyed." Judah patted his bulging briefcase. "Facts. Always the best argument."

"With such facts, we have had too much practice." He leaned back on the leather seat. How gray his hair had become, Judah noticed. How drained his face. The skin beneath his eyes couched leaden shadows. "For today we can have hope. Joseph Chamberlain is something more than Secretary of State for Colonial Affairs."

"More, sir?"

"He is an Englishman with a bottomless conscience. In it, he will find us an answer."

"Uganda?"

Mohamed Hammadi looked properly amazed.

"Kenya . . . British East. That was Joseph Chamberlain's

offer," Judah Nouari replied. "Either that or . . ." he hesitated a moment, ". . . the Sinai Desert."

The sounds of a small orchestra drifted from the ballroom. They had both escaped into the conservatory of Mohamed's mansion in the Avenue Malenkoff.

Mohamed warmed his brandy snifter between strong, slender hands. "What did Dr. Herzl say to that? The Sinai, I mean."

Judah chuckled. "He told the Colonial Secretary that the Jews had been to the Sinai once before—and although they spent forty years there, they hadn't found it much to their liking."

Clatter of conversation and bursts of laughter drifted in. The two men moved farther down the aisle of growing things. "So it's to be Uganda, then?" Mohamed asked.

Judah's face turned serious. "Afraid Herzl and I don't see eye to eye on that one. He gave an emphatic no. Insisted that the Zionist Congress wouldn't consider it."

Mohamed fed a bit of apple to a bright blue and yellow macaw. It nibbled at his finger and squawked. "And what did you say to Herzl?"

"I said what Zosia would have said." He paused by a pot of African violets. "The members of the Congress don't have to live there. It was not they who were slaughtered at Kishinev—and it won't be them next time."

"So, Judah. It all sounds like more talk. Talk, and no action. I've been hearing the same tales from you for years. In the end, what did Chamberlain and Herzl decide?"

"Nothing," came the disgusted answer. "But the door is still open—from Chamberlain's point of view. And I intend to enter it." He turned suddenly to his partner. "Mohamed, the railroad project is nearly finished, isn't it?"

"Yes, and thanks partially to you. Even the Baron was saying yesterday that we both deserve congratulations. Yes, he included you. Said you were a changed man. Changed into some strange word he used: a 'mensh'?"

Judah laughed. "Could the 'mensh' be spared for, say, four months?"

"What for? Do you intend to cross the Sinai in the footsteps of Moses?"

"No. Explore Uganda."

In his mind was the echo of Herzl's argument with the

Zionists when he had presented them with Chamberlain's proposals. The Russian Jewish delegates had walked out at the very mention of Uganda.

"These people have a rope around their neck, and *still* they refuse!" he had complained to Judah. "They call me a traitor. Say I depart from the ultimate aim: a home in Palestine. I told them, 'Money you do not give me. There remains only diplomacy. Now I can see how you help me with that!' "

Judah turned back to Mohamed. "If there's even a slim possibility that Uganda could offer a feasible homeland, I don't give a damn what the Zionists think or decide in their hired halls; I'll persuade Herzl, and he'll persuade them."

"Uganda . . ." Mohamed mused. "Not a bad idea. Marvelous game, they say. Best hunting in Africa." He'd made several hunting trips with Von Bülow in the Bavarian mountains and was developing a passion for blood sports.

The glass conservatory door almost shattered open. "You neglected to say good-bye to our guests, Mohamed. It's customary for the host to appear at his own party." Jacqueline swayed in, arms linked between two men. Behind them, the sounds of the party evaporated.

"Sorry, I didn't know they were leaving. They generally stay all night," came the acid reply.

She threw Judah a fetching smile. "Ah, Judah the mysterious. You didn't even arrive in time for dinner. You were invited, you know."

"Forgive me, Jacqueline. The boat train was late."

"You and Mohamed—always dashing from country to country, while the rest of us have to struggle to amuse ourselves as best we can." She detached herself from arms. "May I present *my* friends to your friend, Mohamed? Or perhaps you've already recognized the Great Petit Joujou? Everybody in Paris knows Joujou."

Her dwarf-short companion, an obscene *cupidon* with a shock of yellow curls, beamed, plucked three small oranges from a miniature tree, and began to juggle expertly. Judah recognized him from the Cirque Pigalle.

"And of course you know Don Jaime de Languadalande, from the Argentine. Three horses at Longchamps this season."

The angular aristocratic reed nodded blue-black plastered hair. "It is the beautiful women for whom I bring myself to Paris, not only horses."

Jacqueline was the most beautiful of them all, Judah thought. Now a woman, no longer a girl, cheeks a shade more hollow beneath elegant bone structure, lips somehow fuller, the same tumble of golden hair. But the eyes had changed. They suggested something more audacious, more inviting. Mohamed was a lucky man. Yet he did not seem to know his own luck.

Her voice skyrocketed excitement. "There is a *cave* opening in Montmartre. The *diseuse* sings lying in a coffin. She is resurrected for the encore. Too amusing! You *might* come along, Mohamed. For a change. You, too, Judah."

Joujou tittered. "The singer is dressed in a shroud. Underneath, she wears nothing but chains. She recites the most mournful poems of Baudelaire, while we spill wine upon her like blood."

"I once knew a man who claimed to have copulated with a camel. I'm afraid my morning starts too early for such pleasures," Mohamed replied coldly.

"I can never drag my husband away from his work." Her voice took on a harsher tone. "Or whatever he finds more entertaining than his marriage."

"Your friends will of course be my guests, Jacqueline."

Don Jaime bobbed his head toward his host. "And you must come as my guest . . . to Argentina. I will send my yacht for you."

"Wouldn't that be fun, Mohamed? A second honeymoon. Don Jaime is from Entre Ríos Province."

"I have ten thousand horses. A hundred thousand head of cattle on my *estación*—and I have never seen it. If you, señores, were to build a railroad in my country, I could ride there. The roads are terrible."

Judah showed sudden interest. "Isn't there a Zionist colony at Entre Ríos? Yes. Founded by the English Baron de Hirsch. Do you know it?"

"I don't even know what is a Zionist!" Lilting laughter trailed them out.

Judah sighed. "A man who would repay a drink in Montmartre with a yachting trip across the Atlantic. And he hasn't even heard of Zionism."

"We need a breath of air. Come, I'll walk you home."

Home was a hotel. Since his student days as Liebermann's house-guest, Judah always lived in hotels. He had thought one day he and Zosia would share a home. Now all desire for personal acquisition was gone. He was living at the Crillon—in a small suite. Several times, Mohamed had tried to discuss this eccentricity of nonpossessiveness, but Judah argued that he cared only for his work and her cause. Zosia. . . . The ghost had become so real that he could almost hear her voice.

"Work, Judah. Carry it forward. Do not let them defeat us. Because what is more important than the salvation of people? It would not be the first time in history that whole races have vanished from the earth. Until the only traces were a broken shard dug up by an archaeologist. Unless we exist in our own land, we may cease to exist at all. . . ."

Or was it only the dialogue he kept holding with himself?

The two men from another land moved along the lighted boulevard without belonging to it. "You're quiet tonight, Judah."

"So are you."

"You are so lucky you never married."

"She looks very well again, your Jacqueline. And always more beautiful."

"Tonight you saw her in one of her high moments of exhilaration. There are days when she stays in her room. Days when she drinks. Others when she disappears. I don't know what she does . . . where she goes . . . and I won't demean myself by having her followed. Or perhaps I'm afraid of what I might discover. Tonight she will listen to the words of Baudelaire—while I live them:

'My breast is a void pit
Sacked by the tooth and claw of woman.
Nay seek not my heart;
the beasts have eaten it.' "

"Mohamed, don't you think that your attitude toward Jacqueline is a little unfair? I can understand how you feel. Her beauty would make any man jealous. But beauty is not a crime."

"She entertains herself with idiots . . . gossips . . . homosexuals . . ." Mohamed complained. "Men who do nothing—and women who'd do anything. All of which might be bearable if we could still reach each other—still touch minds."

Judah paused. They had come to the Crillon entrance. Around them, the boulevard danced with lights. "How would you like to go with me . . . to Uganda?" he asked suddenly.

"What? Why the devil would I do that?"

"There's a new railroad being finished there. Maybe you'd like to have a look at it. Maybe I'd like the company. Maybe you need a change."

"Oddly enough," Mohamed mused, "a few years ago Von Bülow talked to me about the possibilities of laying track there. But the British got in first." He turned the collar of his coat up against the rising wind. "You know, Judah, it might be just what I need: the chance to get a shot at some big game. Just bought a fine pair of Mannlicher bolt-action rifles. Sometimes the cleanest way to get rid of the poison in the mind is to shoot at some poor, defenseless wild creature," he added wryly.

"Then, it's decided," said Judah. "We'll go together. You . . . to find your cleansing bullet. Me to find a bit of real estate."

Mohamed laughed. "What a strange bird you are, Judah! I remember when we were children and we went together to the marketplace in Jerusalem. There was a white donkey—the largest anyone had ever seen. You said you wanted to buy it. Remember? But your father wouldn't give you the money. So one day I got the money from my father, and I said, 'You want it? Here, buy it. We will ride to the sea—or Bethlehem, or somewhere we've never been.' But you refused it. Why, Allah only knows. You said it was more important to have the wish . . . than the fulfillment."

"Why do you remember that now, Mohamed?"

"Forgive me—but your Zosia was the wish. . . ." Then he added bitterly, "My wish was fulfilled. And now I wish I could turn time backward—to relive that first moment I saw her—and have the sense to walk away from it. And so, I would have kept the purity of my wish. As you have."

Judah thought in this moment that he knew his friend less than at any time in their lives.

He could hear her moving about in her room—the clothes falling on the floor, the splashing of water. The door connecting their bedrooms had never been locked.

When he entered, she was standing before her mirror, naked. Just standing. Her hands moved over her breasts, down the curve of hips and thighs. The fall of hair over her shoulders reminded him of that long-ago night in Liebermann's garden when she had played water nymph and he had been so wildly in love. His image behind her in the mirror didn't turn her. She didn't take her eyes from herself.

"Am I still beautiful, Mohamed?"

He came close enough to catch the faint pungent smell of wine. Wine—and perfume. "You're drunk!"

She swayed around to him, lacing arms around his neck. "Make love to me. I'm not too drunk for that."

Aroused although he hadn't wanted to be, he took her to bed. Her kiss was hungry. She moved his hand gently over the points of her breast . . . down across her stomach. Then, inexplicably, she pulled away.

"No. I won't make love now. Go back to your bed."

He held her down. "Whore bitch!" She struggled and clawed at him, making him savage. Her manner almost demanded rape. He lost all control, overwhelmed by desire.

Afterward, he felt only self-disgust. "I'm sorry," he said. "Sorry. It won't happen again. You can lock your door if you wish."

She lay back on the disheveled bedclothes, in the dirty first light of dawn. "The comedy is over," she said, a smile curving the corners of her lips.

An upside-down image of the narrow harbor swam toward Judah through the lens of his new Gandolfi camera. It bulked above its tripod spidered on the deck. The steamer made a tame entrance into the Strait of Macupa.

"Dashed fine view of Jesus Fort you've got there!" The Englishman's voice boomed Judah out from beneath the black hood. "Portuguese chaps knocked it together in 1593. Only thing in Mombasa that hasn't been knocked apart since."

Judah took in the clipped mustache, rumpled whites, narrow black tie, pith helmet. Craggy features of the colonial, honed on a thousand "chotapegs." He withdrew his photographic plate. This picture was no mere souvenir of an ancient fort; it was meant to record harbor installations that would have to cope with crowded shiploads of refugees. Mombasa— official entry port for Uganda.

"Country's a paradise. Except for the people and the diseases. First trip?"

Judah nodded. "Safari." He had no intention of revealing

his purpose to anyone in the Protectorate. Only Chamberlain
knew why he was there. Chamberlain and Herzl.

"Let me know if you run into any problems. And you
will." The Englishman extended a hand. "I'm McCulloch.
Principal medical officer. Find me at the Colonial Office."

"Thanks." Judah began folding away the cumbersome
equipment. They would be landing soon. He looked again at
the approaching land mass.

Mombasa. . . . *Kisiwa m'vita,* in Swahili. Isle of war.
Not an inviting name for someone seeking a peaceful homeland. An Arab dhow swerved dangerously close to their
vessel, cursing guttural shouts at them above an almost motionless sea. The day was crystalline, the country greener than
Palestine. A cardboard cutout of dazzling white buildings,
flat-roofed amid outcroppings of coconut, baobab, mango,
and the thatched huts of the native quarter.

"How far in are you bound?" the doctor demanded.

"Uganda Protectorate."

McCulloch hoisted an eyebrow, clenching false teeth.
"That'll put you on the new British train across to the main-
land. Over Salisbury Bridge. Then it's thirty-six hours by rail
to Kavirondo Bay. Shores of Victoria Nyanza—and a dead
coolie for every quarter mile of track. Mind you keep clear of
the islands when you get to the lake."

"Why?" The doctor was becoming an overdose of information.

"Sleeping sickness. For a start. All those little islands—
empty as graveyards now. The whole area around Victoria,
since the last epidemic."

"What causes it?"

"Tsetse fly. And no bloody cure. And rinderpest—wiped
out all the bloody cattle. Who's your guide?"

"Mr. Baxter. He's to meet us here."

McCulloch snorted laughter. "*Mister* Baxter? Bugger's been
promoted. Don't expect he'll meet you at the quay. Find him
at Kilindini, more likely. Other side of the island. And don't
expect him to be what you expect. A *gharri*'ll get you across."
The doctor turned back to see to his own luggage.

The quay was crowded. Porters, boatmen, railroad person-
nel, blacks, whites, East Indians—all under assault from
assorted vendors peddling everything from copper jewelry to
fruit and bolts of cloth.

Mohamed's eyes searched for Baxter among the groups of sun-bronzed British in topees and faded khakis.

"Told you he wouldn't be here," rasped McCulloch triumphantly. He eyed Mohamed's fine leather gun cases. "Probably too light for rhino. Bullets flick off their hide like a drop of sweat. Aim for the neck, below the ear, and stay upwind." He shoved his way past them. The customs official saluted him through.

"You'll find anything here in Mombasa from a needle to an anchor—except what you happen to need." McCulloch climbed into a rickshaw and waved himself away.

"I hope I don't get sick enough to need him," Judah breathed.

The *gharri* proved to be a small trolley, two seats under a canopy. Porters hoisted their luggage aboard. They climbed in and sat back to back. Powerful Swahili boys pushed the vehicle flying down the track.

Judah was annoyed that Baxter hadn't met them. It was a poor start. The guide had been arranged through Chamberlain's office, via Sir Harry Johnston, head of the British Commission. Chamberlain had been delighted that Judah was willing to investigate his proposal at his own expense. The British had earmarked an area east of Lake Victoria about the size of Belgium.

Judah had studied the map carefully with Mohamed. The territory had a great potential. It included forests, rivers, the Eldama Ravine, the N'gisha Plateau, Mount Elgon, and Thomson's Falls. A steak carved out of the rib cage of Uganda Protectorate.

The *gharri* squeezed through narrow streets of the town, barely clearing walls. Little boys dodged it like matadors. Mohamed's voice came over Judah's shoulder.

"Something I haven't told you. Perhaps I should have."

Through the long journey from Paris, eighteen sea days from Marseilles, Mohamed had seemed unusually indrawn. Judah respected the wall of silence. Now, because they were facing away from each other, words came more easily.

"When we were about to leave Paris . . . the day we left. Almost the hour—Jacqueline told me she is expecting a baby."

"Why, that's wonderful!" Judah knew from the tone of voice that obviously it was not. "But surely you should have stayed . . .?"

"Should I?" came the metallic reply. "Why did she wait until I was almost through the door before telling me? Because she knows—and I know—that I am not the father."

"You still share her bed." It was more of a question than a statement.

"I and how many others?"

Tall, strongly built, in neatly pressed, collarless safari khakis, their guide was, as McCulloch had predicted, awaiting them at Kilindini. He made no apology for not meeting them at the quay. Ian Baxter was a black with a clipped Oxford accent.

Aboard the train, Baxter regarded them in critical silence. Smoke steamed from the tall stack of the little engine dragging its toy cars through the heat of the Taru Desert. Through a scrubland Hades of stunted trees, through forests and across muddy rivers, past villages of red dust where the Wanyika, "Children of the Wilderness," watched the puffing passage with undiminished wonderment. A veritable zoological garden—backdropped by the looming presence of Mount Kilima N'jaro.

In the past few days, it had become apparent that Baxter nursed a collection of prejudices. First against Arabs, whose slave-trading antecedents had scattered his ancestral seed across oceans. His attitude did not exclude Mohamed. His affection for the British was hardly warmer.

"Where did you learn your English?" Mohamed asked finally.

"My father, Kasanga, is King of the Unyaros. Perhaps I failed to mention it. In the first days of the Protectorate, he proved his friendship to the British. The reward: my education. An investment not without self-interest. The British thought I might be useful to them."

"And are you?" Mohamed wondered.

"One day I shall be King. Then we shall see." There was a curious ambivalence in Baxter's attitude—even toward his own people. He viewed them from the heights of his education. It left him a man in limbo, between two worlds. Unacceptable among the colonials, and no longer at one with his fellow Africans.

Mohamed knew he would have to prove himself to Baxter.

"And your name?"

"Ian Baxter? My British schoolmasters could never learn to pronounce Indanga Balingalali."

They had come some eighty miles from the coast, passing through level uplands, when they noticed a giant ostrich striding parallel with the rails, as though racing the train. Baxter's glance challenged Mohamed.

"You came to shoot game, Mr. Hammadi, did you not? Shall I stop the train?"

"No need." Mohamed took up his rifle, drew the bolt, slapped it home, and aimed through the open window. As though sensing danger, the huge bird sped into a zigzag.

The rifle cracked once. The ostrich dropped.

"Now, Mr. Baxter, you may stop the train." Mohamed levered out the shell case.

Baxter stuck his head out the window with an explosion of abusive Swahili. The small engine braked suddenly, then backed up to collect the trophy. Judah watched with some distaste while it was dragged aboard.

"What the devil will you do with it, Mohamed?"

"The feathers will make a fan for Jacqueline."

It was the first time he'd mentioned her name since leaving Mombasa.

"*Simba* . . ." the King said.

Simba. *Sher*. Lion. Four days' travel from Kampala through rain forests, over plains, across a wider river, had brought them to King Kasanga's village. A wily old potentate, Baxter's father was Chief of the second-most-important tribe in the Protectorate. The Unyaros were less sophisticated than the Bandangas, whom they had seen trading in the marketplace in Kampala wearing loose robes beneath shading umbrellas.

King Kasanga's kraal stood amid thatched beehive huts in a dense thicket of thorny jungle bordering the grassland. He greeted them, a leopard skin slung over one shoulder, fanned by a small boy with a long feathered frond.

Judah reckoned they were dead center of the area offered for Zionist colonization. A reasonably happy, healthy place compared with some they'd passed through. Along the river, they had encountered whole villages blinded by some mysterious disease. Waterborne plagues on jungled banks. But here all seemed different. Judah tasted the Unyaro flour, made from m'tama. Sugarcane, sweet potatoes, and tobacco flourished. And kraals of cattle. . . .

Oh, he could see how, with modern agricultural methods, the Zionists might indeed make the land flow with milk and honey. For the moment, hope outweighed rinderpest, with doctors, and . . . what was the Chief calling the marauding king of beasts? *Simba*. Yes, *simba*.

"They have grown shrewd and fearless." Baxter translated his father's words. "They come in the dark of night. Steal people from their huts." Baxter stopped translating to argue with his father. Finally he turned to the foreigners. "My father says they are not lions. The *simba* are devils wearing the skins of beasts."

Another argument erupted immediately between father and son. Baxter sighed. "He insists there is something supernatural in their cunning. That they cannot be killed by one of our hunters. I have offered to try myself. He refuses, because I am an Unyaro. The lions slip right through the boma—the thick thorn fence which surrounds the village. In the morning the surface of the ground is covered by their pugmarks. I've told him this proves they *are* lions. But he says devils are able to leave pugmarks when it suits them."

During the building of the railroad, *simba* had claimed more than thirty victims in Tsavo. It was rare for lions to become man-eaters.

Kasanga led them to a hut where naked human heels marks could still be seen scarring the earth. Two nights before, the man had been dragged away before his wife's eyes. Her shrieks brought the others. In the darkness they could see nothing, but they could hear the crunching of bones plainly enough. *Simba* feasting on another victim.

Kasanga enjoyed the effect on his listeners. The King fixed his attention on Mohamed as his son translated. "The man who will kill *simba* is not among the Unyaros. I know this from the witch doctor." The old man closed mahogany-bead eyes couched in blue-black folds, leaned on his knobkerrie. "Now the great hunter has arrived."

"Are there no guns in the village?" Mohamed asked Baxter.

"Only one. A trade musket. Left by slavers long ago." A word to a bodyguard produced the crude firearm from the King's hut.

Mohamed fingered the rusty flashpan. "Flintlock. At least a hundred years old. No wonder the lions are so daring."

Baxter did not share his father's enthusiasm. The travelers were his responsibility. *Simba* was his father's.

But Mohamed had made up his mind. Suddenly the man-eater seemed his whole reason for being there.

He directed the construction of a small platform, up a tree at the edge of the boma. Beneath it, he ordered a goat tethered for bait. Judah insisted on sharing the vigil with a bull's-eye electric torch, since the lion attacked only after dark.

And the night was moonless.

As Judah started up the tree, a bough moved under his hand. A boa constrictor slithered down the trunk and away into the night.

"Harmless," Baxter assured him. "Unless he feels affectionate enough to embrace you." Mohamed followed him up with the Mannlichers.

Baxter left them to their vigil and returned to his father's hut.

It seemed hours before the snap of a twig alerted them. Then a definite movement in the darkness. Mohammed's rifle blasted toward the sound. From among the huts, screams of terror told them that the predator had slipped by unscathed, ignoring the bait in favor of human flesh.

Next morning it was not difficult to follow its trail. Pools of blood marked its halting places.

"He must have paused several times before beginning his meal," Baxter said grimly. "Man-eaters lick the skin off to get at the fresh blood."

They followed the pugmarks for a few hundred yards and found the body of a woman. The skin was gone in places. The flesh looked as though it had been sucked. The ground was covered with fragments of flesh and bone. Only the head had been left intact. It lay a short distance away, eyes still recording the horror of the night before. Judah turned away and was sick.

"You can tell your father, King Kasanga, tonight it will be our turn," Mohamed assured Baxter.

●   ●   ●

The forest creaked and whispered like a ship in the trough of night. Although only inches separated them, the two men felt intensely alone.

"I killed a man once."

"I know."

"A man whose name I never learned."

"What did it mean to you?" asked Judah.

"I carried him in my mind for a while. Then he went away. If one lived under the weight of every experience—you would never go on."

The night sounds were now falling into familiar patterns: The village. The forest. The birds. The goat tethered beneath them.

Judah's mind drifted to another forest, in France: Fontainebleau. A tapestry glade of trees that remembered the hunting horns of the Bourbons. He had gone picnicking with Zosia when she had permitted him to take her out of Paris for an entire day and night. The little hotel across from the palace had packed them a lunch. Twenty-four hours together seemed a lifetime. Looking back, it was.

"I cannot think what it was ever like before knowing you. We are a world here. Nothing can touch us." They had found the perfect spot some distance off the main road, a mysterious landscape of smooth-faced boulders set into the sandy floor of the forest, shaded by gnarled giants. Just as they were finishing their lunch, it had started. At first it was only tears falling through the leaves.

"It's a storm. . . ."

"A few raindrops. . . ."

"God is angry . . . because we have dared to be too happy."

Suddenly the cloud burst, pelting hailstones, building throbbing lakes with golden flashes above the trees. Zosia was frightened. Dauntless Zosia—wrapped in the protection of his arms, a rain-soaked child, water streaming down face and hair. They gathered the debris of the picnic. Zosia took off her shoes, and the two ran laughing and splashing to the protection of the car. Water inched high around the tires.

"Impossible to try to drive," Judah said, helping her into the back seat.

Zosia's blouse clung to her. She unbuttoned it. "We are prisoners of the storm," she whispered.

"If only it were forever, my darling." He drew her to him, hailstones pounding a rhythm above their heads; he found the sudden softness of her lips. Zosia in his arms, giving, wanting. They made love and it was more than everything. If only it had been forever. . . .

Forever. . . .

The thunder crashed an artillery burst. She shuddered in his arms. "I wonder if it will be like this?"

"What?"

"The moment of my death. . . ."

Always he had wondered if her words had revealed a flash of precognition. The thought chilled him in the hot African night. Mohamed's voice cut through the dark. "Have you fallen asleep?"

Judah forced himself back to the present.

"What's the matter?" Mohamed asked.

"Always the same thing. And I haven't yet found any answer, Mohamed. I'm not sure there is one. But you have something sure. You will either kill your lion, or you will not. The perfect simplicity. No dangling doubts."

"It's only a question of steadying a rifle. Peering across a sight. If I do or if I don't . . . what have I really proved?"

"Maybe that witch doctor was right. No Unyaro would kill him. And wrong. He was no devil."

Mohamed silenced him with a gesture, flicked off the safety. The padding of feet? The swish of a tail?

Wind in grass. No more. Not yet.

They felt it first, rather than seeing. Then the darkness produced a low, stalking shadow. Mohamed held his breath, steadied the butt into his shoulder, part of him now, the extension of purpose.

Again the lion ignored the easy bait, launching itself in a sudden rising spring directly at their platform. Mohamed crashed out the first shot. With the heat of the beast in their faces, he yanked the bolt and fired again. The tree quaked, the roaring shook the platform, nearly tumbling them. The lion dragged itself off. Mohamed fired again at the retreating form.

The shots had silenced jungle noises for an instant. Now the night pulsed with the din of small creatures.

Judah's torch fixed the lion halfway through the boma, where it had fallen.

"Simba . . . simba!" A villager danced forward shouting, exultantly. Others followed more cautiously. Kasanga appeared, Baxter at his side. The others made way for them.

It happened so fast nobody saw it. A tawny streak slipped through the boma and seized the shouting villager. His shouts became a scream.

Three shots cracked from the tree in rapid succession, fired directly into the struggling mass of cat and man. The Unyaros watched, transfixed in horror.

Mohamed's shots had found a mark. The wounded lioness dropped her victim, dragging herself back through the boma. No one was prepared to take up the chase in the dark.

Kasanga shouted an order. Men hurried to the fallen villager. He was mauled but still alive. They carried him to the witch doctor's hut.

Mohamed and Judah climbed down to be confronted by a furious Baxter. "What you did was downright reckless, Hammadi! You could have killed the man. You had no right to risk his life!"

"If I hadn't fired, the lion would have killed him anyway," Mohamed replied coolly.

Baxter spat on the ground. "Arab logic," he said bitterly and turned away. Mohamed chose to ignore it, but somehow the triumph of the kill had been diminished.

Kasanga refused Judah's offer of his medicine kit. The witch doctor preferred his own remedies.

Morning saw two lions carried into the village. With a solemn gesture, the Chief picked up a handful of grass, spat on it, and scattered it over the lions' heads. This would avert the evil from his village. That night, they would celebrate the hunter's victory. Had not the prophecy been fulfilled? A stranger freed them from *simba*.

Judah set up his camera to photograph Mohamed and Kasanga posing beside the two beasts. He stuck his head beneath the black hood. His flare exploded in a puff of white smoke. The Unyaros crowded around, almost collapsing with laughter.

"What's wrong?" Judah asked.

"I told them you took a picture," Baxter explained. "But since they can't see it, they think your magic has failed."

"They might be right! All my plates must wait for Paris to be developed."

The clearing blazed firelight and glistening ebony bodies beating a rhythmic path across the dusty enclave. The travelers sucked down *pombe* from gourd cups. Judah had seen Kasanga's wives preparing this brew in a hollowed-out tree stump, stirring it, adding sugarcane and herbs. But this victory brew must have been fermenting for months. The stuff was more potent than absinthe. . . .

Judah's head spun. He was possessed by the rhythm of drumming, the gyrations of the dancers. In the power of *pombe,* almost everything seemed wonderfully possible. His mind merged into the images of Old Testament prophets whose staffs could strike rocks and bring forth water, open seas, raise pillars of fire, or be cast down into the forms of wriggling serpents. With all these men Judah now became one. A leader of his people—a discoverer of the Promised Land. Faces circled around him. The adulation of black eyes and gleaming grins was not just for Mohamed, but a shared heroic. Victory belonged to all.

He rose, body swaying to the urgent rhythmic command. "Look at me," he cried aloud. "I am he, friends. I am the giver . . . the leader . . . the bringer of hope of the future. I am your Moses. Their Moses . . .!"

He threw off Mohamed's restraining hand. "No, don't question, Mohamed. The vision is clear. From all the corners of the world—I see them. They will come! The miserables. The persecuted. 'Cry, oh, cry, my people. Let your voices echo in all the caverns of the land. . . .' Because I will bring them to their land. Here, Zosia—this piece of Africa shall flourish and bloom on the face of the dark continent. . . ."

Again he shook off Mohamed's arm. "No! You will see it—the descendants of the old tribes: Reuben. Dan. Judah. Issachar. Levi. Zebulun. With their asses and their women and their cattle. With all they bring out of Egypt—marching as a mighty nation to this new homeland."

He staggered. His knees were jelly. Images spun in his brain. The Tablets of the Law exploded in his skull. The Ark of the Covenant weighed him down and he fell into Mohammed's arms.

Baxter had long since stopped translating the words to

his father. He removed the drinking gourd clutched in Judah's hand, and tossed it into the fire. His eyes flashed anger.

"So that is the true purpose of your journey? To bring an invasion of strangers? But you will fail. My people are the only ones who can live in this land. Who can survive in it. One day, all my people will unite. All tribes. Into one mighty nation. No more Protectorate. No more British—no more Germans—no French. No colonizers! We of Uganda will teach the world one day what Europe has forgotten. True democracy. True justice." His feet, too, were unsteady as he rose. His father watched his growing anger with some concern. "I am grateful to the British for my education. Through their eyes I have been able to see my own people. And I see what they can become. A united federation of African republics. Tribe by tribe—nation by nation. We will bury the memory of the Arab slave traders who raided us for human booty. We will forgive the Europeans who drained our land of wealth. We, in Uganda, will teach the world the lesson they forgot: true brotherhood, whose only enemies are poverty, starvation, ignorance, and disease. This will be the message of the new Uganda!"

His words fell on one pair of unhearing ears: Judah had passed out. Mohamed heard, but kept his counsel.

The tent surrounded him like a canvas womb. Judah could feel the icy chill that brought a castanet dance of teeth. He mastered it, soaked in a clammy sweat. Weeks had passed since they had left King Kasanga's village. Behind them lay rivers, rapids, flights of arrows from hostile tribes. . . .

Weakly he reached to the bowl of cassava leaves. Baxter's purgative treatment, when twenty grains of quinine had failed. Was this how it would end—shuddering in a tent, entombed in the silence of African night?

Only, there was no silence, ever, in this rain forest. Armies of insects were marching, warring, feeding, migrating through this dark eternity. He could hear their humming murmur in this primeval dusk, their sawing mandibles, their myriad wings beating—until the jump of a single mantis crashed to his ears like the fall of a mighty tree. Chant of cricket, zoom of ant lion, thunder of bull frog—to the accompaniment of leaf falls, branch creaks, pitch of treetops wind-stirred.

But never silence. . . .

This land—this place, secret and terrible—this Eden haunted by the ghosts of savage deeds. The slave cries of the anguished seemed to pierce every dawn.

Could this be for any but those born in it . . . a homeland?

The steamer edged cautiously out into the Indian Ocean. Wrapped in a heavy blanket, Judah leaned forward in his deck chair. They had carried him back to the train in a litter, most of the time delirious. In Mombasa, McCulloch had taken charge. The British doctor told him how lucky he was it was only malaria. It had left him weak, but at least it had left him.

Mohamed glanced up from a letter that had awaited them at the Colonial Office. It brought news that Judah's grandfather, Abraham, had collapsed in the street and wasn't expected to live. Abraham of the cart, who with his brother Jacob had met Musa so long ago on the road to Jerusalem.

Mohamed had decided to keep the news to himself until Judah was stronger. All he had said was they'd stop over in Jerusalem on their way back to Paris. Give Judah time to recover completely. He would find the right moment to tell him about Abraham.

"Feeling better?" he asked.

"It won't work, you know." Judah's mind was still in Africa.

"What?"

"The Germans and the British have been competing for Uganda for years. Farther north, the Sudanese have already converted the blacks to Islam. Then the Germans converted the Bagandas to Roman Catholicism. And along came the British with Protestantism. One can see that the Ugandans need a Jewish state in their midst like the rinderpest."

Mohamed fingered an ivory amulet at his throat. A parting gift from Baxter. A mark of final respect. "Then, I've brought back two lion skins . . . and you've brought back a decision."

Judah nodded. "Anyway, how could the British offer the Zionists a land that belongs to somebody else?"

"Where, then?" Mohamed asked. "Sinai?"

"No. Palestine."

Mohamed tucked the letter into his pocket. "But, Judah, you and I know better than anyone. We, who were born Palestinians. Are there not people already living there?

Judah did not hear. He had fallen back into a deep sleep.

Seven _____

"IF I forget thee, o Jerusalem, let my right hand lose its cunning!" The ancient vow of those heartbroken captives dragged away to exile in Babylon. The words so often repeated to dose flagging spirits in times of turmoil when the Diaspora scattered them over the face of the world. Herzl had not forgotten. The dreamer had tried to renew the ancient dream. Now the dreamer was dead.

Summer of 1904. . . . Judah peered out the dusty window of the scorched train bearing him from Vienna back to Paris. One more death. . . . Zosia in Paris, Grandfather Abraham in Jerusalem. Now Herzl, at Edlach, in Semmering, Austria. A parade of dyings of those most loved, most admired, most needed. It was the way of this world to steal like a thief, loved one by loved one. But the loss of Herzl, that was the whole world's loss. The tribe of man was as impoverished as the tribes of Israel.

The dead lay behind him like the summer-burned fields slipping away beyond the train's window. Villages clustered beneath spires thrusting upward like dagger blades through onion shapes toward a well-behaved God, bearded and enthroned above a glass-still sky. "Mind and body—body and mind," the wheels sang over track. Time's scythe cutting away Judah's pillars of love. From death to death we walk through life. . . .

The problem was always the same: to go forward while looking backward. Mohamed had understood it more perfectly than he when they were in Jerusalem.

"Accept it, since you cannot change it, Judah. What has happened to Abraham happens to everyone. Give him the respect of prayers, the silence of tears. Then let him rest—

and get on with your own life." Mohamed had said it to him in the darkened room where candles sweated wax and the family "sat shib'a," everyone on low chairs as though to leave space for the passage of the Angel of Death. The two men had arrived too late from Uganda for the funeral.

The Hammadis, too, had taken part. Mohamed's grief-stricken grandfather pushed Jacob Nouari's wheelchair. Abraham's son-in-law, Rabbi Horovitz, from Safad, had come to read the service. Cloth had been rent in ceremonial anguish, ashes strewn upon heads. Judah fixed the memory of Abraham's face smiling down from the great height above childhood. Grandfather Abraham presiding at seders, formidable as a living Jehovah, weighing decisions for the Company, and accepting another relative's mistake without grudge. Oh, Judah had learned much from Abraham.

His grandfather had completed his full span. But Herzl was only forty-four; in the prime of his life and work. *O God, is it the mark of your chosen people to be chosen for trial by loss—trial by punishment?* Judah swallowed back his bitterness. Herzl would never have thought like that.

"Don't do anything foolish while I'm dead," the Zionist leader had said smiling—only three days after his heart attack. That was when Judah knew he couldn't say the things he had come to say. Nor tell Herzl the decisions he had reached in Jerusalem after listening to the vehement arguments of his family.

Heart attack, pneumonia, coughing, spitting blood, exhaustion. Herzl's physical body had reached a final protest against the act of living. Lean, emaciated, he had spoken with the tongue of a prophet: "The bell has rung for me. I can face it calmly, as I have not spent the last years of my life uselessly."

Uselessly! The man had worked right through the last nights of his life, dictating those interminable letters, even preparing a memorandum to none other than Count Plehve, offering to loan money to Imperial Russia—if that country would look more kindly on its Jews. Where would he get the money? That would have been Judah's problem. Herzl and Plehve. How that bizarre coalition would have shocked Zosia. . . . .

But how could he have told the idealist that Uganda was out of the question—and that in Palestine nobody wanted Zionists?

Judah had merely chided, "Is this how you expect to regain your health, sir?"

"No time to lose," Herzl insisted and went on dictating letters—to Italy, Austria, Germany. A final effort to enlist friends to the cause that must not die with him.

"In the midst of life there is death," he told Judah, referring to Judah's personal family bereavement. "And so, in the midst of dying, there must be work," referring to himself.

At his bedside, Judah suffered with him through the brief, troubled snatches of sleep. Suddenly Herzl sat straight upright, fixing Judah with a piercing glance. His fist struck the bedclothes as though it were a gavel and he presiding again at that first Zionist Congress. *"Ad loca! Ad Loca!"* he shouted. Then, later, calmly, "They are good men, my folk brothers; you will see. They will settle in their homeland. When I am gone, you must go to London. There is also someone I want you to see in Manchester." He gave Judah a letter to deliver personally to a chemist at Victoria University.

Judah would deliver it. But he would also deliver a message of his own. A message of personal abdication. A difficult decision, but there was no alternative that he could see, after all that had been said in Jerusalem.

When can families gather without arguments? But, in the discussions, there had been a new note of concern for Judah's activities. It was almost as though he were a traitor in their midst.

"The Turks are masters of Palestine, as everyone knows. There's no reason to believe that this will ever change. But if it did, what would the Zionists expect to do here? Make their own country? The ones who have come already have nothing to do with us. They are not even our kind of Jews," Uncle Jacob complained.

Izak Nouari nodded agreement, glancing darkly at Judah. "Why here? Why should they come here?"

Judah had not wanted to become the spokesman for Zionism. He had dismissed Uganda and the Sinai from his own thinking, but how could he face the concern of the Jews of his family? These natives of Palestine were even more vehement than their Arab associates about the prospect of any change in the status quo.

The Arab partners had certainly been more reasonable. "We must look at all sides," Sayid Hammadi, Mohamed's father, advised thoughtfully. "The settlements near Jaffa have provided employment for Arab laborers. Many have come down from the hills and settled. Prosperity makes customers—for Arab and Jew alike. And we are in the business of trade."

"I myself am against Zionism," David Nouari said. "It is no cure for anti-Semitism. If anything, it proves its success. These people who want to come here, they are strangers to Palestine. Strangers from Poland, Russia, Romania, Austria-Hungary. People different from ourselves."

"Why do you say different? Many are skilled craftsmen, some highly educated, Father. These are people who could improve the life in our country," Judah argued. "You should put out the welcome mat."

"Some professionals, maybe. But how many city dwellers can our land swallow? Already some quarters of Jerusalem are so crowded you can't pass through the street. Why, always, do they head for the cities?"

"Because most grew up in ghettos. They know nothing of the land," Judah replied. "Give them farms and they will be farmers."

"Who gives? Nobody gives. The truth is, Judah, that their poverty will make conflict. Raise the crime rate. Upset the balance of our community life. That is the truth that can destroy us all." Izak Nouari had spoken. Now in his forties, age had not improved his sour disposition.

"The Jews don't need enemies as long as they have you, Uncle Izak!" Judah exploded.

"Then, you don't need me to listen!" Izak rose angrily. The others placated him, and he returned to his seat.

Mohamed had been listening in silence. Now he spoke quietly. "One question I must ask, Judah. How much land will the Zionists consider enough? And from whom do they expect to get it?"

"They will buy it, Mohamed, from anyone willing to sell. My God, you sound as though they're coming here to steal it!"

"I didn't invent the question."

That's how the conversation had gone in Jerusalem. He could not even answer his best friend's question to his own satisfaction. Judah could not—had not told Herzl the resolution formed in his mind.

The news of Herzl's death struck all like a second destruction of the Temple. Judah stayed on in Austria for that funeral. Thursday, July 7. Herzl had requested "a burial such as is customary among the poorest classes. No flowers. No speeches." He wanted to be laid beside the metal coffin of his father . . . "and to remain there until the Jewish people shall transport my remains to Palestine."

When the Jews went up out of Egypt, they carried Joseph's remains with them to the Promised Land.

Amid the six thousand mourners gathered so hastily to pay last respects, Judah had walked alone. Around him in the blazing heat, the silence was punctuated by thousands of footfalls. They followed the carriage bearing Herzl's wife and mother. Like children who had lost a father, the multitude mourned. Handsome, modest, regal Herzl, who had negotiated with princes and leaders in every land; the dapper dress, the noble face, pale above the black Assyrian beard. Judah could still hear the words "If you wish . . . it will not be only a dream."

Where else was there? They were almost running out of world. Maybe, just maybe, in England there would be an answer. At least Judah could tell this chemist in Manchester how they felt in Jerusalem.

"Why do you involve yourself, Judah?" his father had finally asked him. "You have a business. You should be thinking of getting married. Planning your future. Mohamed says you live in a hotel. Is that a life?"

"Whether I'm involved or not will change nothing, Father. Herzl has always said it must be here."

"It? What is 'it'?"

"The homeland."

"And you would give us—the members of this family, who belong to this country—no decision or choice?"

"Me? Why me?" Judah shouted angrily. "I am only one among thousands. I make no decisions."

"You raise money. Money makes decisions."

"In the name of Jehovah, Judah. In the name of peace. Leave it alone. Leave us alone." It was the oldest Nouari speaking: Uncle Jacob.

"In all conscience, I cannot," Judah had said. But then he had changed his mind.

•　　•　　•

"A difficult birth," the doctor conceded, polishing his beribboned pince-nez. "It is often this way with the first."

It was six o'clock in the morning when Mohamed brought Jacqueline to the Hospital of Le Sacré-Coeur. She had been twelve hours in labor—and the water sac had not broken.

Why should birth be so difficult here in Paris? In Palestine, Mohamed had known of women who gave birth under a tree, or in the fields, and went on with their work. The easiest thing about life there . . . was entering it. The doctor had asked Mohamed's permission to perform a Caesarean section. Mohamed refused . . . for the moment. These Catholics would risk losing the mother to save the child. Yet Jacqueline had been half delirious for hours. If she didn't give birth soon, he'd have to let them operate.

Doctors and nurses came and went, looked in at her, exchanged whispers, but gave her nothing for the pain: it might harm the child. His ears were filled with the sound of her moans. Women's moans were all he had been hearing for weeks, it seemed.

First a death—now a birth.

How they had moaned for that death in the Nouari household in Jerusalem! Formal grief for Abraham Nouari. They all shared this bread of sorrow. Some even seemed to enjoy it. Even his grandfather, Musa, sitting in bedroom slippers because one wasn't supposed to wear leather shoes. Sitting on a low stool because one wasn't supposed to be too far above the dead. Sitting by Jacob Nouari's wheelchair, fingers massaging amber beads large as pigeon eggs, saying his own prayers from the Koran.

For seven days after the funeral, the *shib'a* lasted. All the Nouaris came, and most of Mohamed's uncles. Out of respect. Mahmood, from Cairo, elegant, grown fleshier, stretching his high starched wing collar against the heat. Abdullah from the Damascus office, who had worked so closely with Mohamed on the German railroad project. Abdullah had traveled with his partner, Izak Nouari, and brought his two sons: Tariq, an imp of eight, and Yassir, a bully of twelve. Occasionally Abdullah would reach out and swat one or the other with the fly switch in his hand. Otherwise he chose mostly to ignore them. This was a mistake.

All were part of the Hammadi-Nouari empire, except the two doctors: Uncle Yusuf and Aaron Nouari. And even they carried on the interfamily tradition by sharing a practice in Bethlehem.

Then there was Gamel Hammadi, whose inclusion had been prompted only out of a sense of suitability. For Gamel, three years Mohamed's senior, had the mind of a six-year-old. He worked as a cleaner in a small mosque. Musa's fourth son had been retarded from birth.

The thought of Gamel brought a sudden chill to Mohamed's heart. Had not Jacqueline's doctor just spoken of using forceps on the baby? Of course, he wanted this child. Any child was Allah's gift of life. His own or not, he would accept it. It was Jacqueline's child—that was enough. But how could he face a damaged child, a simpleton like Uncle Gamel?

He got up from the hospital bench and stepped over to the sister at the desk. "My wife . . . there must be some news by now?"

"When there is, monsieur, you may feel confident the doctor will inform you."

"At least may I go in to see her?"

"Not possible. They are trying to induce the birth."

"How?"

"That you must leave to the doctor, monsieur."

He returned to the bench, removed a cigarette from his case, slashing a match nervously across the striker.

"No smoking, monsieur." The tower of starch had spoken.

It would come out all right. It had to. . . . She was in the finest hospital in Paris, not a dark back room where flies hummed below the screens and women crowded close around the midwife to do what must be done.

He forced his mind back to Jerusalem. They were met at the train by their younger brothers, Benjamin and Anwar. It was like shedding a skin, this coming back. The death of Abraham seemed to demand a return to fundamentals. Mohamed put on his fez, Judah his yarmulke.

Later they stood together in the tomb-crowded Jewish cemetery and wept for Abraham, returned to his earth. All that wisdom and humor, now confined to one small rectangle— the space that relieves the human spirit of pride, prejudice, and acquisition. All this earth paved with bones—what did it signify? Merely a coin of time spent carelessly or well. Mohamed was surprised how much Hebrew his father knew when Sayid joined his Jewish partners chanting the Kaddish.

He was also surprised to find that Judah's family showed more concern than his own about Judah's Zionist activities, and what they referred to as "disruptive European influences." For centuries the Nouaris had belonged to the Middle East in style, culture, and custom. David Nouari's great house was furnished to the "Damascus" taste: heavy, dark furniture inlaid with mother-of-pearl, and a profusion of hammered brass.

His own father welcomed the European influence. Tables, chairs, chests of drawers, armoires, shipped from France, Germany, Italy. A great brass bedstead for his parents' bedroom. Most Arabs placed their mattresses (if they used them) right on the floor.

His father and uncles were inclined toward mustaches, neatly trimmed beards, frock coats, and trousers in the Turkish fashion of Constantinople. The Nouaris followed suit, only omitting the fez in favor of the traditional yarmulke.

When Mohamed announced the impending arrival of his first child, mother and aunts exploded curiosity. How would a baby be delivered in a European hospital? Was it true that a *man* would deliver it? How were such things permitted? They whispered behind his back: "What sort of woman would allow a man to touch her at such a time?" They touched their heads with a forefinger. Opinions of Mohamed's wife had been formed long before.

The Hammadi house swarmed with kinsmen and leading Palestinian citizens who had traveled to Jerusalem for the funeral. They could accommodate such hospitality explosions. Kitchens and dining rooms were immense, beds enough to sleep twenty-five guests in the main house. Business associates and favor seekers were customarily housed in the "Diwan," a separate guesthouse with its own kitchen and staff.

What horizons of youthful memories flooded back to Mohamed. . . . Breakfasting soon after dawn in the garden with his father, mother, and brother Anwar. The taste of hot bread, fresh goat's milk, cheese laced with thyme oil, crisp cucumbers, and tomatoes. And tea. Even today, Mohamed's mother still considered tea a luxury. After breakfast Sayid would make his way to the Diwan. Each day, he'd pass a few hours there with his visitors. Young Mohamed and Anwar would accompany him, listening quietly to the conversations, uttering never a word of their own—inhaling, as their father suggested, wisdom.

Sayid sat in an alcove at the end of the room. The visitors, on long divans that lined the walls and gave the room its name. Some wore frock coats and fezzes, but most still wore dingy white shirts, loose, baggy trousers, cloaks, and turbans. They would converse, then taste long silences (a social custom hardly comprehended by Europeans). They would sip coffee and depart, with or without conclusions. Others would drift in and take their places. Finally Sayid would go into the city to the office of Hammadi-Nouari. Later, his wife would send a servant with the lunch she had so carefully prepared.

Mohamed's mother supervised all cooking for both the main house and the Diwan. It wouldn't have occurred to her to allow a servant to touch the complicated dishes, some of which might require six hours poised above steaming kettles. Nor did she dine with the male guests. She spent long hours preparing dinner parties she never attended. Generally, the only meal she ate with his father was breakfast. Mohamed could recall that during the fasting month of Romadhan, a "breakfast" would always be served after the sundown prayer. A hot meal would also be required before 3:00 A.M., when fasting would begin again for the several dozen guests in the main house and the overflow in the Diwan. As head of the house, Sayid was expected to remain with his guests. Throughout the month of Romadhan, his wife barely saw him at all.

As slender as Sayid remained in his forties, Mohamed's mother, like most Arab women, seemed to expand after marriage. His mother veiled only her face when in the street. Since the death of her own father and brother, she always wore black. Mohamed had sent her several silk gowns from Paris, which she prized. She wore a black silk scarf around her head, tied at the back, its tails hanging over her shoulders to the waist. Despite weight, her face was still handsome, her eyes still beautiful, and her smile always cheerful.

No, Jacqueline would never allow herself to get fat. But then, she didn't even know how to cook, and although extremely particular about the quality of food, she scarcely touched it.

In the Hammadi family, a death was treated in much the same way as in the Nouari household. Relatives and friends overflowed into the garden, and sometimes beyond, into the homes of neighbors. The formalities of funerals were a male responsibility. For the women it sufficed to wail behind the screens of their own quarters.

That was one difference between the two families: the separation of the women in the home. Yet the Jews separated their women in the synagogue.

Mohamed had denied his mother her traditional right to select his bride. Perhaps that had been his mistake. With an Arab bride, things would have been so different. In Palestine, his mother would have presided over this birth while Mohamed presided over the household. Catered to, waited upon, pampered, and obeyed. Like his father.

But here, in Paris, he could only hope that this Christian wife would survive the ordeal of a hospital birth, that the child would be born with the prescribed number of fingers and toes.

And if the child were a son? Mohamed shuddered to think he might grow up to be like Uncle Abdullah's Tariq or Yassir.

"Boyhood pranks." Abdullah's words came back to him.

"You are far too indulgent with those two," Sayid always complained.

"You want to change them? I give them to you. Change them," Uncle Abdullah had offered almost too eagerly that day in Jerusalem.

"When the pot has been flawed, it is too late to apply the glaze, my brother," Mohamed's father had replied.

That day in David Nouari's house, Gamel had squatted on one of the low stools, wearing his carpet slippers and a respectful, if oafish, smile. That smile was his sole contribution to any occasion. The Nouari women brought in food, setting it out on the table, beneath which Yassir and Tariq were busily engaged in tying Uncle Gamel's leg to the table. After a few giggles, they slunk across the crowded room. Then, when the moment was opportune, they piped, "Come here, Uncle Gamel. We need you . . .!"

Ever eager to oblige, Gamel hastened to follow. With a great crash, down went the table, exploding crockery fragments like shrapnel, splashing hot, sugar-thick coffee to the fine Turkish carpet, where Gamel sprawled. The boys collapsed with gales of joy. Gamel got to his feet babbling apology.

Abdullah's fly switch whisked a saber sting across Yassir's dark cheek. The lad's howl erupted through the embarrassed silence. Servants hurried to clear the debris.

"And you do not even beat them!" Abdullah's partner, Izak Nouari, chided. "Too easy on them, I warn you."

"It is a sign of spirit in the boys," Abdullah replied.

"What do you say, Mohamed?"

"I say, I'd cut off their ears!"

And then the minor comicality was followed by a small catastrophe. Mohamed had been talking to his younger brother, Anwar.

"I don't understand why you won't come to Paris. There's more than enough room at my house. It's like a palace. And you—how old are you? Twenty-three, Anwar?"

"Twenty-four."

"Not too late to attend the Sorbonne. Polish your education."

"Why should I want to live in Europe? I do very well here. Besides, I don't see that it's made you very happy," Anwar countered.

Mohamed found this difficult to answer. He wondered how well he really knew his brother. Not as well as he knew Judah, certainly. As brothers, they differed physically and mentally, Mohamed thought. Anwar, more slenderly built, better-looking. More serious-minded than Mohamed had been at the same age. Both he and Judah had been disappointed that their brothers had preferred to attend the École des Frères in Jaffa.

Ben, at twenty-two, was even more intense than Anwar. For a time, the Nouari family proudly thought he might become a rabbi. But Ben seemed undecided about his future. Except in one area: "Palestine is my home and I intend to remain here," Ben echoed Anwar.

The two Hammadi brothers sat talking in the great family room. Around them it had grown dark. Then they heard an awful sound. A body tumbling downward. A sickening crash and a howl of pain rising from the stairwell in the hall. They hurried in, to find Gamel lying at the foot of the stairs, grotesquely sprawled like a rag doll. Mohamed caught a glimpse of Tariq and Yassir vanishing into the upper corridor.

Members of the family appeared. Lights went on. Poor old Uncle Gamel. Never knew which foot to put in front of the other. Little wonder he has fallen down a flight of stairs! And only a leg broken? Lucky. If it had been his head, perhaps it would have made no difference anyway.

Mohamed knew that Gamel had not fallen accidentally. He had been pushed. He went to Grandfather Musa and told him what he had seen. "You are still head of this household, Grandfather."

The old man nodded, munching a soft Turkish candy on a toothless gum.

"It is your duty to speak to your son Abdullah about his boys."

Musa did. He, too, was concerned. But, as always, Abdullah only fingered his worry beads and shrugged. It was his wife's fault. She had produced them. "Besides, one cannot take the responsibility for bad offspring. One does one's duty, and Allah will do what pleases him."

Allah will do what pleases him. . . .

In the early dawn of the Paris hospital waiting room, the doctor shook Mohamed awake.

"You have a son, monsieur."

"My wife . . .?"

"She will be fine."

"May I . . . see them?" Mohamed followed the doctor to Jacqueline's private room.

Never had she looked so frail, so vulnerable, skin paler than moonlight, hair spread across the pillow in damp, gold ringlets, and, tucked against her breast, a small object. She pulled back the coverlet to reveal a little red wizened clown mask of wrinkles, eyes tightly closed. Topping its head was a surprisingly thick growth of bright red hair.

He bent to kiss her. "Congratulations, my dear. He is a beautiful son. Thank you. What shall we call him? I give you the choice."

"Maurice," she whispered.

He nodded. "Our son shall be Maurice." He drew a velvet box from his pocket. It was the gift he had feared he might never have the chance to give her. Now she made no move to take it.

He opened it for her. It sparkled a circlet of emeralds. Gently he fastened it around her wrist. A tear grew in the corner of her eye.

"Thank you, Mohamed. Thank you. . . ." Her voice held more than gratitude for the gift.

• • •

There were those who called Manchester "England's least attractive but most prosperous city." The observation, if not precisely accurate, could not be totally dismissed by Judah as he progressed through the labyrinth of basements beneath the city's Victoria University. In this hot summer of 1904, it seemed Judah seldom managed to pass more than a few days out of motion. The motion of travel. By ship, train, rocking Channel steamer. By carriage, automobile, and hansom cab— and now by foot through unending mouse-colored corridors of frequently cracked tiles. Depressingly empty. Students and faculty had taken flight to greener summer settings. But Judah had promised Herzl to deliver in person his wearily scrawled letter.

"They'll all be contending for my crown," the dying man had observed. "Wolffsohn thinks it'll fit Max Nordau best."

"And what do you think, sir?" Judah had asked him.

"That the throne of Zionism would be a platter on which he'd be served up like St. John's head. They'd eat him alive."

But the father of Zionism had not named his choice of successor. Judah had wracked his brains all the way to this Godforsaken city. There was Moses Gaster, of course— powerful rabbinical claimant. Dynamic, London-based Gaster had even raced over to Herzl's funeral, to be seen and counted. And Judah had followed Herzl's wishes to visit Gaster in London, where the rabbi made no secret of the fact he was prepared—which was to say, ready and willing to accept the reins of leadership. Still under fifty, a man of imposing presence, a thinker, an eloquent speaker, there was much to recommend Gaster besides himself. As religious head of the Sephardic community in England, Gaster's claim could not be ignored.

But there were other claimants as bountifully endowed. Judah knew that the ambitious rabbi didn't get on with Herzl's leading disciples—who did not exclude themselves from the race. Israel Zangwill, Joseph Cowen, Leopold Greenberg. How could Gaster expect to bring harmony to the angrily divided movement, to patch up furious quarrels between Russian, Polish, Austrian, German, and British factions? Quarrels raged even over the leader's grave.

"I'm heartily sick of the political contention," Judah had complained to Mohamed. "So many of these men seem disposed to use this cause as a pedestal for their personal careers. Let them sew up the rents in the Zionist garment. Let them bring their own warring factions together, if they can."

"Get out of it, Judah," Mohamed counseled.

"I shall!" On which note of resolve, Judah had left for England.

Because he saw no worthy heir and because his heart was sickened by the way the would-be leaders maneuvered for position, Judah was glad that after this one last mission for Herzl, his conscience would allow him to give it up. Let somebody else attack the hearts and pockets for a dying cause. He had promised Mohamed and himself: from now on he was devoting full time to Hammadi-Nouari Trading Company and their banking interests.

"I'll believe it when I see it," Mohamed had replied.

A faint tinkle of glass rang through the rabbit warren of gray-white corridors. Judah pushed his way into a half-open doorway and saw the back of a man nursing a test tube over a burner. The man's concentration was so total he didn't turn.

"Are you by chance Dr. Weizmann?"

The head came around. "Not by chance. As a chemist, I am the result of cause and effect." Chaim Weizmann was at once handsome and enormously magnetic, with lively eyes storing humor, wisdom, practicality. He was prematurely bald, with the blackest of small trimmed beards and neat mustache. "Who are you?"

"Your postman at the moment." Judah drew out the letter he had carried across four countries. "Putting this into your hand was one of Dr. Herzl's last requests to me. And with its delivery, I have acquitted myself now and forever of further service to Zionism."

The chemist perched on a stool, read the letter carefully, then folded it away. "Dr. Herzl recommends you to my use, Mr. Nouari." His eyes dissected Judah. "He calls you one of the strongest pillars of the Temple."

"Dr. Herzl's personality engulfed us all. His chief weapon was audacity, but I can no longer work for Zionism, Dr. Weizmann."

"Nonsense! Herzl knew the value of every coin in his

pocket. And you appear to have been a very large gold piece."

"I've lost my value. I'm not sure I even believe in it any more."

"Of course Herzl leaves an empty space none of us can hope to fill. But we must carry on, within our limitations—or the root will die with the branch. So . . . we shall put science to bed." Competent hands corked retorts, emptied test tubes, extinguished Bunsen burners. "And decide how best to serve his memory." Weizmann removed his white smock, took down a shiny, worn black jacket from a peg on the door. "Come, we have a lot to talk about." He guided Judah out.

"Dr. Weizmann, I have weighed my decision thoroughly, and I hope I lack Herzl's capacity for self-deception," Judah began.

"Don't lack it entirely," Weizmann cut in. "Deception can be a useful weapon, particularly when the arsenal is low. At the moment, I'm sure it has not escaped your attention that we Zionists find ourselves in the midst of civil war. It is always so when a strong man falls. But one day soon we shall get our cart out of the mud. . . ."

"It no longer concerns me."

Weizmann ignored Judah's abdication. "Have you met Menahem Ussishkin? He tries on the crown before his mirror, they say. Fortunately the crown is nonexistent, or he'd have a dent in his head from sleeping in it. Yes, Mr. Nouari. We Zionists are likely to become an army of generals. But Ussishkin's merits must not be underrated. He was in the fight even before Herzl. He is a walking library of Jewish culture. A synagogue of commandments." Weizmann frowned. "And I feel he would be totally wrong."

"Who do you feel would be right?" Judah asked in spite of himself. He found himself rushing to keep up with the man's brisk stride down the corridor.

"Myself." The chemist laughed. Judah couldn't be sure if he was serious.

"I was born in Russia. That makes me geographically acceptable. In a small shtetl, in a village you probably never heard of. Motol."

"I can't say that I have. Well, I wish you luck, but—"

Weizmann cut him off again. "It's situated in 'the Pale of

Settlement,' where the Czar permits Jews to live and conduct a few regulated occupations. My father was a timber merchant. There were twelve of us children. Fortunately he insisted that we learn to speak Russian. You must understand, that is unusual for Jews there—since hardly anyone but Jews speak to Jews anyway. At school in Pinsk, I discovered chemistry— and Zionism. From there I moved on to Berlin. Then Switzerland. Now . . . here. So, Mr. Nouari, you have a 'potted' version of my background and qualifications. Do you think I'll make it?''

"Manchester seems a bit out of the mainstream for you, Dr. Weizmann.''

"Would I be teaching chemistry here if I'd been offered a post in London? I don't mean to sound ungrateful, mind you. My starvation has been postponed by a part-time consultancy. For a dyestuffs plant owned by the leading Zionist here. Three pounds a week, he pays me. More than I'm earning at the university.''

Judah had been so riveted by the man's personality, he'd failed to notice their steps had carried them into Manchester's poor Jewish quarter. Around him, thick, pungent sounds of Yiddish came from time-warped faces scarred by isolation and the intensity of the survival struggle in a world that might at any instant turn hostile—even murderous. Even here, in this friendly land, the fear still remained.

" 'Cheetham Hill.' The only *goyisher* thing about this district is the name. It's no ghetto, but it might just as well be. Jews here lock themselves in with the keys of habit. There is no gate and no wall, except Yiddish. And in a way, I can't blame them. So, to come to England, I learned English only to discover that here the locals speak something called 'Lancashire.' Now. . . .'' He paused. "How soon can you start making yourself useful, Mr. Nouari?''

"I thought I made myself clear, Dr. Weizmann.''

"Forget that. I need you.''

"Dr. Weizmann, I came personally to tell you that I am through working for the movement. I *have* told you. . . .''

"Somehow, I didn't hear you. Anyway, you cannot leave. You must remain at least a few days.''

"Impossible.''

"But tomorrow is my thirtieth birthday. And I'm giving a

talk at the Zionist Association. 'Political movements of the
Jews in Russia.' ''

"Sorry I won't be here to hear it."

Weizmann paused. "Mr. Nouari, a leader should be financially independent. My sin is impecunity. I am a threadbare
professor who can't even afford to get married."

Several small children ran by, wearing yarmulkes and prayer
shawls.

"On their way to school. They're the lucky ones. They'll
still be alive in six months. In Poland the chances are not so
good. I'll want you to make a short journey—on our behalf."

"There will be no more journeys for me, Dr. Weizmann."

"Did you tell that to Herzl?"

"Herzl was dying."

"Zionism is dying, Mr. Nouari."

They stopped before a gracious residence on a tree-lined
street. Weizmann pulled out Herzl's letter. "Here, in this
letter, he tells me—there is no one else who can do the job
that you can do: 'Where there is a need, Judah Nouari will
serve,' he writes."

"There are always needs, Doctor."

"Mr. Nouari, in a few minutes I shall walk through the
door of this house—to plan a mission of mercy. Of salvation.
Whether I walk through alone, or you go with me, will be
your own decision—after you have heard what I must tell
you."

"I've heard it all, Dr. Weizmann."

"We have just had information of a workers' revolution
brewing in Russia. That means the pogroms will increase.
Hundreds of towns and villages will be locked into total
repression. My own brother and sister have already been sent
to prison. The gateway to freedom is Poland. In Warsaw I
have a brother-in-law: Chaim Lubzhinsky. . . . He works
with a group who help get people out. Some manage to reach
England, or France, or the United States. But most still look
toward Palestine. We need silver persuasion to put into the
right hands. It is necessary for you to go to Warsaw. Thousands of lives depend upon it."

"Surely I'm not the only qualified banker—or fund raiser.
Let one of the contenders go. Let them earn their crown in
Poland."

"Gladly, Mr. Nouari. Gladly. If you will name me that

one person who has the financial experience, who knows
Palestine, has dealt with the Turks—and—how shall I put
it?—has a Polish connection.''

"I have no 'Polish connection'—as you put it, Doctor.''

"I have seen your file, Mr. Nouari. It is my business to be
familiar with all the important friends of our cause. As well
as its enemies. And so, for the new rescue operation we have
chosen the code name "Zosia.' ''

Judah froze. "Where did you learn it?''

"From Herzl. This is the only way we can honor her
death.''

If only the sound of the name hadn't brought the image into
mind. The terrible last instant of horror. The slight body,
seeming to be borne aloft, the blinding, numbing concussion
of the burst. . . .

"Who did you say lives in this house?'' Judah heard
himself ask.

"My mentor. A man with another name you may not have
forgotten—though no relation. A Mr. Dreyfus of Manchester.''

Judah walked up the steps with Chaim Weizmann.

For two days now, he had been in Zosia's city. Smoke-
colored buildings seemed in the gray anguish of their stones
to record a thousand years of wars, miseries, occupations,
struggles, rebirths.

Warsaw—the rancid smell of its ghetto scorched his nostrils. Hunger was in that smell, and the burnt tallow of
guttering candles. Though many families had lived there since
the Middle Ages, all Jews were considered aliens in this
prison of a city within a city. When Europe emerged from her
dark-ages nightmare of wars, plagues, and terrors, Poland had
invented the first walled ghetto—at Breslau.

"They were pagans until the thirteenth century,'' Zosia had
once told him. "Christianity came so late that the Jews
represented a special challenge there. After all, we, too, had
only one God—and He was the same as theirs. Anyway, how
could we expect the *goyim* to love us when they claimed we
killed our own Messiah?'' Her words stuck in his mind, like a
bone of the past. "But our ghettos—which were to keep us
from contaminating them—also kept us together. In faith,
customs, and language.''

Her words seemed more alive here, where she had grown up. Her pale beauty was the ghost he met around every narrow street corner. She drifted to him out of the shadow in filtered light. . . . How close again she had become, here in Warsaw. Her city. The very feeling of that nearness filled him with the ache of wanting her again. Weizmann's mention of her name had been enough to change all plans and resolutions. Enough to return Judah to her cause. Oh, the man had been persuasive enough, but it was she who had brought him to Warsaw, not Weizmann.

And now Judah sat in a dingy basement lit only by candles, walled in by heat, sweat, and conspiracy. He sat facing Lubzhinsky and the others.

"Persecution here is every bit as bad as in Mother Russia. Here, there are as many massacres, confiscations, restrictions," Weizmann's brother-in-law insisted. Judah felt exhausted, adrift among a strange breed of people born to danger.

"How does a Jew make a living in Warsaw? He claws up the wall." Kalman, the chairman of the gathering, did not smile at his own joke. Yet humor was the bread of their survival. Kalman was large, powerful, with the sense of great bones pressing out the tight, sallow skin. His hair looked damp and dark as printer's ink, glued in ringlets down the long hollows of his cheeks.

"You tell us that it is impossible to make the Turks raise this quota imposed on Jews. Then, we must proceed despite it, Mr. Nouari. It is my understanding that there exist already eighteen settlements." Kalman shrugged. "And most are illegal, if it were put to the test."

"Anyway," Lubzhinsky added, "it is not only for permissions, documents, seals on paper that we require your help. It is for money. And for finding it you have a fame that has walked in front of you. A very fine ability, Mr. Nouari. Very important."

A fame that walked in front of him. He was developing a shadow—that led him.

Lubzhinsky continued. "I myself have sent funds to my brother-in-law, Weizmann, to keep him from starvation. A brilliant chemist—but no skill at money."

Kalman sucked on a cigarette butt held between nicotine-yellow fingers. "It is not everyone who can persuade people to give to those they do not know, to go to a place that they themselves will never see." His words brought an approving murmur from the others. They needed Judah. Perhaps he needed their need. Zosia had urged him toward the extraction of money with the admonition: "A magnet does not attract gold, Judah. The rich ones, whose pockets are lined with it, will not be drawn to Zion. All we need from them are their contributions. Let them water their consciences with the tears of generosity, and stay home."

With the help of men like Rothschild, Von Hirsch, Montefiore, the golden seed had sprouted into colonies at Gedera, Rishon Le-Zion, Petach Tikvah. Now there was an agricultural school at Mikvah Israel run by members of the "Bilu," who believed that redemption of the soul of Israel would come only through redemption of its soil.

"We cannot be martyrs for our country, because we do not yet have one. We are not looking for a glorious death; we are seeking a life, Judah." Thus had argued Zosia—but she died nonetheless, for a land she could only dream of. Perhaps all lands were better in dreams. Anyone who could believe enough could bear enough. A quality Judah had never found in himself. Judah felt a wave of weariness pass through him as he walked out into the ghetto street. He had refused an invitation to dine with Lubzhinsky. He had another destination.

First darkness was falling early between the tall, scarred walls of the ancient houses. Voices, cries, the drone of prayers came to his ears. The dust of dying summer powdered his fine leather shoes. Poland: crisscrossed by conquerers, traditionally dedicated to the achievement of liberty, yet historically chained to the Russian bear. Poland, of all lands, should have been understanding of the plight of her Jews. But now they, too, faced extermination unless means could be found to get them out.

A water carrier passed Judah, two long wooden pitchers strung from the ends of a pole balanced across his right shoulder. His ragged jacket was belted with a bit of rope, fur cap pulled down over his ears, even in summer. Judah gave him a handful of coins, took a long drink. Water of captivity. . . . "By the rivers of Babylon, there sat we down, yea, we wept." There had been enough weeping now. It was time to turn a page of history.

But how? Who had the answer, now that Herzl was gone? A handful of men in a dark cellar in a ghetto—counting on him to produce the miracle of money? He passed a group of old bearded Jews in long ragged coats and yarmulkes. They glanced toward him as their forefathers might once have looked upon the Persian troops of Cyrus come to rescue them from another captivity.

"There are three million Jews here, most of them near starvation," Kalman had told him. "You represent escape." Judah had agreed to raise funds and to help with the quotas. But only within the limits permitted by the Sultan. As a Palestinian, that was all he could promise Kalman and the others. They could not look to him for more than that. Salvation must remain within the law.

Judah fingered the slip of paper in his pocket. For the third time that day, he drew it out and read the address. He knew it by heart. It was to this address that he had written Zosia's mother after her death. A brief note, saying little. Promising to come to Warsaw one day and explain in full. She had answered in Yiddish, the lingua franca that could once again unite the tribes. Since the sixteenth century, Jews of central Europe chattered their bastard German east and west in *buba meintzas*—those grandmothers' tales of their own folk history. The humor that sustained them through the Diaspora, and could laugh at itself. "When you baptize a Jew, hold him under the water for at least five minutes." Well, Baron Liebermann's certificate of baptism may have been his admission ticket to the lower rungs of French society, but he still remembered his Yiddish, if not his faith. Many like him preferred the Talmud's advice: "Be obscure that you may endure."

The house stood in a street of older residences. Narrow, plaster peeling, a *baleboosteh* of endurance, this house where Zosia had grown up. His heart echoed his knock. What was he afraid of, a ghost? No, it wasn't fear. It was eagerness. Need. He ached to speak to those who had known Zosia. To tell them how she died. How she had lived. He hadn't come empty-handed. He'd stopped in the Jewish food market, bought what he could: potatoes, onions, cabbages, apples, and a chicken.

There was a murmur of voices from within the house in Vilna Street. A note of fear at the unexpected knock. He hadn't warned them he was coming. Now he realized how thoughtless that had been. Eyes peered from behind a heavily curtained widow. The door opened an inch, then widened to reveal a young girl. Judah was unable to speak. He just stood there, feeling himself beginning to tremble inside. She was . . . Zosia, come alive.

"What do you want?" she said in Yiddish. The image of Zosia blurred into this other, younger person. Her voice was not as husky, her hair darker. And now he could see that her eyes were not gray but hazel, though they were formed in the same almond shape. The cheekbones, too, were the same. She was like a portrait of Zosia as a young girl; a portrait by a careless artist, achieving a semilikeness.

A man appeared behind her. Heavy, guarded in manner—suspicious. The two pairs of eyes scanned him from dusty shoes to well-cut suit. "Well?"

"My name is Nouari," Judah began, his own Yiddish faltering. In Palestine he spoke only Arabic or Hebrew. In Europe, only French or English. "I was Zosia's friend in Paris."

"Come in," the man said briskly. "Don't stand in the street. It attracts too much attention, which is a thing we do not need here."

Judah followed them into a small, gloomy sitting room smelling of chicken soup and cabbages. The room was threadbare but clean. A battered piano stood in the corner. "I have brought a small gift—for Madame Halevi. . . ." He indicated the sack of provisions. A sharp word from the man dispatched the girl swiftly to the back of the house. He gestured Judah toward the best chair.

"I am Mordchai Cukor. Mrs. Halevi, my wife's sister, lives with us, a widow."

An old man peered around the doorway, then ventured into the room in carpet slippers, wearing a prayer shawl and carrying his Torah.

"Grandpa Zuckerman, the father of my wife," Cukor grunted. "I have many relatives to support, as you see. But who complains?" he complained.

The old man came forward, nodded, sat on a rocking chair.

The girl returned with two women. Cukor introduced his wife and her sister, Zosia's mother. There was an uncomfortable moment of silence. Judah handed the groceries to Madame Halevi.

"Just a thought on my first visit to Warsaw," he said, unable to take his eyes off the girl.

"My daughter, Ruth. A player of the piano."

"You are very like Zosia," Judah said.

"Why not? A first cousin," Cukor allowed.

Zosia's mother regarded Judah with a curious kind of unease, as though sensing that she would not want to hear what might be told. She was painfully thin, hair wrapped in a black shawl, cheeks hollow, face gray, with something of Zosia staring out of the eyes. Her sister, Ruth's mother, was sturdier, younger. But the family resemblance among all the women was marked.

"You recall, Madame Halevi, that I wrote you after Zosia's death."

"Yes, yes. You were—her friend—the banker. Ruth . . ." she said, "our visitor might wish some tea. Bring a glass of tea. With lemon. We have lemon?"

"No lemon, Aunt Hannah," the girl said.

"So—no lemon. Everything today is hard to find. Thank you for the food."

"Lemon, yet. The women consider me a millionaire," Cukor grunted.

Madame Halevi settled herself against the back of a stiff, wooden chair. Judah felt that no matter what happened in her life, be it death or the lack of a lemon for tea, it would be faced with the same fatalistic resignation.

"In Warsaw we do not meet many bankers. I have always respected a man who commands money but does not serve it," Cukor added.

With a glass of tea in hand, Judah told the family what he knew of Zosia's death. How he could not risk writing the details at the time, because the French police had never succeeded in identifying the "Polish countess" who died on the steps of the Russian Embassy. The authorities had not tied her death to Zionism. Best for all concerned. There could have been reprisals against her family. But she was not forgotten. A rescue operation, of which he was a part, had been named for her. "The word 'Zosia' will mean freedom to thousands of people," he said.

Judah told what he knew—but it was far less than the whole truth. That had died with Zosia and Alexei.

Ruth broke the silence that followed his story. "It was a heroine's death," she said. "I have always wanted to be like my cousin."

"And get yourself killed?" Ruth's mother put in.

Madame Halevi sighed. She spoke with the same husky tone as her daughter. "Who can tell a young person how to lead her life? She said in her last letter—we might not hear from her again. Then, when your letter came, we knew. So we did not question. She took the risks for our people."

"I would never have let her take that last risk—had she told me about the bomb. You see, we intended to be married, Zosia and I."

Her mother exchanged a glance with her sister.

"That is a thing that she never wrote us," Madame Halevi said. "But then, Zosia was always a secretive girl. She had to be, in the work she did."

The old grandfather, Moses Zuckerman, looked up from his Torah. "Zionists! Better she had married this banker! Zionism is against the will of God—that is why she died. The land of Israel—Eretz Israel—cannot be achieved by human methods. Only when the Almighty is ready will He lead us back to our land. Not before. The Jews will return to Zion . . . by the will of God. Never by the will of man. Never!"

The family ignored Grandfather Zuckerman; but Judah knew very well that many Orthodox Jews throughout Europe felt as the old man did—and would do nothing to help themselves or others in the quest for a Promised Land. They would wait through starvation and death for the Messiah to lead them by the hand. The Messiah promised in the Bible. To Jews, a promise still unkept.

Judah had already delayed his return to Paris by a week. Every day, he came to the Cukor house bearing gifts, and always a special toy or sweet for Ruth's baby brother, Olek. He ate dinner with the family, and sat admiringly silent while Ruth played Mendelssohn. The candlelight above the keys reaffirmed her haunting likeness to Zosia. It was easy to feel through the music the poetry of his lost love. He let himself drift into the mirage of melody until the music and the girl seemed to have become one with memory.

They left him alone with Ruth after dinner—each family member with an excuse. Ruth and Judah sat stiffly on the sofa. She seemed to be waiting for him to speak first.

"Have you ever thought of leaving Poland?" he asked.

"Oh, yes. Like cousin Zosia—I would like to travel everywhere. Do important things."

"Like what?"

"Like her."

"You admired her so much?"

She twisted the corner of the handkerchief crumpled in her hand. "Since we were children—I wanted to be . . . Zosia. For her, it was always so easy to say things. Write things. And make people do what she wished them to."

"Why do you think that was?"

Ruth groped for explanation. "In the world, I think, she was the most wonderful person. Didn't you think so too, Mr. Nouari?"

Judah closed his eyes, letting the image of Zosia materialize. It brought a thickness to his throat. He could not, at the moment, speak.

"She was—" Ruth continued, "I mean, like people in books you read about." Then, with a sudden stumble of perception, "Mr. Nouari. . . ." She blushed slightly. "Could I ask a question, a little personal, maybe?"

"Of course."

"Were you fond of her?"

"Yes," he replied. "But life goes on. It is a continuation. It is a river."

"Oh, how I wish I could be like her!" Ruth sighed.

"You are. Very like her, Ruth."

Ruth twisted her handkerchief ringing her finger. "Oh, do you think so, Mr. Nouari? But I cannot use a typing machine. No, I have no head for such things."

"You have talents of your own. The piano. Have you a desire to continue with your music?"

She averted her eyes. "For me, to have a home of my own. . . . And children. It would be enough."

"And a husband, of course?" he suggested.

She blushed a deeper red. "A husband. Well, I suppose. . . ."

"You have a great deal to offer a man, Ruth. A loving nature. Beauty of soul. One can see that you are very like your cousin. The closest woman I have ever known—to Zosia. . . ."

He knew then that he could not leave without Ruth, and finally, a few days later, he told her father so.

It was appropriate that he approach Cukor before broaching

the subject to Ruth herself. Mordchai Cukor restrained his
delight. "My daughter is a very smart girl. Talented and
pretty. But also very young. Not too young, mind you. In our
family, brains go with looks, hand in hand. That is why at
twenty-four she is not yet married."

They had been left alone in the sitting room, sipping the
cherry brandy Judah brought when Mordchai had expressed a
fondness for it. In the kitchen the women were busy with the
dishes. Mordchai removed his small ivory toothpick from its
golden scabbard, worrying a tooth as he spoke.

"But who am I to advise a banker? On the one hand,
marriage is a step that should not be taken too quickly. On the
other hand, the Talmud says, 'He who marries a worthy
woman is kissed by Elijah and loved by the Holy One.' And
after all, for a Jew, Warsaw is not the capital of finance. You
must return to Paris. So decisions cannot wait."

Tactfully Judah suggested that he must first know how
Ruth felt about him.

"The young are not always the best judges of their own
minds," Cukor warned, but obligingly brought Ruth in and
left her alone with Judah. Grandfather Zuckerman's entrance
from the kitchen was hastily detoured to the bedroom.

The kitchen door closed behind the family. Judah could
almost sense the ears pressed against it. The silence was alive
with them. Ruth regarded him shyly.

"You would like me to play some Mendelssohn, Mr.
Nouari?"

"No Mendelssohn tonight, Ruth. I'd like to talk to you."
He led her to the worn sofa. "We have only known each
other for a short time. But I have come to care for you.
Yes—to love you."

She blinked at him with mild disbelief. A faint blush
touched her cheeks. "Is it too warm for you in here? I could
open a window."

"Ruth," he said. "Do you understand? I'm asking you to
marry me. I don't want to go back to Paris without you."

"Paris? But we would live in Palestine, would we not?
That has always been my dream, ever since I first heard
cousin Zosia talk of it. The sun, the fresh air, the fruit, the
open hills, the sea. The homeland that will be ours."

"We can live anywhere you wish." He hadn't the heart to

tell her that Zosia had never seen Palestine. "The important thing is . . . could you be happy living with me?"

"I always dreamed that someday I would open the door and my whole life would be changed. Now it has come true, Mr. Nouari. Changed by you."

"Ruth . . . could you love me?"

"How could I not, my dearest, Mr. Nouari? Even my father loves you. He told me."

He bent toward her, kissing her gently on the lips.

In the kitchen, Mordchai Cukor straightened up. "It's time to go in there," he told his wife with an expansive smile. *"Mazel tov!"*

But, to Ruth's disappointment, marriage did not lead immediately to Palestine. Mohamed couldn't spare Judah from the Paris office.

Mohamed's investment on behalf of the bank, in the Laville-Darlan Tool Company, had paid off handsomely. He plowed back the profits. For Hammadi-Nouari, he made an outright purchase of a failing French tool company and appointed Henri St. Rimaud, his wife's cousin, as managing director. Then Mohamed acquired majority interest in a firm producing tractors and farming equipment in Germany. These projects required more and more of his own attention. Judah had to carry the load in Paris.

It was a time of expansion for the Company, and Mohamed's genius for industrial adventures was being given full play. He found the opportunities. Judah found the money.

Mohamed was delighted by Judah's marriage. "I trust it will mean an end to an episode. Now, once and for all, that chapter of your life with Zosia can be closed." He refrained from mentioning Zionism.

After a short honeymoon in Baden-Baden, Judah moved out of the hotel. He and Ruth bought a house complete with all furnishings down to the last stuffed bird under glass. Even the staff came with the house, which spared Ruth the difficulty of hiring servants in a language she hadn't yet learned. Since nothing in the house had been choosen by either of them, Judah remained as impersonally detached from his surroundings as he had been at the Crillon.

Ruth talked vaguely about redecorating but seemed at a loss where to begin. She was reluctant to touch anything in the house, and just walked about staring at things, as though it were a museum where nothing belonged to her.

Judah insisted Ruth begin French lessons at once. She couldn't even exchange a word with Jacqueline, or any of Judah's French associates, which made entertaining next to impossible.

"You must try a little harder, my dear," he urged impatiently. "It's no more difficult than Mendelssohn."

"But I won't need French in Palestine."

"We're still in Paris. Yiddish is not sufficient."

Actually, it almost was. Through the Synagogue de la rue Notre Dame de Nazareth, Ruth had been introduced into a group of young Jewish girls who sewed for charity and called themselves the Atelier du Couture. They were part of the Alliance Israèlite Universelle. It was one place in Paris where she could chatter away in Yiddish over the throb of sewing machines. She marveled at how freely Jews moved in the French community. Judah explained that anti-Semitism, though always an undercurrent, had been officially abolished by Napoleon I. He had melted the chains of the ghettos for cannon.

But she wasn't listening. She never did. As the months passed, Judah realized that he had married a girl he didn't know. They seemed unable to communicate in any language. How had he been foolish enough to think that he was marrying another Zosia? The cousins were nothing alike. Where Zosia had been brave, daring, adventurous—Ruth was reticent. Where Zosia was wise and shrewd—Ruth could be tactlessly aggressive. Where Zosia had been passionate—Ruth was docile.

There was no other Zosia. There never could be. Yet there was no turning back, no putting together the broken glass that had been crushed under foot in the Warsaw synagogue beneath the wedding canopy.

While he was pondering these imponderables, Ruth brought him the news that she was expecting their first child. In a way, it was a relief. For the time being, he would not have to go to her bed. When she complained that his ardor had cooled, he countered that he didn't want to endanger the child.

On Christmas Day, in 1906, Ruth gave birth to twins. She had wanted them to be born in Palestine. The boy was named for Judah's grandfather, Abraham, the girl for Ruth's cherished cousin Zosia. It followed the custom of keeping alive the names of the dead. The twins soon became nicknamed "Abe" and "Zed."

Now Ruth had another excuse to neglect French lessons. She was too busy with the children.

Eight _____

"HURRIYA!"

"Hurriya! Hurriah!"

"Freedom!"

A harsh orchestration of youthful male voices bounded off medieval walls. Once, this same cellar had been crowded with crusading knights of fortune, opportunists in armor, partitioning this ancient land into feudal fiefdoms. Then and now, above the arched stone vault, Damascus slept under a star-swollen sky. Damascus—oldest continuously existent city on earth. Old before Macedonians and Romans filled their waterskins at its oasis. Tonight minds were being filled with revolution as the cluster of savage-eyed young men drank in the leader's words.

This leader—his face had a certain hawklike beauty, a face underscored by passion and poetry. His blue eyes seemed impassive. His sudden smile was disarming. His voice incited, his intensity seduced their reason, forging them into instruments of his will. Two years at Cairo's Al Azhar studying theology had developed his ideology. A tour of duty as a cadet officer in the Turkish Army had taught him the uses of authority. And yet, this leader was scarcely older than the young men who followed him.

" 'Whosoever of you sees an evil, let him change it with his hand: and if he is not able to do so, then with his tongue, and if he is not able to do so, then with his heart—and that is the weakest of faith.' " His glance swept the faces of the eager young men. "Who in this chamber knows who said those words?"

Silence.

"No one among you?" he queried. "I speak the words of

149

His Messenger: Abu Said al-Khudri. Memorize them. Live by them.''

Bodies seemed to sway toward him through a slight tobacco haze in the dank cave of wine casks and dedication.

"If a man kills a tyrant, it is not murder. A tyrant is one who has been dead from the beginning. And has not Allah prescribed proficiency in all things? Thus, if you kill, kill well. And if you slaughter, slaughter well. Let each of you sharpen your blade like your mind. . . . Make this the sixth pillar of your faith. Your *hajj*—your pilgrimage to the Mecca of your dedication.''

His words reached out to his listeners, touched the core of their deepest yearnings. To belong. To be led. To believe. In this Arab they had found their *mullah*, their lodestone. One to be followed through flame, and blood spilled like the weavers' dye between the cobbles of the medina. Through him was spoken the message of the only true God.

In the full flower of his nineteen years, Yassir Hammadi could appreciate the look and manner of this organizer of Al Fatat—The Young Arab Society. The very timbre of the man's voice brought a singing to his blood.

"Hurriya," the leader repeated, dropping his tone three octaves into a note of sadness for lost Arab conquests. With a quick, almost mincing step, he moved down among them, clasping shoulders, forcing them one by one to look deep into his eyes.

"Only three years ago you heard this cry of freedom in the streets. You saw strangers greet each other, embracing, rich and poor alike. Scholars, illiterates—you saw them drunk with joy, with passion and hope. They, perfect strangers, became brothers in expectation, holding each other in a wave of exultation. And why?" He stopped in front of Yassir, making the young man feel the privilege of being chosen. "Because after hundreds of years of Ottoman tyranny, Sultan Abdul Hamid granted us a constitution! He abolished censorship, released political prisoners. And you and I believed! Naïve as children who hear the word of the father. All would be different. For us, a new time was dawning. . . .''

Yassir's head nodded, reponsive to every nuance. The leader moved gracefully back to the front of the gathering. He took his time, stretching pauses into mystical silences. His voice droned like a sadness of wind, sobbed through cedars of Lebanon.

"What happened then? I will help you to remember back only three years, my brothers. To April of 1909. To the counterrevolution that dethroned Abdul Hamid and placed his brother Muhammad Reshad V on the throne." There was a grunt of response. "And what did Reshad do with his new imperial power? He let it fall into the hands of the Committee of Union and Progress. What beautiful words. . . ."

The leader's voice was a caress, like the hum of devotion in the high, sun-filtering dome of a mosque.

"Union. Progress. Words to embrace. Like 'love. . . .' " His voice hardened. Candles flickered tall shadows on damp walls. "And what happened to this *earthly paradise?* What happened to our feast on the fruits of freedom within the perfumed gardens of the Ottoman Empire? It faded away like the mirage. We Arabs found ourselves pushed back into the old serfdom of Turkish superiority. We—who once conquered to the gates of Vienna—through Spain, through France, through every land where the hoofs of our horses wrote victory carrying the pages of the Koran on our lances—we! became again . . . a subject race."

There was a rumbled murmur of shame. The leader did not waste the moment.

"No, my brothers. Do not spit out those words. Taste them. Savor their bitterness. Say them in your minds. What are we? Say it!" His voice rose to a wail. "Let the poison pour from your lips. Release it from your hearts!"

"A subject race. . . ." Yassir chanted with the other young members of Al Fatat.

"What is the prize? Independence. And how is it to be found? Handed down as a gift to us from the Turks? No! Independence is no gift. It is a thing to be seized." His eyes attacked them. "Is that not why we are here?"

Yassir was not certain what had brought him to this moment. Abdullah's son had grown tall and straight, and embittered. With the others, he had sworn the oath to work for nothing less than complete Arab independence in Syria and Palestine.

There were so many things in this world for a young man to despise. His father, first of all: sucking sweets and administering discipline with a fly switch. If Abdullah had beat him, Yassir could have respected him. But how could you admire a man who allowed himself to be bedeviled by a shrewish wife?—for Yassir's mother was certainly that. Nor did he hold much affection for his father's sour-faced partner, Izak Nouari. To Yassir, home was the perfect springboard from which he might hurl himself into worldly causes. And having discovered an attitude, Yassir could list all the things that made the world around him a despicable place peopled by tyrants and victims, bullies and slaves.

And high on his hate list was cousin Mohamed. Even as a child, Yassir could remember Mohamed Hammadi advocating harsh punishments for Tariq and himself. Righteous cousin Mohamed—greedy and santimonious, with his French whore wife and his power in the Company. It was easy to equate his cousin with the Ottoman Turks, who dangled little carrots of liberty—then plunged their Arab subjects deeper and deeper under the tyrannies of their corrupt reign.

Let the young Turkish officers pretend to new horizons of political "awareness" after their brush with German *Kultur*. Let them boast of their new railroad from Baghdad to Basra contracted with the Germans, assisted by cousin Mohamed. But when it came down to the lot of Arabs in Syria or the Lebanon, were they not, as the leader said, still second-class citizens? Yassir remembered with rage the leering face of a Turkish lieutenant in the café who had knocked a hot cup of mint tea into his lap, then stood over him laughing.

"Look—you have pissed your pants, boy! Do you also wet your bed?"

Yassir had risen, hands knotting into fists. The lieutenant's quirt slashed twice across his cheek. Yassir fell back, palms trying to contain the blood. The lieutenant lifted the remaining tea, pouring the steaming liquid over Yassir's testicles.

He had felt castrated. But now it would be different. He had found a leader: a man he could believe in and follow.

"What are we speaking of tonight, here in Damascus? We talk of national rights. Human rights. Independence for the Arab nation. Yes, and the restoration of the caliphate to a son of the Arab Quraysh tribe. Our strength grows with brotherhood, unity, and secrecy. What we must do to achieve our aims, let it be done. All things will be justified in the name of Allah." Taut, dark-skinned faces leaned across.

Not that Yassir could much admire his compatriots. Sheep who had strayed into the field of a protecting shepherd. But he knew his own worth. So did the leader, for he had selected Yassir as a group organizer, responsible for six others. The leader's face glowed hypnotically in the gloom of the cave.

"From now on you have no father, no mother—only Al Fatat. No land—only Al Fatat. No home—only Al Fatat . . . Al Fatat! We are sworn together that we shall build a new state upon the bones and bodies of the old." His voice broke off. His eyes fixed strangely. Yassir held his breath. Surely he was witnessing a man in the throes of a holy vision. Slowly he turned his head to see what the leader was seeing.

The ancient door of the cave had opened. In the entrance, shadows moved. Ghosts out of the darkness!

One . . .

Two . . .

Three . . . and more and more!

Turkish gendarmes—armed, befezzed—moved purposefully into the guttering candlelight, mustached faces strangely impassive behind carbines and German automatic pistols.

"Lie with your foreheads touching the floor! Do not worry about facing to Mecca. You will not see it in this lifetime."

With sick horror, Yassir saw the leader's knees fold under the butt of a carbine. On his forehead a dark crimson stain flowered like an opening rose. Then Yassir could see no more. The cold, damp stone floor kissed his own forehead. The pressure of a boot twisted into the small of his back. He heard his own curse merge into a scream. The candlelight blurred. A wave of cries. The sickening crack of iron on bone.

His mind's world shrank from a volcano to a spark. The last firefly of a dying universe. And somewhere from the black hole swallowing consciousness, a single sound gibbered back. The confusion of an idiot tumbling down the stairs.

Yassir had no clear memory of the trial. It had been swift and conclusive, a military tribunal with convictions for all. For most, there was a long-term sentence with hard labor. For the leader and the group organizers—Yassir and two others—the sentence was death.

During the trial, Yassir had been flattered to be branded as one of the leader's chosen. But now fear had replaced pride. From a cistern someplace above his cell, water dripped or seeped down the wall. He had nothing left but time. Time in which he could reconstruct the events of the past few months. At first the others who shared his fate and his cell had seemed to have a need to talk endlessly. Then, as the trial wore on, a sense of hopelessness engulfed them all. They were plagued with flies and questions. They were taken out of their cells separately and each told that one of the others had loaded all the blame and guilt on him. When tricks, hunger, and beatings failed to produce a confession from Yassir, he was dragged to the captain's office by three troopers, who threw him, stomach down, across a hard wooden table. They tied his hands to the front legs, ripped down his trousers and bound his ankles wide apart. Tears of shame filled Yassir's eyes at the memory.

The captain showed him the whip and assured him that Yassir would take pleasure from it. Almost as a favor, the Turk began to stroke the whip across his bare buttocks. Gently at first; slowly. Then harder and faster until the stinging blows made him numb. Then the captain's hand smoothed oil across the lacerated cheeks. The hand slid down to penetrate his anus. He caught a glimpse of one of the troopers watching with relish. The face was bearded, curiously monastic. Then Yassir's whole frame shook with the sudden plunging jolt, the terrible thrust of the captain's penis. The pain made him sob and curse. The bearded soldier stuffed a rag in Yassir's mouth.

When it was over, they left him alone in the room, still bound to the table, his trousers hanging around his ankles. In his deepest moment of degradation, he realized that he had had an orgasm. And in this same instant of horror, he vowed that no man or woman would ever touch him again.

If he lived.

"You plotted to overthrow the government—yes? Yes . . .?" This Turkish judge had a nasty habit of touching Yassir lightly with the brass tip of his cane. Only the leader and Yassir had managed a stubborn silence. Neither confession nor denial. . . . In the night, he broke down and wept. The weeping began after the episode with the captain, but he didn't relate it to that, or even to the first announcement that the four would be publicly executed. He had taken that with icy calm.

And then there had been the dream. He was a child again,

and Uncle Gamel was pushing him from the top of a tower. Only, it was not the pathetic, smiling half-wit he and little Tariq had tormented. This "dream Gamel" was sinister: an avenging angel of strength and hatred. And Yassir had fallen and fallen endlessly downward without ever crashing to any bottom, because his own scream had awakened him.

The leader had listened to Yassir's dream. Had been sympathetic. He was a poet, an idealist, a historian. He had felt his purpose mystically communicated. "When I am marched to the scaffold, I shall kill one of the jailers," he assured Yassir. "I shall become the fist of Allah. The sword of Saladin. You must do the same."

One day, the leader was taken out of the cell. He did not return. Rumor was that he had escaped. Nothing more was said, but the remaining prisoners were beaten and given no food for twenty-four hours. It was then that Yassir managed to find within himself a new strength. He stopped crying. He gave himself totally to hatred. And he lost all feeling of admiration for this leader whose voice had sung with the music of persuasion. There was in Yassir's mind a suspicion that the leader had been released. Had he not, after all, once served in the Turkish Army? Escape from this high-walled, well-guarded jail seemed impossible. The leader must have provided the Turks with the evidence they wanted.

For the first time, Yassir could see clearly. This leader was weak. Ineffectual. A man of words who had failed at the real level. Surely Allah would provide stronger men? Yassir dreamed of a room, and the power to see through its closed door. Within this room was another leader. A man so skilled that any strategy must be totally successful. A man capable of conquest, who would strew dead and maimed upon the earth by the shrewd and ruthless clarity of his planning.

Yes, he would be there behind that door. Awaiting Yassir, who knew that he would serve this man—and bring death to all enemies of the true Arab destiny. Even those Arabs by whose weakness betrayal had been made possible.

"I will serve you, and I will know you, though you wear a hundred masks," he pledged, and in his vision the stranger's lips had touched his own. Their hands had met upon the hilt of the curved sword.

In his awakening he was almost calm. He would not cry

again—even on the steps of the gallows. He would laugh—
and he would be saved for the work he was born to. And for
the true leader he was destined to serve.

Djemel Pasha, Turkish governor of Syria and Palestine,
could perfectly well order a stay of execution—if sufficiently
subjected to temptation. He was in some respects a sad man,
because he knew that all pleasure was, alas, fleeting. How
tragic, for one to whom all pleasure was so frequently and
easily available. That his enemies called him a madman and a
sodomist did not trouble him. Perhaps it was partly true. But
in all events it was an oversimplification.

"It is no good just to tuck a few gold pieces under his
pillow," Abdullah Hammadi reasoned. "If Yassir is to be
saved, we must be cleverer than that." He was speaking to
Solomon Nouari, who had hurried from Jerusalem to Damascus at the urgent request of his brother, Izak. Abdullah, never
before overly noted for family feeling, had been strangely
metamorphosed by his son's predicament. Suddenly he blamed
himself. It had been his fault that Yassir had let himself be
drawn into such evil company. Why had he not watched the
boy more closely? Tried harder to understand him? Directed
his youthful energies in a more constructive path?

Solomon Nouari did not quite share Abdullah's feeling of
paternal failure to make the world a more interesting place for
his friend's eldest son. But he, too, strongly felt the need to
save Yassir, if for no other reason than that the lad was a
Hammadi. Standing by each other in personal tragedies was
to Solomon the very essence of the relationship between the
partner families that produced such long-term success. It
would be a mark of failure for the Company if they could not
rescue one of their own.

"Our best argument is Yassir's youth," Abdullah continued. "Even Turkish authorities must respect that. They should
not hang a boy of nineteen years for his first mistake. Besides,
what has he done? This secret society—what did they do?
Was it so dangerous to smoke cigarettes in a wine cellar and
talk rubbish?"

"A reasonable man might agree. But His Excellency, Djemel
Pasha, is crazy, my friend," Solomon reminded him.

Abdullah wiped sweat from his forehead with a clean

handkerchief. The two men were jouncing through the streets of Damascus in a plain open carriage. Ostentation was not a habit of the Damascus partners. It could even hurt bargaining. "I know the whole Company is dedicated to saving my Yassir. But how, when the Pasha is spoiled by bribes already?"

"Spoiled, but not satiated. He knows what we will ask, and he knows our means of persuasion. If there were no hope for us, he would not have granted this interview." Solomon's still-powerful frame belied his fifty-one years. The mane of gray hair was thick as always, and as always, both families respected the good sense of Jacob's son. But today Solomon would need the wisdom of his royal namesake to save Yassir.

"It isn't enough. It isn't enough! Gold, yes. Youth, yes. But we must think of something else." Abdullah's hands waved vaguely. "We must find the invisible hook."

The hook was a nose—hardly invisible—on the face of Djemel Ahmed Pasha, Turkish Governor-General. He appeared deceptively bland, exposing no clue to the unstable emotional climate behind the veiled eyes. Even his vocal tone, thickened by the inhalation of clouds of hubble-bubble smoke, only hinted at the potential rage that lay just under the surface. The Pasha was, as his worst enemies would quickly concede, no fool. The administration of provinces as large as Syria, Palestine, and the Lebanon for his distant master in Constantinople required a precise blending of tact, opportunism, and an instinctive knowledge of every man's strength, weakness, and vulnerability. At the moment, he appraised the two specimens before him with keen measure.

"As Your Excellency well knows, my misguided eldest son, Yassir, is a mere boy." Since it was the weakest argument in Abdullah's arsenal of persuasion, it was therefore first to be used and discarded.

"Not too young to plot the overthrow of the government! No, I warn you, if you are here to waste time pleading for a stay of execution, this audience is quite pointless." The Governor's glance flicked to the superbly uniformed officer who served him as military aide and *ami du chambre*. "Captain, I think these gentlemen have completed their business."

The aide's dashing appearance, in flaring breeches, polished boots, and tight tunic, hid a skill in extracting confessions, useful in the Governor's service.

Well versed in the ritual of Byzantine bartering, Solomon

had bided his time. "The matter that brings us, Excellency, is separate from our natural hopes for clemency for my partner's son. A boy, yes. But a boy from a family important throughout the whole of the Middle East—to say nothing of Europe, where the Company's banking interests are not unknown." Solomon paused to gauge the effect.

The Governor lifted a hand just slightly, as one making a subtle gesture to stop traffic. "Continue. . . ."

"In gratitude for the cooperation of Your Excellency is the completion of the Baghdad-Basra railroad, and in commemoration of its anniversary, the Hammadi-Nouari Trading Company has requested Mr. Hammadi and me to present you with a small token of remembrance. . . ." He glanced at the aide, who laid a box of polished ebony before the Governor. On its lid was a gold plaque inscribed: PRESENTED BY THE HAMMADI-NOUARI TRADING COMPANY TO OUR COMPASSIONATE AND MERCIFUL DJEMEL PASHA.

Due to the gift's special nature, the aide had taken the precaution of removing it from the givers. Abdullah offered a small golden key with which the Pasha unlocked the box. Couched in crimson velvet lay a pair of superbly engraved automatic pistols, their mother-of-pearl grips inset with rubies.

Djemel Pasha's lower lip trembled just slightly. He permitted himself a nod of pleasure. "You may convey our thanks to your Company. We are grateful that our services resulted in benefit to your diligent associates—and the people of our provinces." He picked up one of the pistols, pointing it casually at his aide, who smiled agreeably.

"I have unloaded them, Excellency," the captain said.

The Pasha shrugged, somewhat disappointed.

"One thing more, Excellency," Solomon continued. "A dagger—presumed to have been stolen from Your Excellency's collection—a superb weapon with solid gold and jade handle in the form of copulating horses—was recovered in Jerusalem by Mohamed Hammadi. He will forward it here at the earliest possible moment by a Company courier. The piece is of no slight value, he informs me."

"And you think it was from my collection? Stolen?"

"It bears Your Excellency's initials."

The Pasha nodded thoughtfully. "In that case it is mine." All waited while the aide relighted the bowl of the hubble-bubble and bore the serpent tip to the Pasha's lips. The movement of a plump official finger directed the aide's ear closer. Abdullah and Solomon were far too skilled to play their trump card yet.

The Governor frowned. His restless eyes settled like flies on Abdullah. "In the case of your son's sentence, we are not without the disposition to be compassionate—but the young man's guilt binds our hands. What can we do, without impairing the very administration of the justice we are bound to uphold?"

The invisible hook was baited.

"It is quite possible that your clemency, if a just way were found to use it, would be looked upon with approval by His Serene Majesty, Sultan Muhammad Reshad V, so recently come to rule in Constantinople."

The Pasha frowned. "The Sultan knows of this case?"

"Not from us, certainly. We would be the last to advance our cause over your head, sir," Solomon assured. "However, Mohamed Hammadi informed my nephew, Judah Nouari, in Paris. Naturally he shared our concern and sorrow with our relative in Constantinople, Mehmet Khassadia. You may have heard of him? An aide to the former Sultan, Abdul Hamid. He now serves the new Sultan as Minister Without Portfolio. It is almost certain that he will have entered his own pleas for our partner's son."

Djemel Pasha's fingers drummed across the hilt of his silver scabbard. If the Sultan should be bribed into clemency by Mohamed Hammadi, the stay of execution might arrive too late. An embarrassing possibility. "Constantinople should never have been brought into this," he worried.

"Oh, we quite agree. Never. It places Your Excellency in a position of—how can one say it?—the middle," Solomon said. He was speaking slowly. "We urged our relatives to do nothing that could embarrass your own decision, sir, pending your full investigation. But communications are so unreliable," he added. "Foreigners are not even permitted to use the same postal service as Turks, and our chairman, Abdullah's nephew, with so many urgent international matters on his mind, may be forgiven for acting impetuously on behalf of family honor."

"The Sultan would not wish to influence any decision within my jurisdiction," Djemel Pasha assured them and himself.

"Certainly. The Sultan will also realize that if you see even the slightest reason to show mercy out of concern for our family honor—and the true noble nature of a young man involved in his single mistake—you would naturally overrule the heartless conviction of your court."

The argument had not been total bluff. With Mohamed absent on business in New York, the problem had fallen squarely onto Judah's desk in the form of a cable from Abdullah. Judah brooded over it for only half an hour. While he knew that Yassir had behaved foolishly, the public execution of any member of either family would have repercussions. More than justice had to be served.

Judah cabled Mohamed to meet him in Constantinople. Then he cabled Mehmet Khassadia. Finally he telephoned Ruth to say he would not be home for several weeks.

Ruth, as it happened, was not even home. It was her afternoon at the Atelier du Couture. He left the message and said good-bye to the twins. How impersonal every instant of their lives had become. This marriage was scarcely different from one of Judah's hotel rooms. He sent a bank messenger for a first-class ticket on the Orient Express.

It was his habit to keep a suitcase fully packed at all times in the office. He never knew when he'd be called away at a moment's notice. His eyes fell on a leather-bound volume. The former Sultan had been a great collector of photographs, avoiding travel as a sensible precaution against assassination. Judah tucked the photos of his Uganda expedition into his suitcase. No doubt Muhammad Reshad V, having achieved his throne by a palace revolution, would share his brother's interest in photography.

Mehmet Khassadia had moved his official shadow a few cushions closer to the new Sultan. As a Turkish Jew, he felt no inclination to overstretch his authority in aid of the son of his nephew, Judah's, Arab associate. Not because Yassir Hammadi was an Arab, but because he was a troublemaker. With troublemakers, you never knew when the helping hand would get bitten.

Since his marriage, years before, to Abraham's daughter, the plump Sarah, Mehmet had enjoyed the benefit of reflected distinction as a Nouari in-law. Yet it seemed to him that as their wealth and power grew, his own position in Constantinople also grew in importance. More and more, the Nouaris made use of his generous nature to solicit favors from the Sultan. For the Trading Company, and now for the Hammadis personally.

Toward his Jewish relatives, Mehmet could feel some obligation that his wife, Sarah, would not let him forget. By no stretch of even her imagination had their union been a love match. Not that his own family had been nobodies. They had been established as shopkeepers in Constantinople for two generations.

Adroit, shrewd, young, Mehmet had greased his way into the Turkish Civil Service, beginning with a posting to Jerusalem—no small feat for a Jew. Then he had met Abraham Nouari. On their third meeting, Abraham invited the young Turkish Jew home for a Sabbath evening meal. Nervous and flattered, Mehmet arrived exactly on time. The rules of hospitality in the Middle East were simple: ask nothing, expect everything. But Mehmet had not expected the carrot that was being dangled before him. Over a glass of wine, Abraham imparted a puzzling bit of wisdom.

"It is not written in the Talmud, but I can assure you, Mehmet, that the only shortcut to success is wealth." He then produced his less-than-toothsome daughter.

Mehmet realized that a whirlwind courtship with Sarah was essential if he was to sustain the nerve to marry. "If she's worth her weight in gold," he assured himself, "I'll be the richest man in the Ottoman Empire."

Abraham watched the young couple appraising each other unenthusiastically. He knew that the man who married his daughter would earn her dowry.

But all that had happened over a quarter of a century—and a thousand "financial arrangements"—ago. Abraham had shored up the union with a princely sum and, through the Company, a kaleidoscope of opportunities. For years Mehmet had been buttering his bread on both sides. What puzzled him was that for all his wily manipulations at the Sultan's court, his greasing of palms and lining of pockets on their behalf as well as his own, the Nouaris, though scrupulously polite, tolerated but never seemed to trust him.

As for the Hammadis, he could not avoid a certain traditional contempt of the Turk for the Arab. His eyes drifted to the desk photo of his son, Kemel, in the uniform of a captain in the Turkish Army, taken on his recent promotion. (He avoided keeping a photograph of Sarah in his office.) Dashing Kemel was heir to his father's fine physical stature. Unfortunately the Almighty had seen fit to equip him with his mother's wits. The apple of Mehmet's eye was a dunce to the core, but in the Army this was no great disadvantage. He looked well in uniform and never questioned an order. His career was assured. A fact that did little to endear him to his Palestinian cousins—or their Arab partners. The Hammadi-Nouari empire might think they owned Mehmet, but they would never own his son.

Yet, when the matter of Yassir had come up over dinner, Mehmet had assured Sarah that he would go as far as arranging an audience for Judah and Mohamed with the new Sultan. But no further. Less would reflect on his own status. More would be dangerous.

"I can see no reason why Yassir shouldn't be hanged," Kemel said, wiping from his mustache the floury sweet *kadin göbeği*, which translates astonishly as "woman's navel." Kemel had no sympathy with treason. He was a Turk first, an army officer second, a Jew last.

His father nibbled a handful of pistachios. "Obviously, they could contact the Sultan themselves, Kemel. You understand that. If they persuaded him to request clemency from Djemel Pasha in Syria, it wouldn't strengthen my position. The Sultan might even consider I lacked in family feeling. A flaw to be considered dangerous in a trusted aide."

Kemel shrugged. The whole matter bored him. "I can see no reason why Yassir shouldn't be hanged. If it were up to me, I'd swing him from a minaret."

"The Sultan may agree with you, but the audience must be arranged."

"In these matters, your father's judgment is always right," Sarah told her son. In a lifetime with Mehmet, though Sarah's only joy had been Kemel, she had learned respect for the husband who had provided neither the money nor the love, but the security, of an unshakable marriage.

Mehmet rose from the table. His son stood with him. "So be it," the older man said. "Tomorrow I shall escort the roosters to the fox, and we'll see how loudly they can crow."

• • •

It is said: when a fox has his hour, bow to him. Mohamed and Judah bowed before Muhammad Reshad V. This Turkish fox had taken over his brother's golden throne in Topkapi Palace, which left him with an understanding of the motivations of revolution. He also had an agreeable financial recollection of Judah Nouari's negotiations with his royal brother in the days of Herzl's efforts to purchase Palestinian land. That affair, however disappointing to the Zionists, had left many purses the fuller in Constantinople. This Sultan's manner was haunted, his disposition variable, because he knew his power to be less than secure. Still, it was he who was sitting cross-legged in this throne large enough to hold three men. Its flat surfaces were picked out in an exuberance of motifs, spiral scrolls, abstract flowers, each bloom encrusted with cabuchon rubies and emeralds. He wore a uniform so heavily braided with gold thread that his tunic dragged him down, belittling him as a man. His epaulets seemed as large as fringed awnings. A wide silk sash crossed his chest from right shoulder to waist. His simplest article of apparel was his fez.

Light filtered through a plaster filigree archway across Mohamed's face, standing beside Judah to plead Yassir's case. Judah's photograph album had been accepted with only mild interest. Reshad had no thoughts of attempting to conquer Uganda. It was enough that his expeditionary forces of ragged troops, verminous and malarial, were still dying in Tripolitania and the Balkans fighting Graziani's Italians without ever knowing why. Mohamed could find it easy to despise this potentate who had added to the incompetence and corruption that were strangling most of the Middle East.

"We make it our policy not to interfere in the administration of justice by local authorities." Reshad's voice was curiously toneless, as though talking in his sleep. Mehmet had told them that Reshad slept in a different bedroom every night to confuse conspirators. Perhaps, Mohamed thought, he did not sleep at all.

The Sultan inclined his head toward his minister, Mehmet, who watched with an air of the utmost neutrality. "What is your opinion in this matter, Khassadia?"

"That Your Serene Highness' decision will be wise and

just." Mehmet bowed slightly, his frock coat swallowtailing out behind him.

Reshad twisted his upper lip, making the thick line of his mustache twist in the air. He concentrated his gaze on Mohamed. "What reason can you give us for sparing the life of a traitor when we are surrounded by enemies?"

Mohamed's cool glance riveted Reshad to the great throne. "We are not unaware of the terrible financial burden you bear, sir. We have heard a report that your officers fighting in Libya have been forced to hire fishing smacks at their own expense."

"Completely untrue . . . except in a few cases," the Sultan grumbled.

"And that your troops suffer a lack of arms and ammunition."

"Where did you hear such a thing?" Anger was beginning to color the Sultan's sallow cheeks. "Such information is classified."

"In Berlin, sir. From a minister of the Kaiser, with whom we have been doing some business."

"The Kaiser, yes. A very good friend of Turkey." The Sultan was growing uncertain down which labyrinth he was being led.

"The Kaiser would like to become a better friend, sir. If he had more confidence in the strength of the Turkish Army," Judah put in.

"It may interest Your Majesty to know the purpose of our visit to Berlin," Mohamed began. "Hammadi-Nouari has been considering investing in a munitions factory in Düsseldorf. This factory has traditionally supplied the Italians. It occurred to us that we would be in a position—by acquiring this company—to cut off Italian supplies. And Graziani's army might have to hire their own fishing smacks for a change."

The Sultan brightened perceptibly. "These weapons—what are they?"

"The finest German quality. Which we could supply to *your* armies at the most favorable terms. Once we control production."

Reshad nodded toward Mehmet. The nod snowballed into a gold-toothed smile from the Minister Without Portfolio.

"And how generous would you be with credit?" the Sultan asked, the glazed look quite gone from his eyes.

"Unstinting, sir. And exert ourselves to speed the movement of supplies—pending final arrangements," Judah added. "Our Paris bank is prepared to make the investment in the Düsseldorf plant immediately—pending our instructions," Judah continued.

The Sultan nodded, inclining his head toward them. "It is said that the Prophet used to have drunkards beaten forty times a day with a sandal. Sometimes with a frond of a date palm, forty strokes. In the time of Caliph Abu Bakr, it was increased to sixty strokes—and to eighty in the time of Caliph 'Umar. In my time, ninety. Since this nephew of yours, Yassir Hammadi, was drunk with foolishness only, we shall alter the sentence. For I could not believe that any member of so illustrious a family would consider treason." His attention turned to his minister. "Khassadia, let our wishes be known in Damascus."

The three bowed and took their departure. Mehmet walked them through the cool white carved corridors of the graceful palace that rode the hill above Constantinople.

"Thank you, Uncle Mehmet," Judah observed tactfully.

His uncle grunted. "Another favor—to be quickly forgotten in Jerusalem, I suppose."

"Oh, I assure you, Uncle Mehmet, it won't be."

"Since my father-in-law's death, Sarah hears from nobody," Mehmet grumbled. "Who remembers Kemel's birthday? Where were the telegrams when he was promoted? To your father, David, we are poor relations."

"You know how bad the mails are, Uncle. Everyone in Jerusalem has only the highest regard for you. And I have brought you a present from Paris. For your wife . . . selected by my Ruth."

It had actually been purchased at the last minute by Judah's secretary. A silver-inlaid letter opener from Fabergé. He handed it to Mehmet, who paused to study it.

"What good is a letter opener, when nobody writes?"

"That one will open a hundred letters of gratitude for the life of my cousin Yassir," Mohamed assured him.

"So we got the little dog off."

Mohamed and Judah were alone in the dining room of the only hotel in the city. They were eating Circassian chicken garnished with nuts, red pepper, pumpkins, aubergines, and stuffed capsicum. Mohamed wiped his lips. "Thank you again, Judah, for coming to the aid of the Hammadis."

"You'd do the same for any Nouari."

"I hope I would." He smiled at the slender Judah, who was cleaning his plate. "Don't eat too much. This food goes to the belly."

Judah laughed. "It's a long time since we sat together except in an office—with plans and accounts of profits or losses before us."

"It is." There was a moment of silence. Of just enjoying being together.

"Tell me: How is it in New York? Do you like it?" Judah asked. He refrained from mentioning Jacqueline, being as always uncertain on the state of the marriage.

"I like it very much," Mohamed answered. "You must come. The food is better than here. And there is more money to be made there than in all of Europe."

"You need me in Paris. If we are really to go into the arms business in Düsseldorf, as you told the Sultan."

"Would an Arab lie to a Turk?"

Judah frowned, putting down his fork. "I still don't like the idea of making a profit from arms."

"Everything points to the Turks making a German alliance, Judah. Hammadi-Nouari must choose the winning side."

"So—then I stay in Paris."

Mohamed nodded. "You're doing a fine job. But you're still living out of a suitcase. What is it doing to your marriage?"

"Ruth is a good woman. And I shouldn't have married her. But that's my fault. Not hers." Judah sipped at his small coffee. "Maybe there's only one truth about marriage. It looks better from the outside."

Mohamed nodded. "The ceremony lasts only an hour, but the trouble last a lifetime." He leaned closer. "You know, I had hoped Ruth would lead you away from Zionism."

"Zionism may be my folly, Mohamed, but it's your blind spot."

"You're the only Zionist I ever heard of who moved *out* of Palestine into Europe."

"Ruth still wants to move there," Judah said. "She sees it as I see it. . . ."

"No lectures, please," Mohamed cut him off. "I know all

your arguments by heart. I still say you're dreaming. And it could even be a dangerous dream.''

The night that should have been an occasion for celebration was growing somehow heavy. They had won a battle together, but their lives had drawn so far apart they were reluctant to ask each other too many questions.

He did not know whether he was going to be hanged, shot, or tortured. When they brought Yassir out of his cell, he did not know, and the jailer offered no enlightenment. It had happened in the middle of the night—or was it early morning? Yassir had lost all track of time. He was hauled up from the stinking straw they called his bed and marched out into the prison yard.

Beyond the bars of the gate, he could glimpse a small crowd gathering expectantly. The riffraff of dawn. Street sweepers, beggars, early-morning merchants bound for the medina. A water carrier, his supply swelling a great goatskin roped across his shoulders; a bread vendor, flat loaves weighing down his basket. Had the word spread around so swiftly— if not to Yassir, then to the very least of Damascus' citizens?

A public execution. A little entertainment before the monotony of crouching in a fly-infested street crying wares through the long, scalding hours.

They manacled Yassir's wrists high above his head to a thick wooden ladder braced against the wall. Leather straps bound his elbows to the ladder. He found unsteady footing on the lower rung. Yassir came alive then, with insane fear.

''Noooo—for Allah's sake—don't kill me. . . .''

He heard himself screaming all the things he had so carefully vowed never to utter. Saliva dribbled from his lips. Tears burst from his eyes. He slobbered and wept in the same breath. His sobs choked him.

An officer whom he had not even seen approach, addressed him: ''Why do you make so much noise? You have been pardoned.''

Yassir's senses steadied. ''I—I—?'' He could not form the words.

The officer looked profoundly bored. He produced a document from his tunic, reading tonelessly. ''By order of His Excellency, the Governor-General Djemel Pasha, the prisoner

Yassir Hammadi shall this day, in in accordance with executive order number 917 11 A3 be taken at 6:00 A.M. to the
courtyard of Damascus Military Prison, there to be publicly
flogged. From there he will be delivered into the custody of
Abdullah Hammadi, and within twenty-four hours placed on a
suitable conveyance to suffer permanent banishment from His
Excellency's provinces of Syria, Palestine, and the Lebanon."

Folding the document, he signaled a sturdily built Turk.
Stripped to the waist, the man stepped forward bearing a
limber cane stick. He swished it a few times, stirring the air.

The first, cutting stroke bit Yassir's flesh with the teeth of
a dog. His shriek of pain became a long scream of hate. He
howled and writhed on the wooden ladder. A second stroke
. . . a third . . . a fourth . . . he lost count—and he could
feel the sticky damp, hear the buzzing of enthusiastic flies
moving to business.

Quwhap! It fell again. Yassir bit deep into his lip and blood
gushed down his chin. Quwhap! Quwhap! Heavenly velvet
darkness squeezed closed his eyes. He felt no more. Not even
when they cut him down.

His father, Abdullah, and Solomon Nouari bore him home
in a carriage, gently as a child, head resting across their laps.
When he awoke, Solomon was gone. An Arab doctor was
dressing his wounds. Yassir lay on his bed, flat on his
stomach. The ninety strokes across his back seemed to have
wounded every nerve in his body.

"It will heal," the doctor told him. "It will not leave many
scars. You will forget."

Forget? What did the man mean, "forget"?

His father looked as though he might weep. "I have telegraphed your uncle Mahmood in Cairo. I will take you. There
you can rest and gather strength. Meanwhile, it will be decided
where is best for your future."

Yassir looked across the room. The bright-colored glass of
the lamp offended his eyes. Hatred rose like an intoxicant to
the mind. It fed on the stripes of pain across his back.

"Only through the efforts of everyone in the Company has
your life been spared. When you are well, your gratitude
must be demonstrated properly. Naturally I shall give gifts.
Write letters. So must you."

How stupid his father sounded! His words offended Yassir's
ears. All this concern for the Company. He could still see

Solomon Nouari's sickening look of sympathy. How could Solomon, a Jew, understand what he had borne for the Arab cause? But, from the Hammadis, he expected some appreciation of the meaning of his dedication.

"My cause will become the cause of all Arabs. I shall use every breath of the life the Sultan has given back to me to work for his destruction. And all who follow him. Death to the Turks!"

Sweat glistened on Abdullah's brow. "Please . . . quiet. Who knows what ears could hear you! Doctor, I beg you, forget what my boy has said. He speaks from a mind full of pain."

"I am only interested in the illnesses of the flesh," the doctor assured him. "My ears hear nothing of politics."

"Cairo. In Cairo, Uncle Mahmood will talk to you. Your cousin Mohamed will be there. It was he who did the most to save you."

"I do not want to go to Cairo, Father."

"Want? Want? You have nothing to say. You will do what you are told."

"Will you beat me with a fly switch if I don't?" The door opened. His younger brother, Tariq, peered in.

"Not now, Tariq," his father said.

"Let him in," Yassir insisted. "I want him to see." The younger boy stepped into the room, eyes wide at the sight of his brother's back.

"Look at it, Tariq," Yassir told him. "Remember. I will not be here to remind you. See what the Turks have done to your brother. Remember we are a subject race, and learn to hate."

Abdullah shook his head slowly. "If two Muslims confront each other with drawn swords, they stand at the abyss of hell. If one kills the other, both fall into the pit. The Turks may rule us, but they, too, are Muslims. That is what you must remember, Tariq."

"Are we to serve them in the skins of dogs?" Yassir demanded. "Maybe you, Father, but not me. Not Tariq, either. Tell him, Tariq. Tell our father."

Tears welled in little Tariq's eyes. His brother Yassir was to him the bravest man in the world. But he could find no words of comfort.

"Rest now," Abdullah said, whisking the flies away from Yassir's back. "Come, Tariq." He rose. In his heart he was glad that he and Yassir would be leaving today for Cairo. There were some things he could not cope with—nor should he be asked to.

The meeting took place in the shadow of the pyramids. It had been Mahmood's idea to soften the consanguineous problems of this gathering with a spectacular backdrop. Luncheon was at four o'clock, outdoors on a long trestle table covered by a fine Egyptian cloth, served by a platoon of servants. There were, of course, no women present. The raison d'être of this occasion—Yassir—had been invited *not* to attend, so that all could speak their minds more freely.

Abdullah and Solomon had escorted him from Damascus to Cairo. Judah and Mohamed had arrived ahead of them from Constantinople. Along with their host, Mahmood, and his son Ahmed, the Cairo office was represented by Gideon Nouari and his son Raphael.

These Cairo partners, Mahmood and Gideon, showed no inclination to share authority with their two eldest sons, who were already in their thirties. Gideon was lean, fashionably dressed, and self-indulgent. He was a man of whom it was said he would do anything . . . for himself. Gideon was as unlike his father, old Abraham, as a man could be. His son Raphael knew he maintained a mistress. He had seen her several times—a henna-haired Delilah with a plump bottom and bottomless brown eyes. Raphael and Ahmed shared the conviction that if they were ever to advance in the Company, it would not be in the shadow of the pyramids—or their fathers.

Most days in Egypt were perfect. This one was no exception. But two clouds hung over this event. The second one was financial. Mahmood, elegantly attired in a white tropical suit that strained at the button across his broad belly, wore tinted glasses beneath his fez. Through luncheon, he had guided the conversation, carefully skirting the problems that loomed beyond coffee. It was the custom that no serious matters be discussed during the meal.

Beyond them, a sharp sun baked the enigmatic forehead of

the Sphinx. The wisdom of the ages would be badly needed today, Mahmood thought. When the last sweet and cup had been removed and the servants had retired tactfully from earshot, Mahmood asked his nephew to open the meeting.

Mohamed extinguished his cigar and glanced at Judah, seated across from him. They had avoided discussing Yassir's future on the journey, reserving opinions until they had the opportunity of discussions with the young man and his father. That meeting had been strained. Yassir seemed neither grateful nor repentant. He regarded them with the look of one burdened with an important secret that made him superior to all. As to his future, all he would say was that he would return, no matter where they sent him.

Mohamed came right to the point. "Abdullah requests guidance in the matter of Yassir. It occurs to him that the best place for his son would be in Cairo."

This brought a brief, troubled silence that almost always seemed to follow the mention of Yassir's name. Mahmood winced slightly.

Abdullah relieved him of the necessity of an immediate objection. "Does not the Prophet say, my dear brother Mahmood, whoever desires that his supplication in time of distress should be heard, he should profusely supplicate in times of prosperity?"

"Please—leave the Prophet out of this," Mahmood said testily.

"It is also said: do not refuse a beggar, but give him something, however small," Abdullah continued, undeterred.

"Yassir is no beggar," Mohamed corrected. "He is your son, Abdullah, but he needs our help. Therefore, Uncle Mahmood, I ask you to make a place for Yassir here in the Cairo office."

The genial Egyptian lifted hands toward the unseen guardian of all destiny. "Am I one to turn down the need of any kinsman? Of ours, or"—he indicated his partner, Gideon— "of a Nouari? Would I?" All quickly agreed that he would not. He went on. "But there is scarcely enough business here—which we will go into later—to occupy my own son, Ahmed, or young Raphael Nouari. As I have confided to our chairman, Mohamed, the cotton market here is bad at the moment. Bad."

"I would not say that we have dined out of begging bowls here today, my brother," Abdullah put in with some annoyance.

"When we members of the Company meet so rarely, would I spare any personal expense?" Mahmood shot back. "But, dear brother, the strength of our Company in Egypt leans heavily on the goodwill of official authorities."

His son Ahmed chewed his lip and held his tongue. The strength of the Company, he thought, would be far greater in Cairo if his father, whose mind was going to fat along with his body, would give him half the opportunities that Uncle Sayid in Jerusalem had given his eldest son, Mohamed—now their chairman.

"In Egypt, we balance on the wing of a butterfly. Politically." Mahmood gestured airily. "If any member of the families were to become involved in secret activities here, it would reflect on the Company. With us"—his eyes fell on his own son, Ahmed, approvingly—"a son obeys commands without question and is guided by our experience."

"You are saying that you don't trust Yassir to reform?" Abdullah exploded, knowing perfectly well that his son wouldn't.

"Abdullah, my brother," Mahmood pleaded. "Can we afford to bet that the leopard will change his spots? Difficult times. Revolutionary movements under the surface. I myself would feel more confident if Yassir were to undertake the continuation of his education . . . in a less sensitive area."

Abdullah leaped to his feet. "Yassir is no more anxious to remain in Egypt than you are to have him, brother!"

Mohamed's hand on his arm quickly pressed him back to his chair. "At the moment he is not a happy young man, but he is no fool. I think he would not be averse to going to study at the Sorbonne." He smiled at Judah. "As we did once. He is perfectly aware that his preparation for the future needs, shall we say, a broader base."

Mahmood beamed. "How wise! Yes! He should go to Paris. Do you not agree, Gideon?"

Gideon Nouari promptly did. Generally, in their business relationship, Gideon was happy to allow Mahmood to make decisions. He preferred concentrating his full energies on his pleasures. "Absolutely," he said. "In Paris, Yassir will transfer his interest from politics to women. Much healthier. For him and for the Company."

"I have no objections to Paris," Abdullah said, brightening.

"Paris is far more than a brothel of pleasures for the young," Judah put in quickly. "It has more underground political volcanos than Syria ever dreamed of. As you well know, Mohamed. Paris is the center of our banking activities. I would consider it the worst possible choice for this . . . high-spirited young man."

A silence fell on the group. "Perhaps you're right," Mohamed agreed.

"What about the United States, then, Mohamed?" Mahmood suggested. "Surely you could make room for him in New York? What do they call it—'the land of operations'?"

" 'Opportunities.' But I fear Yassir might find too many opportunities there. A country born from revolution can be touchy about revolutionaries," Mohamed replied.

Abdullah was impatient. "Where, then?" His voice rose. "My son deserves some place on this earth . . . with your permission, Mahmood."

"It was not *my* son who joined a secret society to bring down the Turks, brother."

"Has anyone any constructive suggestions?" Solomon asked from the end of the table.

"In his own interests," Judah offered, "I think we should consider a university with a strict code of discipline and honor. It was because of Yassir that we are opening new business interests with the Germans. Surely a German education would prepare him to be of useful service, and provide him with an important future in the Company."

"An interesting idea." Abdullah was relived by this first sensible suggestion.

Judah smiled. "At Heidelberg he'll soak up philosophy, the poetry of Goethe, the music of Strauss."

"Good idea, Judah," Mohamed said. "The worst trouble he'll find there will put an honorable saber scar on his cheek." He glanced down the table. "Any objections?" There was no voice of dissent.

Abdullah rose to his feet. "I pray Allah my son may never again be the cause of further troubles to our families. I accept Hiedelberg on his behalf."

"So be it," Mohamed said. "Next in the order of business?"

"As I confided to you earlier, Mohamed, there's been a

drop in the cotton market," Mahmood said. "My son Ahmed has compiled the figures for us."

Ahmed opened a folder resting beside his chair and passed a list of statistics down the table. "We are involved rather too heavily," he said with a slightly disapproving glance at his father. "We bought too much, too high. Our warehouses are too full. If the price fluctuates any lower, or if we should get torrential rains, it will cost the Company millions of piasters."

His father signaled him sharply. "My son, in his inexperience, is inclined to be too pessimistic. However, I believe it would be advisable to sell now. The market is low. It could go lower. Do you not agree, Gideon?"

His partner preened, polishing perfectly manicured nails on the heel of his hand. "It is true we overbought. Somewhat. Who could anticipate that our market would dry up? But I agree we should swallow our losses."

Gideon's son Raphael exchanged a glance with his fellow junior associate, Ahmed. The two younger men had discussed the situation privately. They knew where blame must fall. Several times, they had urged moderation in buying, having carefully studied the market reports left unread on their father's desks. The partners had not even troubled to read their sons' carefully prepared suggestions until their warehouses were bursting at the seams.

"Swallowing losses always sticks in my throat," Mohamed said quietly. "Unless the market rises, I suggest you wait four months. Your cotton won't rot in that time. America is the biggest potential market in the world. All we need is to open the right door. I will make that my responsibility."

"Suppose the market drops further?" Gideon asked.

"Suppose you suffer a heart attack while servicing that entertainer who dances lying down?" his partner laughed. Gideon's peccadillos were common Company knowledge.

"I don't get heart attacks; I give them," Gideon boasted.

Solomon leaned forward in his chair. "Mohamed, I must ask you: have you something concrete to go on, or are you gambling? It wouldn't be fair to our Cairo partners to risk a further drop in the market. Besides, as you well know, the cotton may not rot, but the investment isn't earning a profit."

Mohamed put his palms flat on the table. "Trust me, Solomon. There is a market in New York."

"You're perfectly certain?" Solomon probed.

Mohamed smiled slightly. "Only Allah is perfect."

Solomon nodded. "You have my vote."

Judah slipped off his new pince-nez. He was still finding it difficult to speak forcefully while having the bridge of his nose pinched. "I propose we give Mohamed the four months he requests—to put his plan in work. I move the question."

"Second it," Mahmood snapped.

"All in favor?" Mohamed's glance swept down the table. There was a chorus of ayes.

On the way back to the Shepherd's Hotel, Judah put the question to Mohamed. "Where is this cotton market you've got up your sleeve?"

Mohamed shrugged. "When I find out, I'll let you know."

"You mean . . . you haven't got one? My God. . . ."

"Not yet. But I will."

Judah laughed, shaking his head. "With your chutzpah, you should have been Jewish. You really deserve your chairmanship of the Company."

They walked into the yellow marble lobby of Cairo's great hotel, its vastness punctuated by clumps of potted palms and aspidistras. A string quartet floated chamber music past a collection of British colonials whose voices barked across teacups.

"Seventh Hussars, wasn't he? Dashed good polo player."

A dying sunbeam reached down across Mohamed's face through stained glass. They paused at the great gilded iron elevator shaft.

"Come to New York," Mohamed said suddenly.

"Ruth still has her heart set on a visit to Palestine."

"Bring her to New York. It might reset her heart."

Judah threw him a sharp look. "You don't need my help in your 'interestless banking.' "

"Not in that."

"What else?"

"Come and find out."

"You're serious?"

"Deadly."

Judah sighed. "You . . . and Dr. Weizmann. He's been nagging me to go to New York. To raise more money."

"No one could accuse me of sharing his reason."

"That's certain."

"And thanks, Judah."

"For bailing you out of the cotton business?"

"For finding the answer for Yassir."

"Germany. Yes. Let's just hope we don't live to regret it."

Nine

MOHAMED was always exhilarated by New York. For him, it was a city bursting with life. The gray dray horses hauling mountains of beer barrels, the helmeted Irish-American police, the blaring German brass bands gave Manhattan a special quality. Fifth Avenue shops were bright with Christmas lights. Hester Street was loud with the shouts of Jewish immigrants vending from pushcarts. Sicilians in tight black suits snaked through the streets of Little Italy. To Mohamed, the avenues were corridors of competition down which contestants raced in unending rushes toward invisible finish lines. New Yorkers were born to the crack of the starter's pistol, born to compete. New York was a city of foreigners, where success was the measure of worth. Here was a habitat where Mohamed felt comfortable. Not like class-bound London society, where people could progress only within the fences of their own accents. Here life wasn't handed down from father to son, but tossed like a gauntlet to be snatched up with the challenge of speeding time. Nowhere did time sound more loudly in the mind. Time to be here. Time to be there. Race. Rush. Hurry. No Paris boulevard café ringside at this parade of life. No spectator sportsmanship. No lethargy of Turkish Palestine, no complacency of Europe. You were in the game and fighting to win.

Mohamed's steps carried him to the bank on Fifty-seventh Street near Sixth Avenue. The brass nameplate bugled the news that Hammadi-Nouari banked without interest. *Shirkat-e-Enan*—the only banking method authorized by Muslim law. A fixed amount of capital, where all partners would work jointly and participate proportionately in profit or loss.

Mohamed drew out his watch—a fine Howard, made in

Boston, inscribed within the case *J to M 1911*. Jacqueline's first gift to him in America. It seemed to betoken a better relationship. Now it told him that he was just five minutes early for an important morning.

The doorman's white cotton glove came cheerfully to a salute. "Morning, Mr. Hammadi. And a fine nip in the air."

He stepped into the ornately grilled elevator cage and gave the rope a sharp tug, surveying the marble staircase of his domain as he ascended past the banking floor to the office suites above. He had purchased this building for the Company the year before—along with some other choice real estate in downtown Manhattan. Now all but one had been sold at a handsome profit. He longed to show it all to Judah. To share his dream of building a skyscraper that would tower above the Flatiron Building. It would become Hammadi-Nouari International Headquarters.

His mail lay in a neat stack beneath a paperweight. The donkey-and-cart symbol of the Company. A larger carved emblem in olive wood propped up a row of books. Hammadi-Nouari would not forget its beginnings. His eyes lifted from it to the hand-tinted photograph of Jacqueline. The colorist had gilded the lily of that angelic smile. So innocent, so deceptive. There was a long scratch down the glass. "You bitch . . ." he whispered, recalling the day in Paris when he had inflicted that scratch after the private detective had left his office.

The detective he had sworn he would never hire.

He could still see the gray, tight skin over the emaciated features, the half-lidded eyes swimming secretively behind gold-rimmed spectacles. The man was a clerk dealing in guilt and dirt.

"Come in, Monsieur Roache. . . ." His own words came back to him from that Paris morning.

"I have set down everything in my report, Monsieur. One copy only, you understand."

Mohamed had examined the thick notebook with its tidy, immaculate entrances. Times, dates, places. At the front, no name: only a number. Like the anonymity of a prisoner. A criminal. Well, wasn't she?

"It is all there, monsieur. The events. Everything."

"I see that!"

The man shrugged. "Finally, Monsieur's suspicions were

quite correct. Madame has—under a variety of names—rented apartments. Rooms in obscure hotels here in Paris. In these places she entertains . . . gentlemen. The word is academic. Persons of different types, monsieur.''

"Go on.''

"Friday—yes—Friday.'' The man's cheeks were mottled, in strange contrast to the gray skin of forehead and scalp under thinning hair.

"Madame entertained a sergeant of the Chasseurs Alpines. Then again, Saturday—ah, yes, Saturday—a gentleman of the Merchant Marine was seen entering. He carried a bottle of inferior cognac, which he had purchased around the corner for a few francs.''

"I'll read the report later,'' Mohamed cut through.

"As you wish, monsieur.'' The detective fished into the inside pocket of a shiny serge suit. "Should you care to glance at our account while I am here in case any charges require explanation . . .?''

"Please leave it. Good day.''

The man hesitated in the instant of departure. He looked as though he might be searching for some suitable word of condolence. Every detail of the detective stamped itself into Mohamed's mind: the snowfall of dandruff to the collar, the nicotine-stained fingers, the hunched-forward stance. Then he was gone. Mohamed had sunk his head on his blotter, and for the first and only time in his life, sobbed like a child.

A soft knock banished the unwelcome recollection of that day two years ago in Paris.

"A cable, Mr. Hammadi. Just delivered.'' Amy Archer entered, serene, neat, in a dark blue dress. His American secretary was tall, slenderly built, but not boyish; her features were too feminine for that, her movements too graceful.

"Thank you, Amy. Oh, and I'm expecting—''

"It's in the diary. Mr. Goldfarb—at ten o'clock.'' Smart, fashionable Amy; her thinness flattered the least-expensive dress. Embarrassed by coltishly large hands and feet, she camouflaged them beneath cuffs, ruffles, rings, and high-button shoes. Amy had been with him since he opened the New York office.

"And I've got your tickets for the Metropolitan Opera. A box on Thursday night. Caruso.'' Her voice was low and soothing beneath the slight New England twang.

Mohamed read the cable with deep satisfaction. Judah, coming to New York for the first time. He swiveled around in his chair and gazed out the window. So much to show him: the advantages—scope for growth. This country was growing, expanding, almost as you watched it. Why, only this year they'd admitted two new states to the Union: New Mexico and Arizona. Mohamed was seriously thinking of taking out citizenship.

"If you do . . . I shall not!" Jacqueline had asserted when he'd mentioned the possibility. "Perhaps for you, it would be a step up . . . but I am quite satisfied to remain French. It is my last link with civilization." She called New Yorkers "provincials." Not that she hadn't found a few to amuse her, he felt certain. Allah only knew what she did with her time. She spent little enough of it with their son, Maurice, now eight years old.

Still, she had a small point. Americans were perhaps more naïvely direct, more straightforward, than Europeans. But that was not necessarily a fault. You knew where you stood with them. Yes, he admired America. It was indeed a land of opportunity. And with Hammadi-Nouari firmly entrenched, one hand could wash the other across the width of the world.

He pressed his buzzer. Amy returned. "Yes, Mr. Hammadi?"

"The cable was from my partner. Mr. Nouari will be arriving early next week."

"I'm sure you must be very pleased, sir."

He nodded. "Is that report ready on the textile workers' strike at Lawrence, Massachusetts?"

"I've brought you the file. Mr. Oliver worked on it all yesterday into the night." She placed the folder on his desk. "It seems these strikes are backed by some radical group called the I.W.W. Industrial Workers of the World. Mr. Oliver calls them the 'I Won't Work.' He's getting more information on their activities."

"OK."

Amy smiled. "Where did you get that expression, Mr. Hammadi?"

"From my chauffeur. Tony. Is it not correct?"

"Oh, absolutely."

He nodded. "I'll also need the file on the Paterson, New Jersey, mill before Mr. Goldfarb arrives."

"He's here already."

"Well, keep him waiting and bring me that file."

"I'll give him a cup of coffee." She stepped out and returned in an instant, file in hand. "He drinks tea—with lemon."

"You'd better put in a supply."

For the next fifteen minutes, Mohamed concentrated his attention on the textile-mill report. When he pressed his buzzer, he had the solution to the Cairo office's dilemma.

The man who walked into Mohamed's office was short, balding and spreading slightly at the belt. He wore thick glasses and an expression of congenital caution. Herschel Goldfarb was a moderately successful man. It was his wife's desire to make him more successful that had guided him to Mohamed's office.

"Good morning, Mr. Hammadi." He rubbed his hands slightly. They always seemed to sweat a little at the beginning of a meeting.

"Sit down, Mr. Goldfarb." Mohamed came around his desk to offer a chair.

They exchanged the usual small talk that precedes a serious discussion, and then Herschel Goldfarb asked, "Well, Mr. Hammadi, have you had a chance to consider my loan? Have you been looking me up? Investigating me? Going into my past? My future?"

Mohamed smiled. He certainly had. He opened the folders on Goldfarb. From selling dresses in the garment district, he had graduated to manufacturing dresses. Expanded to linens, sheets, towels, tablecloths, and even sacks for farm produce. He had "made money." It was a solid business, and it was growing. Attracted by the bank's no-interest policy, Goldfarb had come to Mohamed to request a five-thousand-dollar loan to expand his factory premises, hire another twenty girls, and purchase more sewing machines. Mohamed had other ideas.

"How much cloth do you buy, Mr. Goldfarb?"

"Maybe two thousand yards a week, all in. Not as much as we'd like to. With more capital, we could double production."

"Have you ever thought of running your own mill? Producing your own cloth from the raw cotton?"

"Have I ever thought about being the mayor of New York?" Herschel Goldfarb deprecated. "In my business, I got no time for daydreams."

"Neither have I. Mr. Goldfarb, the bank has been investigating a situation in Paterson, New Jersey."

"Please, Mr. Hammadi, don't talk about Paterson. The mill I buy from is on strike there."

"Four mills are on strike there, Mr. Goldfarb. One of them is about to close down."

Goldfarb bobbed his head. "I hope it isn't the one I buy from."

"It could be the one you *buy*."

Goldfarb blinked at him through thick lenses. "I don't understand, Mr. Hammadi. I'm asking you for a loan to increase my factory. More seamstresses, more sewing machines. I like the terms your bank offers: no interest."

"When the bank puts up money, it is an investment in your business, for which we take a percentage of the profits—or share in your losses. An Islamic banking principle called *Modaarbah*."

"Whatever you call it, for me it makes sense. But what is this about a mill?"

"How old is your son, Mr. Goldfarb?" Mohamed asked. "The one who works with you."

"Barney? Twenty-three now. A good boy. Good salesman, Barney." He shifted nervously in his chair, uncertain where Mohamed was leading him.

"Your business shows a steady rate of growth. The bank feels you could expand into a national company if you owned your own mill. We are willing to make an offer on your behalf for the Paterson mill. For which we would take a 25 percent share of your business. You go out there. Have a look at it. Take your son, Barney, along."

Goldfarb looked staggered. "How much could such a mill cost? Ten, twelve thousand dollars, maybe. I wouldn't like to run up such a debt."

"The mill will cost double that, Mr. Goldfarb. Do you think your son could learn to run it—if we keep the general manager of the plant on, to teach him the business?"

"Barney went to college. From Columbia, he could learn anything." His eyes began to glow with excitement. "What are you, anyway, Mr. Hammadi, Santa Claus?"

Mohamed smiled. "Saint Nicholas has no place in either of our religions. And this bank is not a charitable organization. We intend to make money."

"OK. So what's in the small print?"

"What we will require from your new mill, Mr. Goldfarb, is the undertaking to buy all the cotton you process from Hammadi-Nouari, Cairo—at a price two points under the market."

"No, you're not Santa Claus. You're smarter. Suppose we get caught? Overproduce? How do we know how much the market will bear?"

"We'll be taking the risk with you, Mr. Goldfarb."

"And the sewing machines? What about the sewing machines?"

Mohamed eyed his prospective associate. "You'll get your sewing machines. And the mill. Mr. Goldfarb, I want you to start thinking on a slightly grander scale."

"You'll pardon my saying so, Mr. Hammadi. You sound like my wife."

The rest of Mohamed's day was spent drawing up agreements and going over figures. Four or five times, he had tried to reach Jacqueline, but she had never been home. He tried again. Five o'clock. She was still out. In the morning, she had said she wasn't feeling well. Going to spend the day in bed. She probably had—but where?

Mohamed slid his file back into the desk and rang for Amy. "Have Tony bring the car around. I'm going home," he told her.

"Mr. Oliver wanted to see you before you left."

"I'll see him tomorrow."

She nodded. "Oh, and I've taken the liberty of asking Miss Duprès—one of the juniors, but very bright—to assist Mr. Nouari while he's here. She's conversant in French."

"Mr. Nouari speaks English, but I'm certain Miss Duprès will be fine. Have her prepare the office next to mine, will you?"

"Already done, sir."

He nodded. Mohamed appreciated initiative in others. He demanded it of himself. Americans seemed to be born with it.

She helped him into his coat and handed him his walking stick.

"It will be your partner's first visit to New York?"

He nodded. "We'll try to make him like it, Amy."

She watched him out the door. It was strange how his mood always changed at day's end. He seemed so happy at his work. Almost as though it were an escape. She had seen the beautiful Mrs. Hammadi. What more could any man wish to go home to?

The Locomobile was waiting. Maroon. Jacqueline had chosen the color—along with Tony's uniform to match. Brooklyn-born Tony, of Italian immigrant parents, wore a cockade on the front of his cap. Twenty-three. Ugly. Unmarried. Tony was totally absorbed by two interests: the motor of the Locomobile, which he half considered his own, and current events, a subject in which he considered himself something of a pundit. When Mohamed could understand his accent, he learned a lot about life in America from Tony.

It began almost automatically as Tony held the car door open. "Hoid de latest, Mr. Hammadi? Some nut took a potshot at Teddy Roosevelt. Now, why would a guy do a dumb t'ing like that?" Mohamed had no answer.

"Newspaper's in de back seat for you, sir." Tony slid behind the wheel, accepting Mohamed's preoccupied silence as an invitation to continue his running account through the speaking horn. "Seems some crank named Shank . . ." he broke off. "Hey! Can you beat that? Crank. Shank. Well, anyways, dis guy shot Teddy in his Milwaukee hotel. De bullet went t'rough a book in his breast pocket. . . ."

"Did you drive Mrs. Hammadi today, Tony?"

"Yeah. . . . I picked her up right after you left de house, sir. Anyways, de bullet went into his chest, alright, but it didn't stop Teddy goin' right on wid his speech."

"Where did you take her?" It sickened Mohamed having to ask.

"Down to de Village. Washington Square." He returned to his subject. "You know, he's announced his hat's in de ring?"

"Who?"

"Roosevelt," Tony declared loudly. "Means he's gonna run again for President. And you know somethin' else? I'm gonna vote for him—just to keep that Eugene Debs out of the White House. Dose 'Wobblies' really get my goat."

The car pulled off Fifth Avenue into Sixtieth Street and stopped in front of the white stone town house.

"Did you collect Mrs. Hammadi later, Tony? From Washington Square?"

"No, sir. She said not to wait. Mr. Hammadi . . . may I ask you a kind of poisonal question?" He held the door open.

Mohamed froze. "What . . .?"

"Mr. Hammadi, sir. I know it's none of my beeswax, but . . . do you have the right to vote?"

Mohamed shook his head and stepped briskly toward the door with near relief. "Not yet, Tony."

The great mohagany door was opened by Gilles, an importation from the house in the Avenue Malenkoff, who was just learning English.

"Good night, monsieur." He relieved Mohamed of pearl-gray gloves, gold-headed Malacca walking stick, Astrakhan-collared winter coat.

"Good *evening*, Gilles. Is Mrs. Hammadi home?"

"Oui, monsieur."

Behind Gilles, a flame of red hair blazed around the corner of a doorway. Maurice, hurtling to be kissed by his father. Mohamed swept him into his arms. The boy, small for his age, seemed strung on taut wires of energy, which sparked from bright blue eyes. Mohamed adored him and spent available moments with him—only, most moments weren't available.

"Papa. . . . Papa!" He squeezed his father tightly.

Maurice wore the short gray pants, thin striped tie, and emblemed green jacket of his private day school. Mohamed recalled the day when Tony had driven him in the Locomobile into Central Park to see the column of little boys marching behind their schoolmaster bearing a soccer ball like a kind of Holy Grail. As the column moved among the autumn-thin trees, another army—the ragged children of the poor—stalked them, occasionally charging out to pelt some straggler with a rock or stick, or even a sock full of unspeakable filth. The rich boys bore the attacks stoically, without crying out. The schoolmaster wisely chose to ignore the raiders. Mohamed thought to interfere . . . then decided against it. It was a grim microcosm of a life pattern wherein have-nots would always harass formations of the establishment. Yet, to Mohamed's mind, the concept of a classless society was fantasy. Nature's law of 'survival of the fittest' was the reality, privilege the reward of effort.

"Did you have a good day, Maurice? Are you doing well in your lessons?" He hugged the boy's warm cheek against his own.

"Fine, sir. And was it a good day in the office?"

Mohamed smiled. "Excellent, Maurice. Making sure the business will grow large enough to have a place for you one day." He caught something of his mother's expression in the boy's eyes.

"Maman says that next year I have to go away to boarding school. Gee, do I have to?"

"Where do you get this word 'gee'?" Maurice's English was flawless now, thought he had picked up an American accent.

"I know a lot of words I'll bet you don't, Papa. Gee whiz. Oh, boy. Golly Moses. Oh, heck. And spondulicks."

"What's spondulicks?"

"You ought to know that, Papa. It's money." He screwed up his face into a mask of objection. "What about the boarding school?"

"I'm certain if your mother thinks you'll like it, you will. We can talk about it later. Has she been home long?" Now he was even interrogating his son.

Maurice nodded. "I guess so. Couldn't we talk about it now?"

"On Saturday. Then we'll have time together." He kissed the boy's forehead. "I promise."

Mohamed started up the curve of stair. Maurice looked after him, kicking at the Persian carpet. "Oh, shucks!" he shouted after his father, and then headed slowly back into the conservatory. Maurice spent much of his time walking from room to room. The house on Sixtieth Street had enough of them.

She was relaxing in a bath when Mohamed entered, hair pinned up in a loose cluster of curls, cheeks flushed from the streaming water—and champagne. The habitual bottle resting on the rim of the tub, one-third empty.

"We don't live in a tent, Mohamed. There are doors on which to knock."

"I know. I paid for them."

Despite thirty-two fully lived years, Jacqueline seemed ever more physically beautiful to him, her body firm as ever, perhaps only more voluptuous.

"Where have you been all day, Jacqueline? I telephoned a dozen times."

"I thought we had an agreement that you don't cross-question me."

"You told me you were going to stay home."

"Gentlemen of the jury. . . ." She waved her arms. "I plead guilty. I drove in the car—I walked in the street—I breathed the air. Anyway, why was it so important where I was? Did you need to consult me on matters of banking? You know I take no interest in your 'no interest.' "

"Judah is arriving next week."

"Vive l'Empereur. . . ."

"With Ruth and the twins. They'll stay here, of course."

"Ruth . . . here? You must be mad, Mohamed. She won't stay here. Ruth doesn't like me. Which I find rather flattering." She sank down under a layer of bubbles, removing the temptation of strawberry nipples.

"I want you to arrange a dinner party in their honor." His voice was sharp. He still wanted her, but in the passing anger of their confrontations he seemed to lose the ability to show it.

"A dinner party? It is difficult enough to entertain Ruth in Paris. But here . . . impossible."

"What do you mean?" he exploded. "You've given a steady steam of dinner parties in New York for your friends. Which, I may add, you have little trouble in finding, wherever you are."

She sat up, soaping a glistening breast with a large sponge. "Some are friends from Paris—in case you haven't noticed. I hope you're not objecting to my having friends now. Fill my glass, will you?" She held it up to him, but he made no move to comply.

"I want you to invite a new client of the bank to the Nouari dinner. I'll put his name and address in your diary. I suggest Friday of next week."

"Who else, Mohamed? Who else would you like me to include in your gala of bores?" She poured herself the drink he hadn't. "They'll have to speak either Polish or Yiddish. For Ruth. It does rather limit the possibilities."

"Herschel Goldfarb will speak Yiddish. So will his wife. They're Russian Jews."

"How exciting!"

"In fact it is. A 'self-made' man, like most Americans. He

started in the garment district. Now he's a successful manufacturer. I respect that.''

"Traded Pushkin for a pushcart?''

"Don't, Jacqueline. You sound like your cousin Henri.
Invite the French consul and his wife. And an extra woman. I
want you to include Goldfarb's son.''

His anger fed her perversity. "Is it to be a children's party?
Animal crackers? Paper hats? Exploding serviettes?''

"Bernard works with his father.''

He forced his eyes from her and walked out. Was she
slipping into a dangerous high—or about to sink into one of
those lows? He could never be sure—the signs seemed so
much the same. Either possibility was frightening. For this
reason, no matter how outrageous her behavior, he knew it
was not malicious. More the devil of possession. There were
still moments—important moments, though brief—when the
virginal Jacqueline of the moonlight emerged, charming, glittering, caring, for him the most fascinating woman in the
world.

When he had left, Jacqueline sank back into the hot water.
Why did she goad him? she wondered. Why did she do
anything she did? He had taken her to so many doctors.
Specialists. Secretly, in desperation, one day she had gone to
a faith healer. "Forgive me, Father, for I have sinned. . . .''
The words had slipped out involuntarily.

"I'm no priest, sister.'' He was a Haitian, in a steaming
little room in Harlem hung with sleazy black blinds. He was
wearing shell beads and a flowing robe. He cut the throat of a
wretched, scrawny rooster and caught the blood in a bowl. He
touched her forehead and cheeks with it, and chanted over her
in a rhythmic sound pattern until she felt faint.

It didn't help. Nothing ever did. There was no treatment
for this sickness of hers. She only knew that when she was
what they described as "at her worst,'' she felt her best. Life
was exciting, worth living. Nothing seemed impossible. She
was driven by cravings and desires. The pace grew faster and
faster. Time sped by until all became a blur and she could
remember nothing of what she had done. "Forgive me, Father,
for I have sinned. . . .'' There were things to apologize for.
Beg Mohamed's forgiveness, for she still loved him better
than any man. But when she thought about it, saying the
words, she seemed to sink lower and lower in her mind, until

all time stopped. . . . And no words were left. How long she would sit locked in her room, she had no idea. She knew only in such times that she lost the volition to live, and what she was experiencing behind the closed door was a kind of death.

"Why me . . .?" she whispered to herself. It all seemed so senseless afterward, but that made it nonetheless real. "I swing on a great pendulum," she had told Mohamed. "Don't let me fall off."

Ruth Nouari did not accept Mohamed's invitation to stay at the house on Sixtieth Street. She told Judah it would be more convenient for her and the twins in a hotel.

Judah glanced across the foam of his shaving mug, straight razor poised in air. "You want them to be offended? That's what they'll be if we refuse the invitation."

"Why should they be offended?" she asked, brushing Zed's long hair in front of the stateroom mirror. "Relieved, they should be."

"Why? Just give me one reason, Ruth."

"Jacqueline doesn't like me."

"That is the craziest thing I ever heard," he laughed. "Why shouldn't she like you? Why shouldn't everybody like you?"

"Because . . . because I—" the explanation of inadequacy was drowned in the blast of tug whistles nursing the great liner into New York's harbor.

They took a suite at the Plaza, which was, after all, "only one step around the corner." It was a step that Ruth promised herself never to take on her own. Jacqueline always made her feel like a lump of matzo dough next to a tureen of caviar.

Since the birth of the twins, Ruth had taken to supervising their meals herself. Tasting, nibbling. It didn't make them eat any better and it didn't make the cook any happier. They'd had enough trouble finding a kosher cook. Abe and Zed loved sweets, so Ruth learned to bake cakes, prepare puddings, most of which she finished herself from their half-emptied plates. She blamed her appetite on the energy it took just to keep up with them. But she refused Judah's offer to hire a governess. She couldn't get used to the idea of a stranger taking care of her children.

On birthdays and anniversaries, Judah bought her pearls

and moonstones, which suited her pale complexion. Her clothes were from Worth, and she relied completely on the *vendeuse*'s judgment. But Ruth was putting on weight.

Abe and Zed were bright, clever, identical, with black curly hair and gray eyes. At six, Abe was hardly more sturdily built than his sister. Sometimes they would play tricks on Ruth, exchanging clothes so she couldn't tell which was which. They had another trick: a private language. Sounds meaningless to anyone but themselves. She complained about it to Judah, but he only smiled.

"You worry too much, Ruth. They're babies. It's a game. They'll grow out of it. Or else you'll learn to speak it with them." He added wryly, "It shouldn't be as hard as French."

If she admitted it to herself (for she wouldn't have, to Judah), she preferred her son. Abe was warm, affectionate, loved to be hugged, cuddled. Zed was silent at times, needing only her own company. She hated to be touched or held and always rubbed her cheek after Ruth forced a kiss on it.

Ruth didn't force many on Judah, who performed his sexual duties rarely and with restraint. Ruth never made an issue of it. What she wanted was love and affection. For her, sex held neither. She had come to realize the life she had envisioned with her marriage to Judah simply didn't exist. Judah was certainly gentle and considerate, but so was her grandfather. Many times, she wondered why Judah had married her. "Surely," she would ask herself, "surely a rich, handsome banker from Paris shouldn't have come all the way to Warsaw to take himself a bride—unless he'd fallen in love with her? So what went wrong?"

It was a question that had no answer. Judah was hardly ever home, anyway. Now that Mohamed was based in New York, Judah had to crisscross Europe for Hammadi-Nouari. He was also spending more and more time in England. For the Zionists. Once, she had said to him, "You should have married Weizmann. He sees more of you!"

Several times, she had taken the children to Warsaw without Judah. Her father, Mordchai Cukor, couldn't understand these solo appearances.

"So, why didn't he come with you?" he would ask.

Ruth always defended Judah's absence, saying how hard he worked. She would present her father and mother, grandfather and aunt with expensive gifts, and clothes and books for little Olek. All evidence of Judah's diligence and largesse.

"God sits above and makes matches below. Who are we to question?" her mother reflected, fingering the large gift hat, its plumage an entire stuffed bird.

Mordchai would shake his head. "We Jews don't believe in nunneries, Ruthele. So maybe you are a little at fault, eh?" He gave her what passed for a salacious wink. "You got a good marriage bed. So don't leave it empty for somebody else to lie in. We love you. We want to see you. But go home."

The grandfather looked at the Sulka robe he would never wear. "In Paris, I hope you don't eat bacon?"

The best moments of her marriage had been the three times Judah took her and the twins to Jerusalem to visit *his* family. At last, she had set foot in Palestine! Once, they made a trip to Petach Tikvah, one of the first settlements. She had stood in awe before Joshuah Chankin, an early pioneer. She wanted desperately to join Judah in his Zionist work. To fulfill that interrupted destiny of her now almost legendary cousin, Zosia. She saw herself—a Ruth among the tractors with tan-skinned settlers all around her, sheaves of wheat in their arms, flinging themselves into instant horas with her in the center, naming their children after her; another Ruth amid the alien corn. They would look to her for guidance as they might have done to Zosia. But whenever she mentioned the dream to Judah, he would only smile, pat her shoulder, and remind her that she had her hands full with the twins.

"Someday, when they grow up," he promised. "We'll see."

She began to study Hebrew in preparation for that "someday"—should it ever come. Her French was finally almost acceptable, and now Judah was suggesting she learn English! Languages. Oy. . . . But, without them, marriage to Judah would be a Tower of Babel.

From the twelfth-story window of the Plaza, Ruth looked out on New York. "Ruth Cukor Nouari, you've come a long way since the night you played Mendelssohn in Warsaw for an audience of one," she told herself. "Suites on ocean liners. A house in Paris, where if you want to change a curtain, you change it. If you want to move a chair, so you tell the servants to move it."

Now it truly was her house. The women friends who came to tea nodded over such richness. They fingered the upholstery when they thought she wasn't looking. But then, why shouldn't Ruth Nouari buy the best? She did. Between the children and charities, she kept herself "occupied." But she suffered from backache and headache. Sometimes toothache. Even at thirty-one, a querulous note was slipping into her voice, though she was unaware of it. Judah was, and it irritated him.

Because it made him feel guilty.

"This soirée will be worthy of the Marquis de Sade," Jacqueline threw across her shoulder savagely. She sat before her dressing table in an open peignoir, powdering her face and body with sharp, angry little dabs, the champagne bucket close at hand.

"I would be pleased if you would remain sober this one evening, Jacqueline. I realize our guests are only business associates, and therefore not amusing—but I should appreciate a small effort on your part." Mohamed pushed a sapphire stud into the front of his dress shirt, stiff as a breastplate.

"I follow your instructions, my lord—and have created the perfect impossible evening. The French consul, who talks through his nose. His wife, who never stops talking. Judah, who talks only Zionism, Ruth who can't talk at all."

"Whom did you invite for the Goldfarbs' son?"

"Marie Courtin."

"Couldn't you have found someone under forty? Their son is only twenty-three."

The moment Jacqueline looked at young Goldfarb, she decided the evening might not be a total waste. Bernard was rangy, athletic, six feet of suntan, blond hair, and blue eyes. Jacqueline quickly shifted the place cards at the table, trading Herschel for his son.

The two years since Jacqueline had seen Ruth and Judah had changed him, she decided. Judah appeared to be seasoned by time from that slightly too ebullient enthusiast into a man who carefully weighed, appraised, and tested his convictions. A Hebrew Hamlet. Perhaps she had never truly seen Judah before. His face had acquired slight hollows beneath the pince-nez he kept putting on and off to highlight a point of conversation with Goldfarb. The shadows made him appear perpetually tired, made his sensitive eyes even larger. He had become almost too thin, but she thought the whole effect appealing.

But Ruth, *mon Dieu,* Ruth! who had the advantage of seeming younger than Jacqueline. In another few years Ruth would look like Mrs. Goldfarb—whose dress could have been fashioned by a Jerusalem tentmaker. She ballooned in, in camel-dung silk.

Jacqueline led Mrs. Goldfarb to a sturdy chair.

Jacqueline, who was not without a certain awareness of human relationships, sensed that there was no real closeness in the Nouari marriage. Far less than in her own turbulent union. Was marriage ever the enrichment of a relationship? Or was it the kiss of finality on the body of excitement?

Dinner was announced. She offered her arm to Bernard, quite ignoring Marie Courtin, allowing him to lead her in.

"Such a fine house you have here, Mrs. Hammadi." Herschel Goldfarb hauled his wife to her feet, offering her to Mohamed. Rachel Goldfarb had already begun a long and intimate conversation with Ruth in Yiddish. They had found an affinity.

So had Jacqueline.

Her arm slid across his blue yachting jacket, nails gently pressing his shoulder. Her body gyrated to the new, syncopated rhythm of a fox-trot. Hips swayed as he pivoted her into a turn on the tiny circle of dance floor.

She could feel a slight tremor in the hand holding hers. A seismograph, recording the earthquake of his wanting. She excited him in a way no other woman had. Magic, did they call it? Spooning, mooning, luuuuve . . .? But what was love? Lust—pure chimera. With him, she sensed it would be an ecstasy, a frenzy of velvet gratification shutting out the mind, the world, in a seizure of repletion.

The room spun. The phonograph record squawked to a stop. Reluctantly Bernard released her, moving to the Victrola and selecting another record. "How about the turkey trot?"

"Oh, my," she said. "We have already wriggled through the crab step, the kangaroo dip, the grizzly bear, and—what was it? the bunny hug." She moved in a cuddly interpretation. "It is too much for an old lady, don't you think?"

"I don't think." His adoring eyes devoured her. Sense of occasion had dictated a navy wool sailor dress, the skirt barely grazing slim white silken ankles above strapped pumps. "You're the kind of woman who'll never be old." In her case, age added an aphrodisiac. It was not just beauty; there were lots of beautiful girls. It was her secret sense of experience that excited Bernard.

When he'd invited her, he hadn't actually hoped or even expected that she would accept. Still, the night of her dinner party, she had paid him special attention. It was indicated through nothing she had actually said or done. A look. A glance. A reaction to someone else's conversation. But it was enough. The message, he hoped, had escaped everyone else. But to him it was clear.

"A sailboat, Bernard? But where do you keep it? Where does one sail, without a Mediterranean?" She had turned to him across a glittering formation of crystal glasses. He was seated on her left, the French consul on her right. His father's voice boomed proudly down the table.

"My son has his own yacht. With his own money he bought it."

"Barney the yachtsman," Rachel Goldfarb confided across to Ruth. "But I ask myself: to a yachtsman, is he a yachtsman?"

"Of course, Bernard still lives at home," Herschel went on. "Why shouldn't he? When he went to college—Columbia, you know, Mrs. Hammadi—he made friends with a boat."

"Friends who *had* a boat, Dad."

"You hear that?" Herschel said proudly. "That's Columbia talking. Anyway, from that he got started."

Bernard was always embarrassed by his father's pride in him. But Herschel, who hadn't had the advantages of a college education or growing up with money in his pocket, took pleasure in his son's pleasures, and Bernard could be grateful for that. Herschel had even slipped him the down payment for the boat as an extra Hannukah present, with the admonition "Don't say nothing to Mama."

"My son belongs to a yacht club, Mrs. Hammadi," Herschel confided loudly. He did not add that Bernard was the only Jewish member. Tall, blond, blue-eyed Bernard, with the broad shoulders of a swimmer and the slightly broken nose that gave him the look of a Roman gladiator—gained on the boxing team at Columbia; Bernard could "pass" in the yacht-club crowd, even with the name of Goldfarb.

The next evening, when Bernard telephoned to thank Mohamed for the dinner, Jacqueline had taken the call. She had brought up the subject of the boat again. "Maybe you'd like to see the yacht club?" he suggested. "It's out on Long Island Sound. You—and Mr. Hammadi."

"I'd love to, Bernard," she breathed into the phone. "Wednesday afternoon, perhaps? Unfortunately, my husband will be in Washington, D.C., that day. Lunching with some college professor who's going to be President."

The January weather had chilled most of the members to their own hearthsides. Only two ruddy-faced gentlemen sea dogs could be seen through an archway downing drinks. The walls of the long lounge sailed with faded photographs of members' yachts. Cup contenders that had braved the Atlantic against Sir Thomas Lipton.

"Which is yours?" Jacqueline had asked.

"My God, none of those. I'm just a minnow on this pond, Mrs. Hammadi."

But now the minnow had her alone in the pond with him. Still, he was playing a dangerous game, and wondered at himself. After all, this woman's husband was about to launch him into the Valhalla of corporate business. There were dozens of girls available for seduction. He didn't need to seek out Hammadi's wife.

Didn't, but had. Because just dancing with Jacqueline made his loins weak with the ache of wanting.

"What made you decide to come with me?" he asked.

"You promised to teach me the new 'animal dances' when we played records at the party. How scandalized Mohamed would be if he saw us now."

"By the dances—or your being here?"

"Both," she replied. "But you promised to show me your ship. Where do you hide it?"

"Boat," he laughed. "And I don't keep it in the club-house. It's moored to the jetty. But it's cold out there. Sure you want to brave it?"

"You will find, Bernard, that I am very brave."

He bundled Jacqueline into her long beaver coat and guided

her out to the wharf. She pulled on an oversize fur hat against the drizzle of cold rain.

" 'O Western wind, when wilt thou blow,/That the small rain down can rain?/Christ, that my love were in my arms/and I in my bed again.' " He put his arm lightly around her for an instant.

"Did you make that up?" she asked.

"Not unless I lived in the Middle Ages."

The Sound looked rough, broken by gray waves beyond the breakwater. Some forty boats of all types and sizes were moored in the safety of a man-made harbor. He led her to a sloop, its sails neatly bedded down under a canvas cover.

"Twenty-two feet," he said.

"How beautiful! I should love to sail with you, Bernard." She threw her hands wide into the rain. "Across the wildest seas. I want to sail through hurricanes to tropical sunsets, to feel the bite of wind and the kiss of spray. Can we take it out now?"

He chuckled. "Not unless you're bent on a watery grave."

"But where do you sail to? And when?"

"In good weather, sometimes to Narragansett Bay. Or up the coast to Bar Harbor. There's a cabin. It sleeps two."

"Show me," she demanded.

He helped her across to the deck and bustled her into the cabin, out of the rain, which by now was beginning to pelt down heavily.

The cabin was freezing. They listened for a moment to the hollow tom-tom overhead. She rubbed her hands. "Rain, rain, don't go away, I wildly love a rainy day." She shivered.

He picked up a heavy pale blue sweater with a white flannel *C*. "Maybe you ought to put this on."

"What's the *C* for? In case of cold?"

He laughed. "My letterman's sweater. For swimming."

"You'll keep me warm."

Bernard produced a bottle of whiskey and two glasses from a small sea chest.

"No champagne?"

"Sorry. Ship's stores: rather limited. If you take up with a seafaring man, you'll have to change your habits, lady."

"Who said I am going to take you up?"

"Aren't you?" He drew her into his arms, kissing her experimentally. She freed herself and sipped the drink.

"Strong," she said.

"It could make a weak woman out of you."

"Is that why you brought me here?"

"Isn't that why you came?"

His boyish confidence appealed to her. Her fingers reached out to caress his rough cheek. "You don't shave close enough."

"Now that I know you, I will." He leaned across, touching her lips again. She drew back just slightly, running the tip of her tongue along his upper lip. The touch was curiously arousing. His arms came around her then. Her tongue slid into his greedy mouth. Greedy, yes. She could feel his need for her, feel his great long frame begin to tremble.

She pulled away. There were two small bunks, one above the other. "How can one make love in such a place, Bernard?"

"How much room do you need?"

They sank down onto the lower bunk. Her hand moved across the front of his trousers, undoing the buttons.

She slid down to the cabin floor beside him, putting her head in his lap. Her lips held him, tongue moving gently as butterfly wings. It was all he could do to restrain the eruption that would bring pleasure to a conclusion. He lifted her up, helped her off with her coat, undid the strings of her middy blouse, revealing the perfection of one rounded breast. His mouth worshiped it.

"Bernard . . . Bernard . . . I lust for you. . . ."

His fingers discovered the warm, damp, secret place he longed to enter.

Whatever either of them had expected it to be, it was more.

"How was Washington?"

"All right. And you, I suppose, went to Washington Square?"

"I went to sea in a cockleshell."

"You must try to control your fantasies, my dear. The doctor says it isn't good for you."

"The doctor is an idiot," she replied.

Flat, dreary marshes, garbage dumps, festering fields of metal scrap, coke, and rust-colored earth. An area of agricultural despair, the Jersey flatland drifted past the window of the Locomobile. Mohamed had been strangely silent ever since Tony picked them up at the bank in New York. His responses to Judah's questions came in terse, bitten-off replies. Judah fell silent. But it was against Judah's nature to allow his friend a private depression without trying to understand or share it.

"Maybe I'm mistaken, Mohamed. But I had the strong impression that you wanted me to come to America."

"Of course I want you here," Mohamed replied.

"What the devil's wrong, then?"

His partner didn't even look at him. "Wrong . . .?"

Judah felt certain that the grievance somehow involved himself. Here they were, side by side—now a pair of hostile strangers. Judah glanced up at the rose Tony always kept fresh in the vase fixed to the car's doorpost. Sensing that the backseat was no bed of friendship, Tony had broken off his usual daily news bulletin and held the car at a steady thirty miles an hour.

And something else: Judah had a sense of portent. When they came off the Hudson River ferry, he had been impelled to glance out and up with the expectation of seeing some form of winged omen. It was there: a great, gloomy hawk beating the leaden morning, its wings like dual scythes. He had not mentioned this to Mohamed. His Arab friend did not deal in portents.

"When are you going to tell me what's the matter?"

Mohamed's glance moved from the vista of rubbish and sooty earth, broken now by crests of reeds, sad against the sky. "Judah—I'm sorry for what I'm going to say."

"You mean it'll hurt you more than it hurts me?" The limp joke brought no mitigating smile. "All right. So I'm guilty. But what did I do?"

"It was a mistake to talk Zionism to Herschel Goldfarb at our dinner party."

Well, there it was, out in the open at last. "Goldfarb was asking me questions about Palestine. I answered. He was interested in the fact that I was born there. He's never met a Jew who was. After all, he came straight from Russia to America. But what has it to do with anything, anyway?"

Mohamed looked at him squarely for the first time since they got in the car. "Judah, I'm not saying we have to agree on everything. Or on anything. But I didn't think it was good

Company policy for you to attack him for a contribution the moment he walked through the door.''

Now it was Judah's turn to feel shocked and angry. ''It's totally unlike you, Mohamed, to indulge in flagrant exaggeration. I'm going to take your statement apart and show you just how irrational you are being.'' Judah removed his pince-nez, cleaning them on a bit of pink cloth. ''First of all, I didn't attack him. The conversation developed perfectly naturally. I merely gave him the address of the Zionist Organization. Did I take money out of his pocket?''

''You talked of nothing but Zionism.''

''We couldn't keep talking about the sinking of the *Titanic* all night. Besides, Goldfarb was keen to learn something about the Rothschild colonies. After all, Zionism is a fairly important experiment—even if you don't happen to be a Jew.''

Mohamed's voice lifted angrily. ''I'm not interested in Zionism, Judah.''

''You've made that abundantly clear. But Goldfarb is.''

Mohamed fished into his pocket for his gold cigar case. His hand shook slightly from the anger he was trying to keep in check. ''Migration into Palestine is something I disagree with. But what I find upsetting—and I speak only from the standpoint of good business practice—is using your first meeting with our new associate to indulge in a lecture on your favorite topic. If Goldfarb were really interested in Zionism, as you insist, why did he choose to come to America? Why isn't he living in one of Rothschild's colonies? Even Jacqueline noticed your zeal.''

''I thought she was too busy learning those new dances from Goldfarb's son.'' The barb had not been premeditated.

Mohamed's voice tightened. ''What do you mean by that?''

''Not a thing. Only, I can hardly imagine that she was absorbing our conversation while bobbing through the bunny hug, or buzzard bounce—or whatever those crazy steps are called.''

Mohamed relaxed back onto the seat and began to laugh. ''You know, just then you sounded like you were getting old, Judah.''

''Old—and bad-tempered. I suppose we both are.''

''Plunging into the thirties.''

''One foot in the grave.''

The air had cleared slightly. "Sorry I upset you, Mohamed. And you were right about one thing: Men like Herschel Goldfarb's only real interest in Zionism is giving money—as a salve to their consciences. For not actually wanting to go there themselves. And why should he? Here, his life is good and getting better. He's delighted to open his checkbook, say his prayers, and let someone else go and dig the potatoes. He needs Zionism like a bellyache. Now—may I ask one simple question?"

Mohamed shrugged. "Of course."

"Why have you become so prejudiced again Zionism?"

"You think I should support it?" Mohamed extended the peace offering of his cigar case. "Take a cigar. Go on—they won't explode."

Judah did. "Anything that develops our homeland—yours and mine—can only help the Company. Aside from providing a place for homeless, unwanted people, it's an experiment in communal living. Don't you realize that, in these little colonies, we are seeing the frontier of the last pioneers? The way of life in these settlements could become an example for other countries."

"You don't really believe that it's the sweat of pioneers that keeps those colonies going? They survive by paternalism and charity! Handouts from men like your Baron de Rothschild. And why does he do it?"

Judah closed his eyes patiently. "Because Zionism is not only survival for those people but a return to their spiritual heritage."

"Don't be a dunce. Rothschild considers it a damned good investment. Palestine is the key to the East, Judah. You and I know that. Alexander—and Napoleon—knew it! It's the sentry box for the Suez Canal. From Palestine an army could swoop across the Sinai and hold Egypt. Secure the lifeline to all Africa." His voice lost its scurrilous edge. "And even all that is not my real concern. Jews and Arabs might not care much for Turks, but under their rule, we've lived as brothers in misery, because we are both of the Levant. Now Zionism is bringing Europeans, people contemptuous of our countrymen. When we were home last time, my brother Anwar spoke of it. Your uncle Izak, too. You yourself have admitted it."

Judah controlled rising anger. "Of course these Jews from Central Europe are different. So are you and I. The smell of

Paris, London, and New York has replaced the sand in our nostrils. Naturally there will have to be a period of adjustment.''

"On whose part? The newcomers aren't trying to learn our ways. Are we supposed to learn theirs?''

"*Our* ways?'' Judah burst into laughter. "Are we selling melons by the Birket as-Sultan? Are we driving goats through Yad Absalom? No, we're sitting in a Locomobile that cost more money than those people will see in their whole lives—being driven by Tony to Paterson, New Jersey. Don't talk about our ways, Mohamed! We lost those long ago—at the Sorbonne.''

Mohamed leaned back. The heat had gone out of his tone. "You're only proving my point, Judah. You and I belong to a wider world now. We cannot even feel the way we used to. Ask your brother Benjamin how *he* feels. Palestine is still his land.''

The argument had been so intense they scarcely noticed that the limousine was now whisking them through the suburbs of Paterson.

Bleak factory buildings were closing in, a smoky prison of brick walls and sooty stacks. The mill district. As Tony slowed the car to check his map, disgruntled strikers eyed the symbol of management with vague hostility. A few blocks farther, Tony slowed the car again.

"What d'yah say, Mr. Hammadi?'' He indicated with his leather glove a loose, broken rank of workers guarding the entrance of the newly purchased mill. "We're here.'' Tony braked the limousine to a stop.

The human barrier wedged tighter in their path. Men came over from murky fires, where they had been cooking up coffee or warming hands. A movement of angry placards bristled above the closing ranks: DOWN WITH THE BLOOD SUCKERS, IWW FOR THE WORKERS, FAIR WAGE FOR A FAIR DAY'S WORK.

"It seems as though we've bought a problem,'' Judah said.

"That's why we bought it cheaply.''

"What time does the picket line break up?'' Judah asked.

"Right now!'' Mohammed replied. "Goldfarb's in there—with the mill manager. Drive in, Tony.''

Tony was uncertain. "Them 'Wobblies' would sooner get themselves bumped off than do a day's work.''

"We've just bought that mill! The pickets may keep Goldfarb in, but they'll not keep me out," Mohamed snapped.

Judah had seen that expression on Mohamed's face once before. In Uganda, the night his friend had fired at the struggling mass of lion and man.

"If you're set on going in," Judah said, "I'll talk to them. Explain that we're the new owners. That we're prepared to consider better wages and working conditions. They're not necessarily in the wrong, you know."

Mohamed totally ignored him. "Drive on, Tony! They'll get out of the way."

"You're the boss, boss."

Tony released the hand brake, geared into reverse, pulled back some fifty yards, adjusted the spark, and opened up to full throttle. "Here goes nothin'!"

The Locomobile plunged forward suddenly. The pickets hastily attempted to weld tighter, clubs brandished, bricks raised. The car sped closer toward the angry faces snarling curses and insults.

"Stop the car! You'll kill them!" Judah cried out.

"Keep going." Mohamed's command overrode him.

The first brick shattered the glass into glistening splinters. Judah felt one graze his scalp. He ducked down, glimpsing in a last flash that the picket line had fallen back. Men sprawled over each other to avoid the onrushing car. There was a terrible, resounding blow on a fender as the limousine roared through. A brick crashed through the windshield.

And then they were slowing up at the mill door, the broken rank of pickets behind the outer wall. Judah was crouched on the floor of the car. He felt Mohamed's hand on his shoulder. He could see a small trickle of blood, surprisingly his own. The car stopped. Mohamed helped him up, inspecting his head. "A scratch. It's nothing."

Judah wiped his head with his breast-pocket handkerchief. "Did we kill anybody?"

They climbed out of the car stiffly.

Mohamed's eyes had gone to Tony, slumped forward on the wheel, both hands over his face. Little worms of blood were crawling out between his fingers. Mohamed pulled open the driver's door. "Can you get out, Tony?" His voice trembled slightly.

"It's OK, boss. I'm hunky-dory." With a ghastly grin, the chauffeur plunged forward into the Arab's arms.

Tony didn't regain consciousness for some forty-eight hours. He was still on the critical list when Judah arrived at the hospital to visit him. A week had passed since the storming of the mill. Poor Tony! The brick had shattered the windshield, and his head. The Locomobile was left eyeless in Paterson; Tony, left with a concussion, victim of Mohamed's impetuousness! Since that day, Judah had scarcely spoken to his partner.

The nurse told Judah that the doctor was with Tony. He was to remain in the waiting room until she called him. Judah had brought a round tin box of hard candies that had a syrupy picture of a Collie dog panting abject affection. After two months in New York, Judah had become fond of Mohamed's garrulous chauffeur, even though he hadn't seen much more of him than the back of a red, weather-beaten, friendly neck.

Curiously, Mohamed's precipitate assault had not affected negotiations with the union's leaders. They appeared to admire him, while ignoring Judah's diatribes on the fairness required by both parties in any dispute. Finally an agreement was signed, and everybody seemed reasonably satisfied.

"Bales of cotton deteriorating in our warehouses and idle mill machinery will be far more costly than giving the thugs what they want," Mohamed confided to Herschel, Bernard, and the mill manager as they entered their final meeting. "They've had their day. Now let them settle down to work." But he beamed warmly around the room as the union negotiators rose at his entrance.

Judah touched his own souvenir of Mohamed's by-now-famous "charge of the Locomobile's": a strip of adhesive three inches long beneath the hair of his scalp. Maddeningly, Mohamed had come through unscathed. Once the mill business was wound up, Judah was anxious to return to Paris. New York was impressive. America was impressive. But there were other things on his mind. He would be bringing good news to Weizmann in Manchester. American contributions had been generous.

On the white-tiled hospital wall, Judah's eyes fixed on a mezzotint of a benign Saviour herding sheep down a lavender hillside beneath a haloed sunrise. The myths men live by. . . .

Insulation of the human spirit against mortality. But mankind, trapped in so uncertain a journey between unknowns, must believe in something. A world full of faiths—hundreds of them, each with its own ensnaring dogma. Which one was right? All, one, or none? Yet people were willing to die or kill for their faith.

What compass had Judah found to steer his own life by? Only one. Immutable—unforgettable—Zosia. Oh, God, how he could still miss her. Even now. Could recapture faint flashes of conversations. A word. A phrase. A tone of voice. A fleeting image. The ache that never goes away. What might have been if she had lived? Might she not have led him back to some lost certainty? Restored the ritual of his childhood faith, the meaning, the belief? God is one. Man is free. Man's highest aspiration is to serve God. And Judaism is the means. A system of communication.

"Salaam aleikum. . . ."

Mohamed's tall shadow broke the light-fall from an upper window. Judah had been too drowned in thought to hear his approach. It brought a return to sharp reality. Mohamed's dark eyes were inscrutable above the neat trident of a new goatee. It made him look a bit like a silent-movie hero, one who would carry the heroine off on a prancing stallion to an enviable fate. But the real Mohamed was no romantic illusion. His chauffeur, lying nearby with a concussion, was ample proof. *"Aleychem shalom."* Judah returned the traditional greeting in the Hebrew form.

Judah had not entered Mohamed's house except for the day when Abe and Zed visited little Maurice. Judah had come to collect them. The partners' sons had developed an instant friendship, rattling away together in French. It made Zed quite jealous. She lured Abe back with a spurt of their private "twin talk," which left Maurice and the rest of the world out in the cold.

It was plain to Judah that Mohamed's son craved more attention than he was getting. He hadn't missed the loneliness in the Hammadi child's bright eyes. Perhaps there would have been a time in their relationship when Judah could have discussed this with Mohamed, but not now.

And he had not expected they would meet here at the hospital, or he would have timed his visit for another day.

Mohamed was also bearing a gift for Tony, wrapped in tissue paper and tied with a blue ribbon. And a stack of newspapers.

"It looks as though we're attending a Bar Mitzvah," Mohamed said. "Can't we go in?"

"Not while the doctor's with him."

Mohamed nodded and settled down on one of the three uncomfortable mahogany chairs, stretching out his legs. He set down the package, glanced at Judah. "I told them to give Tony the best room."

"Very generous." Judah hadn't meant it to sound as sarcastic as it came out.

Mohamed frowned. "You are right to blame me."

"You thought you were doing the right thing, I suppose. What happened, happened."

"I'm not like you, Judah," Mohamed countered tersely. "You think first, then you act. Too often you don't act at all. I do what seems necessary at the moment. If it turns out to be wrong, I can regret it later."

It was the nearest Judah could ever remember Mohamed coming to an apology. In Judah's mind, it was not near enough. "Tony could have been killed. We all could."

The two men were silent. The clock ticked hollowly through the distance between them. A phantom floated into Judah's mind. Another waiting.

Long ago, when they were boys in Jerusalem. Ten and twelve years old, maybe. Sitting in silence, feeling the sun on their bronzed bodies, munching a paperful of Turkish delights pocked with pistachios. The two boys sat just outside the Jaffa Gate watching the world go by. Bab al Khalil. High feudal arches beneath square, crenelated towers. A long awning above the place where the merchants clustered. The Cook's Tourist Office sign in the English neither of them could read. The parade of overladen donkeys, diminished by great sacks of grain across their backs, bumping like corpses of sacked giants. A smart Turkish officer from the garrison, trotting his well-groomed horse amid the camel drivers, who pulled their knock-kneed, lumbering beasts out of the way. Shrouded Arab women, prodding pyramids of melons or shrilly debating the price of a pinch of saffron. The air reeking with newly tanned leather and hanging carcasses from the butcher shop, sweetened only slightly by the pungence of spices. *Jerusalem—if I forget thee. . . .*

Then—Mohamed's dare. The Arab boy led the way, climbing down crablike into the long-disused, dry moat beneath sloping walls and towers. A descent into a Gehenna of rubble and rubbish where not even a beggar would have bothered to scavenge. Judah followed more slowly, picking his way down with tentative feet, balancing his weight against the crevices and protrusions of the wall. So much steeper than it had looked! At one point, a large stone gave way under his toe and he lost his foothold, dangling precariously.

The rock had barely missed Mohamed's head. "Idiot! Watch your step!" he called from below, ignoring Judah's plight.

Judah prayed for someone to notice them and order them back. Nobody did. High above, life hummed and swarmed, and was never its brother's keeper. Merchants, shoppers, beggars, and Turks in their jackets and sashed baggy trousers—all too occupied to note the descent of two small boys into hell.

When they at last reached bottom, Judah didn't let Mohamed see how shaken he was. His friend was already busy prowling the fallen masonry, disturbing the sleep of lizards.

Then Mohamed's hand lifted something from the debris. He raised it so gingerly it might have been a serpent. Judah stared in awe at an ancient bronze cross. It was green with antiquity, formed of a single piece of metal. At its very top, a crude loop had been twisted so someone could wear it, maybe on a leather cord.

"You'd better put it back," Judah whispered nervously. He almost expected the sight of it to destroy them with some kind of invisible flame.

"Why? I found it. It was just lying there among the stones."

"Leave it there."

"I will not! You know what it is?"

"Of course I know. A cross." Even the uttering of the word could be a dangerous blasphemy. Rabbi Baal Shem had turned pale above his long white beard on the day that little Judah had asked him why the Jews didn't have a cross. Judah had been forced to sit for hours listening to tales of armed men slaughtering his ancestors, wiping out whole populations in the name of the man who had died on a similar symbol.

Descriptions so vivid, they seemed to evoke the smell of conflagrations and drying blood on corpses in lands he had never seen in times unknown.

"A crusader's cross," Mohamed pronounced, rubbing a fleck of earth from it. He, too, had been exposed to old tales of armed pilgrims who had come from far away to wrest this city from his ancestors. The men whom Saladin had fought and killed, but who always returned in their flaming, sun-bright armor beneath dirty white robes with crosses in red, and huge horses and straight swords that flailed his people for being infidels and unbelievers.

"Go on. Look at it." Mohamed brought it closer. "Hold it; it won't bite you," he goaded.

"It's not a thing we should touch," Judah insisted.

"Why?"

"I'm not sure. But it's against my religion. I think yours, too. There's evil in it."

Since both knew their parents wouldn't permit such an unholy thing in their homes—and because it made them nervous even staring too long at this forbidden object—it became important to both of them. A dangerous secret that only they would share. When Judah held it, he saw that it had a dot within a circle on every tip. Clutched tightly in the hand, it exuded a kind of tingling sensation. It was a thing of fire and ice. A talisman. A power of evil perhaps, but a force that might even work wonders.

"We'll hide it someplace," Mohamed said. "Nobody but us will know it's even there. Then, when we want to, we can come and look at it. . . ."

"If we held it and made a wish . . . maybe it would come true. Like Aladdin's magic lamp."

"There's no magic in it," Mohamed said sensibly. "But it's seen a lot of blood. The Christian who wore it could have gotten his head cut off. Right here on this spot."

"But there was water here. This was a moat."

"Well, maybe he fell in. And drowned in his armor."

Judah considered the possibility. "What about the"—he didn't want to say the name—"the man who was nailed to . . . the big one?"

"Jesus? Oh, he was one of our prophets. He's in the Koran. Along with your Moses and Abraham. Jesus was a Christian."

"No, he wasn't! He was a Jew. Rabbi Baal Shem told me so. And he ought to know."

Mohamed dismissed that. "If he was a Jew, why don't the Jews follow him?"

"I'm not sure," Judah answered. "Maybe it's because lots of Jews don't like other Jews. You can't even mention his name in Grandfather's house." His voice lowered. "If Grandfather Abraham caught me with this cross, he'd lock me in the cellar."

"Well, he won't catch you," the older boy said reassuringly. "And nobody is going to make us throw it away. We found it, and we're going to keep it."

They hid it under a loose stone near the Ma'muniyya State Primary School, in the Muslim Quarter of the Old City, north of the Dome of the Rock. Then they made a crude map so only they would know where it was. It bound their friendship more closely.

Once or twice, they went back to look at it and hold it. But one day they went back and couldn't find it.

"It was gone . . .!" Judah said suddenly, not even realizing that he had spoken aloud. Others in the hospital waiting room glanced over at him.

"What was?" Mohamed said.

"The bronze cross . . . we found in the moat in Jerusalem. Don't know what made me think of it."

Mohamed wrinkled the corners of his eyes in a hard search through memory. "Yes. Now I remember. And the map. The map—as though it were buried treasure. I wonder who has it now?"

"Let's hope it's someone who needs it. Anyway, it never brought us any wishes."

"It did, you know," Mohamed said suddenly. "I made a wish on it: that we would be friends all the days of our lives."

Judah stared at him. Then he said, "Your wish has come true." Their hands met and clasped.

The nurse's voice exploded through the moment. "You may go in and visit your friend now."

The men took up their gifts. "You know what I envy about you? Your decisiveness. It's better than never being sure. If one stops to see both sides of every question—the dangers, the advantages—sometimes one doesn't do anything at all."

"That is why we make a good team, Judah."

They found Tony wrapped in a great white turban of bandages, one eye covered. The other peered dully at them. Greetings were exchanged. The presents were placed by Tony's hand, but he made no move to touch them. No one could think of anything important to say.

Mohamed opened one of the newspapers. "What do you think of this, Tony? Mr. Henry Ford is going to bring out a new car. He's naming it the Model T."

"Nobody'll buy it," came the weak reply. "No room for a chauffeur."

"You may be right. They're calling it a Tin Lizzy."

A faint smile touched Tony's lips. "Where'd we 'a' been if we'd tried to bust that picket line with one o' them, boss?"

The atmosphere eased. Mohamed went on. "And this might interest you, Tony. They've sent a wireless message from Arlington, Virginia, all the way to Paris. Now when I want to contact Mr. Nouari, I can reach him by wireless."

Tony only nodded. "Who won de Kentucky Derby, boss? You got a bet on it for me."

Mohamed glanced at Judah. The 38th Annual Kentucky Derby had been run almost a year before. "Remember, Tony, we picked the winner: Worth. He won on a muddy track. Don't you remember, you won twenty dollars?"

Tony was upset. "Dat was last year, wasn't it, boss? My brains is scrambled. Worth. Oh, yeah. His time was two minutes, nine and two fifths seconds." He seemed to pull at the bandages. "But I can't seem to remember de name of de jockey."

The nurse signaled them to leave.

In the hall, Mohamed said suddenly, "Judah, will you do me a favor? Say a prayer for him. I will."

"I'm not sure anyone listens any more," Judah replied. "Anyway, I think my system of communication has broken down."

"What about that Jewish prophet neither of us believe in?"

Judah smiled. "He might help. Tony's Catholic. For Tony, somebody might be listening." Then he changed the subject abruptly. "Remember the Ma'muniyya State Primary School?"

"Of course. What made you think of it?"

"That cross. That's where we hid it. Next time I'm in Jerusalem, I think I'll have another look for it."

"You're crazy," Mohamed said with affection. "Let's go have some good American coffee."

The argument had begun before lunch. It continued on down Fifth Avenue. Jacqueline's fox jacket dangled over one shoulder of a lavender silk dress. It was June, but there was a slight chill in the air. She paused in front of a shop window, but her attention was on her own reflection.

"I've told you, Bernard, that I did not want this discussion again."

"But, Jacqueline," he began. He had deliberately taken her to lunch instead of to bed, so they could talk.

"Why can't you leave us the way we are? We are happy. I am happy—yes. You do make me happy, you know. Keep the dark shadows away." She turned slightly. "But I have no stars in my eyes—and I will not leave Mohamed. I love him. There! I've said it again."

He turned her to him in the street—tall, powerful, earnest, persuasive. So youthful, so nearly irresistible.

"You can keep on saying it, Jacqueline, but it just isn't true. We couldn't be together the way we are—holding nothing back. . . ."

"That *is* the way I am, Bernard," she said. "The way I always am. And the way I am is how I need to be. How I can be happy. But it is not the beginning and end of all. Only part."

"I couldn't feel about you the way I do," he insisted, "if we weren't in love."

"Love. . . ." She started down the street again swiftly. When he caught up with her, she turned on him angrily. "It is not love, Bernard. It is lust that we share. Lust . . .! And it is very good." She sighed, brushing back an imaginary curl in her neatly coiffed hair. Now he had the look of a whipped dog nursing his hurt, and she was sorry for him.

"Jacqueline, I am begging you to marry me."

"And you think he will divorce me because you beg it?" She laughed. "You think because he is a Muslim, he need only say three times aloud, 'I divorce you'—like that—and we will be divorced and I will be free to marry my nice Jewish lover?'' Her voice flattened. "We were married in *my* church, Bernard. A Catholic wedding. 'Till death do us part.' ''

"It doesn't have to be. I'll speak to him. Make him understand.'' His voice lifted excitedly. A woman walking her dog stared at them. They moved on more quickly.

"Oh, Mohamed understands. Better than you, Bernard. Besides, what would you do with me if you had me all to yourself? Would you 'understand' me too? Could you pick up all the pieces when I come apart?'' Tears flashed into her eyes. Blindly, she ran away from him on down the street.

Bernard came after her, jostled by Saturday shoppers. He was stopped at the street corner by the cross traffic.

"Jacqueline, wait!'' he shouted.

She glanced back wildly, like a pursued animal, then hopped onto a green double-decker bus, mounted to the open top, and took a front seat as it started off.

Bernard sprinted across the street and jumped aboard. He came up and dropped into the seat beside her.

"What the hell was all that about?''

She didn't answer. They rode on in silence for another block.

"Your trouble is, you think I don't understand you, Jacqueline.''

"One part of me, you do.'' She closed her eyes, considering it distantly. "Better than anyone I've ever known. My physical needs—yes, that you understand. With you I am satisfied. We are like two fine instruments in perfect tune, playing with full stops out, all the vibratos. And I think that if I must give you up now, I will have to join a convent. Because it has been so complete, so fantastic, so perfect with you.'' Her voice dropped. "But where is the cadenza? The grand finale? The final fall of the baton? After all, what does it add up to, Bernard? Only a string tune of moments in a lifetime.''

"If we got married, then it would be forever,'' he insisted. She seemed far away. "Aren't you listening to me, Jacqueline?''

"How often do we meet? Two or three times a week? When Mohamed is away and you can escape from your mill. We are less than the changing of the moon, my love.''

He tried to interrupt, but her words rushed on with a new shrillness. "And what does Bernard know of my other needs? Do you know what I do the times I tell you I am busy? The times when I won't see you? Where are you when I drop through the bottom of the world?"

"I trust you, Jacqueline, whatever you do." He tried to take her hand, but she pulled it away with a strange, harsh laugh.

"That, Bernard, is the thing you should never do. Fuck me, yes. Trust me, never." She looked at him sharply. "Have I shocked you? Good! It is what Bernard needs. All little boys should be shocked. And then, when they grow up, they can sit in their electric chairs and nothing will hurt them, ever, ever again."

"Jacqueline," he began, "why must it all be so complicated between us?"

"Because I need you," she said.

"Yes, and I need you," he insisted with some relief.

"And because—I need Mohamed."

"Why?" he almost shouted. "Just tell me, why?" Several people on the bus stirred uncomfortably.

"Oh, God," she screamed, rising to her feet. "Why? *Because*. . . ! Why can't you stop asking why? *Because*. . .! That is the answer I give little Maurice, to his impossible questions. Because . . .! Because, my dear little son, mother is a whore!" Her fur jacket went sailing over the railing. "A whore!" she shrieked, tearing at her dress as though it had caught fire. "Why? Because I am a whore!" She ripped off the dress. It was burning her skin. Scalding her to the bone. It was crawling with invisible vermin. He tried to restrain her, begging her to stop, but she flailed him with her arms, striking out wildly.

"A whore . . . ! The bitch of the boulevards."

Her hysteria was out of all control. Other passengers on the bus were standing now. Someone called out to the conductor. An old man seemed hypnotized by the excitement. A woman buried her face so as not to see. The bus stopped with a jolt.

"A whore bitch . . . !"

Children were pulled to the stairs.

A mounted policeman tied his horse to a lamppost and climbed aboard. When he reached the top, she was completely naked, still screaming. Bernard vainly trying to calm her. It was all he could do to stop her from throwing herself after her possessions.

In the street, someone picked up the fox jacket. Someone else retrieved the torn silk dress. A young man collected the handbag from the gutter. The policeman's shrill whistle sounded above their heads as more and more people gathered.

She was still shouting. Bernard was grateful that it was now in French. He and the policeman managed to help her down from the top of the bus. A woman tried to hand her back the dress, but Jacqueline didn't seem to see it. The young man gave the policeman the handbag. Bernard wrapped the fur around her. By now, two other policemen had arrived. One telephoned from a call box on a lamppost. She had stopped shouting, and they guided her into the entranceway of a store. Bernard wrapped the dress around her, doing his best to cover her. She stood numbly beside him, oblivious of the gathering crowd.

"All right, get moving; show's over," a policeman ordered. The crowd gradually thinned. They waited in the doorway until the police wagon arrived.

On the way to the station, she sat beside him, shivering, Bernard's arm about her. *"Ne dis pas mon nom"* were the only words she spoke.

At the station, they emptied her purse. It contained no identity, only a roll of hundred-dollar bills. Because she refused to answer their questions, they placed her in a cell. She didn't mind. She seemed oblivious to her surroundings.

Bernard reluctantly gave his own name but refused to identify her until he had made one phone call. The Irish police captain rubbed his broad jaw. "To a lawyer, is it?"

"It's to her husband," Bernard replied. "A very important man."

Making that telephone call was the most difficult task Bernard had ever undertaken.

It was nearly seven o'clock when the phone rang in the house on Sixtieth Street. Mohamed took the call in his library. The frantic babble of Bernard's voice came through the black receiver.

"It's your wife, Mr. Hammadi. Jacqueline's had some kind of nervous breakdown. She—just went all to pieces . . ."

Bernard and Jacqueline? That was a combination he would never have thought of. "Where are you?" he demanded.

"At the precinct station on East Seventy-fifth. But I haven't given the police her name, Mr. Hammadi. She . . . she doesn't seem able to talk."

Mohamed asked no explanations. "I'll be right there." Bernard thought he sounded strangely unsurprised at the news of his wife's breakdown.

Bernard sat on a bench and waited. He knew he was in over his depth. There was too much he didn't understand. For the first time in years, he actually prayed—for Jacqueline and himself. Then he paced the room, ignored by the desk sergeant, until Mohamed arrived.

"I don't know what to say, Mr. Hammadi," Bernard began.

"Later," Mohamed cut him off, heading directly into the captain's office. When he finally emerged, Jacqueline was led from her cell. Bernard was relieved to see that a matron had dressed her. He could never have faced Mohamed with her naked.

Mohamed guided her out, speaking softly in French. She came without argument.

In the Locomobile, she sat between the two of them, eyes fixed on some inner horizon. Tony, now completely recovered, drove the car in discreet silence.

At the house, a doctor was waiting. He and Mohamed helped Jacqueline up the stairs.

"Wait in the library, Bernard."

The younger man sat quietly in the comfortable wing chair, trying to make sense of the previous few hours. He blamed himself. Surely his passionate demands on Jacqueline were the cause of her collapse. He had intended to tell Mohamed the truth of their affair, but his responsibility for her illness weighed more heavily.

In the half hour of waiting, he went over it in his mind a hundred times. He stared at the walls lined with leather-bound books. Millions of words all around him, and he could not find even the few to begin. His lips and throat felt parched, but he was reluctant to ring for a glass of water. His eyes reviewed the ranks of framed photographs. Hammadis and distinguished friends: kings, sultans, presidents. And this was what Bernard wanted to take her away from? To share a little room in a strange city, where they would have to hide from their present "past"?

"The doctor's given her a sedative. She's asleep." Mohamed's voice sounded weary behind him. He rose quickly.

"I've tried to go over it—and find the words to tell you . . ." Bernard began.

"That you've been sleeping with Jacqueline?" Mohamed showed neither anger nor surprise.

"It wasn't like that, Mr. Hammadi. I love her," Bernard insisted.

"And for how long has this great love been going on?"

"Almost since the first night we met—here in your house." He could see the hurt in the older man's eyes, and he knew that every word he said would make it worse. "Six months ago," he confessed. "I assure you it was the last thing in the world I intended. But it wasn't just a cheap affair. I want to marry her." He stiffened slightly. "I ask you now, Mr. Hammadi, to set her free." The words sounded unbearably melodramatic.

"Did Jacqueline say she would marry you?" Mohamed's face seemed carved from stone.

"No, Mr. Hammadi. . . ." Bernard's voice collapsed. "That's why I blame myself for her breakdown. I put too much strain on her. You see, she says she's still in love with you. But I can't see how that's possible—after all there's been between us. . . ." He couldn't look at Mohamed when he said that.

Mohamed poured a brandy and handed it to Bernard. How impersonal Mohamed seemed! Had the man no feelings? In his place, Bernard might have strangled her lover!

"My wife has been very ill for a long time. You didn't cause her breakdown—you're only a result of her illness. You—and others. Don't flatter yourself you were the only one." His tone hardened into anger for the first time. But the anger wasn't directed at Bernard. "She could have ten men like you between lunch and dinner . . .! Delivery boys. Cab drivers. It makes no difference. If she weren't my wife, she'd be rotting in some bedlam."

"It's a lie! She was perfectly wonderful—until today," Bernard insisted.

"And when she recovers, she will be perfectly wonderful again. Her doctor has a new name for it. Manic-depression. He can name it, but he can't cure it. He can't prevent the times when she hides in her room—sees nothing, eats nothing, says nothing. A shadow drops down across her mind, and she's a stranger, in a place no one can reach. She has touched the bottom of her soul. Then there are the times in between. The hysteria. Times when she's capable of anything. There are no rules in that world she lives in. Only pendulums. She could kill. You, me, herself—it would be all the same."

"Jacqueline wouldn't hurt anyone," Bernard said. "She loves people . . . loves life too much."

Mohamed took an ornate Turkish dagger from his desk, drew it from its silver sheath. He raised it toward Bernard. "I woke up one night . . . to find her standing over me . . . with this. Make no mistake, she would have used it." He tossed it back on the desk, sank wearily into a leather chair.

Bernard put his hands over his eyes, trying to blot out the picture of Jacqueline as Mohamed's murderer.

"Of course there are the good periods," Mohamed continued, "—though they become fewer—when she seems the loving, gentle creature that I married." He paused, feeling the hurt. "I find it harder to wait for those times, and can only hope that I'll never abandon her. Certainly not to you. You wouldn't have a clue how to take care of her."

"I've told you I love her," the younger man assured him.

"How long would that last? Could you put up with it for twelve years? Could you collect her out of all the gutters? Take her home and make her well? She needs men as a kind of purge. I can live with that. Because they're affairs of the body, not the heart." His eyes hardened. His voice took on the familiar note of command. "But you are dangerous to her . . . because she has seen too much of you. Today proved that. You are never to see her again."

Bernard couldn't remember afterward how he had left the room or the house. Or what else was said. The whole meaning of his life seemed to have been stripped away. He felt pity for Mohamed, but more for himself. In a way, Jacqueline was dead for him—and even if he could, he did not wish to see her. Mohamed was right. Bernard couldn't live with that other Jacqueline. And if Mohamed could, he had a strength Bernard could not find in himself.

On the following Monday, when Bernard went to the mill, he half expected to see his desk emptied, his name scraped from the glass door. But all was the same.

His father and mother were aware their son was going through some emotional crisis. "Probably a *shiksa*," his mother decided. "No nice Jewish girl would make a fine boy like Bernard so miserable."

Jacqueline's depression lasted longer than usual. The doctor recommended hiring a nurse. Mohamed hired two, around the clock. He had to go to Paris and Düsseldorf and would be gone almost a month.

The nurses bathed and dressed her, combed her hair, and fed her like a child. She was content to sit staring into space, twisting the chain on a beaded handbag she insisted on holding. They would seat her at the window to look out, but she seemed not to see beyond her own reflection in the pane of glass.

And then, one day, her eyes seemed to see again. They followed the passage of an autumn leaf beyond the window. When Mohamed returned, that evening, he thought she scarcely seemed improved.

Next morning, Mohamed had breakfast with Maurice. The boy seemed withdrawn. Mohamed felt a pang of concern that he might inherit his mother's illness. But he dismissed the thought, reasoning that any child would be depressed in this big house with no other children and only the occasional sight of either parent. Boarding school was surely the answer. Jacqueline was right about that. He would investigate Blair Academy. Someone he knew had a son there.

"I've heard of a very good school, Maurice . . ." he began. "Ice skating in the winter. Lots of sports. They have a very fine football team."

"I hate sports," Maurice said. "I like chess. Gilles is teaching me. I can beat him already."

Mohamed smiled. It was true the boy seemed to have more of an interest in mental things than physical competition.

"You'll make a great banker one day, my son."

Jacqueline came down the stairs, almost floating, beautifully dressed, skin fresh, eyes glistening. The cloud had lifted in the strange, miraculous way it always did, leaving no trace that it had been there.

"Praise Allah," Mohamed whispered.

She kissed Maurice's forehead and then kissed Mohamed on the lips. "Good morning." Her voice was bright, cheerful.

Maurice gulped down his last sip of milk. Several times in the past month he had glimpsed her through her door when one of the nurses had left it carelessly ajar. Once, his mother sat there like a wax doll with her hair hanging over her face. He had thought she was dead! "Maman . . .!" he had screamed. She gave no sign of hearing. The nurse slammed the door. Then there was another time when the door was left open. He had sneaked up silently and peered in. There she was—on all fours, crawling, sobbing. The nurse was struggling to get her back into bed. Maurice ran to his own room and hid his face under his blankets. All night in his sleep he saw her, moaning, crawling toward him—begging for help he could not give.

"I'll be late to school, Maman. Glad you're feeling better." Maurice made a hasty exit, pulling up one long sock as he left.

Jacqueline turned to her husband across the breakfast table. "Have I been very bad this time? Have I hurt anyone?"

Mohamed shook his head. He had managed to keep the entire incident of her arrest out of the press by a bit of judicious Byzantine bribery, which he found worked just as well in New York.

"No one to whom I should apologize?"

"No one. Jacqueline, I'm so very glad to have you back."

That night, he took her to Delmonico's for dinner. They drank Veuve Cliquot 1900—the year of their marriage. They laughed and danced. It wasn't necessary to put into words the reason for the celebration. For the moment, however brief, she belonged to him.

After Tony drove them home, she said, "Come to bed with me, Mohamed." They ascended the curve of staircase, arms around each other like young lovers.

When he came into her room, she was wearing the thinnest of pale blue chiffon nightdresses. In it she looked so fragile he thought she might break if he touched her.

But in bed she drew him to her with savage hunger. "Give

me a child, Mohamed,'' she whispered. He made love to her, holding nothing back.

Later, she lay peacefully against his shoulder, humming a little tune.

"Why tonight? Why a child tonight, Jacqueline?"

"Because it will bind us together forever. So that you will never leave me, and I will never leave you. And because . . . Maurice is not yours."

Mohamed arose from the bed. He turned to the window, slipping on his robe, staring out. When he returned to the bed, he kissed her on the forehead.

"He is *your* son. I love him, and that will always be enough. So be it, Jacqueline."

Ten ─────────────────────────────

MOHAMED and his cousin had been brought to the square to watch an austere procession of reverent men, faces stern with holiness, moving in stately cadence between aisles of local Spaniards. *Castellanos,* parading their faith through Toledo's narrow, slanting streets and spacious, noble squares. It was the day of Corpus Christi. The plains below the city, beyond the river Tagus, seemed to sing to the blades of the windmill that felled Don Quixote de la Mancha.

Mohamed watched respectfully. But his mind was filled with the purpose of his journey. And the gnawing concern for the future of this troublesome cousin he had rescued from Germany.

None too soon. Germany was going to war—with brassy, goose-stepping pride, sanctified by the memory of Bismark's policies of blood and iron. How much of this Germany, wondered Mohamed, had been absorbed into the impenetrable mind of Yassir? He could not even guess. Through most of the journey, the younger man had been silent.

Now he seemed oblivious to the stark nobility of this land, oblivious to these passing *hidalgos*, whose robes swayed limp in the windless afternoon.

Yassir's arm waved vaguely over the whole of Spain. "Even in this dead country you can see the greatness of our Arab past. Look at the churches where these men go to pray. How many are built in the middle of Mudejar mosques? *We* ruled Spain! And France, too."

"Not all of it, please," Mohamed said, glad they were speaking in Arabic, so their host could not understand.

Yassir ignored the interruption. "The Moors are remembered here only by palaces and mosques. They have forgotten the mathematics, medicine, astronomy we taught them. The forests of columns from the graveyards of Romans and Visigoths we raised here. We celebrated our conquests with a thousand spurting fountains. The Moors brought culture to this land.''

Mohamed clapped his hands gently. ''Congratulations, Yassir. Heidelberg has taught you to lift an argument into rhetoric. But you must look upon Spain with a little more tolerance. Moorish-Spain also taught the world religious coexistence. Here Arabs, Jews, and Christians lived in peace.''

''For how long, cousin? Only until Ferdinand and Isabella. Then . . . finished! The cross and the sword. What a choice they gave us! Convert or get out.''

''Do not dwell in the past, Yassir. In this place you can make your fortune.''

The young man beside him barely troubled to move his glance. ''Spain provides the coffin, and you provide the body, cousin Mohamed.''

Mohamed was grateful their host couldn't follow this conversation. Don Jorge del Almegraro was, in any case, occupied with the procession. It moved him deeply. He crossed himself as effigies and relics were borne past. Their enormous open Fiat, gleaming lemon-yellow in the sun, its top fanned down into folds behind them, was parked in the place reserved for distinguished citizens, in the Plaza de Zocodover. The cousins fell silent. Don Jorge turned from his place beside the chauffeur to offer a box of marzipan.

''Very good—try it. Very typical of Toledo.''

''Brought here by the Moors,'' Yassir said in French.

''This I did not know,'' Don Jorge confessed. ''But what you are seeing was not brought by the Moors,'' their host continued in stilted French. Mohamed saw that it would be essential for Yassir to learn Spanish. Easy. Languages were Yassir's subject at Heidelberg. German, French, English. . . .

''A spectacular sight,'' Mohamed acknowledged politely. Don Jorge drew their attention to another group of black-garbed men plodding gravely by, green-pompommed square black hats held respectfully in front of them, their long, El Greco faces framed by starched white ruffs. Close behind them came the monstrance, soaring above all, an ornate, jeweled steeple of silver and gold sustained aloft on the shoulders of the elite, who walked that much closer to God. Don Jorge crossed himself again. If he had not had such important guests, he himself would have been one of the bearers. When it had passed, he turned to Mohamed.

"I think perhaps your cousin has hunger? Soon we go to my house, where your associate will meet us. Yesterday, when he made his inspection of the factory, we were all impressed with his technical knowledge. What a cataclysm that has happened to his factory in France."

"An act of sabotage, Don Jorge," Mohamed said quickly. He was referring to the factory near Paris run by Jacqueline's father and her cousin Henri de St. Rimaud. For many years now, the majority of stock had been owned by Hammadi-Nouari. It had been destroyed by German agents. Heartbroken, Jacqueline's father had retired to the country. St. Rimaud was out of a job.

One factory down. The second, in Düsseldorf, had just been appropriated by the Germans for their own use. Yassir urged they blow it up, rather than let the Germans take it over. The proposal was promptly rejected by Mohamed. But if Hammadi-Nouari were to continue to supply arms to their customers, a new munitions plant had to be found in a neutral country. Spain was ideal.

"Now that Germany is allied with the Turks, they'll have your record from Damascus, Yassir. You could be arrested as a dangerous alien," Mohamed had warned his cousin in Germany. "Who would have thought, when we sent you to Heidelberg, that such an alliance would be formed? But, then, who would have thought the Germans would invade Belgium and France?"

"Anyone at Heidelberg could have guessed it, cousin," Yassir replied. "But nobody bothered to consult me."

How exasperating Yassir could be! Still, Heidelberg had improved him in some ways. He wore the beginnings of manhood with more ease.

"I think you can have a fine career here in Spain, Yassir. Henri de St. Rimaud will be an excellent teacher. He's a bit pompous, but no fool. France awarded him the Legion of Honor."

Although Mohamed was giving St. Rimaud a buildup for the benefit of Yassir, his personal opinion of Henri hadn't altered much. The man was a social and political climber who'd had his eye on the Chamber of Deputies until Paris came within range of German heavy artillery. It was Jacqueline's suggestion that Mohamed help her cousin. Nepotism laced with convenience, and conveniently providing for Yassir, too. Two difficult relatives disposed of with one stone.

"I am trying to forget your troubles in Syria, Yassir," Mohamed had said to him in Düsseldorf. "We all make mistakes."

"Only Allah is perfect," Yassir replied, quietly mimicking his cousin's favorite maxim. "My mistake was being caught."

The family *enfant terrible* seemed unrepentant as ever. "The young pick up ideas like germs. They carry the disease of their convictions through life, dormant, yet always ready to flare up," he remembered saying to Abdullah. Now he glanced at Yassir, so impassive, so stubborn. One could but hope that time would work a miracle.

The procession was ending. The crowd stirred beyond the winged patent-leather hats of the Guardia Civil. Don Jorge glanced around. "Today you and your cousin will dine on the greatest delicacy of northern Spain: roast suckling pig, cooked on a spit."

"Pork is not permitted by our religion," Yassir replied.

Mohamed cut in quickly. "An honor, I'm sure. But one which we must decline. Please forgive us."

"Dios Mío! It is myself who must be forgiven, señor," Don Jorge apologized. "It is something I have not even thought of."

Del Almegraro's house turned out to be a small castle. It was set on a rise of ground with a fine view of Toledo across fields of blood-red poppies.

"How many of our forebears have been slaughtered under these walls?" Yassir grumbled when his host was out of hearing.

"Perhaps, Yassir, it was the Moors who occupied the castle, welcoming enemies with scalding water or boiling oil, arrows, and even baskets of poisonous serpents. The Moors imported more than the abacus and backgammon." Mohamed strode ahead of him into the castle.

"Tortilla a la Magra." It was nearly ten o'clock when Doña María beamed from beneath her feast-day mantilla of black lace supported by a towering tortoiseshell comb. The hostess had managed an instant addition to the menu.

"Excellent," Mohamed praised, hoping it didn't have shell-fish in it. His glance lifted to her portrait on the high dining-room wall. A dark maiden of shadow and sorrow. He smiled inwardly. Perhaps it had been painted at the moment she learned of her family's choice of Don Jorge as her *novio*.

Henri de St. Rimaud raised his wineglass. "I drink to the birth of our new enterprise, Hispañola-Nacional. Success and profits." Age and indulgence had thickened Henri's middle, and perhaps his mind. Jacqueline's flamboyant cousin wore the ribbon of his newly bestowed Légion d'Honneur on his jacket, overcoat, and Mohamed was certain, even his pajamas.

Earlier that day, when they met in the courtyard, Mohamed had questioned his own decision in appointing Henri to this position.

St. Rimaud was extracting himself from his oversize touring car. "My dear, dear Mohamed!" His greeting had been followed by a buss on both cheeks. Two "dears" in gratitude for the appointment that got him out of France as the Germans moved in. "And how is our dear [one 'dear,' in case there might be a grain of truth in the rumor that all was not tidy in Mohamed's wedlock] cousin Jacqueline?"

"More beautiful than ever, since the birth of our daughter," Mohamed said truthfully. "She sends her love."

"And her health? She never writes, although she has done us the honor of naming your daughter after her dear cousin, my wife."

"One has heard reports that she's been unwell from time to time?" Madame de St. Rimaud added a verbal hook of curiosity that failed to catch Mohamed.

Don Jorge's servants in aprons and livery were busily transporting an incredible cargo of pigskin luggage from car to castle. Plainly, the St. Rimauds had left little for the invading Germans to find in their small château on the road to Paris.

At dinner, Henri, whose religion prevented him from nothing, sampled the suckling pig. Now he was tucking into a local partridge, on having been assured that "Don Jorge has shot himself," by Doña, whose French was not quite perfect.

"The Boche," snarled Henri. "I would give all I possess to be your age, Yassir—so that I could stand in the front lines and fight beneath *le tricolore!*"

Yassir did not reply.

Henri wiped his lips, brushed an invisible speck of sauce from his scarlet decoration.

"I salute your cuisine, Doña María. Magnificent." He made a sort of French farting sound with his lips, meant to confirm the excellence of the dish.

"*Perdiz*, stewed in the red wine of Méntrida," Don Jorge said proudly.

"If I close my eyes, I could believe myself in a quite reasonable restaurant in Paris," Henri conceded.

"At least here we do not dine to the sound of French artillery in retreat," Don Jorge retorted to the slur on the honor of his chef.

"I assure you," Henri assured pompously, "the Germans will never gain one *centimètre* of the soil of our beloved France." His florid face formed a burgundy barrier to invisible hoards of spike-helmeted enemy.

His wife, who in the candlelight appeared skeletal beside him, had taken a secret vow that she would defend the wisdom of her marital choice, since each passing year more clearly revealed her mistake. "Henri does not let a day pass without the wish that he could take up his rifle for *La Patrie*," she advised the gathering. "But he has at least the satisfaction of knowing that if he cannot himself bear arms, he will still be serving his country by manufacturing the weapons and munitions our gallant French *poilus* will lift in her defense. With your assistance, Don Jorge," she added graciously.

Her host looked at Mohamed. "But, madame, we are producing arms for the Turks!"

There was an embarrassed silence. Yassir pushed back his chair. "Is that what I am to do here, cousin Mohamed? Assist in making arms for Turks? The enemies of the Arab people? Is this to be my fine career in Spain?"

"This is not a place for a political discussion, Yassir," Mohamed replied firmly in Arabic.

"What better place, cousin Mohamed?" Yassir suddenly stood up, spilling a glass of red wine. "Do you think I went to prison, faced the hangman—do you think I still bear the scars of the lash, so that now I will help the three of you bowelless profiteers arm my enemies? No! I am wrong. You are not bowelless. You are full of shit."

Doña María rose from the table and left the room. Henri's wife reached for her smelling salts. Mohamed stood, enormously controlled.

"I ask pardon, Don Jorge, for my cousin's unforgivable behavior at your table. Come, Yassir."

"I will not move a step until I have been answered," Yassir insisted.

Mohamed faced him coldly. "Before I ask you to apologize to these people, I will say this: Hammadi-Nouari *must* fulfill its commitment of arms to the Turks. Not only because we contracted to do so to save *your* neck, but because if we don't, the Turks have threatened to close down our Jerusalem and Damascus offices. Djemel Pasha has threatened our families! They are in the gravest danger—which you, of all people, should understand."

Yassir turned to the Spaniard with a certain dignity. "I ask pardon for my language, Don Jorge, but not for my anger. *That* I keep in my heart until the Turks no longer rule Palestine."

Don Jorge nodded. "We will speak of it no more. Please—sit down, young man, and you, Señor Hammadi."

The Arabs took their seats, Yassir still nursing anger.

Almost automatically, Mohamed picked up his wineglass, swallowing the fine red Rioja. Don Jorge beamed relief.

"Always my guests find much character in the wines of Rioja, which I think are of more similarity to the French wines than the wines of Valdepeñas. It is not true, Señor St. Rimaud?"

Henri pursed his lips forward, rolling a mouthful of wine over his tongue. "Modest. It makes no special promise . . . but like the kiss of a virgin, it is agreeable without the ripeness of experience. Yes, agreeable. But finally, señor, one must say . . . Spain is not Burgundy." He smiled apologetically.

"In France wines are a religion," Henri's wife, having recovered her composure, put in. "Isn't that what you always say, Henri?"

"I am still a Frenchman, Françoise. No matter in what land I find myself."

Yassir came suddenly to life again. "And you, cousin Mohamed? What do you always say? You drink the wine. How is it you don't eat the pig? Surely it cannot be a question of religion? You have no religion but the Company!"

"Go to your room, Yassir!" Mohamed's command cut the silence that followed Yassir's second outburst.

Yassir rose, pale, trembling. "A child is sent to his room."

"You're acting like a child." Mohamed spoke in Arabic now.

"I grew up when the Turks put ninety strokes across my back. And I would bear it again for what is to come. When the Arabs are finally a nation, we shall remember our enemies. The first to be slaughtered will not be the Christians, nor even the Turks. They will be our own people who have lost the purity of their faith and the strength of their purpose. They are the dead leaves that must be pruned from the tree." He turned quickly to his host, switching back to French. "Don Jorge, Monsieur and Madame de St. Rimaud, my anger is not for you." He walked out stiffly, banging into a chair. They heard his footsteps pounding up the staircase.

Mohamed closed his eyes for an instant. He saw the face of a difficult little boy being chastised by Abdullah's fly switch.

"I had nothing to do with it . . . nothing . . . Uncle Gamel is clumsy," came the piping voice back across the years. Mohamed felt a deep sadness.

Above the battlements of Don Jorge's castle, the moon hung full and ripe. In the distance across the plain, Toledo's spires were tipped by stars. From somewhere in the courtyard came the soft throb of a plaintive guitar. "One of my servants—from Andalucía," Don Jorge observed. "There, everyone is a musician." The quick flutter of plucked notes was smothered in a deep throbbing chord—dark as the end of life. *El canto hondo.* . . .

Henri bulked heavily behind Mohamed, brandy in hand. "It is not for me to question your judgment, Mohamed. And God knows I am more than prepared to help you in this new venture. Why, I have even left my own country to serve you with the benefit of my vast experience, and always my honest advice. And I am certain that Don Jorge will agree with what I am about to say."

Don Jorge nodded.

"Let us be perfectly candid, Mohamed," Henri swept on. "We are not making pastry here. To have such an explosive young man working with us would be like throwing a match into a keg of gunpowder."

"And we can be sure he wouldn't?" Don Jorge interjected, taking him literally.

"Personally, I think you must reconsider." Henri leaned

against the balustrade, warming his brandy. "Yassir's presence here would not inspire harmony."

If Mohamed had been honest with himself, he would have been forced to agree. But he was angry. "This has been a shock for Yassir. By morning he may be more used to the idea. But if he isn't, I'll make other arrangements for his future." He turned rather abruptly and headed down the narrow, circular staircase.

For a moment, he paused outside Yassir's door, undecided. Then he moved on to his own room. It would wait. Better to talk after they had both slept.

But, in the morning, Mohamed's knock on Yassir's door brought no answer. He opened it. In the tower bedroom, light shafting through a slit once used for archery, fell across a bed that had not been slept in. On the pillow was a note.

"You supply the Turks with arms, cousin. I will supply them an Arab target."

Yassir's valise and all his possessions were gone. On the floor by his bed was an Arab newspaper—*Filastin*—published in Jaffa. Across an editorial, Yassir had scrawled: "Arab Independence for all Syria!" Mohamed scanned the article quickly. It was bland enough. In support of freedom and equal rights for all citizens in the Ottoman Empire—Christian, Jew, and Muslim. It criticized Turkish racism but suggested that any reform movement against the Turks could provide Zionists with the opportunity to further infiltrate Palestine. His eye traveled to an underlined article beside the editorial. It complained that Arab land was being sold to Zionists and reminded that the Koran warned that the Jews were a people not to be trusted. Mohamed crushed the newspaper in his fist. He could recall no such warning in the Koran.

"Probably he has caught the train to Madrid," Don Jorge suggested, not without a note of relief. "By now he could be on his way to anywhere. North to France, south to Africa. I think we must wait until he contacts us."

But Mohamed guessed where Yassir would head. He telegraphed Abdullah in Damascus, in the Company's secret code, that his son was adrift. No doubt on his way back to Palestine. Every precaution must be taken. If the Turks picked him up this time, there'd be nothing anyone could do to save him.

The gnawing part of it was that, aside from the fanaticism,

Mohamed himself could not entirely dismiss the cause his cousin had so ardently embraced. He wasn't yet sufficiently informed on the many currents now flowing under the surface of Syria and Palestine. There were too many outside pressures on this one small corner of the world: the French interests; the British interests; the German alliance with the Turks; the Zionists' objectives. And beyond all this—the Arab destiny. That shining vision beyond the foreseeable future. A mirage in the mind's eye—or the will of the Maker?

When Mohamed asked himself why he had not informed his partner about the Hispañola-Nacional purchase, he excused the omission on the grounds that the news would come better from Judah's own father, in Palestine. David Nouari was the one who would suffer if the Turks closed down the Palestine office. And Mohamed knew that Judah's sympathies were with the Allies.

David Nouari didn't have the opportunity to tell his son about the Spanish arms factory. Besides, he was certain Mohamed would.

"This damned war in Europe seems to have sponged up all our resources for raw cotton!" Mahmood Hammadi complained, adding an extra smoothing touch to black-dyed, polished hair. Hammadi-Nouari Cairo was having its troubles filling orders in the world market. The problem had once again brought Judah Nouari to Cairo. New suppliers had to be found and transfers of finance arranged.

The meeting seemed to drag interminably, while the partners' two sons, Raphael and Ahmed (now promoted to junior partners), insisted on presenting Judah with fully detailed financial statements for the years 1913 and '14. Judah guessed their zeal was meant to demonstrate their tonic effect on the business. They were now virtually running it for their fathers. Mahmood kept dozing off, managing only an occasional nod to assert his presence. Gideon fidgeted with his amber cigarette holder. Smartly turned out as ever in a shoulder-pinching gray silk frock coat, feet strangled by highly polished kidskin shoes, Gideon inspected his narrow waistline in the mirrored office wall and compared it to his partner's, encased in a tight corset under a silk shirt. Two peacocks, losing a few tail feathers with time.

It was nearly nine o'clock when the meeting finally broke up. Gideon Nouari insisted on taking his nephew to dinner at the Shepherd's Hotel, where Judah customarily stayed. An opportunity to introduce his delicious mistress at last, confided Gideon.

Judah paused at the hotel desk to scrawl a telegram to Ruth. He was worried about the twins. Both had come down with mumps, and the doctor hadn't allowed him to see them before he left Paris. He had urged Ruth to take the children to London when they were well enough to travel. But she had replied, "As long as you call Paris home, Judah . . . I shall be here."

Home. . . .

Judah made his way to the table, past waiters in baggy, colorful pantaloons, short jackets and fezzes—a parody of the ethnic dress. Then he saw her. Mignon, Gideon's open secret, a slightly overblown half-French, half-Egyptian lady of uncertain age. Hardly the femme fatale of Judah's expectation, although at one time Mignon must certainly have been a beauty.

Gideon ate sparingly, fed tidbits to the spreading Mignon, and preened himself. It was the lady's birthday, he confided, although the years were not to be counted. Gideon had arranged for the chef to hide Mignon's gift under the crust of a sticky pastry. As always, she feigned immense surprise, though he did the same thing every year. A bracelet of sharply blue turquoise and pearls set in a thin gold band was forked out of the crumbly dough. Mignon slipped it on with the look of one expecting greater things.

"Enchanting. But too large for my wrist, Gideon. And far too narrow for the size of my arm. See how it makes my hand look like a lump! And everyone says my hands are one of my best features—after my eyes." She flashed Judah a collaboratory look from kohl-lined orbs.

"Every part of you is perfection, Chérie," Gideon soothed.

"Well, then, what's to be done?"

She waved her hand on high, bringing three waiters scurrying to the table. The bracelet jangled down the shapely arm, coming to rest midway. "No doubt they charged you too much. Which shop? I'll take it back tomorrow and exchange it." It was the little trick Mignon played whenever Gideon bought her anything. He correctly suspected that she pocketed a profit from the exchanges, but he was content with the arrangement. Gideon picked up the thread of his conversation with Judah.

"Yassir's disappearance has been a great worry to all members of both families. One is never certain where next that hothead might turn up. Wherever, it is positive, he'll cause trouble. Not that we've had any shortage of that."

"I heard that Djemel Pasha was threatening to close down both our Jerusalem and Damascus offices," Judah said.

Gideon stole a forkful of Mignon's pastry. "The Pasha was so mad when we stopped supplying arms from Düsseldorf, he whipped three little boys. Doubtless he felt better after that entertainment."

"He seems to be leaving our Company alone now. Tell me, who is supplying him arms?"

"Who?" Gideon stared at him. "We are, of course. Thanks to a stroke of genius by Mohamed, shipments are reaching the Pasha regularly again. From Spain."

Judah put down his coffee cup. "Where would Hammadi-Nouari get arms in Spain?"

"Where? Where we make them, of course," Gideon said. "Our own factory: Hispañola-Nacional. Mohamed set it up five months ago. H-N. He kept our initials. Where have you been, nephew? Not sleeping at home too often these days?"

Mignon tittered. It was the only part of the conversation that interested her.

"It was from the Spanish factory that Yassir disappeared," Gideon added. "Surely you knew that?"

"No. I did not. But I appear to be the only member of the Company who didn't. Could you explain that to me?" Judah's face had hardened.

Gideon shrugged. "Surely Mohamed told you? As managing director, the decision was his."

"Nobody's paying any attention to me—and it's my birthday," Mignon complained.

Gideon smoothed his mustache. "The rest of the evening is yours, my dear. The night, in fact." He winked at Judah and waved for the check.

It was nearly one-thirty. Judah dispatched a cable to Mohamed in Company code: HISPANOLA-NACIONAL GRAVE MISTAKE STOP IMPERATIVE H-N MAINTAIN ABSOLUTE NEUTRALITY STOP URGE YOU CEASE SHIPMENTS IMMEDIATELY STOP JUDAH.

Exhausted but too troubled for sleep, Judah made his way into the saloon bar past a convergence of British officers beneath portraits of George V, Queen Mary, Edward VII, and dominating all, Queen Victoria. British troops had occupied Egypt since 1882, and although the country had been nominally a dependency of Turkey . . . if the sun did not exactly set on Egypt, it did not rise without the aid of a British bugle.

Judah slid into a well-worn leather chair and ordered a whiskey and water, no ice. He felt the magnetic pull of a stranger's stare. It came from a bantam-built young man at a near table jutting a prominent jaw at him across an untouched vodka. He was studying Judah through gold, round-rimmed spectacles with the air of an inquiring academic. As their eyes met, he leaned forward, resting his hand on the top of his walking stick, and tapped the polished basalt three times sharply. Like a signal to himself to take the stage.

"Judah Nouari, aren't you? The man who went to Uganda." Heavy-lidded eyes in a tight, serious face. Linen suit, wrinkled and travel-worn. Elegance of manner. A long cigarette pinched between thumb and forefinger, Russian style. The man seemed suspended between ceiling and floor, from the rising wisp of gray smoke to the tip of his cane.

"Should I know you?" Judah asked.

"It depends on your memory. But I think you will have heard of 'Altalina'?"

Judah had. "Altalina" had built an international reputation as a journalist in his early twenties. In Russia he'd been praised by Tolstoy and Gorky as a man of "burning ideas." One thing more Judah knew about him: he was Jewish and a rabid, almost fanatical Zionist. "Altalina is your pen name. I've heard you speak at several of the congresses. Strange we've never met. Jabotinsky, aren't you?"

The response was an almost courtly little nod. "Vladimir. Jabotinsky. A man who believes more than he is believed."

Now Judah could recall those speeches. One in particular, in Basel. Jabotinsky had risen to speak in the debate on Uganda—a passionate, eloquent monologue on the necessity of a homeland and Jewish state. But after the sound and fury had died down, his oratory left one not really sure whether he was for or against. In questions of policy, he seemed to float somewhere above the fence. Perhaps the better to know which way to fall?

Judah knew something of Jabotinsky's background: that he came from Odessa—a city that sprouted the movement's foremost thinkers and philosophers, giants like Achad Ha-am. Yet he seemed quite different from other Russian Jews Judah had met, even Weizmann. Distinctly more Russian than Jewish—yes, that was it. There was also something in his style and attack that was oddly, almost aggressively, theatrical. The way he sat back in his chair staring past the vodka like a footlight, walking stick now propped against his leg. He reminded Judah of the great English actor Sir Henry Irving playing Chekhov.

Goyish, Ruth would have said of Jabotinsky.

"I've come to beard the lion, in fact. The British High Commissioner. Kitchener himself," the journalist confided. "Actually I'm posted in Alexandria now. Perhaps our meeting is fortuitous, Mr. Nouari. I'm after something very particular which will require your help."

"Do I have a choice?" Judah inquired with some amusement.

Jabotinsky rose, bringing his untouched vodka over to Judah's table. He had already sat down when he asked, "Will you permit me?"

"Curiosity impels me."

The journalist downed the vodka in a gulp. Then he began to talk. It was a performance. And it centered on one idea. Astounding. Original. Revolutionary. Impossible. This spindle-shanked journalist with no military experience had set himself the task of building an army to fight for a country that didn't exist! He proceeded to expound his ideas in great detail. When he had finished, Judah told him, "There's only one man to help you: Dr. Weizmann."

"I fear I'm not too popular with the able doctor," Jabotinsky replied. "Too often we've found ourselves on opposite sides in the Congress."

"Should that stop you? If there are two Jews in a room, there are always three opinions."

"Weizmann doesn't like me."

Judah sipped his whiskey. All this arrogance, and a sense of insecurity. "He'll like your idea, I'm confident."

"You think so."

"I know so."

"But I feel his Zionism is minimal."

Judah laughed. "You might as well call the Pope anti-Catholic."

"Weizmann plays politics. Perhaps for the good Zionists, but seldom with their consent." Jabotinsky's voice rose with self-conscious resonance.

"Mr. Jabotinsky," Judah began, "you've just outlined an impossible plan. It has no chance of success. Unless of course it finds the right friends in high places."

"I have one already: you." The journalist smiled for the first time.

"Weizmann's your man. Because he knows the game of politics as it is played in England. In the drawing rooms—like whist."

When they parted, it was nearly four o'clock in the morning. Judah had extracted a promise from Jabotinsky not to discuss his plan with Kitchener—yet. Not until Judah had time to set up a meeting for the journalist with Weizmann in England. The chemist could get him to bigger fish. Even the Prime Minister.

Judah couldn't sleep. Beyond the mosquito netting, he could hear the hum of frustrated insects. A faint whiff of night-blooming jasmine drifted through shuttered windows. Almost morning. Almost time for the muezzin's ancient summons of the faithful to prayer. He knew he had to help Jabotinsky's dream toward reality. Zosia would have wanted it.

Zosia—never far from his thoughts, always haunting his dreams, haunting his decisions. She was the star by which he steered. He could not change that, nor would he ever want to. It kept her alive, close—in a place where he could never lose her, and where she would never grow old. Yes, Zosia would want him to back Jabotinsky with all the energy he could command.

"I hear you've taken over all the distilleries in England, Scotland, and Ireland . . . in aid of the British war effort," Judah remarked. "Are you perhaps trying to keep the troops sober?"

"The distillers aren't too happy about it," Weizmann confessed.

Judah hadn't seen the chemist since his move from Manchester. He found him working at the Lister Institute, in London's Chelsea district. His growing role as "statesman without a state" had brought Weizmann a sense of self-assurance. The small financial security of his new position relieved some of his personal stresses, but he seemed to have replaced them with a thousand new ones. The émigré provincial chemist had metamorphosed into an almost dapper, rather English figure. He walked Judah through the laboratory, where a dozen young men and women were busily occupied over test tubes, retorts, and miles of winding copper filtering equipment. Judah noted huge sacks of maize, other grain, and chestnuts stacked against the wall.

"What are you making?"

"Acetone. They'd rather be making whiskey, I assure you."

Weizmann's private office was small as ever and more cluttered than usual. Judah cleared some books from a chair to sit down. "The Zionist Action Committee aren't too happy with you either, Dr. Weizmann. When I was in Copenhagen, Ussishkin, among others, harangued me with tales of how you had the First Lord of the Admiralty in your pocket."

"A slight exaggeration." Weizmann removed his white coat, donned a new swallowtail frock coat and adjusted his cravat on a wing collar.

"They also accuse you of violating the avowed Zionist policy of neutrality."

"They're right." Weizmann sank into his desk chair, which swiveled with a squeak. "My meeting with Winston Churchill was something of a personal triumph. But it was certainly brief and to the point. Churchill's a man who wastes no time—yours or his. I barely got myself through the door when he barked at me from behind the longest cigar in London: 'Dr. Weizmann, we need thirty thousand tons of acetone to beat the Boche. Can you make it?' Absolutely terrifying! It seems he knew all about my patent. I tried to explain what it would mean in practical terms. What I would require. The material—the labor. And would you believe it? He's given me carte blanche."

"Congratulations," Judah said.

"Condolences might be more appropriate. I've had to set up a pilot plant. Now I'm training this group of young chemists to go out and run the distilleries. Converting vats from scotch to acetone.'' The profound look of inner satisfaction on Weizmänn's face was shaded by weariness.

"Why do they need so much acetone?" Judah asked.

"For their naval guns. It's a solvent. Without it, Churchill would be forced to modify all existing equipment. It would set them back to the Battle of Trafalgar.''

"No wonder you're such an important man," Judah chuckled. "Which returns us to a sore point. The Zionist Congress considers that you're flouting their official position."

Weizmann well knew that his actions were causing a serious rift in internal Zionist affairs. The "Old Action Committee" headquarters, which had been situated in Berlin before the war, had now moved to Denmark—as visible proof to the world of their rabid neutrality. But since a good percentage of the members were German Jews, Weizmann was aware that the Allies believed Zionist sympathies lay with Germany.

"Neutral they may be, Judah. But they are convinced Germany will win this war—and that I'm helping the wrong side. It's a predicament. To remain neutral while conducting Zionist internal policy is like walking on eggs. And besides, I don't agree with it.''

"Why do they think Germany will win?" Judah asked. He hadn't missed the patriotic Kitchener posters in the lab.

"Most of the members from Berlin are Germans first and Jews second. Thousands of Jews are serving in the Kaiser's army. Hundreds have been killed for Germany, many decorated. The Action Committee knows how efficient the Germans are. What they're capable of. On the other hand"—he leaned back, putting his feet up on his desk—"the Russian members know how corrupt, how incompetent Holy Mother Russia is.''

"Neither holy nor maternal, I'd say," Judah agreed. "So they count on Russia losing the war for the Allies?"

Weizmann nodded. "Losing wars has become a habit with the Czars. But what neither side of the Congress has taken into consideration—I suppose because none of them are British—is that the British will win. And if we contribute to that victory, the British may help the Zionist.''

"Wishful thinking?"

"We can't presume that God will grant our wishes, Judah. But a sea of wishes may produce a pearl if we have the courage to dive for it.''

Courage was the one thing Weizmann had never lacked. He was carrying the work load of three men, still spending several days each week in Manchester teaching at the university. His wife, Vera, couldn't leave there anyway. She was medical officer of the Infant Clinic. "And not delighted that she sees so little of me," the chemist added bleakly. Beneath the debonair façade, weariness casts its shadow. Judah hesitated. Could Weizmann shoulder one more challenge?

"Dr. Weizmann, you've always said that you believe Zionism to be a force for life and creativeness—something inherent in the Jewish people," Judah began tentatively.

Weizmann nodded impatiently. He was too busy to sit and listen to his own philosophies thrust back at him. "So . . . ?"

"I've told you often enough—we argued about it—that to me it has meant only an answer to the needs of a displaced people. Exiles from countries that didn't want them."

"So, Judah, come to the point."

"I've met someone who's changed my opinions. Someone who makes me believe it's all possible."

"You know, Judah, there is not in the Mosaic law a single command. 'Thou shalt believe.' Who is this prophet who has opened your eyes where Herzl failed and I failed?"

"Vladimir Jabotinsky."

"Oh. . . ."

"I appreciate you may not like him, but it's unlike you to disapprove without knowing the facts."

"A man I haven't too much sympathy with, I'll admit. A useful man, yes. A born orator. But I didn't think you were a person to be seduced by oratory."

"It wasn't words, it was ideas, Doctor."

"Ideas, yes." Weizmann sighed. "He's never short of those. The trouble is, Jabotinsky thinks of himself as a politician—and that is the one thing he is not."

Judah smiled inwardly. But men seemed to think they had cornered the market on politics. "Will you listen to what he has to say?"

"With him you can *only* listen. He never stops talking. But now I haven't got time."

"I brought him from Egypt—to tell you the craziest idea he's ever had."

Weizmann closed his eyes. Then he rose and put a hand on Judah's shoulder. "All right, all right. Bring him to my rooms in Chelsea tonight. Number 3, Justice Walk.'' He smiled. ''The price is right.''

"Price?"

"It costs nothing to listen.''

"We will not be dismissed as dreamers aspiring to some vague Jewish Valhalla!'' Vladimir Jabotinsky's words soared in nasal crescendo. ''We will offer ourselves as brothers in arms—their champions—their angels of victory.'' He sneezed. The change of climate from steaming Alexandria had given him a raging cold. He balanced elegantly on the edge of a straight-backed chair, throat wound in the long muffler he'd declined to remove. Weizmann's sitting room was icy cold; a small coal fire barely punctured the creeping fog.

"Personally I've always been of two minds about angels,'' Weizmann said. Up to now, the conversation had taken the form of a monologue. Jabotinsky's words seethed and boiled up with a fervor that allowed few interruptions. ''But you live up to my expectations, Mr. Jabotinsky. I find your ideas impossible.''

Judah rose angrily. ''Dr. Weizmann, you don't live up to my expectations. I promised Mr. Jabotinsky a fair hearing. His ideas are *not* impossible. In fact—they're politically sound. If that is your opinion, we're quite prepared to move forward without you.''

"Opinion? It was a comment. Sit down, Judah,'' Weizmann said. ''And you, Mr. Jabotinsky—drink your tea. I've squeezed a little lemon in it. Very expensive. Don't waste it.''

Judah sat.

Weizmann regarded Jabotinsky thoughtfully. At close quarters he exuded a certain charisma. Young men would follow such a leader. ''If anyone but you had come to me with such a proposal I'd have called for a straitjacket. Because, you know, you sound a little crazy. No offense, please.''

"At least we're all agreed on the fact that Zionist neutrality plays into German hands,'' Judah said. ''Their agents have even approached American Zionists with wild promises. If the Kaiser wins, he'll make an open declaration in favor of a Jewish Palestine.''

"The Germans are quick enough to give away land they don't own,'' Jabotinsky interjected.

"I believe them," Weizmann replied. The two stared at him in some surprise. "I believe them—but I don't think they'll get the chance."

"The British aren't fools," Judah began. "They know that unless the Turks are utterly defeated, the German alliance will threaten them long after the war is over. Their Suez Canal can be renamed the New Rhine."

Jabotinsky blew his nose and recaptured the floor. "Which means the moment has come when we must make it clear that Zionists are prepared to take sides! Prepared to fight for our beliefs. Prepared to be a political force. Then the British will see the necessity of supporting a Jewish state." He leveled an accusing finger at Weizmann. "And if we don't take sides . . . the Turks will bury us along with the Arabs!"

A picture flashed into Judah's mind from his recent visit to Palestine. After he'd left Jabotinsky in Cairo, he'd traveled on to Jerusalem. There he had witnessed a horrifying scene. A madman—or so Judah had thought—staggering through dust thick as strings outside one of Jerusalem's gates, leading an emaciated camel. The man called aloud: "Hear me, O seed of Mecca. Hear me, O children of the Prophet. I bring you a promise from the Messenger of God. Independence for the Arab nation! Restoration of the caliphate to the son of the Arab Quraysh tribe. . . ."

Judah had stood transfixed by the staring, wild eyes. The face was young but already leather-creased, wind-blackened beneath the rag of turban. A hushed crowd of Arabs were gathering.

"Hear me . . . hear me . . . Palestine must be returned to the Arab nation. . . ." The staff in the skeletal hand seemed to point directly at Judah.

Then, from beneath the turban, a wave of blood turned the gaunt features into a crimson mask. A blow from behind had brought down the mad prophet. Suddenly the place swarmed with green-turbaned "qadris"—a patrol of the Turkish Police. They were rounding up everyone in the crowd, Judah included. Looking for deserters from the Turkish Army, they said.

Judah's European clothes elicited a certain amount of respect. But it was just as well he'd left his passports at his father's house. He carried two: one French, one Ottoman. Either could have put him in real trouble. One as an enemy, the other as a draftable Turkish subject.

The demand for papers had him fishing through his pocket. He brought out a receipted hotel bill from Copenhagen, flourished it importantly. Happily, the Turk couldn't read. Judah groped for and found the magic word: "*Almanca*"—German. The Turk nodded toward the bill respectfully. It was stamped in three places. Certainly an official document.

As they dragged the unfortunate prophet away from his camel, one of the "qadris" shouted to the crowd. "Here is a prophecy! The Turks will march with the Germans to the ends of the world!"

Badly shaken, Judah entered the city. He found himself walking through the old Jewish Quarter. He knew these streets by heart. Knew many of the families, though few would remember him from his youth. Some of these families had lived in Palestine since the Diaspora. There were a handful of *Ashkenazim* who'd come in the nineteenth century from Central Europe, but most were *Sephardim*, expelled from Spain in the fifteenth and sixteenth centuries. These still cherished the ancient keys to houses in Córdoba and Toledo that no longer existed. Some even still clung to their Spanish nationality, since in all those generations they'd avoided taking out Ottoman citizenship. But wherever they'd come from, they shared Arab ways and Arab dress. Black caftans and skullcaps, hair dressed in the Arab fashion, in long ringlets.

By the time they were three, boys began to study Hebrew. Most could read and write by the age of six. Here, in the Old City, children regularly attended *cheder*—the elementary Hebrew school. If they hadn't already learned it on their mother's knee, the *melamed* taught them the alphabet. Judah recalled his own mother rewarding him with a honey cookie baked in the shape of a Hebrew letter when he'd finally managed to say it right. Was he four years old? At thirteen, after his Bar Mitzvah, he'd joined boys from the Old City to pray at the synagogue three times a day: *Shaharith. Minhah. Maarib.* He studied and prayed. Listened to the older men's endless discussions on some complex enigma of the Torah. Opinions voiced. Reasons stated. Theological pyrotechnics displayed by men from every walk of life. His father, David, happily argued some perplexity of Talmudic law with the cobbler. Or the tailor. One's social position—pocket empty or full—made no difference to one's education, intellect, or right to equality in the House of God. Because they had the advantage of their own schools, most Jews in the Quarter spoke and wrote Arabic better than Muslims of equal station in life. Muslims attended government schools run by the Turks. But Arab families in the Jewish Quarter lived in perfect harmony. After all, the boundaries were self-imposed. It wasn't a ghetto.

And when a Muslim businessman needed a secretary or an assistant, he sought out a Jew, because of his reading and writing ability. In rural areas, itinerant Jewish workmen and craftsmen traveled a circuit, staying in each village for a night or two, welcomed by the Arab villagers, who housed and fed them. Jewish women were prized as dress-makers, because often they were in touch with Western fashions through relatives abroad.

How many of these old Palestine Jews, Judah wondered, knew or cared about the aims of Zionism? He also wondered how well he understood these people any more? How much he cared about his own religion any more?

And that ascetic—that nomad prophet. Ranting about an Arab homeland. A sun-cooked deserter from the Turkish Army—or something more? Had Judah lost touch? Surely Arab and Jew shared one aim now: to rid themselves of Turkish oppression. In this lay the continuation of a brotherhood that must be stronger than the rantings of fanatics— Arab or Jew.

His attention moved back to the present argument. Jabotinsky was onstage again. "Doors are opened to you, Dr. Weizmann. Use them. Walk through them. Start speaking of our state as though it already exists. The British need us—and that makes us their equals."

Weizmann leaned back in his chair and laughed heartily. "The British empire needs a bunch of Jews? Another crazy idea, Mr. Jabotinsky." His voice sobered. "As absurd as your proposal to help them win the war with a Jewish Legion. A legion . . .? A thousand men, maybe? From Poland— Romania—Russia—without overcoats? Without training? What can it mean?" He paused.

Jabotinsky started to his feet again.

"Why is everyone always jumping up?" Weizmann asked. "I listened to you. You should listen to me."

"I'll tell you what a Jewish Legion could mean, Doctor," Judah put in. "The sympathy of every Jew and many Gentiles in the United States. If the Germans think that's so important, the British should too.''

Weizmann rose, dropping one large coal on the fire. ''You think I'm too soft, eh? Well, I think it isn't just in *our* interests to help the British. It's in *their* interests to help us.''

Jabotinsky's spectacles focused on the back of Weizmann's head. ''All this time you've agreed with me? Why didn't you say so? What have we been arguing about?''

Weizmann turned, tongs in hand. ''Because, my dear Mr. Jabotinsky, I wanted to hear what you had to say. I've fallen in love with the sound of your voice—which I think you yourself are already a little bit in love with. As for taking sides, I've *done* that. As Judah knows. As everyone knows. As you would know if you would also listen to the sound of *my* voice.''

''For you, taking sides is not enough, Weizmann. Making acetone is not enough.'' Jabotinsky was shouting in a hoarse whisper. ''Use your contacts, Doctor. Be a country. Be a state! *I'll* be an army.'' His cheeks were flushed with the fever of ideas. ''Tell that to the British War Office. Tell them that the Jewish Legion will march beside them to free Jerusalem from the Turks.''

Weizmann moved to his window, looking out into the damp street. He had come a long way from the little village in the Pripet Marshes: Motol. He has lost his Russianness. Left it behind him like a balalaika hanging beside the hearth. He was becoming an Englishman. He was beginning to understand these British—wrapped in their little brick castles—walled behind their Anglo-Saxon reserve. Cool-eyed card players— ever dealing from that mysterious inner confidence—and generally winning over unbeatable odds. How well he had begun to know them—even love them. Let them face as they now did certain defeat, horrible losses—they must never be sold short. Never be underrated, never pressured or they'd balk. Show them their weakness, their need of you, and you fed their bulldog obstinacy. But join them on the battlefield, and they would honor your banners—with their respects. He looked back at the Russian journalist who had conceived the idea of offering them a Jewish army he didn't have.

That took courage—even *chutzpah*. A very Jewish trait. Insolence honed on suffering. Swagger based on desperation. How could he make such a man understand the British?

"An Englishman is a very private person, Mr. Jabotinsky. He masks his deeper feelings out of terror of your sympathy. Raised voices and shouted slogans only make him uneasy. He minimizes his disasters. . . ." Weizmann's voice took on a parody of an old Etonian: " 'Ship went down with all hands? Hard luck, old chap.' The Englishman calls his favorite sweet a mere 'trifle.' Yes—the Englishman . . . he understates where the Jew inflates. For we, like our Arab brothers, are cut out of a more garish, Mediterranean cloth. We cry out. We wail at a wall, for a temple we never knew. We forgive God for having made us such weak sinners. We are hypersensitive, excitable, thin-skinned—and want everyone around us to itch when we scratch. But, Mr. Jabotinsky, if we play the Englishman's game by his rules, politely, quietly, modestly— we may win a partnership that can give birth to a homeland. Even a nation."

He came back to the fire and spread his hands above the dying coals. "To achieve our goals—which appear to be the same, Mr. Jabotinsky—we need to apply 'quiet' diplomacy. Rash acts will only hurt us now."

"Quiet, maybe. But not dead," Jabotinsky's voice was shaded with disappointment.

"Dr. Weizmann, we put a flag in your hands, and you give us back a lecture on English manners," Judah said.

"What good is it if we agree and take no action?" Jabotinsky demanded, moving to get his coat. "I thank you for listening."

"Wait, Vladimir. . . ." Judah had been the catalyst to bring these two volatile forces together. Now his mixture was fizzling out. "I ask you, Dr. Weizmann, will you present the idea of forming a Jewish Legion to the War Office?"

"Of course I'll present it. Where are you staying in London, Mr. Jabotinsky?"

Jabotinsky came back from the door, suddenly a little unsure of himself. "At Judah's hotel. But my finances won't keep me there long," Jabotinsky admitted.

"Stay here with me; there's plenty of room," Weizmann offered. "And I'm here only three days a week."

Jabotinsky glanced around the modest accommodations. Weizmann's bedroom was scarcely larger than a cupboard. The sofa in the sitting room would presumably be his. "Do you think you could manage to keep the place a bit warmer?" he asked.

"I am producing acetone, not coal, Mr. Jabotinsky. But you—you are producing an army . . . without even planting dragon's teeth."

Three weeks later, three disappointed men emerged from the British War Office. The sentry eyed them curiously, deciding they didn't merit a salute. Jabotinsky was the first to speak, voice harsh, bitterly mocking.

"They have no time for 'fancy formations.' Oh, very good. What did they think we were offering them—a corps de ballet?"

"I think they were a bit worried about how they would pay for your army," Judah said. "And I think we were unprepared. We had the idea—or rather, you did. But we haven't worked it out. We need a soldier—a professional—to lead the legion. We need a warrior, Vladimir. A warrior. Then, I promise you, I'll help you raise the money to finance the legion. When we go back to the War Office again, they'll accept us."

"What would you say if I told you that I know the right man?" Jabotinsky asked.

"Why the devil didn't you mention it in there?" Judah asked.

"I haven't yet had his letter of agreement," Jabotinsky admitted.

Weizmann leaned on his cane, his polished silk hat perched at a jaunty angle. "You've been staying with me three weeks, Vladimir, and this is the first I've heard of this 'Joshua' of yours."

As they headed down Whitehall toward Trafalgar Square, Jabotinsky told them of a man he'd met in Alexandria. The only Jewish officer in the Czarist Army—a hero who had lost an arm in the Battle of Port Arthur, then drifted to Palestine, where he had lived the life of a pioneer. A strange man. A vegetarian, a pacifist. Yet Jabotinsky was sure that Joseph Trumpeldor would be the right person to command and train the Jewish Legion.

"One arm, eh?" Weizmann mused. His glance traveled up to the figure of Nelson, high on the column above Trafalgar Square. "If a one-armed, one-eyed sailor could win the Battle of Trafalgar—Joseph Trumpeldor has my vote. Raise the money, Judah. Then we'll bring the War Office more than an idea.''

"There's enough raw material in Alexandria to form the basis of our legion. Trumpeldor's not the only Jew who fled from Palestine to Egypt when war broke out.''

"It makes a change,'' Weizmann observed. "Jews, fleeing the Promised Land, *into* Egypt.''

The three laughed together as they boarded a bus bearing a large recruiting poster of Kitchener pointing his finger at every Englishman in sight—and three foreign Jews.

Eleven ─────────────────────────

BERNARD Goldfarb shoved his way through the crush of young men jamming the doorway of the Bronx Presbyterian Christian Endeavor Society Hall.

"No more tickets!" the man yelled after him. Bernard brandished a yellow pasteboard and pushed on.

When Judah Nouari had invited him to the lecture, he hadn't expected to see a turnout like this. He'd never heard of this guy Jabotinsky. Who had? Still, Bernard had a lot of respect for Judah's opinion. A man with so many interests. No question about it, Judah was a great businessman. Bernard's father was thrilled when Judah delivered the contract for their mill to supply cotton and burlap sacks and hundreds of bolts of cloth dyed khaki color to the British. The cotton they were buying from Egypt was traveling from America to England, then going home to Egypt—on the backs of British Tommies who'd be fighting Turks and Germans in Palestine and Mesopotamia. The Goldfarbs' New York factory was even turning out some uniforms for Canada. Bernard had tried on one of the new tunics. He liked the way he looked in it.

The amazing thing about Judah Nouari was how he seemed to have time for everything and everybody. The last time he'd been in New York, Judah had taken Bernard and his parents to a couple of Zionist meetings. When the hat went around, Bernard's father dug deep into his pocket. But Bernard found something deeper. Something that had brought him here.

Now Judah was introducing Jabotinsky to America—and it looked like everybody in the whole organization had come to listen. Which didn't necessarily mean they'd buy it. But they all wanted firsthand news of the war in Europe.

Across the hall, Bernard spotted a couple of young men he knew who had talked about getting into it. Still, nobody was really serious. They were too intent on careers and getting on in the world. Bernard wasn't the only one who felt America was wrong in not getting involved, but nothing seemed to shake President Wilson from neutrality.

"Hey, Barney—what are you doing here?" It was Ike Blumenthal, ex-Columbia first-string halfback.

"Same as you." He sat down by Ike. "Heard you were thinking of getting married?"

"Yeah. That's why I'm here. Looking for a way to get out of it." The two laughed.

Judah had told Bernard a little about Jabotinsky's Jewish Legion. The idea had stirred Bernard. Maybe he needed something to dream about—something to erase the memory of Jacqueline.

It had been well over a year since that last, terrible day he saw her. He knew she had another child now. In his heart he wished her well—hoped she'd be happy. But he knew that no one would ever take her place, even though now he could go whole weeks at a time without thinking about her. The anguish of those months had turned him toward a second look at his religion. His mother was delighted when he started going to services. But a long beard didn't make a rabbi, and attending synagogue didn't make you religious.

Bernard's days at the mill seemed to be taking him nowhere. At night he'd go out for a couple of beers and a club sandwich with one of his friends. He'd postpone going to bed, because he knew Jacqueline would be waiting. He would dream they were making love—and it would be almost the way it had been. Too real. But somehow the climax would be interrupted. Or, inexplicably, she would merge into a girl he'd been madly in love with when he was fourteen. Dark-eyed Maria, fifteen and Italian. Sometimes she'd let him walk her home, or take her to the vaudeville. Once, he'd kissed her outside the candy store. Once, she let him touch her breast. Then, for no reason, she got angry with him and wouldn't let him take her out any more.

"*Shiksas,*" his mother had said, as though that explained everything. "Someday, Barney, you'll meet a nice Jewish girl." That was the trouble: he had, and they were.

But why did his dreams mix up that faraway Maria with

still-too-near Jacqueline? Sometimes he'd wake up from a wet dream. He really would have to move out of his parents' apartment. Find a room of his own. Hell, he could afford an apartment now! Did he have to put up with his mother's voice soaring into the breakfast room: "What's the world coming to, Herschel? Again, this morning, Bernard has made his own bed!"

And his father's sour retort: "At twenty-five, what an accomplishment!"

Bernard's attention was jogged back to the present by the arrival of Judah Nouari on the podium. He was introducing Jabotinsky: dressed in paramilitary uniform—wraparound puttees bound spindly calves beneath flaring breeches. He wore no ribbons, but a Sam Browne belt crossed his chest. Jabotinsky carried a walking stick, which Bernard thought very affected. Still, he was European. The speaker removed his cap with a slight flourish. His features were small, upper lip long, chin jutting slightly forward. But, however short of a warrior image Jabotinsky might fall, nobody in that vast hall cared, once the man started to speak. His presence ignited excitement.

Bernard realized that all his life he had been a searcher. Now perhaps he had found what he was looking for. And somewhere beyond that goalpost—a battlefield worth dying on.

"Like I told Mrs. Hammadi: 'Sure I can teach yah to drive. But it's the other guy I can't teach. Besides, I can't do it widout I tell the boss. 'Cause suppose somethin' went wrong? Some gink bangs into your car—what happens to me?' What I mean, Mr. Hammadi—I told yer missus, 'When yer behind the wheel, it's just like sittin' on the tail of a comet.' Hell, these buggies can do nearly forty miles an hour! You don't know what's comin', and what's comin' don't know nei-ther." He glanced over his shoulder. "You want I should teach her, Mr. Hammadi?"

"I'll let you know when I've decided, Tony." But Mohamed had. He would never allow Jacqueline behind the wheel of a car.

"And another t'ing," Tony rambled on. "You got these new taxicabs all over the road. Anyone can ride for a 'jitney.'

But them hackies'll never catch on. If a guy can't afford a chauffeur, he oughtta walk.''

Mohamed smiled. "You're a born snob, Tony—and what's a 'jitney'?''

Tony took that as a compliment. "A nickel, boss. Five cents. What Vice-President Marshall says this country oughtta pay for a good cigar.'' He pulled up in front of the house on Sixtieth Street. Mohamed drew a cigar from his breast pocket.

"Here's a fifty-cent one, Tony. Smoke it slowly. And pick me up at six-thirty tomorrow. I'll be taking the morning train to Washington from Penn Station.''

Jacqueline heard Mohamed come in. But he went directly to the library to take a phone call. From Washington—as so many were these days. This Jacqueline found odd. Even suspicious. Mohamed had only just come back from Washington the day before. He was returning there tomorrow. Seeing somebody called Colonel House. Now House was calling him. Another house call. . . . It made her giggle. Then it troubled her.

There were so many things she found odd and suspicious these days. In Mohamed. In herself. When she could stand outside herself, as the new psychiatrist was trying to make her do.

Mohamed had come in the front door and walked directly to the library. He hadn't come into the drawing room and so hadn't seen her uniform. Yes, uniform. The gray and white of the Red Cross Auxiliary Unit. She opened the carved wooden drawing-room doors in time to see his back disappear. She wanted to tell him how she would knit sweaters of trench-colored brown for their Canadian neighbors. And mufflers, and socks, and helmets, and roll bandages. When she would attend the Red Cross sessions at the Astor Hotel. At her convenience, of course, they had assured her. But the uniform was "divinely flattering, darling,'' everyone insisted. This was no fantasy. Every mirror she came near confirmed it.

Neat folds of the headdress fell to her shoulders. Like a holy order. A Sister of Charity. "Mrs. Hammadi, the Generous,'' everyone said . . . "the Beautiful,''—"the Giving.'' But to Jacqueline, her consecration had meant something more: an exit from boredom. She might even join an ambulance unit. In France—for wasn't she French? And wouldn't she become a truly superb driver under the tutelage of Tony? Françoise was two years old now. Quite self-reliant. Nanny could cope with her. Maurice was eleven, and at boarding school most of the time. They didn't need her. But the warriors did. In the theater of her mind she was already speeding down a shell-pocked road between decapitated trees and gutted farmhouses in a war-maimed landscape—with a load of heroes fresh from Flanders Fields. Heroes—all handsome—all grateful to their heavenly angel of mercy when they recovered consciousness in some field hospital to an orchestration of rumbling artillery fire. And then there might be a day when the encroaching shell bursts disintegrated her vehicle in a puff of German smoke and she would awaken among her maimed heroes—with a Croix de Guerre pinned to her blanket and Mohamed leaning over her, his tears spilling down to fall on her cheek. As all the love he felt for her overflowed into one grand final *mea culpa* plea of forgiveness for neglect and infidelities. And each would finally know there had only been the other. . . .

And this had become for her more and more true. After Bernard, her desire for erotic adventuring seemed to have diminished. After Bernard . . . . After Mohamed gave her Françoise . . . Forgive me, Father, for I have. . . .

"Nanny wishes to know if Madame will go up to say good night to Mademoiselle Françoise?" Gilles's voice brought her back to the realities of time and place.

She nodded. "When I have spoken to Monsieur. If he ever gets off the phone!" Bad form to reveal sarcasm before the servants. The doorbell pealed. Gilles moved sedately to open it. She followed him into the hall.

Judah. . . . In a uniform. Without insignia. Carrying a small overnight case.

"What have you joined?" she asked.

He smiled at her, setting the bag on the floor. "I'm only in training. In upstate New York."

"Is America in the war? They didn't mention it at the Red Cross."

Judah laughed. "And *you* look fetching. How long have you been doing that?"

"Long enough for Mohamed not to have noticed." She put an arm through his, leading him into the drawing room with a confidential air. "I'm going to drive an ambulance."

"In New York? Isn't that dangerous?"

"Perhaps . . . but Tony's going to teach me to drive."

"That *is* dangerous." He sat facing her. She favored him with an extra warmth in her smile. Nothing special. Just what happened automatically in the presence of men. Judah was pleased to see her looking so well. Quite (that awful word that one had come to apply to Jacqueline in her good times) normal.

"You've come to see Mohamed, of course. I quite understand it isn't me that brings you to this house. . . ."

Perhaps "normal" was premature. . . .

"Mohamed lives on the telephone these days. And now they've started transcontinental service, it's become an obsession." She lowered her voice. "Sometimes I think he's a little mad. You know," she confided, twirling a finger beside her temple.

Judah smiled politely. "I've been on the receiving end of a few of those calls, Jacqueline. All important business, I assure you."

"Just like men to stick together. How's Ruth?" she asked. "She does write, I suppose?"

"Can't get her to budge out of Paris. She says she's keeping the home fires burning. But I'm going to arrange to move her and the children south, to Bordeaux. Von Kluck's drive was barely stopped in the suburbs. Would you believe it? They had to rush French reserves out in taxicabs!" His face turned serious. "It's bound to get worse."

Her hand moved spontaneously to touch him.

"What is your uniform, Judah?"

Firm steps moved in from the library to the accompanying beat of young feet. Maurice, home for the weekend, claiming his brief moment with his father.

"Papa's brought me a gun, Mamam. . . ." Maurice held up a fine scale model of a machine gun. "It's exactly like the real ones!"

"I hope it doesn't shoot," Jacqueline said.

"The real ones will, Maman." He aimed it at a crystal chandelier. "Hock the Kaiser. Bang bang blam!"

Mohamed regarded Judah with some surprise. "Hello! What are you dressed up for?"

Judah glanced at Jacqueline and the boy. "Could we go to your study?"

"You might allow my husband to notice my existence before you take him away." Jacqueline was in one of her coy moods.

Mohamed kissed her on the cheek. "Gray suits you, my dear. But pouting doesn't." Judah noted that the dark points of Mohamed's temples were touched by the first frost of silver gray. The chairman of Hammadi-Nouari showing an early hint of autumn in the years—and both of them just past their thirties.

"Sorry, Jacqueline," Judah said.

"Stay for dinner," she urged. Standing in her stiff gray-and-white uniform beneath her own vivid full-length portrait, painted wearing soft creamy lace, posed between two greyhounds, the real Jacqueline seemed diminished, fragile. But, as always, beautiful.

"Love to, but I can't," he replied, patting Maurice's shoulder as he followed his partner out.

She looked after the retreating Mohamed. Tears came into her eyes. *"Ay! je vous aime! Je vous aime! Vous entendez? Je suis fou de vous. Je sui fou. . . ."*

Maurice drifted toward the butler's pantry, pausing to point his model gun toward an imaginary attack, rattling a blast in his throat. "Yuk ka kuk ka kuk ka kuk!"

"Please, Maurice—my nerves aren't very good today."

"But, Maman—it's a working model of the ones Papa makes in Spain. Look what it can do." He pulled the trigger, aiming it at her with a series of small, rattling clacks. "Bang!" he shouted.

"Don't point that at me! Ever!" Jacqueline seized it and slapped him hard. He stepped back, stunned. She stared at him; then her voice came under control. "Go play chess with Gilles. That's quiet." Then, in a sudden panic, she rushed out into the hall, heading up the stairs. Her gray cotton headdress fell unnoticed.

He heard the door of her room slam closed and started slowly after her. On the staircase was the fallen headdress. Maurice picked it up, wiping a tear on it. Then he caught his reflection in the staircase mirror and put the headdress on. Adjusting the folds carefully around his shoulders, he regarded himself with curious concentration.

"Go play chess with Gilles." His mother's voice echoed from his lips as though she had spoken through him.

In the library, the partners faced each other for a long moment. Mohamed broke the silence.

"What do you want me to say, Judah? I couldn't agree with your request; I found it ill-advised. I had to make a decision. I made it."

"And that's the end of it?" Judah swallowed his drink and some anger with it.

"I'm still chairman."

"The Turks are our enemies," Judah said.

"Not mine, Judah. I intend to honor our deliveries of arms. I must. Turks still rule Palestine—and they are clients of Hammadi-Nouari."

"But you're living in America now," Judah protested.

"America isn't in the war. This country hasn't taken sides. In fact, some people in Washington are saying the United States should come in on the German side." Mohamed's face was passive.

"I thought I knew you, Mohamed. As a Palestinian—do you want the Turks there forever?"

"Maybe not. I'd prefer an Arab government," Mohamed replied. "But, for the present, we must live with the Turks. You know as well as I that unless we honor our Turkish commitments, Hammadi-Nouari could be wiped out of the Middle East."

Judah rose. "Mohamed, you asked me about this uniform I'm wearing. I'm going to serve in the Zion Mule Corps. We'll be fighting beside British troops. Against the Turks."

Mohamed burst into sharp laughter. "Your Zionist version of the Foreign Legion? So you finally managed it! And do the mules wear *yarmulkes*? Or doesn't it matter whether they're Jewish? Really, Judah, you should visit Jacqueline's doctor. Take some pills. A holiday in Atlantic City. Forget it."

Judah was upset by the strength of the anger he felt. "You're the one who's burying your head in sand, Mohamed. The British War Office is taking us seriously. Very seriously."

"Who's in command? Baron Rothschild—in a saddle behind his desk in the bank?"

"There's no necessity to be insulting."

"If it will bring you to your senses, there is." Mohamed frowned at his friend. He saw that Judah was serious. "Does Ruth know about this?"

Judah shook his head. "Not yet. But it may be the first

thing I've done that will really please her. She is a dedicated Zionist, you know."

Mohamed's tone changed. "Now you want to turn Palestine into a rubbish bin for the refuse of Europe with the support of the British Government? I intend to see that Hammadi-Nouari remains neutral. It's good business. It makes sense."

"You call Hispañola-Nacional's exports *neutrality?*" Judah's voice was rising.

"The British can buy from us, too. They already do. Egyptian cotton for uniforms."

"And shall we sell them cedar coffins from Lebanon to bury the dead from your Spanish-made bullets?" Judah rose. "I intend to bring this before the board."

"Don't do it, Judah," Mohamed replied grimly. "I'll skin you alive. Jerusalem and Damascus are 100 percent behind me. Ask your father what the Turks would do if we cut their lifeline."

Judah paused. He knew Mohamed was right. That was always Judah's trouble: seeing both sides.

"In that case, I offer my resignation as of now. I want nothing more to do with the Company."

"And that means, presumably, your family and your friends." Mohamed faced him. "You're backing the wrong horse, Judah. In the end the British won't support the Zionists, you know."

"Why not? Why do you think not?"

"Because we Arabs won't let them."

"It has nothing to do with Arabs!" Judah flared.

"Oh, hasn't it? If you weren't so blind in your worship of Weizmann—the great Zionist who's never been to Palestine— you'd realize that Arab military aid is also an important issue to your British playmates."

Mohamed's voice softened with the decision to reveal more than he had meant to. "There's something I haven't told you. I've been appointed as personal consultant on Arab affairs to Colonel House, President Wilson's unofficial ambassador at large. So I don't have to lie on the desert with my ear to the sand to hear the rumble of another army. An Arab Legion, Judah. Who are also shopping for a nation—from the highest bidder."

There was a knock on the door. Annoyed at the interruption, Mohamed stepped to open it. It was Gilles, offering a sealed envelope on a salver.

"Thank you, Gilles." He turned back as the butler closed the door behind him. "One of the dividends of my Washington connection. News dispatches before they reach the press. Curious, they missed noting your Jewish mules." He slid his paper knife under the sealed flap, drawing out a slip of paper. It contained two sentences. Mohamed's face was grim as he passed it to Judah. A curious smile twisted his lips. "It seems you win, Judah. By a German torpedo."

"MAY 7, 1915 . . . STEAMER LUSITANIA TORPEDOED AND SUNK BY GERMAN SUBMARINE STOP 1,100 DROWNED INCLUDING MANY AMERICANS STOP," Judah read.

"Even Wilson won't stay neutral now," Mohamed acknowledged.

Judah's eyes lifted from the report. "Then, you'll stop supplying the Turks?"

"Of course. On the day Wilson declares war."

"I wonder how long that will take."

Mohamed came over to his partner, resting a hand on his shoulder. "Forget the war games, Judah. Put on a business suit. Come back to the office. We'll need you now more than ever."

"I can't. There are answers I've got to find. And I don't even know the right questions. It's like when I was young—in *shul*—and we had to argue with the word of God. You just couldn't accept. You had to oppose every side. To find the truth. Hit it with a hammer—like a miner trying to find a vein of gold in a rock. You kept hitting, hitting, until the sound was right, and you knew. This"—he touched his new uniform—"is my way of searching."

Mohamed sighed. In his heart he knew he had never been able to change Judah's mind about anything. Judah was the only one who could do that. "You crazy *Yid*," he said. "Just don't get your ass shot off."

He refilled their two glasses and passed one across to Judah. Judah lifted his in toast. "To the Jewish Legion."

"And its most stubborn Hebrew mule. And to the truth—which I hope we both find—out of all this. Allah protect you." He started to lift his glass, then slowly emptied it into a bowl of flowers. "An Arab—even a renegade like me—can't pray and drink in the same moment."

"Take care of yourself, Arab." Judah clasped his hand.

"Come back safe, Jew."

The rowboat pulled away from the transport riding at anchor in the Gulf of Saros north of Gabatepe, off the shore of Gallipoli. It was the fourth transport Lieutenant Judah Nouari had visited that evening. He was discouraged.

Bernard Goldfarb, khaki military shirt sleeves rolled up to his armpits, dragged the oars expertly through the dark waters.

"Where the hell has the British quartermaster hidden our mules? I wonder." Judah grumbled. He'd been looking for them since the fleet sailed from Alexandria—and before.

Bernard glanced up at the waning moon. "Don't think we can make it to the next ship, Judah. Tide's against us."

"All right. Head back."

Bernard dug in one oar, neatly swiveling the bow around. Dimly in the fading light, Judah could just make out the silhouette of their own ship, its stacks like miniature skyscrapers against the evening sky. His glance came back to Bernard's face—almost glowing in the moonlight. To the American, this invasion seemed more like a college game. One in which he could earn another white letter.

But Judah was feeling gnawing doubts. How had he gotten himself into this? He, a cool-headed banker, swept away on Jabotinsky's words. Mohamed was right. He didn't belong here. He should be sitting behind a desk, summoning a secretary with a touch of his buzzer—instead of searching through a fleet for a shipload of missing mules. His involvement with Zionism should have been limited to the magic art of raising money. Wasn't that what he did best? And since the *Lusitania*'s sinking had failed to stir the United States from outrage to action, Mohamed (maintaining the neutrality of the Spanish arms factory) was continuing to turn out weapons for Turkey. Weapons that could be shooting at Judah in the morning.

What neither of them could know was that it would take another two years for American pacifism to give way to a declaration of war. Two more years of sinkings, sabotage, and intrigue. But this was still 1915. The Western Front had fallen into a paralysis of trench warfare. Britain and France were deadlocked with Germany. Italians and Austrians, snow-bound in the Alps. The Russians reeling after losing 750,000 men—thus tempting Bulgaria into the arms of the Central Powers. Allied hopes languished in confusion and despair.

This was the climate in Britain when a rising young ex-journalist, ex-soldier, now First Lord of the Admiralty, had a vision. How to pick a deadlock by a daring thrust through a lightly guarded back door. The Dardanelles—that narrow passage to Constantinople. What a convenient "needle's eye" through which to thread a fleet. Slip through it, and one might reduce Turkey's feeble forts, capture her capital, thereby cutting off the source of supplies and knocking Turkey off the plate.

Of course the Dardanelles. . . .

As a sensible insurance policy, the floridly handsome states-man, with Kitchener's blessing invited Russia's participation. However, the Grand Duke Nicholas saw fit to decline a combined Allied operation. Much as the bear might require rescue from his current attack of "German measles," the invalid feared the doctor's bill more than the disease.

Strapped as they were for manpower and equipment, Brit-ain and France had been forced to take on the venture alone. Their combined fleets sailed in, blasted the Turkish forts, and sailed out—straight into an unobserved minefield. In less than three minutes, they'd lost some six ships, with three more put out of action. Churchill turned back to Kitchener. No passage through the Dardanelles could be safely effected without army assistance. An amphibious operation was essential.

And that was what had brought Judah to Gallipoli. . . .

They had sailed from Alexandria, where Joseph Trumpeldor, commanding the Zion Mule Corps with the modest rank of captain, had joined the British Fleet staging for Gallipoli. Judah and Bernard, traveling together from New York along with other volunteers, had joined the ex-Russian officer to board one of the transports. Well recommended by Jabotinsky, who was Trumpeldor's acting adjutant, Judah was given the rank of lieutenant and the assignment of quartermaster and intelligence officer in charge of supplies and information. He did not feel qualified for either task.

Judah first glimpsed Captain Trumpeldor emerging from a companionway onto the deck, one jacket sleeve pinned closed on his chest beneath a cluster of faded Russian decorations. He was a giant of a man: tall, with a large head, enormous eyes, upper lids chiseled deep into the sockets, a straight nose, full lips, and a strong jaw. The effect was impressive—features on the heroic scale, as though carved by destiny.

Trumpeldor surveyed the chaos of loading. "A porridge of mismanagement," he sighed. "They've separated wagons from horses, guns from ammunition, even fuses from shells. And most important, us from our mules." Trumpeldor shook his head. "If the Germans were in charge of this loading, they couldn't have done better to ensure an Allied disaster." His voice was a charcoal deep rumble. "The first thing I want you to do, Lieutenant Nouari, is to find our mules. They appear to have been left off the manifest. Let's hope they weren't left off a ship."

Find the mules. This Judah had been trying to do for over a week. When he reported his failure back to Trumpeldor, his commanding officer was surprisingly sympathetic.

"The fault starts at the top, Nouari," he said.

He was referring to Sir Ian Hamilton, the commander-in-chief, who had not himself made a very impressive entrance on the stage of operations. The rumor had gone around that Hamilton had left London so hastily that not a single member of his staff had come with him. "Hamilton carries a three-year-old handbook on the Turkish Army, an outdated map of the area, and no intelligence reports. They say the War Office's last-minute search of London bookstores for informative material about our enemy was not blessed with success," Trumpeldor said bleakly.

Jabotinsky, who had been standing with Judah, looked across at the Aussie troops lounging on the lower deck, playing cards and one up. "Kitchener has been generous to this expedition, Captain Trumpeldor. He has donated his greenest Australians and New Zealanders. Raw fellows, fresh from the Outback. Still, I wish we had another division of them."

Trumpeldor eyed them. "They're rugged men. They'll do well."

"We've also inherited a division of unseasoned British Infantry—and I understand the French have donated their dregs," Jabotinsky went on.

"What more could we expect? Their best *poilus* can't be

spared from the trenches.'' Trumpeldor exhaled smoke through flaring nostrils. ''We must make do, Ze'ev, we must make do.'' It was the nick-name Jabotinsky's friends always used.

''There's one division of British regulars,'' Judah put in. ''The 29th, from India, were just arriving when I came.''

Trumpeldor nodded. ''We'll be in good company. Not one of our own corps has ever been in combat—including the mules you haven't found, Lieutenant.'' He looked across at the groups of Jewish volunteers. Among those playing cards and cleaning rifles could be seen a few wrapped in blue, white, and gray *tallisim*—the fringed prayer shawls—praying or reading the Torah. ''Look at them—our warriors. Now they study. But the Torah is like this sea. You don't study it—you swim in it.''

''Doesn't the Torah say the purpose of learning is living?'' Judah asked.

Trumpeldor's face warmed into a smile. ''You're right, Nouari. And I wouldn't trade one of my men for the Coldstream Guards. We won't just be fighting Turks and Germans. We'll be taking the first step to Zion. For this we must be . . .'' Trumpeldor paused ''. . . historic. And in Palestine we will father a generation of men who will be like bars of iron. Elastic, but of iron.''

A bar of iron, Judah knew he definitely was not. And the expedition had progressed with great difficulty. Having steamed out of Alexandria—they had steamed right back again. The initial loading had been so disorganized that Sir Ian Hamilton properly ordered, ''Go back and do it all over again.''

But they had reached the eve of battle. Still muleless, Judah and Bernard Goldfarb rowed their small boat through the Gulf of Saros. It bobbed among the tall ships of the Royal Naval Division in a night warmed by gentle seductive breezes.

Finally Bernard pulled alongside their own transport. ''What do they call this place, the Gulf of Sorrows?'' Bernard asked, shipping his oars. ''Tomorrow we'll make those Turks shed a few tears.''

''If Trumpeldor doesn't kill us first. My God, we can't tell him we've failed again.''

''What else can we tell him?'' Bernard grinned. ''To use dolphins? There are plenty of them.'' He seized the bottom rung of the rope ladder. ''After you, Lieutenant.''

Judah scrambled upward. He wished he could share Bernard's buoyant enthusiasm. For Bernard, destiny lay over on that shore behind the strip of sand beach—the rough cliffs, the brush-clad hills.

On deck, they made their way through crowds of uneasy troops to the railing. "Aren't you looking forward to tomorrow, Judah?" Bernard asked.

"Not particularly," Judah confessed, spotting Jabotinsky. They joined him.

Jabotinsky's manner was crisp. "The mules—where are they? What ship?"

Judah shook his head. "Ze'ev, I wish I could invent them. So far, we're still a mule corps without mules."

"My God, what a mess!" Jabotinsky's field glasses made a sweep of the shoreline. He was finding it both hard and easy to imagine the presence of an enemy. Hard, because the unknown shoreline appeared so empty. Easy, because the endless reloading in Alexandria could not have failed to alert every Turk and German. "It won't come as a surprise—that the British are coming tomorrow," he grumbled. "Sir Ian has seen to that."

Judah nodded. "One of the British staff officers even gave his postal address as 'H.Q. British Expeditionary Force, Constantinople.'"

Jabotinsky shook his head. "Then, it won't take Clausewitz to figure out where we're heading.

"I wonder how many divisions they've got waiting for us." Weaving his binoculars along the darkened landfall, Jabotinsky could find nothing. He lowered them again, turning back to the others. "What do you think happened to the mules?"

"Somebody may have got them mixed up with the cavalry mounts—or the supply wagons. They'll have to put them ashore somewhere. Wherever—I'll find them. Mules eventually let you know where they are."

Jabotinsky turned his attention back to the dark mass of cliff above the pale beach. "Zion Mule Corps. What a support unit we'll be! We'll have to carry supplies up to the perimeter on our backs!"

Behind, they heard Trumpeldor's deep voice. "Our forces will be hitting five beaches before dawn."

"How can Hamilton land seventy-five thousand men unexpectedly? At this very moment, a hundred, maybe a thousand pairs of German field glasses are trained on us." Jabotinsky was exasperated.

"Then, they must be an army of owls," Judah said. "We're over five miles from that shore."

Trumpeldor nodded. "And our worst enemy could be the dark. Darkness makes confusion."

The heavy, deep splash of the two anchors chopped through water. Trumpeldor mounted a box of life preservers to address the men. "I've just come from a staff meeting. A volunteer is dead. A strong swimmer. It's a dangerous mission. Whoever volunteers may not make it. He'll have to cover five miles through strong currents."

There was a silence.

Bernard stepped forward. "I swam for my university, sir. I could make it."

Trumpeldor eyed him. "Goldfarb, aren't you?"

"Yes, sir. And I've swum farther than this off Long Island—currents stronger than this."

Trumpeldor nodded. "You'll be carrying your equipment and a sack of flares on your back." He stepped down, taking Bernard aside. "I want the flares spaced out on the beach. Light them, and get yourself into a hold in the cliff—if you can find one."

"I'll dig one if I have to, sir."

Watching Bernard clamber down the landing net, Judah wished he could have found some exactly right words to say to his American friend. Nothing seemed appropriate. Bernard descended swiftly rung by rung, knapsack bound to naked shoulders. A sailor steadied him into the stern sheets of a bobbing boat. He'd be rowed a distance from the ship.

Oars stirred murky water. Judah whispered a brief prayer for the swimmer. Beside him, a Cockney corporal shook his head. "There's a bloke who never learned the first rule of war."

"What's that?" Judah asked.

"Never volunteer."

For days, Judah had been trying to fathom his own feelings. He'd even made a mental list. Excitement? Yes. Fear? Yes. But more, the fear that he might fail the others. He hadn't even been able to locate the mules. Eighty mules. . . .

And so for combat, he knew that he's be scared enough when things began to happen. He just wanted to be up to it. In his life he'd never been able to kill anything. Could he now—when his life might depend on it?

And something else: There was a sense of unreality. It seemed to surround them all—separating them from their personal pasts into one joint present. These fledgling fighting men of the Mule Corps—perhaps they had the least to lose, the most to gain. For them alone, the stakes were clear. The prize, Zion. He had listened to Trumpeldor talking to the men about the future in Palestine.

"If there is a need to dig the earth, we will dig. If there is a need to defend ourselves, we will be soldiers. We will follow only one rule, one law: to build. A road—a house—a village—a farm—a nation."

How Judah envied Trumpeldor and Jabotinsky their certainty! To see past the sowing—to the harvest.

Judah knew in his heart that those few weeks of training—marksmanship, bayonet practice, calisthenics, logistics—couldn't turn him into a soldier. All theory, until you lived it. Practice was never performance. But tonight, sometime before dawn, he and all the others would find their own reality. He gazed over at Jabotinsky leaning against the rail, peering through his binoculars like a man in the forest box at the opera. The small Russian dropped the glasses to his chest, glancing across at Judah—a man in search of an attitude. Jabotinsky was about to go onstage, and the director had not yet handed him his role.

The familiar silhouette of Trumpeldor could be seen on the upper deck beside the troop commander. Had they buried his arm at Port Arthur, where he had performed such acts of courage against the Japanese that his Russian colleagues chose to forget their gallant brother officer was a Jew? Trumpeldor. . . . His very name conveyed a distant sounding of bugles, battle cries, the crackle of wind-stretched flags. Trumpeldor. . . . Almost a prototype. The perfect man-at-arms. Aloof, confident, wise in the art of conquest and survival. A breed unchanged through a hundred incarnations on centuries of battlefields.

He came down to them. "We'll be loading into the boats soon. Everyone should have two canteens of water." His eyes found Judah. "Nouari. . . . Those mules? When you get ashore, you'll have no excuse for not finding them. Detail three men with you. If you *can't* find them, you might as well join the Turks."

"Yes, sir."

Judah nodded to a young private he'd come to know. "David Grien—you'll go with me. Do you know what a mule looks like?"

"It's larger than a needle in a haystack, sir," Grien replied.

Judah detailed two others to join them. The young private stepped up to him. "Could I have a word with you, sir?"

"What is it, David?"

He offered Judah a letter. "It's to my mother and father. In Plonsk. I'm giving out ten copies. Somebody—in case I don't make it—should see it gets mailed. You see, I left against their will to go to Palestine."

"Why did you do that, David?" Judah asked.

The reply came with youthful pomposity. It was a speech he had no doubt rehearsed on his parents. "Because I intend to build a model society—based on social, economic, and political equality."

"Single-handed?" Judah smiled.

The young man was embarrassed. "Naturally, I'll only be a part of it. If I live. Oh, and incidentally, if you see my name's different on the envelope. It *is* mine. You see, I've changed it. From Grien."

Judah glanced at the envelope in the faint light of a swaying lantern: Private David Ben-Gurion. Jewish Legion. British Expeditionary Force.

"Ben-Gurion. . . ."

"It means . . . son of the lion."

Judah smiled again. "A lion may be very useful by morning. Particularly to find a mule. Oh, and incidentally, we're not yet the Jewish Legion, David. Our British Army designation will be 38th, 39th, 40th battalions of the Royal Fusiliers."

"Some of the troops are also calling us by another name, sir."

"Really? What's that?"

"The Judeans."

Judah glanced out across the dark water toward the distant shore. Bernard had been gone nearly an hour now. If he didn't make it—Judah blamed himself already for having brought the young American into it. He hadn't expected such an enthusiastic response. But then, after all, wasn't that why he'd taken Jabotinsky to America? To kindle fires in the mind. Oh, it was easy to sway young men with brave words. But had anyone the right to become the compass of another's life?

Bernard couldn't tell how long he'd been in the water. Powerful strokes brought him, it seemed, no nearer. He felt the persistent drag of the heavy current, like a black element trying to swallow him. Arms and legs fought to oppose the pull. Beyond the rocks, before the steepening cliffs, the beach seemed to waggle a pale finger of encouragement. On the water behind him, the moon was a drowning ghost. Off somewhere to the right, a naval barrage rumbled lightning flashes at the next beach. Bernard tried to concentrate on the shore, but words drifted into mind. . . .

Oh, the moon is a golden galleon. . . . The image of his lit. prof. reciting verse—large-boned, pedagogic, a brainstormed fanatic in bifocals. *Doubt, Bernard. Only the dead or the sleeping accept gently.* Or the drowning . . . ? *Melville, Bernard. Until you have wept for his whale, humanity cannot touch you in the heart. Awake, Bernard. Learn to feel. Then think.* . . .

Awake, Bernard. . . . He was falling asleep. *I am in the process, sir, of awakening. My arms and legs are moving. Wake up, sleeping beauty, in the Rip of a Winkle.* . . . He had never expected the tide to be this strong. The pack on his back weighed him down.

Big white C on its field of dusty blue. Letterman. *Roar, lion, roar.* . . . *Awake the echoes in the Hudson Valley. Fight on for victory ever more. While the sons of Knickerbocker rally 'round Columbia.* . . . He shortened his stroke. Columbia swimming team—against the Gulf of Sorrows. . . . Slow crawl. Breaststroke. *Stretch those arms, Bernard. Kick! Kick! Kick!*

He was tiring. He had been mad to boast. Piece of cake. . . . The pain again. In his arms. In his chest. Ache. Ache. Ache. Shoulders. Leg. Oh, God, a cramp. . . . Float. Don't panic. He flipped over on his back. Guns thundered from the next beach. Hear, O Israel, the Lord our God, the Lord is One. . . .

He forced himself to think of all the girls he'd known. But they all blended into Jacqueline. Oh, God, if she had only not been what she was. Or if they'd met in another time. He swallowed a gulp of salt water. Liquid serpent of death. Muscles beyond aching now. Sleep. Sleep on the tide. The womb of waters. And yet so near that the sea beard foamed upon sand.

They cast loose from their tows. Each group, with a steam picket boat as its head, was drawing in to shore.

"The flares . . . !" Ben-Gurion shouted.

Trumpeldor stood up in the stern sheets for a better view. A low cheer went up from the boats.

The green, gold, orange, red fire blossoms blooming upward showed them where they were to land. But it meant something much more to Judah. Bernard was alive.

Nearly dawn. Judah glanced at his watch. Four twenty-five. Forty-eight boats breasted the last fifty yards to touch grinding bottom. Judah found himself sprawling out among a crush of men crazy to get ashore. Men splashed over the gunwales, cursing and sloshing toward dry land. Screams of agony came from behind him.

"Underwater barbed wire . . . !"

"Christ, get me free . . ."

Judah helped drag one man from the submerged, rusting, ensnaring coils, the legging torn, the leg a crimson protrusion. Soldiers were being dragged down by their frantic efforts to free themselves. A body floated in, bumping against Judah. Somebody shouted for a stretcher bearer, but they weren't yet ashore.

Then it came: the terrible stutter of machine-gun fire and the crack of rifles. Deep coughs of mortar fire and geysering bursts. Judah staggered onto the beach. He could not explain his own sense of exhaustion in those first moments. A spatter of tracer fire came off the cliff, marking the direction of the bullets.

"Get your bloody heads down," somebody yelled. He found himself on the ground in a pile of bodies. Some of the Mule Corps men began firing back. He freed himself to move on. He'd lost sight of Trumpeldor but felt relieved to see Ben-Gurion and his detail still with him.

"Landing craft—coming in down the beach," he called. They stumbled on in search of the mules.

But when they got to the barges, they found only a few terrified horses rearing and plunging as cavalrymen tried to lead them ashore.

"Seen Hare's 86th, Lieutenant?" a British soldier called over.

"They're supposed to have landed on 'W' beach."

"This is 'W', isn't it?"

"It better be 'Y'." He moved on with his detail close behind. The gunfire was heavier now. A soldier dropped right across his path. Judah stopped long enough to pull the man behind the shelter of a beach boulder.

"Second wave coming in," Ben-Gurion shouted. "Maybe they've got our mules."

The wounded Anzac was clutching Judah's arm. Judah looked down at him and met eyes filled with terror. A New Zealander. Scarcely eighteen. Judah turned back at his detail. "Keep going!"

The lad was trying to reach something under his shirt. Judah unbuttoned it. There, on a chain, a silver crucifix was tinted with the boy's blood. Judah pressed it into the lad's hand. He was dying. A prayer came to mind, memorized so long ago. Judah repeated it now. "I am thy Rock, thy Rod, thy Staff. Through Me shall ye walk through darkness into the light of life eternal. For by My death—all men may find salvation. And by My blood that fell from the Cross, all men shall be washed clean. . . ."

Farther down the beach, out of the line of fire, Judah caught sight of several medics moving about lazily, bringing empty stretchers ashore. "Over here!" he shouted. Two came at a trot.

Judah headed back to find his own detail. A shell screamed overhead as he loped along. He flattened, waiting for the burst. It came, covering him with sand and rubble. He picked himself up and moved forward again.

Where had he learned that prayer? Certainly not in any synagogue. Was it on the sheet of paper the priest had given them in Jerusalem, that day so long ago? He remembered that it was after he and Mohamed lost their crusader's cross. One afternoon when the sun scalded the streets, they wandered into the Christian Quarter, pausing before the Church of the

Holy Sepulchre, gazing up at its domes and crosses. Out of the heavy frame of doors, black-robed monks streamed past them. An ominous procession of mysterious figures, faces shadowed by cowls.

"You know what's in there? Crosses ten times as big as the one we lost," Mohamed pronounced.

"Have you been in there?" Judah demanded.

"Of course not. It's forbidden."

"Then, how do you know?"

"I'll show you." Mohamed grabbed Judah's arm, pulling his reluctant companion through the great doors. It was there the priest found the two small boys staring up at the polychrome figure of Jesus on the huge altar cross. Seeing the fear in their eyes, the father had taken them into his study and explained the meaning of Jesus and the cross to Christians. And of salvation.

"But this salvation—could a Jew or a Mohammedan also get it?" Judah asked him.

"If you believe in your own faith and follow it, I am confident that salvation will not be denied you," the priest replied. "We are all children of the same Father." That was when he gave them the copy of the printed prayer. Mohamed hid it in his pocket and took it to the moat outside the city wall where they had found the cross. Then they sat on the wall until they had memorized it. Finally, they dropped the torn bits of paper to flutter downward into the dry moat. But Judah had not thought he would ever use that prayer. And yet tonight he remembered it.

Pouring sweat, throat so dry he couldn't swallow, he paused to take a deep swig from one of his canteens.

"Save that, Nouari. It'll be a long day." It was Trumpeldor. Judah had reached the Mule Corps men at the base of the cliff. Day was lifting a slow curtain no a nightmare landscape. Great flashes filled the sky where the British sixty-pounders bashed the cliffs. Bodies—and parts of them—were strewn across the beach. He fought back nausea.

"The mules?" Trumpeldor asked.

"Not yet, Captain."

Ben-Gurion came up. "I've just heard. The mules. Landed on the next beach with the remounts. Picketed safe in a canyon."

"Get them."

A single rifle bullet kicked up sand against their legs. A stream of falling stones and dirt slid down from above. Trumpeldor swept his revolver up, fired three times. A human bundle crashed down out of the brush. Dawn light reflected in staring, dark eyes of the dead Turkish sniper. Judah headed away with his detail, now following Ben-Gurion.

A half hour later, they had left the beach far behind and were moving through a notch of hills toward a dry lake bottom. They saw a long picket line of horses and mules staked out in the ravine.

"They'd been loaded with the horses, Lieutenant," Ben-Gurion said. "I don't think the quartermaster knows a horse from a mule."

Here there was no firing, nor had been. In the morning light, the British troops looked too relaxed wandering about like boy scouts on a picnic. One or two were actually picking wild flowers—while only a couple of miles away, on the next beach, their companions were being slaughtered. They seemed to Judah to be dazed by tranquility. He led the way into the ravine.

"The mules look a little seasick," Judah said. "Well, now we've found them, let's start moving them to where they'll do some good."

Bernard Goldfarb had taken cover in the hills with the 29th Division—the first British unit ashore. They'd been under fire for several hours and had dug in to hold the perimeter until they were reinforced. During a lull in the firing, Bernard left them to locate his own Mule Corps.

A steep descent brought him down into a strange terrain of huge, pumpkin-shaped rocks—a nightmare landscape where the faint morning light revealed no certainties. Then, out of the dimness, footsteps and voices forced him to take cover behind a cluster of rocks. It was a Turkish patrol. They came forward in spurts of movement. He could make out the officer leading them: a major in a well-fitted tunic, binoculars on his chest, pistol swinging from lanyard. Bernard was close enough to distinguish the Turk's features embellished by a fine, flaring mustache. The officer paused, barking an order to his patrol. They pushed on down the slope ahead of him. He lingered, pulling out his map case to take his bearings. His lips moved as though memorizing contours, landmarks.

The bolt of Bernard's rifle lay cold in his hand. He lifted it, slid it back. It spat out the brass gobbet of an empty shell case.

A glittering clue.

The major spun around. Even in this wild terrain his shoes and puttees were polished to glossy perfection. Bernard raised his rifle. But not before the Turk's revolver bit off a slice of sound. A red hot poker stabbed into Bernard's thigh. With nimble reflex he rolled back into the crevice, rocks and brush briefly masking him. Hunched, waiting, he lay there.

But the rifle was under his body. What an idiot! He should have held onto it. Now he squirmed to free it; the pain in his thigh swelling through his head almost blinded him. He clamped his teeth against it, continuing to work the rifle clear.

Find the trigger. His only chance. . . .

His leg was numb now, dying its own, separate death. The puttees came nearer. The leather mirrors bent toward him. Peering closer, the Turk saw what could not be hidden. A trickle of blood, red from the artery, as though the rocks were bleeding. With a metallic click, the Turk recocked his revolver.

The bullet from Bernard's rifle hoisted the officer in a wild, jerking contortion—and then down again to lie still on the gray earth.

Having retrieved the lost mules and the respect of Trumpeldor, Judah Nouari dispatched his detail to escort the mule train back to the beachmaster and supply dumps. Then, in the rising heat of midday, he headed up a gorge after several animals that had broken loose. He paused upon hearing a pistol shot. It was followed some minutes later by the crack of a rifle, which echoed from every rock surface of the hillside. He waited again, not wanting to wander too close to the Turkish outpost. When all was quiet, he started once more after the mules. Then some instinct moved him toward a strange formation of rocks some distance up the hillside. It was from there the rifle shot had come.

Without moving, Bernard could just see his leg. Sticky red from the hip down. Beyond him, flies were beginning to investigate the corpse of the man he had killed. Then he froze. Footsteps again. The Turkish patrol coming back for their officer? No. It was only one pair of footsteps. They crunched nearer. Bernard knew that even if he had the chance, he wouldn't have the strength to fire again. His mind swam in that endless distance of sea he had crossed; only, now there were fireflies dancing in it.

The curtain of pirouetting sparks was broken by a single figure—calling him by his own name.

"Bernard. . . . Bernard! It's Judah."

"Judah. . . ."

"Yes, Barney. Hold on." With shaking hands, Judah manipulated a hasty bandage. He had found two of the mules. Now he dragged Bernard clear of the brush and hoisted him up over one. It took an enormous effort. And Bernard lost consciousness. Judah hitched his friend tight to the packsaddle and started the mules down the slope. He had gone only about a hundred yards when a sound turned him.

A Turkish corporal, a carbine in the crook of his arm, was bending over something on the ground. One of Judah's mules brayed. The corporal whipped around, carbine at his hip. Judah drew his pistol. The eyes of the two men met. The Turk fired. His shot hit one of the mules. Before he could squeeze off a second shot, Judah fired. The Turk dropped.

For a moment, Judah was too shaken to move. Finally he started back up the hill, pistol in hand. The Turk was dead. Then he saw what had drawn the corporal's attention: a second body. A Turkish officer, the face angry under heat and buzzing flies.

With sinking horror, Judah recognized the dead man.

Sarah and Mehmet's handsome son: Major Kemel Khassadia, from Constantinople. Judah's own cousin. . . .

Judah dropped to the ground beside the body, weeping. Kemel was their only child. Handsome. Straight. Pride of Mehmet. *My son, the Major, you know. You will see how far he will go. A Colonel. A General. Anything is possible—with the right backing. Yes, he is much admired. . . .*

After a few moments, Judah pulled himself together, reaching into Kemel's pocket for wallet and papers. A letter to Mehmet and Aunt Sarah—yes, he would have to write to them himself.

Judah closed his eyes, wiping back hot tears. But what could he write about this death? That Kemel had fallen, a

Turk, fighting against the British? A Jew against Jews? A cousin against cousin? Oh, God of our fathers—is a man to be slaughtered by his own kin? Where is the angel who stopped the hand of Abraham?

Sounds echoed through the narrow defile. The patrol returning. Judah scrambled down the hillside to Bernard and the mules. Bernard was still unconscious, tied across a mule. The other animal was losing some blood from his flank. Judah freed the wounded mule. Let the Turks find him. They'd patch him up if they could.

A Royal Navy search party found a mule and two Z.M.C. men on the beach. One badly wounded, the other suffering from exhaustion.

Major Kemel Khassadia's body was not discovered until the following day, when the Turks recaptured the few miles of rocky, useless wasteland they had so briefly lost.

As for Allies, they had lost Gallipoli. And with it, reputations as high as Kitchener and Churchill. Both sides would count the loss of tens of thousands of brave men.

Bernard Goldfarb was sent to a base hospital in Cairo. His leg was saved, but he would carry the limp as a remembrance of a day he wanted to forget.

Judah was given medical leave. He headed home for Paris, not quite the same man. Perhaps he never would be.

For three days, Sarah Khassadia didn't speak. She sat in her house in Constantinople, in front of the photograph of her son, her head covered in black cloth, wailing softly. Every so often, she would throw back the cloth and tear at her graying hair. She took nothing to eat or drink. The envelope bearing her son's personal effects—along with the note from her nephew, Judah Nouari—rested in her lap. When Mehmet came to her, she seemed not to recognize him. On the fourth day, she went to her bed. She never left it again.

The doctor told Mehmet simply that she had died of grief. A pain too great for the heart to bear.

Mehmet Khassadia's grief exhibited itself in a rage so deep that he was not sure where to focus his hatred. His hands bled from beating the wall. His normally immaculate frock coat was damp from perspiration, his winged collar stained and soggy. He had not trimmed his mustache for two weeks, nor

touched comb to head. Without Kemel there was no destination. Without Kemel what could still be important?

One thing. Yes, one thing only: revenge. But against whom?
The British? The Zionist? His nephew, Judah—who of all
people had no right to take up arms against the Turks?

Certainly the Zionists were to blame. He—a Jew—would
be the first of all to say that. *A noble death,* Judah's letter had
said. *Leading his men against—I am heartbroken to say—the
area occupied by our own Mule Corps.*

And where was this Zion Corps born? Out of the pockets of
the Hammadi-Nouari empire. Their money had bought the
bullet that killed his son.

Mehmet Khassadia arose like a man in sleep. For the next
few hours he shuffled through every cupboard and drawer
with trembling hands. He sought for and found every letter,
every plea for favors, every begging scrap of paper so neatly
filed away, from any member of the Hammadi-Nouari clans.
For in his mind they had always been one.

With ritual ceremony, he lit the coals in the great brass
brazier, then systematically began dropping the letters and
documents, feeding the blaze. He found solace in the flames.
But not forgiveness. Then his hand took up the last communication. It had arrived the same day as the letter from Judah,
and in the anguish of the news, it had been forgotten. Now he
slashed it open with the silver-inlaid letter opener from Fabergé,
in Paris. The one given him by his nephew when he came to
Constantinople with his arrogant Arab partner, Mohamed. To
implore assistance. To save the life of Abdullah's worthless
son, Yassir.

Whom could Mehmet implore to bring back Kemel? And
what new favor would these Arab-Jews beg of him?

The letter was from Izak Nouari, in Damascus. His wife's
first cousin, that sour rind of a man he could never abide. He
had not been wrong. Nobody wrote unless he wanted something. He read with anger—and then with growing interest. It
seemed that swine Yassir was adrift again. He had vanished
from the comfortable berth they'd provided for him in
Spain. Mehmet looked at the date on the letter. Five months
ago, it had been written. He read on. Abdullah had reason to
believe that his son might be somewhere in the Turkish
provinces. Or possibly hiding in Constantinople. Izak begged,
on behalf of his partner, that his dear Cousin Mehmet would

do all in his power—should the lad approach him for aid—to convince Yassir to go to Switzerland. Money would be provided by Hammadi-Nouari. And Mehmet would not be forgotten. After all, was he not himself a father?

He closed his eyes. Kemel's words drifted back to him. *"I can see no reason why Yassir shouldn't be hanged. . . . If it were up to me, I'd swing him from a minaret,"* Kemel had said.

Kemel, Kemel, my son—what would you say now?

Mehmet Khassadi took up the letter opener. He made a vow. Then he lifted the palm of his left hand upward above the flaming brazier and drove the knife into it, letting his blood drip down on the flames.

Mehmet took up a pen. He addressed an envelope to Djemel Pasha, Governor-General of Syria and Palestine. Then he forged a last postscript to Izak's letter. Forgery was a talent Mehmet had cultivated in the service of the former Sultan.

Yassir Hammadi is still working for the overthrow of Djemel Pasha, and much as we in the Company might share his feelings, we deem it unwise to assist his efforts at this time.

Next, Mehmet wrote his own letter to Djemel Pasha: *As a loyal servant of the Sultan, it is my duty to pass this communication on to Your Excellency, in confidence that in your wisdom you will not include my own relatives when justice is taken against the perpetrators of this diabolical conspiracy.*

He signed it *Mehmet Khassadia, Minister Without Portfolio to His Most Excellent Serene Highness, Muhammed Reshad V. Father of Major Kemel Khassadia, died in action 26 May 1915. Gallipoli. Hero of Turkey.*

Abdullah Hammadi's fingers flew over the abacus like a harpist's. His lips moved silently with each click of the beads. He prided himself on counting faster with this ancient tool of mathematics than on the new, cumbersome adding machine his partner, Izak Nouari, had purchased in Paris. They were embalmed in the heat of this Syrian summer. Following their afternoon sleep, they had returned late to the Damascus office. It was now ten-thirty. Dark enough for Izak to pull on the single electric light dangled above their rolltop desks. On the ceiling, the blades of a great fan stirred fitfully.

An invention of Izak's, before the installation of the electricity. The fan was powered by a shaft-and-rope arrangement that traversed a hole in the outer wall. It was affixed to the yoke of a small donkey in the courtyard. At the urgings of an urchin with a stick, this useful animal worked his rounds, day or night.

The partners were deeply engrossed in the monthly accounts. Since the chaos of war weighed heavily on Damascus, Izak and Abdullah had taken the wise decision to transfer all Company profits to Hammadi-Nouari's Jerusalem bank. This was not easy, or entirely legal; Djemel Pasha had blocked all transfer of funds from Damascus. Even in Jerusalem, money wasn't entirely safe from confiscation. But David Nouari was managing to move considerable sums to America via a bond issue floated by Mohamed's New York bank.

There was a third witness to the night's proceedings, a young Turk recently discharged from the Army. Lamed by a war wound, Rustem got around with a stick. He had worked for David Nouari before the war, as had his father before him. Now, once again, he served the partners as a trusted courier.

Rustem waited respectfully, sipping a mint tea while Izak recorded Abdullah's calculations. Since the war, he always kept two ledgers, and insisted that all monies be paid in gold. Paper currency was hardly worth more than its splendidly engraved portrait of the former Sultan.

The Company had been doing profitable business in Turkish Army contracts. All arms from Hispañola-Nacional passed through Damascus. Flour and other foodstuffs were still coming in from Jerusalem. With a final click, the last bead flew across the wire. Abdullah mopped his brow.

"How much do you make it, Izak? The total?"

Izak handed him the ledger to study. "Good. Good," Abdullah said. "Up 10 percent over August of last year."

Izak glanced at his stout partner sweating profusely in the heat. "I tell you, Abdullah, you should lose weight. What good are profits when you dig your grave with your fork? And what did the doctor say about your heart?"

"He says it is lazy. That it wants more rest. But why should it rest when I cannot?" Abdullah, getting on toward seventy, would indeed have retired some years before. But with Yassir Allah knew not where, and Tariq conscripted into the Turkish Army, how could he retire? Who would replace him? Izak had no children to plague his old age, but with his sour disposition, what kind of sons might he have had? Worse even than Yassir and Tariq. Yet, for all Izak's lamentations, the understanding between the partners was deep.

Izak moved the last gleaming stack of gold coin to a small strongbox. There were two keys to the intricate lock: one in Damascus, one in Jerusalem. On the floor stood an open wooden crate of figs. The strongbox fitted exactly into a scooped-out hollow in the layer of fruit. Izak neatly arranged rows of purpling figs over the box. Abdullah watched, from time to time popping a fig into his mouth.

"That's the last thing you should be eating, Abdullah. Pure sugar."

Abdullah took another from the pile of leftovers. "If Allah did not wish me to be tempted, would he put temptation in my way?"

Izak nailed the box lid shut. Each slat was stamped with the H-N insignia of the Company. He glanced up at the young Turk. "Every day of this war brings more thieves, Rustem. Take care with this shipment."

"Nothing to fear, Mr. Nouari." Rustem opened his jacket, patting a shoulder holster. "And our permits are quite in order. Passage for two freight cars of fruit. I shall not sleep until they are unloaded."

"Solomon. My brother Solomon will meet you in Jerusalem." Izak paused. "One thing still worries me. These 'permits' cost more than the fruit is worth. It could make someone too curious," Izak worried.

"My third trip, Mr. Nouari," Rustem assured him. "No one ever looks further than the ten-*dirham* note in my identity papers."

"No doubt they find the face of Sultan Abdul Hamid irresistible. We have many art collectors in the civil service," Izak replied. He paused, having noticed that the faint wheezing of the fan had stopped. Izak glanced at the clock. "Did you tell the boy to stop the donkey at eleven?"

Abdullah shook his head, a look of fear coming into his face. "No. . . . Why would I do that?"

They waited for the knock. It came.

A gentle knock. Nothing sinister, but it paralyzed the three men.

"Open it," Abdullah whispered.

Izak glanced at the leftover figs on the table. With a quick gesture, he swept them into the wastebasket. Then he opened the door. Lieutenant Kumem of the Pasha's Special Police stood smiling in the doorway.

Abdullah breathed relief. This was an official with whom they had always been on the friendliest of terms.

"Welcome, Lieutenant Kumem," Izak said. "Did you come for your usual game of backgammon? I'm in a mood to lose a little money."

The officer mopped his neck with a large silk handkerchief. "This weather—what a summer! I swear I would prefer to be in the garrison at Aqaba." Stepping in, he casually searched his pockets for a paper.

"Some license fee we forgot to pay?" asked Abdullah. "Of all things that age badly, memory is the worst."

"Sit down, my friend. Sit down," gestured Izak. "It's too hot to stand up."

But the lieutenant did not sit. He continued his pocket search with exasperating slowness.

"Ah, here it is," he said, at last fishing out a document. "Two warrants. For the arrest of Abdullah Hammadi and Izak Nouari."

Abdullah turned pale. "My friend, it is surely a mistake. An unkind joke."

"The charge?" Izak asked.

"Treason. I regret, but I must take you both into custody." He lifted a small whistle from chest to lips and blew lightly. Four police with carbines entered behind him.

"Oh, that will not be necessary." The lieutenant's voice was almost indolent. "These people were my friends." He sighed. "If only they had been better friends of Turkey."

"There must be some mistake . . ." Abdullah began almost hysterically.

"Why must there be a mistake?" The lieutenant's attention shifted to the young Turk. "And who is this?"

"Our courier from Jerusalem. He accompanies all shipments," Izak said.

"Your papers?"

Rustem promptly produced them. Army discharge. Identity card. Birth certificate. "One is obliged to carry so many documents these days."

"All quite in order," the lieutenant replied, removing the ten-*dirham* note tucked into Rustem's identity card. He returned it with the documents. "If I were a man to take a bribe, that amount would be insulting."

Izak clenched his teeth. This lieutenant had his own method of collecting bribes. The partners were expected to lose large amounts to him regularly at backgammon.

Kumem began to prowl the room, noting the ledgers and abacus. "Doing your accounts, I see. But where is the money?"

"Gone to the bank. We do not keep it here," Abdullah put in hastily.

The lieutenant held out his hand. "Then, you have the receipt of the bank?"

"Yes, receipt. . . ." Abdullah mumbled unsteadily. "I can look for it in the file, if you wish. . . ."

"But you may not find it, and so much time would be wasted." Kumem peered at the figs in the wastebasket. "Throwing away the merchandise?" He fished one out.

"Fruit flies. Ruinous this year," Izak said.

The lieutenant put one in his mouth, chewing thoughtfully. "Has the Company become so poor that you must pack your own crates—one by one?" He picked up the hammer and bent to the box, prying the wood slats open with the hammer claw. "And since when has there been a shortage of figs in Jerusalem?"

With a sudden, savage motion, he kicked over the crate, spilling out the small strongbox in a tumble of fruit.

He straightened, snapping his fingers. One of his men picked it up, "I presume there is a key?"

The two partners seemed unable to move or speak. The hammer crashed down on the abacus, sending the counting beads flying in all directions.

"Key . . . !" he shouted.

Izak took it from around his neck, but his hands shook so badly he couldn't fit it into the lock. The lieutenant opened the box. He sighed. "I presume you have a permit to transfer gold? But I see by your faces you do not. In any case, it is not *this* crime that you will hang for."

They were handcuffed with heavy manacles.

The young Turk looked on incredulously. "I am free to go, sir?"

''Why not? I have no warrant for you. You are a hero of Turkey.'' He touched Rustem's crutch with his stick.

''But my son Tariq is serving in the forces of Turkey!'' Abdullah pleaded.

''Was. He has deserted. And your other son, Yassir? Where is he? That is the question the Pasha's interrogators will wish you to answer. Where is Yassir?''

Twelve ─────────────────────

SOLOMON Nouari entered Damascus in a tinker's cart drawn by a donkey. In his loose-fitting rags, he imagined he looked very much as his father had when Jacob first entered Jerusalem, in the middle of the previous century. Jacob and his elder brother, Abraham, with their cart, and their new friend with the donkey, Musa. Now Abraham and Musa were dead—and Jacob had crossed his eighty-second year in his wheelchair.

When the courier, Rustem, returned to Jerusalem with news of the arrests, two things were urgently obvious. A rescue mission must be organized. And Djemel Pasha was for once beyond bribery. The governor was riding on a wave of executions of Arabs and Jews. The breath of a pro-British leaning was justification enough. His Excellency was definitely a man to be avoided at this time. Furthermore, it could only be a matter of weeks—maybe days—before the Pasha's wrath stretched to Jerusalem, confiscated the Hammadi-Nouari Bank, and closed the Trading Company.

Even before the news, David Nouari had been preparing a means of escape for the two families. Judah's father had arranged that two Company freighters would be unloading at Haifa. On one of these, he and Sayid Hammadi could move their families safely to Cairo.

One member of the family refused to budge. "Would the Turks waste a bullet on an old man in a wheelchair?" asked Jacob. Nor would he listen to Solomon's pleas. "I have lived here too long to die anywhere else." He laid a hand like a blessing on his son's graying head. "And why must it be *you* who goes to Damascus?"

"Izak is my brother," Solomon replied simply.

"You're too old for this rescue mission, Father," Jonathan insisted. "Let me or Nathan go."

But Solomon was an intransigent as Jacob. Stubborness ran in the family. "A young man will attract suspicions. But an older man dressed as a tinker will attract no attention. Besides, Jonathan, it's a mission on which experience may be more valuable than courage."

"What good is experience when the bullets start flying, Father?" Nathan demanded from his eighteenth year.

Old Jacob put the final word on the argument. "The loss of a father is a sorrow—but it is the harvest of time. The loss of a brother is a deep hurt—for it is not in the order of events. But the loss of a son—that is tragedy. It is you who must go to Damascus, Solomon."

While Solomon made his plans, the two families prepared for their departure to Cairo. So many files to be packed away or burned. In one envelope, a railroad. In another, the purchase of a harvest. Bonds from half the banks in Europe, many now worthless.

Mohamed's brother Anwar was now serving in one of the six Arab divisions of the Turkish Army. He had sent a coded message; Arab troops were preparing to rise in revolt and join the desert Prince Faisal ibn Husain. Most younger Arabs were already members of Al Fatat or Al-Ahd, and dedicated Arab nationalists.

Solomon's sons, who worked in the Trading Company, had been temporarily excused from military service since the Company had been supplying the Army. But now that the winds of change were blowing hot and angry from the Governor's palace, no one would be safe. Nothing, and no one. Jonathan and Nathan would travel to Egypt with their sister Naomi and their mother. When Solomon's mission was completed, he would join them in Cairo.

Solomon tried to remember: What had he been like, this brother Izak, now locked in a jail in Damascus?

As boys, they had shared few interests, never seemed to have much in common. Izak was a dreamy child. Quiet, with a love of poetry. How had he grown into the man who read only ledgers? Young Solomon had always been filled with the need to know the reason for everything. How things worked. What made plants grow. For Izak, it was enough to see the color of a flower. He didn't need to know how the pistil is pollinated to enjoy its scent. Still, the brothers had shared good moments. Nights sitting on the flat, open roof together listening to the cicadas in the garden, picking out constellations in the sky above the minarets, domes, and towers of the Old City. Or watching falling stars trailing firework tails through that enormous silence. Then they had seemed very close indeed. Izak relied on Solomon. Maybe too much. Solomon always had an answer to every problem. And if he didn't, he'd invent one. Every problem except the big one: When Izak had fallen in love with Musa's daughter Bethena, and the harmony of the two families was threatened.

Then Solomon's answer seemed the only one, right or wrong. "You're still young. You'll get over it," Solomon had assured him with conviction. "Accept their offer. Go to Damascus." Izak had. But he hadn't gotten over it. And something became stale and dry inside him. If now flowers had lost their scent and poetry its music, if now one found him cranky and cantankerous, it was living without Bethena that had changed him.

Yes, it was Solomon who had told him to go to Damascus all those years ago. It must be Solomon who would go to get him out.

His wife, Miriam, had wept. Then she had quoted a Hassidic saying: "Remember, my husband, we must also pray for the wicked. We must love them, too. If we do not, the Messiah will never come." Miriam found many opportunities for a good cry. Now she was wasting her tears on Djemel Pasha. How could you understand such a woman? But then, Miriam was the daughter of a fifth-generation Hassidic rabbi—of that mysterious religious movement that found a message of hope even in the darkness of the eighteenth century and produced a spirit of love, joy, and forgiveness in the hearts of suffering Jewry. Hassidim. Men and women intoxicated with God.

Solomon's love for Miriam had never waned. He could count the blessing of a good wife and mother to his children; but that was not the reason he loved her. A housekeeper and nursemaid could have done as much. It was Miriam's quiet support of his decisions that built his confidence, and stoked his wisdom. But when her ideas were not his own, she could, in her gentle way, make him see another point of view. It was

Miriam who had taught him to search beyond the quick answers of his youth.

Three nights had passed since Solomon's uneventful entry into Damascus. Under the east wall of the city's prison, he squatted behind a selection of pots and pans. For three days, the managing director of Hammadi-Nouari Trading Company, Jerusalem, had been peddling copper and brass while studying the layout of the prison, the movements of guards. During the nights, he had made contact after contact, until finally he had reached the right night warder. Enough money changed hands to ensure the Turk's retirement to his own date farm after the war. There was a promise of more to come—if the rescue mission proved successful.

"The *effendi* must understand what he is paying for," the guard said. "The door of a cell left unlocked. Possible, yes. But from there, it will be up to the two prisoners. And yourself."

"The note—you must not forget to deliver the note," Solomon reminded him.

The warder fingered the gold coins. "There will be questions. How was the door left open? It is plain I will have to make certain my assistant is not available to deny the blame. You understand?"

Solomon did. Too well.

So far, everything had gone a little too smoothly. It was worrying. Solomon had traveled without being stopped as far as Al Mazzah, driven by Rustem uniformed as a Turkish military chauffeur. The car, appropriately if hastily painted khaki, bore the pennants of a Turkish major general on its fenders. Easy to come by. H-N supplied all flags and insignia to the Army.

At Al Mazzah, Solomon had transformed himself from major general to minor tinker. In his closed cart there were also tinkers' rags for the escapees. They would have to travel the short distance to where Rustem would be waiting behind a Roman ruin outside the city gate. The car, with two staff-officer uniforms hidden under the backseat, would be their means of final escape. The timing would be delicate. The escape had to be accomplished precisely at the changing of the prison gate watch, when keys were exchanged and security lax.

A curling sliver of new moon had long since vanished behind the triangle of roof topping the dirty brick prison building. Iron shutters were bolted closed for the night. Almost time. . . . Solomon could only hope the warder had delivered the instructions. He glanced down the street. Deserted, except for the two beggars he had stationed to keep watch.

Miriam's parting words came back to him. "I know you will risk your life, Solomon, but do not be afraid. Courage doesn't ride with fear—and fear can make you careless. Come back to me, my husband." He drew a deep breath and mounted the reinforced roof of his cart. Then he hauled a rope from a coiled mass inside the wagon. It was fitted with a cargo claw at one end and a strong rope ladder at the other. Solomon whirled the claw around his head, letting it fly to the top of the wall.

The claw caught. Feeling his fifty-four years as he had not expected to, he tested his weight against it. Perhaps Jonathan had been right. This was work for a younger man. Short of breath—and he hadn't even started the climb! Laboriously, Solomon began to pull himself up.

At the top, he lay still for a moment, panting. He could feel his heart pounding against his chest. *Courage doesn't ride with fear*.

In the prison courtyard below, all seemed quiet. At any moment they should be coming out—Izak and Abdullah. He drew the ladder up after him layering it at the top, where it would be ready to drop down the inner wall. Solomon hoped he would not have to use the small pistol strapped to his forearm. He'd never been a good shot, nor needed to be. Solomon was a cerebral man.

In the Paris bank, Baron Liebermann scrawled his signature on the complicated document. "Personally, I think you're crazy, Mohamed," the Baron confided. His lawyer hovered above the impressive signature that completed the sale of the Baron's banking interests.

"Why, Baron?"

"Why crazy? Why should you want to take over the assets and liabilities of this bank in wartime? It proves that you have learned nothing from me in all these years, Mohamed. How many? Eleven? Who can keep track of time?" But he had. It was exactly that. The aging banker pushed his great humidor across to the Arab. It was empty.

"My dear Baron, you've run out of ammunition."

Liebermann looked, nodded sadly. "This war. Would you believe it? You cannot at any price find a good Cuban cigar in Paris. Only yesterday I said to the Count de Lisselles. . . ."

"I believe it," Mohamed cut him off gently. "Any more signatures?"

"No, monsieur, it is finished. Here is the list of bonds, securities, negotiables, loans, debts."

"Thank you. I've already looked through it." Mohamed tucked all the papers into a tooled morocco portfolio. The lawyer took his departure.

"Where will you go, Baron?" Mohamed inquired politely.

"Where should I go? Where everyone is going: Switzerland. The last sane country on earth. I will give you, my friend, one piece of free advice. Now that you've bought—sell out. As I'm doing. Buy yourself—as I'm doing—a small chalet on the shores of Geneva's lake. Learn to play croquet. Because when this war is over, whoever wins, you will see money become worthless. Good restaurants, nonexistent. And civilization . . . *kaputt!* Do you know what the Marquis de Ronval told me on Sunday in the Cathedral? Three of his race horses— bought for nothing, to pull caissons! 'You call this war?' the Marquis said. 'Gentlemen digging with shovels in trenches? No bugles. No cavalry charges. No columns advancing under flags. No, my dear Maurice'—the Marquis always calls me by my Christian name— 'If we make war like pigs pushing truffles out of the mud, what do you think will come after?' "

"There will be changes, of course."

"And your partner, Judah. He is crazier than you. What did I hear? Commanding a regiment of Jewish mules?"

"I don't think the mules are religious, Baron."

Pearl-gray gloves were taken up by one manicured hand; a walking stick by the other. Its gold head bore a discreet coat of arms. For the last time, the Baron's eyes swept his throne room. Then his head seemed to lower like a turtle's into his winged collar. His shoulders hunched. His hands rose and spread slightly—in the age-old gesture of mere man on the precipice of uncontrollable events. His lips moved softly, unconsciously forming the words. *"Vey is mir. . . ."*

He was gone. Mohamed sat alone. The office looked strangely bare. His mind raced back to that first day the Baron had interviewed him and Judah. "Learn. Learn the business. Every word you hear in this building will be for you a textbook . . ." Well, he had learned. Man is mainly corruptible. Money is living matter. Without it, a bank is only an empty building. Time is of all things the most easily wasted, the most expensively bought.

The Baron's old secretary stepped in with mail on a silver salver. At the top was a cable. Mohamed opened it—stared in disbelief. The Damascus partners—sentenced to death. For what? Treason? He could see their faces. Indulgent, lovable Abdullah. Lean, ascerbic Izak. Treason. Those two? He rose.

"I have to go to Damascus. From Marseilles—or any southern port where you can get me on a ship. Any kind of ship."

"When would Monsieur wish to leave?"

"Today."

Abdullah lay in the corner of the prison cell on the straw that served as a bed. His breath was sucked in sharp intakes, gasped out against the dank, sweaty wall. "I can't do it. I'm not well enough, Izak. No, you must go alone."

"What choice have you?" came the angry whisper. "If you stay here, you die on the gallows. Better we die out there in the courtyard from a bullet." Izak heaved his partner up to a sitting position. Abdullah's cheeks were putty gray, damp as the wall.

"You look fine," Izak lied.

Abdullah shook his head. "It is my heart. I'm not sure I can walk. My knees. . . . No, Izak. I will only slow you down. You must go alone."

"If we die here or there it makes no difference to me, Abdullah. But we will do it together. Just as we have made every decision for twenty years now. We will not give the Turks the satisfaction of making this decision for us."

Abdullah nodded. "All right. Help me up, then." Somehow Izak managed to get the larger man to his feet. Abdullah leaned against the stones, steeling himself for the ordeal. "Yes, I'm better now. But how will we know when it is time? They have taken our watches."

Izak's voice was almost gentle. "It is past time, Abdullah. It was time when the warder unlocked the door. We must go now. This minute."

Izak pushed the cell door. It opened with a rasping creak magnified in his mind to a thunderbolt. He peered out. All was silent and dark. "Come."

Izak guided Abdullah, sometimes pushing him, sometimes pulling, nearly carrying him down the dark passage.

Abdullah leaned against the wall. "Is this the door?"

"No. The second one, he said." They moved on faster now. Abdullah paused again to catch his breath. "Your brother. How do we know he is really waiting?"

"If Solomon says he will be there—you can count on it."

They had reached the second door. Izak tried it. It came open. He pushed it a few inches. From his position, he could see little of the courtyard, bounded by a rectangle of shadows. He could not even see the wall, nor was he certain exactly where Solomon's ladder would be waiting. But, for once, he did not let his own doubt show in his whispered words. "It looks easy, Abdullah. We have only to cross the courtyard. The wall is not far. I will help you up the ladder. Together . . . we will make it."

From his position on the wall, Solomon could see the door where Izak and Abdullah should appear. He could also see the gate. The new guard had already arrived. Now was the moment! But where were they? They must come out before the old guard went off duty. Then too many eyes would be moving across the courtyard. Then would be too late.

The door widened a few inches. Two bent shadows emerged. Solomon eased the ladder down, tried to make out the forms. Izak seemed to be dragging Abdullah. They moved forward with no sure direction, then came to a stop. He let down some more ladder. Why hadn't they seen it? He longed to cry out to them.

They were stumbling forward again, clumsy as two men in a horse costume, movements uncoordinated. He could see them more clearly as they reached the center of the courtyard.

Something was wrong with Abdullah! Solomon looked toward the gate. Three prison guards came out of a doorway, glancing into the courtyard. They saw the escaping prisoners and began to shout. Lights flashed on. In the circle of bob-

bing illuminations, Izak and Abdullah stiffened into statues.
Behind them, the bribed warder emerged from the doorway.

"Run!" Solomon shouted. "Over here!"

Somehow the two old men stumbled on, to the ladder.
Abdullah's hands reached to clutch the heavy ropes, Izak
pushing the thick body from behind. The warder was shouting
too, pistol in hand. Solomon reached for his own but could
not free it from its holster and still hold the ladder.

At the bottom of the wall, Abdullah seemed to disintegrate
into a heap on top of Izak. The ladder danced free.

The warder's pistol lifted high to find its mark. Solomon
felt the hot sting in his chest. He toppled from the wall,
landing near his brother. Izak dragged himself free of Abdullah. "Solomon . . ." he wailed. "Solomon."

"Izak . . . life is a fatal disease . . ." Solomon said,
dying.

It moved on its rope—a contortion of frozen finality, a
flesh pendulum, stiff and grotesque. It hung among six others
gathering flies and the attention of awed Damascenes beyond
the prison gate. The face no longer belonged to Izak, it was
a mask for all the shortchanged, all the cheated who had lived
their lives receiving only the half portions—accepting the
crumb for the loaf.

The face swung slowly away again. Mohamed saw the
darkening, shriveled neck collared in rope beneath the thinning hair. He turned away, sickened. Then he noticed a
man whose attention was also fixed on the corpse of Izak.
A man, in the uniform of the Pasha's Special Police, who
seemed to grant the hanging corpse something near compassion.

A tear dampened the corner of Lieutenant Kumem's eye.
He would miss those backgammon games, the profit and the
pleasure. Yes, he would miss Izak and Abdullah. Noting
Mohamed's attention, Lieutenant Kumem quickly turned away.

In the next few moments, Izak would be cut down. There
was nothing more to be done for him except bury him in the
old Jewish cemetery outside of Damascus, next to Solomon,
whose body waited in a wooden box. Mohamed had seen to
the arrangements. The brothers would lie side by side, in

Syrian earth—much deeper than their Muslim partners, who in accord with their religion, were buried in mound graves that rested aboveground.

> "Come by darkness, O my brother,
>   Hand toward hand through layers of time. . . ."

Words spoken by old Jacob Nouari at Musa's death. Now Mohamed spoke them for the death of Jacob's two sons.

> "I'll not find thee in another—
>   Break the glass that held the wine. . . ."

Now there was only one task left for Mohamed before leaving Damascus. Uncle Abdullah still lay in the prison hospital, where he had been carried after the failed escape. To save him would mean facing Djemel Pasha again. And what means of persuasion were left?

A week later, Mohamed was ushered into the private quarters of His Excellency's Turkish bath in the Damascus palace. Sandalwood vapors rose in smoky streamers around the bulk of authority languishing in a steam fog. Two boys bucketed water onto the hot coals of a gigantic brazier. The Pasha's handsome military aide lounged naked except for his revolver belt.

One towel draped over his belly, a second turbaning his head. Djemel Pasha swiveled toward Mohamed. "And so you come to me again, Hammadi? Brave of you. Brave."

Indeed, this wasn't the safest of encounters. Mohamed knew the Governor was executing thousands of Arabs and Jews, right and left. He didn't need reasons, or proof or guilt. All he needed was his own fear. But today Mohamed needed him. Mohamed inclined his head in the slightest of salaams. The steam was already soaking through to the small of his back, but he managed to appear completely at ease.

"Pasha, I am a man not without some power in the world. Here, in Syria—whom would I come to but to you?" Mohamed permitted himself a smile.

The Pasha grunted. "When you requested this interview, I was of two minds. . . ." His voice held a slight challenge. "My first inclination was to ignore it, don't you know?" He rose suddenly, dropping his towel. It wasn't a pretty sight. Even his aide averted his eyes. The Pasha plunged into a sunken cold bath, gouting water over flowered tiles.

"But you agreed to see me, Excellency. I am honored."

"Honored? You chose the right amulet for safe conduct."

He took up a glittering decoration in a velvet box, weighed it in his hand, snapped the lid closed, and tossed it back to Mohamed. "Your insurance policy, Hammadi. The Order of the Star of Crescent. You thought I wouldn't execute a man so honored by our Sultan, eh?"

"One of several tokens of appreciation I have received from our Sultan—for arming our brave Turkish troops."

"*Our*, Hammadi? Arabs are subjects of the Turks."

"And allies, sir. As Palestinians."

The Pasha pouted. "Some members of your family forgot that. Didn't they, Mustafa?" he called to his handsome aide.

"And paid for their bad memories," the aide smiled.

The Pasha's face twisted in fury. "Our troops defeat the British and French . . . only to have the traitorous daggers of our Arab subjects thrust into our backs!" He slapped a pudgy, ringed hand at an intrusive fly that made no distinction between regents and rebels in Damascus.

Mohamed's silk suit was clinging to his body now, outlining strong, muscular shoulders. "Sir, Abdullah Hammadi, my old uncle, is dying. What use can it serve to send his corpse to the gallows?"

"Should I make state funerals for traitors now? Is that what you expect of your Pasha?" He oozed up from the pool, water sinking behind him. "To honor our enemies?"

One of the boys hurried forward to spray the room with attar of roses. They draped the Pasha in a clean thick towel. He stepped toward Mohamed with surprising friendliness, taking his arm, leading him out of the steam to the antechamber. The Pasha's hand caressed Mohamed's sleeve, then traveled to the middle of his back, fingers investigating muscle beneath thick silk.

"A fine suit," the Pasha said, lips puckering. "It is impossible to get good cloth these days."

"I'll order you one—next time I'm in Paris," Mohamed replied, discreetly disengaging himself. He eyed the Pasha's rotundity. "If Your Excellency will provide me with your measurements."

"Before dinner—or after?" A gust of laughter shook the Pasha. He settled himself down on the marble slab. Waiting to oil him stood a Turk with the bunched muscles of a wrestler.

The Pasha winced slightly beneath the masseur's fingers, then cocked an eye at Mohamed. "Perhaps I shall be in Paris before you. Riding with Von Falkenhayn when our German friends march through the Arc de Triomphe."

"I'll be there within the month," Mohamed assured him. "If the Germans have arrived, I'll present your compliments."

"You know, it's remarkable, Hammadi," the Pasha mused. "You are a businessman. You go everywhere—where you wish. Why should *you* enjoy more freedom of the world than I?"

"But not your power, sir," Mohamed assured him. "Now, may we take up the question of my uncle?"

The Pasha frowned, snapping his fingers. His aide lit a long black cigarette, sucking the paper tip wet, and placed it between the Governor's lips. The Pasha puffed pensively, comparing his aide's supple figure to Mohamed's more virile dimensions. "Since you left your regiment, you've become scrawny as a chicken, Mustafa. You must take more exercise." He cast dreamy eyes at Mohamed while the wrestler continued to knead the borders of his master's spine. "Tell me, Hammadi, world traveler, have you ever seen a man rape a mare? It's possible, don't you know—if the horse is not too big and the man is strong enough. Do you think you could manage it?"

The aide snickered. "If his head was not kicked off too soon." He tossed Mohamed the angry look of a cat about to spray his territory, and lounged back on a pile of cushions.

Mohamed's jaw tightened. "Pasha, you have sentenced my uncle on an unspecified charge. May I know the grounds?"

The Pasha's eyes looked suddenly haunted. His color seemed to rise. "There was an owl in my garden. It came with the dying of the moon. These are ground enough! I have traitors in my provinces. Thousands of them. Arabs and Jews—who fight beside the British. How many of your people ride with El Aurence, the white Arabian? And that double-faced Prince Husain, who listens to British promises that they will form an Arab nation when we are defeated?" He raised himself on his elbows, his voice shrill. "I tell you, we will grind them into the desert until there is not a grain of sand left to remember them. And you—an Arab—knowing all this, still come to me for favors? Why, Hammadi? Is there something between us that I have not noticed? Some affection?"

"Friendship for Turkey, sir," Mohamed replied, seeing the madness in the Pasha's eyes.

"Your request is denied."

There was a moment's pause. The aide, the wrestler, even the boys knew Mohamed had lost. They could see him already dead.

"You are a fool, Pasha!" Mohamed said steadily.

"What . . . ?" The eyes grew even wilder.

"To ignore a friend. Today you can threaten me and my family. But tomorrow—where will you look for support?"

"*You* are not the only source of arms, Hammadi! Do you think it matters to us if you hold back a few cases of Spanish cartridges? With one word I will close every remaining office of Hammadi-Nouari in the Middle East. That is my power."

"Including Cairo?" Mohamed challenged. "You'll need General Allenby's cooperation to remove the British Army."

The Pasha purpled with fury. "You dare to plead with insults?"

"I plead with truth." Mohamed's mind raced ahead of his words. "You say the Arabs are rising with Lawrence. They are. You say the Jews are sending regiments to the English. They are. The world is changing sides, Pasha. Germany is drowning in a sea of Russians. Italy is growing stronger in the Alps. The French are an iron wall at Verdun. And America will join the winners. There will be millions—turning from defense to attack. The British will sweep to the gates of Persia. The Greeks will march into Constantinople. Today you can still choose. Tomorrow, the choice will be made for you."

The Pasha's eyes bulged. "Your pistol! Pistol, Mustafa!"

The aide swiftly offered it, butt forward. The Pasha cocked it and aimed it at Mohamed's head. "Mustafa, you may give the order this time. . . ."

Mohamed slipped the long, crimson ribbon of the Sultan's decoration over his neck. "With your permission, sir, I should like to wear the Sultan's Star and Crescent when you fire."

The pistol wavered.

"Fire!" shouted the aide.

The Pasha's eyes went suddenly blank and wide. A strange, cackling sob came from the back of his throat. His hands clenched into fists. The gun crashed a bullet wildly. It struck an alabaster vase, spraying bits of stone across the room.

The Pasha's mouth lolled open, then his jaw snapped closed. Foam formed on his lips. His eyeballs rolled back, showing only the whites. The aide leaped forward, prying the gun from his master's hand. Then he turned the Pasha's head to the side, forcing a towel between his teeth. Jaws ground against it with animal grunts. The body contorted in quivering paroxysms.

The fit lasted for five or six minutes. Then the leg muscles relaxed, the back unarched. The Pasha lay quiet again. The aide removed the towel from the thick lips. Color returned to the heavy face. He rolled over on his back, eyes slowly focusing on Mohamed. A smile twisted his mouth upward. His voice was hoarse and low.

"Before you entered this room, Hammadi, I had forgiven your uncle. Why else would I have seen you? And you know why? Because it was a member of the Nouari clan—Mehmet Khassadi—who revealed to me the perfidy of your cousin Yassir. Once, I spared that boy's life on the understanding he would never set foot in my provinces again. Now I am informed that Yassir has violated his banishment." He sat up, voice cool and steady now. "You can have the father, Hammadi. I will get the son."

Abdullah Hammadi took a long time dying. For most of two days after Mohamed brought him home to the white stucco house on the hill overlooking Damascus, Mohamed's aunt sat by her husband's bedside. He found her there in the last darkness before morning, weeping with two women servants, faces heavily veiled. Abdullah stirred awake, speaking softly to the three figures huddled beside his bed. Then he closed his eyes, never to open them again.

Mohamed urged his aunt to join the relocated relatives in Cairo, but she refused to leave her home. Since there was nothing further he could do, Mohamed made arrangements to return to Paris.

That afternoon, when he came to say good-bye, he found his aunt in quiet conversation with the same two women servants. They stopped talking when he entered the room. But not before Mohamed caught the sound of the taller woman's voice. He seized her by the arms, ripping the veil from her face.

"I'd have thought this was the last place you'd dare come, Yassir."

Tariq had already removed his veil. Mohamed turned on him. "And the deserter from the Turkish Army. A worthy addition to any household."

"What will you do—that you know, cousin? Sell us back to Djemel Pasha—along with your Spanish rifles?" Tariq challenged.

His aunt moved between Mohamed and her sons. "Please, Mohamed, you must not give them to the Pasha." She burst into tears again.

Yassir put a protective arm around her. "Cousin Mohamed won't turn us in, Mother. In matters of family honor you can always count on him. Our disgrace would only reflect on his dubious fame."

"You have never been fair to my brother," Tariq complained.

Mohamed studied this younger cousin. Shorter than Yassir, heavier built, but very much a man now. "Yassir's antics I know too well. But I'd have expected better from you, Tariq. Didn't it occur to you how much you endanger your mother by being here? How long do you think it will take before the Pasha has this house searched?"

"We're leaving tonight," Tariq assured him. His manner was less arrogantly hostile than his brother's.

"Where is your family feeling, cousin? Would you have kept sons away from their dying father?" Yassir asked with heavy irony.

"Sons who have to dress as women, yes." Mohamed turned back to Tariq. "You said you were going. Where?"

The two brothers exchanged a look but did not answer. Mohamed considered. "I might be able to get you both to Switzerland. But we'd have to move fast. . . ."

"Thank you, cousin Mohamed. But this is our country." Tariq cut in. "We don't intend to leave it now—when we're most needed."

"Needed—for what?"

"We intend to fight for the new Arab nation," Tariq said simply.

Yassir put a proud arm around his brother. "Yes—we will learn to fight. At evening we will not expect to see the morning. And at morning we will not expect to live until nightfall. We shall use our strength while it is still ours, and our lives while we have them, for the service of Allah. We shall see the caliphate restored."

"You needn't quote me the *haddiths,* Yassir. I'm still a Muslim," Mohamed replied testily. But he found himself strangely moved.

"Of course, cousin Mohamed," Yassir replied. "Although sometimes you make it hard to remember."

All anger had drained from Mohamed. Now he felt only concern. "Do you think you'll get ten miles from Damascus without help? Police spies are combing every donkey track for deserters, Tariq."

"We'll take our chances on getting through," Yassir answered.

"So far, we've been under the protection of the Sharif of Mecca, Prince Husain. Any true believer in Syria will open his door to us. We hope to join Colonel Lawrence," Tariq said.

"And what do you think they'll do to your mother?"

"She'll be safe enough here," Tariq replied. "The British have promised to take Damascus."

"The British make a lot of promises. Which ones will they keep?"

"They have guaranteed Husain an independent Arab state. This is the promise *we* will help them to keep," Tariq said quietly.

Yassir eyed Mohamed. "Go back to your countinghouse in Paris—or New York. Forget you ever saw us. Part of being a good Muslim—as you say you are, cousin—is to leave alone that which doesn't concern you. *We* don't concern you now. We concern the British. We will be their right arm against the Turks. And they will reward us with Palestine."

"The British will never give independence to Arabs in Palestine. They can't. Once they win it—and they may—they'll keep control of it. Why? Because Jerusalem contains all the

Christian holy places. This isn't just a war, Yassir. For some, it's the last crusade.''

He kissed them each—and his aunt. ''Allah be with all of you.'' Mohamed turned and walked out of the house. He was troubled, and yet he almost envied their dedication.

Thirteen _____

THEY sat together in the front rank of tables in the Paris street café. The first moments of the reunion between Judah and Mohamed had been somewhat strained. Neither had been sure why. They ordered two *"bocks"* and let time ease down between them like a third guest at the table.

"How is Jacqueline?" Judah asked.

"Jacqueline?" All right. She's coming over to join me."

"That's brave of her, isn't it?"

"Caution isn't one of Jacqueline's failings. I've tried to tell her a German breakthrough could still come. . . ." He fell silent, leaving something unsaid.

"You must be glad she wants to be with you that much," Judah offered.

"Jacqueline has always loved Paris," came the oblique reply. "It's more than a city to her. It's life. I think she wants to be sure it's still here."

Judah nodded. There was a moment of silence. They were both keeping an eye on the old Liebermann Bank building, just across the crowded boulevard.

"And Ruth . . . ?" Mohamed asked.

"I've moved Ruth and the children to Bordeaux for the duration. I don't expect the Germans will ever get that far."

The great brass nameplate that had adorned the bank for over thirty years was being lowered on ropes into a wagon. Its metal would be a Hammadi-Nouari contribution to the French war effort. Metal was almost as rare as manpower these days. In fact, the workmen on the building appeared unusually old to be balancing so precariously. The first phrase of work completed, they teetered against the belleépoque facade higher up on the scaffolding like aging trapeze artists, lowering huge letters molded of black glass edged in gold leaf.

"Where did you find those fellows, Mohamed? At Les Invalides?"

"You try finding able-bodied men in Paris these days. I'm the only one I know still out of uniform." He appraised Judah's now well-worn tunic, face enigmatic.

Judah looked across at the building with something like wonder. "So now we own it?"

"Lock, stock, and barrel—as the Americans say."

"We began in that bank—the day we left university. And now we're hiring our fathers to run it for us," Judah marveled.

"With the Jerusalem office closed, me in New York . . . and you playing soldier, nepotism in reverse seemed the logical step."

Judah nodded thoughtfully. "My father's French isn't very good."

"My father will keep yours out of trouble."

"They have for a number of years. David and Sayid," Judah said.

"Judah and Mohamed," the Arab added. "Only, what's happening to us?" They were silent for another moment.

"It was insanity for Solomon to go there by himself," Judah finally said. "Who did he think he was, Douglas Fairbanks?"

"Brave old Solomon. And Izak and Abdullah." The three dead faces marched through his mind. Mohamed regarded Judah with great seriousness. At least one barrier of strangeness seemed to be dissolved. "It may surprise you—but, in a way, I almost envy you." He paused. "How was it . . . in the war?"

"I hardly know where to begin," Judah admitted.

"You never used to have problems beginning. It was always conclusions that bothered you," Mohamed smiled. "But I'm glad at least you didn't get your ass shot off."

"Not for lack of trying. After Gallipoli, there was Egypt. Then Magdhaba, Rafah, and Gaza." Judah held his breath as the two venerable workmen nearly dropped a huge glass *A* being lowered to its new position. Then he relaxed into a long sigh. "They almost shortened your family name."

Around them, the tables were sprinkled with uniforms. French infantry officers in sky blue with shiny Sam Browne belts and puttees. Belgians in a darker hue. Exuberant Italians in superbly fitted olive tunice with red velvet collars on their capes. Casual British with walking sticks, looking as though they had just come in from a country hike. The hike had been across no-man's-land in France. No second lieutenants in evidence; nearly all of them had been killed. Most of the men here had been wounded. Two aviators lurched in wearing the insignia of the Lafayette Escadrille—Americans who'd volunteered to fly for the Allies because their country was still making up its mind. They were eyed by a pair of noisy *poules*, who would try to win them away to sleazy bedrooms—and succeed.

Mohamed watched the women move toward the pilots. "In this war, the whores will be the only winners."

"No one will win this war—except the profiteers," Judah said.

"Like me?"

"Of course, like you. Every time a bullet missed me, I thought, 'Thank you, Hispañola-Nacional,' " Judah half smiled.

Mohamed chuckled. That bone of contention could finally be buried. "If you hear bullets again, you can thank Krupp. Our supplies all go to the Allies now."

The old waiter came over, set down two more yellow beers, collecting the empties. He wiped the table carelessly, knocking Mohamed's tip to the floor. Judah picked up the coins, passing them to the old man.

"My sons, they are at the front. Two, monsieur," the waiter grumbled. "For months I've heard nothing. But each day the post does not bring a black-edged letter from the Ministry of Defense, I thank God."

"I hope you'll have good news soon," Judah told him.

He eyed Judah's insignia. "And what regiment are you, monsieur?"

"Zion Mule Corps."

The waiter spat on the ground. "Jews. It is they who started this war!"

Mohamed sprang to his feet. "This man has been facing bullets for you and me, you bastard!"

The waiter blanched, then shuffled off to the aviators, whose women were setting up a clamor because their champagne was too warm. Judah put a restraining hand on Mohamed's arm. "Sit down," he said.

Mohamed dropped back onto the wrought-iron seat.

"At least he didn't accuse me of making matzos out of babies' blood," Judah said lightly. "But maybe he will help you to understand. Don't you see, Mohamed? Until we Jews have a country of our own, it will always be the same."

"You are an idiot, you know," Mohamed sighed.

"Why? Because I believe I've found something worth fighting for?"

Mohamed met his friend's eyes squarely. "Because you trust the British to be grateful. Grateful enough to give you that country."

Judah stiffened. "You seem to forget that I've been serving with the British. I think I know how they feel. By making their cause ours, they will make our cause theirs."

"Rot!" Mohamed exploded. "While you were out getting shot at, the British have sold you down the Euphrates. You're living in the world and you've learned nothing about it. Nothing."

Judah rose, pushing back from the table. "I don't think there's much point in continuing this conversation. . . ."

"Now *you* sit down," Mohamed told him. "You seem to forget we Arabs have our dreamers and patriots too. Including my two cousins, who are even more idiotic than you. They're also eagerly offering themselves as fodder for the British war machine. Oh, yes, the British butter their bread on both sides. But they intend to double-cross everyone."

Judah sat down again. "Where did you hear that? In Washington?"

"No. Right here in Paris." He reached into an inner pocket and drew out an envelope. "This piece of paper was put into my hands a few days ago. It's a secret agreement—between Britain and France. Spelling out exactly what they'll do with Palestine when and if the Turks are defeated."

"If it's so secret, how do you happen to have it?"

"I still have a few friends in high places. There's nothing much higher than a bank. You know that. It's a copy, of course. The original was signed months ago. By the French Foreign Minister, Georges-Picot." He passed it to Judah. "Have a look. Maybe it'll knock a few stars out of your eyes."

Judah unfolded and scanned the document.

"As you can see, it sections off the whole of Palestine into red and blue zones. The British and French have turned our country into a game board. 'I give you northern Syria all the way to Saint-Jean-d'Acre. You give me everything beyond Lake Tiberias. I grab Haifa and Acre. You guarantee water from the Tigris and the Euphrates.' " He paused. "Is that enough?"

"Damn. . . ." Judah said. "They haven't left out much."

"Not much," Mohamed agreed. "And they dangle the same carrot before the gullible Jews and Arabs."

Judah sagged with sudden emptiness. "Can I keep this document, Mohamed?"

"Why not? Maybe you should show it to your friend Weizmann. It might wake him up." His voice took on sudden urgency. "Leave Palestine alone, Judah. Leave it to remain the peaceful land we grew up in—where Jews and Arabs lived in harmony, even under the Turkish flag."

"Times have changed."

"Have they? What difference does it really make if we have a French or a British flag waving over us? People don't live by flags. They don't eat flags. They don't sleep with flags. They don't grow flags in their fields. I tell you the only hope for our land—yours and mine—is to let the strong protect it. Let them police it. Let them keep the peace. It began with the Romans; let it end where it will. But not with a struggle between your people and mine. Neither are fit to rule it. That's the truth."

Judah returned his pince-nez to the breast pocket of his tunic, voice thoughtful. "I can't speak for my people, Mohamed. And you shouldn't speak for yours. We are, after all, only observers from a distance. We may join events, but we can't control them. Will your Arab nationalists hang up their expectations with their uniforms? I doubt it. Whatever happens, the dreamers and patriots struggle on. And if the choice should finally fall between Arab and Jew. . . ." His glance shifted toward the waiter, keeping his distance from their table. "Well, I think our need may be the greater." He stood up, folding the copy of the document into his pocket.

"What will you do?" Mohamed asked, rising with him.

"See Weizmann. Then go back."

Mohamed sighed. "Some people never learn. Knowing this, you're still prepared to search for your Jewish Holy Grail? Your Golden Fleece? Your philosopher's stone?"

Judah nodded. "Until I find something better."

"I suppose if there were no madmen there'd be no legends." Mohamed put his hand out and Judah took it. Behind them the new glass letters blazed in the sunlight: HAMMADI-NOUARI BANK, black and gold against the gray marble façade.

"And what will you do with your sanity?" Judah asked, suddenly feeling very close to his old friend again.

"Make money," Mohamed said.

The whistle shrieked. The hissing, sneezing steam engine pulled into London's Victoria Station. On the congested platform, glistening with dawn rain, wounded men were disgorging from the coaches into the confusion of arrival. For some, nurses and attendants waited with wheelchairs and stretchers. The more fortunate walked off carrying rifles and packs; Tommies, and officers in trench coats, scarcely out of their teens, with pencil-thin mustaches and battle-glazed eyes. Wives and relatives surged forward to embrace loved ones in the chaos of a hundred reunions.

Through the rain-spattered train window, Judah spotted a familiar face emerging out of the steam. A tall, dapper apparition in fur-collared overcoat, top hat worn at a slight angle, neatly rolled umbrella swinging along with the dancing verve of his stride.

Musette bag over shoulder, Judah hastily descended the platform. The two men embraced briefly, intensely.

"Thank God, I say thank God," Weizmann breathed.

"You look well, Doctor," Judah said. "Happy, well, and tired."

Weizmann grabbed his arm, dragging him forward through the crowd. "So much to tell you, I can hardly wait." They were pressed back against a baggage cart by a passing file of military police.

"Good news, Doctor?"

"Good news," came the jaunty reply. "Would you believe it, that I, Chaim Weizmann, a Yid from Motol, and an *almost* professor from Manchester—which, let's be honest, isn't exactly London—have finally managed to open the hallowed doors of Whitehall? Judah, you can tell Jabotinsky: stop worrying. While he's being an army, I am definitely becoming a state!"

He glanced at Judah as they moved out toward a waiting taxi. The face looking back at him didn't smile. It was sun-tanned, taut, hair clipped into a new sparseness, the ever-lean frame toughened into truncheon hardness.

"The Lister Institute—in Chelsea," Weizmann told the driver. They climbed in and settled back against the quilted leather seats.

"I've made a conquest," Weizmann confided excitedly. "This you won't believe. Sir Mark Sykes, Chief Secretary of the War Cabinet." His flat features widened expansively. "We have passed from the days of theorizing into the 'now' of hard reality, Judah. Even Lord Balfour is taking our aims seriously."

"Is he?" Judah asked. Weizmann was too filled with his accomplishments to notice the nip in Judah's tone.

"Of course, we are only amateur state builders with no experience in government," Weizmann went on. "After all, Judah, we are a people divorced from our homeland for over eighteen centuries, and only a few generations from the ghetto." He recaptured Judah's arm with enthusiasm. "Now we find we are addressing a world that's ready to listen. Now is the time to put in our claim for restitution."

"Have you a knife on you, Doctor?"

Weizmann regarded him quizzically. "No. Why?"

"Good. Because when you hear what I have to tell you, you will cut your throat."

"May I ask what you are talking about?"

"Politicians, Doctor. Their lies, their snares, their tricks. Their promises."

"Defeatism, from you, Judah?" Weizmann regarded him with hurt disbelief. "I'd expect to hear such talk from my enemies—and believe me, there is no shortage. Now, are you going to listen? Or are you going to make disparaging remarks?"

"I'm listening."

Weizmann leaned back, slightly vexed. "Sir Mark Sykes has my memorandum. He asked me for it himself. Outlining Zionist aims. What's more"—his voice lowered, with an eye on the cabbie—"he told me confidentially that from the strategic point of view, a Jewish Palestine—rebuilt, developed agriculturally, modernized—could be of great importance to the British Commonwealth. I'm quoting."

They pulled up in front of the Institute, and the conversation broke off. Judah paid the driver. They headed inside through the familiar laboratory building to Weizmann's office. Coats and hats removed, Weizmann sat down facing Judah across the desk, swiveling around in his chair until the springs creaked.

"Now then, Judah, just to be clear: Sykes has promised to persuade Lord Balfour to make some sort of open declaration in our favor. Maybe not entirely official. But *officially* unofficial. Perhaps only a letter of intent—for after the war—from the Foreign Minister. Along the lines of my memorandum. An agreement. An offer. Yes," he leaned back ebulliently. "An offer."

"I wonder if Sykes is as generous as his confrere Georges-Picot, in Paris."

Weizmann cocked an eyebrow at his friend. "Frankly you surprise me, Judah. One must live with politicians, fallibilities and all. Believe me, it was no small achievement winning Sykes to our side. I've been getting more shrapnel from anti-Zionist Jews than from the government."

Judah knew the chemist was referring to the Conjoint Committee, led by Sir Aaron Montmarsh. These English Jews, mostly rich, partly powerful, and totally assimilated, had launched a vigorous offensive against Weizmann.

"I tell you, Judah, anti-Zionist Jews do more harm to our cause than anti-Semitic Christians." The chemist cleared his desk top, sweeping all into a drawer. He salvaged a few scraps of paper into his pockets. "Notes. If I don't write myself notes, I tend to forget things." Weizmann's tone changed. "So! What was all that business about cutting my throat?"

"Good news first, Chaim." He reached into a breast pocket. "I've brought you this—from Baron Edmond."

"You've seen Rothschild? When?"

"In Bordeaux. I stopped on my way to Paris. He's quite fit. Over seventy now, but vigorous as ever." He handed an envelope to Weizmann. "This is for your federation. 'To fight the assimilationists,' Rothschild told me. That means Montmarsh's crowd."

Weizmann pulled a check from the envelope. £250. "Gratefully received." He tucked it into an already bulging breast pocket. "Ruth. I forgot to ask you, how is Ruth? She must be glad to have you out of it."

"I'm going back, which doesn't please her much. Rejoining Trumpeldor in Palestine. The Mule Corps is being brigaded into the Jewish Legion. We'll march with Allenby—to take Jerusalem."

"Please God, I wish I could go with you." He closed his eyes for a moment. "I've never been there, you know. I've never seen it."

"I hope one day you will."

"Hope? It's more than a hope."

Judah was silent. His eyes drifted off through the glass partition toward the long tables where chemists in white smocks were working. "I know how much you've put into this cause, Chaim. How much of yourself."

"All right. What have you been holding back, Judah?"

"This." Judah took from his pocket the envelope Mohamed had given him. "Sykes seems to have neglected metioning it to you. Although he should have, since he drew it up sixteen months ago—as you can see by the date of the letter. It's known as the Sykes-Picot Treaty."

Weizmann read in silence punctuated by the creak of his chair. He drew a long breath.

"So you can see why I am not impressed by his offer to you. The piece of cake has already been given away, Chaim. All of it. For an independent Arab state—or possibly a confederation of Arab states, strictly supervised by the British and French. The Russians have already approved it. They've even informed the Japanese. It would seem Sir Mark Sykes thought you should be the *last* to know."

Weizmann paced the small office, pausing to watch the movements of two fan-tailed *Carassius auratus* specimens circling each other in a fishbowl. "The fallibility of politicians. First, the McMahon letter, in which the British High Commissioner in Cairo promised to support Husain ibn-Ali's bid for the restoration of the caliphate. In return, the British got Arab support for Colonel Lawrence. That letter caused us enough trouble. But, fortunately, McMahon didn't actually mention Palestine by name. So what he gave away, no one can be too sure of. But this . . ." He waved the document Judah had brought him. "This spells it out all too clearly."

Judah nodded. "It won't benefit the British, letting the

French in as partners. It won't help the Arabs, and it's the last *kaddish* for us."

Suddenly Weizmann began to laugh. It rolled out of him, exploding the tension. "And I thought I was doing so well! Only the Jews against me. Did you see Montmarsh's letter to *The Times?* No, of course you didn't. As a staunch British Jew, he feels *personally called upon* to rescue Judaism from the clutches of Zionism."

"Montmarsh has been made a member of the War Cabinet, hasn't he?"

Weizmann nodded. "A Jew on the War Cabinet. Such an honor, and look whom they picked."

Judah weighed this. "In that case, he must have known about the Sykes-Picot Treaty all this time?"

"Another dagger up his sleeve."

"Why are they so antagonistic, these British Jews?" Judah asked.

"Even the House of Rothschild is divided over Zionism, Judah. Here, in England, old Leopole and his wife consider me no better than a poacher."

Judah looked at the man he most admired in the world. A man torn between faith and doubt, hope and despair, friend and enemy. An average man would have surrendered to disappointment a hundred times. But Weizmann had never been that. Even now, Judah could sense that mysterious rallying of ideas into the optimism that made it possible to continue the struggle. Weizmann had actually begun to smile again.

"Oh, they're not all against me. I still have Lord Nathaniel, Walter, and James Rothschild. They've opened important doors. To the Crewnes. Ever heard of them?"

"Lord Crewne, yes."

"Staunch Liberals. Great friends of Asquith and Lloyd George. Invited me to their country estate this weekend. Montmarsh will be there. Pity I can't go. I might have dropped a chamber pot on him."

Judah perked up. "Have me invited in your place, Chaim."

"That's possible. But why?"

"As a home-grown Palestinian, perhaps I could pull a scale or two from Montmarsh's eyes."

Weizmann considered it. "You're a born salesman, Judah. Sell him on leaving us alone."

"I can try. And you, Chaim. Will you throw a chamber pot at Sykes?"

Weizmann was watching the goldfish again. "These gilded 'gefilte fish' can teach you something. Keep circling. Never force someone into a position from which he cannot retreat." He turned back with brisk decision. "As long as Sykes pretends to be our friend, I shall pretend never to have heard of the Sykes-Picot Treaty." He handed the document back to Judah. "I never saw it."

"A bit of your 'quiet diplomacy,' then?" Judah smiled.

Weizmann eyed him with a mysterious twinkle. "Did you ever know the meaning of the word 'Israel'? It's in the Book of Genesis."

Judah shook his head.

Weizmann sat back at his desk, a look of serenity returning to his face. "It means: he who struggles with God and man—and wins."

Down the sky the clouds marched in procession before the soft English breeze. Beneath it, a ragged rank of beaters moved between shooters, assailing the undergrowth with sticks, panicking winged creatures into a storm of pellets.

Sir Aaron Montmarsh had already bagged two pheasant and a woodcock. The morning was loping along. He regarded the man walking beside him with measured coolness, his words a telegraphic compression.

"Met your partner, Hammadi, once," he said. "Hunting with a German chap. Count von Bülow. Bavarian mountains. Splendid lodge. Nice spot of scenery. Decent game. Jolly good marksman, your Arab friend. Got a buck at three hundred yards—first shot. Rather put us all to shame." He strode on with brisk steps, nursing a fine double-barreled Purdey in the crook of his arm. Behind him, his bearer carried its mate, breech open. "Bad show if we got a blast of buckshot in the backside, what?" He snorted a chuckle. "Nothing like a rough shoot."

Sir Aaron's balding crown was tucked under a tweed hat, his legs encased in diamond-patterned Argyle stockings and plus fours. An oversize mustache, still very black, underscored a small nose. Eyes large, cheekbones high, it was an aristocratic English face, from which any trace of the middle-

European Jew—in mannerism or expression—had been expunged by three generations of boarding schools and gentlemen's clubs.

Judah had not found it difficult to launch Montmarsh into a discussion of Zionism. The man was only too eager to voice his views. The disputation began the night before, behind the closed doors of Lord Crewne's paneled library. Judah and he collided over port, after most of the dinner guests had retired to bed or billiards. Now they had brought it out into the open of field and stream, had progressed past some of the older chestnuts such as that Zionism was the empty dream of a few misguided Eastern European fanatics.

"Never in a thousand years, my dear chap. Never will Weizmann swing respectable British Jewry to his way of thinking," Montmarsh announced flatly, scanning the cover being rattled by beaters' sticks.

"By 'respectable,' I take it you mean rich and powerful, Sir Aaron?"

"Confess it, Nouari, most of that chemist fellow's followers are from London's East End. Believe me, I'm not without compassion for our homeless Russian brethren. Pogroms—all that. Though Russia *is* our ally. Religion and nationalism don't mix." He peered sharply across at Judah. "Surely you'll agree to that as a democratic principle? Hasn't been a church state in England since Henry VIII. Pity you didn't bring a gun, dear boy."

The war had not diminished Judah's distate for blood sports. He had come along only to shoot down Montmarsh's view—hoping to provoke the War Cabinet minister into a target position.

"You see Zionism as a religious posture," Judah suggested. "I see it as a permanent escape from thousands of years of persecution. Not so much a religious state as a state of survival." They stepped over a fallen tree trunk, moving along the edge of a wood. "Surely you consider it something of a miracle that a homeless people wandering so long through the nations of history have survived?" Judah asked.

Montmarsh grunted, pausing in stride. "Miracle, perhaps. But Jews are bound together by religion only. *They* are not a race. Ergo, they have no claim to a national homeland." Having delivered his final word on the subject, Montmarsh drew an arc with the muzzle of his shotgun. Bang. Bang. Two shots—one bird.

"Well shot, Aaron," his host, Lord Crewne, called over.

"Thanks, Gordon." The beater dispatched a dog to retrieve the feathered corpse. Montmarsh traded for his second gun. They waited. The dog came back in a tail-wagging rush, a quail couched gently in wide jaws. It was dropped into the bulging bag.

"When you speak of Jews, you always say 'they,' Sir Aaron," Judah challenged. "Don't you consider that you are one?"

The War Minister winced slightly, striding on. "Jew, of course. But British first. That is where my loyalties lie, and that is where I stand. I view my religion precisely as Churchill or Balfour see theirs. No more—no less. I certainly have no objection to homeless Russians going to Palestine, or anywhere, if the locals will have 'em. But the most that Zionists can demand is religious and civil liberties. Not their own nation. Why, by that token, Nouari, the Presbyterians could demand a country of their own. Or the Baptist—or those Mormon chaps."

A winged flurry rattled up the sky ahead of them, Montmarsh fired again.

"Damn! Missed."

Some feet away, Lord Crewne's gun banged twice, bringing down a brace. "Bad luck, Aaron," he called over. "Try one of my guns?"

"Not the gun, Gordon. Didn't give 'em enough lead," he bellowed back. They moved forward again, a soft rain beginning to settle on their tweeds.

"If I'm putting you off your shot, Sir Aaron, we can postpone this discussion until after lunch," Judah suggested.

"Not at all. But you've been asking all the questions, Nouari," Montmarsh snapped. "My turn now. As a native-born Palestinian—where would this Russian-Jewish invasion put you and the Arab chaps? In the borscht, I suspect."

"You seem to think Zionism is only the result of pogroms in Russia," Judah replied. "That's far from true."

"Oh? Where does your Weizmann get his ideas? From Smolenskin, Pinsker, Mohilever, Achad Ha-am." They sloshed on through a muddy patch of moor. Several members of the party lagged behind to inspect a field nest.

"Come, come," Montmarsh goaded. "Admit I have you there."

"We've all read Pinsker and the others. Even, it seems, you." Judah smiled. "But the dream of a national Jewish life goes much deeper than the ideology of a few Russian intellectuals. Even Palestinian Jews share it. . . ."

A sudden downpour drove shooters and bearers to shelter, some to an old mill. Judah and Montmarsh dashed for the cover of a hump-back bridge. Drenched, cold, breaths steaming, they peered out. Montmarsh placidly lit a pipe, exhaling aromatic Dunhill smoke. "Most beautiful country in the world, England. How I love this land!" Judah went silent. "Run out of steam, Nouari?" Montmarsh leaned back against the damp, mossy stones, puffing contentedly. "The floor is yours, old man."

A slight frown creased the space between Judah's brows. "Well, then, even if you *were* right—that Jews are not a race—we can't all be dismissed as merely joined by religion. If we *are* 'the chosen,' it's because we are the unwilling instruments of God. 'Chosen' because we, through Abraham, answered God's call. Moses came along to renew Abraham's covenant. Moses set out the terms of the contract. God promised to make Abraham's seed an eternal light to *other nations* of the world—if the Jews obeyed His laws and commandments. It was those laws that bound them as a nation."

Montmarsh knocked the ashes from his pipe. "Score one. You got 'nation' in there, all right." He dipped his pipe into a pouch, thumbing in more tobacco.

"Sir Aaron, if we are to believe the teachings of our religion at all, we must believe that, for the first and only time, God revealed himself at Sinai. It was His word that gave the Jews a guidebook through the Diaspora. A law to live by. A Bible full of stories—some certainly history, some perhaps only fable. But a code of living."

"Laws and commandments of a *religion*. My point," Montmarsh asserted.

"Not at all. One doesn't have to be religious to be a Jew, Sir Aaron. I'm certainly not. But to most Christians, there are no ex-Jews, only lapsed Jews. As some of your friends in the War Cabinet, what was Disraeli's religion? He was a staunch member of the Church of England most of his life, but I'll lay you a guinea they'll refer to him as a 'converted' Jew."

"Now you're seeing *my* point, dear boy," Montmarsh pounded. "Although you don't *see* that you see it. If Zionists get a homeland of their own, whenever Christians feel a bit anti-Semitic, they'll be able to say, 'Now they have a homeland, pack them off to it!' "

"Lord Balfour has assured Dr. Weizmann—"

Montmarsh cut him off. "Balfour's enthusiasm for Zionism is strictly dilettante. The man actually considers it would be a fascinating experiment to reconstruct the Jewish kingdom. I said to him last week, 'Arthur, d'you know it's written somewhere, that when the Jews have a king again it'll be the end of the world?' Imagine what he answered me: 'Even more interesting, Aaron.' " Montmarsh relit his pipe, talking through the smoke. "No, my dear fellow, that sort of mysticism won't do."

An hour later, the shooting party had completed a full circle and was homeward bound. Borne aloft on a slight rise, Crewne Castle loomed Gothic turrets into a freshiening sky. Down to its left, the ruins of an abbey twice destroyed; once by Henry VIII, later by Cromwell. On the right crowning another rise, the silhouette of an ancient druidic stone circle. Across the pastures, church bells called. Montmarsh filled his lungs with tingling air. "English countryside on a Sunday morning. Nothing like it." He paused. "To be a Jew . . . and an Englishman is a rare privilege. One I don't intend to jeopardize."

They crossed the road, taking the turn into the long drive to the castle. "One point of history you've forgotten, Sir Aaron," Judah said. "Spain, Portugal, France—even your beloved England—at one time or another drove out their Jews, massacred them, or kept them as Russia does today, as a scapegoat people. It could happen again. Anywhere."

"Stuff and nonsense, Nouari. We're in the twentieth century." Montmarsh paused, passing over his shotgun to the bearer, who had come up. The Purdeys would be cleaned, oiled, and returned to their velvet-lined box. He turned back to Judah. "If any country were to begin such a policy, the rest of the world would soon deter them, starting with the Pope. You're suffering from nightmares. You might as well fear the black plague. Haven't had one of them either, since the Middle Ages. Torquemada is dead, my friend. And I, for one, feel quite safe from the flames of Berkeley Square."

"Sir Aaron, no one's threatening to drag you out of Mayfair and ship you off to Palestine. Zionism was never intended as an *enforced* homeland." Judah drew breath. He hadn't meant to lose his temper. "The point is, Dr. Weizmann speaks for Jews everywhere. You and your Conjoint Committee speak only for a privileged minority. Your opposition puzzles the Christian world. It could do irreparable harm to Weizmann's great act of faith—if you still intend to oppose him."

Montmarsh's face was unyielding. "I do, Mr. Nouari. With every means at my command. In the columns of *The Times*. In the War Cabinet. Because I firmly believe a nationalist movement such as Weizmann proposes will *provoke* anti-Semitism. Because I *am* a Jew, I feel its's my obligation to stop Zionism—now and forever."

Lord Crewne came ambling over. "Doesn't the British Army teach its junior officers to shoot any more?"

"It wasn't my day to add to the bag, Lord Crewne," Judah replied.

Failure. Yes, that was what Judah had to admit to himself as he stood on the station platform at Clangford waiting for the London train.

How to face Weizmann with it? Weizmann had called him a good salesman. Maybe he was only capable of convincing someone who was already believer. Converting the converted. Montmarsh had half convinced him! Judah knew how Mohamed would react to the offer Weizmann was trying to extract from Balfour. No, of course it didn't take into account Arab dreams and aims. But dreams and aims were nothing weighed against needs—and what he'd told Mohamed that day in Paris in the street café had been right. *Their* need was greater.

Zosia's cause—and his need to preserve her ghost by dedication and action. Zosia had given her life to further Zionism. To destroy its worst enemy, she had sacrificed herself. Judah was bound to serve her memory. He had only to close his eyes—evoke the pale face, the intense expression, hear her voice in his mind's ear—and he was rededicated.

And Ruth. She, too, had made of Zionism a dedication of her heart. How mistaken he had been to imagine he could ever give to Ruth the love he'd felt for her cousin Zosia. The well was dry. What an injustice he had done her, by love

withheld! What small pleasures had he given her . . . except
the children?

Yes, the twins—ten now. Abe. And Zed, so serious. More
like her namesake Zosia then he could have imagined possible. The gray, deep-set eyes. The same serious look. What
future would Zionism offer them—these new Nouaris? French-
born. Would Abe and Zed want to live in the New Jerusalem
he was working to create? Or, like Montmarsh, would they be
tied to the land of their birth? He, too, loved France—but he
had not forgotten Dreyfus, or the frenzy of the crowd. What
was there about the Jews that could cause such rancor, bitterness, hostility? Might his own children not one day . . .
require some haven of salvation? A Zionist state? Weizmann
was right. A homeland of their own must be the only answer.

Yet Montmarsh firmly believed that such a homeland would
cause more anti-Semitism, more conflict. With whom? wondered Judah. Surely the Arabs would welcome development
of their homeland. The jobs it would bring. The boost in the
general economy. The stride of Palestine into the twentieth
century.

All these were truths—but where within himself was the
true believer's fire? He knew his failing: the ability to see
both sides. That some part of Montmarsh's arguments had
won his consideration, he could never admit to Weizmann.
Nation building requires fanatics.

The engine puffed forward and Judah climbed into a first-
class carriage, more than ever in his life feeling an urgent
need to be alone. To put some order to the chaos in his
thinking before coming to confess to Weizmann, "I've failed."

The chemist was in a high state of suppressed excitement
as he entered the lobby of the Ritz. Weizmann threaded his
way between tea drinkers and sat himself down in an over-
stuffed chair. "Did you order tea?" he asked.

Judah nodded. "And sandwiches. Hope you like cucumbers."

"And lemon? I take lemon with my tea."

The waiter arrived and set down cups, pot, and all before
them. His tailcoat looked slightly moth-eaten.

"No lemons, sir. The war." He moved on toward a major

general entertaining his mother. The string quartet had launched into "Smiles."

"Well, are you going to keep me in suspense?" Judah asked.

Weizmann took a gulp of tea. "Sykes and I talked in careful circles. Then I let it fall lightly that I knew of a secret letter—drawn in the earlier stages of the war."

"So Sykes knows you know."

Weizmann nodded. "But he'll forget he ever made that treaty with Picot if we get our declaration from Balfour." He sipped. "No lemon. Uncivilized."

"What did he say, Chaim? Can you trust him?"

"Sykes is a great Arabist, you know. Quite an expert on the Middle East. And he made the point, with which I don't disagree, that he doesn't see our national homeland as some sort of painless substitute of Jews for Arabs."

Between bites of sandwich, Weizmann described the interview in some detail. His confidence in the chief secretary of the War Cabinet had not been shaken by knowledge of the treaty. Sykes had led him into official channels and taught him how to swim with the tide toward friendly shoals like Ormsby-Gore, Cecil, and Amery, all members of the Cabinet.

Sykes had told him: "Within a generation, the Arabs will come into their own. As a people they have intelligence, vitality . . . and most important, Dr. Weizmann, they all speak one tongue. They'll come to terms with the new Jews. Yes, the two peoples will get along—if the Arabs receive support from your Zionists. Emir Feisal believes it too."

Judah nodded. "You'd think Sykes was doing the Arabs a favor by giving Palestine to us. But what about Montmarsh's continued barrage in *The Times*?"

Weizmann brandished a cucumber sandwich like a victorious banner. "He can fire away with my compliments. It's those letters from the Conjoint Committee that are forcing the government to action. Oh, the British may have their own explicit form of lethargy when it comes to red tape—but unlike your Turkish friends, when they *do* move, you may count on them to do the right thing."

"Right for whom?"

"Balfour's declaration will be right for us, Judah. I drafted it myself. At Sykes's request. It comes up before the War Cabinet for the second time next week."

"What happened to the first time?" Judah asked.

"Montmarsh got it removed from the agenda."

"God save the Jews from Jews."

"Don't worry. Lloyd George himself has put the declaration back on," Weizmann assured him.

"Can you be certain the Cabinet will approve it?"

Weizmann allowed himself a chuckle. "Off the record, Sykes thinks Montmarsh and the entire Conjoint Committee are undisguised 'pro Turco-Germans,' angling for a separate peace for Turkey."

Judah regarded him with some amazement. "Montmarsh? Sykes can't be serious. The man's more British than Dick Whittington's cat. Sorry to say it, Chaim. I don't share your confidence."

"Montmarsh got to you, did he?"

"Perhaps a little," Judah acknowledged. "Anyway, I won't be here to see the outcome. I must go back in a few days."

"Wait."

"Why?"

"Because I want you to carry the news."

"Even if it's bad?"

"It won't be."

Weizmann leaned back against the gold damask chair. The quartet slipped into a spirited rendition of "It's a Long Way to Tipperary." People began to wave cups in time to the music. Weizmann's face breathed confidence, overconfidence. His characteristic failing, Judah thought. But a trait that could also make him a winner.

"Lord Balfour has assured me that an offer will be made," the chemist said. "He told me he knows that he'll please one group of Jews and displease another."

"And we get the bride's bouquet. Why?"

"Because—and I quote—we represent a worthy idea. With British support, Zionism is the future of Palestine."

Officers and ladies were joining voices in "Tipperary." It rose like an anthem among the teacups.

Weizmann hunched forward, taking a mouthful of cucumber sandwich. "And I told Lloyd George: we don't intend to go to Palestine to become Arabs. Or Druses. Or even Englishmen. Only to become a Jewish nation."

"I'll quote you—to Jabotinsky. He'll love that," Judah

said. All around them now the voices rose: "It's a long way to go. . . ."

"And you, Judah. You don't love it?"

Unease blurred Judah's glance. "There is an old saying, Chaim: You should be careful what you wish for. Because you might get it."

The Prime Minister's promise has been kept. Once again, the declaration so carefully worded by Chaim Weizmann was on the agenda of the War Cabinet—for further revision and final approval. East End London Jewry, led by Rabbi Gaster, were out to demonstrate support. They clustered in the street at the entrance to Whitehall, lashed by rain, cut by the icy blast of wind, and restrained by the presence of a pair of sedate bobbies, impervious to man or elements. Among the crowd were bemedaled war wounded and older men in their best black usually reserved for *shul*. "Is this day not in some measure an expression of the will of God?" Gaster had told them. Above the little pool of hats and faces and black umbrellas, soggy placards proclaimed:

YES—TO A JEWISH HOMELAND
ENGLISH ZIONIST FEDERATION
ERETZ ISRAEL

Their chant rose bravely above the growl of traffic: "Where are we going?—Jerusalem, Jerusalem . . . Jerusale-e-e-em!"

Judah Nouari found himself pressed against the rope cordoning off the demonstrators from the arriving ministerial limousines. For almost an hour, he'd been waiting in the rain to make one last stab at dissuading Montmarsh from blocking the declaration again. The minister had been 'out' to all Judah's phone calls.

A procession of ministers had already been police-saluted through the official doors when the Montmarsh Rolls drove up. Montmarsh climbed out.

"Sir Aaron!" Judah shouted, his voice loud in his own ears above the chant of the crowd. Montmarsh squinted over. Recognition came with displeasure.

"Nouari. . . .Thought you'd gone back to your Jewish Legion."

"You know I've been trying to get hold of you. . . ." Judah ducked under the restraining cordon. Montmarsh waved back the police. "It's about the declaration to be presented today. . . ."

Montmarsh took a step toward the entrance. "This is most irregular, Nouari. Afraid I cannot discuss restricted information." Judah blocked his way.

"Please, I must talk to you. Look at all these people. . . ." His gesture swept the rain-soaked crowd. "They've brought you a petition."

At the head of the crowd of protesters, a stocky, white-bearded little man with the air of Santa Claus pressed a dank document across the cordon into Judah's hand. Rabbi Gaster.

"Tell him there's more tears on this than raindrops. Tell him!"

Judah passed it to Montmarsh. "Four hundred and fifty-seven names, Sir Aaron. All British Jews. All Zionists. How many can you number on your Conjoint Committee, sixteen? The voice of the majority, Montmarsh. Are you prepared to ignore it?"

The chant rose from the little cluster: "Eretz Israel . . . Eretz Israel. . . ."

Anger clouded Montmarsh's ruddy face. "Mr. Nouari, I do what my conscience dictates. Neither you nor that crowd, nor anyone, can alter that. I shall speak out against it today with all the force of my convictions. I am not blinded by Weizmann's schemes. I am not gullible. When I'm finished, Dr. Weizmann and his demonstrators can take their declaration and try it on the Americans! I understand he has a friend there in Supreme Court Justice Brandeis. Good day, Mr. Nouari."

Montmarsh started forward. Judah put a restraining hand on his arm. "Weizmann has given a lifetime to reach this hour. . . ."

"Stand aside!" Montmarsh ordered. He signaled the "bobbies," who stepped forward.

"Please, Sir Aaron, give me another moment," Judah protested, seizing his arm again. "Listen. . . ."

Montmarsh pulled free, heading into the building. The bobbies were politely firm. "I would suggest, sir, that you return to the other side of that barrier." Reluctantly Judah obeyed.

Rabbi Gaster, wide-brimmed hat jammed low over his forehead like a crazed cowboy, grabbed him by the shoulders.

"Judah!" he shouted. "Wasn't it me who told Weizmann not to count on anyone? Would he listen? Would he?"

It was always like this. The intense, arguing, differing, demanding, yes, embarrassing brotherhood from whom Judah could feel as separate at times as from Norsemen. Yet they claimed him with their words, their voices, their exaggerations, their passions. You fought with them—and for them. Was there not in this a portion of the punishment of being born "chosen"? He turned wearily to the angry leader beside him.

"Rabbi," he said. "I have a friend. You've heard of him. Jabotinsky. He has a favorite saying: 'Hope always. Desire much. Expect little.' " Judah looked back at the government building, closed now against all outside intrusion. "From Montmarsh I didn't expect very much."

Judah made his way through the demonstrators, heading out toward Parliament Square. Big Ben boomed the hour in muffled, dolorous tone. The hour the cabinet meeting was to begin.

Fourteen _____

JUDAH had no way of knowing that at that moment Weizmann was sitting in the waiting room of Lloyd George's office. To the Prime Minister's secretary, he was an unwelcome addition to the decor. But the chemist was determined to remain until the War Cabinet meeting was over. Knees apart, hands cupped over walking stick, he appeared to have taken root in his chair. His eyes were fixed on the secretary.

"Suppose, Mr. Kerr, before reaching a final decision . . . they should want to ask me some questions?"

"My dear sir," the secretary assured Weizmann patronizingly, "since the British Government has *been* a government, no private individual has ever been admitted into that room. Not while the Cabinet is in session. I suggest you'll be more usefully occupied in your laboratory. You'll be notified in due course." Kerr returned his attention to a sheaf of letters. Reluctantly Weizmann rose.

Inside the War Cabinet Chamber, Sir Aaron Montmarsh had taken the floor to launch into one of the most impassioned speeches of an eloquent career. At one point his words so moved him that tears ran down his cheeks.

"His arguments were so vehement, his tirades so rampantly anti-Zionist, that both Lord Balfour and Lloyd George decided in all fairness they should call on *me* to reply. For this, they sent a messenger to Lloyd George's office. I had just been sent away—by his secretary!" Weizmann's voice shook as he recounted the day's events to Judah that evening, in the modest house in Addison Road. The chemist had rented it for his growing family. Across the room, Vera was spooning applesauce to their youngest son, whose chubby legs protruded from a high chair. Her fine, sensitive features

318

showed deep concern, more for the anguish of her husband than the outcome of his cause. "They telephoned me. But I didn't know where Chaim was," Vera said.

Weizmann nodded. "They tried here—they tried the laboratory." He was almost beside himself with gloom. "And all the time they were looking for me, I was only down the hall from them, two offices away. I had gone to Ormsby-Gore's office. I thought when he returned from the meeting, he would bring me the news. Such news . . .!" Weizmann drew a slow breath. "Because they couldn't find me to reply—to argue—to defend—Montmarsh got the declaration reworded."

"But he didn't get it struck off, Chaim," Judah pointed out. "It's still alive, waiting to be voted on."

"Watered down! A disaster! If we agree to Montmarsh's rewording, it will plague our future for the rest of time." Vera came over to her husband, offering a glass of sweet red wine.

"Drink, Chaim. Calm down."

He waved it aside. "How can I drink, Vera? Is this a happy occasion? An occasion for blessings? Give me instead a cup of tea."

"You have one in your hand, Chaim." She smiled across at Judah. "With lemon."

"Exactly what words have they changed in the declaration?" Judah asked.

"Enough. My draft read quite specifically: 'Palestine shall be reconstituted as a National Home of the Jewish *people*.' "

"Lloyd George had approved that, hadn't he?" Judah asked.

"He did. But now Montmarsh has got it changed to: '. . . the establishment *in* Palestine of the National Home *for* the Jewish *race*. . . .' " He pushed the paper into Judah's hand.

"Don't you see?" Weizmann said. "*People* implies a nation. Nations are made of people."

"And *race* only expresses ethnic origin," Judah mused. "Descendants of a common ancestor. A peculiar breed. In other words, Chaim, Montmarsh had gone against his own beliefs in order to prevent any idea of nationalism creeping into this declaration. Political expediency at its most pragmatic."

Weizmann's face was drained of color. "He went further.

It also introduces the subject of civic and religious rights for the existing non-Jewish community.''

"Afraid I don't follow," Judah said, scanning it. "Aren't they entitled to those rights?"

"Of course they are! Who's denying it?" He stabbed a finger almost into Judah's face. "The *implication* is what's wrong. The implication that Zionists might possibly have oppressive intentions. It's practically warning the Arabs that they could need protection from us. That we might just be dangerous to them. Implication, Judah. What's written between the lines.''

Judah rose, pacing the small room. "Chaim, the Jewish code of law forbids a husband to beat his wife. Does that imply that he intends to beat her?"

Weizmann came over to Judah with decision. "We must turn it down flat. Stand firm, Judah. Demand a clearer statement."

"And if you do, Chaim, what then?" Judah asked. "The government could weary of this tedious wrangling—and throw out the whole thing. With the war beginning to swing to the Allies, this is the moment to get what we can. Take what we can get."

Weizmann looked stunned. "Accept their offer—in this form? Knowing of the Sykes-Picot Treaty? Of the McMahon letter? Accept a declaration open to a hundred reinterpretations?"

"Yes. Take it," Judah said quietly, surprised at his own decision.

"Take it?" Weizmann stared at him.

"I'm a banker, Chaim. I don't separate entities under a microscope. I see the project as a whole. And I say, get it in your pocket. When you've got it, you'll have something. Now you have nothing."

"What have we worked all these years for, from the days of Herzl? For compromise? Equivocations?" Weizmann demanded.

"It can be clarified later. Refined in stages, like that acetone you're cooking in your distillery. Don't turn down the offer."

Weizmann turned to Vera. Their eyes met across the child cradled in her arms. "And you, Vera? You agree with Judah?"

"What do you believe, Chaim?" she asked. "In your heart?"

Weizmann was quiet for a moment. Then he spoke. "Judah is right. We have to take it."

"Taking it" was not as easy as it sounded. Having dickered further with the wording, Lloyd George's government was still reluctant to issue Balfour's declaration without the approval of their newest ally, the United States. Though President Wilson considered any statement premature, he was finally persuaded by Justice Brandeis to cable: SUPPORT IN PRINCIPLE.

"Nobody in politics likes to make a clean statement," Judah told Weizmann.

The cable was enough to break the deadlock. But Judah Nouari couldn't wait to see the last act played out. He had to go back to Paris before rejoining Jabotinsky, and so he wasn't with Chaim Weizmann on November 2, 1917: the day the chemist found himself again seated in the antechamber of the War Cabinet. Waiting. This time, nothing could have removed him. The Cabinet was in session to vote on issuing the declaration.

The door was opened by a handsome man in his late thirties. He wore a wide brush mustache beneath gentle blue eyes. His gray silk cravat divided a starched white collar. An image of the timeless gentleman-statesman of England, manipulating the subdivision of continents on which the sun was supposed never to set.

"Dr. Weizmann—it's a boy," smiled Sir Mark Sykes, offering a single sheet of paper to Weizmann: the Balfour Declaration.

Weizmann took it, eyes clouding. Perhaps this wasn't the child he had expected. But it was a birth. The declaration—in the form of a letter addressed to Lord Walter Rothschild. It meant a land for a people.

Yes, a people.

Weizmann's eyes scanned the letter, picking out the words: "His Majesty's Government view with favour the establishment in Palestine of a National Home for the Jewish people. . . ."

People—with a National Home. A nation. A land. A sanctuary, where all could forever live in peace and security. A future.

"I must telephone Vera," he said.

Maurice propped high-heeled boots on the brass cherubim that decorated the fender of Madame Mimi's hearth in her Paris brothel. The old *maquereau's* career had positively seen better days. When he took stock of his situation, which was seldom, it put him in a foul mood. Like this afternoon. His polished footwear was almost the last vestige of that crass elegance once flaunted on the boulevards. In those days, the girls had fed his pockets from swinging purses and silk stocking tops with their night's takings. Maurice had aged into scruffy forties, lean muscles plumping into fat. Now he served Madame Mimi as general dog's-body and occasional bouncer—when girls or clients grew obstreperous. Evil days—but at least it was a billet out of the damp. And if his services took him less often into the bed of his lady boss, and if her tantrums and temperaments burst upon him like unpredictable storms, at least the vocation kept him in tobacco, cognac, and cocaine. He hoised a glance to a gilt-mirrored reflection bathed in the glow of wine satin curtains. Gone, the brick-red hair—now balding and threaded with gray. Gone, the spark in blue eyes—now watery, faded, pouched in caves of self-abuse. Not much left, he had to admit. But still a better finish than those poor, stupid bastards whose names swelled the casualty lists each day.

Maurice flipped through the pages of a newspaper, hunching above the small grate into which Madame Mimi doled chunks of coal as though they were nuggets. Bitch! And if he complained that she was deliberately freezing his testicles off, she'd rasp back in Pernod tones: "No loss to be missed, chéri." Oh, he'd show her if only he could get his hands on a windfall. A lottery win. A horse. He read on. . . .

Three American infantrymen killed in the first engagement where American troops took part. Buried in France. A wreath hung—the article said—inscribed: *Here lie the first soldiers of the great Republic of the United States who died on the soil of France for Justice and Liberty. November 3, 1917.*

Died to make the world safe for Maurice, he thought. Poor,

stupid bastards. He folded the newspaper over. Nothing but war news any more. Then a photograph caught his eye. He sat up, holding the paper to the madam's frilly lamp for closer inspection.

A woman and a young boy looked back at him framed in print. Something familiar about the woman's face—expression. Something that had lingered on, through all the women's faces he had known. Something memory couldn't quite put name to. A beauty, no doubt about it. Twenty-five? Thirty-five? Hard to tell her age. Yes, that face. . . . It sucked at his mind like some orgasmic ghost. And the boy—familiar too. Maurice's eyes lowered to the caption:

MME. HAMMADI ARRIVES WITH SON, MAURICE

Maurice? He read on: *Wife on the renowned international industrialist Mohamed Hammadi, Mme. Hammadi confided to this reporter that she had no fear of returning to France during wartime, although she has left her small daughter in New York with a French governess. "The Germans will never take Paris," she told me. "It is already captured—by the Americans." Traveling with her is thirteen-year-old Maurice Hammadi, a charming lad with bright red hair and flashing blue eyes. . . .*

Maurice stared at the boy's image. Thirteen . . .? How many years ago—that girl? He tried to recall. Poured himself a cognac. He'd met her shortly after he inherited the Quarter from Jules—who had accidentally run into the spring blade of a knife. The one Maurice still carried, strapped to his armpit.

Suddenly he knew why the boy looked so familiar. He was looking at some part of himself.

"Still got that yellow dress with the black fringes, Madame Hammadi?" The voice on the telephone spoke in the patois of the Paris underworld. For the moment, she could not think. She looked across at her son thumbing through an illustrated edition of a book on snuffboxes in the corner of her private sitting room, upstairs in the house on the Avenue Malenkoff. She tried to keep her voice casual.

"Who is this?" she asked. Young Maurice glanced over with a flick of curiosity.

"You should remember," the man's voice insisted. "Yes, you really should. I gave you quite a souvenir." The voice hardened into a faint threat. "I want to see you. Now," he said. "Bring the kid."

Along with the visceral sinking came an awareness. "I can't do that," she insisted, lowering her voice.

"You'll find a way. I'll be in the avenue du Général Lemonnier—across from the Pont Royal. You've got one hour." The phone clicked. She could feel her son's eyes on her again and forced her voice into a lightness, speaking into the dead phone. "So good of you to call. Yes, my husband I would love to dine." Jacqueline returned the instrument to its cradle, her mind fuzzed with a jumble of thoughts.

"Who was that, Maman?"

"An old friend, Maurice. Imagine, the sun's come out. Such a fine day! Wouldn't you like to walk in the Tuileries?"

"Are there any antique shops near there?"

"Dozens—along the Quai."

"Perhaps I'll find something for my collection," the boy said.

"Stamps, dear?"

"No, Maman. I've decided to collect snuffboxes."

"Bizarre. Take your allowance, then. Maman will have a bit extra. Just in case."

Her son hurried out to ready himself for the expedition. Jacqueline put on a small hat with two feathers projecting at an angle. She thrust a long pearl hatpin through it, and tied a thick veil across her eyes. But it was not her own face she was seeing. Rather, a hazy, half-remembered image. Nearly fourteen years—but she hadn't totally forgotten him. How could she, daily confronting his reflection in the boy?

"I can't understand you, Jacqueline," Mohamed exploded in exasperation that evening. "I told you this morning, twice, that my father was coming this afternoon for no other reason than to see his grandson. You have little enough to think of. For once, you could have been home where you belonged, instead of dragging the boy sight-seeing or wherever you went."

"I bought a snuffbox, Father," Maurice said. It frightened him, seeing his father so angry. Instinctively he felt it better not to mention the man his mother had spoken to in the park. He had left them sitting on a bench together, while he wandered across the street to inspect the shops. In one, he had found his treasure: a Louis XV gold-and-enamel *tabatière* signed *J. Moynat*. The maker's name was listed in his book. The *antiquaire* had undervalued it; of that young Maurice was sure.

"Go get your hat and coat, Maurice," Mohamed ordered sharply. "I'm taking you to see Grandfather Sayid."

"Yes, Father." Maurice hurried to his room.

"Don't trouble about dinner, Jacqueline. Maurice and I will dine with my father."

"He'll think it odd—yes, won't he think it odd if I'm not with you?"

"I will explain that you're unwell. I suggest you have an early night—and avoid champagne." He walked out, joining Maurice in the hall. She could hear the excitement in her son's voice telling his father of his purchase. The closing door cut off all sound.

Jacqueline sat very still in her chair so that the shaking would stop. She was not ill again—Mohamed was wrong. And she hadn't been drinking. But she couldn't tell him why she had not been home for Sayid's visit.

The man she had met in the Tuileries had been scarcely recognizable. She could not imagine that *she* had changed that much. But she had been grateful to the man for pretending to be an old acquaintance in front of her son. His son. His son because of the dropping of a seed. The thought almost made her ill. But Mohamed's son now in every important way. Such a gentle nature, such taste and sensitivity the boy was developing. A love of beauty. A sense of elegance. She could see that as young Maurice grew to maturity she would be closer and closer to him.

But now their whole world was threatened. All three. And the last thread that she had to Mohamed's love would be broken by this pimp's demands.

The doorbell jolted her to her feet. Would he dare to come here? And if he did, how would she get rid of him? Call the police? She hurried to reach the door before Gilles, who had traveled with them from New York.

Judah Nouari stood in the doorway, in uniform. She looked

at him with such relief that Judah had to laugh. "Who were you expecting—the Huns?"

Behind her, Gilles shuffled in, slipping into his jacket. "It's all right, Gilles," she said. "It's Mr. Nouari."

"Will you wish anything, madame?"

"No, Gilles. Nothing. Nothing." The servant left. She stood indecisively in the hall. "Where are you staying, Judah?"

"At the house."

"I thought you'd closed it," she said.

He shrugged. "I've taken the dust cover off one bed. Mohamed not home yet?"

"Gone out. Took Maurice." Her cryptic tone seemed to suppress panic.

"Anything wrong, Jacqueline?" he asked.

"No—nothing. Except everything." She stood glued to the spot. "Stay. I don't want to be alone now. Would you, Judah, please?"

"Of course, if you wish." He took off his trench coat. "But can't we—sit down somewhere?"

She came to life again. "You must forgive me. I'm a perfect fool. My sitting room upstairs—if you don't mind." She lowered her voice. "They listen, you know. They hear every word down here."

He followed her up the stairs, leaving his coat on a chair.

She perched nervously on a flowered chaise across from him, trembling a cigarette into an ivory holder. He reached over, lighting it for her.

"I can't tell Mohamed," she said suddenly. "It's not that he doesn't know already. It's that he's chosen to forget. I told him in the beginning. I *was* honest with him. But the boy is *his* now, so how can I remind him now?"

"Are you sure this is something you should be telling me, Jacqueline?" She looked so fragile and helpless he would gladly have helped her, but that was something that nobody ever seemed able to do.

"Can't tell him anything any more, you know. He only shouts at me these days. Just blows up. It hurts Maurice. It's so upsetting to Maurice." She twisted the pearls at the V neck of her dress.

Judah settled into a chair. "Mohamed is under great pressure, Jacqueline." He was thinking of his friend's bitter reaction to the news of the Balfour Declaration. God knew

Judah had tried to break it gently—but they'd had a violent argument that afternoon. That was why he'd come to the house tonight—to patch things up. It would seem that Mohamed had brought something of his anger home to Jacqueline.

"You must try to make allowances for him. Whatever it is that's troubling you, I'm sure Mohamed will come around." It seemed a safe enough assumption. Mohamed had certainly been understanding of her in the past. But how could one not? She was so vulnerable—and hardly to blame for her own feelings.

"Understand, Judah? About Maurice?" Her words skipped in staccato rush. "Mohamed knows he's not his child. But you didn't, did you? Well, it's true. And I wish to God it wasn't. Now the real father wants to claim the boy. The boy or money, he says. Or both. That's what Maurice's father says. Are you shocked?"

Judah wished in that instant that she had not taken him into her confidence. Certainly, they had never been close in the past. Jacqueline was desperate—that was painfully clear—and she had called on him for help. Because he was here—and because she knew he would not refuse.

"How much does he want—this man?"

"Twenty thousand francs. Only, it wouldn't end there. It wouldn't end until he's ruined all our lives. Maybe I've done that already."

"Mohamed has to be told," Judah urged. "You must tell him, Jacqueline."

"Don't you see that I can't? For God's sake, Judah, it's for Maurice as much as him." She broke into uncontrollable sobs. "What a mess I've made of everything. . . ." He came over, putting a calming arm around her.

"All right, Jacqueline. "I'll help you. Who is this man? I'll see him. Talk to him. Pay him, if that's the only way. Twenty thousand? I can arrange that."

She brightened. "You'd do that for me?"

"I'll be doing it for Mohamed, too. But he won't know it's from me."

She leaned against his shoulder, her hair rousing his cheek. He felt heat at her touch as though he'd brushed against a loose electric wire. He'd read of the great courtesans of history who, by the mere brush of a fingertip on a man's shoulder, could stimulate desire. What was it about certain

women—about Jacqueline—that made her exude this unique
sexual energy? Always he'd been aware of it with her, and
always he'd put it out of his mind.

Now the sensation of her touch was too real, tangible. A
magnetism he imagined few people possessed. And being in
possession of it, who could blame her for passions fulfilled?
It was a feeling that had nothing to do with love, he was quite
aware of that. More like a chemical explosion in the blood
caused by proximity. Too close to Jacqueline, one could get
very seriously burned. He freed himself gently and closed his
mind to the feelings she had unconsciously awakened.

"I'm only sad this had to happen for both of you, Jacqueline." He turned away from the slender figure huddled against
the arch of the chaise. "I want your promise that you will not
see this man again. Under any circumstances. Where do I
find him? What's the man's name?"

At first Judah could make out no one. The lamp on the
embankment was haloed in yellowing rain—beyond it, the
dark arc of the bridge. He approached alone, trench coat
buttoned to chin, peaked military cap pulled low. Two forms
drifted past, a Senegalese and a scrawny lady-of-the-night.
Their figures were swallowed in mist.

What kind of a man, however depraved, would ask a
woman like Jacqueline to keep this murky rendezvous with
her purse bulging franc notes? Judah walked forward to the
center of the span above the slow, whispering river.

The man turned; a bantam rain-soaked form.

"Are you—Maurice?"

"Depends who's asking."

Judah stepped nearer. He needed a better view of the
face—wanted to see expression. That could be important. "A
friend of Jacqueline's."

The man turned his collar up against the drizzle, hooking a
finger through his belt. "She was told to come herself.
Alone." Maurice started away. Judah grabbed his arm, turning him back.

"Careful, soldier."

Judah could make out the pasty features, sallow skin, eyes
slightly bloodshot. And in that drunken, dangerous face, the
gentle features of young Maurice seemed caricatured.

"She's not coming here. Forget that. I'm here for her," Judah said.

"Where did you arrange that, cock? Between her legs?"

Judah repressed the impulse to smash his face. He knew, in his place, Mohamed would have done so. "I'm here to do business, not exchange insults."

Maurice shrugged, exuding a whiff of cheap cognac.

"Fine—if you've brought what I asked for."

"We'll talk first."

"Nothing to talk about. Show me the money," the man demanded.

"First you'll listen," Judah told him. "If you trouble her or the boy again—ever—I have the power to put you away. So far—you won't be seen until the day you're buried."

Maurice shifted his weight. "I'm not interested in all that shit. You got the money? Pass it over."

Suddenly Judah heard the sharp metallic clicks of the opening of a long-bladed knife. It glinted through mist and rain. "You won't be the first bastard this put away," Maurice said.

Judah was almost surprised by his own icy calm. He could feel the blade low against his belly.

"You think I'd hand over the money—let you walk away, and that would be the end of it? I've brought something for you to sign. A statement of how and why you came into sudden wealth. If you ever try to contact her or the boy again, the sureté of police will get your confession of blackmail."

"You bastard," Maurice spat. "I sign nothing!"

With sudden fury, the knife drove at Judah's stomach. Judah seized the wrist, instincts sharpened by combat training. The steel-fanged hand twisted, wrenching upward. The man's other fist struck hard into Judah's temple. The knife rose and slashed through his coat sleeve. Judah put his weight against the bantam Frenchman, pushing him back across the stone balusters.

For an instant they were locked in struggle. The knife blade slashed down into Judah's shoulder again. He drove his head into the man's chest, freeing himself. A low animal cry burst from Maurice. He lost balance and went spinning backward over the parapet—down, down through the murk—until even the splash was smothered in distance. The knife arced high and fell into the water.

Judah peered down but could see nothing. He ran back to the embankment, down the steps, a heart-pounding dash to the river level of the Seine. Rippling circles, made by the body, were already wide, vanishing in the flow. Judah waited, watched for Maurice's head to rise, poised to plunge in. There was nothing. All traces of the man who had fathered Mohamed's son were erased beneath black water as though he had never existed.

The first rays of dawn glazed the sky as Judah turned the key in his lock. For hours, he'd been walking. Hours of self-recrimination and soul-searching. He moved through the hall, past the open double doors of the drawing room; shrouded white ghosts of furniture glowed dimly.

Mounting the stairs, he noticed a light somewhere in the upper hall. Left on for him by the caretaker, no doubt. Then he realized the light was coming from his open bedroom door. He moved toward it as silently as possible. With the toe of his shoe, he gave it a violent kick open.

Jacqueline awakened, sitting up in his bed. "Judah—you're back. I was so worried."

He came toward her angrily. "What are you doing here, Jacqueline? This is the last place you should have come."

She ignored his anger. "Tell me quickly, what did he say? What did you do?"

Judah slumped down on the foot of the bed, his shoulder aching. He sank his head into his hands. "He won't trouble you any more, Jacqueline. He's dead."

"Dead? You killed him?" She stared in disbelief.

"It happened so fast. He came at me—with a knife. We struggled. He fell into the river." He turned to her. "I'll have to report it."

"Report it?"

"To the police."

"Judah," she began, a voice deadly calm, as though the crisis had given her strength. "Did anyone see you? Were you seen?"

He shook his head. "No. That is, I don't think so. No. I'm certain not."

She sighed relief. "Then, there's no need to report anything. In fact, it would be crazy to."

"I'm responsible for a man's death, Jacqueline."

"Ethical, Judah. How typically ethical of you." She leaned

toward him. "How many men have you killed in war? Men whose only crime was fighting for their country. Were those killings more honorable than ridding Paris of one blackmailing pimp? Was killing soldiers less of a crime because somebody gave you permission? If so, I miss the moral." She moved closer to where he sat on the edge of the bed. "If you went to the police, don't you see you'd undo all you've done and only put yourself deep into it? Until it leads right back to me. And Maurice and Mohamed, of course."

He lifted his eyes to her. "What are you asking me to do, Jacqueline?"

"Forget it. Forget it, Judah."

"How can you ask that?"

"You've got to." She slid down, putting her arms around him. Underneath the coverlet she was wearing nothing. Soft breasts tormented the rough wool of his uniform.

"You've been cut!" she exclaimed, seeing the blood on his sleeve, then kissed his cheek, trying to turn his face to her lips.

He buried his head in the cup of her shoulder. "Oh, Lord," he sighed. "Oh, Lord. . . ."

She pulled him down into the embrace of her whole body. "Judah, you've done this for me. I'll make you forget. I'll take the hurt away." Her lips pressed his, and he found himself sinking into the oblivion of her soft mouth.

He wrenched himself free, then rose and moved across the room, voice harsh. "Get dressed, Jacqueline. You're going home."

"You don't want me, Judah? Can you put your arms around me—and tell me that?"

He kept his glance averted, voice steady now. "Don't ask any more of me than you already have. I promise you what's happened will remain between us. I won't report it. And hope to God the police don't trace him back to me."

A pounding on the front door silenced them. A man's voice was shouting.

"Don't answer it," she whispered.

"I must. If it is the police, it would only make it worse." He looked back at her from the doorway. "Stay here. Be quiet. And for God's sake, get dressed."

The heavy knocker crashed against the oak door. Judah

opened it to face Mohamed. The two men stared at each other for a moment. Ashen-faced, his partner entered the hall.

"It's Jacqueline. She hasn't been home all night. I'm worried, Judah. You see, we had a quarrel. I walked out—and took Maurice. When the boy and I got back, she had gone. It's not like her to stay out all night. She's never done that before. Even in the worst times of her illness. . . ."

For a moment, Judah hesitated. Mohamed took a step past him into the hall. "I'm sorry, Judah. I shouldn't have brought you this trouble. But I don't like to go to the police."

"She's all right, Mohamed. Jacqueline is all right," Judah said.

Mohamed gave him a sharp look. "How do you know that?"

"Because she's here."

"Here . . .?" Mohamed stared in disbelief. "Here? With you? Where?" He paused. Judah's silence brought a surge of disgust and fury. "Upstairs in your bedroom, is she? Even *you*, Judah? Even you . . . !"

"Mohamed—I can't tell you what has happened. It's not what you imagine."

Mohamed reached into his pocket and took out his wallet.

"I've heard that before. From Bernard Goldfarb. But I never dreamed I'd hear it from you." He removed all his currency and tossed it at Judah's feet. "This will take care of her expenses for the moment. Tell her not to bother coming home. And not to try to see the children again. Because if she does, I'll have her put away."

Mohamed turned and walked out.

PART 2

Harvest of a Twice-Pledged Land

Fifteen ──────────────

"KADIMA" . . .

Forward . . .

Hebrew letters blazed from brass emblems on uniforms of the newly formed Jewish Legion, consisting of the 38th and 39th Royal Fusiliers. They were heading for combat under the commands of Colonel Margolin, a Jew—and that same urbane, courtly Irishman, Lieutenant Colonel Patterson, who with Trumpeldor had led the Mule Corps at Gallipoli.

In the molten Egyptian sunlight, the troops detrained into the roaring arena of Cairo's railroad station, El Qahira. Judah was hardly prepared for the pandemonium their arrival was creating. Jewish locals had poured out to greet the Legion as though the Messiah had finally arrived. Stiff as a flagstaff above their waving banners, a less enthusiastic British High Commissioner took the salute.

Behind Judah, Bernard Goldfarb shouted in his flat American accent: "Over there, Judah. That guy's waving at us like he was your brother!"

Judah squinted through the copper heat. "It's Cousin Jonathan . . . and Nathan!" He wigwagged his military cap at the young Nouaris elbowing their way through the mob.

Nathan pressed forward behind his brother. "It's Judah," he cried, coming up. "Judah the soldier!" Bernard Goldfarb watched the cousins embrace. Home seemed very far away.

A formidable collection of relatives included Gideon, his son Raphael, and assorted wives and children gathered for the welcoming dinner for Judah and his comrades at Miriam Nouari's house.

Cooking, for Miriam, was an expression of love that overflowed from heaping platters to mouths and hearts. Even in wartime, she could make a banquet from a few scrawny chickens.

"Everyone this side of the cemetery wants to join up," Nathan announced, digging enthusiastically into his soup. "Me, I'm ready to shed my last drop of blood for the cause, cousin Judah." He blinked good-humoredly. "It's only the *first* I'd like to avoid." Judah's cousins were built like their father, on strong, muscular frames. Jonathan was five inches taller. "They left me out in the rain and I shrank," Nathan always complained. Since Solomon's death, his sons had remained in Cairo with their sister Naomi, who was still at college.

"And how many men are there in the Legion, Mr. Jabotinsky?" Miriam asked, passing the bread.

"We're five thousand strong, Mrs. Nouari," Vladimir Jabotinsky replied expansively. He tasted the chicken soup like an approving chef. "Excellent. Excellent."

She nodded thoughtfully. "The Scripture prohibits an aggressive war. But to fight for our lives and our laws—that is something else. There is a long history of Jewish armies. Ask my son the archaeologist. He can tell you." She patted Jonathan's arm with pride.

Jonathan looked embarrassed. "I'm not an archaeologist, yet, mother."

"She's the quickest university degree in the world. She graduates you if you buy a pencil," Nathan put in. "With an eraser, you could get a Ph.D." Cousin Gideon laughed louder than the joke deserved. He had a special affection for Nathan, who managed to keep any conversation from becoming serious. Naomi helped her mother serve the chicken when the servants had cleaned the soup plates. Conversation hummed above clicking forks.

"There's a petition going around," Jonathan told Jabotinsky. "Nathan and I put our names on it. Since the Balfour Declaration was published in the local Jewish paper, thousands of the *Yishuv* are ready to join up. In Tel Aviv, Jaffa, and Jerusalem. In the North, too—where the Turks are still strong."

Jabotinsky poised his fork like a baton. "If only Trumpeldor could have been here to see the welcome Cairo gave us this morning. . . . Soul-stirring, Mrs. Nouari. Soul-stirring."

"Eat, Mr. Jabotinsky," Miriam prompted. "To fight a war, you need strength."

Gracefully, Jabotinsky selected a chicken leg from the platter being passed. "A home-cooked meal. It's something I don't get very often. And kasha, Mrs. Nouari. It takes me back to Russia."

"Hmmph," she said. "A place nobody should be taken back to."

"But, cousin Judah, why are you only a lieutenant?" Naomi's voice came suddenly through the silence. She had freckles and a dimple in her chin. Soft auburn curls teased the nape of her neck—and Bernard Goldfarb's imagination. She flushed slightly capturing the American's glance, and returned her attention to Judah. "Cousin Gideon said you'd been promoted to something important."

"That's what you wrote me," accused Gideon.

"We were all demoted when the Legion was formed," Judah explained. "But nobody minded the loss of a pip or two, as long as we got here. The British wanted to send our Mule Corps to Ireland." Judah reached across for a slice of the braided loaf of *challah*.

"Ireland?" Raphael asked. "That's a place for Jews?"

"Anti-British riots are going on there," Judah added. "Mule Corps refused. That's why they disbanded us."

"You're well rid of the Mule Corps, Judah," Gideon put in. "I never took to those beasts."

Nathan gave him a wink. "Right, cousin. One end's stubborn and the other's dangerous."

"But why isn't Joseph Trumpeldor with you?" Jonathan asked. "We keep reading about him in the Jewish press. About you, too, Mr. Jabotinsky," he added.

"Captain Trumpeldor has returned to Russia," Jabotinsky replied. "They've made him commissar for Jewish soldiers' affairs."

"What kind of affairs can Jewish soldiers have in Russia?" Miriam wanted to know.

Nathan looked up from his dish. "Maybe things are better since they got rid of the Czar, the Czarina, and all the little Czardines."

Jabotinsky frowned at the quip. "Captain Trumpeldor hopes to persuade the provisional government to allow him to lead regiments to the Caucasian front."

Raphael shook his head dubiously. "The greatest Jewish soldier in the world should be *here*, where he's needed!"

Jabotinsky flourished out his cigarette holder with the air of an actor who'd been upstaged. "The Legion is not without experienced officers. Is it permitted to smoke?"

"In the sitting room, Mr. Jabotinsky." Miriam rose. "There's coffee waiting. And we are fortunate to have sugar."

"I never take more than three teaspoons," Jabotinsky allowed, having not tasted sugar in months.

They moved into the sitting room. Bernard found a place beside Naomi in the corner. A box of stereoscope slides and a viewer lay close at hand.

"We've got one of these at home," he said.

"Not scenes of Egypt, I should imagine," Naomi replied.

"Niagara Falls and the Grand Canyon. I've never been to those places either. Anyway, I never expected to get this far from New Jersey."

"I don't know where that is."

"You're not missing much."

She dropped a slide into position, handing him the viewer. "Cheops." He peered in. She selected another slide. "Why is it you are only a private, Mr. Goldfarb. You, an American."

"I was a sergeant. I guess there was nothing lower they could demote me to. After Gallipoli they handed me the St. George's Cross—and took away my stripes."

"Was Cousin Judah with you when you were wounded?" She had not missed his slight limp.

"Judah was the one who got me out alive. I owe him a lot. Especially meeting you."

She flushed slightly. "Do you like Cairo?"

"All I've seen is the railroad station. And your mother's cooking. Which, I might add, is delicious."

She put in another slide. "The pyramids. But you must see them in person before you go to the front. They're just outside the city."

"Tomorrow I've got a pass. How about you acting as guide?"

"Oh, no. I couldn't do that. Unless, of course, my brothers were free to go with us." She paused soberly. "In fact, now I think of it—they'd better take you. I don't think I'd be able to go. I'm certain you understand, Mr. Goldfarb."

"I don't. In America, girls can go almost anywhere."

"It's different here. Besides, I'm engaged."

"To be married?"

"That's usually what it's for," she replied.

"Who is he? And where's he hiding?"

"Moishe is not hiding from anybody. He's in Jerusalem, finishing at the *yeshiva*."

"What's that?"

She glanced at him with some amazement. "You *are* Jewish, aren't you? It's rabbinical college. You *do* know what a rabbi is?"

"Oh, yes. We have them in America, too. So your fiancé's in Jerusalem?"

She nodded. "I haven't seen Moishe for three years."

"Three years? How old were you when you got engaged—ten?"

"Fourteen. Moishe's father is a Hassidic rabbi. A friend of my grandfather's. It was arranged between our families."

"And you had nothing to say about it?"

She shrugged. "I'm sure my mother knows what's best for my future. She wouldn't choose anyone who wasn't right for me. Anyway, Moishe's a good man. As I remember him. Extremely thoughtful and serious."

"I'll bet. Has he ever kissed you?"

"Of course not!" she flared. "Now I think we'd better change the subject, Mr. Goldfarb. This really isn't anything that concerns you."

He smiled at her, eying a stray curl blown against her cheek. "I wouldn't make a bet on that, Naomi." He reached for another slide. Photographed Egypt spilled over the thick, jewel-bright carpet. Miriam glanced over from across an inlaid-wood-and-brass tray-table. The others were sipping coffee and nibbling halvah, listening to Vladimir Jabotinsky, who was holding the stage with his account of the Legion's departure from England.

His voice rose, capturing Bernard and Naomi's attention. He was like a Shakespearean player introducing a cast of thousands with a mere handful of actors. "Through the East End of London we marched—five thousand of us. Tailors and merchants from Whitechapel, quartered overnight among the royal ghosts at the Tower of London. I, for one, felt we were becoming part of English history!" He drew neat little puffs on his cigarette, balancing the amber stem deftly between two fingers. Jonathan and Nathan listened spellbound. To them, England was only a name on a map.

"In the morning, we marched in full kit through Whitechapel. They even gave us permission to carry fixed bayonets. A band of Coldstream Guards led us, playing 'Rule Brittania' and Blake's 'Jerusalem.' "

Carried away by his own performance, Jabotinsky broke into song with nasal abandon: "Till we have built Jerusalem, /In England's green and pleasant land." He broke off. "Our Jewish flag—our blue and white Mogen David—moving aloft beside the Union Jack."

"Inspiring, Mr. Jabotinsky." Miriam clapped her hands.

"The Lord Mayor of London himself took the salute. Tens of thousands in the streets singing, cheering, weeping as we passed—bayonets perfectly slanted, heads high. 'An army of tailors,' Colonel Patterson called us. But he said it with pride. Yes, I do believe he was proud of his tailors that day."

Jabotinsky's words turned Judah's thoughts back to the nightmare of Gallipoli. While artillery ripped the skies above them, he had found himself crouching with Colonel Patterson in the same Turkish trench, ludicrously comparing notes on Uganda. Judah recalled that the much-traveled career soldier had his own views on that African paradise: "As a homeland, impossible, my dear fellow. Man-eating lions and all that. Spent too much time out there."

Judah was glad Patterson was commanding them again here in Egypt. Patterson, an Irishman, well understood yearnings for national identity. He could sympathize with the sense of personal elation felt by his Jewish troops about to enter the Holy Land.

Judah glanced around the roomful of family faces. How deeply joined to all of them he felt! Miriam—gentle, wise woman. The silver-framed photo of her brave husband. Sons. Uncles. Cousins. Were not their lives all woven into some pattern like these carpets on the floors and walls—he, Jabotinsky, Bernard, and all the rest who would march with them toward Jerusalem? Judah's attention focused on Miriam's words. She sat, eyes slightly closed, a prophetess at the gates of mystery, a seer into darkness.

" 'Be strong and of good courage, for thou shalt cause the people to inherit the land. Only be strong and very courageous— and ye shall pass over before your brethren, armed. All the mighty men of valor. And ye shall return unto the land of your possession and possess it, which Moses, the servant of the Lord, gave you beyond the Jordan toward the sunrising.' The Lord's words to Joshua. All of you follow in his footsteps, Mr. Jabotinsky.''

"Why are you not more careful, uncle Gamel?"

Gamel's question was asked of himself. Not that it was really Gamel asking it. The happy simpleton of the Hammadi family was merely echoing the words of his important nephew, Mohamed. When Mohamed came to Jerusalem, he never failed to visit his uncle, and Gamel's excitement would be so great that he would sometimes fall over chairs and furniture in his rush to greet the head of the family.

Gamel had not seen Mohamed for some time. He could not tell for how long, any more than he could tell the meaning of what everyone called "the war," which filled the city with Turkish troops and police and ambulance loads of wounded. But repeating bits of Mohamed's phrases helped to keep the nephew close.

"Be careful, uncle. Look, always look where you are going!" When Gamel said the words, he could almost see the nephew. The smiling sadness. Oh, let others say what they liked, Mohamed was hard, Mohamed was ruthless, Mohamed never forgot a wrong. . . . The childlike mind of his uncle loved and missed the great man in the way a dog might miss an absent master.

Let the troubles of Jerusalem swirl past the old mosque Gamel tended as caretaker and janitor. The arrests, police raids, bedraggled files of dusty troops. The ambulances hooting their way between donkeys, camels, and merchants bearing goods on their heads. Gamel's world paid them no heed. His war was against spiders and mice, come in from fields beyond the walls. And if Mohamed had not visited them for a long time, there were still relatives from both families left in Jerusalem. Where had the others gone? Where did they tell him? His brother Sayid was in Paris. Or was it Cairo? No, that was Abdullah. Or wasn't he the one killed in Damascus? It made Gamel's head dizzy trying to keep them all straight. "Uncle Gamel. Uncle Gamel," he muttered to himself. "You are a no-good man!" His voice sounded through the dark, cool cellar beneath the old mosque, amid the cracked Roman sarcophagi lining one wall. The broom in Gamel's hand danced to the rhythms of his mutterings. His slippers shuffled holes through to the leathery soles of his feet. At forty-seven, Gamel looked more like sixty. His hobbling limp was a memento of the wretched trick once played on him by his nephews Yassir and Tariq. He had never known they had pushed him down the stairs. All he knew was that the now grown-up Yassir was off somewhere in the war. And Tariq, a sober twenty-one-year-old, came and went with other members of the two families who so often seemed to visit this underground chamber. How thoughtful they were! How kind! They even brought him sweetmeats sometimes.

His broom moved up the side of the long stone boxes. In them were kept the bundles of clothing that Tariq and the others would bring. "Old clothes for the poor," they would always explain. "The poor. The poor. The poor." Gamel was not sure who the poor were. Himself, and the blind beggars led by small boys calling for alms in the name of Allah? And the cripples with twisted limbs, and the lepers? "Take care of the old clothes—and don't say anything to anyone," they warned.

"Not even the poor?"

"Not even them."

The heavy bundles would be brought by Tariq or by Dr. Simon, or Anwar, or Judah Nouari's brother Ben. Generally one of them would have a sweet for Gamel. The Turkish delights with the green nuts were his favorites.

His broom pursued a larger than usual spider that spiraled down on a silken thread to drop through a crack in the marble and into the long box. "You spider, I fix you! They told me, 'Gamel—don't let nobody know of the clothes.' I get you. Get you. Get you!"

Gamel's broom made a stab at the broken bit of stone lid. Down it fell to the floor, cracking into more bits. But no spider.

Gamel poked down into the bulging sacks of clothing. That spider would not escape! He had nothing against spiders, but, over and over, they had warned. They—Ben, Tariq, Dr. Simon, Anwar. "Don't let anyone touch the clothes!" And that certainly included spiders. He leaned over the open box, broom poised for a coup de grâce.

Something metallic made him forget all about spiders. It

was blue steel and formed into a shape that he vaguely recognized as an object worn by the Turkish police. He pawed into the sacking and brought it out. It bulked in his hand, as he turned it over and over. Yes, now he recalled where he had seen one like it. They had told him not to speak about the old clothes. But nobody had said anything about this thing in his hand. Gamel would take it to his friend.

Most of the Turkish police always treated Gamel in a kindly way. They would make circular gestures with a forefinger at the temple, which Gamel took as a sign of friendship. He would make the same gesture back. And everyone would have a good laugh.

He pushed the object in his waistband and trotted off to the coffeehouse, so excited that he even forgot to lock the cellar door behind him.

In a patch of sunlight in front of the crowded coffeehouse sat one of the officers Gamel knew. Drinking coffee with him was another man, in black suit and European-style hat. The two were talking quite intensely as Gamel came up. They didn't trouble to notice him. Gamel was tired of being ignored and always being kept waiting. He took the object from his waistband, held it up in the air.

"Look at me! Everybody look at Uncle Gamel!" A thundering crack of a shot sent the whole front of the café diving for cover. Gamel himself was so terrified that he let the thing fall from his hand. The man in the black suit swept it up, then seized and twisted Gamel's arm behind his back until he cried out in pain.

"Let him go. He's harmless." The Turkish constable examined the pistol. "But this isn't. Where did you get it, Gamel?" He held up the Luger almost gently.

Gamel could not speak. The awful noise still rang in his ears. Pain wracked his arm. "Uncle Gamel . . ." he whispered.

"I think you'd better show us," the constable said. The dark-suited man completed a search to be sure there was no second weapon. Gamel began to sniffle. He didn't himself know why, but he was afraid now. He had a sense of something going terribly wrong, like that time just before he had upset the whole tray of glasses of hot mint tea. Yet he hadn't mentioned the old clothes.

They walked on either side of him to an automobile parked across the street. "Mohamed . . ." he muttered. "Help Uncle Gamel." The policeman assumed he was praying to the Prophet.

In their small house in Bethlehem, young Dr. Simon Nouari sat across the dinner table from his wife, Sephora. He was wishing they would hurry to collect him—and end her cross-examination. If anything went wrong, the less she knew the better. For her. Bad enough, his wife knew the business that took him out nights was not medical. Bad enough, she complained that as a family man and physician he had no right to take risks. Simon knew how Sephora's mind worked. It read his. He diminished her suspicions and warnings by accusing her of having a prodigious imagination. Such defenses brought on rows. Like tonight.

"You're going to wake up Daniel. Lower your voice, Sephora," he whispered hoarsely.

"I'm sorry if my voice isn't as soft and honeyed as your charming nurse's. But Zuliekha doesn't have to live with you." Anger fired sparkling blue eyes. Her lips, so seldom in repose these days, formed a perfect cupid's bow. The toe of one white-strapped pump tapped impatience on the red-tiled floor. Sephora confronted her husband across their six years of matrimony. "How convenient for you—that her apartment is just behind the clinic!"

"The way you talk, Sephora, you'd think I was Casanova!"

"Not with me, you're not," she accused. "You're always too tired."

"Sephora—for God's sake. All over Palestine hundreds of Jews and Arabs are waiting to join the British. I've got to do something."

"Since Dr. Yusuf made you his partner, you seem to have time for everything but medicine. Do you think that the Turks will be defeated one hour sooner because you and the Hammadis go rushing around at night instead of sleeping in your beds? With your wives?"

Simon glanced at his watch, wondering what was keeping Zuliekha. "Even my cousin Judah is in the war. He's at least thirteen years older than I am. And a banker."

"Maybe he wants to get away from his wife too!" She poured herself another cup of coffee.

Simon sighed deeply. Much as he loved Sephora, he couldn't bear these new-sprung harangues that led nowhere. Nowhere? Well, that was the worst of it. They didn't lead nowhere. They led to crazy conclusions. Jealous fits. Groundless suspicions. Like now.

"If you are honest with yourself, my husband, you're doing a lot more than you think I *think* you're doing!" That same mysterious accusation darkened his wife's eyes again. "You, who know every symptom of illness, why don't you take your own pulse? Tap your own chest? Beat a finger where your heart is and see if it's still beating for me?"

"What the devil are you talking about now?" he demanded, knowing exactly what. Ever since Dr. Yusuf Hammadi had hired Zuliekha to work in the clinic, Sephora had been devoured by the green-eyed monster. Not that Simon didn't consider himself attractive to other women. He knew that he was. He also knew that he was vain—and that Sephora knew it too. She complained about the minutes he spent pruning his thick black mustache and disciplining his curly hair with pomade. He looked more Turkish than Jewish, which at present was very useful. Furthermore he spoke Turkish, which not all Jews in Palestine troubled to learn. As for Sephora's accusations, Zuliekha's love life was something he couldn't discuss with his wife. It was clandestine information.

"And you expect me to believe that when Zuliekha collects you this evening, it will be to meet *them?*"

He knew she was trying to start a row. Engage him in a field of battle from which he could not retreat. Simon rose from the table to put on his jacket, and accidentally knocked over the salt cellar. "You're being irrational, Sephora. We're working for a Palestine where our son, Daniel, can grow up free and proud. *You* seem to think I'm doing this just to get out nights."

"You've spilled the salt," she said throwing a pinch over her shoulder. He took her in his arms and kissed her with some passion. She felt soft and warm, and he longed to stay home. To feel the curve of her come alive under his touch in their small bed.

"There," he said. "Does that finish Zuliekha?"

"Come to bed with me, then, and we'll see." She ran a

hand under Simon's shirt against the hairy skin of his chest.
The automobile horn bleated gently in the street.

"I can't. She's here."

She released him with exasperation. "Go, then," she told
him. "Go to your woman."

"My God," he protested. "There's Ben, Anwar, and . . .
others involved. Why must you always pick on her?"

"Because it's she who always collects you."

"I'm not interested in anyone but *you*," he said wearily.
"Though God knows you'll nag me to death." He took up
the small satchel that profession dictated should never be far
from his hand. His lips brushed her cheek. It brought him a
familiar electric response. She drew back, opening the door.
"Don't keep your friends waiting, then." Past Simon, she
could see the touring car with Zuliekha at the wheel.

Simon glanced back at his wife, framed in the doorway.
The lamp glow formed a corona edge to her cotton dress.
Buttercups and little blue cornflowers that matched her eyes.
And she imagined he could ever love anyone else!

"Keep the bed warm," he said, and was gone.

Zuliekha. . . .Sephora knew all about Zuliekha. The woman
had escaped from the Arab inevitability of purdah via marriage to a French doctor from Damascus. His death conveniently launched her into the freedom of widowhood. Sephora
had decided that Zuliekha was much older than she looked
(which Zuliekha wasn't). Life was so damned unfair, Sephora
concluded. Trapped in Bethlehem with a five-year-old son to
raise and the boredom of household chores—while the Zuliekhas
of this world rushed about playing romantic roles in careers
and conspiracies. Zuliekha had eyes like seductive almonds
flaked with green, and the easy manner with men that came
naturally from close working relationships—which must of
their very nature lead to bed. Such daydreams tortured Sephora
between bouts of training little Daniel. She worried so much
about Zuliekha that she had no time for the more real fear of
the potential dangers she knew Simon risked. He told her
little, but she'd overheard whispered conversations with Ben
Nouari. Ben, the dedicated. Ben, who had no wife to deter
him. Mysterious Ben, always conveying an air of excitement
and adventure that Simon seemed to find irresistible. The
word they whispered most was *Nili*—a spy ring operating in
Palestine throughout the war. A secret known to all—even the

Turks. *Nili* provided the British with details of enemy troop movements and battle strength. Almost everyone had some part in it—even wives and children. Anyone who could count when he or she saw marching men or trucks. Everyone, it seemed, but her.

Sephora sighed, brushing the food from the dishes into a copper pan in the stone sink. On his earnings, Simon couldn't afford a regular servant for his wife. How different it was for women like Zuliekha. But since Sephora was superstitious about harboring evil thoughts, she said a small prayer for the safety of all of them tonight. Yes, even Zuliekha. . . .

"The Eternal One of Israel does not lie," she whispered. From these words, in Hebrew, the name *Nili* had been formed. Sephora blew out the candle and tiptoed into Daniel's room to kiss him good night, even though he was asleep. A good child. So serious. And already so tall for his age.

Zuliekha drove slowly. Her face had been grave since Simon climbed in.

"Something wrong?"

"The Turks intercepted a message. They've snuffed the section at Atlit."

"My God . . ."

"*Your* God?" she snapped angrily. "Everybody's God! Six leaders of *Nili* caught and hanged. What has God to do with that?" Silence settled on the cigarette smoke in the car.

"Is tonight still on?" Simon asked.

"Who can be sure of anything?" She shrugged. "We'll know when we get to Ramat Rachel."

They drove on through the flat, rolling countryside, too brightly lit by a full moon, alert for any sign of a Turkish patrol. Finally she slowed the car toward a dark mass of crumbling masonry: the remains of an old tomb. Tiers of arches protruded above heavy blocks of stone steps. Two small bats completed a fluttering swoop as Zuliekha bumped the car across a patch of sandy earth. When they were hidden from the main Jerusalem road, she braked and cut the motor.

Only then did two figures emerge from shadow. Ben and Anwar loomed beside them, glazed in moonlight.

"You're late," Ben said tautly.

"Dr. Yusuf had a patient," she replied. She looked around. "He's not here yet?"

"He'll come," Anwar said.

"You've heard about Atlit?" Simon asked.

Ben nodded. "The Aaronson woman. . . . Remember her?"

"Of course."

"Killed herself before they could question her," Ben said tonelessly. "If we're safe, it's because of her." His words hung in the cold night air like a judgment.

"What she did was the right thing," Zuliekha said.

Anwar looked across at her. "Maybe. Maybe not. It is still a sin to take one's own life."

"I'm sick of heroes," she said.

They waited. Ben puffed a cigarette cupped in his hand.

"If he doesn't come—what then?" Simon asked.

"He'll be here," Anwar assured him. "Nobody is better at moving through the lines. . . ." He broke off, listening. Coming toward them, they could hear the mechanical growl of a motor. Ben drew his pistol. Zuliekha stayed behind the wheel. Ben moved out to the edge of the wall.

A Turkish military ambulance ground to a stop in the road. The uniformed driver climbed down from the cab. Ben leveled the pistol, ready to fire. The driver lit a cigarette, passing the match twice in front of his face, then dropped it, still lit. Ben lowered his pistol. The driver moved around to the rear of his ambulance and opened the double doors.

Two bandaged men on stretcher cots arose quickly and climbed down. They dragged open a panel in the floor of the van and began removing heavy, rag-wrapped bundles. The driver turned back, striding swiftly to the group moving out to meet him. Anwar put his arms out to embrace him. "Cousin. Allah is merciful."

"It was not easy tonight. There's a watch on all the roads," Tariq said.

"What did you bring?" Ben asked.

"Rifles. Forty of them. Mosin-Nagants. Turks captured them from the Russians. We've borrowed them from the Turks." His eyes went to Zuliekha, who had been standing back from the others, waiting.

"How is it with you?" he asked.

"All right," the woman replied. Her face was shadowed by the *shaytha* drawn over her head.

"There's also a German Maxim," Tariq said. "7.92-milli-meter. That's for you, Simon. For Jerusalem."

Simon let out a low whistle. "Have you got ammunition for it?"

"Some. We'll get more."

The "wounded" men carried the bundles of rifles to the two waiting cars. Ben and Anwar helped them load the trunks of the cars.

"You'll take the ambulance, Simon," Tariq said. "When you've made your delivery, bring it back to the clinic." He handed over the ignition keys.

Simon placed his medical bag in the cab and climbed in.

"Is there enough petrol? I'd hate to be stuck halfway."

"Four extra liters in the back." Tariq's face was grooved with weariness.

"When did you last sleep?" Zuliekha asked him.

"Somewhere north of Al' Aqabah—after I left Colonel Lawrence. Come here. . . ." He led her behind the shadow of the wall. They stood so close, for a brief moment they formed a single silhouette.

Ben closed and locked the trunk of his car, getting in behind the wheel. Anwar came over to his young cousin. "Where do we make this drop?"

"At Motza. They'll be waiting for you and Ben," Tariq said.

"When will we see you again?" Anwar asked.

"Zuliekha will know."

"*In-Shallah*. And Yassir. Is he all right?"

Tariq nodded. "He is more than all right. He is magnificent."

The cousins embraced briefly. Anwar climbed in beside Ben Nouari. The car moved out of shadow, gathering speed, heading down the road away from Jerusalem.

The two "wounded" men remounted to their cots in the ambulance. "At least you'll get some sleep," Tariq said, closing the door after them. He came around to the cab. "How is Uncle Gamel, Doctor?" he asked Simon, who was putting on driving gloves.

"Never a problem," Simon said. "He takes good care of the 'old clothes' and doesn't complain." He glanced at his watch. "I should have your men back to you by 3:00 A.M. Get some rest. You look like you need it."

Tariq nodded. "After Zuliekha and I have made our delivery to Ein Faskha."

Simon started the motor and headed the ambulance toward Jerusalem.

Tariq waited for a moment like a man catching his breath. Then he put an arm around Zuliekha. "Come on, you're my chauffeur."

At the wheel of the ambulance, Simon suddenly felt terribly alone. A clammy sensation dampened his back against the leather seat. He had never considered himself a brave man. This was just something he had to do. That's what he had tried to explain to Sephora. The deeds they did now, the plans, the conspiracies, were deposits into the bank of their future. But on nights like this he sometimes found it difficult to control his nerves. It was all always too easy—these nocturnal forays. Planting arms caches in various squirrel nests throughout the countryside—for the time when they would be needed to support the advance on Jerusalem. When it came. Which could be almost any day. Or week. Or month. *Nili,* working for the liberation of the Jews. *Al Fatat,* for the liberation of the Arab world.

Bedfellows with a common enemy: the Ottomans.

Simon had been driving for over an hour. His feeling of unease wore off as he passed the city gates. As usual, the sentry waved him through. The doctor and his ambulance were a familiar sight by now. He drove on into the Muslim Quarter, down darkly silent streets. No patrols tonight. Yet the creepy feeling returned. He shrugged it off. The Turks were growing lax in the care of their jewel of cities.

Simon pulled the ambulance in behind the old mosque, climbed down, and walked across the street. He hurried down the steps to the room where Gamel slept, rapped, calling, "Gamel. Wake up! Old clothes. . . ."

No answer. He knocked louder. "Gamel . . . ?" Had the poor simpleton fallen into so deep a slumber? He turned—then felt his heart plummet. Three men stood at the top of the stairs. He had not even heard the crunch of a foot. He spoke to them in Turkish.

"I'm a doctor. Come to see Gamel. The poor fellow is ill. . . ." Simon started to search for his papers.

"Do not put your hand in your pocket," the police officer ordered. The other two moved to drag Simon up the steps.

"Let us see what you have in your ambulance." The officer nudged him forward with a Luger automatic.

"Wounded men," Simon replied.

"Open," the Turk ordered.

Simon's hands shook as he pulled the rear doors wide. The Turks peered in. "Two wounded soldiers," Simon repeated. "I'm taking them to hospital."

"And you stop here to wipe the nose of an idiot? Truly, Dr. Simon Nouari, you must do better than that."

One of the police officers climbed in to examine the wounded men. He peered closely at the bandage, then ripped it off. "What did you use? Sheep's blood?"

The "wounded" Arab's bullet tore through his thin covering of sheet. The Turk buckled over on top of him. Before the Arab could shoot again, the other Turk sprayed a burst of fire into the two cots.

Blood spattered the walls of the ambulance.

A police officer ripped open the floorboard and lifted out the wrapped machine gun. He turned, cracking the barrel of his pistol across Simon's face.

Sephora had been dreaming that she was in bed asleep and couldn't wake up. Her body was rigid. She couldn't make a sound or open her eyes. With great effort, she managed at last to free one hand from beneath the covers. She held it in front of her face, trying to focus on it, but could not.

The hoot of an owl awakened Sephora. She opened her eyes to discover both hands still tucked tightly under the covers. She had only dreamed that she was awake.

Heart racing, Sephora reached out for Simon. But his side of the bed was empty. She sat up, groping for matches. "Simon . . . ?" No answer. Nearly four-thirty. He had never been this late. A twinge of fear brought her to her feet. She thrust feet into shoes, crossed the hall to peer into Daniel's room. The boy was sleeping soundly. Her mind pounded worry.

Coat over nightgown, she hurried out of the house, running down the road—reality the worst nightmare. On past a field of shabby corn, past gnarled fig trees reaching toward her. Minutes more and she was in the little town, moving between tall, flat-roofed buildings. The questioning stone eyebrows of

arched double windows glared down sightlessly. Her steps
sped through the marketplace. By day it would bustle with
buyers and sellers. Villagers, travelers, neighboring Bedouin
hawking icons, crucifixes, rosary beads, and Dead Sea stones.
Now the square echoed only her running feet. Sephora turned
past the pale brick façade of the Christmas Church, looming
above her on stanchioned pillars. Around the corner of the
rear of the clinic, where Zuliekha had her apartment.

The sight of Zuliekha's car parked casually in the street
drained the blood from Sephora's head. The same car that
Zuliekha always collected Simon in, and delivered him home.
Sephora paused for a moment to catch breath and sort her
thoughts. No lights from Zuliekha's window. They'd be lying
there together in the dark, making love. She didn't have to
think any more. She knew what to do.

Sephora pounded on the door with all her strength. "Open
up! Open in there, you Arab whore bitch. You hear me,
Zuliekha. Open up!"

Someone was moving inside. Footsteps came to the door.
Tears of fury stung Sephora's eyes so that she could barely
see Zuliekha's face. Zuliekha, pulling a dressing gown over
nakedness. Sephora gave her no chance to speak. She flew at
her in a searing rage, striking out with both hands.

"In your bed, is he?" She pushed her way into the room.
"So here is where he spends his nights? His secret meetings. . . ." She could make out the form of a man stirring
himself awake. "Filthy bastard!" she screamed at him. "Rotten, lying bastard . . . .!" The naked man climbed out of the
bed and lit the oil lamp.

Sephora Nouari collapsed in a flood of tears. "I'm sorry,"
she stammered. "Sorry. . . . Oh, forgive. . . ."

Zuliekha led her to a chair. Tariq Hammadi looked at his
wristwatch. A gift of the British military. It read twenty
minutes past five.

"Simon should have been back with the ambulance two
hours ago! Oh, why did you let me sleep so soundly?" Tariq
groaned, pulling on his clothes.

"Because you've not slept in days," Zuliekha said.

"Sleep? Who cares about sleep? There may still be time to
intercept Ben and Anwar on the Motza road. I've got to keep
them from returning to Jerusalem." He tucked shirt into
trousers. "I'll need your car, Zuliekha."

She passed him the keys from her handbag. He kissed her briefly. "You may not see me for a while. I'll get word to you—somehow. If I find them, I'll take them to a safe house." He turned his attention briefly to Sephora. "Simon knew the risks. He's a brave man. Sometimes the bravest are those who think they are not."

Tariq was gone out the door.

"Let Allah be a watcher over you," Zuliekha whispered as the car sped away. She turned back to the other woman, putting a comforting arm around her. First dawn light was striping the louvered shutters with golden glare.

"Will he be all right, my Simon?"

"*In-Shallah* . . . God willing," Zuliekha answered. "Now you must find strength. Return to your home. Act as though nothing has happened. When they come to ask questions, you know nothing. Nothing. Simon is a doctor. He often goes out at night. That is all you know. And many children are born at night in Bethlehem."

The train puffed through the night-clad Sinai Desert. Within the carriages, the men of the Jewish Legion talked, slept, or prayed. Judah half-dozed. Voices ebbed and flowed around him in an orchestration of wheels over rails. A name formed in his mind. The phantom always waiting in the wings of memory to be summoned by a word, wish, perhaps a note of music, or merely a fleeting expression seen on the face of a stranger. Or maybe just the old wanting.

More than mere recollection of something that had been and was gone. Zosia. . . . Zosia. . . . Eternal presence. Guardian angel of desire. No matter that she was now fragments of decaying flesh in an unmarked grave. Still she drove, guided, and directed him like a lodestone, a compass. His need for her had re-formed itself into his *fatima*—his fate.

Their moments lay close—beads always waiting to be taken up, refingered, relived, recalled. That first warm summer in Basel when the interminable droning days of the Zionist Congress finally ended. He had insisted and prevailed. They would have *one* day for themselves. Completely. No Herzl. No bearded prophets in frock coats. No arguments and dissensions about the tribulations of world Jewry. Only the communication of feeling. The language of lovers. He had bought them both walking boots and a knapsack and they had hiked up the flank of the mountain range just beyond the city; high up into the carpet of purpling wild flowers, beneath the snowy crest, past spurting waterfalls diminished by summer's end to languorous music. A whole lifetime was compressed into hours.

The sun fell golden behind their mountain, tinting clouds to salmon, then draining them to gray. Then night crept in with explosions of stars. He wound her into a blanket, and they became each other's worlds. Her young body firm beneath the linen skirt and blouse, nipples growing hard as wild berries under his lips. The hunger he felt in her, matched by his. The wanting fulfilled and wanting again. All this was still fresh in mind after so many years, after so many other sunsets, darknesses, and sunrises. They had made love, yes. But it was not only with their bodies. They had spread before each other the feast of all the days before they had found each other.

He recalled the strange moment when she took his hand and pressed it under her own to the ground.

"What is it?" he'd asked.

"The pulse of the mountain."

He had laughed and kissed her. "It's only our hearts' beat."

"No, feel. With your senses. It's there. Stronger and deeper than our hearts. It's the mountain. The mountain is more than our bed, my love. It's our judgment."

Wind combed the branches above them. "Shall you forget me?" he asked.

"What?"

"You and your work. Shall we lose all this?"

"How small we are—on the crust of this mountain. Our lives are no more important than the flowers hiding their faces from the moon. We are not important. Only what we do."

He held her tightly until dawn awakened the sky. "Will you love me? Always?" he had asked.

But she had not. She had left him. Blown to bits on the steps of an embassy in Paris. "Zosia . . ." he whispered from the heart emptied now for all time. Living without her was a walk through a kind of sleep searching for he knew not what. . . .

He stared through the dusty train window, watching the

great jet of flame spouting from the engine's funnel. The flame seemed to be leading the train. Jonathan Nouari noticed it too. Face bathed in wonder, he turned back to Judah on the wooden bench across from him. "What does it make you think of, Judah?"

Judah spoke without effort. The old words surged to mind: "And the children of Israel went up armed out of the land of Egypt," he said. "And the Lord went before them by night in a pillar of fire to give them light. . . ."

There was a hushed silence as others became aware of the symbolic fire. For most, it was their first trip into Palestine.

"At least this time we haven't got Pharaoh's chariots chasing us," Nathan said. The railway car chattered back to life again.

Judah probed the faces of his young cousins: Excitement. Enthusiasm. And no real idea of what fighting a war would mean. He could not wipe from mind that last act of the Mule Corps before pulling out of Gallipoli. Every man had been ordered to slit the throat of his mule. Wouldn't do to leave them for the Turks. Kill the mules. . . . Seven hundred fifty mules left stinking on the shores of Asia. And bury the dead with a final prayer. Nine months at Gallipoli. Long enough to create new life. Instead the British lost a quarter of a million men. That was the truth of war.

But the deeper truth was the necessity. It was as though men's little world became periodically diseased from the evil of its creatures, and purgings were required to expunge guilts and sins. Guilts and sins . . . how seldom men felt their weight. Catholics had their confession, Muslims their ritual purification, Jews their Day of Atonement. And nothing changed anything.

The sins of the mind. The sins of the flesh. His own private darkness—a poison of memory with no antidote. Maurice on the bridge. Falling . . . falling. Judah had not killed him. Hadn't meant it to happen. It wasn't *his* affair. His anger. Yet he had allowed himself to be drawn into the sordid mess. Jacqueline's cat's cradle of misadventures. If only he could have explained to Mohamed. Told him the whole story. But his friend had given him no chance.

After Mohamed had stormed out, that dreadful night, Judah had returned upstairs to find Jacqueline sobbing. He'd only taken her in his arms to comfort her. He, who thought he had such firm control of his emotions. But the touch of her skin twisted compassion to passion. He hadn't intended to make love to her, but her body was a magnet.

Love had nothing to do with it. The woman was an Aphrodite, consuming senses. He had discovered things about himself he didn't understand. His love for Zosia had been a kind of worship. For Ruth, an obligation. Jacqueline had led him through a door he hadn't meant to open.

For three days, Jacqueline had remained in his house, not knowing where else to go. He'd removed himself from temptation by retreating to Bordeaux to visit Ruth and the children. He returned to the Paris house hoping to find Jacqueline gone. She wasn't. She showed him a newspaper clipping. Maurice's death, reported as suicide.

"We can forget it now," Jacqueline told him.

"You, perhaps. I'll never forget it."

She looked up at him through a curl of cigarette smoke. "You can't carry the burden of everything you've ever done, Judah. That way leads to madness. No one knows that better than I."

Then she told him she was going home. "Mohamed will forgive me," she said. "He always does."

Two days later, the same day Judah got his orders to proceed to Cairo, he received a letter: *I understand what you did—and why. I owe you thanks, not anger.* It was signed *Mohamed.*

He and Mohamed, born within a mile of each other, had talked the same language, breathed the same air, understood each other so well. Even Jacqueline had not divided them. But this war . . . this cause he was fighting for. Could their friendship survive that, too?

The troop train jolted Judah's attention back to time and place. Across from him, Jonathan's face under his forage cap seemed suddenly as clouded as his own. Judah leaned toward his cousin. "Want to let me in on it?"

"Just thinking—" The younger man broke off.

"Think aloud. It might help."

"I should never have let father go to Damascus alone."

"Solomon was a stubborn man. You couldn't have stopped him."

"If I'd gone . . . I might have succeeded. And he'd be alive. What was he doing, climbing walls at his age?"

"You can't live by 'ifs,' Jonathan."

"And we don't even know if Grandfather Jacob is still alive."

It was true. Nobody had heard from any of the Jerusalem family for nearly a year. The last letter had come from Judah's brother Ben . . . to their father, David, who was still co-chairman of the Paris bank. Then nothing. But private mail was extremely restricted. Judah forced his attention back to the letter he'd started days before. Nothing more difficult than writing to Ruth, but it had to be finished and mailed at the next military collection point.

Her letters always included notes from Abe and Zed. Abe's in French—comparing himself favorably with Renoir. He'd taken up watercolors. *Landscapes, they're called,* he informed his father grandly. Zed's letters freely borrowed from Charles Dickens and Washington Irving. She wrote in an English with a decided nineteenth-century flavor. *Once again I give myself the pleasure of addressing myself to you, dear Father. . . .* Twelve years old. Ruth never trusted her French to the pen. Ink-scratched Yiddish, bearing no surprises: *You have no idea of the shortages we endure, Judah. . . . My back kills me in this damp climate. . . . No one here understands why you abandon your family at such a critical time. . . .*

It will thrill you to know, dear Ruth, that we are traveling now in the footsteps of Moses. Don't worry too much about me. I'll probably be in command of a desk. Anyway, we are far behind the front lines. Remember Nathan and Jonathan? And Bernard, of course. They're all with me—the gantse mishpoche. *. . .*

He glanced along the crowded car, trying to think of something more to say. . . . *After the war, Jonathan plans to be an archaeologist. But now the past must wait on the present. . . .*

Farther down the aisle, Bernard woke up with a smile. He had been dreaming of a girl's face in Cairo. A girl whose hair curled at the nape of her neck. *And Bernard has met my cousin Naomi. He is not expected to recover. . . .* He was interrupted by the laughter of a cluster of recruits around Nathan. The young man's voice rose through the hilarity.

"So you *mazikim* think *our* uniforms are shabby? You should see some of those *Yishuv* from Jaffa," Nathan told them. "Their shoes are so thin, they can step on a coin and tell you whether it's heads or tails."

And Cousin Nathan keeps everyone laughing. . . . But I think he ought to be the archaeologist, he digs up such old jokes.

The door at the end of the car slid open. Jobotinsky swayed in with the motion of the train. "Gentlemen!" he pronounced, capturing their attention. "I bring news . . . from Colonel Patterson." He savored the silence, his slight presence dominating the car. "Tomorrow . . . we join Allenby's army . . . for the march on Jerusalem. *Aliya!*"

There was a cheer and a rising chant of voices. Judah hurriedly finished his letter. *It looks as though I'll soon be saying a prayer for you and the children at the Wailing Wall.* He signed with love and folded it carefully into an envelope. There would be no more time for letters for a while.

Kadima. Forward.

Sixteen ─────────────────────────

THE cell where they put Simon Nouari was deep in the body of the prison. Its walls crawled with vermin. Into this Jerusalem cesspit the Turks dumped the refuse of rebellion.

The doctor did a head count. Twenty. Twenty-two. Twenty-four. . . . He paused. No, that poor bastard was surely dead by now. Simon made his way between sleeping bodies to the still form. He felt the scrawny wrist thin as a chicken's neck. No throb of life left.

A voice chanted from across the cell. "Allah is great, Allah is one, and Mohammed is His Prophet. We are the noblest nation that has ever been raised up for mankind. We enjoin justice and forbid evil. We believe in Allah. . . ."

"Help me with this body, will you?" Simon called out to the one Arab still strong enough to perform prayers. The bundle of rags stirred up from his knees and came over. Less than two months ago, nearly a hundred men had been herded down here. At first there had been regular firing squads in the courtyard. Jailers and soldiers would swoop down, sort out a few victims by choice or whim, drag them up the steps, and stand them against the bullet-pocked wall. If the prisoners climbed upon each other's shoulders, they could watch the executions through the narrow slits of high, barred windows.

Simon couldn't remember how many times that pattern of events had taken place—or how many of his cellmates had gone to meet the "bastinado" and been returned, flayed to unconsciousness. Dr. Simon had acquired a broken nose from the pistol-whipping at his capture, and a scar down one cheek from an interview with his captors. He had babbled, he supposed, names and places, knowing that his disappearance would have alerted the others to take cover. If they'd been

359

caught, they'd be dead. Or here. Now he was glad that he'd kept so much about his activities from Sephora. She and Daniel were probably safe. He had to believe that or lose his mind.

But the curious thing was that for weeks the men in this cell had seen nothing of their jailers. They hadn't been fed or given water—or "interviewed" or taken out to be shot. The prisoners had become a collection of living skeletons. Forgotten. It would seem their jailers had gone. But where? And why did no one else come? From somewhere beyond the outer walls of the city, they could hear distant artillery. But who could know whether the British were winning or losing?

The abandoned prisoners had tried to join voices into great shouts that might reach the street above and beyond the prison. But their windows looked only into the courtyard. No sound penetrated the thickness of four layers of stone wall. Nobody heard. And finally there was no energy left for shouting, or even conversation. The Arabs touched foreheads to the slimy stone, facing, they supposed, toward that great citadel of faith far away across miles of sand. The Jews and Christians seemed equally out of touch with their Redeemer.

Simon surveyed what must be his last ward. No powders, unguents, or morphine left in the medicine bag he'd been permitted to bring with him. A sound of breaking glass caught his attention. One of the wretches was trying to slash his wrist. Simon lunged at the man, wresting the jagged fragment of broken bottle away.

"Forgive me, friend. Perhaps I've no right to intervene. I can't even find a last pill to ease your pain. But we must still hope."

He turned back to his own acrid clump of straw. "No, I am not God. My name is Simon," he repeated silently to himself. "I am—or was—a physician. But if I take a pulse now, what can I prescribe? A sound meal? Bed rest? Tonics to build back strength? Antiseptics for wounds? No loaves and fishes at my disposal. Only the meat of mice for those stout-stomached enough—and water sqeezed from bits of rags we hang out beyond the bars to catch the first December rains. . . ."

He began to weep softly. He, who had been vain, who had thought too much about the trim of his mustache, who had made a mirror of the eyes of men and women in which to survey himself. He, who had bestowed healing like charity. A physician who could not heal himself.

The ancient city of Jerusalem held its breath. It had done so, many times, at the armed tread of entering strangers—from Babylon, Macedonia, Rome, Persia, Byzantium. Its cobbles had resounded to the dancing hoofs of the horses of Seljuk Turks, the chargers of Christian knights, Saracen light cavalry, Tartar hordes, and Mamelukes, as conquest after conquest was memorized by the faces of its stones. Mostly, the battles were fought outside its walls. Only the victors entered.

The events of this December day were scarcely different. More tentative, perhaps. More stealthy, this handful of British infantry that formed the advance party of the newest conquering army. The inhabitants of the city—Turks, Jews, Arabs, Christians, Russians, Greeks—remained cautiously indoors. It didn't do to rush too precipitously into the arms of conquerors. This battle for the city had also raged bloodily beyond the walls. Who could be certain it might not again erupt around some corner in the narrow, tangled streets? Or in the covered bazaars? Eyes watched from behind iron grilles or through narrow slits of shutters as the small patrol prowled forward street by street. Occasionally a soldier paused to batter open a suspicious door. Or a lone advance scout reconnoitered before signaling his comrades.

It all seemed too quiet. Too easy. In the open area near the Damascus Gate, the patrol halted. From far off, a sound was growing. An advancing of hoofs. The flinty ring of iron on stone. Sergeant Hawcombe signaled an alert. Rifle bolts slipped home. The troops joined their still breath to the silence of the city. The sergeant's hand was frozen in air. He called to the man at the most forward vantage point. "See anything, Corporal Lamb?"

The noncom squinted into the reddening sun through the pointed arch of the gate. "Horsemen!" he called back. "Ay-rabs."

Sergeant Hawcombe signaled his patrol to deploy into positions covering the entrance of the gate.

They waited. Watched. And saw, leading the riders, a

slender, graceful man in white burnoose mounted on a white horse. Incredibly, he carried an ancient Arab bow lashed to his saddle. One hand supported a ready carbine, butt balanced against knee.

Yassir Hammadi reigned in through the gate, lowering his gun, an impressive, arrogant figure, skin darkened to mahogany by desert sun.

A fiery red horse carried Tariq to his brother's side. Clattering against one booted leg was a long, curved sword. Two bandoliered horsemen behind watched narrowly, each a mobile arsenal. The British sergeants stepped out to meet the cavalcade, rifles ready.

Yassir called to them in English. "We're from Colonel Lawrence's command. The army of Prince Faisal. Have you taken the city, then?"

Taut vigilance relaxed slightly. "We're not bloody sure ourselves!"

A movement in an upper window sent two doves winging into the copper sky. The third horseman tossed a scaling iron from the saddle of his black mount to the top of the wall, swinging himself from horse to parapet. Atop the roof, he drew an automatic from a shoulder holster, covering the window. "Come forth," he cried in Arabic.

The last rider, an awesome figure in black, dusty robes, spurred forward. Sergeant Hawcombe was surprised to see a human skull gleaming against the acrid green saddle blanket slung across his tawny mount.

Something poked from the window above. A white flag. It hung limp while its bearer waited.

"Come out!" called the sergeant. "Hands where we can see 'em!" Nothing happened. Yassir echoed the command in Arabic. Then in Turkish. "Come forth!" he shouted. When there was still no reply, Hawcombe ordered soldiers forward to kick in the door.

The great bolt gave way. A bedraggled collection of Turkish civilians emerged, haggard faces beneath fezzes, white flags trembling above heads. They glanced fearfully at the mounted Arabs, then turned almost eagerly to their British captors.

"I am the Mayor of the city," announced a man in a long black coat, leaning heavily on a cane. Yassir translated his words.

"Sergeants Hawcombe and Sedgewick. British Expeditionary Forces."

The Mayor nodded. He wore a black necktie as though in mourning and looked as though he hadn't slept for a week. "Sergeant, I have the duty to offer you the surrender of the city." The Mayor put forward his hand. It held a sealed document of office and a collection of large keys. Hawcombe broke the seal and glanced at the document. It meant nothing to him. No manual offered any instruction for such a happening. "Save that for General Allenby," he told the Mayor and turned to his men. "Jenkins. Kalpin. Get back to Company HQ at the double and tell Captain Viner . . . we just captured Jerusalem."

Field Marshal Viscount Allenby of Megiddo—as the victorious Commander of the British Army in Palestine would soon come to be known—waited in silence in his open military touring car. It stopped a small distance from the arched Jaffa Gate, which broke the symmetry of crenelated walls. The General was a handsome, usefully aloof man with features that begged to be commemorated in marble—a man with a sense of history and a superb tactical ability. But, for all his success, Allenby could be humble. When word that the city was taken reached him, he chose to decend from his automobile and lead his army on foot into the Holy City.

Captain Judah Nouari and other members of the Jewish Legion had been granted permission to join Allenby for the final march. With him was Bernard Goldfarb, proudly sporting the pips of a newly minted lieutenant.

The clock on the tower read seven-thirty. Troops lined the streets as Allenby walked in alone, his staff following. Soldiers and townspeople cheered the liberators from balconies and rooftops. Keys of the city were offered and accepted. The military band played "God Save the King." Jerusalem had joined the British Empire.

"This is a city I never expected to see in my life," Bernard said to Judah. "Quite a feeling."

"We're here because the greatest power on earth is behind us," Judah said.

"God—or the British?"

Judah's eyes were drawn to a tall young Arab on a fiery chestnut horse. The rider looked somehow familiar. "Tariq . . . ? Tariq Hammadi?"

The Arab turned with surprise. "Judah Nouari? Well. . . . Not a grain of sand is ever lost." Tariq dismounted in a graceful bound. "Your brother Ben said you were with the British. So am I—as you see."

"The last time we met, you were. . . ." Judah made the time-honored gesture measuring the child who has since grown up.

Another Arab robed in white came over, leading his horse. "So it's Judah Nouari." A half smile touched Yassir's lips as he took in the uniform. "I hear you call yourselves the Jewish Legion."

"So do the British, Yassir," Judah replied.

"We haven't met since you and my dear cousin Mohamed packed me off to Heidelberg." Yassir's voice was acid.

"It *has* been a long time. And a matter of some speculation as to where you were," Judah told him.

"Where I was needed. In Palestine. However, it might amuse you and Cousin Mohamed to know that one of our objectives for Colonel Lawrence was to raid and destroy the railway that Hammadi-Nouari built with the Germans."

"The fortunes of war," Judah said, deliberately switching from Arabic into English. "Perhaps we'll build it back—for the British."

"With the aid of your *Jewish* Legion, Captain Nouari?" Yassir also spoke in English.

"You're serving with an Arab unit, I see."

"We are grateful that you Jews are helping us defeat the Turks. But this *is* an Arab land," Tariq put in.

Bernard Goldfarb moved toward the two Arab brothers. "Sorry to contradict you, friends. But the Holy Land has no nationality. Today we've gotten rid of the Turks. It's under the British flag. Soon it will offer a homeland for Zion. Lord Balfour has promised that."

Yassir's glance darkened. "We have heard of the British Lord's declaration. A scrap of paper from an English dreamer to a Jewish banker. It means nothing." He eyed Bernard with some curiosity. "But you are not from Palestine, I think?"

"From the United States."

"You come a long way to fight for a cause that is not yours. Why? American Jews do not need a homeland."

"All Jews aren't in America," Bernard replied carefully.

Yassir laughed. "You have misplaced your loyalties. Palestine has nothing to offer world Jewry. As for those who live here already, let them stay.'' He remounted his horse, turning his attention back to Judah. ''We'll meet again, Nouari. Before you go back to your Zionist interests, you must show your American friend the Wailing Wall. The last stones of the Temple of Solomon—knocked down by Titus when he threw your people out of Palestine. Come, Tariq,'' he called. ''The prison. There may still be some of our people there.'' He trotted his horse across the square to join the other Arabs.

Tariq hung behind. ''Judah . . . your brother Ben. He's been working with us. A good man. I wanted you to know he's safe. Hidden in Hartuv. Anwar is with him. But your cousin Dr. Simon. . . .I'm afraid he's missing.'' He added, ''It was good to see you, Judah.''

''And you, too, Tariq. Keep safe,'' Judah said. Tariq remounted and rode off after the others.

Judah turned to Bernard. ''Yes. Let's go to the Wailing Wall.''

Propped up in one of the narrow beds in his Bethlehem clinic, Dr. Simon Nouari tried to smile at little Daniel; but the taped bandage across his nose pulled the expression into a grimace. It had been eight days since Dr. Yusuf had rebroken and set Simon's nose for him. A few more days would be needed before bandages could be removed. The nose he'd always been so vain about. . . .

''Thank you for the figs, Daniel. I'll enjoy them very much.''

''I picked them myself, from our own tree, Papa.'' Sephora had dressed the boy in a clean blue-and-white shirt. He stood by his father's bed, shifting his weight from foot to foot, one shoelace untied, brave against the hospital smell that was making him a little sick.

Sephora was trying her best to look cheerful, an emotion she did not feel. Happy, yes. Cheerful, no. She planted a kiss somewhere in the area of Simon's chin, carefully avoiding the burn scar on his cheek. Every time she saw it, it plucked at her conscience. He seemed somehow a stranger, alienated by changed appearance. She longed to have him home again the way he had been. She had sworn to herself that she would never, no matter what the circumstances, ever distrust Simon again. Even if she found him in the arms of another woman.

"Dr. Yusuf says if he lets you come home too soon, he knows you'll get no rest, Simon. He wants you to stay here and recover completely." She held back tears behind a brave smile. "Look what I've brought." She lifted a huge kettle from a basket, opening the lid. Aromatic steam assailed his nostrils.

"Chicken soup," he said listlessly. "You've made enough for the whole ward, Sephora."

She ladled some into a bowl and thrust a spoon toward his lips. "Still hot. Get it down you."

He tried to show enthusiasm, but the act of swallowing was still difficult. At least it avoided the necessity of conversation for which he wasn't quite ready. There were too many things unclear to him. Things he had to sort out for himself.

He was still hazy in his mind about his rescue. It was a somnambulant memory, a kind of vision. A foreboding. Perhaps even a revelation. He could remember lying on his accumulation of straw, too weak to move, the air heavy with the stink of death. There had been a banging, crashing, breaking open of the cell door. It burst in with a sharp, painful ray of blood-red sunlight. A figure in flowing white robes entered like an Angel of the Lord. Behind him, three others formed an angelic army. The figure in white gave a command that seemed to ring like a clap of thunder against the high stone walls. Simon thought he said, "Come forth."

The creatures moved about the cell, carrying out the living. Then the white-robed Avenging Angel stood over Simon. He heard his own name spoken like a great earthquake. "Simon? Simon Nouari . . . ?"

It seemed as though the heavens were wrenched apart, as though the constellations fell to earth around him, like a fig tree shedding its winter fruit when shaken by a mighty wind. The face above him came into focus. He saw that it was Yassir Hammadi. He couldn't remember any more. He had lost consciousness.

". . . be in here?"

"What?" Simon asked, bringing his mind back to the room and the concerned face of his son, Daniel.

"I said, 'How long will you be in here?' Papa."

"Another week or two, Daniel. Been taking good care of your mother?"

The boy nodded. "Your face. Does it hurt, Papa?"

"A bit. I'm afraid you'll have to get used to me with a few scars."

He had said something of the sort to Ben and Anwar when they came to see him. They'd brought Judah and news. Tariq had disappeared again, Zuliekha with him. They were beginning to call the husky-voiced Arab girl *El Agrat,* "The Scorpion," for her daring in striking Turkish targets. It was assumed that she and Tariq had joined one of the *Al Fatat* groups working to clean out pockets of Turkish resistance in Syria.

Simon reached out for Sephora's hand. He could sense the concern she was trying to hide behind gentle cornflower-blue eyes. In that moment, he loved her more than he ever had in his life. "My wife, from now on, things are going to be different."

"I don't understand politics," Sephora said. "A free Palestine—that's what you've all risked your necks for. But Dr. Yusuf says the French will occupy the North. Syria, Galilee. . . . And the British are in Palestine to stay. Do you think they will be better for us then the Turks?"

He patted her hand. "The French are the most civilized people on earth . . . and the British have offered us a homeland. I can settle down to being what I was meant to be: a country doctor. Keep my nose—broken as it is—out of politics. We will sit under our own fig tree, grow our melons, and live in peace."

Sephora shook her head. "There's never been peace for our people . . . since the Children of Israel escaped from Egypt."

Daniel, who was feeling left out, interrupted. "Why was it only the children, Papa? Didn't their fathers and mothers escape too?"

Simon tried to laugh. But it hurt too much. He put his hand on the boy's head and spoke a little blessing in his mind.

The Jerusalem offices of the Hammadi-Nouari Trading Company had been closed tight, its great door sealed since Solomon's death. Today the key made a rasping sound as it

awakened the lock. Cleaners had arrived hours ahead of the
meeting to prepare the dusty boardroom.

This conference, convened to decide the Company's future
in the Middle East, had gathered in directors from across
the world. From Cairo: Mahmood, Gideon, and his son Raphael, leaving Ahmed behind to keep things ticking. From Paris:
Sayid and David, who had been running the French bank for
their sons throughout the war. From New York: Mohamed on
a sprinting schedule, his arrival timed almost to the hour of
the meeting.

The first sight Judah had of him was when the two partners
arrived at the office. Neither had seen the other since Paris,
two years before. Mohamed made the first gesture; sincere,
but cool. "You look well," he said.

"And you, Mohamed."

"Ruth and the children?"

"You'll see them after the meeting. Father has reopened
the house here. We're all staying in it."

"I was sorry to hear about your mother."

Judah nodded. He couldn't quite bring himself to ask about
Jacqueline. The taste of her name would burn his lips.

Mohamed saved him the need. "And Jacqueline. Quite
recovered from her breakdown. Home again from the sanatorium, I'm glad to say," Mohamed dropped casually.

"I'd no idea." Judah absorbed the shock.

Mohamed went on: "It was necessary to commit her when
I brought her back to New York. . . ." He broke off.

"I'm glad she's better," Judah said.

He was saved from further dialogue by Gideon Nouari,
who came up and took his nephew's arm and led the way into
the conference room with a whisper in Judah's ear. "Judah,
Judah, my little Mignon sent you her very fond regards.
Remember her? She has never forgotten you. I should be
jealous." Gideon, beginning to bulge slightly at the middle,
hair thinning but black as the dye bottle would still permit,
debonair as ever, the family peacock hooting sexual achievement. His son Raphael followed a few steps behind, watching
his father with customary disapproval.

As a gesture of respect, Jacob, in his eighties and more
than thirty years retired, had been invited to attend. His
grandson Jonathan, still in uniform, wheeled the old man's
chair to the center of the long table, where a pad and pen

were placed before him. No one expected Jacob to use them. Mohamed took his place at the head, pushing an open box of cigars toward his father, Ben, and Anwar on his left. David Nouari took a place to his right, next to Judah. David and his two sons wore black armbands. Judah's mother had died peacefully in Paris two days before the armistice. Osmon Hammadi, handsome young son of Dr. Yusuf, was seated next to Nathan. Both were attending their first Company meeting.

"Yes, grandfather," Nathan went on with a conversation that had been drifting. "I do want to get married. I assure you. Only, it's a different girl every time."

Jacob, a little deaf, murmured, *"Mazel tov.* You should bring her to the house soon. So I should see her before I die." Nathan exchanged a glance with his brother over their grandfather's wispy crest.

Mohamed called the meeting to order. "Well," he began, surveying the faces down the long table, "most of us seem to have survived the war. Now we must bind up the wounds of the Company as quickly as possible. I believe it's the opinion of everyone here that the Damascus office should remain closed permanently." This was not exactly news. Since the death of Abdullah and Izak—and the conspicuous absence of Yassir and Tariq—the decision on Damascus was unanimous.

Next came points of policy. Postwar problems of supplies still available, markets to be reopened or investigated. An immediate resolution was taken to gear up the Spanish factory for the production of farming equipment, with a sideline in sporting guns. Although the Jerusalem bank had staggered along throughout the war under the direction of Anwar and Ben, it was now proposed to reopen the head office of the Trading Company. Judah nominated Raphael for the post.

His cousin received the idea with great enthusiasm, and was delighted when it was passed by the board. For Raphael, it meant escape from the stagnation of working under his father in Cairo. He felt sorry for Ahmed, who would be left behind to cope with the two fathers. But Raphael had a wife and two small daughters now.

"Diedre will welcome the change of climate," he enthused. Part of his responsibility would be training Jonathan and Osmon into the business.

Ben requested and was given the floor. His expression was

more intense than his brother Judah's. Ben was a man who knew what he wanted, who could make up his mind in an instant.

"I wish to announce a personal decision. Officially. I've already discussed it with Anwar. I am giving my resignation. Leaving the bank."

There was a hum of surprise around the table. David regarded his younger son with deep hurt. "This is something you have not discussed with me—or with Judah. May we know the reason?"

"It has nothing to do with the Company, Father," Ben said. "It's just that I have other plans that I find closer to my heart." He turned appealing to his brother. "Judah, you'll understand. Nobody could have lived through this war without being changed."

"What is it you want to do, Ben?" Judah asked.

"To be a farmer. Work the land."

There was a moment of silence. It was unthinkable that a member of either family would wish to leave the Company. Except for Yassir Hammadi—which, in his case, everyone felt was for the best.

"Where do you propose to do this farming?" Mohamed probed. "Perhaps the Company can help. We intend to expand our citrus orchards in the South."

"I'm grateful for the offer, Mohamed. But it's not my purpose to become a commercial farmer." Ben turned back to Judah. "As my brother knows, new settlements are being formed up North. It's my intention to join one of these."

"The Company can ill spare you now," Mohamed said sharply. "There's much to be done if we're to recover. Your experience is needed."

Ben shook his head. "The land needs me more. I don't have to tell you that aside from the towns and farms owned by *effendi* landlords, this country's still a wasteland. But it needn't be. It's crying out for pioneers to develop it—and I don't see why they should only come from abroad. Why foreigners, when our own people should be working this land?"

Mohamed bit the end off his cigar. "Which 'people' do you mean, Ben? Only the *Yishuv*—Palestinian Jews?"

Ben was silent.

Mohamed went on coolly: "I presume you plan to include Arabs in these settlements?"

There was a muttering around the table among the Hammadis.

"Well, Ben?" Mohamed prompted.

Ben lowered his glance. "No, Mohamed. There will be no Arabs in the *kibbutzim.*"

"And may I ask why not?"

"Because . . . they're Jewish settlements."

Judah tapped his glass with a pen to quiet the table. "I think we should avoid political issues, Ben."

Ben hunched his chair forward. "It's important that our Arab partners understand that the *kibbutz* movement is a whole new social structure. Not like the old settlements. Individuals will work as part of a group. Self-supporting. Sharing a way of life for the good of all."

"All but the Arabs!" Mahmood observed.

Old Jacob suddenly perched forward, tapping his pencil on the white pad. "From such an idea, where comes the profit?"

This brought a chuckle of relieved tension.

"Profit is not the motive, great-uncle," Ben replied. "Not personal profit, anyway." He turned back to the head of the table. "Maybe you can understand this, Mohamed. We Jews belong to a people who have lost their souls in the strife of commerce."

"My dear fellow, if it weren't for commerce, we wouldn't be here at all," Gideon Nouari exploded with exasperation.

"I'm talking about a national renaissance, cousin Gideon. I don't ask you all to abandon your ledgers. Commerce, capitalism, and the working-class movement can exist side by side."

How pompous Ben was becoming, Judah thought.

"And what about Arabs and Jews? Can *they* exist side by side?" Sayid demanded of Ben.

"The *kibbutz* will be founded on equal rights, cooperation, and brotherhood. Which can only improve racial relationships."

"Never!" blazed Mohamed's father. "You're asking for a bloodbath, my friend. Everyone at this table knows what the British have promised the Jews. That's what we're really talking about!"

Judah stood up. "Permission to speak, Mr. Chairman?" Mohamed waved assent. "The British have made promises. True. And I'm proud to have played a small part in the negotiations. But there's no reason to believe these concessions will conflict with Arab hopes in Syria or the Lebanon. There's room enough for everybody in the Middle East—if no one group gets too greedy.''

Argument exploded around the table. Mohamed's gavel banged the room to silence. "This discussion has moved away from the issue: Ben's resignation. Judah, you know this as well as I; we've discussed it often enough: Most of your Zionist communities before the war were charity-supported colonies, sustained only by Jewish philanthropy from abroad. They angered the *effendis,* corrupted the *fellaheen,* and ennobled nobody." He turned back to Judah's younger brother. "If I could with a single stroke abolish every Zionist settlement, I would do so, Ben. For the good of Palestine, I would do so . . . !''

Judah interrupted, choking back anger. "Point of order! I'm aware of our chairman's opinion on this subject—with which I disagree heartily. But I do concur that this isn't the place for such a discussion.''

"Then, for God's sake let's drop it!" Raphael urged, wondering what his transfer to Jerusalem would bring.

"I'll only say," Judah went on, unhearing, "that these new *kibbutzim* are to be based entirely on communal effort. They will not be employing cheap Arab labor.''

"You mean, they won't employ any Arabs at all?" Mahmood cried out angrily, rising.

Ben stood up again. "That's true, Mahmood. Each member of the *kibbutz*—men and women—will share the work. As for our Arab neighbors, I see no reason for conflict on economic, religious, or racial grounds.''

Sayid rose for attention. "And what about immigration? Do you intend to flood our country with Poles and Russians?''

"The Jews must get their homeland, Sayid. The Bible has promised it. And the British have guaranteed it," Ben said.

"Then, I'll make you another promise: a hundred years of war!" Mohamed's father turned and walked out of the room.

There was a silence. "I move the question," Judah said, voice husky, "that we accept Ben's resignation.''

The others grudgingly agreed, but the air was charged with emotion. Mohamed held Judah's glance tightly. "The resignation of Benjamin Nouari is accepted. I propose that we ask David Nouari to transfer from the Paris bank and return to

Jerusalem to work with my brother Anwar.'' He paused. ''And that Judah—now that he is demobilized—take up his old post in Paris.'' His eyes returned to his partner. ''Unless he, too, intends to push a plow.''

Judah's face softened to a smile. ''No plow. I'm a little old for that.''

''Life is an hourglass—but the sand is the color of blood. . . .''

Nobody heard old Jacob, which was hardly surprising, since he had said the words in his mind. Some things that he meant to say aloud sounded in his mind—and others in his mind would sound suddenly from his lips. And everyone would be surprised at how clear his thoughts and memory could still be. It was a penalty of age to be either ignored or overadmired for small accomplishments.

He looked around the crowded room of his rambling Jerusalem home. Here were faces of children grown into almost strangers. But others seemed wonderfully close, returning from the land of memory.

''So, Miriam, you have come back to Jerusalem to watch die an old man in an old house. . . .'' His hand fluttered up, gesturing off in the direction of the city beyond the walls. ''In an old country. . . .''

Well, there wasn't much to answer to statements like that, Miriam thought.

''Solomon. Izak. I miss my two sons,'' he droned on as though she didn't miss her husband. Every minute of the day and the night. But Miriam, daughter of a Hassidic rabbi, lived by values of piety and godliness. Her father had taught her that the Hassidim exult in glory, they sing for joy upon their beds. They have the high praises of God in their mouths and a two-edged sword in their hands. Miriam still believed it.

''I've come home,'' she told Jacob gently. ''With Naomi. To take care of you, Papa Jacob. And share the shining of the sun upon us all—after such a long night.'' She tucked the blanket around the old fellow's thin knees protruding from the wheelchair like broken stalks. He was always cold now. One could wonder if he would see another year. Probably. Old Jacob had a way of outliving everyone's prognostications. Especially his own. He could be grumbling, complaining, using his age to spank their consciences into greater attention. Or he could be venerably august, a gentle sage tinged by the

sorrow of his own transience. As the last of the three founding fathers of Hammadi-Nouari, it would be Jacob's duty
tonight to tell the story of the *Haggada*—the exodus of the
Children of Israel out of Egypt—retold at every Feast of
Passover.

Jacob's house had undergone the ritual spring cleaning
tradition demanded. Every nook and cranny was spotless. All
leavened bread searched out and burned, except for token bits
hidden for children to find and destroy. All metal cutlery had
been boiled, special china used to lay the table. Ruth and
Miriam were preparing the dinner together. Matzos, bitter
herbs, chopped apple and nuts, and the paschal lamb. At
fourteen, Abe and Zed, though a bit old for it, would dutifully hunt for the leavened bread.

But the guests of honor were not the visiting relatives from
Paris. Joseph Trumpeldor had arrived from Russia. He was
seated on the low sofa next to Vladimir Jabotinsky, his old
comrade-in-arms. Clustered around them were the men of the
Nouari family.

"This Passover nearly caused a mutiny in the Jewish Legion,"
Jabotinsky explained to Miriam. "For no reason at all, the
British military suddenly decided to ban Legion troops from
Jerusalem."

Judah nodded. "Even Colonel Patterson called it an unthinkable act of provocation."

Judah's mind was scorched by the memory of August heat
the year before. After all they had fought for! The Legion was
dug in deep in a boulder-strewn ravine in the Jordan Valley,
protecting the right flank of the British Army's northern front.
Crouching in the shade of the wadi's craggy face, waiting for
Jabotinsky to return from a meeting with Colonel Patterson.
When Jabotinsky finally appeared, he spoke with a confidence Judah knew he didn't feel.

"We're surrounded on three sides by Turkish divisions.
We've been given the task of holding against an attack. And
although we will be the first target, we will ford the Jordan
River—at Umm esh Shurt. Almost the very spot—almost
exactly—where Joshua led the Hebrews into the Promised
Land."

But that was all in the past. They had won. The fighting
was over. Yet now British authorities had dared to put

Jerusalem—the focus of the Passover celebration for over three thousand years—out of bounds to Jewish soldiers!

"Even Christ came to Jerusalem to celebrate the Passover," Bernard Goldfarb remarked.

"Maybe it would have been better for us if it hadn't also been his *last* supper," Nathan put in. "Alive, he was an influential Jew."

Miriam gave her son a sharp look. "It isn't proper to make jokes about such things, Nathan."

"But surely our soldiers have been permitted in Jerusalem today?" Naomi asked.

Judah patted her hand. "Thanks to a cable from Colonel Patterson to Lord Balfour; the order was rescinded just in time."

"Where are we safe from anti-Semitism?" Jabotinsky demanded. "In our graves?"

Trumpeldor turned to him. "Nowhere, my friend. Until we have a country. When I was recently on the Caucasian front, I saw something I never would have believed. The Russians were circulating copies of the *Protocols of the Elders of Zion* among the British troops."

"Why are you surprised at anything from the Russians?" Jabotinsky exclaimed.

Trumpeldor took a glass of tea from Naomi. His handsome face looked drawn. In his beloved Russia he'd received a few honors and a great many disappointments. "Never mind," he said. "Their lies will not defeat our truth. But I fear that, though the war is over, nothing is over. At this moment, ten thousand Russian Jewish soldiers are waiting to reinforce our Legion here—but the British won't let them set foot in Palestine. Yet we're still a quarter of all Allied infantry stationed here to keep the peace. I've told them these troops are a matter of life and death to us if we are to create a national existence. And still they refuse to allow them entry!"

Ben turned from peering out the window toward the city wall. "You don't have to look far for the reason, Captain Trumpeldor. The British fear trouble with the Arabs. Faisal's troops plundered Turkish arms and hid them. They're not going to give way now—to the British or to the French in the North. Or to us."

"We are all victims of promises nobody keeps," Jonathan said.

Judah peered from his uncle's window, across the spire and minarets of Jerusalem. "Politics, Jonathan. When the British took Damascus, they put Faisal on the royal rocking chair. The French moved in and tossed him out. Churchill picked him up, dusted him off, then drew a line on the map right down the Jordan River. East of it, he named 'Transjordan.' Just think how easy it was! With a stroke of a pencil, Churchill could create a country. West of that river—the British Mandate. Us."

"The Arabs were also promised a free Arabia," Ben reminded him.

"Nobody will get anything unless they fight for it," Trumpeldor pronounced. "The Arabs know that. That's why they've stockpiled weapons. We, too, must prepare."

"Where, Captain?" Jonathan wanted to know.

"In Galilee. The northern settlements. I've been asked to reorganize their defense. The task is impossible. Never mind. Anyone care to go with me?" He drew a map from his pocket; his finger stabbed points below the Lebanon. "Tel Hai . . . Kefar Giladi . . . Metula . . . Hamrah. Outposts. Pinpricks on this map. But they are the footprints in which we must make our stand. Defend them, and the Jewish nation will be born."

"I'd like to go with you, sir." It was Bernard Goldfarb who spoke first.

"I'm with you too," Jonathan said.

"I guess that means me, too," Nathan decided. "Who could my brother blame for his mistakes if I weren't around?"

"Good!" Trumpeldor was pleased. "Your war experience will make you useful to train others." Naomi stopped pouring tea. In Bernard's face as in her brothers', she read what she had feared yet already knew. One war would not be enough. Trumpeldor's words were making that clear enough.

"Our outposts are caught between French designs and Arab frustrations," Trumpeldor continued. "Galilee is bedeviled by armed skirmishes. We'll be underequipped, underarmed, underfed: The land itself isn't enemy enough—dry, sandy, rocky soil, not even blessed with rain."

"What can you plant there?" asked Naomi.

"How about a flagpole—flying a blue-and-white flag?" Nathan suggested.

Actually, Bernard had made his decision weeks before with

Ben. Since Gallipoli, Bernard would have followed Trumpeldor anywhere. Looking at the man now in the soft, warm lamplight of Jacob Nouari's comfortable home, Bernard caught a 'flash' image of that same Trumpeldor moving casually through a rain of bullets and bursting shells to seat himself on a rock. The Captain had been studying a map then, too—incredibly humming a little tune as though the shells were only bees buzzing around his head on a summer afternoon.

> *"Through fields, through forests,*
> *To meet my love . . ."*

went the words.

"What song is that, sir?" Bernard had asked.

"An old Palestinian folk song," Trumpeldor replied. "One that I'm particularly fond of."

And suddenly the American hadn't felt afraid any more.

"Ever scared, Captain?" Bernard had asked him. The man always seemed so cool, so unruffled.

Trumpeldor folded the map back into his pocket. "It wouldn't do, would it? A leader is meant to be calm. Hard as iron. Danger is my old friend—though I certainly don't court death. But I doubt even he could say I fear him." He smiled at Bernard. "Someone must set the example."

At that moment, a hand grenade had burst near their feet, showering them with rock splinters and sand. "Never mind, Goldfarb. It wasn't close or we'd be dead. But I think we've given them enough target." Bernard had followed Trumpeldor down into a trench in Gallipoli.

Now he would follow him to an outpost in Galilee. Tonight he would write his parents of his decision. What had made him decide, anyway? His eyes went to Naomi. It was nothing she had said or done. He'd scarcely seen her since she and her mother had arrived from Cairo. He knew that her engagement was still as firm as ever. Her fiancé was expected any moment. Bernard was curious to inspect the man. See if he was good enough for Naomi. Not that anyone would consult him—or that his opinion or desires would make a shred of difference. He tried to catch her eye, but Naomi's attention was riveted on Joseph Trumpeldor's words.

"By conviction, I'm really not a military man," the soldier said. "But until the day when we can beat our swords into plowshares and our spears into pruning hooks, I see no other course." His eyes drifted to the table so beautifully laid for the Passover Feast. "Yet we have much to be thankful for. Another springtime. The time to plant seed, the time when things begin to grow. For us, this Passover has special meaning. For it is *we* who will be sown. *We* who will grow."

Ruth Nouari emerged from the kitchen with Miriam. The women's faces were flushed from the cooking, which they had seen to personally.

"Hasn't he come yet?" Miriam asked. "The children are getting hungry."

Jacob, who had been half dozing, opened his eyes. "Who are we waiting for? Elijah? Leave a chair for him. He's never showed up yet."

The bell peeled beyond the front door, interrupting further speculation. "At last—Moishe," Miriam said, hurrying to the door, removing her apron. Bernard noted that Naomi did not move.

The young man who entered wore a wide-brimmed black hat above a pale, bearded face. The fringes of a prayer shawl hung from beneath the jacket of his dark suit. His quiet, studious manner contrasted sharply with the ebullience of the Nouari men. Naomi greeted him shyly, barely speaking. Introductions were exchanged all around. Ruth summoned them to the table. The children were getting impatient.

Jonathan came around to push his grandfather's wheelchair to the head of the table. Judah put an arm around each of the twins, leading them in.

"Aren't we too old to hunt matzos, Papa?" asked Abe.

"Probably. But you'll do it anyway."

"What are they for, Papa?" Zed asked.

"Every year I tell you, and every year you ask again," Judah sighed. "For Passover, a Jew gives up the pleasure of eating soft, doughy bread."

"Why?" the twins chorused.

"Because it was the bread they ate in Egypt as slaves. These dry matzos sustained our people through their forty years of wandering. It was the hard bread of our freedom."

Jabotinsky took his place next to Miriam. "And if it takes us forty years, we'll have a country again."

And so the Feast of the Passover began, for the first time in years in a Jerusalem no longer under the Turks. It gave new meaning to the question: "Why is this night different from all other nights?"

Bernard looked across the table at Naomi, captivated by the sweetness of her expression and her gentle eyes. Yet one could feel a strength in her. Opposite her sat Moishe. Bernard noted that, throughout the meal, the betrothed pair scarcely exchanged a glance or a word. They hadn't even touched hands when Moishe came in. But then, customs were still archaic in this land. "Get used to them, and don't draw quick conclusions," Bernard advised himself.

After dinner, they returned to the sprawling, spacious living room. Naomi led the one-armed soldier to a comfortable lounge chair. "Don't make me too comfortable, my dear child. I'll never go," Trumpeldor protested.

"Captain," she asked softly, "you said earlier that there are women in these outpost settlements?"

He nodded. "It is a good thing to have four or five women in the groups. There is plenty of work for them."

Naomi perched on a stiff chair beside him. "Since my brothers are to go with you, I would like to come too."

"Naomi!" Miriam's voice was stricken. "It's no place for a young girl, northern Galilee. Such a wilderness!"

"I am not a girl any more," Naomi replied firmly.

"And you're not a woman, either, until you're married," her mother decreed.

Naomi turned to her fiancé—a stranger to her more than anyone in the room. "When Moishe and I are married, it will be for a lifetime. And he still has another year at the Yeshiva. It may be the last time in my life that I can do something on my own. When I'm a *rebbetzen,* I will have to live for my husband and his congregation."

Trumpeldor, who had not yet answered, looked across at the girl's mother. "Mrs. Nouari, the youth of Israel will be needed—both men and women—to build our new state. If your daughter wishes to go with her brothers, we will be grateful to have her."

"We'll look after her, Mother," Jonathan said.

Nathan sighed with resignation. "Just our luck, Jonathan. Thousands of nice Jewish girls in Palestine. And who do we end up with? Our sister."

Miriam turned to her prospective son-in-law. "You, Moishe.

You would let her go . . . to a frontier place where anything could happen?''

The pale young man, already hollow-chested from hours bent over the Torah, lifted dark, luminous eyes to Miriam. ''Naomi has her own life, Mrs. Nouari. I have not yet the right to make her decisions. But what is the old saying? Before you marry a girl, study her brothers. They have made a decision I envy. If Naomi wishes to go with them, she will go with my blessing.''

Old Jacob spoke up suddenly. ''Who could stop my son, Solomon, when he decided to go to Damascus? His daughter, too, is a Nouari.''

All eyes in the room had turned back to Miriam expectantly. She looked toward Judah, now the accepted head of the Nouaris. ''Cousin Judah, maybe she'll listen to you.''

Judah, the twins sitting at his feet, considered the question. ''Perhaps Naomi will go like a lantern—so that we can all endure the dark.'' It was a thing Zosia had once said to him.

And so it was decided. Miriam nodded a wordless assent. Jonathan and Nathan came over to kiss their sister. Bernard watched, heart soaring. He would be going with them.

''It is written,'' Miriam said, ''Of everyone whose heart makes him willing; ye shall take my offering. . . .' ''

Seventeen _____

FROM a rooftop in the Transjordanian village of Chalsa, two armed Arabs watched a veil of yellow dust approach along the singlelane road. Their rifle sites leveled on the sun-flared windshield. Only when the black Packard touring car was closer did they recognize the officer seated beside the driver. They lowered their weapons.

Colonel Bakr Hafez stepped out, returning the salute of Bedouin sentries in the army of the newly crowned King Abdullah of the Transjordan.

Inside one of the recently confiscated houses, Yassir Hammadi was growing restless. His war experience with Lawrence had changed the troublesome bluejay into a hawk, lean and predatory. His brother turned from the window. "He's here. Shouldn't we go out to meet him?"

Yassir clucked his tongue, Arab fashion. "When a leader sends for you, you do not seek out his messenger."

The third person in the room also wore a man's *kafaya*. But the head covering hid long black hair. Zuliekha's uniform was completed by a black *abaya* and heavy cartridge bandolier. Since she and Tariq had been working together, she had worn men's clothes. It saved a lot of questions.

Outside, a shrill warbling battle cry rose like the echo of ancient Islamic warriors.

"Ealululu . . . ! Ealulululu . . . !"

"We must go out," Tariq said.

Yassir shrugged. "Very well. Now that he has made his entrance, we will make ours."

Musket puffs powdered the sky with a salute of gun smoke. Villagers made way for the three members of Al Fatat to approach the Colonel. Traditional salutations were exchanged.

381

"We will go, then," the officer said. "He is waiting."

The three climbed into the back seat. Colonel Hafez took his place beside the driver, and the car rumbled away. Somewhere in that wilderness of hazy boundaries, the Galilean hills, the Colonel passed three black scarves to his passengers. "I must ask you now to cover your eyes."

Yassir wound the cloth around his head. The others followed suit.

"You must understand," the Colonel explained, "the Imam has been sentenced in absentia by the British, for the Easter riot at the Jaffa Gate, in Jerusalem. Fifteen years' imprisonment if he is caught."

"He is our greatest Arab nationalist." Yassir spoke respectfully.

"An example to us all! Haj Amin knows how to turn the grumblings in the souks and coffeehouses into a holy rage," Hafez told them. "Six Jews killed in that riot!"

"Were not an equal number of our own people killed in that same riot?" Tariq asked.

"Nothing can be gained without spilling blood, Tariq. We will see that it is the Jews who drown in theirs!" Yassir hadn't invented the phrase. He remembered it from a newspaper article, in *Syria el-Jenoubra:* It was headlined ARABS ARISE! THE END OF THE FOREIGNERS IS NEAR!

The Colonel tested their blindfolds. "I regret the precaution. Even loyal Palestinians like yourselves are not permitted to know the location of Haj Amin's headquarters. If you were caught, the information would be in the hands of the enemy."

"I would kill myself before talking!" Yassir protested.

"Many have said that."

Zuliekha spoke for the first time. "I understand that wherever he goes in the villages, Haj Amin is received like a saint."

"Oh, he is," the Colonel assured her. "Children are brought forward to be touched by him. People kneel to touch the hem of his garment. He is like the coming of the Mahdi."

An hour later, the car jolted to a stop. "We will get out here," the Colonel ordered, "and approach on foot."

Still blindfolded, the three were helped out of the car by armed Bedouins who guided their stumbling progress up the flank of a steep hill to the mouth of a cave. Only when they were deep inside were the blindfolds removed. Yassir blinked his surroundings into focus. The Colonel had entered ahead and was whispering to a robed man seated incongruously at a modern desk. The dank chamber was illuminated by oil lamps and tallow candles.

Pale blue eyes lifted to fix hypnotically on Yassir. Eyes that he had seen before? Impossible! Maybe it was only that he had always known such eyes existed, eyes that could penetrate to the innermost part of his thoughts.

"So. You are the Hammadi brothers. We congratulate you on your activities on our behalf." The leader rose, came to them. There was something in his movements—graceful, gliding, something familiar.

Suddenly Yassir knew: This Haj Amin—this fugitive patriot—was the same leader who had once, long ago, galvanized students in another dank cavern. Yes, in Damascus. The same leader with whom Yassir had spent months in a Turkish jail. The same leader who had been dragged out of their cell and not seen again.

And yet the man looked at him without recognition. Could it be possible that Yassir was wrong? "Imam, we have met before, have we not?"

Haj Amin's expression was impassive. "There are many pages in the book of life. Nothing befalls us but what Allah has destined."

Even the voice was the same, only softer. Yet if this *was* the same leader Yassir had come to doubt, the man did not wish to be reminded of it. This man with the blue magnet eyes, lips fixed in a beguiling half smile, wearing neither beard nor turban, attractive, still young. This man wished to keep his past an enigma. And yet if this was the same leader, he had become so skilled in strategy, so capable of conquest, that he could strew dead and maimed upon the earth by the shrewd and ruthless clarity of his planning. . . .

It was as Yassir always knew it would be.

"Your record shows you served with the Englishman during the war?" A man bulked forward from the shadows, features obscured by metal-framed smoky glasses and thick mustache. Yassir recognized Aref el-Aref, journalist, propagandist—also a fugitive with a price on his head.

"I was very close to Colonel Lawrence."

"This is hard to believe"—the leader noted Yassir's surprise—"since you are a Palestinian. Lawrence of Arabia—

as he preferred being known—informed me that he was not happy with the Palestinians in Faisal's army. 'Unreliable, undisciplined,' he called you.''

"He lied, Imam!" Yassir flared. "It was the Hashemites whose loyalty could never be trusted. The followers of Faisal.''

"Lawrence did not always comprehend the differences that exist between our tribal brothers. Perhaps that is why his devotion to our cause became . . . confused. He refused to appoint a Palestinian to any political position.'' Haj Amin sighed. "He failed to understand that we Palestinians will never submit to being ruled by Bedou-Hashemites any more than we would be ruled by French or British. Or Jews.''

"He is a Jew lover, all right,'' Aref el-Aref exploded. "He called the Balfour letter 'a good thing.' 'To tame the Levantines'—for so he calls us—'with a Jewish rod!' Those were the words of your Lawrence.''

Haj Amin's attention had turned to Tariq. His voice became sad. "But you Hammadis—your family still continue their partnership with Jews. Do you share Faisal's friendship with Zionists—like Judah Nouari, your cousin's partner?''

"My brother and I have no part in the Company, Imam.''

Haj Amin nodded sideways. "If you had, you would not be here now.'' He turned his attention to the silent Zuliekha. "You, young woman, have achieved recognition beyond your sex. 'The Scorpion' has set a valuable example to all women in our struggle. I understand that you are responsible for tossing a grenade through the window of a French military headquarters?''

She inclined her head modestly. "I was once married to a Frenchman. I knew with what contempt his family held our people.''

"And the episode of the hands. You had some part in that?''

"No,'' she replied.

"It was I alone, Imam,'' Yassir broke in. The report sent to Haj Amin had told of the ambush of a French patrol. The hands of the French soldiers had been cut off, arranged in odd pairs and left stuck in the sand in attitudes of prayer.

"We do not shrink from the use of terror against those who stand in our way.'' Haj Amin moved placidly back to his desk. "And now you shall help me drive a wedge between the British and the French. Between the British and the

Jews." He smoothed a map across his desk and pointed a long fingernail at the area above the Sea of Galilee. "The Zionist outposts must be kept under constant attack. Metula. Kefar Giladi. Tel Hai. Harass them. Frighten them. Allow them no restful sleep." He leaned on his elbows, gently touching fingertips together. "Yassir Hammadi, it will be your responsibility to organize and command those raids."

Yassir touched forehead, lips, and heart. "I am the obedient of Allah, Imam. I will serve you and bring death to all enemies of the true Arab destiny."

The light of a smile flickered across Amin's lips. "Colonel Bakr Hafez will place troops at your disposal. They were to have invaded Syria under the Emir Abdullah. But now that he has been given the throne of Transjordan, that invasion has been called off. We are stronger, better armed than these Jewish farmers. We will force them back to their ghettos in Jerusalem and Haifa."

"Let each man kiss the blade that has slain an enemy," Aref el-Aref said piously. "Let hatred be taught our children, for that is sacred. Let violence become the most positive form of prayer."

"Please, my dear fellow. Save these splendid quotations for your newspaper headlines. We are discussing tactics."

Something in Haj Amin's blueprint of aims troubled Tariq. It was one thing for his brother Yassir to pose as the scourge of the infidel. But what was being planned here in this cave would include the destruction of old friends, neighbors, partners. Ben and Simon Nouari, who had worked so closely with them in the underground. How could he look upon such men as enemies? Tariq drew a slow breath. "May I speak, Imam?"

Haj Amin gestured him on, one hand tracing the line of the beard he had at that moment decided to grow.

"It is true, sir, the Versailles Treaty has left the Arab nation with only the Transjordan. But the British have earmarked only a few thousand square miles for this Jewish homeland. Even with the Anglo-French treaties, our claim is to a million and a half square miles. I agree, we must curb the increase of Jewish settlements and immigration. But Jews in the towns have lived peacefully as our neighbors since the Middle Ages. In Hebron, Tiberius, Safed, and Jerusalem itself. They have never harmed us. Isn't our national dream big enough to include them?"

Haj Amin smiled almost benignly, a sadness in his eyes. "If it were only the Jews who have always lived here, my brother Tariq, we could remain at peace with them. But we are confronted by an invasion. A plague. The debris of Europe from the dung heaps of Russia and Poland. The followers of Zion who wish to breed a new Jewish race on this soil, and so claim our country. We cannot hold softness in our hearts for old neighbors, because they carry the disease that will destroy our children. And now I must have your answer. Will you serve with us in this cause, Tariq Hammadi?"

"He will, Imam!" Yassir said quickly.

"No. Let him speak for himself."

"I am with you, Imam." Tariq's words were barely audible. "I will serve without question."

"And you?" Haj Amin looked at the girl. She glanced at Tariq, but his eyes were lowered. She shared his feelings for old friendships, but she had no doubt that Haj Amin was right. "I am prepared to sacrifice all personal loyalties to the struggle," Zuliekha replied.

Haj Amin inclined his head. "I am assigning you both to Jerusalem. Make the Jewish Quarter a battlefield of terror, riots, and demonstrations. Until the British become weary and feel compelled to end further immigration. We Palestinians will yet inherit Palestine. And we will protect it—even from our Arab brothers." He looked sharply at Tariq. "You still have arms hidden?"

Tariq nodded. "We use the old place again. Since the Turks have gone, no one would think to look there."

"I wish one private word with Yassir."

The Colonel led Tariq and Zuliekha out. Haj Amin turned to Yassir.

"Is your brother to be trusted?"

"If the moment ever came when he were not, Imam, I would kill him with my own hand."

Haj Amin drew his fine curved saber. Their hands met upon the hilt of the weapon. Haj Amin smiled.

"Go—and serve me in Galilee—*Major* Hammadi."

With a sudden impetuous motion, Yassir threw off his robes, revealing the scars on his back, now burnished to a grille of tissue. "These marks, Imam. They keep my memory of Damascus fresh. Can I be wrong, that you share no part of that memory?''

Haj Amin closed his eyes. *"Shirridna bi-'irdna;* we ran away with our honor intact.''

"Harass them. Frighten them. Allow them no restful sleep.'' That was the order Haj Amin had given. And the garrison of Kefar Giladi had been under steady harassment by Bedouin and Arab troops for the past four months.

Joseph Trumpeldor grappled with shortages. *Everything! Ammunition, flour, beans, oil, clothes, blankets, and most of all boots strong enough to stand up to the leg-aching terrain,* he had written to Judah Nouari. He hoped that the famous fund raiser could build a fire under Zionist relief organizations who sent no relief. Yet, despite all problems, to the men and women of the settlement Trumpeldor somehow managed to present a cheerful, optimistic front. *Maybe supplies are low, but spirits are high. If the Gogols and Dostoievskys could see my bold young people they would certainly have described their Jewish characters of fiction quite differently,* he had written. His "bold young people'' had managed to recapture Metula, taken by the Arabs several months earlier.

Trumpeldor had arranged communication links between the three surviving outposts. For delivering written messages, dogs had been trained as couriers. For emergencies, a series of signals. Danger: two rifle shots. All quiet: three. Arabs in the area: four. For an all out attack: a salvo of shots.

The Arabs accused the outposts of harboring French military. It wasn't entirely untrue. However, despite the fact that Arab troops had pushed the French north into Syria, the harassment of the outposts still continued.

Then, only two weeks before, Ben Nouari was surprised to recognize Yassir Hammadi approaching the stockade of Kefar Giladi with eight officers armed with rifles and hand grenades. They came under a white flag with the offer to help the settlers fight the French.

"The settlements are neutral,'' Trumpeldor told the Arabs. "We wish to live peacefully with the French—and with you.''

Yassir spat on the ground contemptuously. "Peace? You have been helping the French to invade our lands!'' Yassir's eyes met Ben's, but he said nothing further. He left with a warning. "Go back to Jerusalem. You do not belong here."

Since that visit, the Arab raids had suddenly stopped. All had been quiet. Quiet enough to send out the field workers again to till and prepare for planting—fields hewn from rocky soil with blistered hands and aching backs.

Watchful eyes surveyed surrounding heights. Kefar Giladi's position was weakest on the boulder-strewn western slopes that fronted craggy hills. From there, marauders could take potshots at anyone venturing outside the stockade. Workers always went out with an armed escort.

Peace and quiet were beginning to tell on the weary pioneers. Vigilance was becoming lax, sentries careless. Trumpeldor felt uneasy.

"Some of the men are asking for time off," Jonathan reported to him. "They're very tired, Captain. And the Arabs seem to be letting us alone."

Bernard Goldfarb watched the commander's eagle glance lift toward the foothills. "That we see no one from here, means nothing," he told them. "They are out there, the Arabs. Thousands of them. And we are three little Jewish islands in a stormy sea of enemies. Being weary, hungry, discomforted—all that does not change our situation."

"You mean things could be worse?" Nathan asked with a jaunty grin.

"They will be."

If Jonathan thought Trumpeldor was being overcautious, he kept it to himself. Trumpeldor hadn't grown up with Arabs, as they had. After all, since Yassir's visit there'd been no further trouble. He could understand, even sympathize with Arab animosity toward the French. Even toward the settlements. But he felt certain that ill feelings would soon blow over. However, he knew he had to relay Trumpeldor's judgment. Tonight, like every other, a full guard must be mounted.

At the open stockade gate, Bernard Goldfarb paused to glance out at the workers in the field. In the distance, he could see Naomi perched on a boulder, reading a book. Sun sparked a russet halo above auburn curls. She was tending a small herd of goats, grazing on sparse clumps of nettle and grass. Between her and the field workers, the cordon of defense lounged half asleep in the shimmering heat of afternoon. The guard nearest Naomi had his back to the foothills, watching the down swoop of a giant hawk circling the field.

"They're out there—the Arabs," Trumpeldor had said.

The afternoon's calm was split by a crackle of shots. Instantly, the chain of guards were on their feet and firing back. Naomi was caught between them and the enemy.

"Hold your fire!" Bernard sprinted out the gate toward her. "Run, Naomi! Run!"

The girl sprang to her feet, yanking at the rope attached to several of the goats stubborn in hunger. The dog barked them forward.

Now all the field workers were running for the gate. The ragged line of defenders fell back behind them, keeping up an intermittent fire at the hills, trying to hold their aim well above Naomi. An Arab's bullet ripped into one of the goats, pitching it into the air.

"Run, Naomi! Leave the goats!" Bernard fired a few covering shots past her. She dropped the rope, heading toward him across the long field until at last she fell stumbling into his arms. Bernard half dragged her back to the gate. Still under fire, the last of the defenders were pushing inside. They forced the gate shut as Bernard hurried Naomi through.

Just in time. Some thirty Bedouin rode into view, galloping toward the stockade with wild shouts and gunfire.

"Women to the loft!" Ben Nouari shouted. "Bernard—take Naomi and Anneliese."

Bernard rushed the women into the barn, steadying the makeshift ladder for Anneliese. Younger than Naomi, the girl had come from Austria to the outpost with her father, mother, and sister. Ben was very taken with her.

"Keep watch at the window, with your pistol ready," Bernard told Anneliese. Naomi started up after her. For a brief second, Bernard held onto her. She looked back, surprised. His sun-bronzed features were strained by an expression she had seen there before. An expression she had chosen to ignore.

"Please, Bernard. Let me go!"

"I love you, Naomi. You're going to have to marry me, you know." The American rushed out. She stared at his retreating figure, then hurried up the ladder after Anneliese.

When Bernard returned to the compound, he saw that the dog had herded the goats back to the gate. They managed to get a few inside. Now the mounted Bedouin were riding in a wide circle around the camp, shouting and firing bursts up into the air.

"Save your bullets!" Trumpeldor ordered. The defenders held fire, watching the exhibition of Bedouin horsemanship with perplexity and distrust. These Arabs were graceful, expert riders—and good enough shots when they wanted to be.

"They seem more anxious to show off their horsemanship than attack us," Nathan called from his perch behind a barracade of sandbags.

"They don't want to destroy us completely. That would antagonize the British," Trumpeldor decided.

Suddenly the Bedouin commander shouted an order, and the group rode off bearing three bleating goats across their saddles, along with the one they had shot.

"Perhaps they were only after the animals," Jonathan said, climbing down from a firing perch.

"Maybe," Trumpeldor agreed. "They, too, are hungry." His rifle slung over shoulder, he turned back to the main building. "It is over for tonight, I think. Come. We sing and make music. Show them we are not afraid."

After the evening meal, Bernard Goldfarb took his sentry post on the parapet. It was still early. He could hear the voices of his comrades inside the dining hall singing, laughing, chattering. Bernard turned up the collar of his old Legion jacket, now bereft of insignia. His thoughts went back to home—a century away. The last letter from his mother was weighted with such wisdom as: *Your father says you are a "mishugana," Barney. . . .You father says come home, the business needs you. Your father says if he had wanted you to be part of the "New Israel," he'd have gone there himself from Russia thirty years ago. . . . How will you ever meet a nice Jewish girl in such a place and settle down and get married? . . . Your father says. . . .*

"Bernard . . .?"

Naomi was standing below in the compound. "Bernard—I must talk to you," she said. "Can I come up?"

"You sure can." The American reached a hand down to help her mount the cleats pounded in the wall.

She came up breathless, troubled, beautiful. "I mustn't stay too long. My brothers will miss me . . ." she began.

"We never seem to be able to hold a conversation without

four other people getting involved, especially your brothers.''
He kept hold of her hand.

She nodded, serious in the moonlight. "They take their
responsibility of watching over me a bit too seriously sometimes. But they were very grateful to you for rescuing me this
afternoon.''

"I know. They told me.''

"Bernard—I'm grateful too. But what you said to me . . .
afterwards.'' She turned her eyes away from him. "I mean
about . . .''

"That I love you? I said it because I do, Naomi. I'd have
said it before, if only I'd had the chance.''

"But that's just it, Bernard. You know that I'm betrothed.
To say such things only makes it more difficult for me.''

"Betrothed? Where do you get words like that?'' Bernard
pulled her face to him and kissed her gently on the lips. She
did not resist. Her lips were cotton soft, her kiss innocent of
passion.

"I want to marry you, Naomi.''

"We mustn't even talk about such things.''

"You don't love Moishe. You know it.''

Long lashes dusted cheeks with shadow. Her gaze was far
away. "Love. . . .Well, that was not the consideration in
our betrothal.''

"That word again. I'll speak to your brothers, Naomi. I
think they like me well enough. Maybe they can convince
your mother that betrothals aren't made in heaven.''

"It won't do any good.'' Her voice was choked. "You
don't understand. Betrothals are almost marriages. You have
to break them like a divorce. That's how things are done in
Palestine.''

"*Were* done, Naomi. We're going to be part of the New
Israel. Why on earth do you think we've come to this
Godforsaken spot, you and I? To bind our lives with archaic
customs—like *tefillin* wound around our arms? You've listened to Trumpeldor—heard him speak of the aims of *kibbutz*
life. Men and women are equal. And they *are*, right here, in
this camp. In future Jewish societies, the patriarchal family
won't exist. When we're married, I won't be your lord and
master. We'll be partners, and part of the communal life.
That's the most important goal of *kibbutz* living.''

"But it's too late for such talk to apply to us, Bernard. The match has been made. With Moishe."

"Your mother made this match, not God. Good marriages depend on people. People as they are—with each other. Not who suits your mother, or childhood betrothals." He took her hands, rough from the hard chores of the camp. He kissed her fingers. "Doesn't it matter to you that I love you? One man—one woman—equal. Joined only by love and the desire to build and share in something totally new. You and I can be the real pioneers. Not the old men. Not your mother. Us."

She came into his arms, so softly, so tenderly. "Oh, Bernard. I *do* love you. If only it could be the way you say. If only it weren't impossible. . . ."

His lips found hers. They clung together. He with desire and determination. She with doubt.

"You know, Naomi. There were a hundred chances I could have been killed at Gallipoli. A hundred more with the Legion in Jordan. If God hadn't wanted us together, I wouldn't be here, holding you in my arms."

"Do you think it could be, Bernard?"

"I've got to write my mother. Tell her I've found a nice Jewish girl—in the most unlikely of places."

A double wedding of two Nouaris! Under normal circumstances, such an event would have gathered in family members from far afield. And many Hammadis, too. But this wedding was to take place in the outpost of Kefar Giladi, in the wilderness of northern Galilee.

When Ben Nouari heard that his cousin Naomi was to marry Bernard Goldfarb, he decided it was time to propose to Anneliese Holtz. Their engagement surprised no one in the settlement. Everyone lived too close together for secrets. They all knew that the tall, slim, blond Anneliese and Ben were in love.

Professor Holtz took time off from his test tubes to give his blessing to the union. The chemist had come with his wife and two daughters from Vienna—in the first quota of Jews admitted by the British after the war. He was a vital member of the settlement, applying his knowledge to the conquest of this unfriendly soil.

It was thought that blessings would not flow as readily

from Naomi's mother. Yet, to everyone's surprise, she had accepted the switch in her daughter's conjugal partner with Hassidic fatalism. "New ideas go with new times," she consoled herself. Miriam hadn't been able to stand up against the persuasion of her two sons on behalf of their sister. The betrothal to Moishe was officially dissolved, causing no hard feelings.

"Why should it?" Nathan reasoned to his mother. "There were no real feelings there in the first place. If Moishe has any sense, he'll see how lucky he is. Naomi's a nice girl. But she'd make a terrible *rebbetzen*. She never could stand listening to other people's troubles."

Besides, Miriam rather liked Bernard. Except that he was an American—and therefore didn't seem quite "Jewish" enough for her. Taking no chances, she asked Rabbi Esau Horovitz to perform the wedding ceremony. The good rabbi readily agreed. How could he not? He was married to Ben's aunt Deborah, Abraham's youngest daughter. Deborah, who was ailing, wouldn't be traveling to Kefar Giladi for the wedding. But the word was that Judah Nouari would come up himself with Ruth and the twins. *And I had resigned myself to you as a confirmed bachelor. Congratulations,* he had written his brother Ben from Paris.

"Wishing it gone will not banish Tel Aviv from the face of Palestine, Mohamed!"

"I didn't say that I wished it gone."

"You didn't have to. Whether you like it or not, Tel Aviv is growing." Judah Nouari faced his old partner across the conference table in the Jerusalem office. The heat between them was almost palpable. Judah wasn't certain which side of the argument Anwar would take. So far, the director of the Jerusalem bank was reserving comment. Raphael Nouari, Anwar's new partner, doodled his pencil across a pad. He'd already spoken privately to Judah and was inclined to support his plan. But Judah didn't wish this Company decision to have a religious or political bias.

Raphael leaned forward, stabbing the pencil into a ring hole of the pad. "Tel Aviv is no longer just a garden suburb of Jaffa, Mohamed. It is a real city, and it is being modeled along the lines of European cities. We cannot afford to ignore it.''

"The first *all Jewish* city is hardly likely to be ignored.'' Mohamed's tone was harsh, angry.

"Jewish city? Well, why not? There are thousands of Zionist pioneers in need of homes. Businesses,'' Judah remarked.

"Pioneers? How do you dare call them that? Pioneers plow the land, open the frontier.'' Mohamed stabbed a finger at Judah. "You know, it's a curious thing—Jews always complain about ghettos. About being herded together. Being separated from the rest of the community. Yet when given the chance of emigrating to a new land—becoming part of its development—what do Jews do? Herd together. In settlements. In *kibbutzim*. And now into their own city.''

"That's unfair.''

"Is it? Where are the Arabs in Tel Aviv? Pushing brooms down the gutters?''

"Who caused the Jerusalem riots on Easter morning? Who is feeding the fires of hate between our people? Who are arming themselves—preaching violence and terror? My people? If you can deny this growing Arab dedication to hostility, you can ask me why Arabs aren't being included in the new city.''

Anwar's gentle voice interrupted the growing clash of opinions. "Haj Amin is not the spokesman for all Arabs in Palestine.''

"Don't you think I know that, Anwar?'' Judah said. "But one mad dog can infect a pack. However, we're not here to discuss politics. I'm proposing a profitable venture for the Company.''

"From a business point of view, Mohamed,'' Raphael put in, "these urban immigrants often bring capital with them. Many are professional people. Businessmen. Obviously they didn't come to plow the fields. And there's only one bank to serve the whole, growing community. The Anglo-Palestine Bank, in Jaffa. Since it opened, twelve years ago, it's been getting all the business.''

"Current population figures don't justify a second bank,'' Mohamed said flatly.

"It's unlike you to close your mind to progress, Mohamed. Look at the facts.'' Judah indicated his report. "The Housing

Property Company has spent one hundred thousand francs to buy a strip of Arab land called Karin Jabale. Just north of Jaffa. Sold for a high price, I can tell you. No bargains are being offered in that area. I think we should negotiate a development loan for the property company. Hammadi-Nouari could put up another four hundred thousand francs to build sixty more houses.''

''Our Jerusalem branch can perfectly well handle such a loan, assuming your figures are correct.''

''They are correct, Mohamed. I checked them myself,'' his brother told him. ''Besides, Judah isn't talking about a single transaction. I agree that we could use a branch bank in the heart of Tel Aviv.''

''There were two thousand people in Tel Aviv before the Turks drove them out,'' Mohamed argued.

''That was in the war years, Mohamed. Those refugees flooded into Cairo and Alexandria.'' Raphael spoke with a sense of expanded confidence. ''But now they're pouring back to Tel Aviv, and more immigrants are arriving in the quotas. These people are being forced to live in tents, because there isn't enough housing.''

Mohamed's attention returned to his partner. ''And you would personally underwrite the construction loan for these houses?''

''With every franc I have in the world!'' Judah regarded the figures before him. ''Tel Aviv now has its own town council . . . municipal court . . . police force. The population has passed fifteen thousand. They need a power station, municipal transportation, a fire station. But, most of all, they need a bank of their own to finance *all* those things.''

''And assuming you're right, whom would you propose to run this Hammadi-Nouari Bank of Tel Aviv?''

''Myself. With Anwar. Divide my time between Tel Aviv and Paris. If Anwar's willing, he can do the same—between there and Jerusalem.'' In the silence, Judah groped for what must be said. ''There is one thing. . . . I think, in the interests of good public relations, the new bank should be known as the Tel Aviv Development Bank.''

Mohamed's hand came down hard on the table. ''You suggest dropping the name of our Company? Removing all signs of Arab participation? Is that your proposal?''

''Even as you did, Mohamed. In Spain.'' Judah's voice

had risen to match the level of his partner's. "When you formed Hispañola-Nacional. You made arms under an anonymous front because you insisted it was the Company's policy to show profit from any legitimate source. Not to take political sides."

Mohamed rose. For a moment, it looked as though he would walk out of the room. He paused at the window, his glance arrested by a detachment of British military police moving on the double to quell a disturbance. Their heavy black boots beat on the old cobbles as they ran. From somewhere farther off, the bell of an ambulance jangled insistently. Would Jerusalem ever again be the city they had known? He turned back to his brother. "And you, Anwar. Are you willing to partner this bank under the conditions proposed by Judah?"

Anwar nodded. "Why not? It's a sensible move. I can only see that it is in the best interests of the Company."

"And do you propose to run this bank by Islamic *Shariat* law—interest-free loans?"

"You are stacking the cards against me, aren't you brother?" Anwar smiled.

"I want an answer," Mohamed said.

"I'll answer," Judah replied. "The new bank will be run on international lines. Charging normal competitive interest rates. As our bank does in Paris."

"A Jewish bank. In a Jewish city. You surprise me, Anwar. You really surprise me."

"An international bank, Mohamed. Serving a Jewish population. I move the question. . . ."

The English tea had grown cold in its pot, the sweet biscuits nibbled to crumbs in the lounge of the King David Hotel.

"Your father promised to be finished with his meeting by six o'clock, Maurice. But he is showing his usual Arab disregard for time," Jacqueline Hammadi told her son.

It always troubled Françoise when her mother said such things. The three had spent the afternoon shopping in the bazaar. Chairs around them were piled high with packages.

Maurice unwrapped an icon he had purchased in the souk, fingering the curved wood. How elegant the boy had become, Jacqueline thought. So selective of clothes and acquisitions.

Sixteen. Hard to believe her son could be that grown already. How old it suddenly made her feel!

Her worried glance rose to a mirrored alcove. It reflected a beautiful woman taking tea with two handsome children. She studied her image carefully. The dress suited her. Red striped silk tied at the waist by a wide ribbon, open to reveal a short sleeved white organza blouse and skirt panel. A tiny row of red buttons marched down the front. She swung a calf against the daringly short hem emphasized by horizontal stripes a full three inches above ankle-strapped patent leather pumps. Her head tilted slightly for a better glimpse of cherry clusters riding at a jaunty angle on a ruffled organza cartwheel hat. Perhaps not quite the thing to wear in the narrow streets of Jerusalem, where women passed like wraiths wrapped to the eyes in winding cloths. Beautiful. . . .Yes, she was still that. At least on the outside.

"Northern Russian, I'd guess. Tempera on wood panel." The boy held the icon into the light. "May well be sixteenth century, Maman." Maurice still called her that, although both children spoke English with an American accent.

"How do you know all that stuff, Maurice?" his little sister demanded.

"*Stuff* isn't a word, Françoise," Jacqueline corrected. "Things. How do you know all those things?" She looked at her seven-year-old daughter. One day, Françoise would be outrageously stunning. Jacqueline could admit with some pride, more beautiful even than she had ever been. That coloring— the raven-black hair, milky skin, and most of all, the lavender blue eyes. Her father's daughter. Features cast in a gentle Arab mold. In temperament, too, so like Mohamed. Proud, strong-willed, down to earth, sure of herself.

"If you would go to museums with me, you could learn something too, Frannie." Maurice exhibited the icon a shade grandly. "I'll bet this was taken from a Russian by some Turkish officer in the Crimea."

"You're just making it up. You don't know for sure. Besides, it's not even pretty," the girl insisted.

"It's St. John the Baptist. He's not supposed to be pretty," Maurice replied. "A treasure. It'll be the showpiece of my collection."

"Junk," Françoise decreed.

"Junk is not a nice word for young ladies," Jacqueline corrected.

"It is so, and that's junk. Look, Mama, the paint is even falling off."

Maurice regarded his sister with the utmost disdain. "That's one of the ways you know its age."

Ever since he'd had pocket money of his own, Maurice had been collecting things. A magpie accumulation from side-street shops in Paris, New York, Jerusalem. Sometimes he would trade one item for another, and he always seemed to come out ahead. By what miracle of chemistry, Jacqueline wondered, had this son of hers managed to obliterate almost every quality of the man who had been his father? Except, of course, the glossy, darkening red hair, the bright blue eyes. Nothing else remained of that shadow buried under a river of the mind.

Even in the heat of this Jerusalem afternoon, the thought of that other Maurice made Jacqueline shiver. Since that terrible night in Paris, she had lived in the garden of the world without touching the flowers. She had learned to hate Mohamed. Hate him for her year spent in a sanatorium—locked away from freedom. Had she really been as ill as he said? As the doctors said? Or was it revenge? Imprisonment for her sins. Locked away with only her own memories for companions. That procession of nameless lovers who had lain violently or listlessly between her thighs to explode their seed, often without the formality of acquaintance. "Fornication doesn't constitute a social introduction," she had told the prying doctor.

And when, finally, the sanatorium could find no further excuse for keeping her—the model patient—what had Mohamed done? Brought her home to be watched day and night. "One glass of champagne, my dear. Remember what the doctor said." Home was just another prison, with Nurse Rowland established as a permanent fixture in the house on Sixtieth Street. Only allowed out when Tony drove her. And then he would wait to bring her home again. Reporting her every move. "The missus was just fine today, boss. We even went shopping. And then we took a spin around the park."

And now Mohamed had brought her to Jerusalem. For a holiday, he said. She laughed suddenly, causing the children

to eye her uneasily. Nothing about this trip could remind her
of her honeymoon.

"Nothing. Nothing. Nothing . . . !" she said aloud.

"What, Maman?" Maurice asked, with the old worry.

"Nothing. Nothing from nothing is nothing."

The children were silent. Even little Françoise was aware
of danger signs in her mother's behavior.

It was nearly 7:00 P.M. when Bernard Goldfarb entered the
lobby of the King David Hotel. He stopped at the sight of the
woman sitting in the corner with two children. . . . So many
years had passed, and yet she had scarcely changed. For a
moment he thought of bolting. Then he surrendered to
temptation.

"Jacqueline. . . ."

She looked up, lifting a curtain of time. "Bernard . . . ?
What are you doing in Palestine?"

"The war brought me. I stayed on. I'm only in Jerusalem
for a few days." He did not mention that he was escorting
Naomi and Anneliese. They were having their wedding dresses
made—staying with Miriam at old Jacob's house. Bernard
glanced at the pairs of staring eyes. "Your children?"

"Maurice . . . and Françoise. This is Mr. Goldfarb. A
friend of your father's . . . and mine." She fought to keep
her voice calm. So many years, maturity—or was it the
war?—that had made him harder, leaner, tanned beyond belief
beneath sun-faded hair. Bernard. With him, sex had been a
glorification of living. Bernard. Who had once dared to ask
Mohamed's permission to marry her.

"Mohamed and I are staying at his father's house. Sayid
Hammadi. Everyone knows where it is. You must come visit.
Of course, Mohamed hasn't changed. He's busy all the time
as usual. You will come? Promise?"

"I'd like to . . . but I'll be going back soon, Jacqueline.
I've joined an outpost settlement up North. I'm kind of a
farmer; would you believe it?"

"And you're staying here? Here at the hotel?"

He nodded. "You look just fine. The same. I suppose
you'll never change."

"You have, Bernard."

He excused himself and picked up his key from the desk,
annoyed to find his hand trembling. Even gunfire didn't bring

that on. Only Jacqueline. She always had. The unnerving
feeling hit him that maybe he still wanted her.

He entered the caged lift, just as the doors clanged shut,
and began to ascend. Then he saw Mohamed enter the lobby.

Bernard was enjoying the luxury of hot running water with
his morning shave, but his thoughts were in chaos. The rap
on his hotel-room door brought him back to the moment.

It was Jacqueline. Nervous. Hesitant. Her arrival didn't
really surprise him. Maybe he had even willed her to come.
She had been the face in his mind all through the night. The
face that crowded out Naomi's.

"You knew I'd come?"

"I guess . . . maybe I did." He wiped the soap from his
chin, closing the door behind her.

"Bernard . . . seeing you again . . . it brought back so
much. Pleasure, yes. But pain, too. Your pain as well as my
own."

"I've never forgotten any of it, Jacqueline. I guess I never
could."

Her eyes were luminous. "Perhaps it is the most we are
meant to have—memories. Luckily, time softens them. Leaves
out the bad parts. It hides the cruelty—the unkindnesses, the
selfishness." She looked away, groping through the attic of
conscience. "I think what I wanted to say most now, Bernard
. . . is thank you. For the happiness. And ask forgiveness for
the pain."

He looked at her through a heart full of remembering. "I
wonder . . . is it ever possible to turn backward, Jacqueline?"

"You were different, Bernard. From the others. The ones I
needed the times when I was ill. They were only a blur of
faces—cutting out the fear. They never meant anything."

He came toward her, wanting to touch her. "Jacqueline, I
understand about all that. Believe me, I have only good
memories. With me, you were always wonderful. I only
wish—" He broke off, turned away, started to pull on his
shirt.

"What, Bernard? What do you wish?"

"I don't know, Jacqueline. Perhaps . . . that we had met
in another way."

"If I had left Mohamed . . . and gone with you then . . .

would it have changed everything? Would it have made me well?''

''Nobody was ever like the two of us together,'' he said. ''That's certain.''

She reached a hand to his lips. ''Will you kiss me, Bernard?''

He had wanted to, from the moment she walked in. He took her into his arms. The kiss was a salute between old friends. He stepped back. ''Jacqueline, I'm going to be married.''

''Oh, but that's wonderful,'' she said. He could almost believe she meant it. ''She is young, of course? And unbelievably beautiful?''

''Only one woman was ever that for me. I love Naomi. But it's not because of the way she looks. We share the same hopes and plans for the future. Not just our future, but this land. We want children . . . to share it with us. We've chosen a way of life that's going to be tough. But it's what we both believe in.''

Tears touched Jacqueline's lashes. ''I shall pray for your happiness. And keep, perhaps, one flower on the grave of memory. Good luck, Bernard. How do you say it? *Mazel tov*.''

For an instant a hand rested on his cheek, as though memorizing his features. Then she was gone . . . and he hadn't thought of any last thing to say.

Eighteen _____

". . . THEE do we worship, and Thine aid we seek. Show us the straight way, the way of those on whom Thou hast bestowed Thy Grace, those whose way is not wrath, and who go not astray."

Always the words soothed him. Anwar had arisen from his opening prayer in the mosque. It brought him tranquillity, and restored confidence in the nature of things as they were. Were, had been, and would be. It was nowhere written that this world could be the same as the paradise toward which men journeyed via obedience.

Farther on down the street, he spilled a few silver coins into the grimy palm of the beggar who haunted the bank's entrance, and stepped inside. Hammadi-Nouari's Jerusalem branch bank was bustling with morning commerce, British officers sprinkled amid merchants hefting in heavy bags of coin for deposit. An *effendi* fingering his well-shaped beard, while his uniformed chauffeur stacked packages of Palestinian currency into an elegant dispatch case. A black-bearded Greek Orthodox priest exchanging rubles for piasters. A Frenchwoman removing a pouch of jewels from a satin garter on a silken calf, passing them over for safety deposit. Business bustling and no one about to eject the money users from this temple of commerce.

Anwar Hammadi entered his office past a salaaming clerk. He closed the door and turned to the large, cluttered table he preferred to a conventional desk.

"Peace to you, cousin."

The words turned Anwar quickly to face a desert Arab in travel-stained robes and well-worn burnoose.

"Tariq. . . ."

402

Anwar repressed the sense of unease brought by sudden sight of his wartime comrade of Al Fatat. "Sit down. Sit down, cousin. It's been quite a time. I'll send for coffee." He reached to the handbell on his table.

"You will forgive me if I do not inquire about all members of the family and come directly to the point. This is not a social visit."

Anwar's hand moved in graceful dismissal of the apology. "Of course. Some problem concerning your brother, may Allah preserve him?"

"Why should you think there must always be a problem with Yassir?" Tariq flared. His head shifted slightly to the side, and he closed his eyes for a moment. "I'm troubled in mind to come here on this matter. Yassir does not know of this visit. I would be grateful if he should never know."

"We have both had experience in keeping silent when it was necessary."

"Thank you, cousin."

"Please . . . go on with the matter that brought you."

"You must get a message to Ben Nouari. He is in great danger," Tariq warned. "There are attacks being prepared against the three Jewish outposts in northern Galilee."

"That's nothing new, cousin."

"This time, they intend to wipe them out."

"They? The Brotherhood?"

"It is not necessary for you to ask that. Or for me to answer. I have come only that Ben may be warned."

Anwar studied his younger cousin. "So you're working with Haj Amin? Taking orders from that fanatic? The riots in Jerusalem—I suppose you are yourself involved with them, too?"

"You know better than to ask that."

"We have worked very closely together. You, me, Ben, and Simon. Yes, and Yassir. I do not expect to be told less than the truth."

"Yes, we worked side by side. But now the struggle has left you behind, Anwar. You grow soft behind that desk. You are an Arab."

Anwar picked up the scrawled page of a letter from his table and passed it to Tariq. "It's from Ben. He writes that he's getting married at Kefar Giladi. Tomorrow. You should have come to me sooner. I hope there will still be time. I will have to go up there." He paused. "Will you come with me, Tariq?"

"You know that is impossible!"

"It saddens me that you have joined the pack of wild dogs that follow Haj Amin."

"You speak of our greatest patriot. A man you should support. Haj Amin stands for the things we fought for together."

"We fought to rid ourselves of the Turks. Ben and Dr. Simon fought with us."

"Our battle is now for an Arab nation—and anyone and anything in our way must be destroyed."

"And still you have come to save Ben?"

A slant of light crossed Tariq's lean, passionate features. He hesitated. "I—I have nothing against him. Although he is a Jew."

"You forget your own heritage, Tariq. We Hammadis became a great family because long ago we joined forces with another family. They needed us and we needed them. Jews and Arabs. Between the families there has never been a lie, a deceit, or an unfair act."

Tariq flicked a disdainful glance at the metal emblem of the donkey and the cart. "To you, money is everything, Anwar. I despair for you."

"Why should I despise money? A nation isn't only built on blood. It is built on trade. On growth. On *true* brotherhood. For that, we Arabs need wise leaders. Men who can see clearly . . . who know how to bargain fairly, give and take. Haj Amin is not one of these."

"He is the hope of Palestine!" Tariq flared.

"More like an infection that can kill us all. Tariq, if you turn your back on your own family, listen only to the voices of hatred, you will destroy all we have built. And what will you replace it with? A land in chaos!"

"You are a blind man, Anwar. You live in the past. I thought you were different from your brother, Mohamed. But you are no better!"

"Better than a false Mahdi! Your *imam* is financed by the rich *effendis*. Absentee landlords, most of them. They want to keep the *fellaheen* poor and obedient, and they use Haj Amin to fill them with lies and cause trouble. Tariq, I prayed you'd be different from *your* brother. But now you run with the jackals—and bless your murders in Allah's name.''

Tariq took a step toward Anwar, eyes blazing, hand resting on his dagger. ''I should kill you. You shame our people. You shame our family. My brother is the bravest man I have ever known!''

Anwar made no move to defend himself. Tariq lifted his hand, but it was empty. It waved in a gesture that seemed to wipe out the image of his cousin, dismissing him forever. Then he turned and left the room.

The outpost of Kefar Giladi was ill equipped to cope with an invasion of visitors. Even relatives heading toward it laden with gifts for the Nouari weddings.

''What a pity your father had to be in Paris at the bank. You should have insisted, Judah. A marriage is a family affair.'' Ruth was always strong on family feeling.

Judah did not answer. Ever since Ben walked out on the Company, their father, David, had not allowed his name to be mentioned. He had deliberately gone to Paris so as to be unavailable for the wedding.

Along with Ruth, the twins, and Miriam, Judah had packed his car with supplies for the settlement. Blankets, flour, oil, sugar, tea. . . . A week's baking by Naomi's mother had produced one giant cake for the two bridal couples. This masterpiece was bumped and juggled in its cardboard box from one lap to another in the crowded automobile, orchestrated by Ruth's admonitions: ''Abe! Aunt Miriam's marzipan frosting! Zed, you're tipping Aunt Miriam's sugar roses!'' With which Ruth would wedge the box more tightly between her children. Scarcely an inch of space left in car trunk or roof rack, where crates squawked with live chickens.

Judah had started off before sunset. He chose to travel by night to avoid marauding Bedouin. An hour outside Jerusalem, he caught a glimpse of his son's expression in the mirror gloomily surveying the barren landscape in the last glow of day. ''Not something you'd care to do a watercolor of, Abe?''

''It's all gray and ugly and angry, Father.''

''Hardly Provence,'' Judah conceded.

"What I don't understand is why anyone would want to come here to live. Particularly uncle Ben," Abe said.

"Uncle Ben wants to help make a place for those who haven't anywhere else to go."

"If this is the Promised Land, Moses didn't get much of a bargain," Zed decided.

"That is no subject for jokes," Ruth reprimanded.

Zed pinched Abe's arm, and the twins traded winks and a few words in their private language.

"Stop that!" Ruth ordered. "You should be proud of your uncle. Someday—when you two children are grown up—I, too, want to do something. Something for this. . . ." She gestured vaguely. "The future. Isn't that so, Judah?"

"Someday, Ruth," he said.

No part of Palestine was much to Abe's taste. Although his father had been born there and his mother in Poland, he considered himself and Zed totally French. The one thing he had enjoyed in Jerusalem was meeting Maurice Hammadi again and hearing tales of life in America. Together the boys had wandered through the souks under the watchful eye of one of Mohamed's office staff. He'd admired Maurice's icon and bought himself some street scenes painted by a local artist. The boys found much in common.

Zed, still something of a tomboy, found this trip to Galilee a great adventure. "Do you think we'll get shot at, Father?" she asked scanning the barren land, imagining armed Bedouin behind every hill.

"I should sincerely hope not, Zed. The troubles are farther north."

"Would your father bring us up here to be shot at, Zed?" Ruth scolded and closed her eyes to catch a wink of sleep. They drove through night into morning.

They unfolded themselves, emerging stiffly into the chill dark before dawn. The sight did not immediately warm their hearts. No more bleak collection of buildings could be imagined. Everything for basic utility, with a concern toward defense, Kefar Giladi looked like something between a barracks and a prison. The wind came wailing down from rocky hills. Dust blew everywhere. The settlers regarded their visitors with delight, grateful for the sight of new faces. Ruth whispered a prayer: "May this become the borders of our nation."

Judah's family were assigned a corner of the loft. They had brought sleeping bags. Nathan moved his bed to the women's house for Miriam. The bearded Rabbi Esau Horovitz, from Safad, arrived with a carload of paraphernalia for the wedding. The rabbi seemed to be blessing everything and everyone as he moved around the camp.

In the kitchen, Nathan appraised the wedding cake with Ben. "The most dangerous thing a man can eat!"

"Don't believe him," Dr. Simon said, coming in, his arm around Sephora. They had been assigned sleeping bags in the kitchen. Sephora was relishing this trip with Simon. They had left little Daniel with her mother. It would be like a second honeymoon. Except that Simon had brought his medical bag.

Later, the men clustered together over the cigars Judah had generously supplied. The prospective bridegrooms were being treated to advice. "After you're married, you can forget all your mistakes. Take it from me, your wife will remember them for you," Simon assured them.

Nathan sighed. "Personally, I'll never get married until the wrong girl comes along. All the right ones turn me down."

Ben escaped to take Judah on a tour of inspection.

"Well, what do you think of our defenses?"

Judah shook his head. "Not much. This place could never stand up against any serious attack."

"You think we don't know? Our ammunition supplies wouldn't last a day. . . . I wish you could get those damned committees of the JNF to send what we need."

"Maybe when I tell them what I've seen, they'll stop arguing long enough to listen."

"Don't take too long, Judah. We may not be here." Ben put his hand on a prewar rifle. "These old relics get so hot after a few rounds you can hardly hold them. They're not even much use shooting rabbits."

"Ben . . . are you happy here?"

"Of course," Ben replied.

"I'm sorry about father not coming."

"He'll get over it."

"Will you? How long do you intend to go on with this *kibbutz* life?"

"As long as it takes."

"For what?"

"To put up a flag."

From the communal room, Miriam's voice wafted out, stubborn in righteousness. "Outpost or no, this is still a community of Jews. So where is the *mikvah?* Could somebody please tell me?"

Judah shook his head and moved on with Ben. This problem, they could do without.

In the communal room, Naomi was showing strain. "Mother . . . can't you see that a *mikvah* here would be impossible?"

"I'll tell you what's impossible: to get married without one."

"But this is a wilderness, not a Jerusalem synagogue."

"It's not the synagogue that is important," Ruth put in. "It is the *mikvah*. Ask Rabbi Esau."

Rabbi Esau Horovitz responded without being asked. "We can only go by the Torah. What does it say? If there is a question of poverty in a community, sell the synagogue and build a *mikvah*."

"But we have no synagogue."

"That's another problem," Ruth said.

Not to be excluded from such an important argument, Sephora brought up still another impediment. "And even if we should figure out how to build a *mikvah,* we mustn't forget the most important part. The time of the bath. The law says it cannot take place until the stars are visible to the naked eye. True, Rabbi?"

"True. Except, of course, if there is a fog or clouds, when the stars are hidden. It is all carefully set forth in the Mishna, Sephora. The sixth tractate of Toharoth—the ritualistic order of cleanliness, including the bath *before* the *mikvah*. Nails clean and short. Hair washed. Then and only then the spirtual bath. That is when the bride-to-be must say the prayer."

"Immersed," Ruth reminded Naomi.

"How can she be immersed when there is no tub?"

"Why can't I just use the women's tub, Mother?" Naomi asked in exasperation.

"The women's tub?" Miriam shook her head in dismay. "Not deep enough, my dear."

Ruth nodded. "The entire body including the hair must be under water at the same moment. Not a strand is permitted to float. That's the problem facing us."

Everyone nodded, unable to solve it.

"I could stoop into the sheep-dip trough."

"To stoop is forbidden. In such a position, certain parts of the body would press too closely together," Sephora pointed out.

"The receptacle can be just deep enough to stoop slightly," Rabbi Horovitz conceded.

"How could all this possibly matter?" Naomi flared.

"Details are everything. They are the essence of ritual," the rabbi insisted. "Consider the law which clearly states: it is not necessary to distend the thighs or hold out the arms. Nor open the mouth. Nor shut it too tightly. . . ."

"In my own experience, I've found it's best if the lips remain close together but not pursed. Just so long as no strand of hair gets in the mouth," Ruth said.

"But if she closes her eyes too tightly it could make wrinkles under them. Or if she opens them too wide her eyelids would fold and the water couldn't reach," Sephora added. "I've always found just *slightly* closed is preferable."

Rabbi Esau nodded. "These things may sound unimportant in themselves, but without them the *mikvah* is not valid. And without the *mikvah*, we have no marriage in the sight of God."

Miriam nodded. "And we must mention the folding of the arms together over the body at the time of saying the benediction. Naomi, you mustn't look into the water when saying the words 'Praised be thou, O Lord—' " Miriam began, then stopped abruptly, staring around.

Naomi was gone. No one had seen her leave.

Naomi herself was hardly aware of the impulse that had moved her from that room. She knew only that she could not bear another instant of those voices pondering the absurd, meticulous detail of rituals.

The stockade gate was still open when she ran out of the building—on out through the cultivated fields beyond the stockade. At first she moved on blindly, without purpose or direction, seeing nothing of the surroundings. It was all so hopeless, so impossible. She knew now that she could never go through with it. Never subject herself to all the ludicrous nonsense that seemed to have no part in the joining of lives, of bodies and minds, that marriage should be.

Beyond the fields lay the wasteland of the wadi, untilled, untamed, dangerous. But danger was not in Naomi's mind. Her future was.

"Isn't Naomi with you?" Anneliese Holtz put her head through the doorway of the communal room.

Miriam Nouari looked up. "She was here. Then she left, just in the middle of discussing the problem of the *mikvah*. Problems that also concern you, Anneliese. And your mother, she should be here too."

"It's my mother's night to cook the supper. We have our own rituals here in the settlement. Anyway I'll do whatever is decided. My family aren't Orthodox. Nor is Ben." She smiled sweetly at the group. "I think I'll try to find Naomi."

"Ben—not Orthodox?" Ruth asked Miriam. "Since when?"

"Since coming here, no doubt," Miriam replied. "The only thing against places like this is, people lose their religion."

"Maybe they're too busy trying to stay alive," Sephora concluded, remembering all that Simon had gone through.

Anneliese made a search of the camp. There wasn't really anywhere for a person to go off on her own. No room for privacy. She continued on to the gate. Bernard was just closing it.

"Have you seen Naomi?" Anneliese called, coming up a little breathless.

"No, but I'd like to," he said. Then he noticed Anneliese's concern. "Something wrong?"

"I don't know. I've looked for her everywhere. She was in the communal room, where everyone over forty is arguing about *mikvahs*."

"No wonder she disappeared." His eyes went to the gate. He lifted back the heavy bar. "I hope she wasn't crazy enough to go out there alone." Bernard headed into the field, calling her name. Anneliese stood in the gateway, worried.

Naomi had reached the edge of the wadi before she stopped running and sat down. She had not noticed how dark it had grown. The crunch of approaching footsteps alerted her. She ducked down into a ditch, praying she'd not been noticed by some passing Bedouin.

"Naomi . . . Naomi . . ." Bernard's voice calling her name started her breathing again.

"I'm over here!" she called back. He came up at a run.

"That was a crazy thing to do." He dropped down beside her. "Why did you come out here, anyway? Don't you realize how dangerous it is?"

"I had to get away from them—somewhere I could think. You've no idea how they went on."

"Come on. We'd better get back."

"Not yet. Bernard . . ." She sounded as though she'd been crying. "I can't go through with it. If it's going to be like this, I don't want to get married."

"What are you talking about, Naomi? Don't you love me?"

"Oh, yes. As much as ever. At least I think I do. That is, I love the things we've planned together for our lives. New, important things. Not lives bound up in old-fashioned rituals that have no meaning out here. And they won't in the new *kibbutzim*. If you could have heard all the things they were saying! Mother, and the others. About your arms. Pursing your lips. It's embarrassing—and stupid."

"Then, why let it bother you?"

"Because *they* will bother us all our lives. With their laws and restrictions. I hate religion!"

"Things will be different for us. You'll see."

"No. They won't. They can't be. Because the older generation won't let anything change. We're trapped into the rules of their world. And there's no escape. I thought, coming up to this outpost, that we'd be part of something new. It was just a delusion."

He took her hands in his. "Let's get things into the order of their importance, Naomi. Number one: we love each other. Two: I'm not marrying your mother. And you're not marrying a rabbi. So, for now, we can afford to make the old folks happy. After tomorrow, I promise, the only ritual in our lives will be kissing good night and kissing good morning."

"They're probably still arguing in there about the *mikvah*," she sighed.

He put his arms around her, drawing her close. "Look, honey, if it's just a bath they want from you, I can rig one up that will be perfect to say your prayers in."

"But I'm supposed to be immersed, and they say there's no place deep enough."

He laughed. "You will be. Say, that rabbi cousin of yours

has even made me agree to put on a *kittel*. He calls it the white robe of purity. He brought a couple with him just in case. And pure is something I am definitely not. So if I can wear a *kittel* you can take a *mikvah*, if I have to dig one six feet straight down. Now how about a kiss?''

She kissed him tenderly, then looked up toward the first evening star. ''I wonder what God thinks of all this?''

''He has more important things to think about. And so have we.'' He kissed her again, moving his hand across the softness of her body. ''I know it's *our* wedding. But, in a way, it has an even deeper meaning for the older generation. Don't you see, to them every marriage means that for the Jewish people there's a future. We're not doing it just for us. For my part, I could live with you in a cave, without getting married.''

''Not a chance!'' she said.

He pulled her to her feet. ''You see? You want all that rigmarole. I can just hear you one day telling our daughter, 'Without the *mikvah*, a marriage is no marriage.' ''

''Well,'' she said, ''Maybe that's something to look forward to.''

He looked around the dark evening landscape with a sense of unease. ''I guess our Arab friends are getting lazy. Or maybe they're getting tired of harassing us.'' They started back to the outpost, arm in arm.

''You know sómething?''

''What?''

''After this wedding, Kefar Giladi will have the only *mikvah* in Galilee made out of a horse trough.''

''Horse trough? Of course . . . !'' She began to run toward the gate, laughing. ''I can't wait to tell mother.''

''My good uncle, you are the only man in Jerusalem who has not had some complaint or problem for me.'' Mohamed embraced Gamel. It had been a long time, but, to Gamel, time lacked fixed dimensions. He beamed up at his important relative.

''Gamel has a new broom!''

After the departure of the Turks, Gamel's position as mosque janitor had been restored. He had returned to his private war against dust and spiders, and really very little had changed for him. True, not all of them still visited him these days. He hadn't seen Dr. Simon or Ben. But the woman whose name he could never remember had come. With Tariq. And the old clothes were filling the marble coffins to overflowing again. Now even Gamel knew what they contained, but there were no Turkish police to see them, so he didn't worry.

"You are keeping well, my dear uncle? Anything you need? Anything I can get for you?" Mohamed surveyed the bent figure. The shuffling feet. "A new pair of slippers, maybe?"

Gamel munched the candy Mohamed had brought. "Slippers. . . ." His mind wandered away from the thought. "Two birds flew in here."

"Oh? When?" Mohamed humored him.

"When Anwar came. When he took away these things Tariq puts into the old clothes." Gamel started to sweep vigorously along the side of the Roman sarcophagus.

Something clicked in Mohamed's memory. "When . . . did the birds fly in, uncle?" There was an urgency in the question.

"The birds?"

"The birds—when Anwar came."

"See!" He pointed up to where a pair of swallows were fluttering together in a corner of the ceiling. "You birds! Too high for my broom. You better come down."

"Show me the clothes, uncle."

Anxious to please, Gamel dropped the broom and began to slide back the heavy marble lid. He fished into the rags, bringing up a pistol. He waved it about, beaming proudly. "Boom," he cried. "Boom."

"You'd better give that to me." Mohamed gently took the pistol from Gamel's hand and tucked it into his trouser belt.

"For a long time. nobody brings nothing here. Then Tariq comes again. With the woman. Now Anwar. But he takes things away. I tell him, 'Nephew, the birds!' But he doesn't care."

"I'll bring you those slippers, Gamel." Mohamed embraced his uncle again and left the mosque in search of his brother.

"What are you planning to do, attack the Jewish Quarter with Tariq?" The words turned Anwar to face Mohamed in the garage at the rear of the bank. "What's a banker doing running around with a carload of guns?"

"Don't get involved, Mohamed."

"I *am* involved. Where are you going?"

"To Kefar Giladi."

"To burn it down?" Mohamed indicated the liters of petrol Anwar had packed into the trunk of the car.

"It's you who are against the settlements, my dear brother. I'm going up there to help them."

"They don't take help from Arabs, I'm told."

"Mohamed, I've had information. Al Fatat, the Brotherhood—they're planning a major attack on all the outposts. Ben is up there. He's got to be warned."

"Judah's there too. For Ben's wedding. And Ruth and the children. I'm coming with you!"

Anwar threw him a look. "You won't be able to stop this altercation by banging your gavel, Mr. Chairman."

A curious smile touched Mohamed's lips. "For brothers, we don't know each other very well, do we?"

How true this was! They had become faces across a boardroom table. Attitudes. A conflict of opinions. Aging in the years between each encounter. Mohamed, worldly, urbane, sophisticated, his silvering hair pomaded and shaped by the finest barber. Anwar—yes, he had to admit it to himself—still a provincial. And yet Anwar could feel that perhaps he understood the conflicts in his own land far better than his brother, whose habits and even faith bore the taint of Paris and New York.

"What about Jacqueline? What will you tell her?"

"We'll stop at Father's house and leave a message. I'll tell her I've decided to attend a wedding." He smiled wryly. "Bernard Goldfarb's."

Anwar climbed into the car. He did not always fathom his brother's attitude toward his wife. But then, Anwar had not been foolhardy enough to marry a European. "Let's get started, then. It's a long way."

They stood in the open field beyond the stockade. Although the sun had almost reached the zenith, the wedding guests held lighted candles.

"Candles in the sun . . ." Miriam whispered.

"What a place for a wedding!" Ruth nodded.

"Where does God live? Anywhere man lets him." Miriam was quoting what her father had so often said.

The two couples took their places beneath twin *huppahs*, the silk canopies embroidered with words from the Book of Jeremiah:

THE VOICE OF MIRTH AND THE VOICE OF JOY.
THE VOICE OF THE BRIDEGROOM AND THE VOICE
    OF THE BRIDE.

In lieu of flowers, the brides carried wild heather and green herbs tied up with white ribbon. Anneliese, slender and fair— Naomi, dark and petite, auburn curls struggling to free themselves from an old white veil of her mother's. White shoes were already flecked with earth. But nobody cared; all brides are beautiful.

As best man to both friend and brother, Judah watched the couples sip from two shared wine cups. Rabbi Horovitz recited the blessing of the betrothal. Wedding rings were slipped on the first joints of the index fingers of the brides' right hands.

"Behold, thou art consecrated unto me by this ring, according to the laws of Moses and Israel. . . ." The rabbi read the *ketubah*, the marriage contract still written and spoken in Aramaic, the everyday language of Jews two thousand years before.

Finally, two glasses were placed on the earth. Ben and Bernard crushed them underfoot. Perhaps it was to keep away evil spirits, or perhaps only to remind them all of the destruction of the Temple in Jerusalem. Judah wasn't sure. It was only a custom. But, for most here, *this* custom was as strong as law.

One invited guest was unable to attend. Joseph Trumpeldor, the commander of the northern settlements, was far too occupied with problems at neighboring Tel Hai. As the celebrants at the wedding congratulated the happy couples, Joseph Trumpeldor, binoculars at his eyes, watched a group of Arabs approaching the outpost gate under a white flag, horses tethered in the distance. He could make out five, one man moving slightly in advance of the others. It was always difficult to tell about Arabs. Robes concealed rank. A general could look like a Bedouin brigand. All wore cartridge bandoliers.

Perhaps this parley would bring things to a head. End the constant harassment of skirmishes and potshots at field workers. In his heart, the Russian-trained soldier wished he could bring these Arab marauders to combat. He felt no confidence in peace overtures from them. Untrained though his settlers were, he was certain they could put up a good fight and win—if not too greatly outnumbered.

He moved the binoculars slightly so that he could see past the approaching figures to the concentration of dark goatskin tents hugging bone-sparse hills above the Huleh Valley. "Houses of hair," the Bedouins called them. This city of tents had mushroomed into view only two days before. Two regiments, maybe? It was because of them that Trumpeldor had received as much ammunition as could reasonably be spared from neighboring Kefar Giladi. So far, he had not been able to detect any troop movements, neither among the tents nor in the wadis. Those natural trenches in the folds of the uplands could hide an army. No movement from the scrubby forest, either. If only he had a trained scout . . . !

Trumpeldor moved his binoculars back to the group approaching under their white flag of truce. In this wilderness the light played odd tricks. A man on a camel could seem to ride toward one for all of a day, never getting any nearer. Only a bullet could properly measure distance through these waves of heat, where the midday sun was scorching the rocks.

"No man is to fire unless I give the order."

The defender nearest him nodded. It was Giv'oni, a Bessarabian graduate of Herzlia High School who had come with Trumpeldor from Kefar Giladi. Giv'oni was sulking because he was missing the double wedding. The wine. The dancing. The music.

"They're not going to make any real trouble, Commander. They never do. They're just coming for some more talk."

"I'm looking at trouble, Giv'oni," the Commander replied flatly.

Trouble had always been Trumpeldor's daily bread. He could turn back through the pages of his closely written diary, all through the months of *Tevet* and *Shvat* on the Hebrew calendar. Raids, sneak attacks, snipings. The settlers had been constantly embattled, but not without their share of success. If only he had more men, more guns, more food.

More everything. His urgent demands to the *Va'ad Hatzirim* had produced almost nothing. That "Committee of Deputies," that supreme body that mismanaged the affairs of Jewish Palestine in the name of the World Zionist Organization. They spent their time in endless debates while expecting him to hold out in the three settlements on buttons and strings.

"Hold out to the last man," they demanded.

"With what?" Trumpeldor had inquired. "With prayers? Or perhaps you can produce Joshua's trumpet."

Only Judah Nouari had been able to organize any supplies. Trumpeldor knew Judah would be at the wedding, and he had promised the fund raiser a tour of the three settlements afterward, with the hope that Judah could stir up some action in the W.Z.O. But action would take time, and time was a luxury of the strong—as talk was a habit of the weak.

Through his binoculars, he could now focus on the faces of the approaching Arabs. No roving bandits, these. Irregulars, or perhaps from the army of the caliphate. The five men paused. Officers, all right. Pistols in shiny leather holsters, carbines and grenades. Armed to the teeth, which were at this instant flashing in some kind of argument. Hands gestured. The throaty growl of debate dissolved into the silence of heat and dust. Trumpeldor made a swift tour of inspection of the outpost. A last check on his defenders. Twenty-five men and four women. Settlers who weren't quite farmers nor yet soldiers, but whom survival decreed must be both.

Yassir Hammadi, with his new rank of major bestowed by Haj Amin, was at this same moment furious with his subordinates. He had been placed in command of this mission by Colonel Bakr Hafez, and yet these army regulars dared question his decisions. He hid his fury behind a patronizing tone. "The objective is to get inside. Inside, brothers. And they will have to let us in if we demand to search for the French."

"But everyone knows the French have gone back to Syria."

"It was your advice, Selem, that lost us Metula. Colonel Hafez has placed me in charge. I do not expect you to question my orders." Yassir bristled.

"Metula is weakly garrisoned now. We should recapture it first. Then make our assault here," Selem insisted.

"By capturing Tel Hai, we cut off the main road to both

Metula and Kefar Giladi." Yassir whipped out his map, hand shaking slightly from anger. "Who holds Tel Hai holds the throat of all the settlements. Not a donkey can move up that road. We starve them out—and so we need fight only *one* battle instead of three. Even graduates of the military school in Damascus should recognize that!"

The four officers swallowed rage and offended pride. Because of a few months at the headquarters of Lawrence, this upstart Hammadi thought himself Napoleon! By smoothing the pillows of Haj Amin, Hammadi was now a major, without even an hour of proper military training. They might all pay for his incompetence.

As for Yassir, he despised these men concerned only with careers, not cause. They looked upon him as merely a political warrior. He knew that. And he knew that they would as well serve the Turks—and had! Even the Syrian captain whom he had at first considered a trust-worthy subordinate. Yassir was not a man to suffer the obstructions of military roosters crowing of their fine training under the Ottomans. Idiots! Shaming him with their bickering, here in the very sight of the enemy. And for all their boasts, they had let themselves be routed by a one-armed Jew captain and his dozen farmers at Metula!

"You will see, my brothers," he goaded. "This day will not end like Metula."

The earth leaped, pounded beneath the wild, rhythmic bounding of the *hora*. Hands linked to hands, settlers and wedding guests surged around and around to the seasaw pulse of bright, wheezing harmony from an old Polish accordion. Bridegrooms, children, oldsters panting and jumping between flushed maidens and muscular, sun-darkened field workers in faded, open shirts and weather-bleached cotton trousers. Judah felt the shedding of years as he held tightly to Ruth's and Zed's hands, abandoning themselves to the dance. In the instant, all seemed joined by the joy of the occasion. Naomi, glowing with happiness. Anneliese, flushed from the sweet red wine. Ben and Bernard outleaping each other in the gladness and rapture of this day of days.

The cry came over from the stockade wall. "Automobile approaching!"

The music rasped to a stop. The dancers, perspiring, laughing, turned their attention to that always eventful happening: the coming of a car. It swept up, long gouts of dust, roaring to a stop just outside the open gate.

Jonathan and Ben took up rifles and moved to meet it. The others watched and waited. The door of the car opened. Ben stared in amazement.

"Anwar?" he called. "What the devil are you doing up here?"

Mohamed climbed out the other side. Judah hurried over. "Mohamed. . . . What's this all about?"

The Hammadi brothers stepped into the compound, still dressed in rumpled business suits.

"We've brought information. Where's your commander—Trumpeldor?" Mohamed asked.

"Over at Tel Hai. Why? What's happened?"

"I've had word—I can't reveal the source but it's entirely dependable," Anwar began. "Sharifian troops are preparing to stage a full-scale attack on your settlements. This won't be just another bandit raid, Ben. They're out to finish you this time."

"Haj Amin's marauders?"

Anwar nodded. "Backed up by at least two battalions of irregulars. And troops from the Emir Abdullah's army."

The circle of settlers tightened around the two Arabs.

"These troops call themselves the 'Army of Vengeance.' Vengeance against the French, because they threw Abdullah's brother, King Husain, out of Syria. It doesn't mean they won't use them against you." Mohamed had already appraised the hastily constructed stockade. "This place is hardly a strong deterrent against any well-armed assault."

"What do you think, Mohamed?" Judah asked.

"I think you should get out. Now."

"We know how to deal with attacks," Ben assured him with more confidence than he actually felt.

"They could put as many as two thousand men into the field," Mohamed warned.

Bernard came over. It was the first time the two men had spoken since that night in the house on Sixtieth Street. Now they were like strangers. "When do they plan this attack?"

"Nobody was passing out timetables," Mohamed told him.

"Your wisest course would be to leave now. Before you're wiped out."

There was a silence from the cluster of settlers. "Does anyone want to leave?" Ben asked. "This is your chance if you want to take wives and children back to Jerusalem."

Judah looked at Ruth and the twins. "I have to stay, Ruth. You should take the car—with the children." She hesitated. Nobody spoke.

Anneliese came up to Ben and put her arm through his. He patted her hand. His eyes went to the rabbi. "Rabbi Horovitz, you can make it back to Safad. It's not that far."

"At a time like this, I am needed here."

"You'll need me, too." Dr. Simon stepped forward.

Naomi looked up at Bernard. "This is our home," she said. "I won't leave it."

Judah was waiting for Ruth's answer. "Come, children," she ordered. "Into the building. We will find ways to make ourselves useful."

"You're all staying, then?" Ben asked. There were quiet nods around the circle. "All right. Prepare the outpost for a full-scale attack. You all know what to do."

Judah saw Ruth and his children safely inside. Then returned to Anwar and Mohamed. "You two had better leave."

"If you don't leave, we will stay too," Mohamed said.

"What the devil for?" Judah demanded.

"You will need all the help you can get."

Judah's glance warmed on his old friend. "Then, bring your car inside." Anwar went to move it, Jonathan, to close the heavy gate behind it.

"I guess I'll never understand you, Mohamed. Coming up here to warn us against your own people—when I know how you feel about these settlements."

"I don't think you *do* know how I feel, Judah. I may not always agree with your Zionist objectives. But fanatics on either side won't settle the future of Palestine. Besides, there just could be a chance to meet with their commander. Stop this attack. Reason, as one Arab to another. I still have some influence."

Anwar was bringing rifles from the car. He handed one to Mohamed, who checked it expertly.

"Those are for reasoning?"

"Maybe my idea of a new Palestine isn't quite how you see it, but it certainly isn't how these rebels see it. More killing won't bring peace."

Judah led his old friend to a vantage point on the stockade wall. They watched across the empty fields to the scarred hills. "It's a long time since we've been on a lion hunt together. Thank you for coming to warn us, Mohamed."

In the compound, settlers were preparing the defenses. All visitors had been moved into the safety of the buildings.

Naomi caught up with Bernard, his arms laden with rifles. "Bernard, I think I'm frightened."

"It'll be no worse than the other times," he assured her.

"Yes it will. This time we're married."

He kissed her cheek. "We'll talk about that later. When I can do something about it."

Ben came up. "Bernard, we must warn the other outposts. We can't be sure which they will attack first."

Yassir Hammadi was a short distance from the gate of the Tel Hai stockade. His manner exuded confidence. Five hundred troops were hidden in the hills awaiting his signal. His eyes lifted to the man on the firing step. A large, handsome head. One arm missing. He knew this man by reputation. But he had no intention of granting Trumpeldor the satisfaction of recognition.

"I wish to speak to your commander," he called up.

"I am in command." Somewhat surprised to be addressed in Hebrew, Trumpeldor was careful to keep his hand away from the Mauser holstered at his hip. He was too good a soldier to precipitate a fight. Not until he was ready for it. "Come a bit closer, where we can have a look at you."

Yassir stepped forward a few yards. "We wish to inspect your camp. We are looking for French soldiers."

"There are none here. You know that."

"Nevertheless, we must see for ourselves. If you have nothing to hide, you will let us in."

"Do we kill them, Captain? Do we open fire?" Giv'oni whispered to Trumpeldor.

"No, Giv'oni. We will talk to them." Trumpeldor called down to the Arabs. "Drop your weapons! Show us your

hands. You will permit yourselves to be searched as you
enter.''

"We, too, have nothing to hide," Yassir called back.
Trumpeldor could see that the Arab leader was again arguing
with his own men, who seemed disinclined to obey. Finally
the group set down their weapons, leaving one man to guard
them. The others walked toward the gate.

"Open it," Trumpeldor called down. His sentry heaved
back the heavy bar.

"Are you sure we're doing the right thing, Captain?"
asked Giv'oni.

"Four Arabs without arms won't attack us. But keep a
careful watch on those tents and wadis." Trumpeldor crossed
to the gate to meet the approaching party, Giv'oni with him.
Again the Arabs were in muffled debate. No matter how
brave they were individually, he thought, they seemed forever
locked in dissension. "If ever they learn to agree between
factions, families, tribes, these people might again conquer
half the earth," he told Giv'oni.

"Which side are you on, Captain?" Giv'oni joked.

Trumpeldor sighed. "Always the losing side. With the
Russians at Port Arthur, the British at Gallipoli. I think it is
time to change such a habit." He came over to the sentry at
the gate. A dentist from Berlin who carried an old-fashioned
double-barreled twelve-gauge.

"What do you think they really want?" The dentist's voice
betrayed his fear.

Trumpeldor shrugged. "I don't think. In war, everything is
perhaps. Perhaps today. Perhaps tonight. Perhaps tomorrow.
Perhaps at this moment the enemy are waiting in the wadi out
there ready to rush the compound. Or perhaps they finger
their worry beads and wait until darkness."

"But why do they want to come in?"

"Again perhaps. A little rudeness. A little threat. But we
must always think of every perhaps. So if it goes wrong and I
am killed, you—what is your name?"

"Schneurson, Captain."

"A terrible name. Never mind. If I fall, you will take my
place."

The dentist looked shocked.

"Merely another perhaps, Schneurson. You know how we
are deployed?"

"Eight in the two stables. One man and three women in the loft. One at the door of the dining hall. Two on the stockade. And me—covering the gate."

"You'll end up a general. Come. Our visitors have arrived."

Yassir stepped to the gate and allowed himself to be searched. "You will leave the gate open while we are inside," he told Trumpeldor.

"You know, of course, that you will not find any *poilus* in this outpost."

"I will know when I have looked."

Trumpeldor tried to gauge Yassir's sharp, explosive personality. There was pride. Fanatical dedication. The man seemed dictatorial in command, and yet he sensed a certain insecurity. And insecurity could be dangerous. Letting them in might be risky, but forbidding entrance could be an open declaration of war. Just the provocation this Arab might be waiting for.

"If I do not return to my men, nothing could restrain them from coming after me."

Probably no idle boast. Trumpeldor measured his answer. "We are here as farmers to settle the land. We wish no hostilities with your people."

"Excellent. We will protect you from the French," Yassir offered.

"We can protect ourselves," Trumpeldor replied.

"Well? Are we to be permitted to inspect the outpost? If there are no French, we will leave."

"We will escort you through, but you will be wasting your time."

With a tinge of triumph, Yassir glanced toward his three officers. Certainly the Hammadi star was rising. They would have to report back that all had gone as he predicted. He was already counting the victory.

The search moved swiftly from room to room until they reached the stepladder to the loft inside the barn. The building jutted out over the stockade wall.

"What is up there?" Yassir demanded.

"Some hay. Some supplies. And some people."

"Farm supplies? Or arms?"

"Go up and look," Trumpeldor offered.

Yassir signaled his men up and mounted after them. Con-

fronting them as they came up were three women and a man
with a British Enfield rifle slung on his shoulder. Two of the
women wore pistols in belt holsters. They stood back and
watched the Arabs poke about the loft. One of the Arab
officers kicked at the hay and boxes of food as though they
might come alive. Still nobody spoke.

And then, in the loft, the Arabs stopped short as the sound
of a salvo of rifle shots cracked from the distance, sending a
bounding echo off rocky hills. Yassir dashed to the window.
"Those shots! They've tricked us!"

"Trapped us up here, without guns," his captain cried out.

Below, in the barn, Trumpeldor, too, had heard the distant
shots. Giv'oni ran in. "What is it, Captain?"

"The signal—from Kefar Giladi. An all-out attack!"

"They're attacking there—while they're pretending to inspect
us here!" Giv'oni cried.

In the loft, Yassir and his men were struggling for possession of the settlers' weapons. One of the girls screamed
down, "Trumpeldor! My revolver! He's taking it!"

Suddenly all seemed confusion.

"Fire!" Trumpeldor shouted up to the loft. Shots blasted
the air. The Arab captain came sprawling down the ladder,
blood pouring from his mouth.

In a corner of the loft, two girls lay dying of their wounds.
The third was already dead. A settler lay groaning, his head
split open. Everywhere there was blood on the straw.

Yassir pulled the cloth from his head and waved it frantically out the window toward the Arab guarding the weapons.
He immediately opened fire on the gate.

High on the stockade wall, Schneurson picked him off with
a rifle blast—the first man he'd ever killed.

"Close the gate!" Trumpeldor shouted, crossing the
compound.

Schneurson called down, "They're coming from the wadi.
Waves of them!"

Through the open gate Trumpeldor could see a skirmish
line of Arabs sweeping forward, weapons streaking fire.

The gate guard was struggling to close it when he was shot
dead.

"Somebody! Help to get this gate closed!" Trumpeldor ran
toward it. He had to get it shut before those lines of advanc-

ing Arabs reached the compound. But now the firing at the gate was so heavy nobody could get near it.

Schneurson shouted to Trumpeldor, "Keep back!" Trumpeldor ignored the warning. He had always ignored danger as though it were meant for somebody else. He was almost within reach of the gate when he was hit.

Staggering slightly he called, "Damnation. . . . I caught one. Take command, Schneurson." A spurt of blood soaked his shirt, but he forced his legs to carry him forward.

The second bullet ripped into his stomach. He buckled, dropping to his knees. Giv'oni crawled up to him, dragging him out of the line of fire. He laid Trumpeldor out on the ground and knelt beside him, sobbing at sight of the ghastly wound. Trumpeldor's eyes were closed. He opened them, managing a wan smile. "Never mind. Keep a covering fire on that gate. Get it closed if you can."

"Still can't get near it, Captain."

At Kefar Giladi, everyone could now hear the firing from Tel Hai. A rescue party was hastily formed under Ben and Bernard—eighteen in all. Some must be left behind to guard this outpost. Mohamed and Anwar insisted on going with the rescue party—in case there was an opportunity to parley.

"I'm leaving you in charge here," Ben told Nathan.

"Why me? You're the bridegroom. You should stay."

"Only one of them," Bernard said, coming up.

"I'll take your place on the wall," Anneliese told Ben. She looked wonderfully cool and unruffled. But that was not how she felt. She wore a bandolier and rifle over her heavy cotton jacket, absurdly large eyeglasses perched forward on her delicate nose. She needed them to take aim.

Ben smiled at her. "Good girl."

Naomi turned a tear-streaked face up to Bernard. "Will this be the ritual of our marriage?" she asked. "Kissing you good-bye?"

Suddenly Bernard felt the years between them. She looked so young, so fragile, so vulnerable. He loved her so much. She threw her arms around him, holding him in a mute embrace.

"I'll be back, Naomi. You didn't go through that damned *mikvah* for nothing." She stood with the others and watched them open the gate. Nathan closed it after the men.

At Tel Hai, smoke poured across the defenders. Trumpeldor whispered, "Make me a bandage, will you?"

"We'll get you inside, Captain."

"Not now. . . ." Bullets whined and bit into the stockade. Giv'oni ran inside the building for the bandage. Trumpeldor tried again to drag himself toward the gate. A third bullet cut through him. Even his incredible will could no longer power muscles. He seemed to shrink into himself, knees bunched toward his chin. Giv'oni came back with another defender. This time, they dragged him into the kitchen and laid him out by the stove. From outside they could hear the defenders keeping up a brisk fire.

Trumpeldor lay still, his intestines protruding from the gaping wound. He focused on his maimed belly. "Push them back in . . ." he said through the pain.

Giv'oni looked with horror. No one could bring himself to touch him.

"Never mind," Trumpeldor gasped. "Wash your hands carefully and I'll show you how."

How could the man remain so calm? How could he guide their ministrations in a voice that didn't waver? Giv'oni bound the wound with a towel, tears streaking his cheeks.

Ben Nouari had led the men from Kefar Giladi southwest of the main road through fields of jagged rock. Among them, Bernard, Jonathan, Dr. Simon. Judah walked beside Mohamed and Anwar. Nobody spoke. The distance was scarcely more than a mile. Rifle volleys orchestrated their journey, speeding them on with the insistence of catastrophe. They circled around the hills above the Tel Hai stockade to a point from where they could see the full attack in progress. Bernard gave the order to fan out. Below them, waves of Arabs from the wadis were pressing forward, firing as they came.

From the window of the loft at Tel Hai, Yassir and his two officers were still firing down into the compound. At last they clambered out onto the rooftop, where they could see the stockade gate still open. Yassir's troops seemed to have slowed their advance. "Why the devil don't they rush that gate?" he blazed.

Then he saw why. Through the lowering dusk, a new burst of firing was coming from the hills. It had the effect of an enfilade, catching the attacking ranks of Arabs in a murderous crossfire.

"Keep advancing!" Yassir shouted to his men. "Forward! Forward!" But they were already falling back under the converging gunfire.

On the hillside above Tel Hai, the relief party had intensified their fire. Judah called to Ben, moving down the slope, heels slipping in the loose rubble. "Concentrate your fire in front of that gate!"

Bernard, slightly ahead of the others, lobbed a homemade hand grenade into the advancing flank. It burst with some effect—but too short. He cursed, reserving his last grenade for a closer target.

Yassir, crouching on the barn roof with his two officers, could make out several of his own mounted troops cantering toward the stockade. They spurred their horses through the crossfire, shouting as they came. One of the horsemen bumped out of the saddle. The riderless horse bolted directly toward the stockade wall. Yassir stood up.

Seeing him, Giv'oni took aim, crying out, "On the roof!" He missed Yassir but winged one of the other Arabs, who managed to drag himself back through the window. The second officer was hit and toppled into the compound.

Alone now, Yassir fixed his glance on the riderless horse coming his way. As the beast came bounding under him, Yassir let out a wild yell and jumped. He fell sprawling across the terrified animal, wrapping himself around it. The creature bucked to free itself from the unexpected weight, but Yassir seized a clump of mane so tightly he almost tore it loose. Then he reined around, circling back to his retreating troops, lashing them with furious commands. "Back to the attack! You shame your mothers!"

Crouching on the hillside, Mohamed leveled his rifle sights at the mounted officer, who seemed to be trying to stop the rout. Along the barrel of his rifle he brought the man perfectly into aim. His fingers started the firm squeeze on the trigger. Then he recognized the face. There was no doubt—it had to be Yassir. He swerved his rifle to another target.

"Why didn't you fire? You had him right in your sights!" Judah yelled over.

"Too dark. . . ."

There was nothing now Yassir could do to force his men back to the attack. It must wait for daylight and reinforcements from Chula. And artillery. He spurred around the base of the hills and caught the silhouette of the men who had come to the rescue of Tel Hai moving toward the now deserted gate. The fading light played strange tricks. Yassir could almost believe that one of them, the tall man moving with the others, was his cousin Mohamed. He dismissed the thought and turned his horse back among the retreating Arabs.

Yassir rode on, eyes closed. All that he had to see now was in his own mind. All the moments of his life searing his vision in a procession of flaming exacerbations. He could feel again the sting of the Turkish whip, the flick of his father's fly switch, the sharp bite of Mohamed's reproofs. He rode down the wadi, into the camp of goat-hair tents. Men were crouched beside wounded comrades or lighting cooking fires. Exhausted men, who had fought their day of battle and wanted only rest. Victory could wait for another day.

Fury rose like an intoxication. Spurs sank into his horse's flesh. At a plunging gallop, Yassir swung past one of the tents, seizing an old, dry mat covering the roof. Wheeling again, he plunged it into a campfire and swung it around, a banner of licking flames.

Now he turned his horse full tilt toward the stockade, the wild ancient warrior's yell ringing from his lips. "Ealulululu . . . !" Yassir felt his hand scorch as flames blazed from the mat he was swinging around his head. Then he let it fly up to the roof of the barn. In seconds, it crackled into a mantle of flame over Tel Hai. Yassir galloped back to the safety of his own lines. However this day's attack might have failed, Haj Amin would hear of his act of bravery. His hand would carry the mark of his courage.

The last thin sliver of red sunset had plunged behind darkening hills. In the outpost of Tel Hai, the survivors were in a daze, a suspension of feeling, emptiness after violence. All the wounded had been brought inside. "The roof . . . !" someone shouted. The flames were licking down into the hayloft.

Schneurson ran into the kitchen, where Dr. Simon was dressing Trumpeldor's wounds. "We're going to have to get them out of here. The building is on fire!"

Simon looked up. "Get stretchers, then."

"There are none, Doctor."

"Folding beds. Anything." Settlers hurried out in search of make-shift litters.

Trumpeldor's eyes flickered open. "The supplies. Everything you can—out of the buildings. We will evacuate. . . ."

"That seems best, Captain," Simon said. "I can operate on you at Kefar Giladi."

"How many dead, Schneurson?" Trumpeldor asked, eyes still closed.

Schneurson felt trapped in a nightmare with a dying commander questioning from the edge of the grave. A commander who even now showed no fear or sign of pain. The roll call came stiff and unnatural from his lips. "Ben Munter. Sarah Chisick. Dvorah Drachler. Wold Sharf. All dead. Kanevsky badly wounded. . . ."

"The list is one short. . . . Never mind. It is good to die for our country. . . ."

They lifted him onto a folding bed and began the trip back, a procession of the survivors and rescue party, carrying the wounded and all the supplies they could. Behind them now, the flames of Tel Hai licked at the horizon and their dreams.

Judah fell into step beside Mohamed. "Why did you really come, Mohamed?"

"I thought the cards were a little too stacked against all of you."

The long column stumbled onward, glad for the cover of darkness that might keep them safe from attack.

"There have been more riots in Jerusalem," Mohamed told him after a time.

"I heard."

"Did you know that your friend Jabotinsky was arrested? It happened yesterday."

Judah tried to read the Arab's expression in the dark. "What on earth for?"

"For leading members of the Jewish Legion in defense of the old Jewish Quarter. It was under attack from Haj Amin's agitators. Cutthroats. They were killing old men at their prayers. Women and children. The British came to the rescue— by disarming and arresting the legionnaires. They'll sentence Jabotinsky and some twenty others to fifteen years imprisonment. That's the standard sentence."

"On what grounds?"

"Banditry, pillage, rapine. That's what they call it. I saw Jabotinsky marched through the streets manacled between two Arab rapists."

Judah's fury scalded his words. "Imprisonment, for the man who organized the Jewish Legion to fight beside the British . . . ? What in God's name have they done with the Balfour Agreement? What has happened to the offer?"

"I warned you many times, Judah. Statesmen write with invisible ink."

They walked on in silence for several minutes. When Judah spoke, his voice was once more calm. "What can save us, Mohamed?"

"Us?"

"Palestine."

"Moderation. . . . Which, after today, may be even harder to achieve." Mohamed looked back at the flames. He could hear the breathing of the dying commander being carried behind them.

Bernard came up. "Judah—it's Trumpeldor. I think you'd better come." Judah walked back. They had set the bed down by a small stream. He looked at the still, ivory face. Dr. Simon had dampened a rag and laid it across the captain's forehead.

Joseph Trumpeldor let his mind float adrift. Was this how it would always be? A land embattled. Moated in blood. No peace ever on earth for the chosen? Was their punishment across the face of the earth to continue through time until finally they obeyed God's biblical command to rebuild the Temple, rebuild the Hebrew nation as a light for all nations? Was their persecution the weapon to drive them back to fulfillment of the Covenant? To the land God had promised them—and they had promised God to make their own?

Or was it all an invention of dead prophets and scribes? Fables for the children and the old. Soon he would know. . . .

He opened his eyes to see Judah leaning over him. *"Ein davar,"* Trumpeldor whispered. *"Tov lamut be'id arzenu . . ."* A convulsion shook the soldier's body. It contorted into a spasm. His head dropped as though he had nodded in confirmation of some secret answer. His face turned to the earth.

Judah looked up at Ben, bitterness in his heart. "Even

Trumpeldor could not save Tel Hai. He couldn't even save himself. . . ."

They walked on again in silence, carrying their wounded and dead. Judah strode back to his old friend. "Mohamed. . . ."

The Arab turned.

"Tel Hai. Do you know what it means in Hebrew?"

Mohamed nodded. "The Hill of Life."

Nineteen _____

"MAY I speak frankly, Sir Herbert?"

"Neither of us has time just for the exchange of formal pleasantries, Mr. Hammadi. Though I believe it to be the custom of your country."

The High Commissioner of the League of Nations Mandate leaned across the English bone-china teacups in his Jerusalem drawing room. Mohamed noted the gold-encrusted sleeves of official formality. Sir Herbert Samuel must have come directly home from some ceremonial function. His eyes were dark, level, probing; his mustache cut to a military precision. He looked, Mohamed decided, anything but Jewish. Yet Jew he was—and dedicated to the fulfillment of the Balfour Agreement. As an Arab, Mohamed had been less then pleased by Sir Herbert's appointment. And yet he knew that Judah, too, was less than pleased.

Samuel pinpointed him with a look. "Do you speak, sir, as managing director of a world-wide company—or as a patriotic Palestinian? You seem to wear both hats, Mr. Hammadi."

"I believe in treading softly. My people are being provoked by militant demagogues. Mischief-makers, rabble-rousers fomenting an Arab frenzy of hate. The Jews have their own fanatics and zealots demanding too much. Too much immigration. Too much land. Too much talk of statehood. The storm that has already risen could destroy both sides."

"Dire predictions. I don't see it that way."

"Then, you are more optimistic than I, Sir Herbert. But then, you don't know this country as well as I."

"I thought you lived in New York?"

"I'm still a Palestinian. By birth and conscience."

A nondescript man in a dark suit appeared in the doorway.

432

He smiled in a tentative fashion. He looked like a man who chose his smiles and his ties carefully. Samuel gestured him to enter and be seated. "My political secretary, Mr. Richmond."

"We've met," Mohamed said. "May I come to the point, sir. I've heard a rumor—"

"That I hold Zionist sympathies?" Samuel smiled.

Mohamed shook his head. "I believe that is no rumor."

"My avowed intention, Mr. Hammadi, is to be impartial. As yours must be, since you have Jewish partners. I intend to show absolute fairness in supporting non-Jewish interests." Samuel raised an eyebrow toward Richmond, who seemed to confirm some unasked question. "What is this rumor you've heard?"

"That you are about to appoint a new grand mufti. I wonder if you understand the significance of the post. One might call it a sort of bishopric. After all, Jerusalem is the third-most-important city in Islam."

"The *first* in Palestine," Richmond put in.

Mohamed drew a paper from his pocket. "I'd like to submit a list of candidates for your consideration. After all, no Moslem in the country can live or die without being beholden to the grand mufti. A *moderate* would receive the type of support you need."

Samuel glanced at the typed list with polite disinterest. "My choice does not appear on your list." He looked up. "While I haven't as yet any clear indication of the desires of the 'turbaned class,' I have every confidence of obtaining the support of your religious leaders for the election of the one man who could defuse this current state of unrest." He turned his glance to Richmond. "Will you be so kind as to ask the next grand mufti to join us?"

Richmond left the room.

"My choice may seem at first surprising, since the man has a history as a troublemaker. Some have called him a mad dog. In fact, I've had to grant him amnesty for this appointment. But I believe he is the right person. He has a strong following among the masses. I am confident the responsibilities of his new office will convert him to moderation."

Richmond ushered in a slender, robed Arab. He had a small red goatee. His eyes were bright blue. The head inclined slightly beneath an oversize pot-shaped turban of immaculate white cloth. Sir Herbert rose to greet him.

"Have you met Haj Amin el Hussaini, Mr. Hammadi?"

Mohamed drew a slow breath to relieve the sudden shock he felt to his heart. "Only by reputation, sir."

"Haj Amin will need the support of your Arab influence."

"My congratulations, Grand Mufti." Mohamed's voice was tight. "If I correctly recall, our Glorious Koran tells that in his last year in Mecca, the Prophet wrote: 'and on the heights are men who know them all by their marks.'" He meant, of course, the opponents of Allah's will. As leader of our Muslim community, I trust you will be blessed by the same foresight."

"You surprise me, Hammadi," Haj Amin almost purred. "One would not expect a business figure of such international stature to retain his familiarity with our simple teachings."

Mohamed inclined his head slightly. "Each Muslim takes from the Prophet's words what he can. But the multitude will look to you, Grand Mufti, to interpret for them. Either you will fan the fires—or, as Sir Herbert believes, through moderation you will calm the current unrest."

"Do not fear, Effendi Hammadi, I shall apply myself with diligence to the needs of the humble, the faithful, the devout. Their need is my cause. And I shall have many strong hands to lighten my task. Men like your own cousins, Yassir and Tariq Hammadi." Haj Amin tucked his hands into the sleeves of his robe, his placid expression unchanged. "Dedicated young men."

"Dedication is a thing I can honestly say my cousins have never lacked. Unfortunately, in their case it has never gone hand in hand with wisdom." Mohamed bowed. "If I may be excused, Sir Herbert. . . ."

Richmond showed Mohamed out. "I gather you have some misgivings about our choice?"

"Some." Mohamed walked on, face grim.

Richmond opened the door for him. The day was crystal clear. The sentries snapped to attention. "I dare say the Jewish population may share them," Richmond conceded. "However, Sir Herbert intends to create good will and trust among all elements of this vast polyglot that is Palestine." He paused, noting Mohamed's bleak expression. "We would hope for your support. And of course, any suggestions you have will be considered by Sir Herbert and myself."

"One, Mr. Richmond. Concerning your new grand mufti. Keep your ear on his prayers—and both hands ready to move to his throat."

For a time, it appeared that Sir Herbert's choice was living up to his expectations. There was a brief respite from violence in Palestine. The grand mufti was putting his house in order, consolidating the assets of position and power.

As president of the Supreme Muslim Council, no part of civil activity escaped Haj Amin's attention and control. Courts, mosques, schools, cemeteries. All civic appointments were based upon demonstration of personal loyalty to the grand mufti. He gained control of all religious funds, but what he spent them on was not particularly in praise of Allah. Mohamed was not the only Palestinian whose distrust remained unshaken.

Anwar, too, when he thought of the events of the past few years, could not feel easy about this *'false springtime of harmony and hope,'* as he wrote Mohamed in New York beneath the scripted date February 4, 1925. *The mufti is carefully ignoring the educated Arabs. Building his following with gifts of alms and arms in villages and souks. Raising an army of the ignorant, the devoted, and devout. I fear the moment when he might decide to launch a bloodbath. It is true the British have curtailed Zionist immigration. But there are more than rumors of clandestine immigration. The British had promised to stop it. But I fear if they don't, the Arabs might. His agitators are everywhere in every city. I see signs even here in Tel Aviv, every time I travel down from Jerusalem.*

Anwar sealed his letter. Was he, after all, becoming too alarmist? He laid the envelope aside as a young woman entered his office in the Tel Aviv Development Bank.

"Sit down, Mrs. Kessler. Sit down. . . ."

Two weeks later, Anwar discussed Mrs. Kessler with Judah, who had just returned from Paris.

"She has excellent qualifications, Judah. She is the daughter of a Berlin banker, and a banker's widow. She co-managed her husband's bank, and she already seems to have a grasp of the problems we face here."

"Why did she come to Tel Aviv—and how long ago?"

"She's been here two months. I do not know her reasons. They are personal. But, aside from German, she speaks English, French, and understands some Yiddish. In my opinion she is just what we need to carry the full-time responsibility when one or the other of us is unable to be here. If you are as impressed as I am, we could start her as an assistant manager."

It was true the city of Tel Aviv had grown in the last five years beyond anyone's wildest expectations. Judah had been spending more and more time there and had finally bought a house near the center of town, off the Allenby Road. Ruth liked it and came to Tel Aviv as often as she could. Judah wasn't totally sure what it was about Palestine that Ruth liked. She still talked about playing a more active role in the development of the Jewish community. She was, she reminded him on every occasion, a dedicated Zionist, lacking only the opportunity to take her part. Well, he would have to think of something. Anything that could fill her hours now that the twins were eighteen and both attending the Sorbonne. He was spending more time with Ruth. That is to say, under the same roof, either in Paris or Tel Aviv.

"How old is this Kessler woman?" Judah asked.

"About thirty, I'd guess."

"Well, all right. Set up a meeting, Anwar."

The woman who entered Judah's office the following afternoon exuded an air of cool composure, as though she nursed some special secret of life. She wore her hair like an ashen helmet in the latest "shingle" cut. Feminine curves were hidden beneath the androgynous silhouette of her fashionably straight dress. The line broke at the knee into a troop of tiny pleats revealing a long length of slim, shapely calf, not in the least boyish. But it was the woman's eyes that captured Judah's attention. Incredibly large, hazel, heavy-lidded with a pencil-thin curve of painted brows. High cheekbones were powdered white, with no hint of the effects of two months in Middle Eastern sun.

"Sit down, Mrs. Kessler." Judah came around his desk to offer her a chair.

"Thank you," she replied in a voice surprisingly low and husky.

He offered her a cigarette. "My associate, Mr. Hammadi, has told me something about you. That you ran a bank with your husband in Berlin. A family bank, I believe."

"Leipzig," she said. "I don't mind telling you what happened. It leads to why I am here." She leaned back, crossing her legs with the whispered rub of silk. He noted how slim her ankles were and how the bone made a sharp angle under the clock of her stocking.

"Before the war, as you probably know better than I, Mr. Nouari, our German banks kept a certain proportion of our funds permanently invested in industrial concerns. Part of my duties included the exercising of control over virtually 'subsidiary' manufacturing companies. . . ."

He found himself looking at her rough mouth as she drew a breath of smoke. Lips formed a perfect bow.

"Naturally always we looked for fresh opportunities for investment," she was saying. "But of course participating in industry can have its good and bad sides. By supplying a ready flow of capital, we sacrificed our own liquidity." She looked up at him sharply, as though he might disagree.

"You risked insolvency, I'd say. However, the collapse of the mark didn't destroy all leading banks in Germany, Mrs. Kessler. What happened to yours?"

"In our case, we have been unlucky, Mr. Nouari," she sighed. "I do not wish to bore you with details of inflation in my country after the war, but the public became frightened of holding onto inflated currency. Paper!" She recrossed her superb legs. "Naturally it meant extra work for our bank, all this money in and out. Extra expenses. Hiring more staff." She leaned forward. "As long as they were measured in paper marks, profits could keep pace with expenses. But when stabilization came, *ach,* my God. . . ." She seemed to suffer with the memory. "Then Germany was faced with 'real' values. Like everyone else, we found ourselves stripped of liquid cash. . . ." She demonstrated with a dramatic gesture from head to toe. Judah's mind flashed a length of white body, as white as the powdered face. "All working capital gone, Mr. Nouari. The ratio between the old, paper mark and the new, gold mark was fixed at—how shall I say? Astronomical!"

"One billion to one, as I recall. What happened to your bank?"

"Ruin, Mr. Nouari. Ruin. But you mustn't think it was only us. Government and other securities fell to the vanishing point. My husband never recovered from this shock. He died six months ago—and I decided I must leave Germany . . . or be buried in the past. And so?'' She spread her hand in the air, buffed fingernails catching the light. "So I am here. Willing to work. I need a job not only for money but to keep my mind busy.''

Holding the door to Nathan's Restaurant in Herzl Street for Lily Kessler, Judah Nouari was aware of the galvanizing effect she generated on every man within her compass. Lily's magnetism spun heads. She was dramatic, polished, arresting, he thought, unique among the women one saw in Tel Aviv.

The room was a Babel of languages: Hungarian, Romanian, Polish, German, Russian, Czech, most of all Yiddish. It was a microcosm of Middle Europe, festering with political argument, ripped by bursts of laughter, charged with negotiation and tobacco smoke. Hectic, over-peopled, and intensely *gemütlich*.

"Welcome to Nathan's Restaurant," Judah said. "One of the bank's more successful investments.''

"The owner is your cousin, is he not?'' Lily indicated Nathan, coming toward them with the wide grin of a cheerful host.

"True, but backing Nathan was no act of nepotism. Just look around the room. Every table is full.''

"Cousin Judah! Such an honor. We don't see you nearly enough." Nathan's words were to Judah, but his eyes were riveted on Lily. Judah introduced them, adding, "Mrs. Kessler is taking charge of all loan accounts at the bank. Any problems while I'm in Paris, bring them to her, Nathan.''

"I'll start thinking some up right now.''

Lily surveyed his heavy shoulders, squarely built, muscular frame—more outdoor athlete than chef. "How did you happen to go into the restaurant business, Mr. Nouari?''

"It seemed the logical choice, Mrs. Kessler. Tel Aviv's full of people who'll go without shoes, clothes—even a roof over their heads. But they've got to eat occasionally. Maybe not every time they'd like to, but every chance they can get.''

"Do they all pay cash, or do you extend credit?''

"Credit!'' Nathan clutched his heart in mock horror. "Not without a blood test. Come. I saved you the window table, Judah.'' He guided them to a table bearing a RESERVED sign.

"By the window, we always serve the biggest portions. Good advertising."

Lily slid gracefully into the chair he held for her, stretching those incredibly long legs between the straight wooden ones. "It doesn't look as though you need much advertising. Where did you train as a chef?" she asked.

"Who trained? I cooked—at Rasnet el Deir. For twenty hungry farmers."

"A *kibbutz?*"

He nodded. "A few hundred years north of here. But *kibbutz* life was a complete waste of my talents. We were always so short of ingredients I had to serve the water from the boiled eggs as chicken broth. My Sabbath Special, I called Masterpiece Stew—because I put everything I had into it. Here, at least, we get hold of a steak once in a while, although we serve it black—out of respect for the cow."

Judah winced. "The food may be better here, but I see your jokes haven't improved."

"The service is so slow, I thought a few fast quips would keep the customers busy until the food came."

Lily glanced at Nathan's wall decorations.

A series of framed signs around the room advised:

CHEW WELL AND DON'T HURRY; WE WON'T.
WE COVER OUR MISTAKES WITH MAYONNAISE.
WE'LL GO TO ANY LENGTHS WITH OUR SPAGHETTI.
WHY GO ELSEWHERE TO GET INDIGESTION WHEN
YOU'RE ALREADY HERE?

And so forth.

"I think you're *still* wasting your talents, Mr. Nouari," Lily said.

"On some of these customers, everything's a waste. Honestly, you'd think they were in a barbershop, the way they tie their napkins around their necks. Instead of taking their order, I feel like asking, 'Shave or a haircut?' "

He rose, picking up their menus. "Don't bother choosing. Today we're out of practically everything. I'd advise the fish. It'll only take about twenty minutes." He favored Lily with his crooked grin. "Depending on the bait I use."

A minute later, he brought them a bottle of wine, then

hurried back to the kitchen. Judah found the wine slightly too sweet for his taste. He sipped it, then lit Lily's cigarette. She leaned forward; pale gray silk sleeves cut like a kimono offered a flash of red lining.

"Very nice. Almost like a Bernkasteler Riesling."

"It's local. From the vineyards at Petach Tikvah."

She looked across at him through a curl of smoke. "A *kibbutz*, of course. I haven't yet visited one. This Rasnet el Deir your cousin spoke of, is it very large?"

"The members are generally kept down to between thirty and forty."

"Perhaps one day you will take me for a visit?"

"If you wish. My brother Ben and several other old friends and relatives live there. But Nathan is right; it's not a life that would suit everyone. A person has to be dedicated."

"Or homeless?" Lily suggested.

"That's the purpose, of course. To provide homes for immigrants. But many of the *Yishuv* have also joined the *kibbutz* movement. One of my jobs for the JNF is raising money for them."

"With that and two banks to look after, Mr. Nouari, your wife must see very little of you." Lily gave him a quizzical look that held more than words.

"I was away so much during the war, she's learned to do very well without me."

"And this makes her happy?"

He refilled her wineglass. "Perhaps not."

"Perhaps now you will have less to do for this Jewish National Fund. Now that the British have cut down on immigration."

Judah frowned. "We keep trying to persuade them to enlarge the quotas. We can only hope they will see it our way."

"But some do *more* than hope, do they not?"

"What do you mean?"

She flashed him the spark of a smile. "Oh . . . you know. Helping people into the country—without always the most official permission."

"That is something the JNF tries to prevent." He broke off, seeing a familiar tanned face above an open collar entering the restaurant.

Judah came to his feet. "Excuse me, Lily. It's my brother."
He waved. "Ben . . . !"

Surprised, Ben started over. "Judah . . ."

The brothers hugged each other. "It has been a long time.
You look marvelous. Tired. But marvelous. How are Ruth
and the twins?"

"Fine. In Paris. You and Anneliese?"

Ben grinned. "We're going to make you an uncle. Would
you believe it? After nearly five years of trying."

"I'll try to come up next week. I'll bring Mrs. Kessler.
She's never seen a *kibbutz*." He turned to Lily. "Ben, this is
our new assistant manager at the Tel Aviv bank."

Lily offered her hand. His powerful handshake nearly crushed
her fingers.

"We've just sat down. Why not join us?" Judah asked.

"Today . . . impossible. I've only come to deliver a
message to Nathan. But when you come to the *kibbutz,* we
will make up for it." Ben spotted his cousin entering the
dining room through the swinging kitchen doors. "What day
next week, then?"

"Wednesday?" Judah asked Lily. She nodded.

Ben hesitated. "Make it Thursday. Wednesday I have to
go to Nablus—to collect some sheep. Yes, Thursday. We'll
give you some dinner. Not up to Nathan's standards, but
Anneliese would love to see you. And Bernard and Naomi. It
would do them good."

He said good-bye and started across the room. Lily and
Judah turned to each other, and while eating the surprisingly
good fish and salad, each began to learn more about the
other. They were enjoying themselves.

Later, Judah walked Lily home.

Footsteps, voices—sounded around them in the warm night.
A new city sprouting up in an ancient land. Streets squared
out like a grid, not sprawling and winding into byways and
alleys like neighboring Jaffa. Judah could almost smell the
young bricks and fresh wood buildings so swiftly risen. No
street seemed quite completed. How big could it grow? he
wondered.

"You are so silent," she said.

"Remembering. Something an old comrade of mine once
said to me. He couldn't stand life in big cities—with their
'host of conventions and artificialities,' as he called them. He

said you couldn't make true friends in a city—because the friends of today would cut each other's throats tomorrow for a lump of gold or a crust of bread.''

"I would like to meet this cynical friend of yours."

"He's dead. His name was Trumpeldor. I wonder what he would think if he could see Tel Aviv now."

She walked beside him, her fingers lightly grazing the crook of his arm. Across the street, home goers fed laughter upward toward the moon-spangled clouds.

"Now," she said. "We are here." Her apartment was only a few streets away from his own house. When she invited him in for coffee, he accepted. The evening had been exhilarating; he didn't want it to end.

While she brewed the coffee, he prowled. Her sitting room. How she wished to be known through the eyes of a stranger. Yet perhaps the impression it gave was not totally complete. A self-conscious portrait. There was a small collection of silver cigarette cases with square enameled pictures of pretty ladies in big hats, officers in German uniforms, and woodland scenes. There were books and personal photographs in silver or leather frames. The dead husband stared from ornate silver, interlaced cupids and flowers. Next to it, a family group taken perhaps fifteen years before. Mother, father, a more innocent, parasoled Lily, and a young man. The mother was blond and blue-eyed, the father bearded, with walking stick. The same young man in another photo, older. "Your brother? The one in uniform?"

"Otto. Killed at Verdun." She fell silent. He could hear her rattling cups and spoons.

"I take my coffee without cream," he called, scanning the bookcase. Most in German and English, a few in French.

"You'll have to take it without milk. . . ." She came in, carrying the tray with a wide smile. "I haven't any cream."

"Save that joke for Nathan," he laughed, taking the tray from her and setting it down on a low table. She poured.

"Some interesting books. You like philosophy: Kant, Hegel, Hermann Hesse—I haven't read him. Or this Kafka." He took up a book that had caught his eye. "What a curious title: *Mein Kampf*. . . ."

"Yes, *My Struggle*. The work of a madman. But fascinating. It was published in Germany last year. I must admit, to read it made my flesh crawl."

"A horror story?"

"Perhaps. On a grand scale. This curious young man has a plan to restore Germany. He calls us the 'Master Race' and blames all the troubles of the world on the Jews."

"Hardly original. *We* are always the scapegoat." Judah scanned a few pages, reading aloud. *"I was transformed from a weakly world citizen into a fanatic anti-Semite.* From hating Jews this man gains strength?"

"I didn't know you read German."

"A bit. May I borrow this?"

"Why not? It will put you to sleep. No one pays any attention to the man; only a few political fanatics. He wrote it in prison."

"What crime did they arrest him for?"

"Treason."

"Against humanity—or just Germany?" He slipped the book into his pocket. Lily leaned back on the sofa, crossing her legs. She took a cigarette from one of the enameled cases. Judah bent to light it. In the close room, her perfume was delicate and musky.

"You said 'us' a minute ago . . . referring to this 'Master Race.' "

"I am only half Jewish. I still think of myself as German. Why not? My mother was Lutheran. She died four years ago. Not so long after my father. But I have always been a person who could take care of myself. Quite independent, as you can see."

"I've noticed. And I admire it."

The next time Judah glanced at his watch, he realized they had been talking for almost an hour. He, about his youth in Palestine and Paris. She, about life in Germany before the war.

He rose to leave. At the door, she reached to kiss him lightly on the lips—the full current of her in one swift brush. The spontaneous action left him in a state of stirred desires.

Lily revived feelings, emotions that seemed to have been lost from his life. But feelings could be deceptive, even dangerous. At fifty, they fed some fleeting sense of "last chance." Judah thought he knew himself. But Lily was one of those rare creatures who exude mystery, leaving a man off balance, disturbing the compass by which he steers his life.

His own hallway mirror told him that the years hadn't

treated him unkindly. Now he had added rimmed glasses for reading. Since leaving the Army, he'd let his hair grow longer. It framed his thin face with an invasion of gray. A weariness in the eyes, perhaps, but he had not yet thickened into the finality of age. Well, there must be something to this woman to make him take such stock of himself. He had thought all personal vanity long since vanished.

Sleep in the small wooden house in Tel Aviv brought her again—a face in his dream. Rouged mouth that seemed to turn down at the corners in a sensuous challenge. Eyes heavy-lidded, sultry, green-shadowed. The silken brush of legs crossing and uncrossing. Wrapping around him in his dream. . . .

He woke with a start and went into the bathroom for a glass of water. "No, Judah," he told the face in the mirror. "It would be stupid. Stupid."

When was the last time they had made love?

Naomi rubbed the soggy clothes against the washboard in the wooden vat large as a kettledrum. The other women had left the building that served as a communal laundry. Gone with their gossip, complaints, or sly boasts of their husbands' prowess in bed. Or their weariness, which nobody lacked here at the *kibbutz*.

Naomi was glad they were gone. She had deliberately stayed on to be alone. To sort out the trouble in her mind. Bernard's trouble, whatever it was. But his trouble was hers when it started coming between them.

So when had they last made love? The communion of bodies, forced into quiet, almost stealthy copulation in order not to wake up the child in the tiny next room. Was it a week? Ten days? A month? Problem enough with the fretting three-year-old cutting his teeth in the two-room clapboard shack. And they were luckier than many. Some had to share even smaller spaces with much larger families. Naomi and Bernard had managed two rooms to call their own.

Marriage. "It should be a lifetime of increasing acquaintance and shared knowledge." That was how mother Miriam put it. But they had known each other better after the first night together than now—after five years.

Because he was hiding something from her. His thoughts. The things that were changing the garrulous, outgoing Bernard into a moody automaton. What preoccupied him? What drew his depressions like a hood across their communications?

And how could she help him if he told her nothing of his problem? Naomi squeezed out the last of the wet laundry—and pegged it up on the wagging line behind the communal kitchen. Then she walked back to their house.

Poor Bernard. What was making him suffer so? He had never before been morose or given to long silences. If she questioned him, he would answer laconically, "It'll pass. Everything does." But what was this "it"? Some disease of dreary possession haunting his mind, making him secretive, bleak?

Each morning, he would rise at the bang of the iron triangle, dress in silence. He would have learned the evening before from the daily rota, or schedule—*Sidur Avodah,* as they called it—on the notice board, what duties he would be expected to perform. It might be guard detail or *G'dud Ha-avodah*—the labor battalion. Or it could be field work, planting, harvesting, plowing—or transport maintenance or fruit picking. Virtually all the men's labor was manual. Then he had to serve on committees, attend meetings. Understandably (they all lived in such close proximity) there was little now to report. The women cooked and patched their clothes and fed them and taught the children, along with field work, fruit packing and washing. Nobody could call it a life of sharp contrasts. Without the meaning behind it, without the purpose, it wasn't far from resembling an army camp. But they were reshaping the land that had existed only in their prayers. Meaning and purpose were everything here. Was it *that* he had lost? she wondered.

Bernard moody? Bernard unresponsive? No. This was not the man she had fallen in love with—with a plow in his hands and a gun slung on his shoulder and the crazy American songs that nobody quite understood. "I want a girl just like the girl that married . . . whom? Oh, yes, dear old Dad." Well, he had a girl—wife-girl-mother—and a strapping three-year-old. Their second son.

Second. Was that when the moods had started? He hadn't said much the day before they left Kefar Giladi. The day, yes, that same day, they had buried their first baby son. Boy who had never breathed, who had never heard his name. Dead at birth. It was certainly something not to talk about.

Then or ever. She had seen Bernard's eyes that day. But how could he feel it more deeply than she?

That was already several years ago. She had to find out what was devouring him—now. She looked up hopefully as Bernard walked in. But he passed her with a nod, and no glad-to-be-home kiss.

Not that this was much of a home. The JNF permitted no construction of permanent buildings. All must be suited to the needs of family communal farms. No private property or economic activity allowed. It didn't exactly make for a sense of personal progress upward in the world. Only participation in mass survival. Was this the cause of the change in Bernard? Monotony? Boredom? Drudgery? He never joined his voice in the occasional bouts of singing any more. Or his limbs in the eruptions of horas, pounding in a circle of battered exuberance—at having lived through another month in Eretz Israel.

"We've got to talk, Barney."

"Something in particular?"

He had sunk down, staring at the wall, which wasn't much to stare at. Bare wood planks interrupted only by the yellowing photo of her dead father.

"We've got to talk about us."

"Us."

"Yes. Us. We. Ourselves. A unit called family. You. Me. Solly. We're all in this."

"What's bothering you, Naomi?"

"What's bothering you?"

"Something I did?" He went to the washbasin and began splashing his face.

"Something you didn't do. Never any more."

He got the message. He came over and kissed her, with the towel hanging around his shoulders like a scarf. First on the lips. Hers soft, his rather dry and broken by all-day and everyday exposure to merciless sun and an eternity of wind. Then on one cheek, then the other. The touch told her: It isn't you, Naomi. The change is not concerned with you.

"Feel better?" He looked straight into her eyes.

"It's not how I feel. It's you."

He nodded almost in recognition that she might indeed have cause to probe. Then it was gone. The shadow descended, taking expression from his eyes, restoring that sense of numbness that left no room for feeling or sharing.

"It's always there," Naomi insisted. "Like a blank wall coming between us. I've got to know what it is."

"Just tired. I've got a right to be, haven't I?"

Yes, he had a right. They all did. Every member of the *kibbutz* shared that. Along with the abandonment of personal gain. Nobody could have much to show for the life they had chosen, except that they were there. And existing. Yes, that's what it came down to when you stripped away the fancy words and idealistic pats on the back. Existence. Another day bought by hard labor—in the land of Zion, where, on arrival, some had knelt to kiss the very soil, some had burst into poetry, prayer, and song. The homecoming across centuries! The fulfillment of the Covenant! Eretz Israel! That was what lay behind everything.

"It's what we've bought with our lives. The privilege of being on this land," she told him softly. "Make another settlement. Build. Plant. Give birth."

"And death," he muttered. "Don't forget death. Because death never forgets us."

He walked back to the washbasin, his face a blank. Now she was even beginning to feel angry with him. "So you're tired. So I'm tired. We're rotten tired. You think the 'services', as they call them here, are an entertainment? Kitchen. Laundry. Clothes store. Nursing. Kindergarten. But you don't hear me complain. Do you hear me complain? Ever? And if I did, what would it change? Make them give me softer jobs?"

"No," he said.

"I'm not trying to sound like a heroine. I don't mind. I don't really mind . . . except what's happening to you." She set down a glass of tea and a slice of bread with honey. He came over to the table, but he didn't touch it.

"Do you know how you look to me? Like there was some kind of storm in your mind or your heart. And the sun would never rise again."

"Mama, Mama, Mama. . . ." The call of little Solly. Solly for Solomon, for her father, whom Bernard had never met. Brave, foolish Solomon, shot off the top of the prison wall—to fall into family legend without accomplishing anything. She went into the tiny second room—scarcely bigger than a cupboard.

Bernard took up the glass of tea she had set by his hand. Edge of the glass chipped. "Everything broken here." Make do. Tea itself a miraculous luxury. Naomi had stopped drinking it so there would be more for him, which she always denied. God, she was wonderful. A jewel for any man . . . if only. . . .

His mind swam a distance of years back to the outpost days. After the burning of Tel Hai, the other settlements had been abandoned. Only a few had clung on at Kefar Giladi. For some insane reason, she'd wanted to have their child there. So they'd stuck it with the others. Even through the time when the Arabs had brought French artillery pieces and shelled the compound. That had seemed the end of everything. But, for some unknown reason, the shelling had not led to a final attack. And the handful of settlers clung on a bit longer. And then another bit longer. Bernard knowing her time was near. How near, he hadn't realized. They had planned to bring a midwife from Safad. Perhaps the shelling brought it on, and no doctor at hand. Only Bernard and the other remaining woman on the post to assist with the birth. Naomi was so small. And she was in pain.

When he looked at his son, the firstborn. . . . No breath. A doll, white and motionless. A doll that had not asked to be made. What was God about, to permit such a waste? Such hope destroyed? Was this a God of justice and mercy? Take the sinners—there were enough of those. Was God a cannibal, devouring his own creatures? Or so busy elsewhere, he could not spare time for falling sparrows? Set up a world and let them run it. And if they destroyed it and themselves, try again. Chalk up one bad experiment—and try a different mixture. Centaurs next time, perhaps. No, they hadn't done too well either. What about minds without flesh—incapable of inflicting pain and sorrow on each other? Go on, God—try another formula, since you've given up with this one! Bernard had felt a hand on his shoulder. Rabbi Esau Horovitz, who had come up for the funeral. He had married them. Now he would bury their first son.

"We cannot know the meanings of everything, Bernard. But if we cannot also accept . . . what is left?"

"I'll tell you what is left! Nothing. Rabbi! Flesh! Rot! Stink! Pain! Take your God and get out of here. I don't want you or him!"

Then Bernard had lain down by the grave he was digging and cried into the earth. "Why not let the innocents have their chance? Why take out our failures on them? Never to grow. Never to take first steps toward out-thrust arms. Never to form first word sounds."

Bernard arose. He had finished the little grave, and he knew himself to be squeezed dry of everything. Nothing left but pity for himself, which the world always condemned. Of course, pity for himself. Hatred of the God that had let him down. Yes. But, finally, these were only postures without feeling. He would preserve his life by caring for nothing. Because that gave ammunition to the enemy. If you cherished nothing, there would be nothing to take away.

The graves were about ten meters northeast of Kefar Giladi. Trumpeldor's. Other men, and women. And one child.

Joseph Chaim Brenner tried to make some meaning out of it before the little group abandoned that last settlement. "Tel Hai has gone up in flames. But the heart of Israel is alive. Our brothers and sisters who were killed . . . have shown us that this heart is alive, refined by fire. . . ."

Nobody had said anything more when they'd climbed into the truck sent to take them south. But Bernard knew that, however alive this heart might feel, his was buried in that patch of Galilee covered with light-colored earth so it might be found again. By any who still believed in miracles. . . .

Naomi returned from the child's room, face placid. "Solly is so irritable with that tooth. I do think you might go say good night to him."

"In a minute." Bernard wished he could feel something more for his second son. More of what? He closed his feelings to everything. He would not be vulnerable to punishment. Not this time.

"I wish you'd come out of that tunnel you've been hiding in, Bernard."

"A tunnel is a place, Naomi. Not a state of mind." He reached out and took a sip of tea. She slapped his hand and the glass crashed down, spilling it on both of them.

"Now—we're going to talk! No more moody silences. I want to know what it is that is getting between us. Between you and everything. I want to know. Now."

"Fair enough, Naomi. You wanted to hear it—I'll tell you. Sit down. Forget the damned tea." She withdrew her hand

from the spilled broken glass and sat beside him on the bench
he had built out of crates.

"I want to leave here."

"What?"

"No, don't start asking questions until I've said it all. I
want to give up Rasnet el Deir and go home to America. I
can't stay here any more."

"Go with us? Solly and me?"

"No. Not at first. As soon as I find a place to live, get a
job, I'll send for you both. You understand. I'm not in my
father's best graces. I'll have to see if there's still a place for
me at one of the mills. Then I'll send for you. We'll make
another start. Live like human beings. Our own house. A
telephone, a bank account. Solly can go to a good American
school. You can have nice clothes."

"And just forget about . . . all this?"

"Yes! Let somebody else do the land-building for the
future. If there ever is to be one. If the British keep Palestine—
or give it back to the Turks. Or the French move in, or the
Arabs take over—or who cares? The hell with it! I want the
present . . . for us both. I want to belong to a place that lets
you do something for yourself! I'm tired of grubbing!" He
got up, taking a few steps around the narrow, bare room,
followed by her eyes.

"And is that all of it?"

He glanced around, a little offended. "You think I'm just
indulging myself? Letting off steam? I'm serious, Naomi.
I've tried—and I'm just not cut out for this. It takes a type of
guts—some sort of dedicated endurance I'm just plain out of.
I want to think of us for a change. But I mean really 'us.' I
must be able to build us a better life than this."

"And what do I do when you go?"

"Stay with your mother—and grandfather Jacob."

"And suppose I don't want to come to America?"

"How can you know what you don't want? You've never
seen it!"

"And Palestine?"

He came over and took her hands. "A land of graves."

She arose and kissed him with a strange finality. "If it is
what you want, go. But take that medal they gave you for
Gallipoli. And the first night you're on the ship, throw it

overboard. You once told me you joined up to fight for the chance to come here. You know what I think of you now?"

"Oh, Naomi . . . for God's sake. . . ."

"You said last week you didn't believe in God."

"I don't. I believe in . . . well, our lives. What we can still make out of our lives."

"Money?"

"All right, money. Is it so terrible to want the best for a change? I mean, admit it. What have we got here?"

"I had a nice comfortable home too. The reason why I left it, that hasn't changed. So when you go back to your country— where the streets are paved with opportunities and you can sit in a real bath tub and turn on hot running water—enjoy it, Barney. But you'll have to enjoy it alone. Because your land will not be my land and your people will not be my people. *They* happen to be here—grubbing, drudging, and working for something besides money." Her voice had lifted to a high pitch, and Solly was crying in the next room. She ran out to him as though escaping from her own ultimatum.

Bernard stood looking after her, the moments stringing together. The front door opened. No formality of knocking in this place.

"Did I pick a bad time?"

He turned to see Ben.

"I guess I did," Ben said.

"It's all right. Just a small disagreement. About everything in the world."

Ben nodded understanding. "A little fresh air, then?"

"Something special on your mind, Ben?"

"I think so."

Bernard paused, eyes on the closed door behind which he could imagine a very miserable Naomi. For that, he was extremely sorry, but his mind was unchanged. He nodded as though in answer to a question he had asked himself, then called: "Ben's here. We're going to take a walk. Be back soon."

"No hurry." Her tone said everything. The two men stepped out into the lowering darkness.

Above the *kibbutz,* a single star pricked the sky. Cooking smells drifted out from the community kitchen. Somewhere a mouth organ was sounding plaintively, lonely as the cry of a lost animal. Bernard could almost sense the exhaustion behind those unpainted walls. They were well out of earshot of anyone when Ben spoke.

"Are you still a man who doesn't mind taking a chance?"

"With what?"

"With your own life . . . to save a lot of others. . . ."

Naomi heard their footsteps drift away, blending with other camp sounds. She looked at Solly. Button eyes looked back. He was a happy baby most of the time. He gurgled a three-year-old's aria of his own creation. Naomi felt like crying. She would, as soon as she had time, but even tears were a luxury here. She rocked Solly in her arms and sang him a little tune. His eyes closed and he fell asleep against her breast.

When Bernard came back, an hour later, something had happened; she could see that. His whole expression had changed. He and Ben exchanged looks of shared confidence. She let him speak first.

"Just been talking things over with Ben, Naomi."

"Oh?"

The neutral "oh" could go either way. To forgiveness or continued hurt and anger. Yet she suspected, even before she knew, that Ben had been the cause for the change in Bernard. Ben excused himself. Anneliese would be waiting. He seemed anxious to leave them alone.

"I've changed my mind about leaving here, Naomi." It came out that suddenly, without any preliminaries.

"Your talk with Ben . . . ?"

He reached out, bringing her against him, lacing her into his arms. "Certain things came up. It really doesn't matter, does it? It's what you want . . . that we stay here. Let's just say that Ben has made me see matters in a different light. There are certain things we have to do, Ben and I. Are you happy?"

"Oh, yes, Barney. But what about America? What happened to America?"

"We'll forget about it. For a while, anyway. Come on, let's go in to supper. I'm getting hungry, and those jackals will finish off everything if we don't get there." He launched into an old folk song that Trumpeldor used to sing.

"Through fields, through forests,
To meet my love. . . ."

It was the first time she had heard him sing anything for months.

That night, they made love. It had been so long that she had forgotten the pure joy of it. The extinguishing of weariness on the journey to fulfillment. She gave herself with eagerness, feeling the hardness of him that she had awakened, the wanting she had stirred. His strong, rough hands slid across smooth skin drawing hips closer in the exquisite rhythm of their passion.

"Let us make another baby," she whispered.

"Yes," he murmured. "Yes—yes—yes—yes—Oh, yes . . . !"

"In a country still struggling to survive, who would have believed we'd see this day?" Chaim Weizmann's question to Judah was rhetorical. They were launching together at Nathan's Restaurant in Tel Aviv.

It had been a long time since Judah had met with the Zionist leader—and neither could have imagined the landmark event that would bring them together in Palestine.

"First the Rothschild Hospital. Then the jewel in Jerusalem's cap: the Hebrew University. And who honored us with his presence at the opening? Lord Balfour himself. The man is in his seventy-seventh year, Judah! Mind you, I've tried to see that this tour of Palestine was not too tiring for him. Which made it extremely tiring for me." The smile of the chemist seemed to embrace the room, the city, the land beyond it still in mind dedicated to statehood.

Weizmann stirred sugar into the tall glass of tea before him. "You know, before I left London, I had a phone call from our old friend Jabotinsky: 'What is this university you are bringing Balfour to? An imitation whale—made of wood . . . !' he shouted at me."

"Everything in the world changes but Ze'ev. He only gets more so," Judah laughed.

"He's been attacking me publicly, you know. For what he calls my 'Fabian tactics.' He thinks I'm bowing out of the battle. Accuses me of trying to cloud the issue, with this new university. Divert attention from the main problem."

"Which to Jabotinsky, I'm afraid, is fighting the British Government."

"Which is exactly what he knows I have always opposed."

Judah recalled the angry face of Jabotinsky the day Judah had visited him in the jail at Acre. He had gone there to convince the stubborn journalist-soldier to accept Sir Herbert Samuel's offer of amnesty.

"I was defending Jerusalem's Jewish Quarter," Jabotinsky had argued. "If that was a crime, I shall insist on serving every day of my fifteen years at hard labor." Jabotinsky—theatrical, emaciated, the clothes hanging loose upon him, looking like a heroic scarecrow—had rejected Samuel's amnesty with contempt, because it also included Haj Amin and Aref el-Aref. Jabotinsky had demanded an appeal of his case, and eventually won it.

"The problem is still immigration, Judah," Weizmann was saying. Judah brought his mind back to the conversation.

"We must convince the British to enlarge the quotas. And then we must find homes for all who come here. Maybe Jabotinsky is right. Maybe the only way is mass immigration."

"That would really stir up the Arabs! Just when things have settled down a bit. But time isn't on our side, Chaim." Judah took the book from his pocket that he'd borrowed from Lily. "Anti-Semitism is on the rise again. In Poland, Romania, Hungary. And even in Germany." He leaned back. "My God, here it is 1925 and we seem to be progressing back into the Dark Ages! This book . . ." He handed it across the table. "You should read it. By a man named Hitler."

"Books? Who has time for books?"

"Well, I tell you: if a man like this ever got into power, he'd make Jabotinsky sound like a prophet. Every Jew in Europe would have to emigrate."

"That's one way to build a nation."

"Jabotinsky writes to me regularly, you know. One line he wrote keeps sticking in my head. *'Everything—all forces of life and death—are converging toward one end. A Jewish state—and a great exodus to Palestine.'* It's a prophetic line, Chaim."

Weizmann nodded. "To you, he's a prophet. To me, he's a prophet. But to a prophet, is he a prophet? Jabotinsky is always a man who is both right and wrong. Right in objectives. Wrong in methods. He has his own splinter group in the W.Z.O. now, you know. The voice of *im*moderation. He wants to resurrect Hebrew as a living language. I'd like to offer him a job teaching at the new university. Maybe that would keep him out of trouble.''

"I'm afraid there is no way to neutralize Jabotinsky. The British are right and wrong too. They'll never permit mass immigration as long as they fear Arab reaction. This new regulation they've concocted—''

"The capitalist category?" Weizmann shook his head in disgust.

"Some capitalists! A colony of Russian Jews stranded in Poland after the war. Anyone with twenty-five hundred dollars in his pocket—which I admit sets him apart from the herd seeking labor certificates. These 'capitalists' can get their settlement visas the same day. And where do they go? To the land? The outposts? No. They're pouring into Tel Aviv faster than we can provide housing,'' Judah complained.

Weizmann frowned. "It wasn't what Herzl intended. It isn't what I believed in. I had been telling Lord Balfour how we were building here for *eternity*. Yes, I'm afraid I used that word. Then I walked him through Tel Aviv. The new city. Everywhere we went, we heard only Yiddish. Everywhere we looked, little groups of shopkeepers haggling. These people might as well have moved from Djika to Nalevki. I thought they'd left the ghettos behind, but they have brought them here with them.''

"What did you expect, Chaim? Marching farmers with sun-tanned faces?" Judah was almost angry. "These people cannot change their ways simply by crossing a sea. Yiddish is the only language they can communicate in. Trade is the only way they know how to survive. They can't understand how to build a new land. But love them for the children they will raise here. If it is ever to happen, it will be their children who will father the nation.''

"All this I know, and yet I still find myself obsessed by the discrepancy between the desirable and the possible.''

Judah glanced across the room. Here were the small shopkeepers—the businessmen. Some of them he had come to know through the bank. Some of them cared no more about the land they came to than the land they had left. It was a living. To them, that was all. He turned back to Weizmann. "Show Lord Balfour the Jewish orange groves and vineyards— growing up out of land that was once swamp. Show him the settlements where they plow with one hand and hold a gun with the other. Show him the wheat fields. Show him the cattle. Show him the harvests.''

"It is true, the answer lies in the land, not the cities. To succeed, we must buy more and more—and more. *We* must buy—the Jewish National Fund, not the speculators. And we need level-headed people to handle these transactions. Above all, we must not upset the Arab population. Not only *be* fair, we must be *seen* to be fair.''

"By whom, Haj Amin?''

Weizmann looked up from his tea with a quizzical expression. "Tell me, Judah. Are you a happy man?''

Judah glanced at his old mentor. The man who more than anyone had seen Herzl's dream reach the blueprint for a nation. What game was he playing now among the chessboards and the arguments in the crowded restaurant? Happy? Was anyone happy? "What does that mean, Chaim?''

"Your home life, Judah. Your marriage. How is it?''

"No worse than ever, I guess. Where does a life go?'' He looked away. "There's not a great deal Ruth and I share—except for our love for the children, and they're growing away from me so fast I barely seem to know them any more. No, Chaim, we're not like you and your wonderful Vera.''

"Ruth is a fine woman, Judah. Maybe—just maybe—some of it could also be your fault. Not that I wish to criticize, but how much chance have you given her? Always you tell me how much Ruth wants to take part in your work here. You're busy with the fund raising, with your banks, your're part of a big company, and still you don't let her do anything. Well, I've got a job for her.'' He paused, seeing Judah's surprise.

"For Ruth?''

"You would have to oversee it, of course. But it would give you something to work on. Together.''

"What kind of job?''

"I need the right person to help with the settlers on land being purchased by the JNF. Joshua Chankin is getting too old to handle it all by himself. Many of the pioneers come from Poland. Ruth speaks their language, knows their ways. She could help get them located. Guide them when they arrive. Settle them into the new farms. Obviously, you will send somebody with her. Give her all the help. But Ruth is the right person.''

"She has always talked about playing a part. . . ."

Judah's mind raced back to Zosia. What part would she have played had she been here now? Was it true that he was holding Ruth back?

"Judah, I know that you personally haven't the time to devote. I also know that the Nouari name connected with land settlement would add weight when I'm on one of my annual fund-raising trips. My policeman's beat, between Jerusalem and San Francisco—which you helped organize. Have you ever tried to explain to American businessmen that we want to rebuild a land neglected for centuries? No trees—no soil. And the money they sink in the cause won't bring them any return. They're convinced that for every dollar they give, ninety cents is wasted. The speeches I make—sometimes I wonder as I'm talking—will it feed a cow? build a road? buy a farm?" Weizmann sighed.

The two men fell silent in the clatter of the restaurant. Judah saw Nathan heading toward them.

"I'll ask her," he said.

"Who?"

"Ruth. I'll ask her."

"Good. Ask her for me personally. Maybe you will find working together for the same things . . . brings you together. That way lies happiness."

Twenty ————————————————————

FOR the first time in her life, Ruth Nouari fully sensed the splendor of the land. Riding in the back seat of Zionist Headquarters' official automobile, beside the spokesman for a group of new Polish settlers, the very air seemed a golden toast to the success of Ruth's first assignment. The immigrants were on their way to their new home-site, an Arab farm recently purchased by the JNF. And Ruth was there to start them off on the right track; their guide, their guardian, their adviser, their counselor, their beacon, their lodestar—their Lady Bountiful.

The spokesman, Mendel Shapira, shoemaker from Łódź (Judah called it the Manchester of Poland), was a solid, square-shaped man. Only in his mid-thirties, yet already slightly hunched, shoulders curved forward from hours of mending other people's soles. Now he was in charge of their bodies and destinies—and Ruth was in charge of him.

The man driving them was a ha-Shomer-trained "watchman"—tough, rugged, dependable. Should any problems arise, Ruth could rely on Yuri's judgment, Judah had advised. Sitting up front with Yuri was Ruth's Arab interpreter. Judah had personally selected Selim, who had been employed by the JNF ever since graduating from university. Selim was reliable, experienced, and intelligent.

"With those two, Ruth, you should encounter no difficulties," Judah had assured her.

Behind the car trailed a motorcade consisting of two truckloads of settlers and a few young men from one of the *kibbutzim* who would help with the construction of the prefabricated timber buildings. Two more trucks carried precut lumber and tools along with farm implements and food enough to last one month. All bought by donations from around the world through the W.Z.O. She could say with pride, and frequently did, that her husband Judah had a strong hand in raising the funds that would put roofs over the settlers' heads. From her description, Shapira the shoemaker might believe that Judah was a one-man fountain of funds.

What more, she thought, could even the revered Zosia do in her place? Zosia. . . . How Ruth had worshiped her cousin in her youth, striven to be like her. And how Ruth had grown to hate her memory through the years of marriage to Judah. Because she had come to realize that Zosia's memory was more sacred to Judah than his own wife. To fight for one's husband against another woman was traditional, to be expected, calamity enough. But to fight for him against a phantom required skill with which few were blessed. Ruth was not among them.

Through their entire marriage, Judah scarcely noticed her. As he scarcely noticed the children she had borne him, her beloved Abe and headstrong Zed. But this day's work would prove to Judah once and for all that Ruth, too, was worthy of the respect, reverence, and love that he reserved for her dead cousin—that paradigm of perfection, Zosia.

For this particular JNF land purchase, Judah had paid a high price to Fawsi el Khader, a wealthy Beirut-based Arab landlord. Judah had personally made the trip to Beirut to see for himself that the papers were in order. The Arab, a friendly, flamboyant fellow, showed no great interest in the vast tracts of farmland he had inherited. In accordance with JNF rulings, Fawsi el Khader had been required to make provision for his tenant farmer's family to be relocated. The JNF insisted that no one be left homeless. On his return, Judah had confided to Ruth that no doubt the money would generously finance the Effendi Fawsi's trips to Monte Carlo, gambling losses, and French women.

And now Ruth bumped along the dusty road, next to Mendel Shapira, on their way at last to the farm site where the new settlement would rise. Ruth had kissed Judah good-bye, overriding his last-minute qualms with the assurance that she could handle everything. "Why should there be problems?" she had asked.

"Because you are dealing with human beings."

"And I have been dealing with them very well," she

pointed out. "Although I expect you haven't noticed." This group of settlers had been assigned to her from the first day of their arrival. She had seen them safely through the British immigration procedures and housed in the reception camp. Seen to their needs—children, nursing mothers, and grand-mothers, who had insisted on kissing the ground on arrival.

"Sarah Schreiber, that nice secretary at the JNF Headquar-ters, said to me, 'Mrs. Nouari, you have a gift. You fuss over these people like a relative.' That's what she said, Judah."

Ruth felt Judah was expecting her to make some sort of mistake. But she wouldn't. She had everything in order. All documents in her handbag. All people and equipment accounted for in the trucks. All signatures on the proper papers.

They turned off the main road to be bounced along a dusty bypath. Beyond them, foothills rose and stretched, lofty and impersonal, above the plain of olive trees and tilled fields: the Arab farm.

Selim turned around to her. "The land begins here, Madame Nouari. It is only a small distance now to the farmhouse."

"Our people won't be using that. We'll be building our own quarters." She turned to the hunched figure beside her. "Well, Mr. Shapira, how do you like your new home?"

He stared out the window with no spark of enthusiasm. "How should I know how I like it? Ask me in a few months, I'll tell you."

"Fresh air, open fields, an outdoor life. It will remove the memory of the ghetto," she said cheerfully.

"The ghetto at least I knew." A note of uncertainty had crept into his voice.

Ruth patted his hand. "It's understandable, Mr. Shapira. You're just feeling the effects of the trip. All the difficulties of your arrival. Tomorrow morning when you wake up on your own corner of Eretz Israel, you will feel reborn." She glanced out, seeing the small, white-washed mud-brick farm-house looming ahead. "All right. Stop the car, Yuri," she ordered, lifting her arm out the window in signal to the motorcade.

They climbed out into the scalding sunlight—Ruth, Yuri, Selim, and Shapira. Behind them, the trucks came to a halt. The settlers began clambering down stiffly, lowering personal luggage, their worn-out satchels, the backpacks of the Diaspora.

Then, to her surprise, she saw the door of the farmhouse

open; a group of Arabs poured out. Men followed by women and children, *fellaheen* moving to meet her. Others came from behind the farmhouse. They looked angry. Some carried sticks. The man leading them held an old musket.

Judah's admonition flashed into her mind. He had showed her a letter from David Ben-Gurion. *"According to my moral judgment we have no right whatsoever to deprive a single Arab child—even if through such deprivation we shall realize our aims . . ."* What would Zosia have done now, at this moment? she wondered. What would Judah do?

"Get the rifle, Yuri . . . !" Ruth said under her breath.

"We don't want to start trouble, Mrs. Nouari." But he went back to the car, to be near the weapon just in case. Ruth turned to Selim.

"Why are these people still here? Ask them what they want. This farm is supposed to have been vacated."

Selim stepped forward to meet the man with the musket. The conversation began quietly enough, but soon the voices collided in harsh exchange. Behind her, Ruth could hear the settler's children beginning to whimper. "What is it? What is he saying?" she demanded of Selim.

Selim turned back with a worried expression. "This man— he says that this is his land. He says you cannot come here."

"His land? His land! He is only a tenant farmer. It was never his!"

Selim shrugged uncertainly. "This is his family. They all live in that house, madame."

She looked at the tenant's face: angry, simple, stubborn. "All—in that one house? Well, tell him they'll have to go. He has no legal rights. Say we have documents of ownership. He can read them himself." She brandished the folder of documents. Selim read from one, translating carefully. The Arab farmer waved his hands in a gesture of dismissal. They meant nothing to him. He couldn't read. The harsh exchange continued.

Selim turned back to Ruth, his manner dramatizing helplessness. "This man—he says that he and his family before him, and his grandfather before that, have occupied this land for over half a century. Each year, they give a portion of the harvest to the *effendi*."

"Ask him—just ask him—does he own the land, or was it not owned by the Effendi Fawsi el Khader?"

Behind her now the Polish immigrants were crowding forward, not fully understanding the problem, since the dialogues were being carried on in Hebrew and Arabic. Complaints and arguments in Polish and Yiddish grew louder around her. The Arab farmer's family added their voices to the confusion. Selim was shouting now to be heard. He turned back to Ruth, his confidence beginning to crumble.

"This man—he admits that he does not own the farm. But he says there is no place absolutely for him and his family to go. And so he will not go anywhere."

A goat protruded its head from the house, its bleat seeming to join in the general protest. Chickens squawked in the dusty heat.

"Now listen to me," Ruth said, voice strident above the din. "The owner, Fawsi el Khader, has made all the provisions for this family. It's all here in writing." She waved another document. Selim took it patiently and read aloud. He pointed at the seals, flourishing it with authority. It made no impact.

"They are all to be relocated in another area! Don't they understand?" Ruth's voice was shrill.

Selim turned back. "This man—he says that el Khader has lied certainly to you. He has made no such arrangements for them. They will not certainly leave."

Mendel Shapira was shaking her arm. Though he hadn't understood the discussion, he got the message. "What have you brought us to?" he shouted. "We had the word of the JNF that all arrangements were made. All! From what I can see here, nothing has been made. We come on a rusty, leaky ship from Poland. We land like cattle. The British count us like animals. We are treated like fugitives in camps of detention—and now you bring us to nothing! We should have remained in Poland!"

A chorus of Polish voices rose in support. Children were crying. In the din, the dust, the confusion, suddenly Ruth felt herself losing her grip. "Nobody asked you to come here," she snapped.

"God asked us."

"Then, complain to him, please. I am doing all I can." She turned back to Selim. "Tell them—tell this farmer—that I am giving him two hours to get off the land. He has to go. That is final."

The interchange of languages continued. "This man—he says it is you who have to get off the land, madame. Which he claims by right of generations of living on it. If you do not leave, his sons will bring trouble."

"Trouble? Trouble? He will find out what trouble is." Ruth placed herself on a box of supplies, calling to her ha-Shomer driver. "Yuri . . . ! Drive back to Tel Aviv. Bring the British Military Police at once! It is their responsibility to see that we take lawful possession. We will wait here until you bring them."

The ha-Shomer defender shook his head: "Mrs. Nouari, it is always better to avoid bringing in the British. We can settle this ourselves."

"Do as I say. I am in charge here." Her voice had taken on a commanding, strident tone.

He hesitated. "But if there should be trouble, I would be needed here. Mr. Nouari said I was to stay with you."

"It is more important to get the police. These farmers won't bother us once they know why you've gone," she assured him.

"And the rifle?" He looked doubtful.

"Leave it here."

Yuri took it from the car, passing it to one of the *kibbutzniks* who had come along to help construct the buildings. "Keep it out of sight unless you need it."

The young man slid the rifle into the truck. Reluctantly, Yuri climbed into the car, heading back down the road toward Jaffa.

Selim told the Arabs of the imminent arrival of the British military. The farmer spoke with his four sons, his brothers, and his brothers' sons. He turned back to Ruth and spat on the ground. Two of the younger Arabs hitched up a horse to a cart and abruptly drove off toward the foothills.

Other settlers crowded closer. "Where are *they* going? Where is everyone going?" Mendel Shapira demanded, not having understood the melange of languages.

"I fear they, too, have gone for help," Selim said. "This is most unfortunate, madame. If I may suggest—"

She stood up. "What? What do you want to suggest? That I let them throw us off the land which we have bought and paid for? This tenant is a liar! And you can tell him I said so."

"That would be unwise." Once again, Selim tried to show the farmer the papers of ownership and guarantee that the farmer's family would be relocated. At last, Selim turned back with some small look of triumph. "This man—he has admitted, madame, that the *effendi did* make arrangements. But he says that the land to which the *effendi* would send them is poor. All rocks. Nothing will grow there. And no house. He has no money to make such a move. No money for a house. No money for the fields. I suggest, madame, that there is a solution."

"Well—what is it?"

"Money."

"Are you saying, we should pay him to let us occupy this land which we have already bought and overpaid for?"

Selim shrugged. "The money that has been paid did not go to this man."

She sat down again. "Tell him he gets no money from us. He can ask the *effendi* if he wants money. We will not move until the British police arrive."

The Arab farmer listened. Then he and his family walked back to the whitewashed hovel they called home. Incredibly, all of them squeezed into the one small structure. The door was closed. Then it opened. A child raced out, grabbed the goat, and dragged it inside. Then the door closed again.

"What are they doing? What did he say?" Ruth demanded.

"This man—he said, madame, that they stay inside—where they will wait absolutely until you leave. Or the Al Fatat arrives to make you go."

Some two hours had gone by. The Polish settlers had fed the children on oranges, bread, and water. The afternoon heat beat down on them with no relief. They clustered in the shade at the side of the trucks. Some of the men had strung up one of the tents for the old ladies and children. Flies hummed around them. No sounds came from the house.

Then a dust haze was seen rolling toward them from the foothills. It held a rattle of hoofs. Six horsemen, well armed, materialized out of the yellow cloud. Behind them, some distance back, came the farm cart and the farmer's sons.

Selim rose from where he had been sitting near Ruth. His

voice shook with fear. "This is very bad, madame. These are men from Al Fatat. There is much danger. It is better we take the trucks and go now. At once. Return with the police later."

"The rifle. . . . Get the rifle!" Ruth cried.

"Most unwise," Selim insisted. "These Al Fatat are armed. And our rifle is only one. If they even see it, they will think there are more. Cause a battle."

"All right. Get all your people into the trucks, Mr. Shapira. Everyone."

"We are leaving?" he asked eagerly. Right now, a ghetto would have looked very good to him.

"No. We are not going to be driven off. Hurry up; get everyone under cover." She stepped forward with Selim to meet the arriving riders. Mendel Shapira gaped at her. This woman might be foolish, but certainly she was braver than he.

The Poles clambered back into the trucks. The three *kibbutzniks* joined Ruth and Selim.

Yassir Hammadi trotted his horse forward, flanked by Tariq and Zuliekha dressed, as always, as a man. This was exactly the opportunity Yassir had been waiting for. The time had come to create "incidents"—particularly in the countryside, Haj Amin had ordered. Although the grand mufti was ruling Jerusalem, he had not forgotten his wider ambitions. It was important to spread the word that land was being usurped. When other Arab farmers heard of it, they would strengthen their forces against these Zionist invaders.

The door of the farmer's house opened. The farmer and his family poured out to greet Yassir, babbling their cries and protests.

Yassir did not know Ruth Nouari. He saw a group of crowded trucks—a stoutish woman standing in front of them with four men. The woman appeared to be in charge.

Selim stepped forward to speak to Yassir, but further exchange of threats and ultimatums failed to break the stalemate. Yassir gave the order to drive the Zionists out.

The farmer's family joined in with clubs and stones. The horsemen spurred forward, laying about them with gun butts and whips.

"The rifle!" Ruth shouted, sorry now she had sent the

ha-Shomer guard away. One of the *kibbutzniks* rushed to get it. Yassir shot it out of his hand.

It was not his intention to kill anyone, but in the fracas that ensued several of the settlers were injured.

Ruth found herself staring up into the eyes of a mounted Arab woman dressed in man's clothes. Her surprise was cut short by the blow of a whip, which sent her reeling to the ground. She sprawled between horse's hoofs, which miraculously failed to touch her.

As she struggled to her feet, two British military trucks led by an officer in a motorcycle sidecar hooted into view, horns blasting, one siren screaming. Yassir gave an instant command to retreat. His little troop galloped back toward the hills. They were out of sight behind the first range of foothills before the police convoy drew up.

The young officer in charge jumped out of the sidecar. Lieutenant Jeremy Meredith was no special friend to the Zionists, but he was a man of consummate fairness, punctiliously attentive to duty.

Ruth pulled herself together as best she could. There was an angry welt on one cheek, and her clothes were covered with dust, but she was otherwise unhurt. She stated their case in no uncertain terms.

Meredith examined the documents carefully, perusing them with exasperating slowness, as though searching for some loophole through which to fire blame at Ruth. Now, for the first time, the Arab farmer showed fear. He stood uncertainly among his relatives, a prophet losing honor. He had tasted authority from the Turks and knew when to give up.

"I am afraid, Mrs. Nouari, that every move made by your people brings a problem." Meredith's tone was glacial. His eyes swept the haggard Poles. "I suppose that every one of these people can produce proof of legal entrance into the Mandate?"

"Of course they can! They are all from the JNF relocation center. We make a great effort to stop illegal entry. Insist on proper visas before locating any settlers."

He folded the documents, returning them to her. "How often, one dares wonder, do other of your . . . people . . . get smuggled into the country without the formalities?" His jaw muscles worked beneath the tanned face. He was a young man, confident. He made meticulous notes in a small book from his tunic breast pocket. Finally he spoke.

"It appears that your papers are in order. They compel me to enforce your claim to the land."

"What about those Arabs who attacked us?"

"It will be reported."

"Aren't you going to try to catch them?"

"We will make an official complaint . . . to the grand mufti, in Jerusalem." He turned to the farmers, addressing them in perfect Arabic. This time they made no move to resist. They went back to their house and brought out their personal belongings. Animals and baggage were loaded into farm wagons. Members of the family were helped into the British Army truck. They would be escorted to their new land. Somehow, they would have to learn to live on it.

An hour later, the pioneers stood alone on *their* new land. Yes, theirs now. Theirs to build and grow on. But no one could feel happy. A gloom and heaviness hung over all. They had won the day, but what was it they had lost?

Ruth climbed into the car beside the interpreter. She was bone weary. There seemed nothing further to say to the settlers, who watched the car out of sight before going into the house.

The hands of the clock moved Judah deeper into worry. Afternoon merged into evening, and still no sign of Ruth. She should have been back hours ago. What to do?

He walked over to the JNF office, where Sarah Schreiber was still wrestling with the accounts. Sarah, born in Russia, grown almost old at thirty-eight from years of toiling in the United States of America as a translator for a professor at N.Y.U. If there were any news, Sarah would have it.

She had. It wasn't good. A report from the British Military Police had just come in. Lieutenant Meredith had taken a patrol up to the new settlement. No details yet. If she heard first, she'd let him know. He turned to go. He didn't feel like conversation tonight.

In the early hours of the morning Judah heard the car drive up outside the small wooden house. He opened the door to see Ruth being helped out by the driver. She came up the

steps alone, disheveled, dirty. As she entered the doorway, he
saw the bruise down one side of her face.

"Ruth . . . what on earth . . . ?"

One look at Judah and she burst into tears. He brought her
into the sitting room and put a glass of brandy into her hand.
She sipped it. "What I've been through. . . . You'll never
imagine what I've been through." The angry, bitter but tri-
umphant account of trials and tribulations spilled from her
lips. She capped the story of the day's events with a description of how she had not given in an inch, held the Arabs at
bay until the arrival of the British police.

Judah listened without interruption, refilled her brandy glass.
But, to Ruth's surprise, he didn't rush to embrace her with
congratulations. "We'd better do something about that bruise"
was all he said, shepherding her into the bathroom and getting
down the medicine chest. Ruth couldn't understand it. For
some inexplicable reason, he failed to see her as a Zionist
Joan of Arc prevailing against their common enemy.

"Well, Judah. Have you nothing to say?"

"It was foolish of you to send the guard away. You could
have been killed. And I'm sorry you couldn't have settled the
problem without bringing in the British authorities, Ruth."

"I don't expect a medal . . . but I think I deserve some
sympathy. And some praise, Judah."

"Of course, my dear. You were very brave. But perhaps a
little unwise," he continued. "You should have followed
Selim's suggestion to offer compensation."

Weary as she was, Ruth's anger brought energy. "Give
them money? Bribe those lying *fellaheen* to leave? Is that
what *you* would have done? My God . . . if I had been Zosia
coming home to you now, you would have been on your
knees . . . ! But all you can say to me is . . . I was foolish!
What do I have to do . . . blow myself up . . . before you
notice I'm alive?"

"Ruth—please, that's quite unfair. . . ."

"Oh, don't tell me about your perfect Zosia. Don't think I
don't know that everything I do is compared to what *she*
would have done!"

"There is no necessity to attack Zosia. She dedicated her
whole life to this work, not just a few days. And she certainly
would have had the sense to settle things with the tenant

farmer without dragging in the British. Too many of them are looking for opportunities to prove us in the wrong.''

"Well, we weren't wrong! Even Meredith had to admit that our documents were perfectly correct.''

Judah frowned. "I know that young lieutenant. He has no love for Zionists. If only you had made an arrangement with the Arab tenant, he wouldn't have called in the Al Fatat. Now those Polish immigrants will have to become soldiers before they can even be farmers. There will be more attacks on that settlement, I can assure you. The Al Fatat will use this to stir up more trouble.''

Ruth began to sniffle. She felt belittled, insulted, and hurt by his unreasonable attitude. He put an arm around her with unexpected warmth.

"Ruth, I know you did the best you could. Everyone isn't suited for this kind of work. Sending you on such a dangerous mission was all my fault.''

"But Zosia was, of course. Suited!'' She pulled away, ran water, and began to wash her face and hands.

"Ruth, I can't talk to you if you're going to continue to bring Zosia into this. Let's talk about this band that attacked you. The woman. She could have been the one they call The Scorpion. She has gained a reputation for acts of terror. You were lucky.''

"You call it lucky?'' She patted medication onto her cheek. "I don't understand you, Judah. You always see the wrong side of things.''

"There are always two sides, Ruth. Sometimes three. For generations, those farmers have known no other home.''

"That didn't stop you from buying the land out from under their feet! This whole thing is *your* fault for believing that *effendi*—and our people are only settled on that land tonight thanks to me!'' She slammed the bathroom door behind her.

Judah walked back into the small sitting room. He poured himself a drink, sank back into a chair. His eyes fixed on a painting by a young *Yishuv*. A city of the future as it might one day look in Palestine. Buildings like the towers of the Temple, laddered to heaven with converging sunrays. How simple for the young to seize on beliefs as he once had, passed like a torch from the hand of a dead woman. Locked into a cause that was producing more trouble than hope. And now he sat in the shambles of a long marriage. Over twenty years, and he had never before tonight realized that Ruth carried a jealousy—as he carried a memory.

She came out in nightgown and robe, face set in stubborn, wounded righteousness. "All the settlers thanked me. Grateful. Crying. The old ladies kissed me on the cheek. And what do I come home to? The loving arms of my understanding husband? Always understanding the other side!"

"Ruth, we'll talk of it tomorrow."

"I don't ever want to talk about it again." She crossed the hall into Zed's empty bedroom.

"Ruth, please . . ." He started to follow her, but she stopped him.

"I'm sleeping in here tonight. I'm going back to Paris, Judah. And I don't care if I ever see this country any more."

"You'll feel better in the morning."

"Better. But not different. Don't ever ask for my help again."

Next morning, Ruth made arrangements to return on a steamer leaving from Jaffa in two days. Judah didn't go with her. It was his month in Tel Aviv.

"I'll see you in Paris soon," he told her on the quayside.

"You can do as you like. You always do anyway."

He watched Ruth being rowed out to the steamer, her full-blown figure looming at the stern behind the rowers.

In a way, it was an ending.

The marriage of Paris with April was bearing a perfect spring. The year 1927 had produced a buoyant moment in the affairs of men. But Mohamed Hammadi, facing a barrage of reporters in his hotel suite, was finding the weight of years unrelieved by the greening of the outer world.

"And how long will you remain in Paris this time, Monsieur Hammadi?"

How long did he ever stay anywhere now? He fought a drift of mind toward the boulevards, the Tuileries Gardens. If only a man could lose himself for the space of a day, step out of his skin, his pack of burdens. . . .

"That question, I think, you must ask my secretary." He smiled over toward Amy. Efficient Amy, elongated guardian of the desk against telephonic interruption. He had promised her this trip and a night out in Paris for all her good deeds. If only there were ever time.

"But, however long," he added, "for Paris one stays never long enough."

They scribbled words on their pads. Amy flashed her boss a brief tentative smile. She could be a bull dog in defense of his privacy, yet was never spoiled by those times when he needed her as a woman. Another journalist looked up from a list of prepared questions.

"You are at this moment also an adviser to President Coolidge, no?"

"I have that honor."

"Do you think his call for the Geneva Conference to limit naval armament will succeed?"

"You must ask your Foreign Minister, Monsieur Briand, that question. My guess is that France and Italy will refuse to join the U.S.A., Great Britain, and Japan. I think none of them will agree on cruiser restrictions."

"Then, there will never be, in your opinion, permanent peace?"

Mohamed glanced over at Judah, whom Amy had just admitted, and signaled him to wait for the press conference to finish.

"Peace? Not in this world," he said slowly.

"But there is a report—a rumor that our Foreign Minister will himself propose an agreement to outlaw war . . . ?"

"He already has. Frank Kellogg, the American Secretary of State, will welcome it. Some American university professors will support it—and there could even be a great effort to expand it to include all nations. Peace pacts are very popular in an election year in Washington."

Jacqueline. . . . What sort of pact would he make with her this year, or any other? There was gossip in New York that she was pursuing another college boy. An image flashed to mind. A photograph last autumn. Jacqueline in the Princeton grandstand surrounded by racoon-skin coats and silver flasks. Perhaps next she'd be taking up the ukulele. Well, nobody grew old gracefully any more.

He forced himself back to the question being asked: "Then, you believe President Coolidge will win again?"

"Why not? If he chooses to run."

"One final question: With your Washington contacts, why have you yourself never considered entering politics there?"

Mohamed smiled. "I do not think it is yet the time for us Arabs to build a mosque on the Potomac. And now—if you will forgive me. . . ." He gestured toward his crowded hotel desk.

Amy rose crisply, moving to guide them out of the room.

Judah came to join Mohamed, as he sank back and stretched, exhaling softly. He was wearing pearl gray spats below the cuffs of striped trousers, and a pearl gray cravat. And he looked exhausted. Judah shook his hand.

"So they are trying to make Mohamed into a prophet?"

"It's always easier to be wise about other people's problems."

"By the last dividend statement, you are not doing too badly with our own."

Amy reentered and took up two bulging, heavily engraved morocco portfolios. "If you won't be needing me for a while, I can get these letters typed, sir."

"By all means, Miss Archer."

Judah had not missed the almost too ostentatious formality in the exchange. It told him what he already knew. They slept together when it was convenient. Well, he, too, had his bouts of illicit joy in Tel Aviv. Part of the trappings of success in business. All appetites easily fulfilled.

"Help yourself to coffee or a drink."

"Thanks." Judah chose coffee. "I'm still surprised you decided not to open the house."

"Jacqueline's in New York with Françoise, and Maurice has decided to share an apartment with your Abe. . . . So why should I wish to rattle about in all those rooms alone? Anyway, I shall have to leave in a week." Mohamed surveyed the spacious elegance of his suite in the Ritz. Louis Quinze, which might even be real. Engravings of shepherdesses being seduced without upsetting a strand of their high, powdered Marie Antoinette coiffures. An accomplishment that Jacqueline, too, would have acquired, no doubt. He turned back to Judah. "How are our boys doing? Have you been over to the Bank since we launched them?"

Judah laughed. "Better than we did. Under Liebermann the Terrible, as we used to call him. Poor old Baron. He never realized his ambition of being elected Pope. I understand he

heads the Catholic community in Basel, however. And goes
South whenever there's a Zionist Congress. The wonder is he
never changed his name.''

"He had to leave something unchanged.'' They smiled as
the image of the old convert whisked through mind.

"I agree with you. Our sons will do better here than we
did,'' Mohamed said. ''Maurice is ready for responsibility.
Twenty-three. Harvard Business School behind him. A taste
for—I'm not sure what. Extravagance, I suppose.''

Judah brought his coffee cup over by his friend. ''So has
Abe. He collects more treasures than Bernard Berenson. Noth-
ing like we were, really. Never gets into trouble with girls. . . .
Sober. Upright. And, I dare say it . . . just a bit stuffy.''

"Should make an ideal banker.'' Mohamed picked up a
steel-nibbed ostrich-plume pen from the small desk. He
smoothed it gracefully between his fingers. ''How old is Abe
now? Twenty?''

Judah nodded. He had spent a trying afternoon the day
before with his son. Being shepherded through some of the
smaller art galleries and exhibitions. They had ended up in
Abe's new apartment with a stack of paintings.

"You shall have to learn to rely on my artistic judgment,
Father.'' (How pompous the young could be!) ''I can assure
you that one of the most substantial forms of investment for
the future will be in collecting art.''

"A Goya, maybe. Or a Rembrandt. But *these*, Abe?''

Abe drew himself up, adjusting the stickpin in his cravat.
"I have deliberately selected some of the best of the lesser
known Jewish painters for you, Father, to hang in your Tel
Aviv bank. This one, Marc Chagall, is already highly thought
of. Chaim Soutine is not to everyone's taste, but his work is
important. Also Modigliani. Poor fellow died seven years
ago, penniless. Now his work is going up like stock.''

Judah stared at the painting, of a girl with raisin eyes and a
long neck. ''I think I prefer stock.'' Still, he didn't wish to
discourage his son's initiative so early in his career. The
paintings were duly crated and shipped. Maybe he would
even get used to them someday. Or maybe the ship would
sink.

Judah brought his attention back to Mohamed. ''By the
way, I talked to Zed about going with you to the New York
office.''

"And?"

"She can hardly wait. I told her if she listened to every word you say, she'll become the first female tycoon."

"Allah preserve her. But I'll do my best. You know that."

"I know. Zed could be useful to the Company. She has, aside from a diploma (which, as you recall, the Sorbonne doesn't just pass out)—strength of character. More, I think, at times, than her brother. Or her father. And the tenacity of her mother."

"She has something else important. Youth."

"I guess we could both use a pinch of that in our thinking."

Mohamed tossed the pen like a feathered javelin to land on the desk. It was as though he were trying to throw off some weight. "Last night, I happened to wander into the Ritz Bar. Oh, not to drink. I've given that up completely. I don't really know why I went in. It's a monkey house. Writers. American tourists. Balkan bandits of finance. British noble ladies trying to act like whores. Whores trying to act like ladies. The zoo of Europe, where the animals feed on each other. And everyone is so infernally young. I think I wanted to see if I could still feel any attachment to . . . well, Paris. I mean the way we used to feel . . . when we were a pair of foreign students. I just have stopped feeling anything much about anything. Does it show . . . this surprising indifference?"

"It didn't at Tel Hai."

"Seven years. Not so lean years, either. Yes, that's a feeling I can still recall. We were alive that night. Why should a person feel more alive when death is around?"

"Poor old Mohamed. I'll take you up to the Bal Tabarin tonight. We'll watch the pretty dancers kick up their long legs. Then go around to the Jockey Club—"

"Like a pair of rich tourists, paying too much for bad champagne."

"Which you won't drink anyway."

"True. Will Ruth let you out?"

"Matter of fact, she barely lets me in."

"Poor old Judah."

"Well, not exactly. I feel a bit younger . . . in Palestine."

"Still dedicated."

"Dedicated? I don't really know. Maybe it's just habit. Happiness is a curious thing. You never know when it can suddenly turn up. Or suddenly get lost. The truth is I can hardly wait to get back to Tel Aviv.''

"And I to New York.''

The taxi bore them to the summit of Montmartre. At its top, the Sacré Coeur presided in white stillness, a jewel of tranquillity above the seething hubbub of night Paris.

"I wonder what our sons are up to,'' Judah said.

"Planning the financial future of Europe, I expect.''

"I wonder what made them so different from us?''

How different, neither man could have guessed. The fledgling bankers were at that moment giving themselves a very special launching party to which they had carefully avoided inviting their fathers.

"Such nice young men. Such interesting people. Where does Abe meet them all? I wonder.''

Praise from the lips of Ruth, spoken with a kind of gratitude to practically anyone who paused to listen. As the mother of one of the hosts, she had found a potential audience. The new apartment being shared by Maurice Hammadi and her son, Abe, was crowded. Afloat in a cloud of smoke, talk, and sound. The chime of clinking crystal mixed with the discord of a curious piano. Nothing like the Bechstein Ruth still occasionally played on.

Abe introduced her to a bull-like young Romanian, Wishnagrodski. She had watched his arrival with amazement. He entered with a pushcart bearing a three-keyboard instrument of his own invention. On it he rendered his single composition, a dissonant fugue of unearthly sound. He paused to explain to Ruth:

"In this movement, I am under the earth. The sound is from a city sunk under the water. It is the sound of the lost Atlantis.'' His eyes narrowed to dreamy slits as he played on.

"Very moving,'' Ruth replied, not knowing what else to say. Abe guided her on through a hectic upbeat of preposterous laughter.

"I don't believe it. He painted them gold?''

"*She* did, darling.''

Abe planted her with two attentive young men and refilled her champagne glass. "Oh, no, Abe,'' she protested. Ruth barely touched a drop of anything but sacramental wine on the Sabbath.

"Tonight's an occasion, Mother.''

Abe drifted lightly away to introduce Maurice from group to group. Maurice, in a snow-white burnoose contrasted with darkening red hair, bright blue eyes, and skin like a well-smoked meerschaum. Abe's loose-fitting white suit seemed a bit startling to Ruth. He had topped it with a crimson scarf knotted at the throat of a white silk shirt. A black cigarette wisped perfumed smoke into the high-ceilinged room, once an artist's studio. Well, young men liked to strike a pose. Why not? Their apartment on the Île Saint-Louis, though still sparsely furnished, revealed a catholic taste in art and people.

Abe and Maurice drifted like mannered lords from group to group. Every so often, Abe would return to Ruth's side and guide her to yet another collection of types totally unfamiliar to her. A wild-haired man who introduced himself as a poet, boasted of his friendship with somebody called Francis Picabia.

"Is he somebody important?" Ruth said.

"Almost God, madame. I quote from his *Dada Manifesto:* 'Art is dearer than sausages, dearer than women, dearer than anything. Art is a pharmaceutical product for idiots!' "

Ruth nodded blankly and turned away quickly, almost falling over a White Russian refugee sculptor kneeling at the feet of an American film producer's amber-haired wife.

"Bessie, I will beatify your husband in white marble," the sculptor insisted.

"Well, Boris, he's actually more interested in racing cars, I'm afraid."

A Japanese artist arrived with his Parisienne wife, with a housewarming gift to his hosts. A large watercolor of a smiling cat. Everyone clustered around it with appreciation.

"Do you like it, Mother?"

She shrugged. "Personally, I prefer dogs."

"I'll tell Foujita."

This was the Paris of Hemingway, James Joyce, and André Lhote. Of F. Scott Fitzgerald and the flowering of the Left Bank, of Le Dôme and La Coupole—the two cafés where the painters and writers gathered. To Maurice and Abe it was the best of times in the best of places. But they couldn't compare it to the Paris of their fathers' youth.

Ruth sipped her champagne, feeling just a bit tiddly. She beamed at a striking young man in dinner jacket of immaculate cut. "I am the mother of Abe Nouari. The one over there in the white suit. He and Maurice are now in their fathers' Company bank. Hammadi-Nouari.''

"I would never have guessed, madame. I thought they were art dealers.'' The voice behind the cigar was husky but light.

"And what do you do?''

"I exist. One can only be free through full consciousness of one's illogical place in a meaningless universe.''

"Is that Dada?'' Ruth asked.

"Existentialism, madame.''

Ruth nodded knowingly. She would tell Judah—if they ever spoke again—that in their son's artistic circles everyone had been interested in her opinions and ideas. Dada and existentialism. "Judah has never heard of such things,'' she assured herself, moving on in search of Abe.

"I really must leave now, dear.''

"So soon, Mother? You're a night owl, everyone knows that.''

"He loves to tease me,'' she confided to Maurice.

"I hope you had a good time, Aunt Ruth.'' Maurice had called her that since he was a small boy.

"Oh, yes. Such nice young people. But . . .'' She glanced around for a final check, "why no businessmen?''

"We get enough of those at the bank. One last glass of champagne?'' She shook her head. Maurice had his mother's good looks, a softness and graceful charm. And such good manners. The girls who got these two young men would be fortunate. Not that she could think of any young woman good enough for her son.

"What a pity Zeb had to miss your housewarming,'' she told Maurice. "But it was very kind of your father to accompany her on the Île de France.''

"She'll love New York, Aunt Ruth.''

Ruth sighed. "And tonight she would have met such nice young men. Like the one I was talking to just now. That thin one in the dinner jacket. We were discussing existen—er . . . Dada.''

Abe chuckled. "That young man is a girl, Mother.''

"Oh . . . ? Dressed in a man's suit? With slicked-back hair and flat . . . ?'' She indicated the appropriate area of her own generous front. "Did she—er—come from a costume ball, maybe?''

"In a way."

"One thing before I go, I must tell you. Not that I wish to interfere, but you really must think about appearances. You don't mind if I am candid?"

A faint flush touched Abe's cheek, but he remained composed. "Yes, Mother?"

"The pictures on the walls. . . ."

The two young men exchanged a glance of relief. "You don't like them?"

She shrugged. "How do I know? They could be very fine pictures, but you've hung them all crooked, every one. A banker should hang his pictures straight."

The two men laughed. "A passing fad, Mother."

"Fad? Is that something like a Dada?"

"You see, Mother," Abe explained carefully, "everyone hangs their pictures straight. So hanging them crooked makes people bother to notice them."

She nodded uncertainly. "Well! So much I'm learning tonight."

"You're right, Aunt Ruth; it is a touch of Dada. Provocation. Divorce from the tradition into which Cubism and Futurism have sunk." Maurice took on an authoritative tone.

"And hanging pictures crooked does all that? Imagine! And does it have anything to do with banking?"

"Actually a great deal, Mother. Some of our most important customers are diverting capital from stocks and shares into art, as an investment. The bank has decided to back certain dealers in making important purchases."

"And your father—what does he think of all this . . . fad?"

"He isn't exactly enthusiastic, but he has agreed to be advised by me in these matters," Abe conceded. "Of course, he has so many other causes that take up his time. I don't expect he'll ever learn much about art."

"How well I know!" Ruth kissed the two good-bye. Abe showed her out to her limousine. When he returned to the party, Maurice tucked a tall glass of milky Pernod into his hand.

"Your parents don't get along any better than mine, do they?"

Abe shook his head. "Not so you would notice. But then, I see very little of my father."

"You'll see more of him now that he's become our guide and mentor into the world of banking." Maurice put an arm through his friend's, leading him back to the guests. "God, I dread seeing *my* mother these days. I wish she were like yours. Aunt Ruth is comfortable."

Abe threw him a sympathetic look. "Your mother has suffered from a terrible illness."

"I wonder. She seems to enjoy it, a lot of the time. I think the reason my father works so hard is not to notice what's happening." Maurice loved Mohamed dearly, and sensed keenly his father's loneliness. Admired, powerful, brilliant, always on the move, alone. Unable, it seemed, to find for himself personal happiness.

"I wonder when it all began to go wrong," Abe said.

"After the honeymoon, no doubt. I shall never marry."

"Nor I," Abe echoed. He brightened. "I think I shall teach our new houseboy how to make a French 75. He did rather well with the pink lady."

"If you get sick, don't call me," Maurice said, turning toward the best-dressed woman in the room—who happened to be a man.

The city put out its tongue of land to meet the breakers, lapping the freshness of the sea. It was early morning when his ship dropped anchor. As always, Judah could almost smell Haifa before he could see it. It sprawled in the bay's curve beneath the contour of low, dry slopes. Coastal humidity lay limp as a sultry shroud. So many departures and arrivals. Yet, light-years away in the cool clarity of Paris, it was always easy for Judah to forget the perverse climate of his homeland.

Ashore at last, jacket slung across one shoulder, he moved swiftly through customs. Here, they knew him by sight and name. Never bothered to look into his luggage any more. The port was hectic with the loading of ships—grain from the fertile plain of Horan, in Syria. Judah took up his two satchels, hailing a taxi into the old town of low-slung white-washed buildings. For centuries, Haifa had been a major center for Mecca-bound pilgrims. Now, as ever, it was teeming, clamorous, alive.

As the driver turned away from the seafront, Judah spotted a familiar figure emerging from the old Jewish Quarter, Harat al-Yahud. Ordering the driver to wait, he jumped out and hurried after the disappearing form.

"Ben . . . !"

His brother rounded a corner into a side street, Judah after him. "Ben!" he called again through the jostle of people.

Ben turned with a look of sharp distress. The same look Judah remembered seeing when they were small; the look that said something wasn't going quite as Ben expected.

The screen of mind caught the flash of a long-ago day. Ben, five; he, eleven. He'd come into his little brother's room to find Ben perched precariously on a thick stack of books piled high on a wooden chair. Ben had been trying to reach the top shelf of the cupboard.

"What are you doing on that chair, Ben?" Judah had demanded.

But his brother seemed unable to answer. Instead he scrambled down, sobbing softly, pointing to the shelf. Judah had climbed up to find a small cigar box. Ben watched in fascinated horror as his older brother opened it. Inside was the black, shriveled corpse of a frog. Ben, it seemed, had put the frog there weeks before to keep it as a secret pet. Then forgot it. The poor creature had simply mummified from starvation.

"What are you doing in Haifa, Ben?" Judah could hear through his own tone the same remembered demand.

"*Kibbutz* business," Ben said. "We're expecting some supplies to arrive today."

"Then, I must have come on the same ship as your supplies. I've got a taxi waiting. We'll find a coffeehouse. Have some breakfast, then check on your cargo. What a stroke of luck running into you here of all places, Ben."

For some reason, Ben acted as though the chance encounter was ill-timed. "Sorry, Judah. I can't go with you. I'm on my way to meet Bernard."

"Splendid. I'm just about to arrange for a car and driver to take me down to Tel Aviv. I can give you both a lift south. Drop you off at the *kibbutz*."

Ben's face tightened. "Afraid we'll be carrying too much equipment. Besides, we have to make a stop. Another *kibbutz*, near Acre. Bring some settlers back to Rasnet el Deir."

"Well, then, I'm in no hurry, Ben. Why don't I go with you? I could make a report for the JNF. Which settlement is it?"

"Judah, try to understand: we have things to do." Ben sounded almost angry. "Business that doesn't in any way involve you. I'm sorry, but we'll have to get together another time."

Judah nodded with some disappointment. "I'm sorry too. Maybe you'll tell me about it sometime."

Ben's face seemed veiled as though almost afraid his thoughts might show. "Yes. I'll do that." He embraced his brother quickly, saying good-bye, and hurried off. Judah called after him.

"Say hello to Bernard!" He stood for a moment looking after his brother. It was unlike Ben not even to inquire about the family. But then, everything in Ben's manner was unlike him today. Judah returned to his taxi and woke up the sleepy Greek behind the wheel. He put Ben out of his mind. After all, he was a little too old for Judah to play the big brother.

It was late evening when Judah reached Tel Aviv. The driver took him directly to his house. He stayed only long enough to leave his luggage and wash off the dry desert dust. Too late to see Lily Kessler? Of course not. Never too late.

But, at her apartment, his ring brought no answer. Judah glanced at his watch. Nearly midnight. He let himself in with his own key.

The sitting room was dark. He switched on a lamp and went into the bedroom. Bed untouched. He came back, feeling a hollow sense of disappointment. With a sigh of exhaustion, he sank into a chair. Where on earth could she be at this hour? He picked up one of her silver enamel cigarette cases. An overripe woman being kissed by a German officer. It didn't make him feel any better. In Paris he had missed Lily more than he could have imagined. Damn it! He was getting to need her. How long had it been? Nearly two years since they had become lovers. And every moment of their shared sensual world was like a photo in a secret album.

Her key in the lock awakened him. Lily froze in the doorway, her face a powdered mask of surprise. "So . . . you are back. You should have let me know when you would be coming, my darling Judah."

"Why?" he asked sharply. "So I wouldn't know how late you stay out? Where have you been, Lily? Who is he?" He was angry with himself more than with her, for the way he felt.

Lily turned away coolly, poured herself a brandy. "Would you like a drink, Judah? You must be tired. I can always tell when you are tired." Her husky voice reproving by its tonelessness.

"Lily. . . ." He rose, suddenly contrite. "I'm sorry. Of course you have a perfect right to go where you like."

She turned back. "So! Then—I shall tell you where I have been. To see an old friend of my father's. He is here with his wife, making a trip through Palestine. They are at the Herzl Hotel. Their name is Knerdler. If you wish to check up on me—please!" She took up the telephone, offering it to him.

He put the phone back on the table and took her in his arms. "Forgive me, Lily. I'm getting to be as bad as a husband. But you're so beautiful, how could any man keep his eyes off you? Naturally I'm jealous." He kissed her tenderly. She ran her tongue along his upper lip. The touch was sensual, and he drew her to him more tightly.

"Come to bed," she commanded. "I like to make love to you when you are jealous."

She changed into a pale silk nightdress and came back into the bedroom. The nightdress was embroidered around the waist with tiny lavender flowers and deep-set lace. Judah had brought it from Paris on his last trip. It was perhaps too feminine for Lily, who preferred Chinese pajamas. After making love, she would move around the bedroom looking for a cigarette in a pajama top, bare longer-than-long legs flattered by high-heeled marabou mules.

Now she came into the bed beside Judah.

"Drop your shoulder straps," he said.

She looked at him with a curious smile and obeyed. He opened his hand. "For you, from Monsieur Cartier." He fastened a thin gold chain around her neck. Suspended from it was one freshwater pearl in the shape of a tear. It fell between her breasts, glowing against the extraordinary whiteness of her skin.

"*Wunderbar* . . ." she breathed. "*Schön.*"

He kissed the dark points of her nipples. Her nakedness

was like a Canova marble, curved, hard, gleaming. "Oh, Lily, you have brought me so much happiness. With you I can feel again. I know I'm alive."

"But you do not *own* me, Judah. I belong to you because I wish it—not because I must."

He moved to enter the warmth of total surrender, the explosion of desire. He had learned to need her, and he could think no farther than that need.

Twenty-one _____

"CAN anyone overhear our conversation, Mr. Nouari?"
Sarah Schreiber glanced around Judah's office at the Tel Aviv
bank, her normally open, friendly countenance disquieted by
deep concern.

"Not unless the walls actually *do* have ears, Miss Schreiber."

"British Military Intelligence have ears everywhere. You
know something? I don't even trust Zionist Headquarters any
more."

Judah had been back about three weeks when Sarah paid
him this unexpected visit. She interrupted him in the midst of
hanging the paintings Abe had shipped from Paris. Six of
them had arrived that morning, to be uncrated and invade his
office. Now, like criminals in a lineup, they awaited judge-
ment as to where or whether they should be hung.

For Judah, this picture-hanging dilemma echoed a similar
moment when he had moved into his first office in the Paris
bank. Hanging the portraits of Grandfather Abraham, Great-
uncle Jacob, and his father, David. He had been no older than
Abe was now. That was the morning Zosia had entered his
office and his life.

Sarah Schreiber recaptured his attention. He knew her to be
a direct person, even at times blunt. A woman without conceit in manner or dress. Her habitual uniform was a cotton
shirt and skirt. She spoke with a marked American accent and
wore no makeup or ever "did anything" (as Ruth used to
say) with her mouse-brown hair other than crop it short and
let it curl where it might. She was no beauty, but she exuded
inner warmth and intelligence. Judah had always liked Sarah
and had worked with her occasionally over the years at

Zionist Headquarters, with growing respect for her opinions. Yet he was still on formal terms with her.

"Is it something that couldn't wait, Miss Schreiber? I'll be at the JNF board meeting next week."

"This *can't* wait. While you were in Paris, we had a visit—more of a warning, really—from Colonel Richard Meinertszgarten. You know him?"

"Oh, yes," Judah recalled. "I met him when he was a political officer on Allenby's staff. An interesting man. Started as a rabid anti-Semite, you know. Now he's grown quite friendly to our cause."

"That may be true, Mr. Nouari. But it is still the Colonel's job to ensure strict adherence to British quotas. He accuses us and the Haganah of smuggling illegal immigrants into the country."

"That is a serious charge. Is there any truth to it?"

"Mr. Nouari, if ever we are seen to be involved in illegal acts against the Mandate, it will give the British the perfect excuse to take away the few privileges Dr. Weizmann has managed to win."

He knew she was right, and he also knew she was keeping something back. "You haven't really answered my question. Is there any truth in their claim?"

"Truth . . . ?" She lowered her voice. "We *know* the Haganah are continuing to help immigrants into the country. To us this isn't smuggling and it isn't news. These people are mostly Jews from the Crimea—delivered by Lebanese sailors who provide transport at a handsome price. Four days they travel on a rough sea in a small boat, to arrive on a lonely beach—seasick, penniless, and confused. Haganah men meet them, slip them into one of the settlements by night, dress them to look like the other farmers. Within a few days they blend into the background. They're safe. Then they're moved on to another settlement. And maybe after that, still another, until how they entered the country is forgotten by even themselves."

"I wish you weren't telling me this, Miss Schreiber," Judah said. "Of course, I was aware of illegal immigration. But I hadn't realized it was such an open secret."

She pierced him with a hard glance. "You want to stick your head in the sand, Mr. Nouari?"

Judah frowned. "There are some things . . . that are better for me not to know."

"The problem is more serious yet—" Sarah Schreiber broke off instantly as footsteps and a light tap on his door brought Lily bearing a folder. Lily scarcely glanced at her.

"The new loan accounts, Mr Nouari. I thought you'd wish to approve them yourself." Lily paused, taking in the row of paintings. "Interesting, Mr. Nouari. Your taste is to be admired."

"My son's taste. Perhaps you'll help me decide where to place them later?" Their eyes made a rendezvous.

"With pleasure. I'll come back to your office when I finish my next meeting." Lily closed the door behind her.

"Now then, Miss Schreiber . . . ? You were telling me that the *kibbutzim* are being used as way stations."

She nodded. "What are we supposed to do—report them? No, Mr. Nouari, we must turn a blind eye. But we must also see that they are not caught. That could be disagreeable for everyone. We can't let Haganah activities reflect on Zionist Headquarters."

"I'm a fund raiser, Miss Schreiber. Why, exactly, have you brought this problem to me?"

"We have promised Colonel Meinertszgarten to make a thorough investigation. We have told him that if it is true— which we have strongly denied—we shall use our best endeavors to put a stop to it ourselves."

"You want me to speak to Meinertszgarten, is that it?"

"No, Mr. Nouari." She gave him one of her special, straight-in-the-eye looks. "We have every good reason to believe that the underground road starts in the coves near Haifa and ends in the *kibbutz* of Rasnet el Deir. Some of your most *personal* friends—relatives—are involved. Do I need to say more?"

His heart sank. "No, Sarah. . . . You don't. Thank you for warning me."

Judah didn't get around to hanging pictures that day. He told Lily he was driving up to see his brother, and left the office after lunch.

At Rasnet el Deir he found Anneliese in charge of the nursery. Ben was away on business, she said. It was obvious she didn't want to be questioned. Judah glanced at the group of children playing in the enclosure. "Which one is my niece?"

Anneliese's face brightened. She picked up a sturdy little girl in pink overalls with a chubby face and blonde wisps of curl. "Rebecca is now two, Judah. *Bubele,* say hello to your uncle." Rebecca obeyed unenthusiastically, wriggling to be set down. "And the little boy in the green overalls—" Anneliese pointed to a robust five-year-old. "That is Bernard and Naomi's son, Solly. And over there in the playpen, their daughter, Ruchel." The tot bounced on the bars sectioning off that portion of play yard.

"Quite a harvest of healthy new relatives."

"The outdoor life. It would be good for you, too, Judah. You look a bit tired."

"And Ben—how is he looking these days?"

"Ben is fine, as always."

"I saw him in Haifa, you know. Is that where he is now?" She hesitated. "He'll be back next week."

"Anneliese, please tell me: is Ben involved in something he shouldn't be?"

Anneliese turned angry eyes on her brother-in-law. *"Shouldn't be,* Judah? You should know your brother better than that. Whatever Ben does is right."

"Like the business that takes him and Bernard away so often? Would it have anything to do with immigrants?"

"If you have more questions, ask Ben yourself." Anneliese turned away. "I am, as you can see, very busy now, Judah. I must give these children their lessons."

Judah kissed her. Ben was lucky to have married such devotion. "All right, Anneliese. I'll come up to see you again when Ben returns."

He left her and went in search of Naomi. He found her with a group of workers out in the fields. She took time off to join Judah, offering him a glass of tea from a table set up in the shade of a clump of trees. She patted her damp brow with a handkerchief, smiling with the inner satisfaction that comes from a labor of love.

Naomi had changed. Before, one might have called her pretty. Now she had real beauty, radiating from within. She seemed enhanced, animated, intensified.

"I saw the children. Solly and Ruchel—a little doll. How old is she now?"

Naomi smiled mother's pride. "One year and two months. Already she wraps Bernard around her little finger."

Judah looked past her to where the settlers were plowing long furrows. "There seem to be quite a few new *chalutzim* in the settlement."

Naomi nodded. "They've moved down from another *kibbutz*, in the North."

"Why?"

"The Kibbutz Artzi policy. To help new settlers become more familiar with all parts of Palestine. It strengthens the pioneer role, and builds the communal spirit, rather than personal aims."

"Where are these settlers from?"

"Russians mostly—from the Crimea."

"Illegal immigrants. It's the Haganah who keeps shuffling them, isn't it? And Ben and Bernard are part of it."

She flashed sudden anger. "You're too soft, cousin Judah! You think a homeland can be built only with money. Don't you realize that every time there is a major Arab riot anywhere in Palestine, the British cut off *all* immigration?"

"Yes, of course I do. But they only close it temporarily, Naomi."

"You think the Arabs don't know that? Don't use it? Cause enough riots and the British will stop the Jews completely! Think how many of our people are prevented from coming here—every time the quota is closed. And do they make up for it in the next quotas? Never!"

A swirl of dust blew up around her skirts. Then the wind moved on. The heat of the afternoon sent dancing waves, visible above the newly turned earth. How many people would find this hard land better than the one they left behind? Judah wondered. And yet they fought to get here. Fought, when they got here, for mere survival.

"We must live by the laws of the Mandate, Naomi, if we are to live at all. The Balfour Declaration was only a first step. We must move slowly."

"Do nothing, you mean? Sit back and wait for Arab hearts to soften and British minds to change? Thank God your brother and Bernard do not agree with you." She looked around. "You will not find one here who does. We will not let the numbers of immigrants grow smaller month by month until this *kibbutz* and all the others fade away."

"Where are Bernard and Ben?"

"Opening a door." She looked at him defiantly. He patted her hand.

"Tell them I must talk to them as soon as they get back."

Her face softened. "You mean well, Judah, but times are changing, and you haven't changed with them. Ben and Bernard are tough. And resolute. They drew their strength from the land."

"Maybe you're right, but deliver my message anyway."

He kissed her good-bye and stood watching as she returned to work in the field. How proud Solomon would have been of this daughter!

"Your brother, how is he?" Lily finally asked. If she had been upset by their canceled dinner date, she didn't show it. That was one of the wonderful things about Lily. Perhaps it was because she wasn't a wife.

"Not there."

"You did not find him?"

"No." Judah had arrived at Lily's apartment after ten. She had a little supper waiting for him, as though confident he would appear. "I know you never eat . . ." she had told him, "unless somebody places the food in front of you where you cannot escape." He ate as much as he could. It postponed coversation. Lily brought the matter up again.

"Do I not recall that you told me you saw Ben last month in Haifa?"

"Yes. Why?"

"He does not seem to spend much time at the *kibbutz* with his wife."

Judah pushed away the half-eaten food. Chicken and noodles. "I think I'd better go, Lily. I'm not good company tonight."

"Come to bed—and then we shall see how good."

She came around, sliding into his lap; kissed him, then drew back with a sharp look of inspection.

"You are still *in* there—I can tell! Hiding somewhere behind your eyes, which are troubled." She kissed them, her hand trailing along his thigh.

He sighed. "All right, Lily. You win." He let her lead him into the bedroom.

But the gratification of desire did not dull Judah's sense of worry. Lily leaned back on the rounded tips of elbows, studying his thin, serious face. One finger traced the silvering threads at his temple.

"What is making your hair gray tonight? Is it Lily? Are you growing tired of me, my lover?"

He drew her face to him, kissing her gently. "Not *you*, Lily. Never you."

"Is it Ben? His marriage does not go well? Or perhaps, like Nathan, he is also tired of the *kibbutz* life."

"Ben loves the *kibbutz*— and Anneliese."

She teased a hand down his still firm stomach.

He caught it in his, drawing her fingers to his lips.

"Then, what is the matter with Ben?"

"He's got himself involved with something he shouldn't. I suspected it when I saw him in Haifa last month."

"Maybe, like his brother, he keeps a mistress hidden away." She nuzzled her head against his chest. "A little Haifa hussy." She laughed lightly.

"This is serious, Lily."

"Is he robbing banks? Smuggling jewels?"

"There are other things to smuggle."

"Into Haifa? The customs there are very strict."

"There are a dozen small coves along that bay."

"So that is why you think he goes there?" She sat up, letting the bedclothes slip from her body. "Surely not immigrants, Judah? Ben would not be such a fool. Put it out of your mind."

"I can't. I'm damned certain I'm right. Certain he's up there now—bringing in more poor souls from the Crimea. God knows, I have sympathy for them. But this is just not the way. If only I knew what to say to Ben to stop him."

"When you were boys together, could you stop him from dangerous games?" She crossed the room, picking up a red silk kimono. It lay like a flame on her white skin. She tied the cord in a single loop. "Even should you wish to stop him, I think you would not succeed." She came back to sit on the bed. "So now, my darling, you must go home and for tonight forget about Ben. Dream of your Lily instead." They kissed.

"I would insist tonight you stay here with me—but I know, as always, you would refuse. So. . . ."

Judah got up, dressing slowly. "Ben has a wife and child. He's too old for these games. Even if he doesn't listen to a word, I intend to tell him."

"What a wonderful brother you are!"

Through the window, Lily watched Judah down the street until he'd turned the corner. She glanced at her watch. Two-thirty. She dressed quickly, throwing a jacket over her shoulders.

Once out in the street, Lily moved purposefully through the little city that was sleeping so quietly.

The last painting was finally hung in its place. "I still can't feel certain which side is meant to be up," Judah said. The blue horse was flying hoofs skyward above the floating bride trailing veil and flowers like a Jewish Ophelia ascending to heaven.

"Certainly by the signature you can tell," Lily insisted.

"How do we know he didn't sign upside down too?" Judah surveyed the splashes of color interrupting the white space of his office wall. He liked them no better.

Lily laughed. "An artist may not wish to understand his painting, but he will wish to read his name."

The phone bell cut through. Judah picked up the shiny black instrument, lifting the receiver to his ear. It was Nathan. For once his voice was flat, humorless, and to the point. "Judah—can you come over to the restaurant?"

"Now?" Judah asked.

"Yes. This minute."

"If it's that important, of course, Nathan."

"It is." Nathan rung off. With a sense of foreboding, Judah replaced the receiver.

"Something is troubling Nathan?" Lily asked.

"He sounded upset. I'd better go over." Judah picked up his jacket and started out.

"Will I see you later?" she asked.

He smiled, kissing her on the cheek. "You couldn't keep me away."

Lily watched him leave, then returned to her own office.

For a while she sat at her desk. Then, finally, she picked up the telephone to make a very private call.

The restaurant was nearly deserted, except for three men in the corner hunched over coffee and dominos. Nathan signaled Judah into the kitchen.

He followed his cousin past the gleaming stove and immaculate cooking utensils, a dishwasher scrubbing the sink, and a cook stirring a pot. Nathan led Judah down into the wine cellar.

At the foot of the steps, Nathan paused, facing his cousin. "I'm afraid it's bad news about Ben. . . ."

Judah felt the breath go out of him.

"Your brother was on a mission for the Haganah. With Bernard and Jonathan."

"Smuggling immigrants?"

Nathan nodded. "He thought you didn't know."

"Were they captured?"

"Ambushed by a British patrol. The soldiers ordered them to halt. Naturally, they ran. Bernard and my brother managed to escape with some of the immigrants."

"And Ben? They captured Ben?"

"He's dead, Judah. Shot."

Judah leaned against a wine cask. The sticky sweet smell of the young wine was almost suffocating. "Why did it have to be Ben . . . ?"

Nathan uncorked a bottle of brandy, handing it to Judah. "Drink. Get hold of yourself." Judah obeyed. "There is no time for grieving now. The police haven't identified his body yet. When they do, and you are informed by the authorities, you must know nothing. Anneliese . . . she hasn't been told yet."

Judah swallowed the burning liquor. It was harsh in his throat. "Bernard and Jonathan—where are they?"

Nathan dragged back a heavy hinged wine rack that reached almost to the ceiling. Behind it was a door, which he opened. Inside were six cots and two figures sprawled in the sleep of exhaustion.

"Judah's here," Nathan said softly.

Bernard sat up, face stubbled, haggard. He pulled on his trousers. Behind him Jonathan stirred, then jumped to his feet.

"Judah."

Bernard came out, putting a hand on Judah's shoulder. "What the hell is there to say? Ben—he was the bravest."

Jonathan put his arms around Judah. "There was no point in going back for him. He was shot through the head."

"He stayed behind trying to cover us, so we could get the immigrants out," Bernard said. "But they caught most of them anyway. They'll be sent back to God knows where. Judah, Ben was a real leader. He inspired us all."

"But don't weep for him. This was the life Ben wanted."

"And Anneliese?" Judah asked. "Did she want it too?"

"Anneliese knew the danger. She accepted it. Just as Naomi would. It's part of what we are living for. Maybe the only thing that makes any sense," Bernard told him.

Jonathan pulled on his clothes. "We had better get back to Rasnet el Deir. They will be coming up there to ask questions—if they identify the body."

Bernard paused. "Somebody talked, Judah. We're sure of that. The patrols were everywhere. It was always safe as houses before. This time they were waiting for us!"

Jonathan nodded. "Now we'll have to find another route."

Judah scarcely heard them. All he could think of was Ben. Brave, stubborn Ben. How he would miss him.

It wasn't until two days later that the police finally came to see Judah. He pretended to be properly shocked, grief stricken. Ben's body was brought back to the *kibbutz* for the funeral. Rabbi Horovitz came down from Safad to officiate. He had married Ben; he would bury him. Their father, David, arrived from Jerusalem. For several days, the British police questioned everyone in the camp, searching it thoroughly, checking all papers. But all of the immigrants had proper documents. Colonel Meinertszgarten and Lieutenant Meredith led the investigation. Zionist Headquarters could offer no assistance. They were cooperative, but, finally, unable to help. Nothing further was done.

Death imposed its terrible charade, a stilted ceremony emptying the heart. Judah went through all formalities, said all that was expected. Finally everything was done that could be done, and Judah, drained, returned to the pattern of normal life.

Judah had seen Lily only briefly in the bank. She understood that he needed time to work out his feelings, talk to his father, Anneliese, and the child. Judah had offered Ben's family financial security. He wanted to set up a trust fund for them. Anneliese refused. In a *kibbutz,* no private money was necessary. If he wanted to give, she told him, give to the cause Ben had died for. Her grief was contained. She seemed to take strength from it.

Lily had said she would be there when he needed her. But a week had passed before he went to her apartment.

There was no answer to his knock, yet he felt certain he had heard noises inside. His key opened the door. Yes, there was someone in the bedroom! He moved cautiously toward it; with a sudden kick, sent it flying open.

Judah saw the back of Bernard's hand slap across the pale face of Lily Kessler. His beautiful Lily, white skin blotched from beating, bound to a chair. Standing over her, the bulky forms of Jonathan and Bernard. He could not believe the sickening tableau.

Judah rushed at the American, seizing him by the throat, dragging him to the floor. Then Jonathan was on top of him, tearing him off. Judah tried to rise. Jonathan held him down.

"Have you both gone crazy?" Judah gasped.

The two men freed him. He sat up painfully.

"Not crazy, Judah." Bernard's face was implacable. "It was this whore of yours who gave us away to the British. She was one of them. One of their spies!"

Judah pulled himself to his feet, staring at her. "I don't believe it."

"Go on, ask her yourself," Bernard challenged. "Ask her how much Colonel Meinertszgarten pays her."

"Tell me, Lily. . . . I'll believe whatever you say."

Lily was silent.

"It was she who reported the operation in Haifa. This bitch . . . got your brother Ben killed. Had the British waiting on the beach at Hayyim," Jonathan said.

"Judah. . . ." Lily's voice was husky with pleading. "How could I know they would kill your brother?"

"Why, Lily? Did you need the money that badly?"

"It is true Meinertszgarten—he paid me. But I have worked for the British before. In Germany, during the war. They ordered me to come to Palestine. Yes, I am their agent. I have worked for order and peace in the world. Surely also to you it must be as important as to the British?''

''And so you let me help you kill my brother . . . let me believe you loved me.'' He turned away from her to Bernard. ''What are you going to do with her?''

''The only thing we can do. She'd identify every one of us now.''

''No, Judah. Please . . . ! I promise you,'' she cried. ''I will say nothing more. I will tell them I refuse to stay here any longer. I will leave Palestine forever. You must believe I did not intend to harm your family. And one thing I did not make up. What was between us was not a lie.''

Judah looked at her for a long moment, tears in his eyes. He had not cried at Ben's death. Now he could. Then he confronted the two men. ''Will you let her go?''

''How can we?'' Jonathan demanded. ''How can we?''

''Is that your decision too, Bernard?''

The American shook his head. ''Can you promise she won't turn us in?''

He looked back at Lily, heartsick. ''No . . . I can't.''

''I am a professional agent,'' Lily said. ''If I make a promise, I keep it. I will tell the British nothing more. I will return to Germany.''

''I believe you, Lily. But I cannot make the decision,'' Judah said. He turned and walked out of the room.

''Why has she left? I was so certain she was happy here. . . .'' Anwar avoided mentioning the 'personal' relationship which he was aware existed between Lily and Judah. They were sitting at the Tel Aviv bank over morning coffee.

''She left. And that's the end of it. I'd really rather not discuss it.'' Judah turned back to the monthly accounts before them.

Anwar let the matter drop. Judah had been nothing like himself since the death of Ben. That was also something he did not wish to discuss.

''If you agree, Anwar, we could ask my cousin Noah to come down here permanently from the Jerusalem office. He's told me he'd like to live in Tel Aviv.''

''Dr. Simon's brother?'' Anwar didn't know Noah very well, but the young man had shown great initiative in the Trading Company. ''A good choice.''

''Then, it's agreed. I'll look for a house for him and his

wife, Rose. You can tell Noah when you get back to Jerusalem. And it will help if the transfer is made as quickly as possible.''

The following week, when Anwar walked into the Jerusalem bank, having dispensed the customary alms to the beggar beside the door, he felt gnawed by unease. Anwar separated his hands slightly in the gesture that implied acceptance of all trials Allah saw fit to impose.

His first visitor of the day was already waiting, and not a welcome sight. His cousin Yassir sat in a corner of the outer office reading an Arab newspaper. He tossed it on a table and followed Anwar into his office past the secretary.

Yassir glanced at his watch. "Well, cousin Anwar, I suppose this is what you call keeping banker's hours."

They had not seen each other for some years, yet neither of them made a move to embrace in the customary fashion. The younger man's features had been sharpened by time, desert winds, and hatred. His eyes were stormy and intense as ever. He wore Arab robes and riding boots. Anwar recognized the bulge at his waist as a pistol.

"I expect even relatives to telephone or write for an appointment," Anwar said, taking his place behind his large, tabletop desk.

Yassir ignored the note of correction, a sardonic smile twisting his face. "Congratulations, cousin. I see your bank is crowded today. Tell me, which does more business—this, or your Jewish bank?"

Anwar sighed. Everything in the world had changed but Yassir. "Forgive me, but I haven't time to exchange unpleasantries this morning. Why did you come here?"

"To report a conversation I had yesterday." Yassir's hand drew a wavy line through the smoke of his own cigarette. "With the grand mufti. It concerned the calamity of a Jewish bank in Tel Aviv that has Arab partners—and yet employs no Arabs."

"Find me an Arab who speaks Hebrew and can do the work and I'll employ him tomorrow. However, I do not think that our business is the mufti's concern."

"Everything that affects Arabs is his concern."

"Yes, I hear Haj Amin has been sticking his nose into the affairs of the new High Commissioner. He had better watch his step. Lord Plumer was one of the finest generals in the British Army."

At the mention of Plumer's name, Yassir's eyes narrowed to points of anger. "Did you know what this High Commissioner Plumer did? Stood at attention for the Zionist national anthem. And when the grand mufti queried him on such a biased action, your fine Lord Plumer told him that we Arabs should go out and get our own anthem—and then he would stand at attention for that, too."

Anwar laughed heartily. "Excellent advice. Maybe you could write one, Yassir. It might keep you out of trouble for a while."

Yassir's face darkened. "The grand mufti warned Lord Plumer that if he allowed himself to continue showing prejudice, the mufti could not be responsible for keeping order in Jerusalem. What did the British imperialist dog have the effrontery to reply? He said it would not be necessary for the mufti to keep order. The commissioner planned to do that himself."

Anwar looked amused. "That should give the grand mufti more time to mind his religious affairs—and pray that Allah will forgive him his sins."

Yassir hooked a finger through his belt, anger thickening his tone. "And who among our people will forgive you, cousin Anwar? You and Mohamed, who allowed your Jewish partners to open that bank? Where is Tel Aviv? Is it not in Palestine? Yet this flood of Europeans who pour into our land, they do not even bother to learn the language of the land. They teach the new arrivals Hebrew."

"You know the reason as well as I, Yassir. The one thing their people have in common with each other is the language of their prayers."

"And what do they have in common with us? They will not learn Arabic, because they look down on us. They want their own language in preparation for their own state. Today they exclude our people from a chance of earning a livelihood. Tomorrow they will exclude us from our own country!" Yassir's voice was an unconscious imitation of the man he most admired in the world. Soft, deadly. "You, Anwar, think yourself a clever businessman—but you do not see what is happening under your nose. The Zionists are buying our country field by field—financed through your Tel Aviv bank. They claim a historic right. But before Moses crossed the Red Sea, Palestine belonged to us! Through the centuries, we were invaded and occupied, but we remained. We won back the land and then for centuries it was ours. So it will be again."

Anwar rose. "I'm weary of this history lesson, which I think comes more from Haj Amin than Heidelberg. Do not come to see me again, Yassir."

Yassir rose in his turn, tall and grown surprisingly impressive. The student rebel had learned to carry himself like a leader. Another imitation of Haj Amin? Yassir picked up the old Company emblem: a bronze donkey and cart that stood near the edge of Anwar's blotter. He pushed it to roll across the tabletop toward his cousin.

"Before I look upon your face for the last time, cousin . . . I will tell you why I came. It has been decided that the Company must be dissolved. Unless every Hammadi resigns from all banks and business enterprises with the Nouaris . . . steps will be taken. I will not be able to protect you."

"I wasn't aware that you ever had." Suddenly Anwar began to laugh. It rolled out of him, filling the room. After all these years to be confronted by the black sheep of the family— the one they had always hidden, got rid of, got out of trouble. And now he stood there calmly threatening to destroy them all.

"You find this funny?" Yassir blazed.

"You have just asked me to dismantle three generations of a world enterprise . . . or you will deprive me of your protection. You have an undeveloped talent, Yassir. For comedy."

"I think none of you will be laughing soon. I would rather be the only member of my family alive than see Palestine become a second Jewish kingdom."

But when Yassir had left the office, Anwar sat back at his desk. His fingers played with the wheels of the little donkey cart and he no longer felt like laughing.

Smothered in predawn darkness, the Valley of Ajalon stretched a dusty snake of road from Jaffa toward Jerusalem. Behind the ruined arch of an old wall, the woman they called 'The Scorpion' stretched her glance through field glasses into the first glint of metallic day. Zuliekha had taken the trouble to learn the habits of the Development Bank of Tel Aviv's armored van. Its weekly trips to the head office of Hammadi-Nouari Bank in Jerusalem always started well before dawn. From the bank's point of view, it attracted less attention. From Zuliekha's, it made the target easier.

They were cold, all of them. They had been waiting all night. Zuliekha glanced up at the youth she had stationed as lookout on the top of the wall. She did not know that this was the same crumbling wall where once, many years before, another guard had been killed by the bandits who had attacked the honeymoon caravansy of Mohamed Hammadi. Had she known, Zuliekha would have found in the coincidence a certain justice.

She whistled a low signal. The lookout waved his hand in the negative.

Nothing yet. She had placed her five men as carefully as chess pieces. Two with her behind the fallen rubble of the wall. Two on the far side of the road by a tall cyprus that had been sawed through and propped to fall across the road.

The newborn day was lightening. No wind. No movement of leaf, weed, or insects cloistered in the cracks of rocks. Zuliekha inhaled deeply, smelling victory in the morning air.

Through the past few hours, she had carefully prepared the explosives. Two mines planted just under the surface of the road, to be set off by the plunging of a detonator. It was a simple arrangement of dynamite sticks wired together and bound into casings. The Scorpion had earned a reputation for being good with explosives. They had buried two packets, then smoothed back the surface of the road, which was, in any case, so rutted that no new bump would draw attention.

From the nearby sleepy village of Latrun, dogs barked up the morning. An old *fellah* came shuffling down the road accompanied by his three mongrels prodding a herd of some twenty goats.

"Get rid of that cigarette!" Zuliekha spoke sharply to the young man nearest her. He obeyed, but looked surly. He didn't like to take orders from a woman. But he would learn. She would see to that.

The *fellah* goatherd turned his flock across the road just at the point where the mines had been laid. Zuliekha held her breath. A goat chose this inopportune moment to mount his mate right in the middle of the road, kicking up dust.

Sniffing strangers, two dogs trotted up the bank and around the wall, barking at the crouching riflemen. The men kicked out at the dogs and drove them off with stones. Instead of making them leave, it started them yelping. The old *fellah* crossed back to investigate, stepping right over the buried mines.

"What shall we do?" asked the surly one.

Zuliekha rose, walked down to the edge of the road. "Grandfather!" she called. "I ask you to get your goats away from here at once. There will be trouble here soon."

The old man looked confused. "In our village there is no trouble."

"Today there will be. We are sent by the Brotherhood."

"The Brotherhood . . . ?" he looked vague.

"Perhaps you have heard of The Scorpion?"

His eyes widened. Even in Latrun that name meant something. He hurried his goats on into the opposite field. In a few minutes they were out of sight. Zuliekha looked across the road to where she had stationed her two riflemen by the tree. A father and son. Druses. No worries about those two. Both were experienced shots. She herself had supervised the loading of all guns and seen that each man had a grenade and knew how to use it. Two for herself, and a submachine gun. Then she noticed that the goats had exposed one of the mines. Zuliekha walked out and smoothed it over with her hands, then returned to her position by the plunger.

From the lookout at the top of the wall came a warning whistle. All grew instantly alert. They knew what they were to do. Now they needed luck. In a few moments they began to hear the low hum of a motor. The lookout signaled again. It was the van, all right.

A closed, unmarked vehicle adapted into a mobile strongbox, a veritable vault on wheels; steel sides with a narrow slit providing an opening for a Sten gun. Zuliekha's hands rested on the plunger. Her timing would, as always, have to be perfect. She knew that the van normally carried three men; one guard beside the driver, one riding inside with the money. Generally sacked paper currency and silver, sometimes gold.

The van came to the rise. It grumbled into a lower gear. Zuliekha whistled. The Druse and his son obeyed the signal. The tall cyprus tree came crashing down across the road. The van ground its gears to a sharp halt. Zuliekha plunged the detonator.

A geyser of dust and rock burst skyward, hurling the van over on its side. The blast had rocketed open its rear door, sending a paper flutter of bank notes into the air. The guard clawed his way out of the cab. Pinned under the wheel, the driver was unable to move. From the back of the van the second guard crawled out dazed, hand groping to his holster. His face was blood-streaked. He fired a wild burst at the hillside, hitting one of Zuliekha's men in the leg. The small band opened fire, cutting him down.

"Hold your fire!" Zuliekha commanded. She loped down the hill, submachine gun ready, slung from a shoulder strap. Across the road the Druse and his son covered the remaining guard. The driver was unconscious, crushed under the wheel. The guard dropped his gun and raised his arms above his head.

"Don't shoot him!" she ordered. Noticing a flutter of flame licking from the hood, she raced to the rear of the van. All but the wounded man came forward now.

"Inside. Get those sacks out!" she commanded, but her men stood frozen, seeing the licking flames.

"It is going to explode any minute," the surly one cried out.

"Coward—who thinks women are only to sleep with!" Zuliekha crawled into the back of the van herself, shaming the others to come to her aid. One by one, they caught the sacks of currency and coin as she threw them out. They hurled them up the hill from man to man to where their own truck was hidden behind the wall.

A shouted warning sent Zuliekha sprawling into the ditch just seconds before the bank van erupted into an explosion of orange flame. Some of the bank notes from the broken sacks sprayed up in burning, curling paper leaves.

The one guard left alive stood trembling nearby. "Don't kill me," he begged. Zuliekha came over to him.

"No. We do not kill you. You are our messenger. To Hammadi-Nouari—from Al Fatat. The Brotherhood. Say to them, they are foolish not to have taken our warning. Tell them The Scorpion sends this message. What has happened today is only the beginning of the end of Hammadi-Nouari."

They left him standing there in the road, beside the smoking wreckage of the van. He waited, weeping. This had been his first job since arriving in Palestine from Cracow.

The small truck, stolen long ago from the British military, roared back to Jerusalem. The men inside half chanted, half sang a victory song. Zuliekha was not singing. She was counting the packages of money. It would purchase arms enough for a regiment.

The Rolls-Royce that arrived at eight o'clock in the morning to collect Mohamed at the Shepherd's Hotel was a brand-new Prince of Wales model—pale gray in color, with upholstery of tooled moroccan leather in red—and it belonged to King Fuad.

Mohamed's arrival in Cairo had been appropriately celebrated in all the newspapers. His close connection to two American Presidents as adviser on Middle Eastern affairs had not escaped the press's attention—nor that of the Egyptian monarch. Since the war, Egypt had been suffering from a series of ailments, one of which was the decline in the cotton market. The quantity and quality of exports had badly hit Hammadi-Nouari Trading Company. As mainly middlemen, they were swamped with orders they couldn't fill.

In charge of the Cairo office since the death of his father, Ahmed Hammadi had cabled for help. Mohamed had been instrumental in organizing an International Cotton Spinners' Congress in Cairo, which he chaired and dominated as principal speaker. He had won a great personal success. Industry hopes were soaring again. After all, he had challenged, wasn't the new Port Fuad recently built opposite Port Said able to handle the sort of shipping needed to embark Egypt into the twentieth century? And wasn't Hammadi-Nouari ready to fill the ships?

But, this morning, King Fuad's limousine was carrying Mohamed back into the Middle Ages.

"So! You have never seen a camel race, Mr. Hammadi?" The King of Egypt brandished a cigar the color of his skin. He filled most of the backseat beside Mohamed in the huge Rolls. The car had taken Mohamed to the palace, where he had joined the royal party. Now three Rolls-Royces were heading deep into the desert outside the city.

"I have the greatest respect for the camel, sir," Mohamed said. "But personally I have been more inclined toward horses where racing is concerned."

Fuad emitted a rumble of laughter. "You have been spoiled by Paris, Hammadi!—And this Derby of Kentucky you have in the United States. My beautiful white Hejins can outrun any horse over a distance—for your horse will tire and your camel will not. You understand, the camels you will see racing today are not domestic dromedaries. These Hejins of mine were brought to Arabia from Persia centuries ago, and then to Egypt. Direct descendants from the Suwarees of India. Specially bred for racing, specially fed, trained, and groomed every day. They are ridden only by small boys—of no more age than eight years." The King's eyes rested on his son, a lad of about seven, perched on one of the jump seats beside a slender young woman. "You would like to ride one of these camels, would you not, Farouk?"

The boy turned his head to his father. "No, Father, I would not. They are mean, those camels. They spit. They bite."

Fuad roared with laughter again. "Mean! And so they are, my beautiful white Hejins. But their feet are soft, and spread out to grip the sand so that they fairly fly over it." He sparkled a mysterious wink at Mohamed. "But although they will live to become fifty years and one trains them every day, you can never really tame a camel. And so you are wondering, how do we make them race? Today you will see this for yourself."

Mohamed was wondering something else. He returned his glance to the silent young woman whose back was to him. Since getting into the car, she hadn't spoken a word except in a low whisper or two to Prince Farouk. Her thick black hair was worn in a heavy braided chignon that rested low at the nape of her neck. She was dressed in pale silk, obviously Paris—with a tiered skirt that seemed to flutter about her legs when she entered the car. The skirt was slightly longer than current fashion's dictate, which would no doubt have offended Egyptian taste. King Fuad had introduced Muna as his niece. Why, Mohamed asked himself, had this girl been allowed the rare privilege of sharing His Majesty's car?

In the automobiles behind them were other members of the

royal family, and some palace dignitaries. They had been driving for nearly an hour now, having long ago left the road to bump over undulating desert terrain. The car stopped abruptly.

"Sir, this is the place," the driver said.

Mohamed glanced out the window. They seemed to be in the middle of nowhere.

"Excellent!" Fuad replied. 'Now, Mr. Hammadi, as you say in America: hold onto your seat, for at any moment the camels will be coming."

Mohamed could see for miles. There was nothing to interrupt the vista of rolling dunes.

"If I recall, sir, you had an Imperial Camel Corps Brigade serving in Palestine in 1917."

"Indeed we did," Fuad replied proudly. "I am pleased that you know this. It fought in many battles, and also took part in Allenby's advance on Jerusalem; in fact, there has been a Camel Corps in our Army since 1884, Mr. Hammadi. But the British have shown their gratitude to us in a very curious way. After the war, we were not invited to attend the Peace Conference. Is this not unbelievable?"

"Shocking, sir. But very believable. Great powers are capable of everything except gratitude."

"How true, how true, Hammadi. I personally sent to Great Britain as minister a man who had been educated in England. One I knew was even liked by Lord Lloyd. But he was snubbed! After that I arranged many spontaneous anti-British demonstrations in Cairo. But the memory of my people is short, and so now we make new treaties of agreement with the British. If ever we should be attacked, they will come to our aid."

"For which Your Majesty will be required to furnish all facilities and assistance—and naturally, not oppose British imperial policies abroad," Mohamed suggested.

The King studied his guest. "You should have been a minister instead of a businessman, Hammadi."

"Businessmen live longer, sir."

Small beads of perspiration were beginning to dampen Fuad's forehead. "I see I have not underestimated you. Yes, some of our people do have short memories, but we do not forget our victimization by the British. We have demanded self-determination and have been ignored."

"At least they didn't saddle you with the Balfour Declaration. A good case could have been made for the Jews having been *here* before *Palestine*."

Fuad's belly throbbed with laughter. Then his expression turned serious. "Ah, but here at home I am faced with intrigue on every side. So I have been compelled to dismiss the Cabinet and dissolve Parliament. So! I am forced to carry on the governing of Egypt by royal decree. . . ."

A wild shout sprang from the lips of the driver, putting an end to further conversation. "Sir . . . ! Sir . . . ! It is the camels! They are coming!"

Mohamed followed his glance through the rear window. Behind them, spread out in a wide arc, galloped ten camels hedged in by some thirty army trucks—all heading full tilt toward the three Rolls-Royces as though about to plow them into the sand.

"Go!" commanded Fuad.

The driver put the great limousine into top gear and took off at full speed ahead of the onslaught. The three Rolls-Royces leaped and bounced over the sand, racing out in front of the camels.

Young Farouk's eyes were wide with excitement. "How fast are they going? How fast?"

"We are moving at least seventy kilometers an hour! Look at them run. They must be reaching speeds of at least forty!"

Long slender legs pounded into the sand, the beasts swaying from side to side. The jockeys clung to their wooden saddle frames behind the single humps as though their very lives depended on it. All too frequently, they did.

The Rolls jounced along at an incredible speed with shouts of exuberance from the driver and the King's private bodyguard, who shared the front seat with him. Mohamed thought the girl seemed strangely calm in all the excitement.

For an instant, the riders were lost behind a dune, then reappeared, their mounts spraying sand from great, flat feet. One small rider lost balance as his bobbing beast hunched into a stumble.

"He is falling . . . !" shouted Farouk.

The rider was a spidery grapple of lost balance, and down he went. On came the race, the front-runners almost even, matching stride for stride, a sandy veil of heat between them and the bumping Rolls-Royces.

Then, suddenly, the car braked to a screeching stop, pitching sand against the windows. There, in the center of no place in particular, a tent had been set up, guarded by armed soldiers. This was obviously the finishing post.

"We get out now," Fuad said.

The bodyguard came around and opened the door. Everyone piled out, eyes on the advancing avalanche of camels and trucks.

The first two racing camels bolted in, to be pulled up to a stop. Close behind them the others sprinted up. These camels were taller, more slender than any Mohamed had seen. They wore special belts beneath their bellies, the boy riders clinging to the seat at the back of the hump, sweat-streaked with dirt, but eyes shining and faces wreathed in broad grins.

"My beautiful Hejins. What creatures in the world are more splendid? A sight you will never forget, I think, Mr. Hammadi."

The motorcade had come to a halt. The race was over. Fuad stepped forward personally to hand out the prizes. The camels were now being led away by attendants. They would be brought back to their stables at a slow walk. The little boy jockeys were being congratulated by their fathers, who had arrived with the military motorcade. They wore loose desert robes in contrast to the King's Paris-styled suit of natural linen, topped by a fez.

An officer came up to Fuad with a large painted box. Fuad took it, signaling the boys who had ridden the first three camels to approach. They were followed by proud fathers. Fuad squatted on a carpet laid on the sand with the boys and their fathers. Ceremoniously he opened the box. Inside were gold coins. Meticulously he doled out ten to the first boy, five to the second, and three to the third. There was a consolation prize to the boy who had fallen, miraculously unhurt. Ten silver coins.

"Quite a display of democracy from a dictator," Mohamed whispered to the girl. But if he had expected a reaction from her, he was disappointed. Muna did not answer. Instead she walked into the tent.

Fuad got to his feet and came over to Mohamed. "Come," he said. "A refreshment is waiting for us."

It was surprisingly cool inside the tent. After the King took up his glass, other members of the royal party began helping themselves to cakes and lemonade. Fuad drew Mohamed aside.

"After the war, the President of America, Wilson, formulated many interesting principles. He has had a great effect on the thinking of our educated classes. It is a curiosity how the Americans can manage to maintain order when so often they change Presidents. Now this new man, Coolidge—I understand he has asked you to report to him personally on our affairs."

"Only in the interests of peace in the Middle East," Mohamed replied, adding, "with a most favorable report on progress in the Egyptian cotton market."

"Have no fear, Mr. Hammadi, whatever you report to the President of America—even our camel race today—will make me most grateful. We should like to see a stronger interest from America in our achieving independence. You could be of the greatest help to us. As you have seen today, I am a man disposed to give prizes for effort." The King's glance trailed across the tent to where his niece Muna stood, surrounded by several small boys of the royal household. "Have you not ever thought of taking another bride, Mr. Hammadi?"

Mohamed looked across at the girl. Her eyes lifted to catch his. They were large as a calf's and jet black. She had a warm, handsome face, and was perhaps about twenty-four, maybe only a year or two older than his son, Maurice.

"I am married to a Christian, sir."

"But a Muslim is permitted to have four wives. You are still a Muslim, Mr. Hammadi?"

"Of course, sir. But, for my part, one wife has seemed quite enough. Too much, at times." He had a sudden vision of bringing a new wife home to Jacqueline.

"My niece Muna is a princess whose dowry would be a rich reward for any man. But Muna is a reward in herself. She is beautiful, as your eye tells you, obedient, and has been educated in Switzerland. A wife like Muna would not be one too many for a man of importance."

Mohamed's eyes remained on the girl. A wife like Muna. . . . He tried to imagine the possibility. It would be like beginning one's life all over again. No more screaming scenes, no more moments of dread as to what the next disaster might be.

Jacqueline. . . . When had she last been a wife to him? He could scarcely remember. He felt certain that this young princess standing so calmly across the tent must have been told by Fuad what he had in mind. Young enough to be Mohamed's daughter, yet from her look she would have no objection to such an alliance.

Tempting as it was, Mohamed dismissed the thought. Then he realized that Muna was smiling at him.

Twenty-two ─────────────

IF it had not been for the death of Ruth's father, she might never have learned the truth. Life has a way of holding back some of the cards—but Ruth had not expected this one to drop into her lap at such a late date.

All that week, Ruth had been apartment hunting with the help of Abe. On Judah's last trip to Paris, she had told him of her decision. It was final. She wanted to sell the Paris house.

"Find a nice apartment somewhere near Abe on the Île Saint-Louis. With Zed in New York and you hardly ever here, what do I need with such a big house?"

Judah could honestly find no objection. It had never made much difference to him where he hung his hat, and it wasn't being hung too often in Paris these days.

"Do as you like, Ruth. Abe will handle the financial arrangements. Anything special you should need, send me the bills."

The reunion in Paris caused no fireworks. Judah had taken Ruth out to dinner and spent the night in his own bedroom. More than ever, they were strangers. On the day Ruth received the telegram from her brother Olek, Judah had already returned to Jerusalem.

Her father was dead. Old Mordchai Cukor. Could she come to Warsaw immediately? Olek wanted to know.

Abe took leave from the bank to travel with her. Mother and son boarded the train that very same day. Traditionally, a body couldn't wait for more than three days above ground, even for a daughter in another city.

Abe was so handsome and so elegant, Ruth felt proud walking through the Gare du Nord with him. He held her arm, guiding her around the mounds of luggage. She was certain strangers were looking at them.

"They think I'm your beau, Mother," he teased, giving her elbow a tiny squeeze. How happy she had always been with Abe. Ever since he was a baby. What a son! Not like Zed, who always went her own way without wondering if she might be needed by her mother at home. What a son, Abe. Life wasn't perfect to be sure, but Abe made up for a lot.

In Warsaw, Olek met them at the depot with his car. It was hard for Ruth to believe her brother was already a grown man with a wife and son of his own. Shimon was seven now. There had always been a deep affection between Ruth and her brother. And for his part, she had done so much for him he could never forget. Her money had put him through Warsaw University, started him in his own law practice, bought him a modest house on a pleasant, tree-lined street for Shimon to grow up on—Aleje Ujazdowskie. Such things had not always been possible for a Jew in Poland. But General Pilsudski, Poland's new Premier, was kindly inclined toward Jews. He had not forgotten that when the Russians came looking for him in 1920, it was the Jews who had hidden him in a synagogue, draped in a *tallis*. Life in Poland was paradise to what it had been before.

When he was younger, Ruth had tried to urge Olek to move to Paris, but he had refused. Why should he? Warsaw was his home. Her urgings had finally been dropped.

"How is Mama bearing up?" Ruth asked.

"Bearing up is something that never happens to Mama. She cries, she's helpless. She cries some more. Only, this time she has reason." He turned the car down the familiar gray street toward the old family house.

"Who can blame her? Papa always made all the decisions. He managed everything for Mama." She wiped a tear from the corner of her eye with an already soggy black-bordered handkerchief. "Such a capable man, Papa."

Abe glanced out at the bleak street. He hated Warsaw. "What a pity Grandpa Mordchai isn't here to handle the problems of his funeral."

She nodded. "What a moment he picked to drop dead. Just when I have my hands full with moving the whole house in Paris." The way she held up her hands, it looked as though she were lifting it herself. She sighed. A procession into the grave of all her relatives. Aunt Halevi, Grandfather Zuckerman. And now Mama would be all alone.

"I'll bring her to Paris," Ruth announced with finality.

"No, Ruthele. For such a change, she is too old. She will move in with Gittele and me. In the house you helped us buy—which I haven't forgotten—we have plenty of room. But, of course, Papa did not leave her much. And to me he left only his gold-and-ivory toothpick." He took it out of his waistcoat pocket and passed it across to Abe in the backseat.

Abe handed it back quickly. "Very fine engraving."

"Never mind the money, Olek," Ruth assured her brother. "I'll see Mama gets her regular monthly amount, the same as always."

The funeral was a reasonably splendid affair. Every friend of Mordchai's who had a job had taken off from work to attend it. When the procession moved down the street, strangers turned and walked for a way with the casket, as was customary in the Jewish Quarter of the city. It showed their heart was with the family of the dead.

"With his last breath, he pronounced the *Shema*," Ruth's mother assured her. It wasn't true, but it comforted Madame Cukor to say it. Every Jew wanted to die with a prayer on his lips. After the funeral, Ruth's mother had a beautiful meal waiting for everyone. She seemed to drift through the day's events on a thread of suspended emotion. And finally, when everyone had said everything that was expected, it was over.

Next day, Olek took Abe on a tour of the city to get him out from under foot. Ruth stayed at home to help her mother, who was busying herself, packing up china and other personal items for the move to Olek's house. Ruth seemed more in the way than helpful.

"In the attic, Ruth. So many papers. Your papa should have gone through them long ago. Burned the rubbish. Who needs such things? Several lifetimes up there, packed away. Mordchai's family. Mine. The Halevis—the Zuckermans. Maybe you could sort through them? See if there is anything worth keeping. Of the rest we can make a bonfire." The old woman intended to put the house up for sale as soon as she had moved out to her son's.

Ruth took an oil lamp and went up to the attic. Just as her mother had said, the clutter of the past had been stored away in boxes and trunks, everything covered by a fine layer of dust. Old chairs, the cane seats broken out, a table with one leg missing. Madame Halevi's violin in its worn-out case. A mattress with a rip in it. Ruth noticed a hatbox with a Paris label. She lifted off the cover.

In it was the hat she had sent her mother at least twenty years before, the feathered bird still intact. Carefully she took it out of the box. Never worn. She placed it on her head, turning to look into a cheval glass. In the flickering light her reflection beneath the sweeping brim reminded her of cousin Zosia. Quickly she took it off and returned it to its box. Then her eyes fell on a large wooden steamer trunk with the name HALEVI crudely stenciled in black letters. It was not locked. She lifted the lid.

A trunk of memories of her aunt and uncle in Russia. Books, an embroidered shawl, a man's shiny black frock coat, faded dresses, a piece of heavy Russian lace, a painted wooden doll, a folder of documents, and a tidy pile of letters.

Ruth took out the folder and sat on a corner of the mattress near the oil lamp; she would go through the papers. Surely now there would be nothing that could still matter to anyone. There were no Halevis left. Passports. A residence permit. A record of her uncle's military service. Her aunt's birth certificate. She paused. None for Zosia? No.

But a marriage license—dated 1895. The names on it made Ruth feel suddenly dizzy. *"Zosia Halevi. Born: Russia. Jew. Leonid Avraham Lesno. Born: Poland. Jew."* Could it be possible that Zosia had been married—that her mother knew it—and that she had never told anyone—even Ruth's mother? But why? What had happened to the marriage? By the date, it was long before Zosia went to Paris.

At least two years before Zosia ever met Judah.

Ruth took up the letters. . . . Something about the handwriting looked vaguely familiar. She ripped open the ribbon that held them together. All were addressed to "Madame Halevi," and all were from Zosia—from Geneva, Berne, Paris. For the next hour, Ruth read by the smoky light of the oil lamp. When she had finished, she knew beyond a shadow of a doubt that the man to whom Zosia had been married, this Polish Jew named Lesno, was the same Russian Count Alexei Lubenov she had heard Judah speak of so often. Lesno-Lubenov was Zosia's secret husband—all the time she had been mak-

ing love to Judah. All the time she had been promising to
marry Judah. *Her* Judah!

Ruth wanted to cry, but instead she began to laugh. What a
trick life had played on Judah! And on her. . . . The laughter changed to tears.

Anwar Hammadi arose from the prayer mat in his bedroom
feeling refreshed. He slipped his feet back into neatly polished shoes. The Jerusalem day sparkled in through thin white
curtains. He was looking forward to his meeting with Judah at
the bank. They hadn't seen each other since Judah's return
from Paris. He wanted to report on how well young Noah
Nouari was settling in at the Tel Aviv bank. That was the
good news. The bad news—the loss of the bank van and
guards—would have to be discussed. He had several ideas on
how to improve security. But finally, none could guard themselves against wanton terrorism.

With a worried smile, Anwar kissed his comfortably plump
wife, Farida, good-bye, took up his dispatch case and opened
the front door. He found himself confronted by a small lad
carrying a message.

It was a hastily scribbled note from Dr. Yusuf. More bad
news. (Was there any other kind these days?) Another disturbance in the Arab Quarter. Somehow Uncle Gamel had
become involved. He'd been injured.

Anwar sent the young messenger to the bank with a note.
He would be late for his meeting with Mr. Nouari. Could
Judah please wait in Anwar's office? He would get there as
soon as he could.

Anything that happened to Uncle Gamel was a double
concern to all members of the family, since he was the only
member of their illustrious family who could not take care of
himself. Anwar hurried through the already teeming morning
streets. To have the chauffeur bring his car would have taken
even longer.

In his dark little room beside the mosque Gamel lay, head
bandaged, breathing heavily. His brother, Dr. Yusuf Hammadi,
sat beside the bed. He arose as Anwar entered. They kissed
on each cheek.

"How bad is he, uncle Yusuf?"

"Mild concussion. A few days' rest and Gamel should be as good as new."

As good as new . . . . As if "new" had ever been very good for Gamel. Anwar came over and took up his uncle's hand. "Some say the simpleminded have been touched on the forehead by an angel before birth. Some see in it a gift of prophecy. Poor Uncle Gamel. He never prophesied anything. His comments deal only with the small creatures against whom he wages his lifetime of broom warfare." He turned back to his doctor uncle. "What happened, Yusuf?"

"Another riot in the old quarter."

"Thanks be to Allah you were here in Jerusalem."

"It happened to be my day at the clinic. Dr. Simon and I alternate from Bethlehem now."

Anwar put down the work-worn hand. Gamel's eyes were closed, head freshly bandaged. "But how did he get involved in a riot?"

"From all I could learn, an old Jew was on his way to teach at the *cheder*. Some of our young men bravely threw stones at him. The Jew was looking for a place to hide. The nearest available building was this mosque. My poor, simpleminded brother saw the Jew running and went out to help him. The gallant students turned their stones on Gamel. For this, they need to go to school!"

"Shouldn't you take him to the hospital?"

The elderly doctor gestured that the question had already been rejected. "It will be less confusing for him, here in his own room. And less crowded. The wards are full of casualties from the riots. I have arranged for a retired nurse to come and take care of him. She can cook."

"What does he eat? A sliver of lamb? A spoonful of rice. He eats like one of his birds."

Yusuf rose. "I cannot stay any longer, Anwar. Every time Haj Amin makes a speech, I have a very busy day. Can you wait with him until the woman comes?"

"For a little while. Unfortunately, Judah Nouari is in my office waiting for me."

"Give Judah my best wishes. It is a long time since we have seen each other. Not since the war." He handed Anwar a box of pills. "When my brother awakens, give him one of these."

"When is this rioting going to end, Yusuf?"

The doctor clucked his tongue, Arab fashion. "Maybe if we could make every member of the Brotherhood have a Jewish partner as we do, they would see things differently." He touched his head and heart in a gesture of farewell, took up his black bag, and was gone.

When Anwar turned back, Gamel's eyes were fluttering open. "Now, Gamel, what have you been up to?"

The face was woefully serious. "The birds . . ."

"Yes, uncle . . . ?" He popped one of the pills into Gamel's mouth and held a glass of water to his lips. Gamel swallowed automatically.

"I think they have been . . . very angry." His expression changed. "I fix them. Bad birds."

"Of course you will. But there's no hurry, uncle."

Gamel began to weep slightly, but not from the pain. "I can't find my broom. I think they hide it. . . ."

"I'll get you another one."

A tear or two coursed down the leathery cheek. "Why do they not like me? I left in the dish . . . crumbs of bread. I put it always outside by the fountain for the washing of hands and feet before prayer."

"Everyone loves you, uncle Gamel."

A strange light—like a flash of knowing—visited the janitor's eyes. "The stone that flew—it didn't love me."

"Wouldn't you like to wait in Mr. Hammadi's office, Mr. Nouari?"

The secretary was new, young, bright. Probably from the Lebanon, by her stylish French look.

"Yes, I think so. Did Anwar—Mr. Hammadi—say how late he would be?"

"No. Only that he would be delayed. There has been some unrest in Jerusalem. Perhaps traffic was held up."

"Yes, I believe so." Judah looked around the familiar office. The air was stifling. He had a list of things to be discussed with his partner. First among them was what could be done to prevent further attacks on bank transfers. He put his hands toward his head, which ached slightly. "Do you think we might have a window open?"

"Oh, yes, sir. Mr. Hammadi keeps it closed in the morn-

ing to keep out the noise of the street when he is dictating.
But if you wish . . . ?''

Judah nodded. The pain in his head seemed to interfere
with his breathing. The open window brought in a rush of
familiar sounds. Vendors. Bearers. Automobiles. Donkey hoofs.
He took up one of the European newspapers. So the Republicans had nominated Herbert Hoover? Well, whoever won,
Mohamed would be busy making friends with the new President. The Republicans were promising "a chicken in every
pot." Did they have to promise so prosperous a nation so
much? What do you give the country that has everything?
Mohamed had told him that the Ford Motor Company was
spending over two hundred million dollars to change over to a
new model from their Model T. And Hammadi-Nouari was
taking advantage of it by buying up some of the fifteen
million discontinued models—to sell in the Balkans. America. . . . Land of the plus and the plenty. Even the street
sweepers and cabdrivers and carpenters were plunging into
the soaring stock market—buying on faith and margin. But
here things were not so bright. He could only hope Mohamed
had been successful in Egypt with cotton-production problems.

The new secretary's voice sounded in from the outer office.
"We have just made a pot of coffee; may I bring you one,
sir?''

"Yes, thank you." Judah glanced at the black armband he
was still wearing. He rested his face in his hands. And that
was where it had all ended—all Ben's drive, enthusiasm,
dream for the future of a new Palestine rising out of the
rubble of the past, the confusion left by every passing tide of
war. . . . Could Judah himself still believe in it? Of course.
Otherwise what purpose had those gone lives served, all who
had departed leaving only prayers and black armbands? Herzl,
Zosia, Trumpeldor, Ben. . . . He turned his mind to the
financial page of the newspaper.

He did not see the car moving slowly in the road beyond
the low wall that separated the office from the outer world. It
was a dusty, nondescript vehicle driven by a nondescript
young Arab with a stubbled face and eyes hidden by dark sun
goggles. In the back seat, a woman was picking through a
basket of fruit. She was dressed in a black *abaya*, her face
concealed.

The car inched forward, paused, tentative, awaiting the

precise moment, its movement synchronized to a clamor of voices farther down the same street. Around the car, people began to run—some toward the disturbance, some away—until very soon the street was empty.

The woman signaled the driver. He knew exactly what he was to do. She was holding a round object from among the fruit in the basket. It looked dark as an eggplant. The car started forward—so close to the wall that the wheels almost grazed it.

Sitting in Anwar's office, Judah began to wonder why Anwar was so late. He put down the newspaper, shielding his eyes in the darkness of the palms of his hands. Then he had a sudden mental flash of Ben. Ben's face, troubled, concerned as though trying to tell him something. It flashed and was gone, just as the Lebanese girl came in bearing an inlaid brass tray with a copper Turkish pot, cup, and glass of water. She was smiling brightly. Judah smiled back, not noticing the dark object that soared in through the window like a bird without wings.

But the girl standing there holding the tray, saw it. A cry sprang from her lips. Now Judah saw it too, rocking on the floor by her feet. He made a lunge for it. His warning was drowned in the explosion.

The girl almost disintegrated before his eyes. Like a slow-motion image mixing spurting blood with the round brass circle of tray spinning into the air. With terrible split-second memory flash, he saw only Zosia being blown to bits on the steps of the Russian Embassy.

The clanging ambulance brought an unconscious Judah to the emergency ward in the Rothschild Hospital. Dr. Yusuf Hammadi was called to surgery. Judah's arm had been almost torn from his shoulder. Dr. Yusuf took three hours to complete the amputation and tie off the arteries and veins. A bomb fragment had lodged in Judah's left eye. Dr. Simon Nouari arrived from Bethlehem in time to help remove the fragment. How much damage there was to the eye was still uncertain.

It was several days before Anwar was permitted to see Judah. He had sent two urgent telegrams—one to Ruth in Paris, one to Mohamed, who was again in Egypt.

Mohamed was first to arrive. He stood looking at Judah in the white hospital bed where for weeks he had been hovering between life and death. Then he stepped out into the corridor with Simon, Yusuf, and Anwar.

"He will survive," they told Mohamed. "The arm had to be taken off close to the shoulder. But wonderful things are being done with artificial limbs. Nobody can be sure how successful it could be in Judah's case."

"What about his eyesight?" Mohamed asked.

"Serious damage to only one. The other will function satisfactorily. With what is going on in the world today, the less one sees the better," Yusuf told his nephew grimly.

"How does Allah permit such things?" Mohamed asked softly.

"He was not killed. That in itself is a miracle for which thanks must be given."

"The bomb was meant for me, Mohamed," Anwar said.

Mohamed turned to his brother. "The criminals are known?"

Anwar's face was bleak, bitter with helpless anger. "They have announced responsibility." He put a copy of a letter into Mohamed's hand: *We the Brotherhood of Al Fatat have struck this blow as an act of war against the company which represents the partnership of Jews and Arabs in Palestine. There can be no end to our war—until Palestine is free of all Jews, and the traitorous Arabs who serve them by friendship.*

"Witnesses in the street have said it was a woman."

"The Scorpion?"

Anwar nodded.

Mohamed's hand closed on the paper with a convulsive gesture. "I trust you have given the original to the British police?"

"And a copy to Haj Amin."

"Who, I suppose, deplored such an act of violence?"

"Oh, to be sure. He was saddened by these horrors, which he sees as the inevitable result of British permission for Zionist immigration."

Mohamed nodded. "He is the fomenter of every trouble that plagues Palestine—and yet . . . if only one could say that he is completely wrong. Before the immigration, there was no trouble between our peoples."

Dr. Simon sighed deeply. "Neither the grand mufti nor any man on earth can change that now. What has begun will continue. And it will grow."

Mohamed shook his head. "You are wrong, Dr. Simon. The British will stop it. Or lose the Mandate."

"And if such a thing should happen? What then, Mohamed?"

"Who knows?" He lifted his glance to Simon's. "May I stay with Judah? If I talk to him, will he hear me?"

"He will hear. But he hasn't started speaking yet."

When they had all left, Mohamed sat down by the bed. "Judah, Ruth will be here next week."

The slight nod of Judah's head told him that he heard.

"Come on, old soldier—it isn't the worst thing. Nelson beat Napoleon with only one arm and one good eye. You've still got *me* to fight—and to love."

A half smile touched Judah's pale face. "Thank God for that," he whispered softly. "But are we strong enough to build a bridge?"

When Judah was released from the hospital, his father brought him home to the family house outside Jerusalem. Although David still kept six servants, the old man insisted on looking after Judah personally, bathing and dressing his son's wound every day. There were so many things that Judah couldn't yet manage—such as buttoning his shirt, putting the stud in his collar, tying his shoelaces. David did everything, trying not to appear too obviously helpful.

Stiff-backed as a cedar at seventy-eight, Judah's father had always remained fit as men half his age. Now Judah could sense the underlayer of anxiety left by Ben's death. It rankled in the heart; it slowed his words; it weighted his movements. He seemed to cling to Judah as though afraid if he turned his back he might lose this son too. They both knew he had come very close to it. Neither spoke of it. David kept a cheerful face and sat for hours by Judah's bed in the early days of his recovery.

"We come from a line of long livers. I can still remember my great-grandfather, tough as a goat, striding across the Valley of Hebron. We are survivors." David took Judah's one hand in his. "You will get over this. It doesn't take two arms to run your business. To sign a check only one hand is needed. And money in the bank."

Letters of sympathy had poured in. When he was well enough to read again, Judah sat out in the walled garden and worked his way through the stack. One letter from Ruth, explaining that she would have to come later because of her father's death. A mountain of letters from Mohamed keeping Judah abreast of Company news and international gossip. Hinting at personal problems and ending with the promise to see him again as soon as possible. From Abe, three short notes: worried, anxious, assuring Judah that banking affairs in Paris were completely in hand. He must only think of getting well. And from Zed, one three-page letter penned by hand in very small, tidy script. Rereading it, he could imagine her expressive, lively face beneath the tight black curls.

New York is so wonderful, Father—I never expected it to be like this. Mohamed tells me I am learning the business so fast, he is afraid of losing me to a rival. As if I would ever leave the Company! He has made me his Personal Assistant and he is sending me on regular trips now, taking over many of his duties, particularly to Florida, where the bank is investing heavily in land and property development. I have just set signature to my first million-dollar deal. The only thing wrong with Hammadi-Nouari all these years is that they've never had a woman in the Company! . . .

There were plenty of other things wrong with Hammadi-Nouari—in Palestine, anyway. Judah was glad Abe was safely in Paris and Zed in New York. He put the letter down. Reading it with one eye still gave him a headache. Ruth was coming today. And he had to admit to himself that for perhaps the first time in years he was actually looking forward to seeing her. Ruth, who had put up with so much from him. Somehow he would find a way to make it up to her. He intended to tell her how he felt; that he wanted to bring them closer together.

He heard the door from the house open and looked up. There she was—coming across the open courtyard with his father, carrying that oversized handbag he had bought her years ago in New York. Large enough for all the necessities of travel, she had said. Her face wore a slightly stricken look. He hoped to God there wouldn't be tears. His nerves hadn't been so good since the accident. Accident. . . . Could he call it that? It was as accidental as a war casualty.

They were talking softly together as they approached him. He couldn't make out what they were saying. . . .

"It won't bother you about the arm?" David asked Ruth. "Some women are squeamish."

"The arm? No."

"It could have been worse. It could have been his life." They moved to join Judah, who was seated beneath the shade of a large date palm. Ruth kissed him perfunctorily on the cheek.

Like a polite stranger, David thought. No real warmth. Well, their marriage had never been his business. He returned to the house to arrange for the tea and see Ruth's luggage taken to her room. He had given her the large one next to Judah's. A maidservant would unpack for her. He would leave them alone for a while. Let them find their way.

When David had gone, Ruth stood there for a moment staring at the empty sleeve. Then she sat down facing Judah. "So, Judah. Have they caught the person who did this to you?"

Judah shook his head. "They won't. These Arab terror squads aren't easy to find. But some people in the street said it was a woman who threw the bomb from an automobile. Difficult to believe."

"Why you, Judah? Because of your Zionist work?"

"That's the curious thing, Ruth. They have already made a few attempts to bomb the JNF office. But this attack was definitely directed against Anwar. They consider Arabs who work with Jews, traitors."

"How like you, Judah. In the wrong place at the wrong time, always."

"It's not deliberate, Ruth." The conversation was going nowhere. She seemed so cold, so matter of fact. No emotional outbursts. It was a Ruth he wasn't used to. "How is Abe?"

"Fine. He went to Warsaw with me."

So that was it. He had neglected to mention her father. "How stupid of me, Ruth. Of course. The funeral. Naturally I would have come to be with you too—if this hadn't happened."

"You weren't needed. Anyway, I've had to learn to do without you through the years."

He closed his eyes. "It will be different now," Judah said.

"Will it?"

"Ruth—that's what I wanted to talk to you about. Maybe, when I am better—things could be different between us."

"When you are better—we will discuss it."

He sensed she was holding back something, but he didn't want to probe. Not now. He still tired so easily. He was relieved when his father returned with the servant and the tea tray. There would be time.

Several days passed without much more being said between them. When they were together, Judah sensed something more than the usual barrier. One day, when they were again alone in the garden, it came out.

They were talking about her mother's move to Olek's house, in Warsaw. How Ruth had helped her with the endless packing, clearing up a lifetime of details, sorting through papers, family documents, letters. . . . He was only half listening, the effort of conversation still wearying, letting her words drone over him.

"That must have been a tedious task," he said.

"On the contrary, Judah. It was fascinating." The words were suddenly edged with acid. "I found something that I think should interest you, too." Ruth reached into her handbag and brought out the document she had found in her aunt's steamer trunk. She set it down in Judah's lap, by his hand. He took it up, somewhat mystified.

"Afraid I never did learn to read Polish, Ruth. What is it?"

"A marriage license, Judah. And you don't have to read Polish to recognize the names. Or the date."

He scanned down the page, then stopped. "Zosia . . . ? But who is this man? This Lesno?"

"*You* knew him as Count Lubenov. But he was a Polish Jew."

So that was it. Ruth thought she had found something that could destroy the memory that always loomed between them: Zosia.

"This document must be some kind of forgery. . . . Something Zosia and Lubenov used for their undercover work. They were always traveling with forged papers, Ruth."

"This one is *real*, Judah. I have every one of Zosia's letters to her mother—that prove it. Zosia was married to him when you met her. For all these years, you have worshiped a lie!" Her voice rose. "For her, you cheated me out of my life! Wasted the days of my years. Yes, Judah—all these years you worshiped a lie!!!''

''It can't . . . can't be true. . . .'' His head was spinning with the pain of her words. But she wasn't finished.

''The only truth was that she never loved you. Never! She belonged to *him* all the time. How she used you, Judah. Got everything she wanted from you. Money. . . . Support for her cause. Devotion, even. And you—you punished me through our marriage for not being your glorious, dedicated Zosia. How I hate her! Hate the memory of her that you still carry even now! But this piece of paper destroys the stupid fantasy of Zosia that replaced the reality of me, your wife . . . !'' Judah had no words for Ruth. He looked away. A hollow silence descended over everything.

''From now on, my dear husband, you can start comparing me to myself.''

Ruth stayed on in the Jerusalem house for another week; then she returned to Paris. Judah volunteered no information to his father of what had passed between them.

Through the next few weeks, Judah answered his mail—to Mohamed, Zed, and Abe—and a long letter to Chaim Weizmann. In it he wrote: *I'm afraid, Chaim, that I don't love God any more—and that I don't know whether I even believe in Him. But if I do, I don't love Him. And if I don't love Him and still believe in Him—then I can't believe in Zionism.*

Weizmann, in London, read the letter through, several times. It was easy, he knew, for a man who had undergone a severe shock to lose his way. He would make the time for a longer visit with his friend on his next trip to Jerusalem, at the end of the month. It hurt him deeply to know that Judah had been injured because of the riots and the general troubles in Palestine. It was, after all, a desperate effort by Arab extremists to scare out the Zionists. They would fail. They could not overthrow the structure being so carefully built for the National Home. It was too late. As for the British—they might try to retract the promises made in the Balfour Declaration, but they, too, would fail. Public opinion was now on the side of the Zionists. No, Weizmann's problems were closer to home. Jabotinsky and his Revisionists, trying to oust him from his seat as President of the Zionist Organization. They were demanding a Jewish State on *both* sides of the Jordan.

He put all this into a letter to Judah, adding: *They want the easy road. The road paved with the promises of others. I said to the Congress, "The walls of Jericho fell to the sound of shouts and trumpets. I never heard of walls being raised by that means!"*

He reread Judah's letter, then added a postscript to his own reply: *Don't worry about losing faith, Judah. Like love—it is something you cannot force. But also like love, it will return to you when you least expect it.*

Can any man plumb his own heart's darkness?

The trellised autumn roses shed a few crimson petals on Judah seated on a bench beside the courtyard wall. Here, once long ago, he had been a child in a peaceful city, in an innocent time. The bench was scarred by his initials. Cut by the knife of that boy lost somewhere now behind a sea of troubles, war, and disappointment. He started to reach out to touch it—feeling the arm that was no longer there, so strongly that it seemed to hold his pulse, his heartbeat. He repressed a sob. But it was not for himself. It was for Uncle Jacob. Brave old pillar of the family, who at ninety-six should have died in his bed. Instead, he had been killed on the eve of Yom Kippur saying his prayers at the Wailing Wall.

A hand fell gently on his shoulder. Judah looked up to see Mohamed, smartly dressed as ever, thinner perhaps, and wearing a new Panama hat.

"Where did you drop from?"

"Cairo. I came as soon as I heard about Uncle Jacob. Sorry I couldn't have attended the funeral. By the way, there was no Company car to meet me at the station. Didn't they get my cable?"

"Jerusalem has been like a battlefield. We don't even know the final count of the dead. The rioting has spread all over. Hebron. Safad. Haven't you been reading the papers?"

"Confusing as usual. It looks as though everyone is blaming somebody else. I hoped you could give me a clearer picture. All I could gather was that somehow the Jews had committed an offense against the Muslim religion."

"Sit down. It's hard for me to look up toward the sun." Mohamed dropped into one of the iron garden chairs. Judah wiped his damaged eye, which tended to tear a little now that the bandage was off.

"It doesn't show, Judah. Hasn't left a scar."

"They say my sight will improve." He smiled. "I still have one good eye to keep on you."

"The rioting—what started it? Does anyone know?"

"The rabbi erected a screen at the Wall—to separate the men and women at their prayers."

"How could that have bothered anyone?"

"It was just the provocation Haj Amin was waiting for. He accused the Jews of violating Islamic property. He spread the rumor that our real aim was to take over the Dome of the Rock. That, of course, brought Lieutenant Meredith to the rescue. Do you know him?"

Mohamed nodded. "A stickler for regulations. But fair." Mohamed took out a string of amber worry beads. They looked shiny new, inlaid with gold. Worry beads so fine, the man who owned them need never have cause for worry. Judah had never seen Mohamed use them before. Now they clicked nervously through his fingers.

"Fair, perhaps. But misguided. Meredith arrived with a platoon just at the most solemn moment of prayer. He ordered that the screen be removed. The rabbi refused, the Arabs protested, Meredith dithered. There was a scuffle—then a pitched battle. There was no containing it. Agitators were everywhere."

"How did Jacob get involved in this?"

"My cousin Nathan had come up from Tel Aviv for the holiday. As a special treat, he wheeled his grandfather to the Wall to pray. They were caught in the thick of it. He was knocked out of his wheelchair. When Nathan managed to carry the old man into a side street, he saw that he was dead. His heart just stopped beating."

Mohamed closed his eyes. In the tranquillity of David's lush garden, he groped for some reason. "The last of the founding fathers. Old Jacob. Old when we were boys." He paused. "The Muslim Inferno—Jehen'nam—has seven stages, you know. The first is reserved for atheists. The last for hypocrites. That is where I feel I belong at this moment. My own personal news seems somehow inappropriate."

"Why? What could you have done to prevent any of this?"

"Nothing—any more than you. But I share your anger,

your pain—and your concern. Because I know it isn't over—just as you do. I'm sad for your loss. But today I am almost ashamed to tell you that for the first time in years I am a happy man."

Judah watched a hummingbird hovering above flowering trumpet vines climbing to the jagged broken-glass ledge atop a sun-parched wall. "Have things become so bad we are ashamed to be happy?"

"In the name of heaven, Judah—how can I tell you? With the whole city like a funeral parlor. How self-indulgent it makes me feel."

"You came here to tell me."

Mohamed got up, pacing over to where a small fountain splashed liquid music. Then he turned back abruptly. "I have fallen in love as no man ever did. As I never thought could again be possible for me. Muna is Egyptian. Muslim. A niece of the King. She has brought me back to life and to my religion."

"Was it she who gave you the beads?"

Mohamed smiled. "And a worry to go with them. She's years younger. Beautiful, gentle, compliant. She is willing to be my wife."

Judah stared at him with disbelief. "Well, of course in Islam there is nothing against your having two wives."

"Don't look at me with such disapproval, Judah." He sat back on the iron chair. "I was beginning to feel dead—like stone inside. Turning into a business machine. Muna has made me recapture some purpose again. She makes everything important to me."

"Everything except Jacqueline?"

He slipped the beads back into his pocket. "My decision is made. No, Judah, not to have two wives. I think that would be more cruel to Jacqueline than a divorce."

"Have you told her?"

"Of course. I've asked her to divorce me—which I think she might prefer from the standpoint of appearances."

"Has Jacqueline agreed?"

"She will, I feel certain. After all, what has our life been together? Naturally, she will have no financial worries."

"She never did." Judah weighed it. "So—you've made up your mind. Well, I above all people cannot blame you, Mohamed. Where will you and this princess live? Cairo?"

Mohamed shook his head. "Never did like Cairo. But from now on I'll spend no more than half the year in New York. I want to be based in Palestine now. Just as you are. I think it is important for the Company if we are to survive these troubles."

"You just said a minute ago there was nothing we could do. How do you think you can help?"

"I intend—with the backing of some important people to whom I've already spoken—to start a countermovement. A tide of moderation. There are more moderates than anyone else here, but they have no voice, no leader."

"If they did, he wouldn't stay alive very long. Anyway, I'm glad to see you're still an optimist."

"And you're not? Not moderate—nor an optimist?"

"I'd like to be. I always was. But recent events are pulling me by my one hand to the other side. I think it is time, for *our* people at least, to meet terror with terror. . . ." Judah broke off sharply. He didn't want to dig into the things beginning to shape in his mind. A secret Jewish army, built to fight back. An eye for an eye. (That was too close to home.) Jabotinsky was preaching conquest by the sword. Weizmann may have tagged him "our own d'Annunzio," but if that would be the only way—maybe Judah would support it. Once he had finally decided. . . . "What about New York, Mohamed?"

"You have a brilliant daughter, Judah. She'll soon be running the office by herself. No, I have no worries about grooming Zed to head up New York one day."

Judah smiled. "My daughter. The first woman executive in Hammadi-Nouari."

At some moment—and Zed herself knew exactly when—she had fallen in love. It had been during the North Atlantic crossing on the *Île de France*, on the night of the Captain's dinner. The first stormy days that had rocked the ship in a violent cradle had now given way to smooth, long, gray-blue distant fields of water as though the nearness of the landfall had converted the ocean to tranquillity.

Zed, for whom clothes had scarcely ever been more than basic necessity, was suddenly aware that the evening dress her mother had packed for the occasion of the ship's gala exactly matched her eyes. Judah and Ruth's daughter could never have considered herself by any stretch a great beauty. Appearance had never much mattered to her. But tonight, awaiting her father's partner on the promenade deck, where he had suggested they meet, she felt a gladness of her own youth—a gratitude that her rather too tight, unmanageable curls had been brushed ruthlessly into a flattering dark helmet above the steel-gray silk of her gown. She wore no makeup, but as her mother always told her, "You'll never need it, Zed. You have what they call 'high color.' "

When Mohamed stepped onto the deck in black tie and dinner jacket, it happened as suddenly as that. Judah's oldest friend and closest business partner ceased to be the familiar avuncular presence at a hundred half-remembered moments through childhood. He became in that instant a perfection of man, seasoned, strong, the timeless adventuring hero of all the books she'd ever read. His voice, his smile, his touch—though no more than the perfunctory shake of her hand—was fatal magic.

It was impossible, of course—for every reason. His age, his religion, his closeness to her parent. All the things that made Mohamed the man he was, made him the man he could never be: her lover.

He was followed by a steward bearing a tray with two cocktails in delicate champagne glasses. "Tonight, my new young associate, I have brought these so we can toast something special. Something I have not yet shared with anyone. You must forgive me that my religion dictates my glass holds only ginger ale. But since this is a special night, I think your father will not mind if I corrupt my new colleague with one of the *Île de France*'s best champagne cocktails." He took the glasses from the silver tray and put one into her hand.

She gazed down at the ambered sugar cube melting in the bottom of her glass and waited breathlessly, unable to speak.

"Since we shall be working together—or at least you will be training to follow things up while I continue to bustle about the world making a nuisance of myself in high places—I now offer this toast: To the new Florida Hammadi-Nouari Land Development Company!"

Mohamed had gone on to explain how he had convinced the board to acquire a controlling interest in new tracts of

Florida coastline. "It will be subdivided and sold, conditional on Hammadi-Nouari supplying all construction material and having total approval on planning. Think of it, Zed. We'll be building whole new communities in that vast, undeveloped stretch of sun-soaked America."

"I've never been there," Zed confessed. It excited her to hear his expansive description.

"No? We'll go next week, you and I—to see the land boom we are going to create."

"I've heard there are hurricanes and tornados. And that much of the coast is swampland. Won't there be tremendous risks?"

"Risks begin with a baby's first breath, Zed. In our business, you escalate or you shrivel. There is no such thing as just holding your own, no middle road. Now! You have had your first lesson in 'tycoonery.' "

She sipped her champagne, thinking him at this moment the handsomest, most exciting man she had ever known of any age.

"And your first assignment, my dear little Zed, will be to familiarize yourself with our new subsidiary. Which, by the way, will be going public. Shares will be selling on the open market. I want you to learn everything there is to be known about land investment." He broke off, chuckling. "Then maybe you can correct some of your father's mistakes in Palestine. . . ."

She had learned. In her New York office in Hammadi-Nouari's new skyscraper building, Zed considered the two photos on her desk. Her father, who was now recovering from the terrible wound of terrorism in Jerusalem—and Mohamed. It was the photo he had given her when she first moved into her own office.

"If ever you are in doubt about making a decision, dear little Zed, look at my photo. If I don't wink—trust your own judgment. . . ." That was what he had said when he had presented it to her. The large, dark, thickly lashed eyes in the photo stared back at her and she could hear other words he had said to her only the month before, when he left again for Cairo.

"I have decided to end my marriage to Jacqueline. I find that I have fallen in love with somebody else. Somebody who has grown so dear to me and so important to my life. . . ."

How her heart had leaped with sudden, stupid hope. She scarcely heard his next words. It took a full minute for them to sink in.

". . . an Egyptian girl. Of royal birth. I'm sure, when you meet her, you will love her too, my dear little Zed."

Dear, but not dear enough. And this Muna was almost the same age as she . . . ! She returned her mind to the rather extensive report on her desk. The Florida Hammadi-Nouari Land Development Company. . . . She wondered if Mohamed—so preoccupied with his Muna—had given this project enough thought. There were rumblings in Wall Street. Unease about the market. The Florida swamps were proving more costly to drain and fill than originally planned. The investors were speculating on margin. Stock had been bought at a fraction of the cost to develop land that was underwater.

She had held this report for three days, not wanting to run scared. But now it wouldn't wait any longer. Her recommendation, carefully detailed in the report, was to liquidate and sell out.

Divorce, divorce, divorce. The word seemed to take over Jacqueline's thoughts. Why had she agreed so readily? Well, after all, why not? Had Mohamed asked her, which he did not, she would have been the first to admit that their marriage, in any real sense of the word, had ended long ago. And if blame were to be laid, it was certainly at her bedroom door. To deny him a divorce on the grounds of her Catholicism would have been hypocritical. She had long since strayed from that religious path.

Jacqueline accepted his request almost fatalistically, and agreed to make the six-week retreat to Reno, Nevada. But she had one stipulation. She was, after all, forty-nine (although everyone insisted she didn't look a day over forty), and though for the past two years her mental health had been fairly stable, she told Mohamed, "I have no intention of going to such a Godforsaken place as Nevada on my own. I shall take Françoise with me."

Mohamed had shrugged. "Do as you like, Jacqueline. Yes, in fact I think it would be a good idea." He was really thinking that having her daughter with her might keep Jacqueline out of trouble.

But Françoise didn't like the idea at all. In fact, she resented it bitterly. Nearly seventeen and finishing her last year at Finch, in New York, she was looking forward to going to college the following autumn. She had made her plans, and now they were being rudely disrupted.

To be sure, the news of the divorce had come as a blow to her, too. It was embarrassing, degrading even, that her father was going to marry somebody *she* didn't even know. A stranger—a *young* woman, at that. She couldn't understand how her mother could take it all so calmly. And she couldn't understand how they could both be so casual about upsetting *her* entire life to fit in with their follies.

"I am really terribly sorry, Françoise. I do see your point about graduating and all that," her mother said across the open suitcase on her bed. "But it is not absolutely vital that you do so instantly. After all, you are at least one year younger than the other girls in your class. And you . . . have your whole life ahead of you."

It was true she was younger . . . and at the top of her class. Except for Delphine, who was a hopeless "wet smack," as all the girls knew. But Françoise had chosen a career that would take years of preparation. Four at university, another three at medical school, then internship and residency before she could earn the title of Doctor of Medicine. She would be an old lady before she got through all that.

"It means I'll have to go to summer school to catch up, Mother. I absolutely *must* enter college next autumn."

"All right, Françoise, if you are that keen. But think of all the fun you'll have on a dude ranch. When I was your age, I'd have given anything for such an opportunity."

Jacqueline had been partly right. When they got to Reno, Françoise spent most of her time riding. She hated having to come back to the ranch house. She could never be sure what condition she would find her mother in. By late afternoon, if her mother was not half inebriated, she would be highly excitable. That was when the arguments about college began.

"Either Vassar or Wellesley, if it's America," Jacqueline

said with finality. "Unless you wish to go to the Sorbonne, which might be better still. I think I'd quite like to live in Paris again anyway. Everything there is so much more—real."

"I don't see why everything *you* do has to affect my life. I want to stay in New York, Mother. To go to Columbia University. I've already applied and been accepted—if I pass my College Boards, which naturally I will do."

Jacqueline stared into her daughter's defiant lavender eyes. Such white skin and black hair—really quite a beauty. Taller than Jacqueline, still a bit gangly, but in a year or two, adolescent gawkiness would be gone. "Why on earth would you want to go there?" Jacqueline did not add that the thought of Columbia University provoked memories of Bernard Goldfarb.

"Because, Mother, they offer an excellent pre-med course, and they accept women."

"I really do not consider medicine a suitable occupation for a girl. Certainly, from all the doctors I have known, it is a profession to be avoided."

Finally Jacqueline dismissed all responsibility for the decision. Françoise had always had a mind of her own. "You will have to take up this matter with your father."

"Why? He has nothing to do with us any more."

"He may not be my husband much longer, Françoise. But he is still your father."

Six weeks later, all Nevada's legal requirements having been fulfilled, the divorce was granted. Mother and daughter returned to New York and the house on Sixtieth Street. Françoise came home to find most of her friends away on their holidays.

Jacqueline had never felt the house so empty. She drifted from room to over-tidy room as though expecting to meet a ghost around the corner of every doorway. Half her mind argued that Mohamed had never, in the best of times, been home very much. But something else stirred. The need to pick up some fragment out of the dust of their wrecked marriage. Oh, how bravely she had faced friends and press on her return. She would start a new life—live it as *she* wanted— not always having to be at his beck and call. And now, how foolishly when it was ended she needed to hear the phone ring and it to be his voice again. She even thought of calling him.

Any excuse or other. But that way lay real danger. Indifference from him might turn into something more. Finally, Jacqueline stopped taking phone calls, spent much of her time locked in her bedroom, even taking her meals on a tray.

Bored to tears and anxious for summer school to begin, Françoise spent days in her father's library determined to read down the length of one bookshelf. She was defiant, resentful, too often disgusted by her mother's behavior. But she was also protective. When her classmates talked about their mothers, she had always described hers as a glamorous, doting parent. She never discussed the illness or the drinking, or the hinted-at rumors about men. Often, she had lied to her father when he returned from one of his trips.

"Mother's never been better, Father. So cheerful. So busy. . . . Drinking? Heavens, no. She seems to have given up champagne."

But now Françoise was worried. Too often, as a child, she had seen Jacqueline slip over the borderline into one of her "spells," as Gilles called them. With Maurice in Paris and Mohamed never to come home again, it would be up to her to look after her mother. Well, she wanted to be a doctor. This would be her first test of responsibility.

Through the library door, she saw Gilles hobbling across the hall carrying the afternoon newspaper up the great staircase. As usual, it was neatly rolled on a silver tray. Poor old Gilles. His knees would scarcely make it to the top these days. Françoise turned back to her book. Zola's *Thérèse Raquin*. A few minutes later, she heard a ripple of laughter coming from her mother's bedroom. The sound was not unfamiliar, and she knew that Gilles was hardly one to crack a joke.

When he finally creaked down the staircase, Françoise went out to him. "What is it, Gilles? Is Mother all right?"

He pursed his lips. "I would not go up there right now, Miss Françoise." He moved slowly back to the servants' quarters, looking very bleak indeed. Françoise returned to the study. The laughter had stopped.

Jacqueline was manicuring her nails when Gilles brought in the paper. She took it from the tray and opened it, skimming the headlines: STOCK-MARKET PANIC CONTINUES, it read. U. S. STEEL BOUGHT AT 205. Then, beneath it:

8,000,000 SHARES DUMPED. . . . Force of habit. She did not really care about the news.

Then she saw it—in the middle of the page. Mohamed's photograph beside a dark-skinned girl with smooth hair and a beautiful, heart-shaped face. The words beneath it stabbed through her. *Mohamed Hammadi, international industrialist, marries Egyptian.* The article went on to describe in some detail the history of Hammadi-Nouari's worldwide enterprises and the beauty and wealth of Princess Muna. The last sentence read: *Mr. Hammadi was recently divorced by his wife of twenty-seven years, the former Jacqueline Laville-Darlin, of Paris.*

Her first impulse had been to laugh. More an explosion of emotion than a release of attic wit. All the hurt and fear she had kept bottled up since that day Mohamed had come to ask for the divorce had been detonated in that laugh. No, it was not jealousy she felt. Just cold fear. The fear that without him there would never again be the steadying hand, the reef to cling to in the stormy sea. If now her mind slipped out of her grasp, where would she turn? To doctors? Nurses? Sanatoriums?

She knew she should occupy her mind more with her children, but it was too late for that. Anyway, Maurice was no child and, she suspected, glad to live one country away from her. Françoise was a good daughter. The fact that they were not close was not Françoise's fault. Or Maurice's. Or Mohamed's. . . . None of it had been theirs.

In her mirror she caught the reflection of a frightened, aging woman. She stared at it, but it only stared back, not liking her any better. She turned away, crossed the room to her wardrobe, and took out a clothes bag that had hung at the back of the closet for years. She laid it across her bed, then unlocked a wall safe and brought out a leather jewel case: the suite of emeralds Mohamed had given her so many years ago when their love glittered bright as the stones.

In the study, the afternoon light was beginning to fade. Françoise turned on the desk lamp. Then she heard her mother's step on the stair and put down her book. She came out into the hall.

A cry escaped the young girl's lips. A phantom was descending the great staircase in a white lace wedding gown, complete with dusty veil.

"Maman. . . ."

Françoise could see the green blaze of emeralds. Her mother's face seemed serenely content. She did not even appear to have been drinking.

"Where are you going, Maman? Why are you dressed like that?" Françoise was trying to keep the alarm from her voice.

Jacqueline reached the last step focusing on Françoise as though from the bottom of the sea. "Do not stare so at your mother, *ma belle*. Because you have never been a bride, you must not find me frightening. I am, you see, dressed as a bride. For once one has been, it is never canceled out—not even by the unkind angels who draw lines in your face and steal gold out of your hair. . . ."

"Maman . . . are you sure you're all right?"

"Perfectly, darling. It's a masquerade. I am not the same bride, perhaps—but only a masked memory to be revealed at midnight in a hall of mirrors. Yes, I am invited to a *bal masque*, my darling. Do you not think I shall deserve the prize? But my bridegroom . . . we won't tell his name, will we? Not in this empty house full of whisperings. . . ."

"But I didn't know you were going out tonight."

"Didn't you? This is an engagement I have had for some time."

"But you haven't been seeing people."

"Does that mean I cannot? Really, Françoise. You are not my chaperone."

Gilles, having heard the voices in the hall, came in.

"Do you wish me to ask Tony to bring the car, madame?"

"Not necessary, Gilles. Get me a taxi, will you?"

"Certainly, madame." A shrewd look came into his face. "But—where shall I say you are going?"

Jacqueline glared at him as though he had appointed himself her jailer. "I am quite capable of giving the driver the address myself. And Gilles, now that Monsieur is no longer in residence, I shall be obliged if you would take your orders from me without question."

Gilles nodded, and went out into the street, more than accustomed to his mistress' moods.

Françoise looked at Jacqueline uncertainly. She seemed dangerously calm. "When will you be back, Mother?"

"Perhaps not for a long while, my darling. You are not to wait up for me. You are nearly a woman now." She reached out to kiss her. A thing she had rarely done.

"Yellow roses. I should like yellow roses at my bedside."

Gilles returned and held the door for her. Jacqueline walked out to the waiting yellow cab.

Françoise stood in the doorway until the cab had disappeared around the corner. She wondered whether she ought to phone the doctor. But she didn't know where her mother had gone. If only Maurice were here, he would have known what to do. She went up to her mother's room to look into her appointment diary. Françoise never got that far. She was stopped by the sight of her father's photograph on the front page of the newspaper.

The Hammadi-Nouari building protruded above the city like a huge phallic altar to commercial enterprise. True, it would eventually look up to the newly planned Empire State Building, soon to be erected; but now, from the roof terrace of Mohamed's skyscraper, one could still enjoy an uninterrupted view of Manhattan.

The elevator operator knew Jacqueline and although somewhat startled by the fact that she appeared to be wearing a wedding gown, he was never too surprised by "white folks' carryin's-on." He saw no reason not to take her up to the roof terrace in the private executive elevator.

"Jest ring when you wants to be comin' down, Mrs. Hammadi."

"What goes up must come down, they say. Isn't that true, Bert?"

"Yassim. The market's sho' been doin' plenty o' dat. But Mr. Hammadi, he say in de newspapers: Long as dey has a donkey and a cart, dey's in business."

Jacqueline stepped out. A light wind whipped at her dress and veil. There were potted plants and trees and a miniature fountain copied after the one in Baron Liebermann's garden. Mohamed had built it in memory of that night so long ago when they had first fallen in love.

In the days and nights of their love. . . . Jacqueline walked across the stone terrace to the railing and gazed around the girdle of rivers. She had never bothered to learn their names. Below, the first streetlights were flickering on. Office buildings sparkled checkerboard illuminations. The breeze was stronger at the railing. It brushed her face and lifted her veil. She took it off, offering it to the wind.

It puffed out and billowed like a white butterfly, drifting up, down, up, and finally sailing far away. She did not see where it landed. Slowly, ritualistically, she began to unhook her dress. It dropped to her feet on the stone tiling. She lifted it up over the railing. The lace was beaded, heavy. It plummeted down, drifting out from the building. Cars screeched to a stop when it landed in the street, forty stories below.

The end of everything . . . relief from pain.

Jacqueline mounted the wrought-iron railing. But when she jumped she did not look down. Her eyes were on the diamond glitter of the first evening star.

In her office on the thirty-eighth floor, Zed Nouari was working late. The newspaper with the photo of Mohamed and his bride lay open on her desk. But there were more crucial matters to deal with. She knew that he and Muna would be honeymooning somewhere in the Mediterranean on King Fuad's yacht. But he had left her an emergency cable address. As much as she disliked doing it, she would have to use it.

The Florida Hammadi-Nouari Land Development Company stock had dropped from one hundred and fifty-eight to forty cents a share. Roughly six million dollars had already been lost on paper. Zed had spent the entire day buying up their own stock as fast as it came on the market. But she knew she was fighting a losing battle, and she wasn't prepared to invest any more of the Company's money without direct orders from Mohamed. Honeymoon or no. . . .

The sirens in the street far below distracted her from pacing. She went to the window. She could see an ambulance and police cars and a congestion of traffic. Probably somebody had fainted or been hit by a car. Zed returned to her desk and started to compose her cable.

A few minutes later, Mohamed's secretary, Amy, came in. "Miss Nouari. . . ." Amy hesitated, face curiously taut.

"Yes?"

"A woman has jumped from the top of our building. . . ."

"The top? Nobody is allowed up there except executives."

Amy nodded. "The elevator man, Bert, thinks it was Mrs. Hammadi. He took her up about a half hour ago. The body . . . well, it's unidentifiable. She was wearing . . . no clothes. Just . . . an emerald necklace. The police . . . they'd like to speak with you."

When Zed had finished answering all the questions, she sent quite a different cable to Mohamed. It was the most difficult thing she had ever had to do in her life. Then she went down and got into her car. She wanted to tell Françoise herself before the press got at her. The poor child. . . . Hadn't she had enough suffering because of her mother? What would become of Françoise now?

Twenty-three _____

FRANÇOISE Hammadi glanced at her wristwatch. Nearly six-thirty. Daniel Nouari would be waiting at her apartment. No matter. The doorman would have let him in. Nothing could have dragged her out of the auditorium before the speaker had finished.

Mrs. Eleanor Roosevelt, First Lady of the United States, was talking informally to a group of medical students and doctors. Her subject was the current civil war in Spain. Since November of 1936, there had been heavy fighting around Madrid. Now the battlefronts were moving north. Françoise had heard about the "Escuadrilla España," André Malraux's mainly French air squadron who were bravely trying to defend Madrid with obsolete Potezes—aircraft nicknamed "collective flying coffins"—his pilots hanging on in Madrid at the Hotel Florida waiting for parts, supplies, money, help, hope. . . .

Françoise tried to form a clear picture in her mind of the map of Spain. All she could imagine was a man's profile, nose placed prominently in the middle of Portugal. A fourteenth-century face wearing a pointed beard and a flat square hat. Madrid was located somewhere around his ear. That was where Malraux was now. Hanging on somewhere in the tympanic membrane. But Malraux did not have the ear of the free world.

Eleanor Roosevelt was guiding her audience through the history of Spain's endless occupations—from the days of Carthage's rule, past the Roman Empire, the invasions by Vandals and Visigoths, conquests by Moslems, reconquest by Christians, political marriage to the German Hapsburgs, who in the sixteenth century helped Spain to carve out a colonial empire from the belly of the New World. And then the wars that, century by century, stripped Spain of her treasured colonial possessions until today she hovered in the Western world like a poor relation, lamenting better days. Poor . . . but free.

Since 1931, Spain had abandoned her fusty thrones and become a Republic. And now General Francisco Franco, military leader of the Fascist insurgents was attempting a coup d'état, to destroy the Republic before liberal influences became a habit. The free world watched and remained neutral.

Yet it seemed that some countries were inclined to be *less* neutral than others. Hitler and Mussolini were backing the Generalissimo with arms, planes, and money, while Russia, safe on the sidelines, watched her "friends" in the Republic and donated some antiquated fighter planes and tanks. America and England rested in their neutrality. Nobody wanted to upset the balance of power. Nobody wanted to start a second world war.

Yet, in the free world some individuals were trying to help the Spanish Republic. Mostly people young enough to join one or another of the International Brigades.

Mrs. Roosevelt paused and drank a glass of water. Her toothy smile warmed to the eager young faces. "In America," she continued, "the only money that can legally be raised for Spain's defense is for medical or refugee relief. That is the cause for which I speak today."

Françoise wondered what President Roosevelt would think of his wife's plea. Although FDR had expressed sympathy for the Spanish Republicans, he seemed confused by Iberian politics. "I hope that if Franco wins, he will establish a liberal regime," he had told the press. His wife went much further.

Listening to Mrs. Roosevelt, and the enthusiasm her words received, Françoise came to a decision. Tonight she would tell Daniel.

When Dr. Simon Nouari's son Daniel had completed his pre-med training at Hebrew University, in Jerusalem, he came directly to Columbia University's Medical School, in New York. Although he had heard about her for years, it was the first time he had seen Françoise Hammadi since she was a little girl. Her great-uncle, Dr. Yusuf, told him that she, too, was at Columbia studying to become a doctor. That knowledge had in some part influenced his decision to travel so far from home to study. It was a decision he had never regretted. He and Françoise had become almost like siblings, with his cousin Zed playing protective "big sister" to the two of them. Daniel didn't feel homesick in New York, but he still looked forward to the day—internship and residency completed—when he could return to Jerusalem and join the staff of surgeons at Hadassah Hospital. Having graduated, he and Françoise were now interning together at Bellevue Hospital, in Manhattan. Her sights were set on gynecology.

"I shall have a practice in New York," she told him. "It's time women had the privilege of choosing women doctors for their more personal problems."

The time would soon come when they would have to go their separate ways.

But not quite yet. And tonight Zed was expecting them for dinner at seven-thirty. Daniel, who had been on duty all afternoon, had rushed home, showered, changed his shirt, and hurried to pick up Françoise. Ever since her father had sold the big house, she'd had an apartment off Park Avenue on Sixty-seventh Street. As Françoise had guessed, the doorman let him in to wait for her.

Daniel was a year older than Françoise. He had inherited Dr. Simon's dark good looks. Taller, more robust than his father, perhaps. Sometimes, as Françoise had observed, he had his mother's quick temper.

"Aren't you going to change your dress?" Daniel demanded when Françoise finally came in. She was tight-lipped, flushed, excited, and not too forthcoming with an explanation.

"Why should I change?" she demanded. "It's just Zed's house and only relatives. Nobody will be there but my brother and Abe. And you, of course." She smiled. "You don't count. Not since you put that pickled hand in my locker."

"A doctor has to get used to shocks," he replied.

She was wearing the same dark blue wool dress with the starched white collar she wore almost religiously. Although Daniel didn't realize it, Françoise owned four, all exactly alike. She considered the dress was a statement, almost like a nun's habit. An abnegation of fashion. Though she never gave it much thought, at twenty-three, Françoise's beauty required no artifice. Her coloring had always been extraordinary. She had grown up slim, graceful, with deep intelligence behind the lavender eyes. But most of all—and this Daniel appreciated—she possessed a naturalness of manner that came from caring more for other people and events than for one's self.

It had taken years for Françoise to get over Jacqueline's suicide. She blamed herself for being insensitive to the emotional upheaval her mother was experiencing. Her father, she felt, had been cold blooded. Now when he came to New York, she saw him and Muna, but they were like strangers to her. Within the boundaries of her academic life, Françoise had become a kind of island, absorbed only by her sense of direction—and Daniel Nouari. They, at least, had much in common: colleagues and comrades. He was her alter ego—mentor, confessor. And no more. And Zed . . . with Maurice living in Paris, Zed had become Françoise's only family.

It wasn't often that Maurice and Abe could leave their Paris bank at the same time. But, this year, Hammadi-Nouari had scheduled its board meeting in New York. Their fathers would be coming over in a day or two and it was giving the sons a chance for a few days' holiday first.

The young men still shared their apartment on the Île Saint-Louis. Their collections of paintings, friends, and objects of art had grown until now the place looked more like a museum than a home.

Abe brought a painting to his twin. A small Miró. Zed had grown to like Postimpressionist art. It suited her apartment, furnished in the slick '20s look. It was smart, cosmopolitan; but then, so was Zed. Tonight, she looked very chic in a peach silk dress with short "butterfly" sleeves, Maurice thought, watching the twins with some envy.

"A little higher," Zed advised. Abe was balancing the Miró with one hand on the wall above a table lamp.

"It shouldn't be higher, Zed. It is supposed to be viewed at eye level."

"By midgets? It's hidden behind the lamp. Move it, Abe."

"Move your lamp." But he complied, sliding the canvas several inches up the wall.

"Perfect," Maurice put in. They were so alike. Occasionally, to his annoyance, they still jabbered in their secret language. He often thought how strange it must feel to have a twin. His sister was so much younger, they really had very little in common.

Zed turned to him. "I do think it's bad of Françoise and Daniel to be so late."

"It is her fault, of course. She has no sense of time," Maurice replied. "Just like our mother." But like her mother she was not. He, too, had brought his sister a present: a dress from Lanvin, in Paris. "I do wish, dear Zed, you could teach Françoise something about style."

Zed took the hammer from Abe and pounded a nail in the wall. "Frannie doesn't care about style, Maurice. She is the most single-minded, uninhibited girl I know. And I love her for it." She placed the picture on the nail and turned back. "You will have to learn to accept her as a woman, you know. Not just a baby sister." She stood back. "There now, how does that look?"

"Like a bad appendectomy." It was Daniel's voice. He came into the sitting room with Françoise. "Sorry we are late. Occupational hazard."

"My fault. I went to a lecture," Françoise said.

Zed gave them both a hug. "Apologize to the roast beef."

"Oh, Zed, don't you look lovely!" Françoise exclaimed, then turned to embrace her brother. She held him at arm's length. "Maurice—you look lovely too. But you smell like a crushed gardenia."

He pulled back, offended. "Really, Françoise. All the fashionable men in Paris wear scent these days."

Abe kissed Françoise warmly on the cheek. He hadn't seen her for several years, and for the first time was struck by her beauty. There was something of Jacqueline in her features, but her entire expression held a controlled calm that Jacqueline had never known.

Maurice brought out a large box. "For you, my dear rude little sister."

She opened it, holding up a pale lavender dress with oversize pearl buttons down the front and long puffed sleeves. She gazed at it as though it had come from the moon.

"It's very pretty, Maurice. I expect I'll find some occasion to wear it."

"What about right now? Go put it on. I can't remember

when I've seen you in anything but that blue poultice you wear for ministering to the sick.

Françoise hesitated. Zed's maid appeared at the dining room door.

"Later," Zed said, to Françoise's relief. "Time for dinner."

"But where is this new boyfriend we have been hearing so much about? Why haven't you invited him to meet us?" Abe asked as they moved into the dining room.

"Frazer was trapped with a special House Committee meeting. Couldn't leave Washington," Zed replied.

Abe noticed she didn't look too happy about it. "The youngest senator in Washington. Thirty-seven, or so Zed tells me. One President, two senators, and a Supreme Court judge perched on his private Plymouth Rock, a gold spoon in each talon."

"All that and still a bachelor?" Maurice asked with just the slightest lift of an eyebrow. "How did you meet this paragon, Zed?"

"On one of my Washington trips for your father. Frazer Innes is the senator from Wisconsin." She did not tell them that, the evening before, the senator had taken the train into New York to see her, arms laden with violets. He always brought them. They were his state flower. They had spent the night together in her apartment and made love—not for the first time. They had been lovers now for nearly a year. Long enough to know that it was his arms she would want around her always.

She did not tell them that there was talk of Frazer Innes running for governor of the Badger State. Last night he let drop that the Party had advised him to get married. Before Zed's hopes could even soar up to the thought that this might be some sort of circuitous proposal, Frazer announced that there was a girl—from an important Milwaukee family. "Sally is pretty. She's popular—and—" He hesitated.

"Protestant?"

"Well, actually, yes."

"And what am I? Your jocose Jewish joyride?" Zed's voice had raised to a pitch unfamiliar to herself.

"Be reasonable, Zed." Frazer stroked her as though smoothing feathers. "I love you. You know that. But naturally I have to listen to my advisers. Give thought to my political future. You wouldn't respect me if I didn't."

"Try me. . . ."

He sat up, lighting a cigarette. "Zed—I hope you're not going to misunderstand what I'm going to say. You see, my state has a substantial German population. There's even some pro-Hitler feeling there at the moment. And there is, let's face it, anti-Semitism. Though that will change if we go to war. Now you of all people know *I'm* not anti-Semitic! And I've really been trying to see how we could work this thing out. Well, Zed,"—he wrapped her small hands in his—"I've come up with an answer. If you would consider changing your religion—give up your job at the bank. . . ."

"Job? Is that what you call it, Frazer? I am a full partner. I make more money than you do. And I'm the first woman to hold such a position in Hammadi-Nouari." She sat up, wrapping the sheet tightly around her slender body. "And as for my religion—well, I'm not very religious, but I *am* a Jewess. Does that word offend your Gentile sensitivities when we make love?"

"Please, Zed. You're being damned unfair. All I meant was I need a wife by my side. Middle Western voters are still damned provincial. I need someone who can share my public image on a Sunday morning in church. In front of the press. As a hostess in the governor's mansion in Madison. Not a woman trying to compete in a man's world in New York. Christ, they weren't even too keen on giving women the vote in Wisconsin!"

She looked at him, almost hating him, and still loving him deeply. "I am what I am, Frazer. Anything else would be living a lie. . . ." Somewhere in the back of her mind, Mohamed's words echoed: *For a woman, you have one of the best business brains of any man I know, dear little Zed. . . .*

She knew, if there were a choice, which it would have to be.

They were halfway through Zed's roast beef when Françoise's announcement dropped into a lull in the conversation.

"I've decided to go to Spain."

It came out as simply as that. All eyes turned to her as though they hadn't quite heard. Maurice was the first to respond.

"Hardly the time for a Spanish holiday, my dear sister. They're having a war—or haven't you heard? A civil war, at that. Which means you can't stay behind the front lines, because there *are* no front lines.''

"If you were half a man, Maurice, you'd want to go too!" Françoise flared. "I'm going because the International Brigades need doctors. They need nurses, ambulance drivers, people to carry stretchers. They're as important as fighting men.''

"So I have heard," Maurice replied. "They're creating an army of pacifists and poets, men with no military training who can serve the Republican cause without their consciences objecting. Someone has called this war—the rebels versus the rabble. No thank you, Frannie. I have problems of my own without taking on those of the rest of the world." He looked toward Abe for approval but did not find it.

"If my work schedule weren't so heavily committed, I might even be tempted to volunteer myself," Abe responded. "However, Frannie, although this war may be just, and even necessary—it's certainly no place for a woman. Even a lady doctor.''

"This isn't war in the old sense, Abe." It was plain that Françoise wasn't going to let the matter drop. It wasn't that she needed their approval, more that she wanted them behind her—in spirit at least. "My God, can't any of you see what's happening?" She searched their faces with angry desperation.

"I can see that my wineglass is empty," Maurice said a shade wearily.

She ignored him. Her words poured out, echoing Mrs. Roosevelt. "Germany and Italy are using Spain to test their weapons and destruction techniques. It's threatening the whole of the Mediterranean!''

"A touch too melodramatic, I think, Frannie," Maurice sighed.

"What about Russia?" Abe demanded. "The only ally the Spanish Republicans have. From the Jewish point of view, it has brought our enemies to both sides. Whoever wins, *we* lose.''

Daniel nodded, putting down his glass. "First the war in Abyssinia—and now this. What worries me is that the democracies are doing nothing to prepare. Nothing! Where will we find ourselves if this epidemic spreads?''

"How would you suggest stopping it, Daniel?" Françoise

demanded. "In an isolation ward? We are seeing the most cynical murder of ideas since the Inquisition. Yes, that's what this struggle is about. The Fascists are putting democracy on trial."

Zed looked at her young friend. She loved her like a sister. "I agree with everything you say, Frannie. But I wish you wouldn't go. Why you? You haven't even finished your internship. What do you want to do? Ruin your whole future?"

"If *they* win, there will be no future, Zed."

Daniel reached across the table to Françoise's hand. "You intend to join the International Brigade?"

"I do."

"And nobody can talk you out of it?"

"Nobody."

"Then, I'm going with you. At least I'll be more useful in Spain than some of those starry-eyed poets."

Maurice banged his glass down on the table. "Histrionics and theatricals. God, I had enough of those from my mother!" He glared at his sister. "I insist that you wait and consult Father before you make such a decision, Frannie. It's only a few days until he's here."

Françoise eyed her brother. "Father didn't consult me when he married his Muna. Maybe you can forget what it did to our mother, Maurice. But I can't. And I never will."

"Pull!"

Judah's command sent a dark saucer of clay spiraling off above whitecaps. The bang of his shot changed it into a black powdered puff. His single arm lowered the twelve-gauge. "Another hundred francs you owe me."

Mohamed shook his head in wonder. "Years ago in Uganda when we were after that lion—and still young—you couldn't hit a tree trunk at ten yards."

"I've had a little practice since then. Pull!"

"You've done it again. It's disgusting. Perhaps you've had a few pointers from that British captain, Orde Wingate?"

"A few." They were referring to the eccentric Englishman who was training *kibbutzniks* into an effective fighting force in Palestine—much to the unease of his superiors. And Mohamed's.

Judah leaned against a lifeboat, squinting into the sun. Stenciled on its side was the name *Île de France*. "I gather you don't approve of Wingate?"

"Certainly not. He's costing me money." Mohamed tucked a shell into the barrel. "And he will cost Arab lives." He snapped the barrels closed and shouted, "Pull!"

The deck steward yanked the cord. Another clay pigeon soared aloft above the Atlantic. Mohamed took a careful lead, then squeezed the trigger. The shot chipped off a fragment of flying target.

"I think I need glasses."

"What are you now? Sixty-three?"

"Sixty-two. I'm still only a year older than you. But thanks for not saying you could beat me with one hand. This is becoming very depressing." Mohamed handed his shotgun to the deck steward, along with a fat tip. "Bring us some coffee, please." He turned back toward the sea. A rag of black, oily-smelling smoke from a stack fogged them briefly. The air was chill, damp.

Judah sighed, moving to the rail. "Where do we go from now?" he wondered aloud.

"What in particular are you referring to? Geography, or destiny?"

"World events. Just when most people were beginning to feel confident that happy days were certainly here again—1937 is bringing grave doubts. The world has conquered its depression, Mohamed. But now it faces a new and even more dangerous delusion: the madness of grandeur."

Mohamed nodded. "There is no doubt that Mussolini's legions have conveyed some of the more dubious advances of twentieth-century civilization to Ethiopia."

"And don't for a moment forget Hitler. While that pair of bullyboys are flexing their muscles, the democracies are dithering. Waiting to see. Hoping for the best. Remaining punctiliously neutral."

"Well, my friend, we cannot solve everybody's problems. We have enough to deal with in Palestine. Which I think your Orde Wingate will make more difficult."

Judah deliberately changed the subject. "I'm surprised you didn't bring Muna this trip. . . ."

"She's following with Jalal and the servants when I've

opened the Park Avenue apartment. It's a strange thing. Jalal is young enough to be Maurice's son. If he had one."

Judah sensed just the slightest note of regret. No doubt Mohamed couldn't understand Maurice any more than Judah could Abe. Could the past ever understand the future?

"We must talk," Mohamed said. "Seriously."

"Yes. I know."

"What do you know?"

"Nothing. Only, it has been sticking out of you ever since we came aboard—like pregnancy."

Mohamed nodded. The sea swelled, a horizon of dancing blue hills of water, changing, timeless. "We're growing old, aren't we?"

"Of course, it happens. Suddenly. You were yourself, full of hope, expectation—promises given, commitments. Then they begin to cut away your flesh in little morsels—starting at the heart. Beliefs. Meanings. Ambitions. Each day I am a stranger to myself. Something lost. Something black—like a badge of mourning worn on the mind."

Mohamed lifted his hands into the Atlantic breeze. "It can also be . . . something found. Or rediscovered. Do you know what I did, after my second honeymoon? Do you know, Judah?"

Judah was silent, waiting.

"I followed the footsteps of my great namesake. He walked to Mecca, as you know. I carried his message on my lips: "There is only one God, Allah.' In Islam, there is submission to God. It's not just a religion, but a code of life. Alms to the needy—the third pillar. Fasting during Ramadan, the fourth. Universal brotherhood. Oh, I am aware of the changes that have closed the gate of interpretation. The rigidity, the inward search, the dogma that has taken hold. I felt all that had come to pass in Islam as though it were happening personally to me. It was Napoleon who felled the citadels of faith. Colonialism separated us from the well where we drank the purity of thought. But, in the end, it is there still in the mind, under the layers of memory. *Alahu Akbar!* Unchanged and unchangeable. The faith by which we live—by which we depart life." Mohamed fell silent. It was as though he had been speaking to no living man, but sharing the inner room of his own mind. His thoughts returned to his recent pilgramage.

He felt again the touch of the seamless white sheets—one wrapped around his loins, the other covering his torso, that afternoon when finally he had stood before Allah on the Plain of Arafat—on the ninth day of Dhu'l-Hijja. He had taken part in the early-morning stoning of the great Devil, Aquabat al Kabir. And then there had been the descent to Mecca, head symbolically shaved by the snipping of a lock. And so, bareheaded, wearing sandals, and carrying a parasol, and in a state of *ihram*, he had performed the circumambulation of the Ka'ba—running between Safa and Marwah seven times, his breath pounding against his ribs in the scorching heat. Without adornment or perfume, and abjuring intercourse, he had entered a state of ceremonial purity through prayer, and had thus been brought to "a freedom from life." A shedding of all sin and guilt. And with it, the phantom of Jacqueline.

After a while, Judah spoke. "I'm supposed to be impressed? Well, maybe I am. You find your faith, as I lose mine."

"Nonsense. One loses youth. But faith, if you ever had it, can only be misplaced like reading glasses—or cuff links. It is there under your hand, waiting."

Judah sighed, then smiled at his friend. "For me it will be a long wait. Because I once believed he who lives by the sword, dies by the sword. Now I have learned . . . who does not live by the sword, will not live very long."

"You are embittered."

"Name me one man with a better right?"

"All right, my 'one-armed bandit' friend. That's what they are beginning to call you, I believe?"

Judah nodded, his eyes far away, on a dark journey into a lost world, where Zosia had once lived in his heart. Emptied now by a flash of truth.

Mohamed let the silence settle between them.

"What else did you want to tell me?" Judah asked finally.

"As you may know, the Company has been expanding widely since Maurice and Abe took over in Paris. We have now acquired controlling interest in a chemical factory in Sweden."

"Yes, I read the correspondence. H-N Chemicals, Stockholm. Used to be a subsidiary of Nobel. It seems a good move." He paused. "But that's not what's on your mind."

"No. I want to talk about our Spanish interests."

"Hispañola-Nacional? Didn't the factory convert to making plows, farming equipment?"

"Briefly, yes. But with the civil war. . . ." He shrugged. "We have begun manufacturing some other items. On a small scale."

Judah started to rise. "You promised me once—"

Mohamed pressed him back to the deck chair. "I know. But it's more than just business now, Judah. It's politics. If the Republic wins, communism wins. You're aware of that I'm sure."

"And if Franco wins, fascism wins."

"We have to think in the long term."

"*Merde!* Spain has a popularly elected government."

"And how long do you think the Russians would let them remain popular?"

Judah was seething inside, but he controlled it. "Come to the point!"

"I'm trying to—" He broke off. Judah glowered across his glasses, his one good shoulder twitching slightly, betraying an attack of nerves. Mohamed drew a long breath, then continued. "Our factory lies in the Republican zone. Two weeks ago, I went to see the Generalissimo. We had a very frank talk."

"Frank with Franco."

"Don't be comic. This is important." Mohamed lowered his voice, almost as though afraid of being overheard even on the empty boat deck. "Franco has guaranteed not to bomb our factory if we will make arms available to him. If and when his army captures the province of Toledo."

"Colossal."

"You like it?"

"I hate it."

"But why?"

"You are ignoring the policy of total neutrality. You are putting the Company squarely into the Falangist camp alongside Il Duce and Der Führer." Judah's voice rose. "I will oppose it with every bit of power I have left in Hammadi-Nouari. I will force a vote at the next Company meeting and defeat it!"

Mohamed smiled almost benignly. "The policy has already been set in motion. However, if Franco fails to take Toledo, we owe him nothing. If he succeeds, we are stockpiling arms, which, I may add, will bring us no small profit."

"Blood money. My God, you must be mad!"

"No. Not even particularly unique. You are the one who is calling the kettle black, my hypocritical friend."

"Oh, for God's sake, Mohamed. . . ." He broke off as the steward arrived with the coffee.

When he had gone, Mohamed went on. "You see, I happen to know that you have been working with the Haganah. And through our Company, have been financing and selling prefabricated stockades and watch towers complete with searchlights, for new outposts. *Homa u Migdal*, they are called. True or false?"

"True."

"Why?"

"Why what?"

"Why do you do it? For money?"

"Not just for money," Judah admitted.

Mohamed smiled sadly. "No, I thought not. It is because these fortifications you are building stretch the Zionist claim to the land. A claim you are backing up with a twenty-five-thousand-man Haganah army. Don't tell me your German immigrants are coming just to be farmers."

Judah pulled the blanket around him in the deck chair. The wind was rising on the sea. "It seems I can't tell you anything. But why shouldn't the *kibbutzniks* fight for their own survival? Since April of last year the strife in our homeland has been at its worst. The British cannot be moved to action, and you, Mohamed—the great moderate—how can you condone this new Arab Higher Committee—whose first action last year was to call a general strike?"

Mohamed drew a thin cigar from his gold case, voice perfectly calm. "I don't condone it. I don't support Haj Amin—or his Syrian friend Fawzi el Kaukji. I know he's been organizing his bandit raiders to waylay and murder Jewish travelers. I know they've continued to attack settlements, burn fields, dig up newly planted orchards. Believe me, I'm doing all in my power to stop them."

"For example?"

"I convinced the British to invite the Foreign Minister from Iraq to negotiate with the terrorists."

"Which gave them an almost official status! A fine help—and a hell of a way to prove your moderation."

Despite his habitual control, Mohamed found himself growing angry. "I have supplied information and records to every official in the Mandate. Named names. Fawzi—*El Agrab*—and . . . the others." He stopped short.

"Like your cousins Yassir and Tariq?" Judah's tone was accusing.

"They headed the list I handed to the Governor."

"Then, why haven't any of them been arrested?"

"Fawzi has trained his raiders to disband—vanish into crowds—take to the hills. They're lightly armed and they can move fast. The British are at a disadvantage. Official forces can never successfully destroy guerillas. You know that."

"Well, I'll tell you something *you* don't seem to know. Behind our mutual troubles in Palestine is Axis money and encouragement. Zionists regard Adolf Hitler as a far more serious enemy than Arab guerillas. Our country must be kept open for immigration because the time may come, Mohamed, when there will be no place else for Jews to go."

"So, for that reason, you continue to assist Weizmann in his new role: chairman of the Central Bureau for the Settlement of German Jews."

"I cannot think of anything more important to do in the world," Judah snapped defiantly.

"All right. Go on—play the Good Samaritan. But remember, Judah, you may be bringing these people out of the pot and into the caldron. I wish for once you could remember that *our* main interest must always be in the growth and prosperity of Hammadi-Nouari. That is why I am right in Spain, and *you* are wrong in Palestine."

Judah got up slowly, feeling the cold. Mohamed started ahead of him toward the companionway. Then he stopped. Sarah Schreiber emerged on deck. She came up with a knitted scarf for Judah and a radiogram for Mohamed, which she handed to him.

"The purser just brought this." She wrapped the scarf around Judah's neck. There was love in the gesture. And concern.

Mohamed read the radiogram. The wind whipped the envelope from his hand, carrying it out across the water. "It's Françoise . . ." he breathed, passing the radiogram to Judah.

It read: FRANÇOISE LEFT FOR SPAIN WITH MEDICAL UNIT TO JOIN REPUBLICANS. DANIEL NOUARI GONE WITH HER. TRIED TO TALK THEM OUT OF IT. NO LUCK. SEE YOU SOON. ZED.

Judah lifted his glance. "Do you still think you are so *right* in Spain?"

In Judah's cabin, Sarah Schreiber turned down the bed covers. Judah lay down, closing his eyes. The glare of the sea made them tear. "Would you like a drink?" she asked. "A whiskey, perhaps."

"No thank you, my dear. You take too good care of me."

"I hope I always shall," she replied.

Ever since Ruth left him, their only communication was via their children. Judah had not seen Ruth since she walked out of his father's garden, seven years before.

Judah's respect for Sarah Schreiber had grown into a deep friendship. From that had come not the burning fires of youthful ardor but the closeness of two people who shared understanding. Sarah had not expected marriage. But she moved into his house in Tel Aviv and was at his side whenever he traveled.

He opened his eyes, studying her homey, comfortable face. She was typing a letter for him on the Remington portable. Nothing spectacular about Sarah—except her genuinely open, giving nature.

"I love you," he said suddenly.

She stared around at him without surprise. "Yes, I know."

"Welcome to Berlin, gentlemen," Hitler's Minister for Propaganda and Enlightenment got to his feet at Mohamed and Maurice Hammadi's entrance. A graceful hand protruded from a stiff bow. Mohamed shook it. The man's face was a polished fox's skull, beaded with lively eyes. His smile drew the lower lip down, revealing a parade of white, even teeth.

Joseph Goebbels' desk could have been the longest in Europe. It was flanked by a silken swastika banner fringed in gold and presided over by a beaming, paternal Führer in life-sized heroic portrait that surveyed all comers, hand thrust upward in salute.

Goebbels swiveled his attention to take in Maurice. "And you are co-chairman of the Paris bank? Is it not so?"

"Quite true, Herr Reichminister. This is my son's first visit to your capital," Mohamed answered for him.

"You are most welcome. Both of you. Please sit down, gentlemen. I trust you have comfortable lodgings, yes?"

Mohamed nodded. "The Adlon Hotel has always been a favorite of mine."

"Excellent. Excellent. So—if you forgive me, we will come directly to the matter that concerns this invitation—which you have so kindly accepted." His hand jerked above a bulging dossier. "Again I must plead forgiveness that the pressure of affairs does not permit us to entertain you more properly during your stay."

"I perfectly understand," Mohamed replied.

"Herr Hammadi . . . what do you know about helium?" Goebbels' question came out of the blue.

"Aside from the fact that it is a gas used in balloons? Nothing."

"Ja. Ja. And perhaps your son could make a guess at the kind of balloon? Since it was his Paris bank who initially interested itself financially in our airship project?"

"The Graf Zeppelin *Hindenburg*, sir." Maurice sat uncomfortably stiff on the edge of his chair in the presence of this runt of power.

Goebbels nodded. The slender hand flicked to touch a model of the great airship on his desk. The gesture was at once affectionate and sorrowful.

"From Germany came the first commercial air service across the North Atlantic. The *Hindenburg!* 1,002 passengers it carried. It flew ten round trips between Germany and the United States. And now the Americans, under the influence of Roosevelt—perhaps I should say Roosenfelt—" His sharp smile glittered slightly. "Now they refuse us helium to continue our air services."

Maurice lifted his glance from the model to the arch features of the German. "Pardon me, sir—but since the *Hindenburg* blew up, last month, I'm rather surprised that you plan to continue the flights."

Goebbels shrugged slightly. "Why not? The *Hindenburg* was not our only airship, Herr Hammadi. Her sister ship, *LZ-130*, will be completed and tested early next year. She is equipped with an arrangement for condensing water ballast from exhaust gases for the helium operation. And now the Jews have talked their President into not selling us this necessary element."

Mohamed carefully clipped the end from his cigar. "Thirty-six lives were lost when your *Hindenburg* blew up, Reichminister."

Goebbels betrayed no hint of annoyance, his smile fixed as ever. "And why, ask yourself, did our airship blow up? Please, yes, Herr Hammadi—why, in your opinion?"

"I understood it was a discharge of atmospheric electricity near some hydrogen leak."

"The excuse, Herr Hammadi. Not the explanation. For that I must use an ugly word: sabotage. On the part of the worldwide Jewish conspiracy."

"Herr Reichminister, such a suggestion is absurd!" Mohamed replied.

Maurice looked uneasily at his father. But Goebbels only laughed softly. "I expected that you—an Arab—would not share President Roosevelt's enthusiasm for Jews. But no matter. The incident is in the past. It is the present and future that concerns the Third Reich. So! Because of your importance in the world of international business—and the influence you still exert in Washington—you are in a position to do us a favor."

"What sort of favor?"

"We wish you to persuade the Americans to sell helium to H-N Chemicals, Stockholm—for experimental purposes, of course. The newspapers will be permitted to discover that this Swedish company—in which you own a controlling interest—is investigating the possibility of building dirigibles."

"Our Swedish company would have no interest in airship construction."

"Ah, but you are the oar that rows the boat. Is it not so? After you have made the purchase, what then would prevent your Swedish group from abandoning their airship project? Thus, being overstocked with helium, which is now to them useless, what prevents them from selling it to a German interest?"

"Ethics, perhaps . . ." Mohamed said flatly.

Goebbels emitted a thin laugh. "What? Do you think it will put a gray hair in the beard of Uncle Sam?"

"It would hardly improve my standing at the White House—if it were discovered."

Goebbels lifted his voice joyously. "Of course it will be discovered! And of course, you will deny it. With passion, Herr Hammadi. The greater the lie, the more people will believe it. Naturally, we intend to pay the Swedish company a handsome profit."

"Such a maneuver would merit a considerable profit," Maurice put in.

"Should we say . . . a hundred thousand shares in our airship company?"

"How sure can you be that the second Graf Zeppelin won't go up in smoke?" Maurice asked.

"We have new designs for the sixteen gas cells which employ hydrogen in the ballonets within the helium. This must eliminate any possibility of another accident."

"I thought the Reichminister accepted the cause as sabotage."

"Touché, Herr Hammadi. Sabotage will also be taken into account—with special provisions to guard against it. Besides, the Jews will soon be less able to make trouble in the world."

"A hundred thousand shares, you said," Mohamed mused.

"Convertible for gold marks. Or if you prefer, gilt-edge bonds." Goebbels rose. "Our government will of course show its gratitude. A decoration perhaps, similar to the one bestowed on Herr Lindberg, the American flyer."

Mohamed returned the cigar to his case, still unlit. "Very generous."

"But I quite forgot. This evening—if you have no plans, you might wish me to arrange some entertainment, yes? Perhaps a small dinner party. Some of the artists of our film industry. You have not met our beautiful Aryan actresses. Rhine goddesses, Herr Hammadi. . . ."

"Very thoughtful, Herr Reichminister. But we have already planned to dine with my very old friend Count von Bülow. Many years ago we were associated in the construction of a railroad. Before World War I, in fact."

Goebbels came to his feet. "Von Bülow. Yes. A very old man. A bit senile in his ideas. He is no friend of our Führer. Time walks by the old, Herr Hammadi. A pity you waste it with such a fossil. Von Bülow's days are numbered. But that railroad. Your part in it demonstrated your friendship with our country. A friendship that can now serve us again."

"The matter will have my deepest consideration, I assure you."

"I shall count upon your good judgment, and that of your son. The young are very sympathetic to our directions, Herr Hammadi. A pure new world—purged of the poisons of the past. Until morning, then? Good day."

Beyond the collection of desks in the outer office and down the long corridor draped with Nazi banners, a large number of people were waiting patiently for appointments. Father and son walked past the groups of petitioners and boon-beggars, ignoring the looks of curiosity on inquiring faces.

Mohamed was stopped short at the sound of his own name in a familiar voice: "Cousin Mohamed. . . ." He turned to confront a pair of sun-darkened, weathered faces.

The brothers were showing their ages. Mohamed made a quick mental calculation; both must be in their mid forties. How long had it been since he had last seen them? Never long enough. The four men stared at each other for an uncomfortable moment.

"Maurice—meet your cousins Yassir and Tariq. Straight out of the family skeleton closet."

Mohamed had never seen either of them attired in business suits. If anything, it made them a little more sinister. Perhaps he might even have walked by them without recognizing them—except for Yassir's eyes. They were as restless as ever. Feverish, angry wells of perpetual hatred.

"What brings you to Berlin? Mohamed asked coolly. "Has Jerusalem run out of riots?"

"It is survival that brings us, cousin Mohamed. For the Arabs of Palestine. I would hope it is the same thing that brings you."

"And you expect help from Goebbels? You must be mad. But then, of course you are."

"It is not a new experience to be insulted by our cousin. However, if *you* have forgotten, Herr Goebbels will remember that we and he have the same enemy."

Mohamed's words bit hard. "I will tell you what is the worst enemy of the Arabs: the past. It handcuffs us—prevents our growth. It forces us to live in two worlds. It obsesses us with the idea of shame. If we can conquer our past, we will, as you hope, survive. And we will be worthy of the true gift of Islam. Our key to greatness isn't just a curved sword."

"You still love to make speeches, cousin Mohamed," Yassir replied tartly. "Nothing changes you."

Maurice knew very well who these cousins were. He had heard of them all his life. He could see that beneath his father's outward calm a storm was brewing, and he had heard enough in the last few moments to know he had no liking for these relatives. He glanced at his thin Cartier wristwatch.

"Father, the Count will be waiting at our hotel."

"Yes, of course." Mohamed turned back to Yassir and Tariq. "I won't say it has been a pleasure to see you again. I only hope your presence here does no more damage than you have already caused. If we were in Palestine right now, I would have you both arrested."

Tariq looked at him levelly. "I wish just for once you would try to understand us, cousin Mohamed. You consider us terrorists, but we consider you a traitor to the Arab cause. Who is the more dangerous?"

"It is not understanding I lack, Tariq. It is sympathy with your methods." He turned away, down the long corridor, with Maurice, their footsteps sounding hollowly on the mottled marble.

"They are worse than I even imagined, Father!" Maurice said. "Vipers in badly tailored suits."

"There is a saying, Maurice. It is always too late to change the habits of a viper. You kill it—or you avoid it."

"With those two, it would be a hard choice. Of course, we might kill them first and avoid them later. They'd hardly smell worse, in any case."

Mohamed chuckled. They left the building and climbed into a waiting limousine. "And Father—about Goebbels' request. What do you intend to do?"

"I'm a decisive person. But this time I will avoid a decision as long as possible." He turned to his son. "Another old saying, Maurice. Nothing is lost by waiting. But many a mistake has been made in haste."

"How long can you wait? The Reichminister only gave you until eight o'clock tomorrow morning."

It was another two hours before Goebbels received Yassir and Tariq. The Reichminister was having a cup of tea when they entered. He gestured them to chairs. The press of a button brought a full-bodied girl bearing a tray of cups. She had ruddy cheeks and superb calves. "I apologize that the tea is British," Goebbels said, voice syrupy thin. "Tea is perhaps the thing they do best, no? Tea—and the manufacture of umbrellas in which to hide from the weather—which is always for our British friends a fog—in the sky and the mind."

Yassir smiled. Tariq watched his brother's eyes, not following the language. Goebbels selected a letter from a folder.

"I have read the message from your grand mufti. Impressive. He commends you highly. You would care to add to it, perhaps? Something he did not wish to put into writing?"

"He is hopeful that the Third Reich will increase the supplies of arms and money to our Sharifian movement. It is in your own interests, Reichminister, to support us, since it buys trouble for the British."

"Tell me, Mr. Hammadi—how is it that you speak German so perfectly?"

"I was once a student at Heidelberg. But my brother does not understand German. Perhaps, if you have no objection—we could speak in French?"

"Certainly. I have just had a most fascinating conversation with two relatives of yours in that language. We should use it while we can. It will soon be a dead language. So! You think by your extermination of Palestinian Jews that you Arabs help us?"

Tariq shifted uncomfortably. "Sir, it is not the Palestinian Jews we attack. It is the European immigrants, who are trying to turn our land into a Jewish state. If you will allow me to say it, Reichminister, I do not understand why your Nazi Party is opposed to the Jews in Germany. They are not taking over a country that does not belong to them. In Palestine we do not attack Jews because of their faith. It is only the land-thieving Zionists who are our enemies. . . ."

Yassir threw Tariq a restraining look. Tariq fell silent. Goebbels had not missed the exchange. After that, he addressed himself to Yassir only.

"I am curious—do you share your brother's opinion?"

Yassir frowned. "What you do with your Jews in Germany does not involve us. Unless it becomes hurtful to our Arab cause. Haj Amin is concerned that your persecution of these people, who are, after all, German citizens—will lead to more and more of them coming to *our* country.''

Goebbels showed the hard whiteness of teeth. ''Tell the grand mufti that the dead do not emigrate.''

Yassir nodded soberly. ''Your message will be delivered.''

''And tell him something else. If he will send us a select group of young Arabs. Fearless. Strong. Dedicated. We will train them in sabotage and the newest fighting techniques, so that each man can become a leader of a group. We will provide him with more finance and more weapons.''

Yassir was swept by a sudden flush of pleasure, a feeling he always had in the presence of strong leaders. Here was a man who could conquer, who was fearless.

Goebbels' eyes traced a path across a map of Europe. ''I myself am not a war maker. But if it should come, no power or combination of powers could stand in our way. Our army is the strongest on earth. Our people are pure in dedication to the Führer.'' His voice had risen slightly. It brought Yassir to his feet.

''Praise Allah! We have found a true friend. Heil Hitler!''

''Heil Hitler,'' Goebbels mouthed automatically.

''And *you* have found a true friend, Herr Reichminister, in Haj Amin, grant mufti of Jerusalem, and those who serve him. If war should come, he is your ally against the British.''

Goebbels rose and came around the desk. Something in his movement drew Yassir's eyes to the Minister's feet. Even in the shiny boot, Yassir could tell that one foot was clubbed!

On their way back to their hotel, the brothers paused to watch a noisy parade. Black-uniformed troops of the SS, silver skulls above the peaks of officers' caps catching the last glint of the fading day. Terrifying, impressive. Yassir's eyes were shining. ''Today, my brother, we have assured ourselves of a place on the winning side.''

Tariq looked soberly after the departing formation. ''I am not questioning your judgment, Yassir. Nor that of Haj Amin. But I think, all the same—we are moving too quickly.''

Yassir came to a stop under a linden tree. ''Why, in the name of Allah? We have come for aid—and we have been promised it. Our mission is a success.''

''It is one thing to take aid from the Germans. But I cannot feel it wise for our cause to make commitments that our people could later regret."

"What is to be regretted? Herr Goebbels is one of the most powerful leaders I have ever encountered!"

But even as Yassir said it, the picture of the German's foot flashed back to mind. Somehow the image seemed in sharp contradiction to the formation of blond Aryan warriors who had just marched by, prepared to die for this Goebbels, as well as Der Führer.

"I only say, Yassir, we must walk carefully with these people. If they hate the Jews only because they are a Semitic race, then couldn't they turn on us? We, who are the fruit of the same branch? Our quarrel is with Zionists, and must never be united with theirs."

"You heard me tell him we are not involved with their Jew hunts."

Tariq nodded. "And also we must not forget that the Germans have always had an eye on Palestine. I say it is one thing to take help—another to take sides."

"And I say we will take sides with anyone who helps us. That is the command of Haj Amin."

They walked on in silence for a few steps. The street bustled with the first traffic of the chill February evening. Tariq paused again, watching a woman crossing the street swathed in red fox furs, calves gleaming beneath amber silk. He was still not used to seeing girls unveiled in the street; he couldn't keep his eyes off them. Tariq forced his mind back to the matters at hand. "Yassir, I cannot help this feeling of unease. I must, for my own conscience, ask Haj Amin to reconsider—before we climb into bed with these Brownshirts."

Yassir regarded Tariq patronizingly. "Open your eyes, my brother. And not only to look at pretty legs in the street. I tell you, we are already in the Nazis' bed, and they in ours."

Maurice's glance crossed the nearly empty bar of the Adlon. There was a woman—hair a mass of tight blond ringlets, mouth a blood-red rosebud. A woman in a pale green dress, the color of her eyes. At least in her forties, he thought, and obviously looking for a man. Their eyes met. He turned his head quickly away with a slight feeling of nausea. She reminded him of his mother.

His glance moved to the crystal mirror etched with stylized flowers. In it was reflected the image of one of the handsomest men he had ever seen. Blond, almost polished hair, pale hollow cheeks, wide-set eyes that gave him a boyish look—although the man must be into his thirties. He was the only other person at the bar except for the predatory female.

From the far end of the room came the moan of a saxophone counterpointed by the sharp tinkle of an expertly played piano and the brush-scratched skin of a drum. The music was good. But Maurice could not enjoy it. His mind was full of worries tonight. He was opposed to the Company's involvement with Goebbels. But no matter what he thought, it would be his father's decision. Stubborn, narrow-viewed, firm—that was Mohamed. Qualities, perhaps, that had expanded the Company, even after the losses through the Depression years. Qualities, Maurice felt, that had destroyed his mother. And yet it was curious to Maurice that he never felt in his heart a part of his father. He knew Mohamed loved him. But in so many ways they were strangers. Maurice found so little in the world to be sure of—starting with himself. He was grateful this evening to be alone, to marshall his own arguments against the German Minister's proposal.

His martini glowed pale golden solicitude. He had first tasted the cocktail in a bar with Françoise the night before she and Daniel left New York to join the volunteer medical unit. She hadn't, as he had urged her, waited for Mohamed's opinion. There had been no word from either of them since their departure for Spain. Savoring his drink, he put his sister out of his mind. He was at least grateful to have escaped from the evening with his father and Von Bülow in a crumbling *schloss*—nobility's fading flower of '83. Thank heaven Mohamed had not insisted upon his going. Maurice would have been subject to interminable hunters' boasts of ancient kills. He could not ever bear the death of anything, even a friendship.

If only Abe were here with him in Berlin. Abe, understanding of every mood, every need. Closer to him than any human being had ever been. Yet there had never been a total commitment between them. He had never been able to express his deepest feeling to Abe. Feelings that were all *for* Abe. He preferred Abe's company to all the young women he had ever met. Yet, in his company, Maurice was never entirely at ease. Sometimes there was the desire to hurt Abe. To stab at him with double-edged sarcasms and darts of poisoned gossip. And sometimes he felt afraid.

The reflection disappeared from the mirror. Maurice looked around with some disappointment. But the man had not left the bar. He was walking over toward Maurice. A slight thrill of excitement touched Maurice's groin.

The man bowed to him slightly. "If you will pardon me, sir, for addressing you? But I heard you speaking to an older man in the lobby, and so I know that you are French, and therefore, a stranger perhaps to Berlin?"

"My first trip, in fact," Maurice replied, keeping his tone casual.

"What have you seen so far of our beautiful city?"

"No more than the inside of one office, I am afraid. My father—the man you saw me with—and I are in Berlin on business."

"And he has left you alone this evening? A pity."

"A blessing, actually. He has gone to a boring dinner. I was hoping to see a bit of the night life."

"What a coincidence! Tonight I find myself with a broken engagement. And so, we are two men at loose ends—in one of the most exciting capitals of Europe. An opportunity it would be a pity to waste. Is it not so?"

Maurice nodded enthusiastically. "You must allow me to offer you a drink, sir."

"Honored, sir." The man dropped gracefully to the bar stool next to him. In close-up, the man's steel-gray eyes were thickly lashed with golden fringe. But beneath them were etched dark lines of dissipation. It somehow added to his appeal. The man glanced at Maurice's glass. "And what is it you drink, please?"

"A martini. An American invention. Gin, lightly shadowed by vermouth."

"Then I shall join you in the same."

Maurice signaled the barman for two more drinks.

"Permit me to introduce myself: Friedrich Wilhelm von Nymphendorf. To my friends, I am Freddiedorf."

"Maurice Hammadi." They shook hands. Maurice did not miss the heavy, gold-crested signet ring—three boar heads crossed by a hunting sword. The German's nails were buffed, his watchband of fine rose gold, his shirt and tie of cream silk. This Freddiedorf wore an elegance bred through generations.

"Well then, where—where shall it be? Have you seen . . . ?" Freddiedorf paused. "But I forget. You have seen nothing. I take you, then, on a guided tour. The parts of Berlin that are not included in the itinerary of Thomas Cook. Tonight you shall—how shall I say?—place yourself in my hands."

They touched glasses, downing drinks at a gulp. Maurice put money on the bar, and they walked out together into the raucous, tinseled night life of Berlin.

The suggestion to go to a homosexual bar had not come from Maurice. It was offered casually—like an invitation to a freak show. They would be voyeurs—observers. What could be more amusing? Maurice had readily accepted.

By the second bar, they were on their third bottle of champagne. The room was heavy with perfumed smoke and eruptions of hectic laughter. Maurice eyed the dancing couples fondling each other. In Paris, they weren't so blatant, so open, so uninhibited. The entertainer in the velvet swing and fire-red wig dangled a tempting, black-stockinged leg into Maurice's face, the song a purple rasp, harsh and inviting. The entertainer swung nearer, leaned gracefully to kiss his lips. It was a man. He could feel the stubbled chin beneath the powder and greasepaint. The sensation was strange, electric.

Only once had Abe kissed him on the mouth. That time when they had both been so very drunk. In spite of what people thought, they had never really gone further—except for that once. Then he had been too drunk to remember much—only that he had been the aggressor. They had both been too embarrassed to speak of it in the morning. Or ever to try it again.

He downed his champagne, feeling suddenly warmed by the memory of Abe. Freddiedorf ordered another bottle. Maurice was swimming in a thick syrup of erotic atmosphere. Freddiedorf's hands touched him lightly on the leg. Freddiedorf's lips brushed his ear. He was wild with excitement.

The two young men moved on to a more private party.

Cocaine was passed around. The snow of summer, somebody said. The winter of dreams. He refused it, knowing it would make him sick after all the wine. He was beginning to feel sick anyway. Freddiedorf took him to lie down in a bedroom—and he found himself being made love to. A sensation of pure eroticism. This time it was Freddiedorf who was the aggressor. It was an experience beyond his wildest imaginings—somewhere between pain and ecstasy.

When the police broke into the apartment, Maurice wasn't quite certain what had happened to Freddiedorf. The police pulled him into his clothes and bustled him into a car between two burly plainclothesmen.

Maybe they had locked Freddiedorf in another cell. Maurice spent the night in the jail, retching, ill, sobbing. No one seemed to hear him when he called out. Men from other cells swore at him.

"You are lucky," the jailer said when he finally came in the morning, unlocking the cell door. "You have friends."

Was it Freddiedorf? His mind groped for meaning. He had a fleeting awareness of stark faces watching from cells, haggard, haunted men—as the jailer led him down the corridor.

It was his father who was waiting. Mohamed with a uniformed officer of the SS. There were many papers to be signed. Words exchanged in low voices; Maurice could feel rats' feet pounding in his skull. They scurried through a terrible emptiness. He smelled his own vomit on his wrinkled dinner jacket. Someone guided him into the lavatory. Maurice splashed water on his face. In the murky light, a grotesque, corrupted clown's face spotted with smeared lipstick leered back at him from the mirror. The jailer steadied him in the walk back to the inspector's office. Maurice was sick with shame—but not for the arrest.

Mohamed said nothing until they were inside the limousine. Then he asked, "How did it happen?"

"I'm not sure, Father. There was a man—at the Adlon bar. He took me around the town, I got very drunk, I don't remember much. It was all rather sordid, I'm afraid."

"You were used."

Maurice stared at him. "What do you mean?"

"I mean they used you . . . to get at me. I was forced to call on the assistance of the Reichminister himself—or you might be rotting there for months."

"Goebbels . . . ?"

"Of course, Goebbels." He did not tell Maurice about the photos. They were too disgusting to him. He had paid the price they had asked. He would burn them when he returned to the hotel. He regarded his son with slight distaste. "You need a bath. You stink. We are catching the train to Paris in two hours."

"You should have left me . . ." came the bleak reply.

Mohamed gave him a strange look. "You bear the Hammadi name. You walk through the world as my son. Anyway, I have had some experience—in getting your mother out of jail."

Maurice suddenly knew what his mother must have felt. "I am . . . so awfully sorry, Father."

"We will not discuss it—ever again. But if you cannot refrain from this sort of private life—at least see that your antics do not in future affect the Company."

Maurice nodded, beginning to understand. "Because of me you've been forced to agree to Goebbels' request. That's it, isn't it?"

Mohamed's face was glacial. "They landed their fish—with you as willing bait."

"I have put you in a terrible position."

Mohamed glanced out the window at the passing gray city he was now anxious to leave. "It is of no matter, Maurice."

"What do you mean, Father? Now you'll have to give them their helium."

"I think not. I will see to it that the Americans refuse my request to sell the helium to Sweden."

Maurice felt a faint brightening of hope. "Then, nothing is really lost, Father?"

"Pride is. . . ."

"I'll never forgive myself—that I have done this to you. My own father."

Mohamed turned cold eyes to him. "Your own father was a Paris pimp who slept with your mother, Maurice. I thought I would never tell you this in my life. I have always loved you as if you had been my own son. I have given you everything. You have been raised as a Hammadi. But today you have made me realize that blood will tell."

Maurice began to shake. He couldn't seem to control his

body as he tried to take in the meaning of Mohamed's words. The image of his mother as he had imagined her plummeting to the street in that last act of contrition flashed through his mind. For the first time, through all the pain and heartache of being her son, he could understand her.

Twenty-four _____

"WE are now in this moment only a few miles from the front," their Spanish driver assured them in his proudest English. "There we find a medical team of the Red Cross. If there are not in the road too many obstacles, we will arrive in half of the hour." Miguel was, as always, unbearably optimistic—and as always, he would be wrong.

For the past month, Françoise and Daniel had been making regular forays into the areas of the fighting, attached to the International Brigade. Their job was to collect wounded, administer first aid, bring casualties to the nearest hospital, and if no more senior doctors were available . . . to perform operations. The Americans had six hospitals scattered near the lines of fire, the British, five.

When Franco found he couldn't take Madrid, he had pushed northward into the Basque country. Fighting was heaviest around Bilbao. The volunteer doctors had been moving behind the ever-changing Republican lines. Casualty clearing stations had been set up in churches and public buildings. The trouble was, the Republicans themselves had been responsible for burning many of the churches. Françoise and Daniel were heading for the Church of Santa María, hoping it would still be there.

They were crowded into the back of the ambulance with six wounded men, bumping along a dirt road skirting the sea, up into hilly countryside, somewhere in the province of Vizcaya. Through the window, Françoise watched isolated farmhouses slip by, seemingly sealed against invasion from either side. Red poppies lay like gouts of fresh blood on the rain-soaked green valley; a mantilla of crocus and lavender wild flowers covered the slopes. Occasionally they passed a field where a *campesino* in worn black trousers and frayed blue shirt was painstakingly cutting furrows behind a pair of donkeys pulling a primitive plow. Nothing more than flint stones pounded into a board. From time to time, the ambulance was forced to dodge knots of refugees and retreating soldiers. Miguel drove like a bull fighter. Fortunately, there were few other vehicles, except for the occasional army truck. They jolted through tiny villages, no more than clusters of gray stone buildings. Françoise noted few signs of life—except for the barking of a stray *campo* dog. No chickens, pigs, or goats in evidence. If the *gente* still possessed such treasures, they kept them well hidden from any soldiers.

Françoise crouched between two stretchers. The young Brit with the chest wound was bleeding heavily. She applied a fresh pressure bandage. It was all she could do until they got him to where they could operate. Her mind swam with exhaustion. The American boy from Colorado moaned faintly. His leg was shattered. It would probably have to come off. No more than nineteen or twenty, she thought. Uniform almost in rags. She glanced back at the young Brit. No uniform at all. He would probably die in that same threadbare tweed jacket, bought so long ago in Cambridge.

The American's eyes opened to focus on her. He was trying to speak. "Two . . ."

"Don't try to talk. You'll waste your strength."

"Two . . ." he said again. "They shot two."

She nodded. He was probably delirious. She had given him a small injection of morphine for the pain. She couldn't spare much. It had to last to the next medical supply center—if ever they found one. At least twenty or thirty men had been killed or wounded that day. Franco was backed by Moorish troops and a fresh Italian brigade. She started to turn away. The American's hand stopped her.

"Two members of our regiment—shot."

"Yes, I know," she replied. "The Falangists are better-armed. But you'll be all right now. We'll be at the hospital soon." Hospital? She could be forgiven a lie under the circumstances.

"Not by Falangists. . . . Frank and Artie—shot by Republicans."

Françoise placed a soothing compress on his brow. "No more talk now."

Daniel made his way over to her. He had heard what the American said.

"Why does he think Republicans would shoot members of the International Brigade?" Daniel whispered.

Françoise shrugged. "His mind's confused."

From all over the world, volunteers had poured in to help fight for the Republic. They had been welcomed as saviors.

Daniel held his canteen to the American's lips. The lad sipped, then spoke again.

"Important . . . you understand, in case I die. . . . They were my friends. We signed on together—for three months. Volunteered. For three lousy months."

Françoise nodded. There was nothing new about what he was saying. "You're not dying," she soothed. "You can tell us later."

"No, Frannie, let him speak," Daniel said. "What happened to your two friends?"

The boy shifted his glance slightly to include Daniel. "Artie and Frank—they had enough. Wanted to leave. Defenders retreating. Cut off. Didn't know where to fire. Shallow trenches. Too shallow. . . . Always being evacuated. We were at a village called Elgeta, up in the hills. Good deep trenches there. We held them off. Then two of our Spanish battalions withdrew. Left us holding the sack. . . . Could I . . . cigarette?"

Daniel slid one out of his pack, lit it, and propped it in the American's mouth. He puffed, trailing smoke up in the coffinlike frame of the ambulance.

"Frankie asked," the boy droned on. "Went to the commissar of the battalion. 'Three months?' he said. 'Can you prove it? Where are your documents?' Commissar told him— if he left without documents—it'd be desertion." The boy closed his eyes. The cigarette dropped from his lips. Daniel picked it up. The boy snapped awake with a start.

"Should have hightailed with them. Too scared. They were caught—by Republican troops. Commissar ordered . . . death penalty. No exceptions for International Brigade. Not for Americans—British. Not for Spaniards. Not for anyone. . . ."

They were bumping into a small town where the road, if anything, got worse. Miguel slowed to an uneven stop near an ancient gnarled oak in the middle of the square. Daniel peered out. Obviously market day. Stalls had been set up. Dried fish—cheese, strings of onions, potatoes, and the like. Refugees from other villages mingled with townspeople and *campesinos* in from the countryside with their donkeys. Daniel climbed down into the cobbled square filled with the steady uproar of barter. Miguel had parked the ambulance right in the thick of it. Daniel helped Françoise out.

"Here they don't seem to have noticed there is a war on," Daniel said.

"I wish I didn't. Let's get these men inside." She signaled to Miguel, who came around.

"You see? I told you, is a church of doctors," he beamed.

Red and black anarchist flags draped some buildings in the square. The Communist flag waved over one. The Church of Santa María bore the banner of the Red Cross, having been commandeered by an American medical unit. Daniel shouted to a white-jacketed orderly smoking a cigarette in the entrance.

"Get some stretchers, will you?"

The orderly jumped into action.

Inside the dark church, pews had been pushed together and covered with straw and sheets to form beds. Several make-shift oak-plank operating tables were being sluiced down with disinfectant as the men were brought in. They were greeted by an American doctor graying at the temples, assisted by a bearded *practicante*, four nurses, and a few nuns.

"We're running low on supplies. Got anything you can spare?" the medic asked.

Daniel shook his head. "We were hoping to beg some from you." He took charge of the American with the smashed leg, cutting away the trouser.

The medic came back to have a look—shook his head. The *practicante* looked too. Said something in Spanish to the medic, who nodded. "Don't think there's enough left below the knee," he told Daniel.

Daniel continued his examination. "What do you advise?"

"Have to come off."

Daniel's heart sank. He had never before performed an amputation. The medic noted his indecision.

"I'll give you a hand. I've had four off in the last few weeks," he told him. "Chloroform, nurse."

A weary young woman with a pale face brought a bottle. "It's all we have left. Use it sparingly, Doctor."

The harassed medic's eyes seemed to bulge with anger. The veins in his temples swelled visibly. Daniel thought he might be losing control. Everything seemed so unreal in the dark, crowded church. "God damn it!" the medic exploded. "I'm not taking off his leg with that kid half conscious!" As suddenly as it had come, the anger passed. He turned back to the boy with reassuring calm.

Françoise, busy picking steel splinters from the British lad's chest, registered the American medic's outburst. She knew the pressures on him must be unbearable, after almost a year in Spain. A dark-eyed nun stood at her elbow, holding the tray of instruments. How lucky *this* boy was, Françoise thought. The wound wasn't close to the heart. Then, suddenly, it seemed as though his whole chest exploded with great clots of blood. "A fragment has severed an artery! Plasma— quickly!" she cried out.

"Of plasma there is no more, Doctor," the nun said sadly.

For the next ten minutes Françoise worked frantically in an effort to stitch up the artery. Before she could complete her task, the boy was dead.

Françoise took off her stained white coat, handing it to the sister. It would be boiled and ironed for the next calamity. She washed and went out into the square, sat on the steps of the church, and began to cry. Some time later, Daniel came out. He and the American medic had successfully managed the amputation. The boy would recover. Daniel sat down on the dusty steps beside Françoise, handing her a lighted cigarette.

"You did your best," he said.

"Is it ever enough when the patient dies?"

Daniel couldn't think what to say to her. All her courage and skill had failed to save a life. As a doctor, it would not be the last time. He tried to find words of comfort. "Fran . . . did I ever tell you? You are the woman I respect most in the world."

"Don't, Dan. Don't say anything."

He drew on his cigarette. The heat of the afternoon was building up. From the road leading south came the sound of marching feet. It brought a platoon of Basque militiamen into the square. They were escorting five prisoners—sad-eyed

Falangists in dirty uniforms with little red tassels swinging from their forage caps. They were unshaven, and complaining of thirst. The militiamen herded them beneath the gnarled oak tree.

From inside the buildings, a fat-bellied official in a shiny black coat and Basque beret emerged into the square. He stood for a few minutes, hands gesturing in argument with the sergeant in charge of the platoon.

Then he seemed to give way to whatever the sergeant was demanding. He shrugged, as though washing his hands of the matter and watched while the militiamen marched the prisoners away. The official returned to the banner-draped building and closed the double doors behind him, shutting out his acquiescence.

The American doctor, who had come out of the church to see what the commotion was all about, shook his head. ''Poor bastards. Those prisoners were from a village near here. That hombre in the black jacket with the beer belly—he's the mayor of this town.''

''What was the argument about?'' Daniel asked.

''The sergeant insisted that the prisoners were traitors—because they joined the other side.''

''Where are they taking them?'' Even as she asked, the air was ripped by a sudden burst of submachine-gun fire.

''I'm afraid that's your answer.''

''But they were prisoners of war . . . !'' Françoise exclaimed.

The medic nodded. ''Sure. Spaniards. Neighbors. Maybe even relatives, for all we know. Last week a son shot his father. Or maybe it was an uncle. Who knows? The hatred between these people goes deep. It's something we can't judge.''

''Then, what are we doing here?'' Françoise demanded.

''Trying to save a few lives.''

''While they go on killing each other? It doesn't make sense.''

''It's a little late for philosophical questions, Dr. Hammadi. You should have asked yourself that back in America.'' The medic turned away into the church. Its bell was beginning to peal out the half hour in metallic throbs. Between four and five o'clock. Françoise stubbed out her cigarette. Suddenly it tasted like straw.

"Would you like something to eat or drink?" Daniel asked her. "I see a dried fish over there that looks friendly."

"No—I'm just tired, Dan. So tired. I've lost all track of time. What day it is—what month. How long has it been since we left New York?"

"It's the twenty-sixth of April, Frannie. We have been here for two months now. And you've learned seven words of Spanish, if you count *buenos días* as two." He paused. The church bells had begun to peal again. Insistent, clamorous.

"What do you think it means?" she asked with a sudden premonition of fear.

"An air raid. We'd better get inside. Hopefully they will not bomb the church. They can see the Red Cross." Daniel helped her up and into the doorway. Everywhere around them people were seeking shelter. Françoise turned back to see a single plane swooping down on the town.

"Heinkel 111," Daniel shouted. "One of the new German bombers. They are fast—carry up to three thousand pounds of bombs!"

The plane dropped its load some distance from the square. A spire of smoke reached skyward. They watched the plane circle away.

"There are no air defenses here," the American medic told them. "Let's hope that it doesn't return."

But, a few minutes later, it did, with three more of the same. Bombs seemed to be dropping everywhere around them—people screaming and running in every direction. Billowing smoke and flames filled the streets.

"*A las montañas!*" people were shouting outside. They began to get the wounded ready to be moved. An old Basque appeared in the church doorway. He wore the traditional black beret, but he addressed them in French. "You must get the wounded and yourselves to the hills. All the people of the village go there now. There is a large cave. Inside, it is safe." Then he was gone into the crowd of running figures.

Now the air was black with planes: Junkers 52, Messerschmitt BF-109 fighters, which were beginning to machine-gun anybody still in the streets. Shrapnel bombs were dropping in waves. Mutilated bodies were sprawled in the square.

Between the barrage of attacks, the stretcher bearers and

nurses tried to carry out wounded and equipment. The medical detachment moved up the hillside with the townspeople, slowed to the pace of women, screaming children, and the aged. Wave after wave of fighter planes descended to strafe the running crowd. Somehow those still unhurt stumbled on up the hill.

In the town, Heinkels continued dropping incendiary, shrapnel, and high-explosive bombs. The ancient gray walls seemed to be decomposing before their eyes. Planes were so thick in the sky, they veiled the sun.

Françoise's arms were heavy with medical supplies. Daniel was on one end of a stretcher carrying the lad from Colorado whose leg he had amputated. A nun was helping him. Behind them the earth screamed, the sky streaked flames, low-flying planes stitching the ground with lead needles, marking the perimeters of horror with sordid precision in blood, ashes, and flame.

A bomb gutted the earth ahead of them and the stretcher with the American on it was blown to pieces. The blast hurled Daniel violently backward. Moving behind him, Françoise dropped her cases and rushed to his aid.

He was unconscious—but mercifully alive. Beneath the dirt it was impossible to tell the extent of his wounds. She had to get him to safety. The old Basque came over to give her a hand.

"The cave—it is close now." He pointed up the hill. "We must hurry—before the planes come back."

A child in short trousers with large frightened eyes picked up her medical supply cases and hefted them on up the hill behind them.

People were crowding into the cave. It wasn't large enough to hold everyone. The mayor suddenly appeared and took charge, herding in women and children, wounded and the infirm.

Françoise found a bit of old blanket, and they laid Daniel on it. He was in great pain. She wiped his face. Minor cuts and abrasions. Most of the damage seemed to have been to his eyes.

The American doctor came over. "Is he very bad? Let me have a look." He examined Daniel, then took out a small flask from his case. "Sterilized water. That'll have to do until we can get him to a decent hospital. God knows where that will be.'' He moved on to attend to more wounded being brought in, calling to her, ''I can use you—when you're finished with him, Doctor.''

Daniel stirred to consciousness. ''Frannie. . . . Frannie . . . ! I cannot see. . . .''

''I know, Daniel. But I'm here with you. We're safe—in a cave. I'm going to wash out your eyes and bandage them— and then you must try to sleep.''

He nodded, and lay quite still while she attended to him. He moaned slightly. She knew the pain must be very bad, and gave him a small injection of morphine.

When she had finished all that could be done, she left Daniel and went to help the American doctor with other wounded. After a while, they heard the planes roar away and all was quiet. When they had finished bandaging the last casualty, Françoise came back to have a look at Daniel. He was sleeping.

The cave was heavy with the smell of blood. Françoise went outside for a breath of air.

The old Basque was sitting under a tree, looking down at the town. Women were sobbing, one cradled a dead baby in her arms. Then they began to wail—slowly at first, then it grew, building into a chant. Men's voices joined in the rising dirge for their dead town. *''Gernika . . . Gernika . . . Gernika . . . Gernika . . .''*.

The old Basque came over to her; his voice held a note of triumph. ''The bastard Germans—they have missed the arms factory outside the town. And more important, the tree is still standing.''

''The tree?'' she demanded. ''There are at least a thousand dead down there—and you worry about a tree?''

''Yes, I know what you say is true. They have killed many of our people. But they have not killed the spirit of Basque liberty. Always—even before recorded history—it has been represented by that great oak tree in the square. These things I know, because I teach in the school. I read in three languages.''

How mad it all seemed to Françoise at this moment listening to this old man go on and on about his languages and the tree!

''Beneath its branches, the parliament of senators has been

held since there has been a Basque people. Beneath that tree
the kings of Castile swore to respect the special rights of the
Basques. And it is because of that tree that Franco's German
friends have bombed our Guernica."

She sat down. "I shall never understand politics. Or wars,"
she told him.

He brought out a bottle of wine from the deep, sagging
pocket of his jacket and passed it to her. "Drink," he said.
She accepted gratefully, the dark rough wine soothing her
parched throat.

"So you do not understand politics—and war?" He took
back the bottle, drinking deeply. "I will tell you. War is
nothing more than politics negotiated by Sten guns—and
achieved by bombs. The dead do not vote against you. Though
we Basques fight beside the Republicans, we still want our
own changes in the government. Everything is not as we
would wish it. All over Spain, there is the desire for a
revolution. Some think it should come now. Others think we
must first win this war—defeat Franco and fascism—then we
can change our country. Yet we are afraid to arm the anarchists who fight with us against Franco—for if he is defeated,
then the anarchists would lead the revolution."

"It sounds very complicated for a country of—well. . . ."
She paused.

"Go on. Say it. A primitive country. Yet primitive as we
are, we have at least five political parties." He smiled,
passing the wine bottle back to Françoise. "This politics of
ours is a labyrinth. It is two much for a foreigner, however
well-intentioned, to comprehend. We do not understand it
ourselves. Now we may need your help, yes—but you do not
belong here. This is not your fight. This is a war that is being
fought in the darkness of our hearts, from the hatreds of the
past and present. Family destroys family—and in the labyrinth, who can finally win?" He arose stiffly, finishing the
wine and tossing the bottle away.

"Take your friend while you can still save him. Get him
away from here. If you stay, you will both die for a cause that
is not yours."

She watched him start slowly down the hill toward the
rubble that had been Guernica.

By morning, Daniel was able to sit up. Françoise bathed
and rebandaged his eyes.

"They look fine," she lied. "You'll just have to keep the light out of them for a while."

"I can walk, Frannie. I'd like you to take me outside."

She helped him up and led him into the pine forest. The air was pungent with the smell of burned wood and flesh.

"What do you see?" he asked.

"Nothing, Daniel. The whole town of Guernica has been destroyed. Some men from the village have gone down to begin clearing the rubble—and dig graves. There is still smoke."

"I cannot understand this bombing—as an act of civil war. Could the Germans have done such a thing without orders from Franco?" Daniel asked.

"There is a lot I don't understand, Daniel."

The American doctor came up the hill. He had gone down to the town to reconnoiter and collect any remaining supplies.

"There's one ambulance still usable. But the driver's been killed." It was their Miguel. "Can you drive, Dr. Hammadi?"

Fran nodded.

"I can't spare any of my Red Cross people. But I think Dr. Nouari should be taken to a decent hospital as soon as possible. And we have a few pretty badly wounded here. Do you think you could make it to San Sebastián if I give you a map? It's roughly thirty miles. There is a base hospital there. You may encounter some fighting. Try to stay off the main roads. What do you say?"

"I can do it."

"Good girl. Tell them we need all the supplies they can spare: morphine, chloroform, antiseptic, bandages. And cigarettes. And tell them about Guernica. Tell them it's a gift to the world's neutrality."

"Are you going to stay on in the church?" she asked.

"For the moment. There are a lot of wounded in the town. Maybe over a thousand dead. We can't move everyone. The church has been smashed up quite a bit, but I think we can hold on there—for a while longer. If the planes don't come back."

"I'll get my bags. We'll start right away."

•   •   •

They had been driving for nearly an hour on rough back roads. Daniel had fallen asleep with his head on her shoulder. In the back of the ambulance were six men she hoped would still be alive on delivery. She glanced at the map as they came to a crossroad, then turned left, heading north along the edge of a small stream. The ambulance jolted and bounced on the rocky lane. Daniel stirred awake—reached toward his eyes, felt the bandage, then sank back.

"Frannie? Everything going all right?"

"No sign of fighting around here. We passed one patrol, but they were ours. How do you feel?"

"The pain is less. Where are we?"

"Somewhere near San Sebastián, I should think. There's a real hospital there. You'll be able to have a proper examination." She pulled a crumpled pack from her shirt pocket. "Want a cigarette?"

"Thanks."

She placed it between his lips. She could tell that the pain was worse than he admitted.

"Daniel, last night . . . I had a talk with one of the nurses. She told me that it was true—what that boy from Colorado said. About the Republicans shooting deserters. Even Americans and British. And you know something else? The Italians are fighting with Franco, but there are a lot of them on the Republican side, too."

"It's all so mixed up, isn't it?"

She drove on for a while in silence, pulling off the road at the clattering approach of a small armored column. "Daniel, I feel so guilty for having gotten you into this. If it weren't for my stupid, overromanticized notions, neither of us would be here. I seem to have lost all perspective. I don't know who's right or who's wrong. All I know is war is wrong. I realize we didn't come here to carry arms; we came to save lives. But democracy, fascism, communism—what does a label mean when you're being bombed? By German planes who have no more right here in Spain than we have!"

The armored column had passed. She started up again. Daniel rested his head back against the seat. He seemed weak, but he wanted to talk. "Don't just blame yourself, Frannie. I should have stopped you back in New York."

"Stopped me? My mother used to say that nobody could

stop me from doing anything I'd set my mind to. I suppose in that way I'm like my father.''

At the hospital in San Sebastián they delivered their wounded. A British doctor took charge of Daniel. Françoise watched while he used a magnet to remove tiny metal fragments from both Daniel's eyes. When it was over, the doctor took Françoise aside.

''I'm not an eye specialist, I'm afraid. I can't be certain Dr. Nouari's sight will ever be anything like normal. It's impossible to tell the damage to the retinas. The sooner you get him to a specialist, the better.'' He shook his head at the absurdity of his own suggestion. ''Madrid, perhaps. You might find someone. If anyone can find Madrid.''

Françoise left Daniel to sleep off the anesthetic and walked down toward the harbor. Beneath the fortress-crowned outline of Mount Urgull, the city lay in the great curved shell of the bay, Bahía de la Concha. Starkly beautiful, the water glittering bright beneath the cleanness of the sky, people promenading; a setting for a holiday, not a war. A setting Daniel might never see. Get him to Madrid, the doctor had suggested. Madrid . . . ? A city under siege, nearing its own death rattle. She took the map from her bag—began to study it. Where, then, if not Madrid? Barcelona, across the width of Spain? Impossible.

The following morning, Françoise told Daniel her plan: She had made all the arrangements. Daniel released himself from the hospital. Françoise had hired a car to drive them east—to Fuenterrabía. That was as far as the heavily paid driver would take them. ''Gusolina! Gasolina! Muy difícil para encontrar!'' he had grumbled, separating the money and stuffing it into various pockets. It took most of the pesetas they had.

At Fuenterrabía they found a farmer willing to sell them a donkey. They bought blankets, a straw hat and ragged shirt for Daniel, and a black shawl for Françoise. It took their remaining pesetas and a few American bills the farmer wasn't sure how to value. They traded their Columbia graduation rings for bread, sausage, cheese, and three bottles of wine. Except for Daniel's bandages, they might have passed for any Spanish farmer and his wife moving through the countryside.

''OK?'' she asked.

''Fine,'' he said.

Françoise got Daniel onto the donkey and led it up the steep, tortuous climb into the Pyrenees. They avoided the main road, only keeping near enough not to lose their way. Once, a patrol passed too close for comfort. Françoise stuffed grass into the donkey's mouth to keep him quiet. *"Silencio!"* she whispered. The beast had no choice but to chew.

They couldn't tell which side the troops belonged to. It hardly mattered. The one would have shot them as enemies, the other, as deserters. After that, they kept farther from the road.

The tapping of rain through pine needles increased with the dusk. She moved them back to the main road, for shelter. Suddenly the rain came pouring down in a torrential sheet. In minutes the earth beneath them was a lake of mud. The donkey's hoofs were slipping in it. "You're going to have to walk for a while, Daniel. All right?"

"Fine."

She helped him off the donkey, holding both his arm and the donkey's lead rope. They moved forward again, along the edge of the narrow road grooved into the mountainside. She didn't want to look down. The drop was precipitous. Daniel stumbled, and she knew his strength was running out. By now they were both soaked to the skin. "I'd better get you back on the donkey," she said, leading him around to mount from a fallen branch. The rotten wood cracked under his weight. He fell, sliding down the edge of the bank into a ditch some twelve feet below.

"Daniel!" she cried. He did not answer. Françoise took the rope from the donkey's pack saddle and tied it to the lead. She clung to it, making her way down to Daniel. He was shivering, and covered with mud. She got him up to his feet, and tied the rope around his waist. "Put some of your weight on me," she said. He was feverish and a little delirious. She managed to move them up the rope to the donkey, which, happily, had remained fixed in stubbornness. She did not try to get Daniel back on it. They walked on, staying near the crest of the road. The rain had not let up.

Then she saw it: a small shepherd's hut dug into the side of the hill. She led them to it up a narrow track.

The door had never known a lock. It hung loose on leather hinges. The low hut, scarcely more than a lean-to, was

deserted, but the shepherd had left wood. Françoise tied the
donkey inside with them and got a fire started. She gave
Daniel a small injection of morphine. It was the last she had.

"Better now?" she asked him.

"Fine . . ." He never said anything but "Fine."

"I've got to get those clothes off you. And me." She
helped him to undress, and laid their clothes out by the fire.
He was shivering again. She took the only dry blanket from
their pack and wrapped them together in it. They lay in warm
closeness and he felt her nakedness that he couldn't see. His
breath came easier, she kissed his forehead, then his cheeks.

"Frannie. . . ." He found her lips. It was the first time
they had kissed as lovers. It drew from him the last of anxiety
and pain, and brought the absolution of sleep.

Morning warmed the air, leaving only the dripping of water
from rain-soaked boughs. She helped him back into clothes
still damp, but to wait longer could be dangerous. The storm
had been their protection, but that was gone, and there were
miles to cover.

She put a flask of water to his lips. "Drink. Can you eat
something?"

"Yes. I feel hungry now."

"That's a good sign," she said.

She broke some of the stale bread, cut sausage and cheese
for them, and they ate. Daniel seemed troubled. Finally he
spoke.

"About last night, Frannie—I had no right to kiss you. It
was taking advantage. I'm sorry."

She smiled, packing away the food. "Dan—I told you I'm
a strong-willed girl. Nobody, even a big brute like you—kisses
me if I don't want them to. Now, forget it."

"I can't forget what you're doing for me, Frannie. I've
never known anybody like you."

"We'll talk about that later. Are you ready to mount your
steed, Don Quixote?" She led the beast out of the hut, made
fast the saddle blankets as the donkey cropped the wild grass
and cool fern leaves.

At noon they came on the ruin of a farmhouse. It looked as
though it might offer ideal shelter, but when Françoise stepped
through the doorway, she could smell death. Inside, there was
a body: a woman stretched across the bed. From her position,

it was plain she had been raped before she was murdered. Françoise left quickly. There was nothing she could do for the woman now.

"What is it?" Daniel asked.

"A dead animal." They moved on. Darkness crept early over the mountainside.

Françoise's shoes were nearly worn through, and her feet were sore, but Daniel seemed stronger and more talkative. From time to time they were slowed because of the donkey— not the most cooperative of animals at the best of times.

"It's curious that our families have always used this beast as part of their symbol," Françoise said. "He is stubborn, malicious, and always hungry."

"The Hammadis supplied the donkey," he reminded her. "My great-grandfather was smart enough to own a cart."

"I wish we had it right now," she said.

They found the winding road again and started down the mountain toward the sea. Waterfalls spurted with the last of the winter snow. When night fell, they were still in the mountains.

"We'll stop here to rest. We can't be too far from the French border."

"I can go on."

"Well, I can't. We both need sleep. We'll start again before first light. By dawn we should be over the border."

Daniel nodded. She helped him dismount and spread out one of the donkey blankets on the flinty earth. Trees stirred with the hoot of night birds and the rhythmic maracas of the cicadas. Françoise tied up the donkey where he could graze, then cut the last of the bread and cheese for them.

Daniel made a pretense of eating, but he barely touched the food. She poured wine and he drank. A shiver ran through him.

"I'm sorry I have nothing more to ease the pain."

"It's strange," he told her. "When you cannot see, all sounds and smells seem so much more important. The frogs are an orchestra tonight. And we are like the English fairy tale I read once: 'Babes in the Wood.' And it is I who am the most helpless." She moved closer to him, wrapped the blankets around them both and held him in her arms, cradled close, like a child.

"Are you cold, Daniel?"

He did not seem to hear her. "Every leaf is alive as if it has its own voice. Every twig moves with its own will. The wind lifts the blades of grass. The darkness is crowded with sounds—and we are its lost children—its prey, Françoise."

"We must sleep, Daniel."

They bedded down by the side of the road.

Another day was well into morning when she opened her eyes. Something black was hovering over them. She looked up and saw with vast relief a young priest.

"Good morning." He was speaking in French. They had crossed over the border and they didn't know it. "You are Spaniards?"

"No," she replied.

Daniel awoke with a start and got to his feet. "Who is it, Frannie?"

"I am Father Antoine, monsieur. I am sorry if I have startled you."

"We're not exactly sure where we are, Father," she told him. "We've come . . . a long way."

"You have arrived just above Hendaye. It is a fishing village not far from St. Jean de Luz. We are, in fact, no more than ten kilometers from Biarritz. But you, monsieur—I see you need medical attention?"

"That's the reason we left Spain, Father."

"Spain?" The priest nodded knowingly. "Hundreds have been coming through here. But if they have not the correct papers . . . they are held by the French authorities in detention camps." He paused cautiously. "If they are found."

"Papers are the one thing we have," Françoise told him. "I carry a French passport. My friend has one from the British Mandate of Palestine. But we haven't any money left. I must send a telegram to my brother in Paris. You'll be repaid, Father . . . . for any help you can give us."

The priest nodded. This was a risk he always accepted. "It is possible to send a telegram from Hendaye. I will take you."

They followed him along a path edging a small river that led down toward the sea and the fishing village. The priest walked with Françoise at the head of the donkey, which had suddenly become docile—as though anticipating the end of his journey.

"There is a fisherman—a good man," the priest told them. "He could provide you with a bed in his house since his son is away."

"We would be grateful, Father."

"Until you have funds to resume your journey."

The fisherman's house was notched into a small cove, his two boats, festooned with dark, drying nets, rested high on the beach beneath the full noon glare. In the ample kitchen, the fisherman's wife clucked around them like an enormous hen serving up plates of fish soup, fresh-baked crusty bread, and a pitcher of light mountain wine. The priest regarded the strangers with slight deference. He had not missed the Hammadi and Nouari names when Françoise sent off her telegram from the railroad station. Names not unknown even in this remote corner of France.

Over the meal, Françoise explained why they had gone to Spain, and told what happened to Guernica. The fisherman looked grave. His father had died at Verdun, fighting the 'Boche.'

The meal finished, they stepped outside. Françoise guided Daniel to a weather-worn bench facing the sea. "Is there anything else I can do for either of you, Dr. Hammadi?" the young priest asked before taking his leave.

"Yes, Father Antoine," she replied. "You can marry us."

The priest looked at them surprised. "Marry? Here, in Hendaye?"

"Please. As soon as it can be arranged. You *do* perform weddings, don't you?"

"Certainly—but—"

"Now, wait a minute, Frannie!" Daniel protested. "I'm not marrying anyone just because she feels sorry for me."

She took his hand, holding it in both of hers. "Don't be so stupid, Dan. Do you think I'd want to marry you if I didn't love you—or know that you love me? So don't try to deny it."

When he spoke, his voice was harsh, angry. "What do you want to do—lead me around by the hand all your life? Pick me up when I fall over chairs?"

"If necessary, yes. We belong together, Dan, and you know it. I'm not marrying a patient." She leaned close and kissed him. "Even if your eyesight is never restored—at least you won't have to watch me grow old."

"Fran . . . I want to go back to Jerusalem. . . ."

"Good. I'll buy you a donkey and cart to ride around in, and go with you. And we'll give the symbol of our two families a new meaning."

He smiled faintly. "Hammadi and Nouari. . . . It was never just a business, it's always been a way of life. But the one thing our families never did permit was intermarriage. You know that."

"Then, it's high time we changed that."

The priest looked at them both. He did not understand English. But he understood the nature of love.

It was Mohamed, not Maurice, who was at the bank when Françoise's telegram arrived in Paris. He stuffed money into his wallet, ordered the bank's limousine, and left within the hour for the South.

For months he'd had Company agents from Hispañola-Nacional searching Spain for the two young doctors. But since they had been behind Republican lines, his agents could learn nothing. A private report had reached his desk about the bombing of Guernica. Now the thought that his own daughter and Daniel Nouari had been caught in it gnawed at Mohamed's conscience. Though he would never be able to bring himself to admit it to Françoise, he was certain that at least some of those bombs had been produced at his Spanish factory. This guilt he would have to bear in silence.

Thirty-six hours later, the chauffeur reached Biarritz. They had paused only once, to sleep at an inn. Hendaye. . . . They would be there soon. He glanced at the morning's papers in his lap. From Biarritz and Paris. On the front page, a photo: Françoise and Daniel. The press had found them before he. They were calling his daughter "a heroine of the Spanish Republic." It brought a wry smile to his face. He could well imagine how this would go down with his Falangist patrons and customers!

Mohamed closed his eyes. A picture of Jacqueline flashed into mind. Jacqueline as she had been when he first met her. Fresh, beautiful, untainted. He was feeling tired from the long drive. What could he say to their child? What could he say?

• • •

"Married . . . ? Have you both lost your senses?" All of Mohamed's relief at finding Françoise safe and well had turned to anger.

"No, Father. Dan and I are perfectly sane and very much in love. In every way we share the things that matter to us both. We consider that the most intelligent basis for a marriage." There was a slight note of reproach in his daughter's voice.

Mohamed studied Françoise's defiant face. Yes, she was like Jacqueline, all right. But also like him. Determined, strong, unswervable. No wonder his words couldn't affect her. At that age, who could have talked Mohamed out of anything? She was so much tougher than Maurice. So sure of herself. Nevertheless, there were words that had to be said.

"You have broken the tradition of our two families. No Hammadi has ever married a Nouari." He did not mention the others who had long ago loved each other and been forced to part. Sour Izak and his lost Bethena.

"If I may remind you, sir," Daniel said, "we are not in the Company. Frannie and I have our own careers."

"And what kind of career will a blind man have in medicine?"

"I don't know, sir. I'll have to find that out."

"Well then, Daniel—what about your religion?"

"We were married by a priest, since your daughter is Catholic. I believe that you married her mother in the same way."

"Yes—and look what unhappiness it caused," Mohamed insisted. He sat down on the fisherman's bench, looming too large and important for his surroundings.

"Really, Father. I didn't expect hypocrisy from you. Your problems with mother never had anything to do with religion. Besides, I don't see that you're much changed by your new marriage and return to Islam. You're just as stubborn as ever."

"So are you!" Mohamed was swept by a sense of depletion. His posture crumbled before his daughter's keen perception. "All right. I will say no more on the matter. You have made your choice and my blessing is unimportant. What do you intend to do now?"

"First, take Daniel to Paris to a specialist."

Mohamed nodded. This was something he could take charge of. "We'll stop in Biarritz and telephone. Maurice will have arranged everything by the time we return."

Daniel nodded his gratitude. "Whichever way it comes out—about my sight—I intend to return to Palestine and Françoise has agreed to go with me. We came to Spain to serve a cause that wasn't ours. Now I intend to serve one that is. We're going to Jerusalem."

Mohamed was silent. Then he spoke. "Any other place in the world would be better for the two of you."

Twenty-five _____

ALL day, anxious depositors had bee-swarmed the marble-lined chambers of Hammadi-Nouari's Paris bank, extracting savings, dissolving accounts. The chief teller, old Émile, gesticulated his helplessness in the sweltering June day—then fled to the inner sanctum past a string of accountants and secretaries, virtually forcing his way into Abe Nouari's private office.

"What can one do, monsieur?" Émile thrust a trembling book of neatly penned balances into Abe's hand. "As Monsieur can see, there is almost nothing left from which to pay out! Our depositors, they have all gone crazy. Do they think there is any place safe to hide their money from the Germans?"

"No need for alarm, Émile. We have sufficient liquidity to meet any amount of withdrawals." Abe scanned the figures with some surprise. "What is this transfer of assets this month—for six million francs? Where did it go?" He flipped over the page. "And last month—eight million. Why wasn't I informed about these transactions?"

"It was authorized by the young Monsieur Hammadi. In my opinion, it is now necessary to close our doors, monsieur. In another hour there will be no more cash left to pay out. Those madmen, they are ready to tear down the bank!"

"Close our doors? Hammadi-Nouari? Impossible. Where is Monsieur Maurice?" Abe demanded.

The teller drew his head down into shoulders faintly snowed with dandruff. A trouble turtle, breath rancid with garlic. He should have been retired ten years ago, Abe thought.

"Monsieur has not yet returned from Switzerland."

Abe glanced at his watch. Nearly one o'clock. Maurice

590

should have been back by ten. "So you suggest we close our doors? What excuse can we possibly offer, Émile?"

Émile reached to the morning paper on Abe's desk, waving it at him. The headline under the date, June 27, 1940, read: GERMAN ADVANCE NEARS PARIS! "Does Monsieur need to find more excuse than this?"

Abe nodded. "All right, Émile. I shall make the announcement."

Abe knew there could only be one person responsible for this disappearance of funds: Maurice. As he stepped out into the main hall of the bank, customers erupted into shouts and accusations. It looked like another French revolution. Abe mounted a chair, raised his arms in a dramatic appeal for silence.

"Ladies—gentlemen! As a patriotic measure—since the Germans may enter Paris at any moment—we are closing our doors! What true Frenchman would wish to remain open to business when the foe is about to pierce the heart of France?"

There was a hue and cry of response. "The money is ours! We demand our money! We want it now!"

His voice rose above the shouts. "We are not closing because of any financial necessity, I assure you. Hammadi-Nouari is as solvent as ever. Your money is safer here than under your mattresses waiting to be skewered by some Boche bayonet."

"That is so," somebody in the crowd agreed.

"Go to your homes. Prepare yourselves for this invasion. And those of you who can, prepare to resist. My friends . . . France is wounded. But she will rise again!"

There was more mumbling. Then cheers. The greatest realists on earth were ever vulnerable to a touch of chauvinism. Abe hurried back to his office. The bank was closed without further incident.

"Very excellent, monsieur. Inspiring!" Émile clapped his hands, following Abe. "Truly it brought tears to my eyes."

Abe kept walking. "Let me know the minute Monsieur Maurice arrives."

A half hour later, Abe's secretary informed him that Maurice had just come in and was in his office.

Abe walked in to find his friend at his desk, his slightly rumpled Italian jacket hung on the coat tree. Maurice was drinking coffee and already dictating to his rather agitated woman secretary.

"May I interrupt?" Abe asked.

Maurice gestured to the secretary. "Please get that typed and into the post immediately. We can't be sure how long there will be a mail service, at least without German censorship."

The woman nodded, flustered. "Oh, monsieur, what will become of Paris?"

Maurice leaned back, loosening the tie on his elegant Sulka shirt. "Paris will survive. It always does. But I strongly advise against taking to the roads, mademoiselle. They are crowded with refugees, renegade troops, and broken-down automobiles. Made my train five hours late this morning. Dirty *wagons-lits* and a wretched breakfast of stale brioche. So take to your typewriter instead, my dear. Then go home and say your prayers."

She retired, clutching her notebook and sniffling. Maurice appraised his partner. "I hear you closed the bank. Sorry I missed your curtain speech."

"Had to. No money."

"Yes, Émile said you were very inspiring. A Joan of Arc rallying her footman. I'd offer you coffee, but it's gone as cold as many French feet today."

"Maurice, do you realize that Italy has declared war on France and Britain?"

"They do print newspapers in Switzerland."

"It's the last straw! When Il Duce takes sides, it means the Allies are finished. Nothing can stop the German war machine now. Nothing!" He leaned across the desk. "Maurice, why didn't you tell me you were sneaking assets over to Switzerland? I presume that's what's been happening to our funds."

Maurice stood up. "You were away. Jerusalem, London, New York. I started when the Germans invaded Belgium, the Netherlands, and Luxembourg. May 10, to be precise. No point in waiting until the jackboots come pounding through the Arc de Triomphe—which could be tomorrow. So when the conquering hordes get around to investigating a bank with Jewish connections, they will find us just a soupçon insolvent."

Abe sat down and leaned his head against the worn leather of the Biedermeier chair. The same chair once used by Baron

Liebermann. "Sometimes I think you're a genius, Maurice. But how does one dress for one's own execution? Mourning bands—black cravat? Or, to be more specific, how does one explain our slightly enormous shortage of funds to the victors?"

Maurice's calm was serene. "The books. I have drawn up an entire new set of ledgers for the last year." From a locked drawer in his desk, he brought out four heavy volumes in well-worn leather bindings. "Especially aged by an antiquary book binder in Zurich. We cannot lose money we never had, Abe. Besides, we've had some heavy withdrawals by nervous customers fleeing Paris. Panic, you know." He sighed. "It has almost bankrupted us, I fear. The misfortunes of war, which I'm certain the Germans will understand."

Abe scanned the books and burst into light laughter. "Brilliant." Maurice rang for his secretary. She put her head in, hat planted firmly on it.

"Yes, monsieur?"

"Please send Émile in before you go. Tell him to bring the ledgers for the past twelve months."

She disappeared. Maurice turned back to Abe. "Now that the good gray warrior Marshal Pétain has replaced Renaud, his first official act will no doubt be to sue for peace, collaboration . . . and survival." Maurice's face grew serious. "However, I don't think Paris will be a safe place for *you*, Abe. Or your mother."

Abe walked over to the window. The street below looked strangely empty. "You're being unduly alarmist. There's no immediate danger. Although I do think you were wise to get the money out."

"I want to get *you* out. Money, I can replace."

Abe looked at his friend, reading his fears. "The Germans will never dare carry out their anti-Semitic policies here in France. Remember what happened in Denmark when they ordered all Jews to sew on yellow stars? Their king was the first to ride out wearing one—followed by practically every Dane in Copenhagen."

"I wish I shared your confidence."

"Maurice, the Germans need the support of banking interests. They need international approval from some quarters. They're still trying to get the support of the American President. They can't afford to put their worst boot forward here."

Maurice shook his head. "You wouldn't be so complacent had you been with me in Goebbels' office in Berlin."

"Well then, what do you suggest?"

Maurice came over to him. "That you and your mother leave for Switzerland. Tonight. I've arranged everything with the Zurich office." He reached into the pocket of his jacket and handed a small envelope to Abe. It contained two rail tickets to Zurich.

"These must have cost you a gold bar right now."

Maurice shrugged. "The date is open. But I wouldn't wait too long."

Abe glanced at Maurice's desk calendar in its gilded Fabergé frame. "I suspect that tomorrow will be a most unlucky day for travel. For my part, I'm content to take my chances here. But I'll have a word with Mother." He slid the envelope into his pocket.

Maurice came beside him. All the closeness between them rose in a spectre of fear for what tomorrow could hold. "Abe. . . . Abe. . . . I want you safe. If anything happened to you. . . ." For a moment their hands touched. Then their arms encircled each other. Abe's voice was reassuring.

"Coward, take this coward's hand. . . ."

"Abe, we stand on the edge of the world. The slightest wind could blow us over the precipice. Tomorrow. . . ."

Abe drew back. "From now on, 'tomorrow' is a word to be avoided." He tapped a cigarette on his gold case, then turned back, more in control of himself. "By the way—I bought you a present at Cartier. To wear on the day they take Paris." Abe reached into his pocket and brought out a ring box.

Maurice opened it. It contained a gold ring worked with letters to spell a single word.

Maurice read it aloud: *"Éternité. . . ."*

Two nights later, Abe was dining with his mother in her apartment on the Île Saint-Louis. He had tried to convince her to go to Zurich, even without him. She wouldn't hear of it. "Your father banished me to Bordeaux for the duration of World War I, which you must well remember. This time, I stay put. Why should I leave? Where should I go? Who do I know in Zurich?''

"Well, perhaps New York, then, Mother." He passed her a cable from Zed begging them both to come.

"What's for me there? Zed doesn't want me around—with her Gentile boyfriends. No matter what she cables."

"What about Palestine?" He tactfully allowed the cable from his father to remain in his pocket.

"Your father now has his own life. With that ugly nothing from Tel Aviv. I have my life, and it's close to you, Abe." Ruth drank a long swallow of mineral water. She never touched wine any more. "You know something, Abe? Since I was a girl in Poland, there hasn't been any place ever for me, a real home. Sometimes I think the mistake was to marry your father. But how could a young girl know? Judah had everything I thought a man should have. A good future. He was handsome." She smiled. "You take after him in looks. And in those days, I believed in the Zionist movement. I wanted to be a part of it, like my cousin. . . ." She broke off, not wishing to go further backward into that memory field.

He sighed. "Very well, Mother. If you want to stay here, we'll stay."

"So what have I got to lose at my age?" She watched him picking at his food. "Eat, Abe. You're looking too thin. Like your father. What you need is some nice girl to take care of you."

He smiled. "Who could replace you, Mother?"

This was something she couldn't argue with. "You know, Abe, today Marie, my cook for seven years, walked out on me! Didn't even give two weeks' notice. Just packed her clothes and left."

"For what reason?"

"I can't remember. Something about her mother had a toothache in Dijon. So that is why I cooked dinner myself tonight!" She brandished a forkful of chicken.

"I'll try to see if I can get you another maid tomorrow, Mother."

They were discussing anything to avoid mentioning what was on their minds. The entrance of the Germans two days before—goose-stepping under the arch that had celebrated an age of heroes. Neither mother nor son had gone near the

Champs Élysées since then. It seemed wisest to stay out of the center of things until Paris settled down. Ruth had even seen a German sergeant at her local bakery. He hadn't looked at all sinister, she thought.

They were interrupted by a loud knock at the door. Abe pushed back his chair. "Expecting someone, Mother?"

"Of course I'm not expecting anyone. Who should I expect?" She took up the plates, scraping the unfinished food into one dish, stacking the silverware. "Maybe it's that crazy Marie, deciding to come back. I told her, I said, you have here a fine job. Only one old lady to look after. . . ." She broke off. The knock sounded again, this time with some insistence. Then a voice erupted sharp with authority. "Open up!"

Abe moved softly to the door. "Who is it?" He called, feeling a sudden bone chill.

"Police. Hurry up. Open it."

Abe looked at his mother. She set down the dishes, suddenly pale. He unbolted the door to three men. Two wore dark suits beneath thick-set, inquisitive faces. Behind them was an SS officer.

"This is the home of Madame Judah Nouari?" the plainclothesman asked.

"What is it you want?"

"Are you Abraham Nouari?"

Abe nodded, producing his calling card with the bank's address. It usually made an impression.

"Then, this woman is your mother?"

"Yes. What do you want with us?"

The men whispered together for a moment, then stepped into the room.

"You will come with us," the plainclothesman said.

"Why? We have done nothing," Abe protested. Ruth seemed stunned into silence.

The SS officer stepped forward. He spoke perfect French. "It is enough you are the wife and son of one of the greatest enemies of the Third Reich—the Zionist leader Judah Nouari."

"My father is no enemy of anyone," Abe replied. "He is a merchant banker and completely neutral. He has business interests in every part of the world—including Germany."

"He is a Zionist Jew. And you are Jews! Now stop wasting our time and come with us!"

Before Abe could protest, Ruth suddenly burst out, "You have no authority to take us anywhere! This is my home!"

The plainclothesman took her by the arm. The shock lifted her voice into a shrill scream. The SS officer drew his pistol.

"No more arguments!" the officer said harshly.

"We have a right to know, where are you taking us?"

The officer had pale eyes and a sallow face. He spoke without expression. "You have no rights. We go to Gestapo Headquarters, Monsieur Jew Nouari."

"May I make a phone call—to my partner? Maurice Hammadi?"

"No."

"But I have to let him know—"

"You are a prisoner—charged with acts of conspiracy. And you are a known homosexual—charged with immoral actions. Put out your wrists."

Abe complied slowly. The handcuffs were clapped on his wrists. He heard Ruth's sob behind him. Then they were walked downstairs, past the silent, wide-eyed concierge. As they passed, he muttered something about "the Jews" and spat on the ground.

One of the plainclothesmen got into the backseat with them. The others rode in front. The car sped out into the oppressed night.

When Abe failed to return to their apartment, Maurice tried vainly to phone Ruth Nouari. Getting no answer, he went around to see the concierge.

The concierge's wife protruded a troubled face into the heat-sogged Paris afternoon. Her husband, she said, was indisposed. She seemed reluctant to talk, but the crinkle of currency in Maurice's hand could not be ignored. Not in times like these.

No, she had not seen Madame Nouari or her son leave. But . . . her husband had. This—in a lowered voice. They had left with—well, some men.

"Who were they?" Maurice demanded.

"These are dangerous times, monsieur. It is not wise to see too much, you understand." She glanced over her shoulder to the bedroom, where her husband was resting, then turned back, lowering her voice even further. "I myself saw nothing. I was visiting with my sister when they came. It is like the *patisserie* down the street. For years I have gone there to buy bread. Monsieur Berman bakes fresh every day, and his prices are always fair. Now they have put a yellow poster in his window, and it is not wise to be seen going in there. Myself, I am very sorry for him. He is a good man. And Madame Nouari. . . ." She shook her head.

"Who were the men, madame?"

Her voice dropped to a faint whisper. "My husband says—the SS."

The cable had told Mohamed to go to the office of the United Press in New York and await a phone call, three o'clock, New York time. It was signed "Maurice." Busy as he was, Mohamed hurried to the news headquarters and waited in the press room. The bureau chief was an old friend of his. He'd given him enough stories through the years.

Mohamed's arrival stirred curiosity. A portrait of him had recently appeared on the cover of *Time* magazine above the caption "International Businessman of the Year." The bureau chief came over with a cup of coffee and a question.

"Well then, Mr. Hammadi, what d'yah think? Is the war in Europe *kaputt?* Will the U.S. get into it? You've got one of the privatest ears in Washington."

"You had better clear this one through the press secretary for the White House," Mohamed said. "The President is about to name a four-man defense board. It seems possible Bill Knudson will head it."

"What are they supposed to do?"

"Prepare U.S. defenses—and speed up aid to Great Britain. What does that sound like to you, George?"

"Like the hawks are flying high. Can you say anything about this phone call you're expecting?"

"I haven't had it yet." Mohamed smiled, sipping his coffee. Not as good as American coffee used to be. One of the private lines rang insistently. A reporter took it up and passed it to Mohamed. "Your Paris call, Mr. Hammadi."

Mohamed waited between clicks and buzzes. Somebody at the other end was probably monitoring. At last Maurice's voice came through.

"Hello . . . Father?"

"How are you, Maurice?" There had been a cool front between them ever since Berlin. But Maurice still called him "Father," when he called him at all.

"I'm all right." From then on, they both kept switching languages from French to English to Arabic. "Abe and his mother . . . had to go away," Maurice said.

"Oh? Where?"

"Whereabouts unknown."

"Did they go . . ." Mohamed asked in careful English, "because of a . . . rest? A . . . rest?"

"A rest. Yes. We think it may be a camping trip. No idea where the camp is."

"I understand," Mohamed said.

"They need their passports renewed—in Washington."

"I can arrange it. Does Judah know they've gone?"

"No. Wiser he doesn't. He might try to join them—and succeed."

"We'll keep it that way, then. I'll bring those papers you want myself."

"Good idea," Maurice replied with some relief. "Give you a chance to meet our new German customers. They're doing quite a business with the Bank. We've still got the donkey, but the cart's gone. . . ."

"I understand. Take care of yourself." The words held some of the old warmth. Mohamed hung up. The newsmen were all sitting on the edge of their chairs.

"A story for us, Mr. Hammadi?"

"Sad news. My son has broken off his engagement."

"Didn't even know he was engaged."

"A French actress. Juliette something or other. She went away—with her mother. Now, would you think he'd go to all the trouble of phoning through the UP Paris office just to tell me that?"

The bureau chief regarded him with some suspicion. "Frankly, no, Mr. Hammadi."

Mohamed smiled. "Thanks for the use of the line. It was a special privilege."

"You're a special person, sir. Say hello to Franklin D. next time you're in the white wigwam."

Tony was waiting behind the wheel of the new Cadillac.

Although several years younger than Mohamed, the chauffeur was showing his age. Loquacious as ever, he still followed hard facts to wrong conclusions.

"I tell you, boss, that Roosevelt is going to get this country into a big mess of trouble. Know what he just done? Traded fifty destroyers to Great Britain for a heap of snow in Newfoundland and some other worthless place—where was it now? Oh, yeah—the West Indies. Now, what does America want with those hunks of real estate, boss, you tell me?"

"Naval and air bases. On a ninety-nine-year lease, Tony."

"Yeah? Well, I'm givin' my vote to Wendell Wilkie. We got enough trouble in our own backyard. You heard about that suspension bridge collapsing in Tacoma, Washington? Fell 190 feet into Puget Sound." It was the sort of detail that warmed Tony's heart. "You oughtta tell your friend Roosevelt to stop givin' away our battleships and build better bridges."

Mohamed chuckled. "Don't worry too much, Tony. Those destroyers were over-aged."

"Like us, boss, huh?"

"Like us."

A half hour later, Mohamed was back in his own office facing Zed. "I want you to promise me that you won't say anything to your father about what I'm going to tell you," he began.

Zed looked worried, but she promised.

"It's a bit of a shock, I'm afraid."

"I'm shock-proof." She smiled confidently.

He launched straight into it. "Your mother and brother have vanished from Paris. There is every probability that they have been arrested by the Nazis. Maurice used the word . . . 'camp.' "

"Oh, my God . . . my God!" Zed burst into tears, collapsing onto the sofa. Mohamed reached a comforting arm around her, holding her as though through his grasp might flow strength and courage.

"I promise you, Zed, I will do everything in my power—and I still have a bit of that left."

"But, Mohamed, I'll have to tell Father. . . ."

"I warn you not to, Zed. He'll rush off to Paris—and end up with them. Use your brains. The Nazis aren't arresting *all*

Jews in France. At least not yet. This may be a ploy to get their hands on your father. For his sake, tell him nothing yet." He rose. "I can handle this alone."

Zed leaned her face in her hands, imagining her beloved twin—and her poor, foolish mother—behind the barbed wire of some concentration camp. Tactless Ruth—dashing Abe. Were they even still alive? "Yes, Mohamed," she said at last. "I will trust you. There's nobody in the world I trust more." Her voice steadied. "What do you intend to do?"

Mohamed's eyes narrowed. "First I must get them American passports. Maurice asked for those. Good idea, too. Back-dated, of course. Have you heard me mention a man called Donovan?"

"Yes, I think so. Military intelligence, isn't he?"

Mohamed nodded, crossing to his desk. He opened the rosewood humidor, extracting a long, dark cigar. "If you recall, we made a few shipments to Canada some time ago. Machine parts that found their way to England. Donovan was extremely grateful. I think I shall give him the opportunity of showing it. He has an extensive passport collection. Locate him for me, will you, Zed? Personally. I don't want my secretary to hear this. Tell Donovan I'll meet him in Washington tonight." He started toward the door in a hurry. "And ask Amy to cancel all my appointments for the next month—and to book me a flight to Lisbon for the day after tomorrow. I'll get to Paris from there."

And he was gone, leaving a ghost of cigar smoke and a sense of purpose.

Mohamed was met by Maurice with the Paris bank's limousine. He found his son looking strained. They kept their manner impersonal for the benefit of the driver as the car moved through almost empty streets of the occupied capital.

"I had a letter from Françoise this morning," Maurice said, breaking the ice. "She and Daniel were worried about me staying on in Paris. I cabled them. Naturally, I didn't mention. . .the situation here."

Mohamed nodded. "How is your sister? She hardly ever writes to me."

"Both still working at Hadassah Hospital. The miracle is Daniel's eyesight. Almost normal now."

"The fools. . . . Why did they do it?"

Maurice was not sure whether Mohamed referred to their Spanish misadventure, or their marriage. He didn't ask. It had been several years since the Paris doctor had treated Daniel. There had been some scar tissue left; but Daniel could see. He could work.

But the scars caused by the marriage reached the families, alienating them from the couple. God knows, Maurice thought, they certainly would have been happier had they chosen any other place to live than Jerusalem. The Hammadis had been outraged further by a second wedding service; this one Jewish.

Mohamed glanced out the window. "A swastika over the Arc de Triomphe. . . ."

"And the Tour Eiffel. And all the best hotels. Crillon, Ritz, the Continental, the Meurice. The Germans have taken over every important French plant. Renault, Citroën, Potez. Converted to arms manufacture."

"Why are the streets so empty?"

"Gasoline shortage. No buses. No taxis. Hardly any private cars. Parisiennes travel on the Métro." He pointed out the window. "Look there. Horse-drawn wagons. Some are even pulled by dogs. Or men. But there's still plenty of life—for the Germans. And the collaborators."

"Like you."

"Of course, Father, like me. I'm trying to save the remains of our French banking interests." He switched to Arabic. "I'm not leaving here until Abe and his mother are safe."

"Then will you come back with me to New York? I don't want you in danger."

"Oh, there's no danger—if you are seen to be with the right side. No, I'll stay on for a bit. But what *you* came to do is dangerous. Did you manage the passports?"

"That was no problem. Who is the civil power in Paris?"

"Jean Chiappe, former prefect of police. But he can't lick a postage stamp without the approval of the German military authorities. You'll have to start there."

"Where, exactly?"

"The *Kommandantur*—corner of Place de l'Opéra and rue du Quatre Septembre. It is generally considered advisable to enter on one's knees. And there's an old friend of yours in Paris, Father. Haj Amin Husseini."

"What's the grand mufti doing out of Palestine?"

"Aside from being photographed with Hitler? Heading an Arab delegation with Fawzi el Kaukji, his Syrian Jew-killer."

"They should be very popular."

"Oh, they are. I attended a reception in their honor, given by the most important Nazi, after the Führer, of course: Heinrich Himmler, Reichsführer SS. Travels on his own private armored train. He is the man who controls all concentration camps. Dachau, Buchenwald, Sachsenhausen, Gross-Rosen, Flossenburg . . . well over one hundred scattered through the satellites." Maurice paused. "What we have to find out is which one."

Mohamed looked around at his son. "I see you already know quite a bit."

"The bank has been very cooperative." He switched back into French. "I'm afraid there is some bad news. The bank— The Hammadi Bank of Paris, as we are now known—is nearly bankrupt. That is, we would have been had not the Germans made some heavy deposits."

Mohamed was about to question this—but stopped himself. He was beginning to know this strange son of his—well enough to comprehend that Maurice was hiding a card up his sleeve.

In the next few days, Mohamed learned how very difficult his mission would be. All routes to Himmler proved dead ends. The Reichsführer simply would not receive him. Even the good offices of Franco's Spanish emissary brought no success. He got as far as Chief of Staff for the Waffen SS Gottlieb Berger. From him he got a hint of his persona-non-grata status with the Nazis.

"The Reichsführer Himmler wishes me to convey his respects. He seems to recall a promise given Reichsminister Goebbels. Something to do with helium, not so?" But something Berger said gave Mohamed a sense of direction. "Herr Himmler is so busy. Every day meetings with the Arab delegation."

Mohamed found himself waiting at Haj Amin's suite at the Hotel Ritz. Waiting. It had been two and three quarters hours. Not that punctuality had ever been among any Arab's outstanding virtues. Mohamed himself customarily kept his appointments waiting—almost as a matter of tradition. It was bad manners to be prompt, except in America. He turned toward the two Arab bodyguards at the grand mufti's door. They looked back at him with curved, scimitar smiles.

It was another hour and a half before Haj Amin himself glided into the sitting room. "Ah, Hammadi—we meet again. What brings you to Paris?"

"I have been waiting several hours to tell you just that."

Haj Amin stifled a faint yawn. "Here, we are all servants of power. . . ." His glance went to an Arab secretary who had come to his elbow. The man handed him a piece of paper. "The Führer himself—and the Reichsführer—are expecting me. Last month we were even photographed together, Hammadi!"

Mohamed stopped himself from asking, in what position? Haj Amin's eyes glazed like an aging falcon. "I have no time today, Hammadi. If you desire any guidance from our Arab delegation, my assistants will grant you a few minutes. You will find them, also—'old acquaintances.' " This latter was delivered with a caustic smile.

A tall, impressive Arab with a warrior's step entered with a briefcase, falling in behind Haj Amin.

The grand mufti made no move to introduce him, but Mohamed recognized Fawzi el Kaukji. "Ah, good—you are here." He turned his back on Mohamed and moved with gliding step out of the room, followed by his Commander of Arab Irregulars and one of the male secretaries.

Mohamed turned to the room from which he had emerged and stepped in.

"Welcome to Paris, cousin." Yassir was seated at a small side desk in the suite-turned-office. Leaning at his shoulder was Tariq.

"Congratulations, Yassir, on your elevation to so important a post. Tell me—what exactly do you do?"

"I am the right hand of Haj Amin," Yassir replied.

Mohamed's eyes went to Tariq. "And that would make you the left hand?" The insult did not pass unnoticed. Traditionally Arabs use the right hand to eat with. The left, for other bodily functions.

"You go too far, cousin!" Tariq exploded, making a move toward him. Mohamed thought he might draw his dagger. Yassir restrained his brother with a gesture.

"Do not take offense at this old man, Tariq. Our cousin has lived too long among foreigners to remember his manners."

Yassir had fleshed out somewhat since Berlin, Mohamed thought. There was a new weight in his voice, self-importance in his bearing. He took his time in speaking, aware that his statements must be received with the respect that his position now merited. Tariq looked much the same, face only more engraved with age. On Haj Amin's desk, where Yassir was now seated, stood the personally inscribed photograph of the grand mufti and Hitler. There was also a nostril-flaring photo of Mussolini, and one of an unimpressive man in SS uniform with steel German helmet and pince-nez. Mohamed thought he had never seen less expression on a human face.

"I see you are looking at Heinrich Himmler," Yassir observed. "Another strong friend of the Arab cause. We have the full support of Germany now, cousin. We are no longer a discarded people scattered over sand dunes—manipulated by French and British imperialists. We are full-fledged allies of the German Reich, the conquerors of Europe."

"As I said before, congratulations."

"You are pleased to find us powerful, then, cousin?" Tariq put in, eyes mocking his older relative's face.

"Of course, I'm pleased. It will make it all the easier for you to grant me . . . a modest request." Mohamed glanced around at a chair. They had not offered him the comfort of being seated. "May I?"

"You used to make us stand in your presence, cousin. But if old age is making your legs tired . . . sit on the floor, Arab style." With a swift gesture, Tariq threw a cushion to land at Mohamed's feet.

Mohamed felt the rush of blood to his temples, but he dropped gracefully to the cushion, crossing his legs. "It is most thoughtful of you, cousin Tariq. A pleasure I rarely enjoy in New York." He indicated the pile of cushions in a corner. "You will join me, of course?"

Yassir and Tariq exchanged glances. Arab courtesy forced the brothers to comply. They took cushions and came to sit beside Mohamed.

"Well, now . . . I will tell you the problem. I know that you will be anxious to help . . . since it is a debt of honor."

Yassir eyed him suspiciously. "What is it you want from us?"

"Abe Nourai and his mother have vanished from Paris. No doubt confined in one of the detention camps. We must find out where—and get them out."

Yassir stared incredulously—then began to laugh. "You ask us to aid Jews?"

"These are not just *any* Jews, Yassir, as you, of all people, must know."

They were interrupted by a discreet knock, which preceded the entrance of a wizened Frenchman and his assistant bearing a long box. "Your fitting, Colonel Hammadi."

Yassir arose, glad of the opportunity. "Come in. You will have to excuse me, cousin. But you may continue to plead your petition while I am being fitted for my SS uniform." The tailor lifted it out of the box. "No doubt you have heard that new divisions are being formed. Many of our brother Muslims from Bosnia. Himmler has made Haj Amin an honorary SS Lieutenant General." Yassir stepped behind a small screen, attended by the tailors.

"And given you the rank of colonel, I gather. Is it appropriate to congratulate you three times in one day?" Mohamed went on. "But one point eludes me. Doesn't an Arab division compromise the Führer's racial standards? After all, our roots are Semitic."

Yassir's voice came through the screen. "Himmler takes a broad view. In the interests of expanding his SS divisions, he welcomes into his ranks Asiatics whom he links with that other great conquering race led by Genghis Khan." He reappeared from behind the screen, resplendent in the black uniform, if just slightly thick through the waistline. The chief tailor handed him a peaked cap with the silver skull and crossbones. "If you will care to look in the mirror, my Colonel?"

Yassir preened before it. He was pleased. His mood even improved. "What do you think, Tariq?"

"Magnificent, my brother."

"And you, cousin?"

"Very handsome," Mohamed agreed. "But I think you have put on weight."

Yassir frowned. "Conquerors dine very well." He turned,

feet apart, striking a pose. "Now, why do you think I should use my power to help your Jewish partners?"

"As I mentioned before, you will be anxious to—as a matter of honor and pride. Which to us all, as Arabs, is perhaps the most important thing. The repayment of a debt."

"What debt?" Yassir asked.

"You surprise me, Yassir. Is your memory so short? Judah and Solomon once used their power to save your life—when you were to be executed by the Turks."

Yassir frowned. He removed the tunic reluctantly, passing it to the tailor. "Too tight in the waist. Have it loosened."

Mohamed forced Yassir's attention back to the subject. "But it was not only *your* life that was saved at great risk by the Nouaris. Surely I do not have to remind you that both Solomon and Izak died trying to save your father, Abdullah." Mohamed paused, gauging the effect of his argument, then went on. "These were not words, Tariq . . . Yassir. They were deeds, written in life's blood. If you refuse to help the Nouaris you will be forever shamed before our family. Before Allah. You would violate every law of our Holy Koran and every custom of our people. You would stand for the rest of your days marked by shame." He rose. His voice softened. "But this of course I know you understand better than I. For you are both men of honor."

There was a silence in the room. The tailors, who had not understood a word of the Arabic, were watching, fascinated.

"I wish to wear this uniform tonight," Yassir told them.

"It will be ready, my Colonel." They bowed their way out as though before royalty.

Tariq regarded his brother with urgency. "Mohamed is not wrong, Yassir. It *is* a debt. One that I cannot forget, since that day I saw the stripes of blood on your back. This debt must be paid. It has nothing to do with our Zionist enemies."

Yassir nodded, going back to the desk. "Very well. We shall help you, cousin. Only one man could save them: Himmler. But he will never see you on our request alone. However, there is a woman—a German who travels with him. His mistress, it is said. She is beautiful—and certainly influential. And she has gone out of her way to be friendly with our Arab delegation." He looked up a phone number and made a call, speaking rapidly in near-perfect German.

When he hung up, he scribbled a name, Hedwig Briemann, and an address, the Hotel Meurice.

"She will see you. And I have made it clear that to help you would be an important favor to Haj Amin."

Mohamed embraced Yassir, then pocketed the paper. "For the first time in my life, I trust you, Yassir."

"If I have lied, cousin, you may cut out my tongue."

The German woman looked strangely familiar. Mohamed felt it the moment he walked into her suite at the Meurice. She emerged from a cluster of uniformed officers; Germans, Vichy French, Italians, Romanians. The place glittered with stunningly dressed ladies around whom small conversational islands had formed.

Her smile as she greeted him gave no sign of recognition. Her age was an enigma; so was her beauty. Her slender curves were sheathed in black sequined glitter with thin straps over white shoulders. Smoky blond curls framed startlingly blue eyes, which missed nothing. Her high cheekbones and wide mouth made her look a bit like the German actress Marlene Dietrich. "Herr Hammadi—what a pleasure to meet you at last. Your cousin was so thoughtful to say I must see you before you leave Paris. How kind of dear Yassir."

"But surely, Madame Briemann, we have met?"

"Surely not. I would most certainly never forget the famous Herr Mohamed Hammadi."

Then he remembered. Lily Kessler! There could be no mistake. He had met her only once, with Judah at the bank in Tel Aviv. Yet there was something changed in her face. A stretched look, a more masked expression. Plastic surgery, perhaps? He had been aware of Lily's relationship with Judah. Later, after she vanished from his friend's life, Judah finally told him that Lily had been a British agent.

She guided him among the guests, introducing him here and there. When the room had thinned to a handful of people, he found himself alone with her on the balcony.

"You know that I *do* know you?" Mohamed asked softly, in Hebrew.

Her eyes were wide with noncommittal. "I have forgotten much Hebrew, Mr. Hammadi."

"Have you forgotten Lily Kessler?"

She glanced back toward the party. Nobody was paying them any attention. "No, I have not forgotten. And Yassir has told me your difficulty. It is possible that I can help. Yassir, of course, does not realize my . . . personal interest."

"He won't know it from me." Mohamed offered her a cigarette, lit it and his own, letting the tiny wax match drop like a slow flare over the roof tops and chimney pots of the occupied city.

"How is he—your partner in Palestine?"

"There was an accident. . . ."

"This I have heard also. I wanted to write to him. But it wasn't possible. You see, Herr Hammadi, Lily Kessler was buried in Tel Aviv. She died in a room in that city when Judah looked at her for the last time. When he convicted her with his eyes and his mind. He was, of course, right." She shrugged, taking a deep drag on her cigarette. "She did what she was employed to do. Because of it, his brother was killed."

"Are you still employed by the same firm?"

Her smile answered nothing. "We must meet again tomorrow, Herr Hammadi. The Church of le Sacré-Coeur. Below it there is a street café where the artists sell bad paintings. There are not many tourists these days."

"Can you find out where Ruth and Abe have been taken?"

"You will buy one of the paintings," she replied. "Yes? And now, if you forgive me, I must slap your face."

Half laughingly, she slapped him across the cheek, just loud enough to draw attention. The remaining guests looked over toward them as they returned to the drawing room.

"Really, these Arab industrialists are impossible!" Her voice rose somewhere between amusement and offense. "Herr Hammadi wishes to make love to me!"

The officers laughed heartily. "He cannot be too well informed," one said. "Or perhaps maybe he is tired of life, ja?"

All laughed, including Mohamed. "Forgive me, Frau Biermann. Your beauty made me careless. I did not realize your affections were already given to another man."

"Man? That is funny, nein? He calls God a man!" The SS officer splashed champagne with a wide gesture. "Herr

Hammadi, you must be the only person in Paris who is—permit me" . . . heels clicked . . . . "so ignorant!"

Mohamed smiled with good grace. "I shall be more careful in the future." He turned back to his hostess with a private look. "In fact, I shall be careful from now on." He bowed. "With your permission—I have an early morning." His eyes met Lily's.

She offered her hand to be kissed. "The hand is permitted. Not the lips, Herr Hammadi."

The café she had chosen was small and deserted except for the corner table, where she was waiting, a thin glass of apéritif before her. He sat down at the table, and she greeted him like an old friend. In the dim light she looked somehow different, ageless, an almost waxen image. Her face was shadowed by a wide-brimmed hat that matched the forest green of her suit. A cherry-red blouse set off the whiteness of her throat. He signaled the waiter and ordered coffee. In front of the waiter she chattered on about the difficulties of buying nylon stockings. When the man left, her manner changed. "Judah's wife and son are in Poland. Sachsenhausen," she said softly.

"Are they safe?"

"For the moment."

"Thank God. . . ." His glance caught a young student painter entering with a large worn cardboard portfolio. He spotted them and headed over.

"A member of the Resistance," she whispered. "They have provided us with what is necessary."

The young man had intense eyes and a slight limp. He opened his portfolio to Lily. She thumbed through a mediocre collection of watercolor street scenes, pausing at one. "Yes . . . the Moulin Rouge. This one I like."

"It is surely the best, madame."

"How much?" Mohamed asked.

"Fifty francs, monsieur."

Mohamed paid the money, and the artist wrapped the painting in newspaper. The headlines read: ARMISTICE SIGNED BY HITLER IN FOREST OF COMPIEGNE. The very spot where Germany had signed the terms of surrender at the end of World War I. The newspaper was several weeks old.

When the artist left, Lily spoke softly. "You may not like this painting so much when you see it in your hotel room. You will find it washes off quite easily. The cheap paints they use these days. However, beneath it you will discover something for which Himmler might be persuaded to trade two lives. For all his great position, he is a man of deep insecurities. A man of humble origins, who rose from apprentice farmer to become top policeman of Europe. But he could use a weapon to protect himself against strong rivals for Hitler's favor. Ley, Speer, Goebbels, Goering, Bormann. They all hate each other. You see, Herr Hammadi, there are some in high places who even now are not completely confident that in the end Hitler will finally win."

"And you, Frau . . . Biermann? How confident are you?"

"If you were to move your hand up my thigh, Herr Hammadi, and I did not again slap you, you would feel under the garter a small vial. It contains my lack of confidence."

"Thank you for all you are doing, Lily. Someday I will see that Judah knows."

"It is better not. When wars end, memories still go on. Scores will be settled."

"You are a brave woman."

"To be brave is easy, when one hates what is happening to one's country."

As he walked back to the hotel carrying the painting, he wondered about Lily. He could see why Judah had loved her. But had it been only a sense of guilt that motivated her help? Or was she ensuring that he would never disclose her identity? Little wonder that she had befriended the Arab delegation. He thought of Yassir posturing in the shade of Haj Amin and laughed aloud. By now, British Intelligence would know exactly how much aid the Germans were giving to Al Fatat, their troublemakers in Palestine.

Rimless pince-nez, a tightly trimmed mustache, weak, receding chin. A face at once dull, almost obtrusively ordinary, above narrow sloped shoulders which not even a German uniform distinguished. And yet Mohamed was aware that behind those porcine features lurked a sense of Messianic mission. At this moment it was possible to imagine that Reichsführer SS Himmler would succeed. A surprisingly unassuming bureaucrat who could have been typecast as a post office clerk empowered no further than to register a letter. Was this the man who planned the mass arrests and murder of millions of Jews? the formation of death camps?

Mohamed knew that he was. Maurice had carefully briefed his father about the Minister of the Interior. Lily had arranged the meeting to take place in a private dining room of Maxim's, telling Himmler that the Arab industrialist had hinted at important secret information.

Himmler was no gourmet. He was dining modestly on sauerkraut and sausage washed down with a glass of pale yellow French beer. Evidently a person of no great pretension beyond the fulfillment of his passionate convictions.

"I am a reader of your Koran, Herr Hammadi."

"So I understand, Reichsführer." Mohamed dabbled with a stringy pheasant leg, feeling little appetite.

"I am told the grand mufti is served by two of your cousins?"

Mohamed inclined his head modestly. "They are devoted to the Third Reich."

"We also know something of your son. There is a dossier of his visit to Berlin." Himmler paused, wiping his chin.

"Somewhere in our Sacred writings it is said that the young can grow a year older each day—with the proper guidance. It is mainly through Maurice's efforts that your officers here in Paris are so well served by the Hammadi Bank."

Himmler looked up from his plate. "I understand you have something to offer me, Herr Hammadi?"

Mohamed put down his fork. "Reichsführer, information has come into my possession that could fortify your position against any rival."

Behind the pince-nez, Himmler's eyes were squints of interrogation. Lips pursed, but he said nothing.

Mohamed continued. "Of all Hitler's subordinates, it is said you alone are incorruptible. You have a reputation of impeccable honesty. For this reason you, sir, deserve to be armed against less scrupulous fellow officers, men who might be tempted into conspiring against you. I can place in your hands a list of all the high-ranking officers, administrators, and diplomats of the Third Reich who have secret numbered bank accounts in Switzerland.''

Himmler's face went pale. He stopped chewing, swallowing hard. ''Such a list exists? And why would any true Nazi have done such a thing?''

''Insurance. In case the tide of war should turn. If ever you should need to demonstrate your own loyalty to the Führer, such a list of names might be of use.''

''And what is your price?''

''The freedom of two Jews. A mother and a son from a family who have been the Hammadis' neighbors and partners in Palestine for generations. They are being held in Sachsenhausen.''

Himmler's lower lip pouted out, bristling the triangle of mustache. ''To free persons already under detention would create a dangerous precedent. Impossible.''

''You have authorized exceptions before.''

Himmler finished the last mouthful of sausage before answering. ''Once before, yes. When Eichmann was in charge of the Office of Jewish Emigration in Austria. It is true I approved his recommendation to permit some hundred thousand Jews to leave. But that was before the war. Naturally we confiscated their property, which they had stolen from the Austrian people. In the case of Baron Louis de Rothschild, his palace in Vienna became Eichmann's headquarters. We took possession of his steel-rolling mills, and he was allowed to leave with the others, carrying a passport that declared him disowned and stateless. But it is no longer necessary for us to make such compromises, Hammadi.''

Mohamed leaned back, lighting a cigar. ''Herr Reichsführer, I understand that you drew inspiration for your Lebensborn Movement from a Teutonic legend: that the ancient Rhine warriors renewed their ranks by copulating on the gravestones of their ancestors.''

''Ja, ja. . . . I prescribed that every man in the SS make it his duty to father a child before going to the front. And every woman has the duty to receive the seed of a warrior. In my scheme, marriage has no importance. I have pledged to care for all children of pure blood, that we may repopulate our ranks for the wars to come! After this war, Germany will be pure Aryan. We will move like a tide across the world until man is perfect and the earth is ours!'' His words had suddenly changed the pedantic bureaucrat into a madman poised on the precipice of his own fantasies. But Mohamed had not missed his Achilles' heel.

''What a pity all this could be lost, Herr Reichsführer by a cabal of self-interested leaders, ingratiating themselves with the Führer. Undermining your great dream with scheming and politicking.''

Himmler tapped his fork on his glass, drumming a little tune as his mind worried the bone Mohamed had thrown him. ''Swiss back accounts, you said? How many names?''

''Twenty-nine. . . .''

''Twenty-nine?'' Himmler exploded. ''Twenty-nine traitors to the Third Reich?''

''It is a wise doctor who cuts out the canker before it spreads.''

The drumming stopped. The mouth pursed. The narrow shoulders hunched together. Finally Himmler spoke. ''You are fortunate, Herr Hammadi, to be dealing with the one member of the Führer's staff who has never broken his word. There is a difficulty. What passports do your Nouaris carry?''

''I have new passports for them. American. A country with whom the Third Reich is not at war.'' He handed them across to Himmler to inspect.

The Nazi flicked through them with some interest. ''The Americans do not even put the word 'Jew' in their passports. Curious. . . .'' He placed them on the table beside his glass. ''Your Nouaris will be freed. Sachsenhausen, you say? And the list?''

Mohamed drew it from his pocket and placed it on top of the passports.

''You take a chance, Hammadi. I could keep the list, and not release your friends.'' He attempted a smile, bristling the triangle above his lip.

''Your reputation is my guarantee, Herr Reichsführer. When the Führer trusts you so much, could I do less?''

Himmler glanced down at the list, eyebrows lifting. ''German officers . . . Teutonic Knights! Hiding their fears in

Swiss banks. Who would have dreamed of such defeatism?''
He tucked the paper, with the passports, into his pocket.

"Personally, Herr Reichsführer, I would have advised Argentina. Excellent banks. And a much larger country in which a man, as well as his money, can become lost.''

Himmler laughed. It came out as a strange high snicker. "You make a joke?'' He extended his hand to seal the bargain. Mohamed was amazed to find it so soft.

Twenty-six ─────────────────────

ALTHOUGH not an extermination camp, Sachsenhausen offered its harvest of victims hard labor, cold, and malnutrition. Cramped human cattle, the truckload of prisoners that included Ruth Nouari and her son Abe had ground in through ominous gates that closed on all semblance of a known world.

They had been immediately separated, Ruth to the women's side of a tall barbed-wire fence. The impact of all that had happened since the night they had been dragged from Ruth's Paris apartment—the dismay, the disbelief, the fear, the offense—had been so staggering as to be almost incomprehensible to either of them.

Abe, the elegant, a man whose tie and handkerchief combinations set a precise harmony between shirt and suit; banker, art connoisseur, generous donator to charities, celebrated host to his friends, now wore the badge of his condemnation: the striped uniform with the yellow star.

Sachsenhausen was officially listed as a labor camp. ARBEIT MACHT FREI, it said above the gate. Work makes free. And yet most soon came to know the mockery of that word "free." Work made pain; work made blisters; work made the whole body ache. Work made illness; work, as often as not, made death.

Abe was detailed with the others to chopping rocks. By the first two hours, his well-manicured hands were so blistered he could scarcely hold the pick. That afternoon, he saw a man beaten to death for not working fast enough. Abe kept at his rock pile, mind numb. As the days passed, he would catch a glimpse of Ruth across the barbed wire that separated them. Usually after the noonday meal his mother would wait by the side of a hut. They would stare at each other for a few minutes, then move on. It was enough for each to know that the other was still alive. And yet all Abe seemed to think about was death. He began to train himself into the habit of non-thought. Since thought led nowhere, he gradually learned to erase it. He made himself an automaton, without memory or expectation. If work made one free, he would be free of fear, of caring, of self-pity.

Ruth grew thinner before his eyes, seeming to shrink. Her expression no longer belonged to her. Some days, he wondered if it was really his mother standing by the hut, or some total stranger without connection to himself or anyone he'd ever known.

Then, one night, a group of men were moved into his hut from one of the others. A contagious infection, someone whispered. Eight had died of it already. The men in Abe's hut shied away from the new arrivals. One of them came toward Abe, gaunt features twisted into a near smile. At first Abe did not recognize the man. Then he knew. It was Olek Cukor, his uncle from Warsaw.

"Abe. . . . No, my God. You here? But how could it be?" Ruth's baby brother—now nearly fifty, the once well-furbished lawyer, appeared like a grinning skeleton. He threw his arms around Abe and the smile melted into a fit of weeping.

"Uncle Olek. . . . Please, sit down. You must get hold of yourself." Abe helped him to his own cot. The man on the next bed picked himself up and moved to the opposite side of the hut, afraid he might catch something from the new arrival. Olek took possession of his bed.

"Your mother—she is all right?" Olek asked finally.

Abe shook his head. "If 'all right' means alive. She is here, uncle Olek. Here—in Sachsenhausen." Abe had broken down and wept with his uncle at the ironic conicdence that had joined them, out of the millions of victims scattered through the quick-death and slow-death concentrations of God's chosen people.

The next day, Abe told Olek to stand by the barbed wire where Ruth would be able to see him. When the guards were at the far end of the compound, he signaled to her and Ruth came forward, eyes dead of expression.

"Mother," he whispered. "Look who is here!"

She shook her head. She had no wish to see anyone.

"Mother . . ." he prompted. "Don't you know him?"

He had not expected the way his mother would react. Ruth cried out and fell to the ground in a faint. Other women carried her quickly inside the women's block. It was dangerous to attract attention.

Next day, she was there again waiting, this time, composed. She stood quietly and stared at her brother, hiding all signs of recognition from the guards. She began to sing a little tune they had shared in childhood, her voice reedy in the chill morning.

> "When we are together
> Nothing is to fear
> Remember, little brother. . . ."

Keeping his eyes carefully averted, he chanted the child's answer: "The Lord our God is near. . . ."

Ruth and Abe had been in Sachsenhausen nearly three months, Olek for almost six. He did not know what had happened to his wife, Gittele, or their son, Shimon. The lad would be twenty-one now. Removed to another camp, that was what Olek had been told. Would they ever see each other again? Would they survive? Nobody could answer such questions. Still they had to ask them.

It was rare that the men talked at any length. Mostly they would fall on their cots with exhaustion and sleep like the dead until the *Appell*—the morning call to work. Olek and Abe did not let it be known they were related, for fear they would be separated. At night they would talk together when the others were asleep. To Abe, life had become a nightmare. He felt himself losing grasp of the old realities. This present was unacceptable.

"What is it we have done—what crimes have we committed—to bring us to this?" he demanded of Olek as they rested up on their elbows in the dark dormitory. Troubled, exhausted breathing thickened the air. A sliver of moonlight carved Olek's emaciated cheeks. His hair had turned quite white, and yet there seemed to be a strength in the man, a tenacity that the younger man found impossible to equal. Olek's wasted arms could heave up the heavy rocks, muscles cording against the unwieldy carts. The cadaverous body could still stand arrow straight in the morning roll call. From where did this man draw his strength? Abe wondered.

"To be born in the wrong religion—to some, this may be sin enough, my nephew. But to keep hold of that religion, live by its laws, that is even more of a sin, maybe."

Abe had never really known this uncle well. Olek had never been more than a few short memories, a framed face on his mother's mantelpiece. A signature on birthday cards. A name in conversations. They had never before talked seriously; but in the gloom of this hut at night, words seemed to flow out of the man as though the necessity to voice thought was a compulsion that could save them both, that could give perspective beyond their hell and misery. To survive, they must find a pattern, Olek said. A meaning. For, without it, the only solution would be the termination of life—of which, as things were, they might have little choice anyway.

"It is not enough," Olek told Abe, "to say that it is monstrous we are here. Disproportionate with our great crime of having Semitic blood. Or to say that it is preposterous—that it cannot be happening. Or that if it *is* happening, God should be punished. Or that some may survive this atrocity." The ex-lawyer scraped mud from the shoe in his hand, tying the loose sole with a piece of string he had unraveled from his sleeve. "Physically, yes, survive. But to remain intact, that is impossible."

Olek's eyes lay so deep in their sockets that Abe could scarcely see them in the slit of light from the window.

His words had become the harsh edge of a whisper. "Yes, many will be destroyed, Abe. Some of the survivors will attempt to forget—wipe the horror from memory. But there are others—and I am one—who will always remember to the last detail . . . live always with the ordeal, like an old friend. This abomination . . . this capacity of man for limitless sadistic cruelty. . . . ?" He looked up, studying his nephew. "You know, Abe, we are all here because we did not expect to be here. When they came to our houses, we did not expect them to take us away. When they herded us into the boxcars, we did not expect them to bring us here. When we arrived, we did not expect that it would be a labor camp. Did not expect to see friends, neighbors, strangers, dying around us from starvation, or beaten to death. That is why we are here, Abe. Because we expected life to continue to have normal, rational meaning. We were not prepared to change our thinking, our way of seeing events. We were passive. When they came for us, not enough of us stood up to fight and die in the streets.''

"Then, where is hope?" Abe asked. "What is the meaning of anything ?"

Olek placed his shoe carefully beside its mate beneath his bunk and lay his head down. "Hope? There is none. Meaning? Here we endure the unendurable.''

The night the guard came for Abe and took him away, his knees began to tremble so badly he thought he wouldn't be able to walk. It was after ten o'clock. The others were all asleep. Only Olek stirred, wide-eyed when Abe was marched away. But Olek said nothing.

Out in the compound, the guard informed him he was being taken to the Commandant's office. When Abe arrived, there was a second shock. Ruth was waiting on a bench in the anteroom. When he walked in, a low cry escaped from her lips. Mother and son threw their arms about each other. The guard pushed them apart; not roughly, just doing his job.

"Inside. The Commandant is waiting." He gestured them forward through the door.

The Commandant's tunic flashed a cluster of ribbons and an Iron Cross. One leg jutted stiffly into the well beneath his desk. His upper lip drooped; the lower one protruded when he spoke, showing cigarette-stained bottom teeth. "Abraham Nouari. Ruth Nouari. *Ja?*" He glared up, a front-line veteran who didn't much relish this present assignment. "There has been a mistake. You were not meant to be sent to this camp at all. You are both to be released immediately! You will collect your possessions. You will depart"—a glance at his watch—"in exactly forty-five minutes." He clapped down a hand on two folders that bore their names.

Abe stared at the Commandant. Was this some sort of a grim joke? Would they be taken to their last departure from this earth?

"Mistake, you say?" Ruth's voice lifted in the muted room into near hysteria. "Mistake?"

"Mistake, *ja*, Frau Nouari. Made in Paris. No doubt, by the Vichy French. And it seems my junior officer neglected to report to me about your passports."

"Passports?" Ruth repeated. Both hers and Abe's were

French. And yet he was reaching into their folders and extracting two passports which she had never seen. The desk-bound officer shoved them toward her.

"Your passports, *ja*, Frau Nouari. Why did you not tell us you were American? Go on, pick them up!" he ordered sharply. "You will need them to board ship in Königsberg."

"But these passports . . ." Ruth began.

Abe flashed his mother a warning look, taking up the passports. He glanced inside the top one. It contained a picture of Ruth taken years before. He passed it to her. "Yours, Mother." The second held a picture of him he had given Zed three years earlier. He could hardly believe it. Authentic American passports!

Mother and son were escorted back to the corridor by the guard. Abe felt as though the fog of the last month was lifting from his mind. Forty-five minutes. . . . They had exactly forty-five minutes. And maybe they would never see Olek again. He appraised the guard quickly. There was about his face . . . a used look. Hard use, in a harder world than he would have wished. Abe wondered what role such a man would have found in a peacetime Germany? A railroad station master, perhaps? Cautioning children to take care as they mounted into the coaches? His was not a face of brutality. All the times that Abe had seen him, he had never noticed him strike a prisoner, even the time one of the older men had hidden behind the latrine wall for a moment's rest. This guard had looked the other way.

Abe attempted a smile at the man. "Well, now—as you can see, they have at last got things correct. Discovered who my mother and I are." Abe flashed open his passport for the guard to see. The German glanced at it quizzically. "We are Nouaris. Of the Hammadi-Nouari Banking interests. I headed the Paris bank. No doubt you would have heard of us?"

"Ah, so? It is why they let you leave here," the guard remarked. "Nouari and the Hammadi. These are names that are known around the world. Banking, *ja*. This I know. Jews and Arabs."

"Are you a married man?" Abe asked suddenly, sliding the passport carefully into the one pocket that hadn't been ripped from his prison uniform.

"Married? *Ja*. My wife and son, they live in Cologne." They had almost reached the outer door of the building when

Abe pulled Ruth down to a bench. She looked at him as though he had gone mad.

"You almost fell, Mother. Sit here a minute." He turned back to the guard. "For a certain favor, I could arrange for your wife to receive a money order in American dollars—ten thousand of them—when I am free. Cologne, you said?"

The guard eyed him dubiously. "Ten thousand dollars? It is a lot of money."

"The favor I ask could be somewhat difficult."

Forty minutes later, Abe and his mother were brought out to a truck waiting in the shadows of the courtyard. A probing beam from a watchtower scanned it. In the rear of the van, they found long crates to sit on. Safely tucked in Abe's pocket was a scrap of paper with the name and address of the guard's wife.

The truck rumbled out through the gates, and miraculously, Sachsenhausen lay behind them. Some twenty minutes had passed before Abe worked his way to the largest of the crates. He pried the lid up—to help Olek Cukor out. Tears of joy filled Ruth's eyes as brother and sister embraced. "Am I awake? Is it possible?" Olek finally explained how the guard came to his cot. "He told me only not to make a sound. Then he brought me to the truck—and told me to hide in the crate. I think maybe he put a dead man in my bed."

"Don't worry, Olek," Ruth said. "Abe took good care of him. In Cologne his wife will be a rich woman."

"Where are they taking us?" Olek asked.

"Mother and I—to Königsberg. It seems someone arranged two American passports," Abe told him. "God knows how. For you, without a passport, Königsberg would not be safe. You'll have to leave us—somewhere here in the forest. Sorry. Olek. It was the best I could do."

"Sorry? For all you've done? I will find some way to cross a border, don't worry." He smiled at Abe. "Now that life has found its meaning again."

Abe moved to the double doors of the panel truck. As promised, the guard had left them unlocked. Abe peered out; only a slender moon, and a light mist veiling the road. Abe turned back. "Wait until the driver is forced to slow down."

Olek moved to the door and crouched, ready. He looked back toward his sister and his nephew as though to memorize their faces. "If I make it—it will never be to return to

Poland. Never. My son Shimon—I don't know whether he is still alive. In Poland, he belonged to a Zionist youth group who believed in conquering the land of Palestine with fighting men. Beter Trumpeldor, it was called. 'Ra Koch,' they would say. 'Only Thus.' '' He shook his head. ''No. Poland will never be for me again. I dream now of one place only. If I live, that is where I shall go.''

He broke off. The truck was beginning to slow. He glanced out. They were on a steepening grade, moving up an aisle of dark pines. ''God only let us meet again,'' he said, and was gone.

When Abe peered out, Olek had already blended into mist-cloaked pines.

Abe and Ruth's arrival in Jerusalem had been anticipated by a cable from Zed to her father, telling him as much as she knew. Zed herself had taken the next boat from New York to Barcelona and on to Palestine, via Cairo. Her mother and Abe arrived the week before her and were recovering in the old Nouari-family house outside Jerusalem, closed since Grandfather David's death. Judah had driven down from Tel Aviv to get the house ready for wife and son.

He had come alone. When Sarah Schreiber heard the news, she told him, ''You must go to them at once, Judah. Whatever problems existed between Ruth and you . . . are now all in the past. She needs you. In the same way that you once needed me. You owe her that. But if ever again you want me, Judah, I will always be here.''

Judah knew that she was right. He drove himself to Jerusalem in his special car, built for a one-armed driver. Once again, the family was under the same roof—one family—yet all now strangers.

Judah found Abe suffering from a sense of dislocation and depression. Ruth was physically depleted, mentally drained, with a chronic bronchitis lodged into weakened lungs. So thin now, she had become the image of her once imaginary complaints. Judah spent his days sitting quietly beside her bed, where Dr. Simon had recommended she stay for at least two weeks before taking up normal life.

Daniel's father was advancing gracefully into his early fifties. The scars left by his adventures against the Turks had given him the look of a man who had lived dangerously. The truth was, he and Sephora had settled into tranquil middle age, the only bone of contention between them, Daniel's marriage to Françoise.

"Good food, plenty of it. And sun, Ruth. Good for the lungs. This climate will bring you back in no time," Dr. Simon had assured her. Privately, he warned Judah that Ruth's heart had been weakened. Not serious—but a condition to be respected.

The sun streamed in through light, billowing curtains. In the low hills above the city there was usually a breeze, even in the hottest days of summer. A vase of pink and yellow roses on Ruth's dressing table added their delicate bloom to the air. Ruth, lunching from a tray, had drawn her hair back smoothly from her face. An improvement, Judah thought, from the crimped-tight waves. She had gained composure and serenity; bony hollows had given her cheeks structure. Judah wondered if he had ever really seen her before—or if his eyes had always been clouded by the vision of her long-dead cousin whose name he could no longer bring himself to voice, even in mind. His heart swam toward his wife.

"And so it was Mohamed who did this for us," Ruth was saying. "This is a thing we must never forget."

At first, Judah had been furious that Mohamed and Zed had kept the truth from him. But, of course, they had been right. Had he known, he would have rushed headlong into the net. And Mohamed had effectively engineered their escape without him.

"Ruth. . . ." Judah's voice sounded hollow to his own ears. He scarcely knew how to begin; so much that should never be spoken. "Ruth, we have perhaps not always shared some of the higher moments of our lives. Not even, for that matter, the disasters. Perhaps the best we can expect is that now we can try to understand and forgive the things we didn't do. Along with the things we did. This way we may bring some happiness to each other and to our children. This is what I want. I hope you do."

"What about Sarah Schreiber?" Her words cut sharply through the softness of the moment.

What about her, indeed? Could a man be faithful to two women? Yet it was Sarah who had urged him to return to Ruth, not just physically, but with his whole heart. "Ruth, I have broken off my relationship with Sarah. We are still friends. We will always be that. Sarah is a good woman."

Ruth regarded her estranged husband across a glass of fresh goat's milk. He, too, had changed physically. Thick hair bristled gray about the temples, horn-rimmed glasses perched low on his thin nose. He gazed over the top of them, his injured eye squinting slightly from time to time. The empty sleeve was tucked into his jacket pocket. With all that, Judah was still a handsome man. And for all her resentment, she knew, a good man. Yes—if hurt pride were not a consideration—it was true that Ruth still cared for him.

"If you have broken off with that woman, Judah, then I will ask no more questions. We will try again to live together. Here in Jerusalem. This time as we really are. You. Me. Not a childish fantasy of what we dreamed we might find in each other." Judah bent over, kissing her on the cheek. He wondered if it was possible to feel more.

And so the days passed. One afternoon, he brought a letter from Weizmann. "This will give you hope, Ruth."

"Hope? For what should I hope?"

"Well . . ." he smiled. "Mankind. In this new 'dark age' covering Europe, there are still a few who carry a light. Listen to what Weizmann writes: *Do you remember meeting sometimes in a Haifa bank—a Swede. A man called Raoul Wallenberg? Well, the J.N.F. has received the most astounding reports. In Nazi Hungary, this Wallenberg, now with the Swedish Embassy, has constituted himself a rescue agency for the Jewish population of Budapest. Men, women, and children, herded together for the Death March to the trains bearing them to the camps. Wallenberg appears like an Angel of Mercy, armed with fake Swedish papers, passports. Any excuse to save them, take them out of the doomed multitudes. He faces the Nazis waving his spurious documents, demanding that Jews be freed and given into his charge. He has taken hundreds into his own house. Thousands owe Wallenberg their lives. Such a man exists, Judah and Ruth; a Christian who cares and dedicates himself at risk of his own life to the salvation of our people. Maybe his courage will inspire others. . . ."*

"Maybe," Ruth said. But her voice lacked conviction.

Judah put the letter aside as his daughter walked into the room. "Well, Mother, you're looking better today." She came over and kissed her.

"Where is Abe?" Ruth asked.

"Out on the terrace."

Zed spent long hours with him there, gazing out across tranquil landscape that showed no signs of the strife and unrest in the country. She sat with an arm around her twin, their heads together, talking in half whispers. Zed seemed to be the only one who could get through to Abe. In the crisis situation of Sachsenhausen, Abe had been brave, enterprising, quick to maneuver. Dr. Simon assured Judah that it was only the shock, the aftermath, that was upsetting his son. "Physically, he is as fit as can be expected. All Abe needs is rest, food, and work for the mind. That would be the best tonic."

Abe confided to Zed but not to his father, and yet, indirectly, it was about Judah that he spoke.

"Because of what I have seen," Abe told his sister, "because of what is happening to millions of our people throughout Europe, I can never be the same person. Do you remember when we were children and went to Uncle Ben and Cousin Naomi's wedding? All the people killed at Tel Hai and Kefar Giladi! I hated Palestine then. Never wanted to see this country again. I couldn't understand why Father wasted so much time on Zionism. I understood it even less in Paris, at the bank. I thought I had carved a personal niche for myself. I thought nothing could shake me out. How much security I expected from life, Zed. . . ."

"I know the feeling," Zed told him. "I feel it in New York. Secure. Happy. I love my work. It makes one gloriously blind to what is happening in other places. To other people."

"Zed, who in the world is coming to the defense of the Jews? I have heard Father say it—and now I know it is true—we cannot rely upon the conscience of the world."

"What do you intend to do, Abe?"

He took his sister's small hand in his. Always so much between them requiring no words. "I have been close to death. It is a powerful force. As powerful as the love of life. Zed, without a purpose, there is only one answer. I have thought about it a great deal. But perhaps for me, there *is* a purpose, after all. It is here in Palestine. I intend to stay and find out."

When Zed returned to New York, she carried letters of gratitude to Mohamed from Ruth, Abe, and Judah, along with her own constant admiration for her father's partner. Her latest "man" would be waiting. He was forty-five, married, and semifaithful. As Ruth had once unkindly remarked, "Another of Zed's Gentile gentlemen." Perhaps Zed thought, leaning across the ship's rail as it passed under the tall arm of Liberty—perhaps she would never marry. Not unless she found a man like Mohamed. A man who was strong in himself, yet could appreciate her for her talents and mind.

Abe wrote a long, fond letter to Maurice, knowing it would be opened and read by the Vichy French censors. He didn't know when they would see each other again. Meanwhile there was news for Maurice: *Raphael Nouari is now sixty-two. He's retiring from the Jerusalem bank. The old cock wants to return to Cairo. Personally, I think he's tired of turmoil and wants to crow peacefully in the shadow of the Sphinx. So now I have agreed to replace Raphael at the Jerusalem bank, working with Anwar.*

Before Zed left, she and Abe had driven to Bethlehem to visit Françoise and Daniel. The married doctors had been working at the clinic, after finishing residency at Hadassah Hospital, since Dr. Yusuf Hammadi was now retired. They had a small house near the clinic, and were blissfully happy, except for their isolation from certain members of the two families. On hearing of the marriage, Daniel's mother, Sephora, had said the prayer for the dead. She hadn't spoken to her son, or seen her daugher-in-law, in the four years since their arrival from Spain. *With much of Europe killing Jews, Sephora ought to be damned glad a "shiksa" had the courage to marry one*, Abe wrote in his letter to Maurice.

Abe and the young couple began spending evenings together hunched over wine, cheese, and conversation—always about the same thing: Palestine. They smoked too much, drank too much, talked too much, and so began to know each other.

Then, one morning, to Abe's surprise, the two doctors arrived in his office in the bank carrying a small wooden crate.

"Abe," Françoise began breathlessly, "we want you to keep this in your strong room overnight."

He looked up with curiosity. "What is in it?"

"Hand grenades." Daniel set the crate down on the floor.

Abe leaned forward, hoping he had not heard correctly. "Hand grenades?"

"No one will think to look for them in the bank," Françoise assured him. "They'll be perfectly safe."

Abe arose. "Good God, Frannie—where did you get them?" He lowered his voice. "I trust you didn't steal them from the British."

"No," she replied with a touch of pride. "From the Haganah."

Abe went to the door of his inner office, locking it. "You stole them from our only defense force? Have you both gone crazy?"

"They'll be put to good use," Daniel replied matter-of-factly, settling his huge frame into Abe's arm chair, small beads of perspiration soaking through his shirt. "Anyway, the British supply the Haganah. When the Haganah find these have been stolen, they will write an anxious, if angry, letter to British Ordnance—who will be forced to replace them. You see, we're very short of arms in certain. . .sensitive areas. Which the British couldn't be expected to supply."

Abe sat back in his chair. "I am truly amazed at the pair of you. Doctors. Professional people!"

Dan shrugged. He couldn't disagree. "Well, Abe, with me it's something of a family tradition. My father used to move illegal arms in his ambulance in the last war."

"And my uncle Anwar worked with him." Françoise beamed.

Abe broke into a smile. "How the devil did you manage to steal grenades?"

"That was no great problem," Françoise said, helping herself to one of his thin cigars. "We work part time training their medical unit."

Abe regarded her quizzically. "I've always been fascinated, Frannie, that you could feel such intensity of dedication to other people's causes." Fascinated and not a little admiring. She was so different from her brother; yet he could see something of Maurice in her smile. In her laughter. A kind of overcommitted gaiety. Like her mother? No, she was more like her father, if anyone. Recently she had cropped her hair like a boy's, which only made her lavender eyes more vulnerable. But the effect was deceptive. Of all the women Abe had ever met, Dr. Françoise was the most durable, most self-controlled, most capable. And the most unpredictable.

"Will you take care of the box for us?" she demanded.

"Think of the consequences for the bank if those grenades should be traced here. Think of my father and the entire JNF!" He could imagine Judah's face if he knew. Judah, who opposed any and all unofficial militancy, who was more in line with Weizmann's moderation than Ben-Gurion's determination.

"We'll have them off your hands by tomorrow night," Daniel assured him.

"Where are they destined for?" Abe asked.

"A *kibbutz*—in the Valley of Jezreel."

"All right, then." Abe rose, ringing for his assistant to carry the unmarked crate to their vault. He unlocked the door. "I'll keep them here on one condition. One only. That you let me go with you when you make the delivery tomorrow."

Daniel exchanged a look with Françoise, then turned back to their friend. "Be ready at four o'clock. It's about time you met Bernard Goldfarb, anyway. It will increase your education in many directions."

Next afternoon, in the car driving to the *kibbutz*, they explained a great deal more about Bernard and the operation he was involved in. Dan was driving. The battered jeep had seen a lot of service, but it had a few good years still under its hood.

"The days when your father and the others used to preach *havlagah* are gone, Abe. Passive attitudes to Arab violence . . . are a thing of the past."

Abe leaned forward from the backseat. The hand grenades were on the floor beside him, covered with a tarpaulin. He had never troubled to learn much Yiddish or Hebrew. He tasted the word: "*Havlagah?*"

"Self-restraint," Françoise told him. "It means passive self-defense. That's what the Haganah used to practice in the past. In short, Abe, if the Arabs attacked a settlement, they were expected to resist with shovels, hoes, and plowshares. And pray the British police arrived before they were all dead."

Abe smiled at her. "Tell me, my half-Arab friend, have you by any chance swallowed the *mezuzah?*"

"What?" she demanded, looking around at him.

"Taken up the Jewish religion. That's what he means,"
Daniel explained.

Françoise threw Abe an impatient glance. "You don't have
to be Jewish to believe in the right of human beings to exist.
Though sometimes, I wonder if God does."

"That all depends on whether God remembers he's Jewish," Dan put in.

Abe shook his head. "Where would you be without a
cause, Frannie?"

"Perhaps sitting in your chair at the bank, angry because of
all you've been through, yet not knowing what to do about
it."

Abe glanced at the sharp outline of distant hills. A land
forever swept by wars and winds. "Tell me more about
Bernard Goldfarb. I haven't seen him since I was a child."

"In order to tell you about Bernard, I should start with
Orde Wingate," Dan said. "The British captain who earned
the name of *Ha-Yedid*. And that means 'friend beyond compare.' Bernard was one of the men specially trained by Wingate to lead a night squad. But Wingate was too helpful to us,
too devoted. So his superiors packed him off to Burma.
Arrested all his night raiders, including Bernard and your
cousin Jonathan. They were all locked up in the jail in Acre.
Until your father, judicious Judah, made a deal to get them
out."

Daniel took a turn off the main road across a track of
bumpy, sandy wadi bed. After checking his directions, he
continued. "Instead of imprisoning Haganah men, Judah convinced the British to use them on dangerous missions against
Axis forces."

Françoise twisted around in her seat, to face Abe. "But
there are those among the Haganah who believe in something
more. Not just service in the British Army, or service *with*
the British Army—but a Jewish Army that can eventually
serve a Jewish state."

Abe studied Françoise. There was much more behind her
words. "Does such a group exist?"

It was Daniel who answered. "If it did, it would have to be
a real striking force. Shock troops. Trained to defend against
Arab attacks, as well as Axis enemies. Such men would have
to know guerilla tactics. Demolition. Sabotage. Intelligence
work. The units would have to be kept small. And completely

secret—even from the Haganah. No uniforms. No glory. No identity.''

From the car radio came a sudden burst of insistent Arab music. It whined up into the reddening sunset. Suddenly the sky was like a curtain of flaming clouds.

''This group that doesn't exist, Daniel . . . has it a name?''

''Plugot Mahatz. The Palmach.''

Abe hadn't seen Bernard since the wedding that turned into a nightmare, in Galilee so long ago. Bernard must be at least fifty; yet to look at him one would hardly suspect it. He was scarcely changed from the way Abe remembered him; rugged and fit as a man in this thirties, long, athletic from strongly muscled beneath faded khaki fatigues, face weathered into pleasant creases by the outdoor life, a white crest highlighting fading blond hair.

Abe's Cousin Naomi was still a pretty woman with a joyously warm smile and happy brown eyes. Life had been to her liking. One could almost feel the radiation of trust and love between husband and wife. Abe envied it. It was something he would never know.

The community room where they were dining was buzzing with animated conversations. On every table stood a large basket of fresh vegetables—cucumbers, onions, tomatoes and the like. The food was simple, home-grown. Wholesome.

''Wingate ate here with us,'' Bernard said. ''He told us that if everybody ate as we do—instead of all that tinned rubbish—our lives would have the freshness and sparkle of the fruits of the earth.'' Bernard took a bite from a spring onion. '' 'Pungent,' he said. Quite an extraordinary fellow, that Wingate! Really irresistible.'' Bernard pushed his plate back satisfied. ''You won't believe it, but he knew this valley the first time he came here—almost as though he'd stepped right out of the Bible. Wingate climbed up on one of those hills where he could look out over the whole of the Emek. Then he began a tirade against poor old King Saul. Pointed out En-Dor—where Saul ran into trouble with the witch. He seemed to have the entire layout clear in his mind at a glance. Almost as though Wingate had been here himself, three thousand years ago. Knew where the fire signal would have been sent from. Where the women would have hidden the flocks

and the children. And talk about military strategy! Wingate
ranted on about how Saul put all his forces into a daylight
battle when, as he put it, 'with a few hundred hand-picked
men, Saul could have surprised the Philistines by night and
changed the history of the Bible' . . .'' Bernard leaned back
on the wooden bench with a hearty laugh. "To him, the
whole thing could have taken place yesterday."

"We shall never stop missing Wingate," Jonathan said.
Abe hadn't remembered Naomi's brother too well. He found
him immediately likable, more like an academic than a soldier or farmer. Yet Abe suspected that he too, was deeply
involved with the Palmach.

"The British have just suffered a defeat in Greece. So now
they take what help we offer," Jonathan was saying. "But, to
us, they make no commitments. They are still holding down
the quotas, turning back death ships of refugees to God
knows where. And they avoid discussing our political situation here with the Arabs. Oh, yes, now they are willing to
train some of our men. Our new *Palmachniks*. Because they
serve the British for no pay, only expenses."

Bernard chuckled again. "And thanks to your father, Abe,
we have pulled a bit more wool over official eyes. Judah
arranged for the British to pay our *Palmachniks* through the
JNF. In that way, the British don't know the names of our
men. They also don't know the amount of expense. So we
collect double, and train twice as many men as they think."

"If ever they should try again to arrest us, it won't be easy
to identify our *Palmachniks*." Jonathan smiled.

"Today they need our help—against the Vichy French.
Even though they don't give us what we ask, they know they
can count on us as allies. And they also realize that the entire
Middle East is about to be axed by the Axis." Bernard
narrowed his glance across the table to Jonathan. "A surprise
attack on Syria and Lebanon could be decisive. For that, the
British need the Palmach. Men who speak Arabic. Men familiar with the country, trained in sabotage." A silence fell on
the table.

Later, they all went outside and joined in the dancing and
singing. Abe found himself circling in a *hora* with Françoise.
He did not hear the conversation among Bernard, Jonathan,
and Daniel. Nor was he meant to. But even as he danced he
caught glimpses of their serious expressions.

Bernard was detailing to Jonathan and Daniel the plan of a British-led sabotage raid. The first in which *Palmachniks* were to be used.

"Twenty-one of our best men will be under your command, Jonathan." Bernard leaned forward; firelight danced sparks in vivid eyes. "Your target: the oil refineries outside Tripoli. That's where the Germans and Vichy French refuel their planes. You'll be on your own. No British troops to back you up. If you pull it off, the most vital Axis base in the entire Middle East will be destroyed."

Jonathan sucked in his breath slowly. "My men had better all speak Arabic."

"I have selected men who do. Even speak French and German." Bernard stood up, eyes drifting away to Naomi and their daughter. Ruchel was fifteen; so like her mother when he'd first met her in Cairo in that other war. Solly, his son, was away training in a secret camp. He would be with Jonathan on the raid. Nineteen: born and raised in a *kibbutz*. Bernard watched Ruchel and Naomi circling in the dance, hands clapping with the others to the stirring beat of accordion, harmonica, and fiddle. "There's only one thing I don't like about this raid," he added.

"What's that?" Jonathan asked.

"The Commander won't let me go. My leg. My age. And my Arabic; it's practically nonexistent."

"When is it to be?" Daniel asked.

"In three days. Why?"

"This one I should go on. You won't be carrying the wounded home in litters. A doctor could be useful."

"You're not trained for a sabotage operation, Dan. It's a little more dangerous than an appendectomy."

"Bernard—you're not my mother," Daniel grinned wryly.

Jonathan looked across at Bernard. "We could use a doctor along. Particularly one who graduated from Spain."

Bernard considered, then turned back to Daniel. "Right. We'll make it twenty-three men."

The music wheezed to a stop. Laughing dancers broke apart, letting go of hands. Abe returned with Françoise. He was aware that his approach stopped conversation. He looked from one to another, feeling himself somewhere on the outside of their plans and activities.

"What is wrong with me?" he asked. "You keep feeding

my interest with tastes of information, but you exclude me from the *'plot' du jour.''*

Bernard smiled slowly. He liked this son of Judah for whom banking would not be enough. But Abe was still weakened physically from Sachsenhausen. ''When you fully recover your strength, Abe, we'll talk some more. Give you something to chew on and digest.''

Pitch blackness of a moonless night blended sky with sea. Departure time minus fifteen. Bernard shook hands with the British liaison officer, a form without face, leading the *Palmachniks*. They were all faceless in this dark—a file of ghosts loaded with arms and equipment, weighted down by boxed explosives—their footsteps heavy on the short jetty.

There was nothing more for Bernard to say. They were the best—these twenty-three. Some, veterans of the special night squads that had attacked and defeated the Arab marauders at Dabburiyah with Wingate, or served with the British guarding the northern frontiers. Some had already taken part in dozens of forays and ambushes—and some, including his son, Solly, were tonight trained for this first raid, proud and glad to be chosen, knowing themselves as Bernard knew them—to be the best.

Nothing to be said now. It had all been said in the countless briefings and training maneuvers and rehearsals for this amphibious operation. They knew their job as well as it could ever be known. Bernard had made sure of that.

He made out the form of Daniel with his medical pack, Solly in a black sweater and pulled-down cap. He had been careful to show his son no more attention than the others.

But Bernard knew that finally, after all the planning, the training, the practice, war was always the dark gamble, needing luck, and perfect timing—which was another name for it. He knew from his own war how many things could always go wrong in the confusion, the unreckoned element. Man, the fragile gambler pitted against his brother, and a hundred accidents, and finally—even nature itself.

Jonathan was last to get into the long open motorboat. A shadow-form, familiar to Bernard, well loved, trusted. He, who in another time would be happily digging through the layered gardens of the past, was now pitted against the future. Tomorrow. Bernard heard the weight of each man rock the long boat—making a faint splash. Then the rhythm of oars creaking against the leather-lined locks—pulling away from the jetty.

And at last . . . the thud-thud of the motor. Then there was only darkness where night blended into water—and the heartbeat sound of the boat was stilled by widening distance.

Judah arose from his desk in the Tel Aviv bank when Sarah Schreiber walked into his office. On his return, he had phoned her to say that Ruth was better and still recovering in Jerusalem. He hadn't suggested that they meet. But any strain between them was now suspended by the look on Sarah's face. She was obviously distressed, and flushed as though she had run all the way from JNF Headquarters, where she still worked. He came around and brought her over to the sofa.

"Sit down, please, Sarah. Catch your breath."

Sarah's pleasant face had creased with the years. Her skin, never treated to the luxury of unguents and creams, made her look older than she was. Such a warm, well lived-in face, one that should have offered comforting guidance to a houseful of children and grandchildren. A face framed in hair that had gone an honest gray. As always, she was simple and direct.

"Afraid I bring bad news, Judah. I—I had to come . . . to tell you in person."

He patted her hand. "Sarah, my dear, you don't need to apologize for coming to see me. Good God, we're still friends. Besides, our relationship—it was never that volcanic . . ."

"Judah . . . it's the Palmach. The Tripoli raid. . . . We've just had a phone call from Yitshaq Sadeh at the Haifa office. . . ."

Judah, of course, knew all about the sabotage raid. He had to know. Bernard arranged finances through the JNF. They had purchased an old motor launch, the *Sea Lion,* for three hundred Palestine pounds.

Sarah calmed slightly as her story poured out. The phone call from Sadeh had given all know details. There weren't many. The men had set out from a jetty near Haifa. That was it. The *Sea Lion* had simply disappeared. Vanished with every man aboard. Gone without a trace.

"Maybe they're dug in—in Tripoli. Cut off, or captured," Judah suggested.

"Impossible. Tripoli is monitored. We'd know. They never

reached there, Judah. The men never left the boat." Sarah
paused. "Judah . . . your Cousin Jonathan was in command
of the operation."

Judah digested the blow, sinking deeper into himself. "That
. . . I didn't know. . . . The names of the men are always
kept secret. Jonathan. . . . He wanted to be an archaeologist.
Now he's a dead saboteur. Not even a wife or a child to
remember him."

"There's more, Judah. I'm afraid there's more. Bernard's
son, Solly, was the youngest member of the raid. And Daniel
Nouari went with them as medical officer. They said he
volunteered. Insisted on going."

"Oh, my God, no. . . . *Yizkor.* . . . *Yizkor.* . . . May
God remember. . . ." The moments ticked away between
them. She waited without speaking. Finally he looked up at
her. "One by one, they are all lost. . . . Is this how we
build a nation, Sarah? By killing off all our finest men? Are
the bricks to be formed with blood and straw?" Judah broke
down and wept.

She put a çomforting arm around him. But there could be
no comfort.

Later, he telephoned Abe in Jerusalem. Somebody would
have to break it to Françoise. "I think it would come best
from you, Abe," Judah told his son. "And then you'd better
go see Dr. Simon and Sephora. They have to be told about
Daniel."

He could sense Abe holding back the tears, voice choked.
"Yes, I'll tell everyone." Judah knew how close his son had
grown to the two young doctors. It had pleased him to see the
strong links in the family.

When Judah put down his receiver, he left the office,
heading for Nathan's Restaurant. He himself would have to
be the one to inform Nathan about his brother Jonathan and
his nephew Solly.

"The only rank in the Palmach is the privilege of getting
killed first," Françoise said to Abe. Now that the initial
shock was over, the tears dried, a certain stoicism had replaced emotion.

He had found her at the Bethlehem clinic. It was, as
always, crowded with patients. When she first saw the look

on his face, she drew Abe into her tiny office. Dr. Simon was away for the day at the clinic in Jerusalem.

"Daniel and I discussed death many times, you know," she said at last. "We saw so much of it in Spain. Dan used to say, 'You shouldn't be afraid until it happens. Then it's too late.' " She went to the sink and washed her face with cool water, then came back and sat behind her desk, eyes far away. "When we finally knew that we wanted to spend our lives together, we also knew that it wasn't a long life we were after. We weren't cut out for declining days in rocking chairs." She glanced up at him. "I'm sure that's something you understand, Abe."

He did. The three of them had sat together through too many long hours of nights trying to make some sense out of the madness of the war and what would happen to Palestine when it was all over.

"What will you do now, Frannie? Go back to New York? Go into gynecology, which is what you used to want?"

She looked up, surprised. "Why should I leave here, Abe?"

"I would have thought that was obvious. I mean . . . Zionism may have been your struggle when Dan was part of it."

"He still is . . . for me. When I married him this became my land. It was half mine anyway. The Arab half. And even a Catholic can see that the world has left no other course for your people. If there were no anti-Semitism, there would be no need for a Jewish homeland. If there were no Jew-haters, there would be no Zionists."

"Then you'll stay on—here in the clinic?"

"There are as many sick people here as anywhere else." She rose and looked out the window, past a row of ancient fig trees, to the suncaked square. "But I shall also make myself useful . . . for the Palmach."

In the next few months, Françoise became extremely useful. She could speak Arabic, French, and English, and had learned quite a bit of Hebrew. As a Catholic, she could pass for a nun. As a doctor, she could wear the disguise of a Red Cross worker.

At her insistence, Bernard arranged that she go on an intensive training program—intelligence and propaganda—at a new Palmach *kibbutz*, set up in the Valley of Jezreel, Mishmar H'emek. Bernard himself was one of the instructors there. The group had been formed in memory of the twenty-three.

What Françoise didn't know immediately was that Abe, too, had begun leading a double life: banker by day, trainee by night. But the course he was taking was more rigorous, and even more clandestine. Abe had joined an underground movement that drew no line between terrorism and acts of war. Their target was not only the Axis powers and Arab raiders, but also the British who blocked entry of illegal Jewish refugees into Palestine, refugees from the concentration camps.

Abe had joined the Irgun Zvai Leumi.

Twenty-seven ―――――――――

The poster lay on the desk in front of Abe Nouari in his
office in the Jerusalem bank. His secretary had placed it there
along with the morning mail.

Five thousand pounds. . . . Abe studied the face above
the first name listed: *Menachem Begin.* A bespectacled youth.
His description was detailed beneath it: *Age: 29. Height:
175cm. Build: thin. Complexion: sallow. Hair: dark. Eyes:
brown. Nose: long, hooked. Peculiarities: wears spectacles,
flat-footed, bad teeth. Nationality: Polish.*

Abe's glance traveled along the rows of faces. Eighteen
men. There was something familiar about one of them, but
the name meant nothing to Abe. *Reuben Kahane.* He studied
the face. Could he be wrong? Above the iron-gray beard
bristled a thick shock of white hair and deep-set, haunted
eyes. No. There could be no mistake. He knew the man.

He read further down the poster. The men were all leaders
of various underground militant organizations. The Irgun Zvai
Leumi (I.Z.L.)—sometimes known as "Etzel." The Lochnei
Herut Israel (L.H.I.), called, after its leader, the Stern Gang.

Abe was already familiar by name with these groups. Often
enough since he had been in Palestine, he had heard Judah
discussing them with Ben-Gurion and others. "The Irgun is the
enemy of the Jewish people," Ben-Gurion had insisted. And

Abe had heard his father echo the attitude, vowing that the Jewish Agency would use all its means to suppress these terrorists. Men who opposed all moderation and endangered the entire Zionist cause. "They defy our official leadership, they provoke the British military, they doom our goals," Judah had insisted.

Abe did not agree with his father. But then, Judah had not been with Abe in the concentration camp. His eyes returned to the familiar face on the poster. He would have to find that bearded man. But where?

Childish laughter splashed sound through the airy, spacious corridors and courts of Mohamed's Jerusalem house. Little Jalal, now a tempestuous eight-year-old, was vigorously pedaling a toy model of an armored car. It was a facsimile of an item Mohamed was repurchasing from Generalissimo Franco's surplus stock. It seemed unlikely that "El Caudillo" would still require much of the vast armament he had amassed to make his revolution, since it had been won almost six years before.

"Blam. Blam. Blam. Kaablaam!" Jalal gunned down the invisible foe.

"Does he not resemble his father? Is he not like Mohamed?" Muna spoke with soft, oiled gutturals, but her French was, of course, immaculate. Françoise was grateful that at least they had found one topic of discussion between them. Their conversations were always starched and desultory. Neither welcomed these unavoidable meetings, but politeness required that, having lunched with her father and Muna, Françoise must now accept a glass of mint tea from Mohamed's wife in the courtyard. She was surprised at how young Muna still appeared. Arab women often aged quickly. Hers was a placid marriage, with only one child to show for it. But, at sixty-nine, Mohamed could hardly be expected to perform Vesuvian exertions in the bedchamber, virile though he might still appear.

"I asked if you think he resembles my husband?"

"As Americans say—a chip off the old block," Françoise affirmed. "The same stubborn chin. The same polished complexion."

"What is this 'chip'? I do not understand."

"Never mind. It isn't important. But, Muna, I wonder if I could ask a favor? No need to bother my father again, since he's in talking business with Judah Nouari—but there used to be an old album of photographs. Children's pictures of me— and Maurice.'' Françoise carefully avoided mentioning Jacqueline, whose name was never spoken in the presence of Mohamed and his second wife. It seemed an unspoken command from Mohamed.

"The books of the photographs. Yes. I have seem them. Your father does not like to think of the past, and I myself am not interested. Now I must try to remember where it is I have put them . . . ?''

Try, indeed. Probably hidden away somewhere in the depths of the cellar. Muna had carefully gotten rid of any photographic reminder of Jacqueline left in the house. Curious, Françoise thought, for an Arab woman who would perfectly well have accepted another *living* wife in her husband's marital orbit. Perhaps the dead presented more of a challenge.

"Yes, I now remember. Old photograph books. They are in a chest outside Mohamed's study. If you wish, I could find them, but it would perhaps be better if you look yourself, Françoise. You know better what you are looking for.''

"Yes, thank you. I will.'' Françoise set down the glass of mint tea. It caught a sun spark in its amber dregs. She felt grateful for the opportunity to escape those long silences that always punctuated these sparse exchanges with Muna. She went into the house and down the wide, tiled hall with Egyptian hangings of camels and dragomen that led to her father's study. The chest, carved and inlaid with bone and colored-wood geometric designs, stood coffin-deep outside Mohamed's closed door. Françoise opened the lid. She could hear her father's voice in conversation with Judah Nouari, words drifting out through the triangular carving of stone lace above the door.

The photo albums lay on top of some blankets. Françoise lifted one out. Mohamed's voice sounded more loudly. Was he beginning to be just a little deaf? she wondered. Or was Judah? She opened the album, turning the pages. She and Maurice on bicycles in the Tuileries Gardens. In bathing suits at Le Touquet. A family picnic in some forgotten countryside in some forgotten country; Mohamed looking bored, Jacqueline petulant. She turned the page. She was looking for a portrait of her mother wearing a cloche hat. Maurice had written asking for it. Not here. She put down the book, taking up the second album. And there it was staring at her; faded, fascinating. Luminous Jacqueline. She studied the face, wondering if it would ever have been possible for her to know this mother. Could any child ever really know its parent?

"What, exactly, is the consignment?" Judah's words drifted out.

Caught up in her own memories, Françoise sat down on the lid of the chest, thumbing through the second album. The conversation inside the study began to sound ominous.

Dappled light in the study filtered through the screens. Otherwise the room was shadowed, cool, faintly fly-hummed. The whirr of fan blades forced them to lift their voices.

"Surplus from Hispañola-Nacional. Submachine guns, ammunition, some revolvers. The shipment has been authorized through Lord Gort's office," Mohamed was saying. "But I have been left in complete charge of the arrangements. There will be a British military truck to unload the shipment from its point of entry. That, you understand, must remain secret until the very last minute."

"Why aren't the British importing them through the usual channels?"

Mohamed's voice hesitated for just the fraction of a second. "They're to go to Arab units in Syria. We don't want to stir up trouble—with *your* people."

"Arab units?" Judah's eyebrow lifted.

"You know there are Arab troops serving with the British. Why the long face?"

"You know damned well, Mohamed, that too many Arabs are supporting the Axis!"

A picture of Tariq and Yassir flashed to Mohamed's mind. "I can assure you, Judah, that these will be used against the Vichy French. Now, as to the unloading point. . . . I've waited to give instruction until the last minute to avoid leaks. But as I'm taking Muna to Cairo tomorrow, I'll leave it with you to confirm the collection point with Meredith. In person. No telephone calls."

"Where is it to be?"

"The containers will be brought ashore by longboat, a half mile south of Jaffa. A cove below the ruins of an old crusader's fort. Do you know the place?"

"I should," Judah replied with a faint smile. "We've been there together. When should Colonel Meredith's people collect?"

"Saturday night. It will be rowed ashore exactly at 2:00 A.M."

"Leave the details to me, Mohamed. And have a good trip." Judah was already feeling sorry he had flared up at his friend.

"Thanks. King Farouk is giving us an anniversary party. He's always been very fond of Muna, since he was a child. By the way, how is Ruth these days?"

Judah's brow creased. "Even after two years, she is still unable to wipe out the horror of that place. Still suffers nightmares. Jumps out of her skin every time there's a knock at the door. And still grieves for her brother, Olek. Ruth is certain he never made it out of Germany, though I keep telling her we have no proof he's not alive somewhere." Judah sighed, rising. "I'd better get back. I don't like to leave Ruth alone too long."

The clock ticked loud, a metallic heart on the long table of portfolios, files, and notebooks.

"What about Sarah? You still see her?"

"When I'm in Tel Aviv. See her. That's all." He rose, and the friends clasped hands.

"I wonder, Mohamed. Have we perhaps been meeting like this throughout the ages—arguing about armaments against Persians, Romans, crusaders, Turks . . .?"

Mohamed smiled. "Probably. And always as stubborn. And always, whichever of us happened to be backing some cause—convinced he must be in the right."

Judah took a step to the door, pulling it open. It framed him in light, bright as polished brass. "And you would have been selling javelins to Carthaginians, and chariot wheels to Alexander."

"No doubt. But this time, Judah, grant me at least a bit of patriotism. The Hispañola-Nacional shipments to Britain's allies . . . will benefit us all."

"Well, perhaps the High Commissioner will put you up for an OBE—to add to your collection?"

"No need. I already have one."

"Pay my respects to Muna."

"She was delighted to see you. As usual."

Judah walked down the empty hall to the front door, and out to his car. Somewhere behind him, he heard Mohamed's voice addressing his son, rather formally it seemed, for an eight-year-old. Perhaps, he thought, his friend had been right. A younger wife seemed to suit him. How well Mohamed looked. The stump of Judah's arm ached as it always did when he was weary—and now, before returning to Ruth, he must try to see Lord Gort about another matter. To make another attack on the British White Paper that had been beleaguering them since 1939. It curtailed immigration at a time when it should be expanded, attempted to set up a territorial ghetto for Jews in their own homeland, putting them at the mercy of the Arab majority. Judah had promised Ben-Gurion to join him at the meeting with the British governor-general.

And as for the arms shipment? Whatever other troubles stirred in the world, Mohamed could still turn an honest penny for the Company—even if it meant guns sold to Franco, bought back and resold to pro-British Arabs for use in Syria. And so the world turned and the galleys unloaded their amphorae on all the coasts washed by Mare Nostrum, he thought, driving through the perpetual hubbub of the timeless city.

They lay hidden in the ruins of the crusaders' fort on the hillside above the beach. There were twelve of them under the command of a wiry, bearded man in his early fifties. Too old for the mission? Maybe in years, but not in spirit. "Reuben Kahane"—his shock of white hair catching a glint of moonlight, had the respect of every member of the Irgun Zvai Leumi. A man with a price on his head and tattooed numbers on his arm.

"How are your nerves, Frannie?" Abe asked. The two of them were slightly separated from the others in the shelter of the old keep. From here, they could see the road and the beach.

"I won't need to take pills for them," she replied. It was through Abe's influence that Françoise had first joined this splinter group, born from the Polish Betar Trumpeldor Youth Movement—whose emblem was a rifle brandished across both sides of the Jordan. But now there were few rifles available to wave or fire, and no legal means to get them. Six hundred men with only thirty rifles and sixty pistols among them. And yet they were determined to teach the world to respect "the fighting Jew."

But despite such lofty aims, the Irgun had become diminished and divided. Jabotinsky, its leader and inspiration, was dead. He had gone to America in 1940, to address a Betar Youth Movement, staunch members of his Zionist Revisionist Party, being given military training before going to Palestine. He spoke briefly to his young followers, then retired to the bungalow assigned to him. All day, he had been troubled by pains in his chest. He felt short of breath. He would lie down for a little while, he said. In the bungalow, he suffered a fatal heart attack. They remembered his words: "I want a state with an army . . . ! Not a 'national home.' The Jewish people are not ready to retire to a home for the aged. . . . They have enemies to be swept aside."

Now some of the Irgun's best fighters had gone to join the British Army. Irgun's very existence was condemned by the Jewish Agency and official defense forces. Haganah and Palmach members readily handed over the names of Irgunists to the British. Yet this terrorist group still clung to its deadly purpose—the conquest of a homeland by violence.

They talked in whispers, trying to keep their minds occupied while they watched and waited.

"What sort of man was he, do you imagine—this Jabotinsky?" she asked.

"A hero—and a fool, I expect. He believed in the 'conscience of the world,' like my father. They were close friends, you know," Abe recalled.

"How much conscience has the world shown against ovens and gas chambers? The Allied Powers refused to divert any military effort to bomb Hitler's death camps. At least that would delay the genocide." She looked at Abe, the dandified banker by day; perhaps, it was said by some, her brother's one-time lover. Had Sachsenhausen been his anvil—fashioning the polished softness into the iron of hate? The more she knew Abe, the farther she saw, he had come from the image of his Paris dilettante days.

"Haven't you learned by now, Frannie, that the conscience of the world is always carried by its rebels? Yes, Jabotinsky is dead. But we have another leader now." Jabotinsky's protégé was a man of many names and identities. Ugly, young, frail, he headed every British "wanted" list. Abe glanced at the illuminated dial of his watch, the only shining thing in the gloom. "Your father's shipment should come in soon, and the British will certainly arrive ahead of it. Hope they haven't brought dogs with them."

She looked at his dark form nursing the carbine. An American military weapon. Who could imagine the trail by which it had ended in Irgun hands? She could sense the tension in the silhouette. "What's bothering you, Abe?"

"My father, Judah. Still believing that Palestine can be won by polishing British apples. He listens to Ben-Gurion, and tries to see everything from every side."

"By our acts we may educate the *Yishuv*—but nothing can put the fire back into the old. Their years defeat them, Abe."

He could see the etched profile of her slender throat. "Do you miss Dan?"

"Dan thought that the rightness of things was there—like polarity. Fixed as the stars. 'Right' will out, he thought. Like Jabotinsky's 'conscience of the world.' Dan was a good man. Too good. Now he's dead somewhere—under the waters, God help him. Yes, of course I miss him."

"What do you expect of God?" a voice spoke from the dark.

It was Reuben, their leader, his angular form dark against a powder of stars. He had come around the wall and had been standing there for some minutes, unnoticed. "You, I think, Doctor, abondoned Him somewhere in Spain. As Abe did—when the wrong tourists marched into Paris. As I did, when they marched into Warsaw. Man only, is responsible for his actions. The coward wills himself cowardly. The hero, heroic. God was a good excuse. Somebody to carry the blame. A more culpable scapegoat then even the Jews. The universe has no more interest in us than fleas on a dog's back. Maybe less. Life is ridiculous. We invent our reasons to act, and act on our own inventions. The rest is a bad joke—which mankind has kept repeating without ever getting the point."

Françoise knew that Reuben and Abe had known each other in Sachsenhausen. He would have had another name then. Names were something no one asked of each other in the Irgun. Particularly of a man whose entrance into Palestine had been illegal. There was a deep bond between Abe and

Reuben; this she knew. Reuben had enlisted Abe into the Irgun. She even knew that when Judah was away in Tel Aviv, Abe took Reuben home to visit his mother, Ruth.

"I'm going down to have a closer look from the shore," Reuben said, turning away to the slope.

Abe called softly after him. "Stay near the rocks."

Françoise came over to Abe. "Maybe someday you'll tell me who Reuben is."

"When it won't cost him his life. As Shakespeare said, 'What's in a name?' "

She put her hand on his shoulder. "Sometimes you are very like my brother."

"So are you," he said. "I suppose he's the only person I have ever deeply cared about. Of all the people I've known, we shared the most."

"And you loved him?" She dared ask it.

"That is a word I have banished. To do what we are doing, one must feel only hate." He turned to face her. "What are you trying to do, Doctor? A post-mortem on my soul?"

"Perhaps on mine. I'm trying to understand what I feel about you. You proclaim yourself a nonbeliever in anything. Yet here you are—here we both are—ready to kill or be killed for a boatload of weapons. And we might not live long enough to discover what might have been between us." She took his hand. It was a fine hand, the muscles well formed. The strong throb of his life force came through the slight touch of his fingers. And suddenly she wanted his arms about her just as she had once needed Dan's arms—and somewhere long ago her father's.

"Frannie . . ." he said, unsure of himself, but responding to her touch.

She came closer. They were drawn into an unexpected kiss. The union was for both overwhelming, tender and ardent. Abe had never experienced it with a woman. He clung to Françoise, trying to hold onto the wonder of the moment. His hands were the antennae of his soul, searching for something that had always before eluded him.

"This is crazy. Completely crazy, Frannie. . . ."

"Abe. . . ."

They kissed again and he knew it wasn't.

The lights of the British military lorry swept a bright zigzag across crumbling masonry. From the sea, a torch flashed four times. Minutes later, the sound of a boat crunched sand. Feet in heavy black army shoes slipped and skidded slightly under the weight of the crates. Six men from the Ordnance Depot.

"What d'you reckon they got in them?" a soldier asked in a husky Lancashire accent.

"No bleedin' cream puffs," the man behind him grunted.

"Get on with it—and don't take all the bloody night," the sergeant ordered.

Up on the road, they slid the wooden boxes into the back of the lorry. The crates made a loud scratching sound as they went in. Two soldiers closed the gate, lifting it up and pressing shut the pins. They were about to mount inside, rifles slung over shoulders, when the first shots rang out— small arms at close range, fired above their heads.

"Drop your guns on the ground—and move away from the lorry. Nobody will be hurt." Abe spoke in crisp English, a voice from the shadowed ruins.

There was a moment's hesitation, then the sergeant swung his rifle around, firing at the sound of the voice. He was cut down by a burst from Reuben's machine pistol. It ripped through his shirt, gouting blood. Another soldier was struggling to unsling his rifle. A shot nipped his shoulder. He dropped the weapon, lifting his hands. Another fired at the shadow shapes now moving out toward them. A shot dropped him to the ground. The driver was trying to start the lorry, rasping the clutch. It stalled before he could get it into gear.

Abe and the others emerged from the dark, running hard toward the lorry. There were a few more shots exchanged before the last soldier dropped his rifle. Reuben came over and pulled the driver out from behind the steering wheel.

Françoise went to one of the British soldiers who was badly wounded. Automatically, she ripped the shirt away, working to stanch the blood. He looked up at her with some surprise, eyes grateful.

The Irgunists tied up the soldiers, leaving them in a ditch, taking away their shoes and flinging them over the cliff. They wouldn't get far without shoes.

Four men took over the lorry with Reuben at the wheel. The rest headed for an old school bus hidden some distance away in a cypress grove.

Françoise was running, stumbling toward the bus. In the darkness and confusion, she couldn't see Abe and couldn't remember if he was meant to be in the lorry with Reuben. The three Irgunists with her were strangers. One was a girl of nineteen or so who had been wounded in the hand. She must have been sucking the wound, because there was blood on her lips and chin. She wore a bandolier and an old revolver thrust into her waistband.

"Give me a hand, Frannie!" It was Abe, helping one of their men who was limping. Françoise breathed a small prayer of thanks at sight of Abe. They helped the man into the bus. Abe took his place beside a bearded driver who looked like a rabbinical student. Abe's face was almost without expression. He thought he might have killed one of the soldiers. "Let's move," he said.

The driver started the bus.

"There are some burlap sacks on the floor. Wrap your own weapons in them," Abe told them.

"Where do we hide them?" the teenager asked.

"About an hour from here. Outside Petach Tikva. There's a dry well. We're to sling them in."

"But we can't afford to lose our weapons," one of the men protested.

"We won't lose them. They'll be collected. Israel Sassover will see to that."

There was silence. It was a name they all knew as head of the Irgun. To the British his identity was only known by his Polish name, Menachem Begin. A man they couldn't find.

"We must get rid of everything to do with the raid," Abe was saying. "Then get rid of each other for a few weeks. Do nothing until Reuben contacts you."

Françoise was examining the wounded man's leg. "I'll have to get this bullet out soon, Abe."

"Can we take him to Bethlehem?" Abe asked.

"Yes. The clinic will be deserted at this hour."

A faint glow of dawn paled the east as the driver rasped the clutch and the old school bus bumped away. Françoise turned to bandage the young woman's hand.

It was after seven o'clock Sunday morning by the time Françoise finished removing the bullet from the wounded Irgunist. She drove him into Jerusalem; then, on a sudden impulse, went to see Abe.

He opened his apartment door in pajamas.

"Sorry I awakened you. Can I come in?"

"Of course." He pulled his robe around him, bringing her into the room. It was a simple place; nothing here of the Paris elegance. Most of the furniture had come from the old Nouari house. It gave the apartment a faded, comfortable look. Her eyes went to a row of photos. A much younger Ruth, a recent picture of Maurice, sent only the month before. There was a picture of Abe and Zed together, prewar. No photos of Judah.

"No trouble, I hope, Frannie?"

"Everything was fine," she said. "The bullet was not too deep. He could be up and about next week, but I warned him to stay out of sight. Wounds bring questions." She picked up the picture of her brother, noting the inscription. *"Eternité,"* she read aloud, a question in her voice. "And has it been?"

"You could do with some sleep," he told her.

She set the photo down, turning back. "Do you think I could sleep, Abe? There's too much unsaid between us."

"We should leave it that way," he told her. "Last night was a mistake, Frannie. Prompted by the excitement of all that was about to happen." He offered her a wry smile. "Surely you're aware, Doctor, of sexual response to the nearness of danger or violence."

"I think it was much more. Very much more, Abe." She came around to face him. "Abe . . . hold me again. Let's be sure."

He hesitated, then took her into his arms, feeling her eagerness. Their lips brushed lightly, setting off an alarm bell of excitement. He drew her closer.

"Abe . . . do you want me to leave?"

"No. You know I don't."

She led him back into his bedroom, unbuttoning her faded blue shirt, dropping her skirt. She wore no bra. She was small-breasted, narrow-hipped, built almost like a boy. Abe stared at her body in wonder. He had seen enough naked women in Paris, but never before felt the wanting. To possess and be possessed. To know every curve and secret place of this body. She sat down on the bed—sheets crumpled from his sleep—and held her arms out to him. "I want you, Abe. I need you."

He moved close beside her, touched the soft smoothness of her skin, felt the hard bud tips of her breasts, fascinated by his own response. Then he pressed her down gently onto the pillow, still warm with the smell of his sleep. His hands drifted along her body, and he knew that what he was searching for was the unknown area of his own being. Something he could find only in another person.

In his mind was still the image of her brother. Maurice's voice, Maurice's touch. But somehow these two, brother and sister, were part of the same body—both nurtured in the same womb. And then he knew that he could forget Maurice. Forget anyone but this woman in his arms.

In that first moment that he entered her, they became as one. Abe had lost the sense of violence and destruction that had haunted him for so long.

Mohamed dismissed all of the office staff before Judah's arrival. It was late afternoon. A cool breath of evening brought a freshness to the air after the heat and dust and bustle of the teeming day. Judah had no idea why his friend had summoned him. Only that it was important enough to interrupt his afternoon rest. He came in and sat down. Mohamed said nothing at first, not even a greeting. No sound broke the silence in the office but their breathing. Somewhere, far away, the voice of a muezzin pierced the dying day. The moment was becoming endless.

"One British soldier dead. Three wounded. Our lorry load of arms hijacked—to use an American gangster term. Not inappropriate, since it was the act of gangsters."

Judah met his friend's glance. So that was it. He could sense that, in some way, Mohamed was blaming him, but he couldn't imagine why. "A terrible thing. Bad for our people. To the British—a fist in the face. I agree it could not have been worse, Mohamed."

"I see you know all about it?"

"How could I not? I heard at the Jewish Agency. We have pledged full cooperation and assistance to the authorities . . . to find these criminals."

" 'Criminals?' " Mohamed's tone was acid. "Is that what you call them? I thought you might call them 'patriots.' "

Judah fixed him with an outraged glance. "How dare you say that to me? I am totally opposed to the Irgun!"

Mohamed pushed the small carved wooden donkey and

cart, the original toy that had become an emblem, toward his old partner. "Two people knew of this arms shipment. Only two, Judah. You and myself."

"That is absurd. The purchase of this shipment was approved by the High Commissioner's office. The Military Police, the Revenue people. The Ordnance troops who arranged the collection. Even the captain of the trawler who made the delivery. All knew some part of what was happening. . . ."

"They knew that there were crates to be collected. No one . . . but you and I knew all the details of the plan: what they contained, where they were being brought in, the exact time. You and I, Judah. We had the whole jigsaw in one piece. The rest were aware of only the bits that concerned them."

Judah slowly shook his head. "This is unthinkable. That I should be sitting here, confronted with such an accusation by the man who knows me best in the world! If the matter weren't so serious, I'd think you were making some kind of joke."

Mohamed's hand brought the donkey and cart to a standstill. "The British have arrested two members of the Irgun. One of them had been wounded in the leg. They'd like to know who took out the bullet. Naturally, they won't talk. And naturally, they'll both be hanged. There had to be an informer who supplied information of the exact time and place, because the Irgun knew the details even before the British! You would agree to that, wouldn't you, Judah?"

"Of course. It is obvious."

Mohamed sat back in his chair. "*You* were the only one who could have told them, Judah."

Judah rose. His blood was racing, his voice choked. "I'll say it only once. I had nothing to do with this. I hate these terrorists as much as you do. As much as the British do! My God, would I sanction the death of British soldiers in a war they fight against the enemies of our people? Do you think I'm a madman?"

Mohamed said nothing for a moment. The accusation remained in his eyes. Then he replied, "I think that after this British White Paper—which you and Ben-Gurion so violently oppose—you could be angry enough to do anything."

"If you don't believe me," Judah said finally, "if you cannot accept my word of innocence, I will resign all connection with the Company—and pray we never meet again. I will go to the British myself and ask them to prove against me; which God knows they cannot—nor any man on this earth. If you don't believe me. . . ."

Mohamed rose to face him. All the years they had known each other lay between them. All the trust, all the differences, the anger, and the affection. And yet, at this instant, neither of them could reach across that moat.

"For the first time in my life, I do not," Mohamed said.

Judah picked up the old olive-wood carving of donkey and cart. The symbol that had always represented the unity of the two families, the seed of their beginnings from which the mighty Company had grown. His one arm sprang out like a catapult, hurling it against the wall. It shattered into matchstick splinters. Judah's voice came as a hoarse whisper. "Never again will I set foot in this office—or any office of the Company. Never again will I speak your name or look at your face." He spat on the shattered emblem and walked out.

Gestapo Chief Heinrich Mueller had served on Himmler's staff for over twelve years. Outwardly he appeared almost handsome, with a rather square-shaped head and eyes that moved as rapidly as a serpent's tongue. His voice could lift as suddenly to a shout as it could drop to a piercing whisper. He was, of all things, to the core a policeman. His hands were enormous, lips thin. His immediate task offered him none of the pleasurable rewards of an interrogation; yet he was applying to it his customary thoroughness and passionate attention to detail.

Before him stood four Arabs, the last of the once proud delegation to the conquerors of Europe: Haj Amin, Fawzi el Kaukji, and the Hammadi brothers.

"I cannot ask you to sit down, gentlemen. Our office, as you can see, is in the process of being moved." The big hand gestured toward a parade of minions bearing filing cabinets out to a waiting van in the courtyard, where, through the now glassless window, others could be seen meticulously burning papers and documents in three small iron ovens. Black smoke curled back through the window into the headquarters. Beyond lay a bleak vista of the German capital: rubble, gaunt bones of buildings protruding upward from mountains of fragmented brick and mortar—the slag heaps of broken power. "Not so pretty, Berlin today." Mueller's hands pawed through the layers of papers and reports on his desk. Reports proclaiming insane optimism—or black dejection. "Yes, it is here." He selected a bit of microfilm of a photographed document and placed it on a viewing box.

Haj Amin's soft smile was fixed as ever as he leaned forward. His beard was grayer below the wrapped turban, but he seemed otherwise unchanged.

"This has come into our hands. It contains the names of persons on a war-criminals list compiled by the Allies. The heroes most wanted by our enemies. All of you gentlemen, along with myself, have the honor to be included. Therefore, by the command of Herr Himmler himself, for your distinguished services to the Third Reich—and you especially, Grand Mufti, for taking personal responsibility for the mass liquidation of the Jewish population of Bosnia—I am authorized to arrange your safe departure from Berlin."

Yassir took a step nearer the Gestapo chief. "Do you, then, consider the situation here hopeless?"

The policeman's eyes danced restlessly. "Hopeless? No. . . . Such thinking is forbidden. But frankly"—his voice dropped in confidence—"it can only be a matter of weeks."

"But we still hear of German successes, Herr Mueller," Haj Amin purred gently.

"From whom?" Mueller's eyes bulged with anger. "From Goebbels—who sits correcting proofs of his latest book, *The Laws of War?* Do you know what he said to me yesterday?" Mueller rose from his desk, chest swelling with exasperation. "Can you believe what he asked? 'Why don't we separate Russia from the Allies? Why not make her *our* ally—and roll back the Western Front?' " Mueller banged his fist down on the desk. "I tell you, that Goebbels has invented so much rot—he now believes it! I said to him, 'Bring your mind to what is now happening. This is the spring of 1945, Herr Reichsminister! The Allies have pushed us out of France, Belgium. Holland! They are sweeping Germany with a broom of armies. Americans have come by the millions. And you, Herr Goebbels, publish articles about the Punic Wars. About Frederick the Great! About Prussian resistance to Napoleon! Is this to be our defense against the Jew-backed democracies of the world?' " His words had risen to an accusing shout.

No one disagreed.

"No, my friends, only the mad or the dead are safe from the truth. And so, we face three possibilities: surrender . . . suicide . . . or escape. Of these, I think you will agree that the last is the most desirable, no?" He paused for a reaction, but there was none. "I have for you passports and letters of introduction to some of our friends who are establishing safe houses in the Argentine. There you will be welcomed, provided with all you require." He pushed an envelope toward Haj Amin, who made no move to touch it.

The grand mufti closed his eyes, lips moving as one suddenly in a trance. "Oh, Prophet . . ." he quoted, "urge on the believers to fight. If there be twenty of you, they will overcome two hundred!" He opened his eyes as though expecting the room to be filled with angelic armies.

"Yes, that's all very well," Mueller replied. "But prayer doesn't work against tanks and saturation bombing."

"Let others do as they will." Haj Amin shrugged, his hands fluttering aloft. "I shall return to Palestine, where I am needed."

"And I," echoed Fawzi el Kaukji. Above his military uniform he wore the flowing Arab headdress ringed by its tight band. "It is our homeland. Our lives draw breath because it awaits us. And if need be, we'll drown the world in blood to gain it!"

Mueller nodded wearily. "Yes, yes. . . . The Führer said something like that himself, once. About the Sudetenland, if I recall." The whip of his eyes flicked to the Hammadis. "And you two?"

Yassir, still wearing his colonel's uniform, answered slowly. "We worked with the Nazis for the future of Palestine. Perhaps it is true Germany has lost this war. But we have not lost our purpose."

Mueller shrugged. "If you intend to return to Palestine, your best possibility will be through Africa. You will still need a hiding place until a crossing can be arranged." He broke off, diverted by distant muttering thunder from the east: Russian artillery. The Arabs looked at each other. The Gestapo chief unlocked a desk drawer, took up an empty dispatch case, and started to transfer the contents. "In that envelope"—he gestured to where it still lay untouched on the desk—"you will find some addresses in Europe. Places you can stay without questions asked. When you have chosen, destroy the list.''

Haj Amin now took up the envelope. "We thank you. And may we ask where you yourself intend to go? Soon, perhaps, we will be able to offer you our hospitality in a Palestine empty of British and Jews.''

Mueller shook his head. "Personally, I never cared for hot climates. I have, however, always admired the police methods of the Russians. Professionally, you understand. Once, long ago—in the days of the Moscow-Berlin Pact—I had occasion to become friendly with some of their military intelligence.'' His eyes returned to the drawer he was unpacking. "You see, gentlemen, the Allies winning this war will not end the conflict. Let them punish a few old men as war criminals. The next war they may lose without a single battle.''

Haj Amin bowed, ready to take his farewell. Mueller started to give the Nazi salute—then, curiously, closed his fist, lifting it in the fashion of the Russians, with whom he had secretly chosen to cast his lot. "Transportation will be at your hotel in precisely one hour. I advise you not to delay for any reason.''

They didn't. It was Haj Amin's decision that they separate. He and Kaukji chose to head for the villa of a Nazi general retired to Andalucía.

Yassir and Tariq disguised themselves as Moroccan laborers and made their way through Austria, Switzerland, and finally France, to cross at last into Spain, to the northern hills near León where there was an old monastery. It had been second from the top of Mueller's list of safe houses. And it was Yassir and Tariq's destination.

El Monasterio de los Padres de Santa Rita was as large as its name, isolated from the nearest village by the rocky haunch of a mountain. Through the ages, these meanderings of sixteenth-century masonry had fallen into disrepair. Frequently it had provided haven and refuge from a turbulent world. Before the present monastic order of silence and self-denial, it had even served from time to time as an impregnable fortress. Napoleonic cavalry had managed to bring their horses up this steep mountainside, later to be evicted by

Wellington's troopers. More recently, it had offered refuge to a group of Falangists fleeing Basque attackers.

Upon their arrival, Yassir and Tariq immediately noted that the current monks in residence had a habit of clicking heels beneath their cassocks when addressed by superiors. They soon learned that the real abbot had been killed for resisting these uninvited guests. Aged monks, the rightful occupants, were imprisoned in some of the older cells, except for those few who were willing to work for these fugitives of the Master Race. The monastery had always been self-sufficient. Someone still had to care for the vegetables, cook the meals, clean the cells for the time when unwelcome visitors would leave.

Yassir and Tariq had received an enthusiastic welcome from the new "abbot," whom they immediately recognized from having met briefly in Berlin. Martin Bormann's short, squat figure was girdled in a brown monk's cassock. Hitler's secretary and personal aide, known as the Brown Eminence, was, it was said, among the last to have seen the Führer alive. He led the Hammadi brothers on a tour of the buildings and the grounds. The view was quite stupendous. Rolling hills of lavender, smoky clouds hovering above the spires of mountains still creased with snow. To Tariq, it seemed a haven where one might stay forever. Forty-nine years of impassioned living had brought him and Yassir to this place. In some ways it was a harbor of finality. It was not easy for him to imagine anything beyond.

Guiding them through the neatly trimmed paths of the monastery gardens, Bormann relayed to them some unfortunate news. Word had reached him of Haj Amin. The grand mufti had been intercepted while trying to cross into Switzerland. "He was forced to surrender," Bormann told them sadly. He moved his bulk stiffly in the unfamiliar cassock. Tariq could see that beneath the skirt he still wore polished boots.

"What have they done with the grand mufti?" Yassir was asking.

"He awaits trial in a French prison." Bormann's coarse peasant features worked themselves into a frown. "His friend Kaukji was more successful. As far as I know, he has not yet been caught." His thick-set body bulged the cassock as he led them to watch aged Spanish monks collecting string beans and peppers. "Here they produce also a quite acceptable wine. But I forget. You do not drink."

Yassir was silent. The news of Haj Amin had struck him like a blow to the heart. This leader, who above all others had been the architect of the Arab cause, a man who at times had seemed to Yassir above mortality, Haj Amin . . . a name to be spoken with the reverence of prayer. "How could such a thing happen?" He trembled as though gripped by a sudden fever. "Is it because we were always too soft against our enemies? Is this the punishment for our weakness—our mercy?" Yassir sank down onto a bench and buried his face in his hands.

Tariq stood over him for a moment, a comforting hand on his shoulder. "My brother is a great hero of our people, but he has been through too much. The months we both spent on the Russian front with the Muslim SS Division. And then the journey here from Berlin. Nights, sleeping on the roadsides—soaked in rain. Begging from the French, like the Moroccan dogs we were pretending to be. You will forgive us, Chancellor, if we are not quite ourselves."

Bormann sat down on the bench, fingers plucking at a thick eyebrow—a habit unconsciously picked up from Himmler. "Do you think for any of us it was easy to come here? I waited in the bunker until the last moment. I was there when he shot himself. I was there when the body was burned. Then" —a smile touched his lips—"I made my little disappearance. I said good-bye to my secretary—and as I had so carefully planned it, I vanished. Somewhere between the Weidendammer Brüke and the Lehrter Station, those who followed, lost me." He sat quietly for a moment, submerged in thought, his mind reliving the flaming bunker he had left behind. "Where shall we be without him?" he asked finally. He rose, strolling on to where a clump of raspberries were growing along a wire fence. Tariq walked with him, leaving Yassir behind on the bench. Bormann picked a handful of the berries, eating them thoughtfully, one by one. Like a man swallowing his worry beads, Tariq thought.

"This hiding place on a Spanish mountain, it is not the end for me, Hammadi. I am not swallowing cyanide, like Himmler. In a few short weeks, when matters have been arranged, I shall be on my way to South America. There, with a handful of loyal Nazis, and a great deal of money, I shall resurrect the

Third Reich." They moved on around the path, coming back to the bench where Yassir sat. "We have some five hundred million pounds in the safekeeping of Eva Perón. What do you think of that, Yassir? Why don't the two of you come with me? I can offer important work for men of your caliber."

Tariq glanced at his brother, then replied for him. "I don't know how or when, but we must return to Palestine, Chancellor."

"Palestine?" The word was spat from Bormann's lips. "That would be as stupid as my returning to Berlin right now. The British would hunt you down like one of their foxes!"

Later, they dined at a long refectory table, served by the monks. There was no shortage of wine for the Nazi officers. The table erupted with loud gusts of laughter. Some members of Bromann's entourage were getting too drunk. He regarded them with disgust, turning to Yassir and Tariq, who sat to his right and left. "*Schweinehunde.* . . . They lose the world—and instead of dedicating themselves to rebuilding it, they gorge their appetites like fat Romans in the twilight of their empire. Well, Yassir, have you reconsidered my offer? Sanctuary in South America and a part in the rebuilding of the Nazi world movement?"

Yassir's eyes were glazed with despair. "I would not exchange a prison cell in my own land for a bed in paradise, Chancellor, if it took me from the work that awaits us. The British, I think, will not remain in Palestine much longer. We shall assist their decision to leave by practicing the terrorism we have learned. By systematically slaughtering Zionists. And when we have finally gotten rid of the British, we will push the Jews into the sea."

Bormann rose. The officers instantly came to their feet. "In ten minutes, we will be showing some private film, gentlemen. For your entertainment." There was a hum of conversation as the officers moved out and down the corridor. Bormann turned back to the Hammadis. He fingered the heavy cross that swung from the girdle of his cassock as they walked. "Pushing the Jews into the sea could be more difficult than you expect, Hammadi. In the battle of the Warsaw Ghetto, we learned to our surprise that not all Jews are meek. When they fight, they can be tough opponents, even without weapons or training. We were forced to divert combat troops

with tanks and artillery before we could finally finish them.
When I told Himmler, he could not believe it! It is something
to be taken into consideration. We have proved that the only
solution is to exterminate them scientifically, as we were
doing.''

Tariq spoke quickly before his brother could answer. ''Arabs
are not concerned with exterminating all Jews, Chancellor.
We must be clear on that point. We oppose only Zionists.''

Bormann's manner stiffened. He led them on down a corridor. ''Forgive me, Hammadi, but you are children in the
playroom of history. You talk of sparing some and destroying
others. Do you not see you can make no distinctions? It must
be none, or all.''

He opened the door to the monk's library. The other officers
had already collected. ''What good is history if one cannot
take lessons from it?'' Bormann reasoned. ''Our methods
have proved that it is not enough to break a few windows, put
yellow stars on doors, beat up old men and women. . . . To
erase a whole people is not so easy. It requires technical skill,
experiment, ad experience.''

They followed him into the room, where a sixteen-millimeter
projector had been set up. The officers had arranged themselves on benches awaiting the screening. Several rose, making a place for Bormann and the Hammadis. ''What I am
going to show you tonight even few Germans have ever seen.
While you were serving with our armies in the field, you had
no opportunity to visit one of our extermination camps. Few
did, except those immediately concerned.''

The bitter stench of wine breath assailed Tariq's nostrils.
Flickering images assailed his eyes.

The parade of horrors opened almost gently. Street scenes
of old men and women forced to scrub gutters, while booted
Nazis strutted and rode them like horses. Bormann leaned
over to the Hammadi brothers.

''What you see are films from my own private collection.
Many unfortunately have been destroyed in the haste of our
departure. Watch closely—and you will see how to handle
your Jewish problem in Palestine.''

Yassir shifted in his seat. The films made little impression,
except when the Jews were hung upside down and flayed.
This brought back a slight twinge of personal memory. He
could feel again the bite of the Turkish whip. But for the

events photographed he could feel nothing. The hollow faces. The bodies piled like cordwood, the naked women herded to the place where they would be shot. The pyramids of wornout shoes of the dead, the boxes of gold-filled teeth. "What a pity Haj Amin is not here to see these," Bormann added.

Yassir heard a gagging sound beside him. "What is it, Tariq?"

"These pictures. I never imagined it was like this . . . !"

"Would you prefer that those people were alive, being sneaked into Palestine—to steal more land from us? Would you like that better?" Yassir's tone was biting.

Tariq could not reply. He could not put any words to his reaction to what he was seeing. He had once read of a Christian hell—where agony was prolonged into a kind of mass carnival of every torture and method of exerting pain on man. This was not just a battlefield where atrocities could be masked by the truth of courage, purpose, sacrifice. This was the butcher's abattoir—in which the desecration of flesh tore away the last vestige of the dignity of all men. And through all his life, this dignity Tariq had believed in. Of man . . . of his brother . . . of himself. Always, a Muslim's enemy was someone to be respected. You met him in the wilderness, you fought, you employed stratagems. And if you destroyed him, you might, in your prayers, remember his courage and take pride in your own skill that had given you victory.

But these poor creatures on the flickering screen, their sheep's eyes swimming in blood, the bones of their little children stabbing through lank skins, the bodies of the women, stripped of any clue of humanity and respect. These shadow creatures were more real than anyone in this room. And Tariq felt shame for all who had shared this time on the same earth and not troubled to know. Yes, they had all been told of the extermination camps. But who could imagine it until confronted by it? And in his small way, Tariq had sanctioned such total evil. By ignoring it, he had played his role in the making of this heinous film. By closing his eyes to the truth of it until this moment. Now, among these Nazis, with whom he was sharing food and haven, the offense welled up in his throat like vomit. He could not look at the screen. He could not bear to see his brother's form beside him, a brother who could watch placidly while the screen showed horror upon horror. If any God or any man could permit such things as he was watching, then surely the act of living was a sin, and shamed anyone who still drew breath. Tariq got to his feet. The bench leg scraped against stone.

"Where are you going? The film is not over," Yassir demanded, rising beside his brother.

"You defile the name of Mohammed, the Prophet. You defile our family, our cause. I will not share this room with you or any here."

"Sit down," Yassir ordered sharply. "You will offend our hosts." This exchange had been in Arabic. Only the tone of anger registered on Bormann and the others.

"What is the matter with your brother?"

"Nothing. It is nothing. Too much food at dinner."

But Tariq's hand had formed a fist. All his life he had followed his brother. Now, in this instant, he realized the times he had made excuses to himself for the poison of his brother's hatreds poured into his own mind. "For the last time I have taken your orders, brother!" The fist crashed squarely into Yassir's face, knocking him back across the seated Bormann. The other officers rose, hands moving to their pistols.

Yassir pulled himself erect, his voice imitating the frigid calmness of Haj Amin's. "You have lost your senses, Tariq. Go to your room and lie down. Cool off."

Tariq turned and walked out. He could hear Yassir apologizing for him to Bormann and the others. "My brother means no offense to you, gentlemen. . . ." That was the last he heard. The obscenity of an apology. His steps sounded hollowly on the worn, tiled floor, carrying him to his small cell. He lit the single oil lamp.

No, pride could not permit. A man who could call himself human, honorable, could not accept this destiny—either as the foundation on which to build the Arab nation or as the means necessary to the end. A vision flashed through his mind: another flickering film of time itself—and what might be to come. He saw the hordes of people he had never hated, driven like cattle into a sea red with the blood of their extermination. He saw airplanes crashing from the sky, plunging human torches. He saw explosions larger than any yet conceived—for what weapons might not be used by future fanatics in the fulfillment of their ambitions? He saw the death agonies of thousands to come, in the name of purification—this time in the land where he had been raised in love and pride.

He saw the face of his father shining toward him, his beloved mother caring for all children, concerned for even a scratched finger. He saw the parade of heroes who had lived for him in the words of storytellers in the open square of the Damascus of his childhood. Saladin and the horsemen who rode at their foes with lance, bow, and curved sword, mindless of odds—gallant enemy to gallant attacker. . . .

And Tariq knew that from his heart had gone the essence that gave all things shape and form. Now there was nothing left but the shame of having seen what he had seen—and having taken part in this sacrilege of life.

He took off his greasy, roadworn rags of disguise and put on the robe of his desert pride: his white burnoose. Then he took the Luger from his shabby pack. It was loaded. He flipped off the safety catch and placed the gun against his temple. For a moment he hesitated, not out of fear, but to savor the sudden feeling of peace. Then he squeezed the trigger.

Twenty-eight _____

"SO, Uncle Anwar, what is all this nonsense about you retiring? You would never catch my father doing such a thing?" Maurice Hammadi was making his first trip to Palestine since war's end. "Besides, you're looking fit as ever." Maurice's words stretched truth. Although six years younger than Mohamed, Anwar lacked the same sturdy constitution. He had begun to look frail, careworn.

"No, I have never had the drive of your father. It is an attribute that I can admire, but one I do not hope to understand, Maurice. Perhaps that is why Mohamed is a great man, and I—well, I am the brother of a great man."

Yes, Maurice was back in Palestine—his ears offended by the sharp, harsh shouts of porters, beggars, travelers, the blur of languages; nostrils assailed by the acrid smells of sweat, dust, and donkey urine. Why had he come now? In the last years since Abe had settled here, their letters had slipped more and more into banality and business; Abe communicating little news of a personal nature; nothing of his private life. There was no doubt in Maurice's mind that Abe's feelings for him had altered. It was to be expected after the time apart. When had absence ever made anyone's heart grow fonder, except in Victorian novels? For Maurice there had been fleeting affairs, brief alliances—but in mind and heart he was still tied to Abe by the fine thread of memory.

So when the letter came from Uncle Anwar asking Maurice to consider taking his place in the Jerusalem bank, Maurice had written back that, in principle, he could be interested. Osmon, Dr. Yusuf's son, had been working with him in Paris for several years now. Older than Maurice, Osmon was quite capable of managing the bank on his own with marginal supervision. Since war's end, it had remained "The Hammadi Bank"—and Abe's refusal to return to Paris was almost understandable to Maurice.

But Jerusalem was different. Jerusalem was still the head office of Hammadi-Nouari for worldwide banking and trading. And here Abe and Maurice could be working together again. Perhaps they could even pick up the lives they had dropped years before.

Yet Anwar, meeting the train from Jaffa, had, to Maurice's surprise, come alone. Uncle and nephew had embraced, exchanged blessings, and moved on with the luggage-loaded porters, who were trading insults with less fortunate colleagues, the din unendurable.

Anwar sank back into the leather seat of the Company car, gazing wearily out at the teeming streets as they pulled away. Ahead of them, a crowd of Arabs armed with sticks were running after a group of Orthodox Jews in *yarmulkehs,* prayer shawls protruding from beneath jackets. A patrol of British Military Police burst out of a side street, heading toward the commotion. Anwar's car turned a sharp corner, ending their view of the disturbance.

"The war wasn't enough. These last few years, Maurice, so many troubles here in Palestine. I feel it is time for me to step down from active life. I am, would you believe it? sixty-six."

Maurice would.

"And who but you is left to fill my shoes? My daughters, Lalia and Ferzan, praise be to Allah, are both happily married. Praise also, they did not wish, like Judah's daughter, to follow a career which, for a woman, can bring only unhappiness."

"I've never heard that Zed was unhappy, uncle. My father tells me that, in her job, she's better than a man."

"Perhaps I am old-fashioned. But it is too late to change the way one thinks." Anwar dismissed it. "Besides, she is not of our faith."

Neither was Maurice, if he wanted to put a fine point on it. But the Hammadis had always managed to close their eyes to his Catholicism. One thing had disturbed him in the interfamilial relationships, to which he had never been able to get a satisfactory answer from Mohamed. Now, alone in the car with his uncle, Maurice asked, "What happened between Judah and my father? Why did Judah quit the Company?"

Anwar shook his head. "This is something the nature of which is not known, even to Judah's son, Abe. There was some kind of argument. The emblem of the Company was found broken. That we know. Mohamed will not speak of it, nor allow the matter to be mentioned in his presence. So we must leave it at that. Perhaps, like Abe, Judah spent too much time on matters away from the bank."

"I rather expected Abe would be with you to meet me."

"As I say, Abe is very busy these days. Like his father exactly, for he seems always to have too many things which occupy his time."

Maurice gave him a sharp look. "What sort of things, uncle?"

Anwar shrugged. "Who knows? Politics. But I do know he looks forward to your arrival and once again to be in partnership with you." Anwar offered a hopeful glance. "Perhaps, with you here, Abe will spend more time at the bank. Be more concerned with the business of the Company."

They rode on in silence for a block or two. "And my sister. What's her excuse for not coming with you?" Maurice asked finally.

"Every afternoon, Françoise works at the hospital. She is busy, like Abe. After Daniel's death, she moved here from Bethlehem, as you know."

"That's about all I know, from her letters."

Maurice felt Anwar was about to add something to his last statement, but his uncle hesitated, then changed the subject. "Tomorrow your father arrives for the annual Company meeting. So! Tonight I thought you would dine at home with Farida and me. Mohamed has opened up the house for you, but you are welcome to stay with us as long as you wish."

"Thank you, uncle." Then, careful to keep his tone casual, he added, "Will Abe be at your house tonight?"

"Yes, surely Abe will come. And Françoise." He began listing the guests on his fingers. "And Salim, Osmon's son. You remember him, of course? And his wife. And Noah Nouari, his wife, and son Micah. Raphael will not come until tomorrow with your father from Cairo. Then it will be a real Company reunion. They are all eager to have you here in

Palestine. To welcome you into the Jerusalem head office. And none more than I, my boy. None more than I."

Glancing out the car window at the filth and turbulence of the city, Maurice wondered if he would be so glad to stay here. As far as he was concerned, it was a cultural wasteland. No art, no theater, no opera, no ballet, and undoubtedly a shortage of witty friends. Well, he would have to see. Everything depended on Abe.

Anwar's home was long, rambling, white stucco with an octagonal inner courtyard and the obligatory splashing fountain. Its terraces looked out on two views: the city, and the plain. The house brought back memories of childhood visits with his mother when they had stayed at Grandfather Sayid's and Mohamed always seemed to be away somewhere on business, and Jacqueline had remained mostly locked in her room. In that time long ago when he still believed that Mohamed was his father. When he didn't know about that other Maurice. How often he had roamed alone along these sloping hills beneath the cypress trees, dressed sometimes in the small loose *abaya* of fine white linen, his red shock of hair covered by the *kaffiyeh* held in place by a gold braided *agal*—exactly like the garments Mohamed still owned but seldom wore. In his belt, Maurice had carried a curved silver dagger, but the blade was not very sharp. He had tried once to carve his initials in a small black ebony table in his bedroom. The wood was too hard or his blade too soft. All that was before Françoise had ever been born. The memory brought a smile.

"I see you are glad to be back," Farida said to him, offering a plate of cakes. He took one, biting into it delicately. It was pungent, with the smell of roses, and tasted of pistachio. Anwar's wife was a comfortable woman and a warm hostess.

"It is really too bad of Abe and Françoise to be late," Salim said, devouring his fourth cake. "They are always late, those two." Osmon's son, now in his mid-thirties, was darkly handsome and, Maurice thought, looked a bit more like photographs of Mohamed at the same age than his own father. His wife, Luana, had large dark eyes and rarely spoke unless asked a question.

"Françoise is a doctor, Salim," Anwar reminded him.

"One can never count on doctors being punctual, as you should know from your grandfather, Dr. Yusuf."

Maurice suddenly felt unbearably out of his element. He jumped up. "I nearly forgot. Your father sent you something from Paris, Salim." Maurice retreated to the hall, where he had left his portfolio. He found himself feeling insanely nervous. Damned silly. But it had been so long. How would he look to Abe? What would he say? He glanced in the hall mirror. No, he had not changed that much. Hair gone darker, more to chestnut. But it was all there and not gray. He looked handsome, elegant. He could say it for himself without conceit. That was his character: knowing his strengths as well as his weaknesses.

He returned to the drawing room with a flat package from Sulka. Salim opened it eagerly. In it was a honey-colored silk shirt with the thinnest blue stripes. A Schiaparelli scarf for Salim's wife. She took it, thanking him softly. Salim held his shirt up, admiring himself in the mantelpiece mirror. "Thank you, Maurice; I'll wager my father did not choose it, though."

"As a matter of fact, he did rely on my impeccable taste." The bell rang. Maurice felt the familiar excitement. Now he would see Abe.

They came in together, arm in arm. At first Maurice didn't know what to think. Then he did. Abe with Françoise . . .? Clearly their being together was no accident. Maurice could also sense that it was the cause of some embarrassment between the two families. Nor could he ever have imagined how such an alliance could have come about.

Abe came over to him, throwing his arms around him in a great bear hug. "Maurice. . . ." He searched for words. "My God, how long has it been?"

"Too long, Abe. We must make up for it." He was trying to sound natural. Françoise kissed her brother.

Abe moved beside Françoise. "We will. It's simply marvelous you're here, isn't it, Frannie? And to work together again. Almost like old times." Abe's words poured out with glib polish, leaving much unsaid. But what more could Maurice expect in front of the barrage of eyes?

"I haven't decided yet . . . about staying."

"But you must." Abe's tone lacked conviction. Farida came up, ushering them all in to dinner. The highly charged moment was broken.

Maurice glanced down the table at the ladies, glittering in jewels and colored silks. And across from him, beside Abe, Françoise, hair falling about her face in an unruly crown. Cotton shirt and skirt, more military uniform than party dress. How Jacqueline would have hated a daughter so totally bereft of style! While his lips continued to move in distracted conversation, his eyes remained on Abe. So changed. Abe now grown sinewy, tough as leather, more robust—and the youthful, boyish grace quite vanished. Lost. Lost to him. Yet Abe's eyes were the same. Wise, like Judah's. Knowing. Missing little. And there was no question that Maurice longed to be with him again.

The dinner passed in platitudes. Afterward, the party rambled into the drawing room for coffee. Salim challenged Abe to a game of chess. Maurice was furious that he should accept. He was sure that after dinner Abe and he would have a private talk. But Abe sat down with Salim in a corner over an inlaid board with carved ivory Saracen warriors and knights. Françoise watched the game over Abe's shoulder, then drifted out to the terrace. Maurice followed his sister.

She turned as though having expected him to join her. "Got a cigarette?" He offered one from his case. "Galoise. Haven't had a French one for a long time."

He lit it for her. "So, Frannie. What is actually between you and Abe?"

"You come right to the point, don't you, big brother?" The wrought-iron railing trailed a scent of jasmine through the night air. She leaned against it.

"*You* always did. Frankness, as I recall, was your most unendearing quality. Next to your total disregard for appearance—or appearances."

"Right. No need to beat about the bush, Maurice. Abe and I are living together. It's as simple as that. The families don't approve, as you may have noted by some of the longer faces this evening. But then, they'd probably like it even less if we got married. Anyway, we don't want to. We're happy the way we are."

"Are you, Frannie? Happy? Is Abe?"

Her look was steady. "Yes, Maurice. I am . . . he is . . . we are."

He managed a thin, disparaging laugh. "The way we are. Touching. And what way would that be? You in your surgery, passing out prescriptions to the locals. Abe coming home from the bank—to a full account of measles and poxes. Or would it be leprosy here, perhaps? Really, Frannie, for Jacqueline's daughter, you didn't inherit any of her many graces.''

"Or her madness. Maurice, I don't blame you for being a bitch. I know what you and Abe were to each other. But that's very far in the past. If you stay in Jerusalem, you'll have to get used to us.''

"And what do you give him, Frannie? What do you offer? The perfect fuck? Nails in the shoulder blades? Writhings in a sweaty bed? Or do you sleep in that outfit too? It does look like it. You are the antithesis of everything Abe once admired. I can't even begin to understand what he sees in you.''

"*You*, Maurice. Yes, first he saw *you* in me. Then he saw me.''

Maurice's hand closed on his sister's arm. "I warn you, Frannie: if I can . . . I'll get him back.''

"Don't try, Maurice. You won't succeed. And it will cause too much pain for you.'' Suddenly she threw her arms about her brother, hugging him to her. "Oh Maurice, truly I am sorry. I never minded what you are. I understand you. Admire you. You were always so good at the things I'm not. You knew how to have fun and style. But it's a hollow world and I don't belong in it. And as for Abe . . . he doesn't belong there either any more. There won't be any going back for him. Believe me. I am only sorry for both of us that it had to be me.''

"How could you, Frannie, how could you?'' Maurice was close to tears. He tried to control himself as Abe appeared on the terrace. Brother and sister drew apart.

"I'll leave you to talk.'' Françoise returned inside. The two men faced each other, the night a barrier between them. Abe broke the silence.

"Well, Maurice, so now you know.''

"Yes, now I know.''

"I couldn't put it in a letter.''

"No, of course you couldn't.'' Maurice twisted the gold ring around on his finger, holding it in the light. The ring Abe had given him before the Germans marched into Paris. "How does one say, 'Eternity isn't forever'?''

• • •

Mohamed felt uneasy. The June morning was sultry, humid, thick with the weight of portent. He watched them taking their places along the lengthy conference table in the Jerusalem head office of Hammadi-Nouari. Familiar faces. Young ones coming of age, attending their first annual board meeting. Older ones, aging almost as you watched them. And the one missing; that was the wrench. Judah, sometimes vehement, sometimes supportive—sometimes rambling amid his mixed convictions, which at least often added up to an open mind—vulnerable as an open window through which would enter any germ of thought to twist friendship into treachery. Wretched Judah. The memory stung Mohamed still. Oh, he was often enough wrong in his thinking. Misguided. Misdirected by overemotional responses—but never, before that day, dishonest!

"Shall we get started, Mohamed?" It was Anwar, pushing his gold pocket watch under his brother's nose, a touch of gentle prompting.

"All here?"

"All who are supposed to be," Anwar noted.

Mohamed let fall the olive-wood gavel, which Company legend suggested had been made from hub and spoke of the original cart. The table of faces swiveled toward him.

"I declare this annual meeting open." His glance slipped down to the agenda, then lifted across the table to Maurice. "There is a new face among us today. One I hope you will welcome from your hearts as much as I do. And one I hope may be here to stay."

A murmur of accord rang round the table. "I'm sorry there is at this time no Nouari available to serve in our Paris branch. We hope that soon the name Hammadi-Nouari will appear above its doors"—Mohamed's eyes drifted to the youngest Nouari present, Noah's son—"and young Micah, here, will join Osmon in its management."

Micah flushed slightly. He had just turned twenty-one. He knew that at the same age, Mohamed and Judah had already been in the Paris bank—training under the legendary Baron Liebermann. And Abe and Maurice had been no older than he when they began. But the war had slowed progress in the Company.

Mohamed took a glass of water and continued. "I hope you will all indulge me, gentlemen, if I take the unusual privilege of praising my own son." His eyes went to Maurice. "It was he who saved not only the finances of our Paris branch, but by his shrewdness and courage in moving our assets to Switzerland under the very noses of the German occupation, he assured us the capital to rebuild. I would like to move a special vote of commendation for Maurice Hammadi . . . my son."

Hands beat against the table in salute. Anwar asked for the floor, and rose, fumbling slightly with metal-rimmed glasses from the snap folder bulging the breast pocket of his business suit. "Gentlemen, I wish to make an announcement, which I think may be generally known anyway. I offer today my resignation from the Company. I wish to retire."

There was an instant polite protest; nobody was surprised. Anwar lifted a hand in equally polite restraint. "I believe the affairs of the Company will require the vigor of a younger man. Therefore I wish to nominate Maurice Hammadi to take my place as co-director of the Jerusalem head office of the bank. But before I put the question to a vote"—his eyes turned to his nephew—"I must officially ask, Maurice, are you willing to accept?"

Maurice glanced toward Abe—who looked down toward the note he was making on his pad. Plainly he wished no part in Maurice's decision. Anwar returned to his seat, all attention concentrated on Maurice. He stood up, elegant in a white silk suit, pale blue handkerchief matching his tie. His sharply blue eyes turned to Mohamed. He had been touched—deeply touched—by Mohamed's remarks. They had erased all lingering remembrance of that awful Berlin episode. "Father . . ." he began. "I must thank you first, for your commendation. And I promise you that robbing our own bank, however pleasurable, will not become a habit. As for my remaining in Jerusalem—yes, if it is in the interests of the Company, and if you all agree, I am willing to accept the post you offer." He sat down, rather surprised at himself. He had made the decision at that very moment.

Mohamed put it to the vote. Maurice's appointment was passed unanimously. "Next on the agenda, a report from our outgoing co-director."

"Yes . . ." Anwar seemed today to be fumbling memory

as well. Allah! how this brother had aged, Mohaṃed thought. Suddenly as a snowfall on Mount Ebal. "The citrus report, Anwar," Mohamed prompted gently.

"Yes." He tapped a folder. "The statistics are available to be studied after the meeting by anyone who cares to. I won't count oranges and grapefruit for you at this moment. I would prefer to discuss the state of our country, which, as an aftermath of the war, is still suffering from a serious economic slump. Some here may not be aware that unemployment figures have mounted to more than 50 percent of our working population. The fact that so many Zionists are still—despite the White Paper—reaching our shores and taking jobs, has been a major factor in causing the current unrest." He glanced toward Abe. "As the Nouaris here present will be the first to agree, this friction between Arabs and Zionists has brought, as we all know, strikes, riots, retaliations. Before the war, our Trading Company owned citrus groves. We let them go because of the difficulties. Repurchasing citrus farms and building the new fruit cannery has enabled us to begin exporting our own produce again. More important, it now offers full employment to hundreds of workers—Arabs and Jews—who, I may add, work side by side quite happily. This has been my special project, which I began not only for profit but in the hope of bettering relations between our peoples. Where better to start than with Hammadi-Nouari?" Anwar sat down, wiping his glasses.

Micah Nouari put up his hand uncertainly. Since this was his first meeting, he felt it important to be noticed. "I would just like to say that I heartily approve of Anwar Hammadi's program. I mean . . . persuading Arabs and Jews to work together. Like us. In harmony. I don't think anyone here could argue against the benefits of that."

His father looked at him with a slight frown. "Well, that's my opinion." Micah sat down quickly.

Mohamed bestowed a benevolent smile on the neophyte. "We thank you for your helpful comments, Micah." He turned back to his brother. "Wasn't there something else you wanted to tell us, Anwar?"

Anwar rose again. "Oh, yes. Now I am pleased to announce that H-N Citrus Limited has received a substantial offer for a huge contract. Our biggest to date. To supply tinned citrus fruits to the British Army. The contract should be worth several hundred thousand Palestinian pounds." He smiled. "You all had a tin of our grapefruit after Ramadan, so you know its quality. But the negotiations for this contract are not complete. I wish to nominate my nephew, Maurice, to carry on in my place with Colonel Meredith, who now acts on behalf of the British Quartermaster General here in Jerusalem."

"Objection!" Abe's voice cut through the general acquiescence. Maurice glanced across at him, hurt, even offended. Voices erupted in anger and amazement.

Mohamed gaveled silence. "If you have something to say, Abe, say it."

Abe's lean features hardened. In anger, there was something reminiscent of the younger Judah in his expression. Was Abe becoming as difficult as his father? Mohamed wondered.

"This meeting is no place for personal attacks," Raphael interjected quickly.

"My attack is not personal. It has nothing to do with Maurice. I wish to disapprove any plan of accepting a contract from the British Army. I don't give a damn if it's for lemons or mortar shells; I oppose the idea of supplying the British at this time. The war is over. Most of us at this meeting, for one reason or another, are beginning to look forward to the end of a British presence in Palestine. If we accept contracts with them for anything, we are accepting that presence." He sat down, face tight.

Anwar thrust up his hand and started speaking even before he was recognized. "I cannot agree with Abe Nouari. If we start to turn down honest business opportunities, we are discriminating politically—and that is against everything this Company has always stood for. I am only sorry Judah Nouari is not here, because I think he would agree."

There was an honest rumble of voices mostly against Abe's position. Maurice said nothing. He was too unfamiliar with Palestinian political views. He abstained when the vote was taken: five to three, against Abe. Abe sat back in silence.

Mohamed turned to him. "For myself, I feel deeply sorry that this question should have even arisen. We are still under a British Mandate, Abe. Perhaps tomorrow this will change, and anyone has the right to hope it will. I, for one, am not yet sure that it should. Oh, I know all the objections—yours, our own—but this land is a divided house. The only thing preventing open warfare—the only thing that keeps more blood from flowing—is a British soldier fairly maintaining the peace.''

"Fairly!" Abe exploded.

Mohamed banged his gavel. "Abe, everyone here is concerned with the problems of Palestine, but this meeting is not an arena for such political contests. Here in this room we must remain neutral."

Noah raised his hand. "How neutral are you, Mohamed?"

Mohamed sighed, then laughed a little sadly. "As chairman, I am completely neutral. As an Arab—of course I am not neutral. A few weeks ago I spoke to King Abdullah in Trans-Jordan. In his eyes, Zionism is a test of Western intentions. He's perfectly aware that the British are passing the problem to the United Nations, and if anybody should partition Palestine, Abdullah has made it clear, he would have no option but to invade."

Abe surged to his feet. "In fact, he's only awaiting an excuse!"

"Not true. His British military advisor, Glubb Pasha, confirmed to me that the Jordanians do not want war. But, in his opinion, if it is forced on them, the Jews would be defeated in two weeks. I quote Glubb." Mohamed broke off, voice weary. He closed his eyes a moment. "I mention this . . . not to give you gentlemen a lesson in history to come, but to point out that we, as members of the Company and as individuals, should ask ourselves: What will become of Palestine if the British leave?"

"Did your friend King Abdullah offer any solution?" Abe demanded.

"One. He told me confidentially, regardless of what the British might say, victory for the Arabs will not be easy. But if the Jews become his subjects, it will save needless spilling of blood. 'This land can be a paradise for us all,' he said. 'We have more in common than what divides us.' The King is a man of many aphorisms. But he is sincere."

Ahmed Hammadi, who had arrived with Mohamed and Raphael Nouari from Cairo, frowned beneath the graying mustache that jutted like sabers across his cheeks. "Tell me this, Mohamed: does your friend Abdullah, to whom Allah has shown such mercy—does this King plan that Palestine become part of Jordan? And if so, how will the Egyptians, the Syrians, and most of all the Palestinian Arabs feel about that?"

"Let us reserve that question for the coffeehouse, my cousin."

This brought an even louder outburst of argument. Mohamed drummed the table with his gavel and finally came to his feet, demanding silence. Maurice saw that Abe's face was the color of parchment.

"I think we should get on with Company business," Maurice said.

"I second that! While we still have one," Salim put in. "Leave political decisions to the Anglo-American Committee of Inquiry."

"Whatever we discuss here will only, in the end, be settled by the United Nations." Mohamed let the arguments mutter on a few moments, then subside. He suspected that whatever his board could or couldn't agree on, the vote of the street would reach one accord. All wanted the British out, and most would take the battle into their own hands. He also knew that when the time came, he would be speaking for the newly formed Arab League. But somehow, at the moment, looking at Judah's empty chair, his mind was wandering backward. He saw a sun-bright street and two small boys exploring together through the Turk-controlled city. It brought a thickness to his throat. He forced his mind back to the room.

"Next order of business. . . . Raphael Nouari's departure from Cairo." There was a buzz of surprise at this.

Raphael rose heavily to his feet. "I am sorry, gentlemen, but I have decided to leave Egypt, and therefore the Company office."

"Why?" Noah demanded. "May we not know why?"

"I think war will come. Maybe from Jordan, maybe not. But certainly between Jews and Arabs. Whoever wins, the Jews of Egypt and all other Arab countries will be the losers. For me, the handwriting is—if you will pardon my saying so—on the pyramids. I shall move to London. I am too old for an internment camp."

His older partner Ahmed quickly put up his hand and was recognized.

"This is nonsense, Raphael. If that war comes, it will be between Arabs and Zionists. You are an Egyptian! By birth. By feeling. By everything!"

"The Jews of Germany were Germans," Raphael replied.

The old man awoke slowly. From dream to awakening was such a small distance. The length of a shadow. His feet, dry as autumn leaves, lowered into worn-out slippers. His eyes blinked into the light of the world. Sound creaked in his ears—a jittery chirping. He searched but couldn't find it. A creaking of light?

"I come now. . . . Uncle Gamel hears." It loudened, piercing some dusty cupboard of mind. Then he saw it: the familiar trespasser; large, blackish, dusty-feathered, pinched head, lightly down-curved beak.

"What you want here?"

"You! You! You!" it cawed insistently against the stone vault of the small sleeping chamber under the mosque. The old man nodded. He understood perfectly.

"Yes, I know. You are the one who put the nest. I tell you how many times, here is no place for you! In this house many people come to talk to Allah. Nobody here wants you."

"You! You! You!" the bird repeated.

"And you not get me! Go now. Find another house."

The bird chirped back, fluttering above a single egg that had fallen from its nest in the rafters. Then it flew up to the ceiling with heavy, beating wings.

"Why you do not go when I say?" the old man pleaded, a slight quaver in his voice, but not for himself. Not ever for himself. For him all troubles of the world were no greater than mice, spiders. Or birds. These were the children of his concern. And surely they must be evicted with sweeping strokes of his broom—that these days brought sharp needle pains to arms and shoulders. He reached to the wall for the great scimitar of his life's work.

"If it were for me . . . I let you stay. But everyone say to Gamel: Bad! Mice, bird, spider—bad." He broke off, eyes fixing on the dappled egg lying on his string-worn prayer rug. The old man looked from it to the dark fluttering above, wildly stirring the shadowed ceiling. His eyes fought gloom and found the small basket-shaped nest lodged in a corner of a rafter.

"What do I say always?" he called up. "The trees—they belong for you. Sky. All this for you. But mosque—for Allah. And Gamel." The needle stabbed higher up his arm, so that he could hardly lift his broom. "All right," he said.

"This one time. Now Uncle Gamel help you. But never other time, you hear?"

He picked up the egg, and in a mounting agony of pain, positioned his rickety stepladder against the wall. It creaked in the slant of a light beam from the window blending with the squawks of the dark bird.

Later that afternoon, when Maurice Hammadi come to pay a call on his great-uncle, carrying a box of Gamel's favorite sweets—Turkish delight—he at first saw nothing. Then, by the fallen ladder, Maurice recognized the shrunken form of his frail relative holding something upward from sprawled stillness.

"Uncle Gamel . . . !" he bent to feel the old man's wrist. No pulse. He felt the heart. No beat. Nestling in the cup of Gamel's stiff, protective hand was a single bird's egg, unbroken.

Maurice stood up. The room was still. Its only other occupant—the bird—had flown away.

In Judah's Jerusalem house, the luggage had begun to overflow the bedroom. Hers, not his. Judah customarily traveled light; Ruth, heavy. She could never make up her mind what to take, since she could never decide what she would or wouldn't need.

"So how is the weather in New York? If somebody could please tell me that, I would know what to pack." "Somebody" was always Judah.

"You've been there almost as much as I have," he sighed. "July. August. It's summer. Heat showers."

"Hmm," she said. "Thunder and lightning. I've got to think of the wedding. The reception. My dress I haven't yet bought. Bergdorf, maybe."

"Zed wrote they don't want a reception, Ruth."

"No reception . . . ? Whoever heard of such a thing?" The tragedy in Ruth's tone was positively Grecian.

"No reception. You read the letter."

Ruth picked up an embroidered lime silk blouse, holding the color against a dark blue suit. "Read it, yes. That's what happens when she marries a Gentile. Is he ashamed of her, would someone please tell me that?"

"Oh, yes, of course. That's why he's marrying her, Ruth.

Out of shame, not love. Shame. She's forty, Ruth. What did you expect? Sir Launcelot? Thank God she's found somebody with whom she can be happy.'' Judah was becoming irascible. He was feeling frazzled, tired; his nonexistent arm hurt. It often did. In a way, he felt a bit left out of things. Another annual Company meeting, and again he had not attended it. No matter that he had taken the step of resignation, himself. He was longing to know what was happening. Now even more than when he'd been part of it.

Judah was grateful when Abe arrived, carrying a bouquet of flowers for his mother. Abe kissed her warmly. Since their internment, the affection between the two had deepened. They seemed to have things to whisper about all the time.

''How did the meeting go, Abe?'' Judah asked casually, returning to the bedroom. He was balancing a small circular tray holding a carafe of whiskey and two shot glasses. Abe took it from him, pouring.

''The usual problems. Nothing special, Father.''

''Problems?'' Judah asked hopefully. ''My ex-partner bad-tempered as ever, I suppose?''

Abe sat on one of his mother's delicate chairs—the only one undraped with clothes. ''Brandishing his gavel like the sword of Islam. I got voted down.''

''Oh? On what? What was the issue?''

Ruth held up her blouse to Abe. ''Tell me, darling, does this go with my suit, do you think? It's no good asking your father. For colors, he has no taste.''

''It's lovely, Mother; very smart. When are you off? Tomorrow?''

''You *know* tomorrow. And I still think it's a terrible thing that a brother won't even go to his own sister's wedding,'' she complained.

''Not a matter of choice, my dearest mother. I'm needed here.'' He put a hand in his pocket, drawing out a small package. ''For Zed—and the bridegroom, what's his name. Françoise picked it out.''

There was a silence at mention of her name. Abe was rather hurt that neither of them ever mentioned Françoise. They were nice enough to her when he brought her to the house, but their warmth was reserved.

''It's a *mezuzah*,'' he said. ''Silver. For their door.''

''But he's Gentile, Abe!'' his mother exclaimed.

"Then, he won't know it's Jewish," Abe replied.

Judah studied his son. So strong, so dedicated . . . but to what? Very like himself, Judah knew. And yet there was something—he didn't know what—that troubled him in Abe's attitude these days. Something preoccupied, secretive.

"What did they vote you down on, Abe?" Judah persisted.

"A contract with the British. I opposed it. No need to bother you with it, Father. Meanwhile, I've got a lot to do, to get Maurice acclimated. And we're very busy at the moment."

"So busy, from what I hear, you're hardly ever at the bank."

Abe digested the incrimination. He had one of his own to throw back at his father. A matter he had not wanted to open up before, but now suddenly with Judah going away, it seemed important to know where he stood. "Father, what in your opinion should be done about last week's British raid on the Jewish Agency?"

Judah drew a slow breath. "Nothing."

"How can you say, 'Nothing'?" Abe erupted. "You've been working with the Agency for years! You, of all people, should know what this means."

"It was unfortunate, of course. But there is nothing that can be done about it, Abe. They had a warrent. We were not immune from police action. Right or wrong, we are still under British law."

"How much wrong are we meant to swallow?" Abe demanded. "They broke in, seized all documents. Confiscated all secret files. Now they've got the names of every Haganah member. Every *Palmachnik*. Every Jew in Palestine who ever served in any paramilitary group. Now they could arrest any man at any moment—for any cause. For *no* cause! They have confiscated our ability to exist—and you say do 'nothing'."

"Abe, please," Ruth said from her packing. "Don't use such a tone with your father."

Neither of them paid her the least attention. Judah shook his head sadly. "All right, so they have the files, Abe. So they may arrest a few hotheads. Underground madmen like the Irgunists do us more harm than the British."

Ruth now stepped in between them. "I won't have this kind of conversation, especially when we're going away to Zed's wedding. And you not coming, Abe."

Abe put his arm around her. "It's all right, Mother. Father's memory is slipping. He forgets he battled beside Weizmann for years. And that he has been the driving force that kept the Jewish Agency alive.''

"I have fought by legal means, Abe. Not by raids and explosions. I will never condone banditry and murder. 'A tooth for a tooth' belongs to another age.''

"Just answer me one thing, Father. What happened to the man who was there with a rifle in his hand the day Trumpeldor died? What happened, Father? Have you grown so old?''

Judah felt choked with hurt. He finished the whiskey in his glass, then turned back to his son. "How easy it is for the young to rant and storm and threaten. Yes, and to act. Blindly, impulsively. Perhaps you're right, Abe. Perhaps I've grown too old. Age doesn't improve us much, I'll admit. But it gives us a longer perspective from the past to the future. Abe, if you could see . . . each retaliation only makes things worse. When the *Yishuv* struck to raise the quota of immigrants, what happened? The British reduced them. For acts of violence, they arrested us. When we struck back at the Arabs, they reduced our weapons. I don't say they were ever right, but time will bring them to our side if we prove we can restrain ourselves. Show ourselves to be deserving.''

"Can you still believe in fairy tales—after Hitler? Can you still think God will hand us back this land because it is our birthright?''

"I never thought that, Abe." He seized his son's hand, voice thick with emotion. "To the world . . . we are still 'the Jews.' And even six million exterminated will not be punishment enough for believing ourselves chosen by God. Nor can they in their hearts forgive us that their Messiah was Bar Mitzvah, kept the Sabbath, spoke our prayers, and pleaded, 'Love thy neighbor.' But then, maybe we aren't always so easy to love.''

"Well, Father, perhaps a generation is too far apart to see eye to eye. Take care of yourself. Perhaps it's better you're going away right now. Because there *will* be a retaliation in Jerusalem.''

"I pray God not!" Judah embraced his son. "And don't worry about us. It's only a wedding.''

Ruth came over, relieved to see tempers cool again. "Some wedding. Who could believe it? No reception.''

Judah forced a smile, banishing the tension. "Your mother

would like them to get married on a float coming down Fifth
Aveneue.''

Abe smiled. ''Getting Zed married would be worth it. I
must go now.'' He embraced his father.

''I'll see you out,'' Ruth said, leading him down the hall.
They paused together at the thickly carved front door.

''What is keeping you here is, I hope, not this retaliation?'' she whispered. ''And Olek—you must beg your uncle
again not to get involved with such things.''

''We are *both* involved, Mother! Anyone who was where
we were, has to be.''

''Then, I will pray each day for you and Olek.'' She
opened the door that led through the front garden. A faint
wind rattled the palm fronds.

''I only hope Father hasn't started putting two and two
together,'' Abe said.

''From me, he doesn't even know Olek is alive. Not one
word. But Olek is getting too old for all this under-the-ground
activities. And you, with a fine career as a banker.''

He opened the door of his small coupé. ''We've got to be
part of what must happen.''

''But will somebody please tell me why it is so necessary
for Olek to stay in hiding just because he entered the country
a little illegally? Why should he be treated like a criminal?''

''Mother, to the British, he *is* a criminal.''

She sighed, clasping her hands together. ''A lawyer from
Warsaw. When will it end? When can Olek stop being this
'Reuben' person and we can have him to dinner?''

He smiled, leaning to kiss her. How much could life
change as long as she was there, reducing tragedy to the
scope of her own small world? ''When the British leave
Palestine—and we finally have our own state, Olek can come
to dinner.''

All morning, Maurice had been trying to reach Abe. He
didn't come into the bank, nor was he at his apartment. No,
this was certainly not the Abe he had known in Paris; Frannie
was right about that. Maurice sighed, leaning back in the
worn leather chair. All the furniture in his office was old and
musty, the walls a flat white. He would have to redecorate.
Blue, perhaps? Cool things off a bit. The white walls glared

relentlessly. He removed his thin jacket, hung it up, and sat back at his desk. Why had he come? Why given up his beloved Paris? For Abe alone? Or was it really for the Company, his father's expectations?

As much as his initial reaction to Jerusalem had been distaste, he had to admit a certain excitement and thrill in being part of the development and growth of new projects. Yes, he was actually enjoying the citrus deal. Anwar had assembled the pieces with the care of a mosaic. Now he was putting them together. The plans for a proposed addition to the fruit cannery at Ramle lay on his desk. Maurice had carefully weighed the cost of additional building plus purchase of new machinery, against estimates of increased output. Gross and net profit. The figures looked good. Excellent, in fact. Just to be certain, he had sent them over to Noah Nouari, at the Trading Company. No harm in a second opinion. Noah was more than enthusiastic. He reported back that, with all factors considered, by the end of the year production could be up as much as 40 percent.

Maurice reread the draft contract with the British Army— designed to accommodate a 25 percent increase in quantity to be purchased over a six-month period. Nothing wrong with that. He lifted a solid gold pen from its lapis lazuli base—one he had brought from Paris. A pen worthy of signing his name to the check and accompanying letter authorizing construction to begin. H-N Citrus Limited would soon be moving up from a bantam business into the world of eminent enterprise. Carefully he folded the letter, slipped the check into the neatly typed envelope with it, and placed it in his outgoing tray. Then he picked up the telephone and dialed British Headquarters.

When Colonel Meredith's voice finally came on, the tone was briskly clipped, words trimmed and varnished in the effortless way of the British military.

"Colonel Meredith? Maurice Hammadi here."

"Ah, yes. About the tinned fruit?"

"It is. Colonel, I have the contract in front of me. I believe my uncle told you I shall be handling the matter."

"He did. Splendid chap. Pity he's retiring. But then, I suppose someone has to give you younger chaps a go?" His manner seemed a shade condescending. Maurice cooled slightly.

"I thought we could arrange a meeting to work out the final details, Colonel?"

"Good idea. Your uncle spoke very highly of you, Hammadi. I'll be looking forward to meeting you. Settling in all right at the bank?"

Maybe he wasn't actually being patronizing, Maurice decided. "Only British. "I think perhaps I shall like it here in Jerusalem, Colonel."

"Why don't we get together, then, tomorrow? Twelve-thirty any good to you?"

Maurice glanced down his desk calendar for the next day. Meetings at ten o'clock, eleven o'clock, and three-thirty. "Twelve-thirty will do fine, Colonel."

"Excellent. Afterward, perhaps we can have a spot of lunch? The Régence Café, below us, lays on a good spread. I'll reserve a table for one o'clock."

Maurice warmed to the invitation. "I'd be delighted, Colonel." It wouldn't do his social life any harm to meet someone besides relatives.

"My office is on the first floor. Come straight up, then. I'll leave your name and a pass at reception."

"See you tomorrow. And thanks." The phone clicked. Maurice entered the appointment into his diary for the next day. He was quite looking forward to it. 22nd July, 1946. 12:30—*citrus contract. Brit. H.Q. Colonel Meredith. Lunch after. 1st fl. King David Hotel.*

Twenty-nine _____

IN the Bustling Street outside the King David Hotel, an Irgun terrorist lounged against a lamppost, unnoticed. But he was noticing everything.

Since World War II days, Jerusalem's British Military G.H.Q. had been housed in the hotel's south wing; six stories of steel, stone, and concrete. Even now, with the war ended, the hotel remained a bastion of British might. The Irgunist looked across at the adjacent building: the Headquarters of the British Military Police and Special Investigation Bureau. His keen eyes scanned the area, separating the two structures. It was heavily protected by machine-gun nests, soldiers on twenty-four-hour guard duty, police, and even rather obvious plainclothesmen.

In the basement of the hotel, beneath the offices of the chiefs of staff, including Colonel Meredith, the Régence Café did a roaring lunchtime trade. Meredith had had difficulty getting a reservation that day, but had finally booked a table for 1:00 P.M. At noon the restaurant was still empty of customers, the maître d'hôtel busy supervising the laying of tables. Arab waiters bustled about with glasses, silver, plates, and napkins, arranging flowers, setting out the cold buffet. When the crowd descended, at one o'clock, they would be hungry as locusts and all expecting to be served at once.

In the large, immaculate kitchen, cooks were putting the finishing touches to soups, gravies, sauces; turning roasts, cleaning vegetables, making pastries. The chef moved from one to the other, tasting, testing.

Outside, in the bustling street, British police paid only fleeting attention to a cluster of hotel workers in flowing robes hefting heavy milk cans as far as the entrance to the restaurant. From one of the machine-gun nests, the gunner watched them idly for a moment. "Gawd, I'm 'ungry," he said.

"Bit of chocolate?" his companion offered.

"Ta." The machine gunner accepted it, losing interest in the Arabs with the milk cans, who had paused for a moment at the restaurant door before entering. If the gunner had been fifty feet closer, he would have heard the Irgun watchman whisper to one of them: *"Abi gezunt."* Had he heard this, he would no doubt have thought this slightly comic Yiddish expression sounded like a curious way to address an Arab.

It was the trigger word of the Irgun. The "Arabs" disappeared inside the restaurant, and the gunner gave them no more thought. He glanced at his watch. Twelve o'clock, straight up. His stomach was growling. The chocolate had only made him hungrier.

In the street outside the Régence Café, the Irgunist lingered. Inside, things were beginning to happen.

"Raise your hands! We mean business!" It was the man they called "Reuben Kahane," in command of this assault unit. At his side was Abe Nouari. There was no resistance from the café staff. There had been too many bombings and attacks in the city. The Arab waiters willingly allowed themselves to be herded into the kitchen. While pots continued to bubble away, cooks were jostled with the waiters to a side room, where they were locked in. Abe led the men with the milk cans down the steps to the cellar. Reuben and several others remained upstairs on guard with Sten guns.

The cellar was small, airless. Pyramids of boxes left scant space to move about. "It's perfect," Abe said. "The less room the better. Set the cans right there—by the foot of the stairs."

"What's in them?" one of the men asked.

"Five hundred pounds of explosives. TNT and gelignite," Abe told him.

"Think it's enough to do the job?"

"In this small space? When the gases escape, the explosion should reach the roof." Abe set a placard in front of the cans so it could be seen from the steps. It read: MINES. DO NOT TOUCH! "Just in case anyone thinks they can dismantle them."

From upstairs, they were alerted by an exchange of shots.

"Hurry; get those things triggered!" a man called Sha'ul told Abe. He did not know Sha'ul's real name. It was a rule. No one ever did. Abe began to pull the pins on the explosive devices. "Should give us half an hour," he said, checking the time. It was 12:05. They started back up the stairway, revolvers drawn.

In the dining room, two British soldiers lay wounded on the floor. Reuben had been hit in the arm. "We go now," he said.

"The staff. We must let them out." Abe headed for the door of the side room.

"Hurry, then."

He unlocked it, calling in Arabic, "Run for your lives! There is a bomb!"

The restaurant staff tumbled out into the street, the Irgunists behind. A British military patrol opened fire. Sha'ul was hit, dropping to the pavement. "Keep going!" he shouted at them. In the street, an Irgunist threw a cracker bomb, which sent up a covering screen of smoke.

"Get away from the hotel!" The shout tore from Abe's lungs to the crowd. "It's going to blow up!" He headed away with the others, followed by a volley of shots. But there were too many people in the street, and the drifting smoke made it impossible for the soldiers to continue firing.

Once beyond the smoke screen, the men shed their Arab robes, separating quickly. Abe caught up with Reuben. "Hurt bad?"

"Not bad."

"Wait at my apartment. Frannie will get there."

Reuben tore off down a side street.

Abe ran on toward a phone booth. Françoise was waiting inside, receiver in hand. As he came up, he signaled and she began dialing at once. Her first call was to G.H.Q.: "Explosives have been placed under the hotel. They will go off in twenty-five minutes. Evacuate the whole building immediately!" She rang off, starting the next call as Abe reached her.

"Olek—at our apartment. Wounded. Go to him as soon as you finish." Abe continued on down the street, slowing his pace to a walk. The *Palestine Post* newspaper office was just answering her second call. Françoise alerted them, then phoned the French Consulate, which was opposite the hotel. They were told to open their windows to lessen the shock. Having completed these warnings, Françoise started back to her apartment, where Olek would be waiting. If nothing had gone wrong.

Maurice Hammadi headed up the steps of the King David Hotel, two at a time. It was nearly 12:30. He knew the British military had a taste for punctuality. He wanted to start his relationship with Colonel Meredith on the right foot. In his dispatch case were three copies of the citrus contract. He paused on the steps, noticing some commotion in the street. A flurry of British police, but whatever it was, it seemed to be over. He continued on through the double doors, entering the lobby. He stopped, to identify himself to the desk sergeant. Meticulously the sergeant began checking down his clearance sheet for Maurice's name.

At almost precisely the same moment, Abe Nouari checked the large wall clock as he entered the Hammadi-Nouari Bank. On the way to his own office, something made Abe pause at Maurice's door. Abe knocked. When there was no reply, he put his head in. The office was empty. Abe stepped over to Maurice's desk, glancing at his daily diary. He read the entry of Maurice's appointment with Meredith.

Hand trembling, Abe picked up the telephone, dialing the King David Hotel, hoping that no one would still be there to answer.

His heart sank as the operator came on: "British General Headquarters. . . ."

"You've been warned—there's a bomb! Why haven't you evacuated?" Abe demanded.

The operator's voice was unruffled. "We don't take orders from the Jews, sir."

"This is S.I.B. Give me your desk sergeant. Hurry."

Abe waited tensely until the sergeant's voice came through. "Inspector Smith here. Special Investigation Bureau," Abe lied. "A bomb's been planted under the hotel. A man calling himself 'Hammadi' is responsible. Have you seen him?"

There was an agonizing pause, while the sergeant checked down his list. "Hammadi? He's still waiting in the lobby, sir."

"Place him under arrest," Abe told him.

"What?"

"Bring him across to us. And get that building evacuated. Now."

"I'll get him over to you, sir. But I have no authority to evacuate the building." The sergeant clicked off.

Abe stood for a few minutes, uncertain what to do next. Then he started out of Maurice's office, moving down the corridor into the bank lobby.

The distant explosion almost threw him off his feet. It was blocks away, yet the bank shook as though struck by an earthquake. A teller rushed over to Abe.

"Mr. Nouari . . . what do you think it was?"

Abe looked at him, mind spinning. "Maybe . . . the end of an era."

"Aren't you even dressed?" Ruth called in from the bedroom of their Waldorf Hotel suite in New York City. "It's almost time we should leave."

"Still forty-five minutes before Zed comes up to collect us."

"Suppose she should be late?"

"To her own wedding? That's why she's taken a room in the hotel."

Judah had put on striped trousers and a white shirt with a starched collar. He was manipulating a bow tie in front of the sitting-room mirror, still in his red silk dressing gown. To hook the ready-tied bow with one hand had become an exasperating challenge. Normally, he had perfected the trick. But today. . . .

He gave up, waiting for Ruth—shifting his attention to the courting of two oversexed pigeons, their puffed-up bodies strutting in ritual dance on the sooty ledge above Park Avenue. A discreet knock announced the entrance of the waiter. He peered tentively around one of the double doors, as though ever hoping to find some orgy in progress. This suite would be his disappointment, Judah thought.

"Good morning, Mr. Nouari." Generous tipping had already bestowed identity. The man wheeled in a white-clothed table bearing silver-covered breakfast dishes. Ice framed grapefruits bulls-eyed by a single cherry.

"Mind signing, sir?"

"You'd mind if I did not." Judah took the pencil from the waiter and scratched his initials on the bill.

"Terrible about that hotel in Jerusalem, Mr. Nouari. That's where you're from, isn't it?"

"What hotel?"

"It's all there in the *Times*—with your breakfast." The waiter left. Judah opened the front page of the paper.

Ruth's voice called in from the bedroom. "Did you remember to order a boutonniere from the florist? Informal or not, I always think a white carnation—" Ruth came in, breaking off on sight of her husband. "What is it, Judah?"

His whole form had begun to tremble; his skin was ashen. His eyes pierced from behind his glasses. "Look, Ruth! Look at this. . . ." He waved the paper in front of her. She looked at the headlines.

"Oh, my God. My God. . . ."

"Ruth, more than two hundred people—killed or injured! British officers. Jewish civilians. I can't believe it. . . ."

"Who could do such a thing?" she whispered.

"You know damned well who could do it! The Irgun." He was shaking so badly now, she thought he would collapse. Ruth took his arm. "You must sit down, Judah. You are getting yourself too excited." She led him to a chair, mind reeling with secret worry for her son and her brother. This thing—in the newspaper—in her heart she knew *they* must have been part of it.

Judah was out of the chair, pacing. "You know what this means, Ruth? The destruction of all our work at the Agency. Now they will be within their rights to cut immigration to nothing. To arrest thousands—because a handful of terrorists have declared war against the Mandate."

Ruth took the newspaper from him. "They can't blame everyone for what a few people do."

"Oh, can't they? The Irgun have already blown up three railroads. Attacked the Jerusalem prison, wrecked power stations. And now this! How can we explain such atrocities to the Anglo-American Commission? How appeal for a homeland to the United Nations? How can we stand before the world and plead our cause after this?"

Ruth soothed him like an upset child. "Don't think any more about it now, Judah. Later we can worry. Now we must

gutteral sound escaped his lips, eyes fixed on her in irrevocable accusation. Ruth knelt beside him. She herself was gasping from the shock. Then she found strength to speak his name. "Judah. . . . Judah. . . . Don't— Please don't leave me."

He was neither responding nor even appearing to hear. Yet his eyes. Fixed. Alive. Piercing through into her mind. His face seemed frozen in contortion—an agony carved in living flesh. Ruth cried out, sobbed, then somehow pulled herself to her feet. Voice barely audible, she had to ask three times to be connected with her daughter's room before the operator could understand.

Zed took a long time answering. Or so it seemed. Time had ceased to exist.

"Oh, it's you, Mother. I tried to phone you before. Almost ready for the human sacrifice?"

"Zed . . . Zed . . . your father . . . I think he has had a stroke."

Silence. Then the quick, efficient, controlled tone. "Just stay right there. I'll call the hotel doctor. Then I'll be there, Mother." Zed hung up.

Ruth looked at Judah's face. She hadn't dared touch him. She could not tell whether he was alive or dead. She began to wail aloud, and words took form, words from the deepest part of her hidden resentment and anguish. "It's unfair. Unfair. Unfair. You even cheat *her,* like you cheated me. Cheat Zed out of the happiest day of her life! But me you cheated every minute after. I hope he takes Zed away from us . . . all of us . . . all the misery, all the suffering, all the poison. God of my fathers, I'm glad"—she wept—"I'm glad you're giving my Zed to a Gentile!"

Sun streaked the dust-layered afternoon. Maurice Hammadi followed the British sergeant across the open courtyard of Acre's military prison. But it was not Maurice who was confined in the old crusaders' fortress. The authorities had realized quickly enough that the phone call denouncing Maurice had been a fraud. But a tip from an informer had led them to Abe, who had been recognized running away from the hotel.

It was Abe who had been confined at Acre, who had been questioned for weeks, who had kept silent under interrogation.

Maurice had great difficulty obtaining permission to visit his friend and partner. Finally, Company influence—and his father's connections—had opened the gate.

The sergeant brought Maurice to a cell isolated from the others, then stepped some distance away, watching them. Maurice was stricken by the sight of Abe's emaciated features, crusted by a thickness of new beard. Eyes moved in deep shadows, yet Abe's expression was somehow benign. On sight of Maurice, Abe came to his feet.

"Thank God. . . . Thank God. . . . They wouldn't tell me whether you were alive or dead."

"Abe . . ." Maurice began. "I know it was you who made that phone call. I . . . I can't bear maudlin scenes . . . but, Abe"—his voice was near breaking—"I'm alive because of you. And you are here . . . because of me."

"Compared to Sachsenhausen, Acre is a holiday camp. And I'll tell you something. Being here has meaning. Jabotinsky was here. And so many others. It's quite a monument."

Maurice studied the face that he had loved better, perhaps, than any in the world. It was all he could do to contain emotion—hold back the flow of words he would never dare speak now.

"Abe, I want you to know we have done everything possible. Even my father has appealed to the highest authorities."

Abe glanced away to the cell wall that bore the hicroglyphics of loneliness. Words in many languages, scratched into the dank stone through centuries of time. He had even added his own, and carved the emblem of a fist holding a rifle across the Jordan. "One thing you never run out of, here, is reading matter." He seemed unconcerned about his fate. "Oh, I'm quite content to stay here until the last British soldier has left Palestine."

Maurice smiled wryly. "And the first Jewish warden unlocks your gate?" His tone grew serious. "But Françoise . . . what about her?"

Abe's lips tightened. For a moment, he said nothing. Then his words came, low and toneless. "She will be . . . all right."

•   •   •

Françoise, at the moment, was not all right. She was facing the harsh anger of her father.

"What are you trying to say to me?" Mohamed demanded. "That you had some part in that heinous bombing? That you became a physician . . . to soak your hands in the blood of hundreds of people?"

"In wars, civilians get killed too, Father. Nobody plans it that way."

Mohamed shook his head. "That attack had nothing to do with war, Françoise. It was an act of terrorism."

"Terrorism is one kind of war. But the intention was not to kill. The Irgun telephoned a warning."

"So they say. If it were true . . . why wasn't the hotel evacuated?"

"I don't know why, Father. But I know the warning was given. I gave it myself."

Mohamed rubbed his forehead between thumb and forefinger. "Françoise. . . . How did you get yourself involved? Was it Daniel? Or was it Abe who influenced you? You . . . my daughter. You . . . half Arab."

"I did what I believe in, Father. The British know now their Mandate can no longer be administered. And so they will leave Palestine to us."

"To whom? The Irgun?"

"Why not the Jews?" she demanded. "If the Arabs win this land, the moderates will be the first to be wiped out. The fanatics will take over—turn back the clocks to the Middle Ages. Put every woman back behind the veil. Shoot every Arab who is less extreme than themselves. But if the Jews win their state . . . with all that's wrong with them, they will develop the land; bring it into the twentieth century. They will be fair to their Arab neighbors. This country will enjoy a good life. And peace."

"You are wrong, my child. Wrong! If the Jews take this land, there will be *no* peace, ever! Only war and more war. Only more destruction, more terror, more hate. The Jews have their fanatics too!" Mohamed knew that nothing he might say could change his daughter's thinking. Still he must try. "By working with the Irgun against our people, you and Abe are traitors to everything I . . . and Judah Nouari ever stood for."

He had spoken the name almost unconsciously. It was the first time it had been on his lips since that day in this very room when they parted. And suddenly he knew the truth. He turned back to his daughter. "Why did you come to me to confess your sin? To gain absolution for the lives of those people? I know you are not a Mohammedan. Now I know you cannot be a Catholic, either. What are you, Françoise?"

"I am your daughter."

"My daughter. . . . Here, in my house. As you were that last day, Françoise—when Judah and I talked here, in this very room. . . . *You* heard us, didn't you? Told your murdering friends where the shipment was to be landed. And all these years I have blamed Judah for your treachery! You should be sharing that prison with Abe. God . . . why do we have children?"

"Are you going to turn me in, Father?"

He crossed to the garden door, stared out at the peaceful scene. A hummingbird hovered above the white-belled flowers of a vine. "A good life . . . and peace," she had said. He turned back to her. "You wanted to be a doctor, Françoise. You ran off to a revolution. You wanted to work here in a clinic. You joined terrorists. You had beauty, wealth, parents who cared for you—yes, even your mother. And you run after trouble like a fifty-dollar lawyer chasing ambulances. What do you want, Françoise?"

"A better world. Not just for today."

He nodded. "I think we shall not see each other again. That is my wish. But I will not turn you in, Françoise. I will go the the mosque, and pray for you. For all of us."

"I'm tellin' yah, boss, nobody recovers from a stroke." Tony was at the wheel, the back of his neck a dried prune of pessimism. His expertise in all areas of human knowledge had not omitted medicine. "You can take it from me, Mr. Nouari is a goner. Just lucky you got here as fast as you done."

Tony had driven Mohamed to collect Ruth at the Waldorf. She was waiting in the lobby. On sight of him, she wept. Ruth wept at sight of almost everybody these days. The Arab held her for a moment in his arms. "My poor, dear Ruth. . . ."

She pulled herself together. "Come, he is waiting. I told

him it would be today. I said, Mohamed is coming. He doesn't show much expression, but he understands everything. You can tell by the pressure when he holds your hand. He doesn't speak. But the doctor says there's no reason why he can't.''

Tony drove them on to the hospital, for once silent. Ruth blew her nose heavily. It was quite red. ''The doctors, what should they say, that he'll get better? It's just a matter of time. They pat your hand and send you a big fat bill. But if you ask me what I think. . . .'' Handkerchief dabbed nose again. ''I think Judah will never leave his hospital bed.''

Tony grunted. His diagnosis had been confirmed.

In the hospital, they took the elevator with a pair of overstarched ladies in white. The strong medicinal odor penetrated the grilled Otis like a whiff of death. Zed was waiting on the sixth floor with her new husband. Mohamed knew Henry Mathews well. He had been the bank's legal advisor for several years. Tall, rawboned, sparse in speech, he and Zed had formed an alliance well before the lawyer's long-ailing wife had died.

Zed hugged her mother. ''The doctors say he's better today. It's just a matter of time.''

''Didn't I tell you?'' Ruth nudged Mohamed with her eyes. ''I'll stay with Henry and Zed. You go in alone. Too many people at once confuses him.''

''He really *is* better,'' Zed insisted to Mohamed. ''Isn't he, Henry?''

''Yes,'' Henry confirmed.

Mohamed kissed Zed on the cheek. He hadn't seen her since his return to New York, and was grateful that marriage to Henry had not taken her away from the bank.

Judah's room brimmed with flowers, a basket of fruit, and on the dresser facing his bed a photo of Ruth that she herself had placed there. Beside it stood the official wedding picture of Zed and Henry, Zed in a frilly hat that didn't quite suit her customarily tailored look. Abe's likeness was noticeably absent from the family formation. A clinically brushed and scrubbed Judah was propped up in the elevated hospital bed. The left corner of his mouth sagged just slightly. His cheeks were hollows, eyes shadowed but open and strongly responsive. On sight of Mohamed, the lips trembled as though trying to form words, or perhaps even a smile. Mohamed knew instantly that Judah would hear and understand his every word.

"Don't exert yourself, old friend." Mohamed took Judah's hand in his own, sensing rather than feeling the pressure of response. At first they were silent, letting the reunion flow through hands to heart and minds. As for Judah, he saw Mohamed as clearly as any time in their lives. He saw how his friend had aged, the mustache white, face weary from the long, difficult flight via Egypt by private Company plane. Judah felt perfectly able to form all the words he wanted to say, but he was not really sure if, having said them clearly in mind, they had actually passed his lips to reach his friend's ears. The trouble was that Mohamed kept interrupting.

"I see you've gone into the florist business. Appropriate for an old gangster, eh? They say you'll be up and about in time for the next Olympics." The sugaring of conversation to cover truths.

Cut the bedside chatter, will you? I'll be damned lucky to ever set foot on the floor again. The words rang only in Judah's head, but Mohamed seemed to understand anyway.

"Look, Judah, I didn't take that rotten long plane trip just to watch you being pampered by beautiful nurses." His face grew serious, "I came to apologize for a terrible wrong I have done you."

Judah's eyes brightened.

"I am asking your forgiveness for the mistake I made in believing it could ever have been you who informed on the arms shipment. That was the stupidest thought I ever had in my life. I know now who was responsible."

Yes, I forgive you, Mohamed. And I agree, it was the stupidest conclusion you ever jumped to. But it's in the past. Everything is now. I bear you no grudge. . . . Only Judah's expression told Mohamed what was needed between them. He smiled.

"Then, we are again friends?"

Judah's head inclined slightly.

"Yes, we have both lost so much. We are a pair of bankrupts in life. Everything given—everything taken away. Who can understand their sons and daughters? We want them to be mirrors of ourselves. Your Abe, my Françoise. And curiously enough, Maurice, who I never quite understood, who was never my flesh and blood, comes closest to being the true child of my heart." Mohamed was finding it easier to voice feelings to his stricken friend, whose glance alone spoke volumes of perfect understanding now.

"Something else," he went on. "I have been asked to represent the Arab League at the UN. Though I am a moderate, it is my duty to speak for the majority. But perhaps not as immoderately as they would wish."

Judah closed his eyes. There was so much to be said. He opened them again and focused on a letter lying on his bedside table. Weizmann had written of his meeting with Ernest Bevin, British Foreign Minister. *Read it, Mohamed. . . .*

Mohamed looked at him, glanced at the letter. "You want me to read it?" he asked. Judah nodded faintly.

Mohamed picked it up, scanning it. In it Weizmann reported that the Zionists had even offered to waive their aims for an independent state—if Bevin would only raise the quotas. As they stood now, it would take seven years for the displaced persons who had already suffered so much to be released from their present "temporary" detention camps.

How many will ever live long enough to see the land? Judah asked in his own mind.

"That's quite a letter, Judah. A generous offer from Weizmann. And Bevin's answer. Cryptic." He read from the letter: " 'They must wait their turn. Many people suffered during the war. The Jews cannot expect to jump the queue.' " He folded the letter back into the envelope and returned it to the table. "A brutal rejection of Weizmann's offer."

If not Palestine, where, then? The moon? The concentration-camp survivors have been barred from almost every civilized country on this earth. . . .

Mohamed brought out his cigar case, squinting into the smoke as he lit up. "Such attitudes, I fear, bar all hopes of peace. And yet now, in spite of everything that has happened, Judah, I still believe our Company can show the way for Arab and Jew to work together for the good of both. I believe it, though fewer and fewer of my own people agree with me. Moderates like you and me are out of fashion." He smiled dryly. "I suppose Haj Amin was a man ahead of his time, Allah preserve us all." He blew a perfect smoke ring, letting it drift upward, changing shape, decomposing. The room smelled of medication and now the more pungent aroma of his fine cigar. Mohamed was annoyed with himself. He hadn't wanted to discuss Palestine. He had come to apologize, not to upset Judah.

Judah's lips worked. There was something he wanted Mohamed to know. Something that had sustained his faith in man's conscience. He tried once more to form words, and in the instant made himself heard. "Mohamed . . . !"

Startled, the Arab brought his head close to the muffled whisper. "There was . . . a man I met before the war. At a bank in Haifa. . . ."

"Yes, Judah. I can hear you!" The smile blazed from Mohamed's face, the even white teeth gleaming. "Tell me . . . about the man in Haifa. What am I to know about him?"

"Swedish. Christian. Raoul Wallenberg."

The name rang familiar. Mohamed searched memory. "The banking family? And in import-export, like our own Company."

"Yes. That one. . . ." Judah broke off, struggling to articulate. His tongue felt strange and thick. Yet now he could actually hear the sound of his own words in his ears. "In the war . . . Wallenberg, a diplomat . . . Swedish Embassy, Budapest. From Hungary half a million Jews being deported . . . to Auschwitz." A tear trembled in Judah's eye.

"You don't have to tell me all this now," Mohamed urged. "It'll keep. There'll be plenty of time for us old fellows sitting in the sun someplace, when we get you out of here."

"No, Mohamed. Must tell you. He gave Jews Swedish passports . . . any kind of document. Forged. Any excuse. Saved at least a hundred thousand people. Hid them. Even in his own house. Faced down their assassins. Risked his own life over and over. He was, this Wallenberg, to the hopeless, the lost, the condemned, their savior angel. He saved first the young ones . . . because he wanted to save a nation . . ."

"Why are you telling me this now?" Mohamed asked. "Surely it can wait."

"Wallenberg was arrested. . . ."

"By the Nazis?"

"By the advancing Russians. I tried to find out where they have imprisoned him. Lubianka . . . Lebadunskya, maybe. . . . Mohamed, you must promise me! Bring his case before the United Nations. See that Wallenberg is freed. He is a righteous man. As long as such a one exists, there is still hope."

Mohamed took his hand again. "I promise, Judah. I will find out everything I can. Do even more than is in my power." He rose. "Now you must really sleep. And without a troubled mind. Once again, you have me on your side." His face wrinkled in a smile, and for a moment he was to Judah the young Mohamed, fearless, unconquerable.

Judah closed his eyes. The talking had been a great strain, and yet he suddenly felt his own strength returning. He knew that he would be well again.

Mohamed moved quietly from the room. Judah was already asleep.

A soft rain had begun to sprinkle the street. The sky had darkened with the weight of clouds. Tony spotted the black vicuña overcoat and pearl-gray felt hat as Mohamed emerged from the hospital. The boss still cut a distinquished figure. Tony climbed out of the limousine to open the door.

"How is Mr. Nouari, boss?"

"Hard to say. Actually, the doctor is much more hopeful than Mrs. Nouari suggested."

"I wouldn't be too sure, boss."

"You never are." Mohamed paused before entering the car, glanced around, sensing a presence. Out of a shadowed doorway, an old Arab woman was coming forward through the drift of pedestrians. She wore the traditional dark garment pulled up over her head. As she came closer, Mohamed saw that the woman was smiling slightly, as though she recognized him.

"You are Mohamed Hammadi?" she asked, in deep-throated Arabic.

Poor soul, Mohamed thought, adrift in so foreign a city. Yet she had recognized him. But then, why not? His face was well known enough. Probably she would beg a little money. His hand started toward his wallet. "Can I help you?"

In the sliver of time that the woman's eyes held on Mohamed, she seemed to be reaching out her hand. "At the United Nations . . . you will not be our voice!" she whispered harshly.

By the time his glance had caught the metallic snout of her automatic, it was too late. The silencer's muffled coughs doubled him forward. Mohamed fell to the wet, slick pavement. The woman was already gone around the corner before Tony grasped what had happened. He bent lifting the dying Mohamed into his arms.

"Boss . . . boss . . ." he sobbed.

Mohamed's lips moved; words too softly spoken to reach Tony's ears. "There is no God . . . but Allah. . . ."

Around the corner, the old Arab woman climbed into the back of a laundry van. Zuliekha, The Scorpion, knocked on the panel, signaling the dark-skinned young man at the wheel. The vehicle sped off, merging into traffic.

Ten minutes later, a siren wailed its cry of havoc through gloom.

"Grandfather . . . if you could see them! A sight you could never forget. Father says there are more than six hundred thousand people in the streets today. All watching. And the planes. You hear them?"

Judah strained his dim vision. Above him, all was a blur of sound. "What do you see, Emmanuel?"

"Fouga Mystére jet trainers. Shaped like arrows, they are. Mirages, with needle noses. Fighter-interceptors. And just now above us . . . American Skyhawks! Behind them, Vatour bombers." Emmanuel's voice lifted in excitement. "And coming now our own, home-built planes, Grandfather! Flying in the shape of a Star of David."

From the streets of Jerusalem, cheers rose for the marching formations, the clattering captured Russian tanks, the columns of suntanned infantry. The emotion was so great that many could not restrain tears. Here they had welded the promised State. Promised first by God, later by Lord Balfour.

Twenty years had passed since Israel had gained independence. Today the rejoicing also marked last year's victory in the Six Day War. Twenty years, and many had not believed they would have lasted even twenty days. Oh, yes, Judah knew this was an occasion for the utmost giving of thanks. A salutation to accomplishment. We were tired of being a chosen people, he thought. We were tired of being permanent guests in the whole world, sometimes welcome, sometimes not. The Nazis showed us how they treated unwelcome guests.

And yet, in his heart—which was by now his only true place of feeling—Judah could feel nothing certain, nothing of assurance, nothing of conviction. Had it all been . . . a mistake? Had Herzl, Jabotinsky, Trumpeldor, Weizmann, Judah, and all the others worked to create a small geographical error on the map of history? "Here the wandering soul of Israel shall reach its haven," Weizmann had said. And if not Israel, then what? What other choices had there been? A melting into all the pots of the world? Oblivion for a faith, a people?

Judah knew now only . . . that he didn't know. But even his gigantic doubts could never be shared with his grandson at his elbow. Emmanuel. Almost sixteen. The name meaning "God is with us." *Was He?* Judah wondered. Were they truly a state by the will of God? But then, even doubt required conviction. Perhaps he had lived too long. Judah's ears rang with the roar of the planes, his mind with the past.

Beside Judah's wheelchair, Emmanuel's parents, Françoise and Abe, shared the roof terrace of the old bank building. By the formation of this State, Judah's son and his wife had become terrorists-turned-respectable. Judah sighed. Animosities, bitterness, were long gone. Perhaps *their* way had accomplished more than his. And his grandson, part Arab, part Jew, was he not the true heir to this land?

Abe leaned over, speaking into Judah's ear above the roar of planes. "May second, nineteen sixty-eight, Father. A day to remember. A day you helped bring about. . . ."

The words washed over Judah along the sky roar and the cheers. True, he had done his small part. And yet, Judah could not feel pride. Had he been wrong? Had any of them been right?

Shalom. Peace. Without it, the quick little wars could grow until their conflagration engulfed the earth. This Zionism, would it finally be the fatal accomplishment? Abe would style such pessimism as the defeatist philosophy of age. A privilege perhaps well earned at ninety-three. And yet Judah knew that these victories would demand more victories—because leaders were stubborn and as blind in their hearts to compromise as he was blind in his eyes. He had always believed: "not by the sword."

"By what, then, *I-AM-THAT-I-AM?* By what. . . ?"

Nobody heard what Judah said. Nobody saw what he could see. Judah could no longer perceive the present, only the past. What one could not discern—not even imagine—was the future. That was God's secret. And so, Judah was afraid.

BIOGRAPHICAL NOTE

Jesse L. Lasky, Jr., and Pat Silver have been writing as a team since 1958. They were married in 1960. They live part of the year in London, part in Spain, and travel extensively. *The Offer* is their third book together.

Jesse, the son of the famous California film pioneer, was educated in Princeton and Dijon, France, and served for three and a half years in the Southwest Pacific during the Second World War in General MacArthur's army. He achieved success as a poet at seventeen, then went on to write novels, short stories, and over fifty film scripts in Hollywood, England, and Italy. Eight films for Cecil B. DeMille included *Samson and Delilah,* for which Jesse received the Box Office Award, and *The Ten Commandments,* which brought him the Christopher Award.

During his period as a student at the University of Dijon, Jesse spent considerable time in Palestine, Syria, and Egypt.

Pat Silver was born in Seattle, Washington, attended the University of Washington, Stanford, and Reed College—where she produced their first play. As Barbara Hayden, she wrote, directed, and acted in the first live dramatic television series from Hollywood, ''Mable's Fables,'' which received an Emmy nomination.

Together, Jesse and Pat have written seven films and over one hundred television scripts, including the award-winning series ''Ten Who Dared,'' for which they wrote the *Colombus* and *Stanley* episodes. Their verse play, *Ghost Town,* received the American University Women's Award.